Acclai[m]

The Evolution *of* B[runo]

"Stuffed with allusions high and low…rich with philosophical interest…an absolute pleasure." —*New York Times Book Review*

"A brave and visionary work of genius…Erudite and affected, bitter, brilliant, and lonely, Bruno's narrative voice self-consciously echoes many of the twentieth century's most memorable narrators…THE EVOLUTION OF BRUNO LITTLEMORE is a major accomplishment. A lively page-turner that asks the big questions head on and doesn't shy away from controversy, Hale's first novel is a noisy, audacious, and promising debut." —*San Francisco Chronicle*

"Sprawling, ambitious, aiming to shock as well as to illuminate… Bruno's narration never fails to provoke and compel…It throbs with energy and boils with passion as it expresses a dark vision of our essential nature that strikes uncomfortably home."
—*Los Angeles Times*

"Bruno's human struggle is what makes him so provocative…He can teach us things. His naiveté and innocence inspire us to admire the beauty of nature and art and great writing." —*USA Today*

"Brilliant. It's a fantastic concept, that something that shares so much of our DNA can have something to say. The book is worth a read for the narrative voice alone—that of Bruno the chimp—who is erudite, arrogant, and more than a bit confused by the emotions humans take for granted."

—Jodi Picoult, #1 *New York Times*
bestselling author of *Send You Home*

"[An] exuberant début...[Bruno's] hyperallusive, Nabokovian confession is the tale of 'a first-generation immigrant to the human species,' encompassing Milton, Whitman, Darwin, Diogenes, and Kafka...Hale's relish for his subject, and his subject's relish for language, never flags." —*The New Yorker*

"It cleverly challenges the reader to explore ancient philosophical themes while sharing a love story between a woman and a chimpanzee...The story leaves you thinking deeply about what it means to be human. Open the book—and your mind—and let Benjamin Hale take you away." —*Columbus Dispatch*

"An epic tale of an erudite chimpanzee with superior language skills who endeavors to become part of the human race...Bruno has been compared to Nabokov's Humbert Humbert, Saul Bellow's Augie March, and Gunter Grass's Oskar Matzerath (I would throw in John Kennedy Toole's Ignatius Reilly, as well)." —*Chicago Sun-Times*

"A funny, sad, and shocking tale of a stranger in our strange world...Hale wraps his prehensile wit around humanity's deepest philosophical questions...When the novel's antics aren't making you giggle, its pathos is making you cry, and its existential predicament is always making you think. No trip to the zoo, western Africa, or even the mirror will ever be the same." —Ron Charles, *Washington Post*

"Told in an eloquently deluded voice reminiscent of Nabokov's Humbert Humbert, the book, a tinderbox of complications, touches on some big topics: animal rights, linguistics, and philosophy." —*O, The Oprah Magazine*

"A hugely ambitious debut novel...What makes it a worthwhile and rewarding one is that Hale doesn't shy away from presenting humanity in all its facets. What could have been an entertaining but saccharine tale of anthropomorphic acceptance instead becomes an enthralling—and still entertaining—examination of man's capacity for good and evil." —*Rolling Stone*

"An eloquent and dramatic writer." —*Time Out New York*

"Audacious...a brilliant new voice...Funny, philosophical, provocative, and irreverent, this controversial debut novel explores what it means to be human." —*Arizona Republic*

"Bruno is indeed a worthy creation, a little like Shelley's Frankenstein, a creature incarnating human hubris (or Promethean ambition), created by us in our likeness from the clay of, in this case, another species." —*Buffalo News*

"Quirky, witty...BRUNO LITTLEMORE enthralls...Hale's descriptions of ape life brim with metaphors for the human condition...[an] intelligent, poignant debut." —*Harvard Crimson*

"Hale often writes beautifully, sending some startlingly vivid images blazing...There is the pervasive sense of an interesting mind lurking behind Bruno's." —*New York Review of Books*

"[Hale is] a terrific talent. He's devised a voice for Bruno that owes something to Nabokov and something to the comic pomposity that John Kennedy Toole brought to Ignatius J. Reilly in *A Confederacy of Dunces*...That language is a grandiloquent wonder."

—Bloomberg.com

"One need only read a few pages to be swept up by the grandeur of Hale's ebullient prose...With his primary Chicago setting, engrossing storytelling, unabashed braininess, predilection for eccentric characters, and long, looping, wonderfully evocative sentences, Hale reminds me of no writer so much as Saul Bellow...Adventure tale, love story, science fiction, novel of ideas—this one's got it all."   —*Newsday*

"Completely different...totally convincing...so beautifully written. The voice of this novelist is so intelligent, so exciting, the language is so rich...astounding...If you liked the book *Room*, you'll love this book...I mean, this is disturbing, but you'll fall in love with it."   —Bill Goldstein, NBC's *Weekend Today*

"One of the more effusive and unrestrained works of fiction in years...It's Bruno's voice that gives this novel the complexity and life it deserves. His stories, although not always reliable, are always abundantly full of the mysteries of humanity."
                    —*Minneapolis Star Tribune*

"Powerful...a debut novel short on arrogance or pretention, but full of confidence and life...By giving us a narrator with so much passion, and so few successes in acting on it, Hale has created one of the most tragic literary heroes in recent memory."
                              —TheMillions.com

"Benjamin Hale is the most talented and intriguing young writer I've met in years. A writer with a capital W...It's like being a baseball scout in Oklahoma in the late 1940s and seeing this young kid running around center field, and you ask the guy next to you, 'Who's that?' And the guy says, 'I don't know, some kid named Mickey Mantle.'"
              —Jonathan Ames, author of *Wake Up, Sir!*, *The Extra Man*,
                    and the HBO series *Bored to Death*

"Stunningly ambitious...a moving meditation on what it means to be human...There is something irresistible about THE EVOLUTION OF BRUNO LITTLEMORE." —*Houston Chronicle*

"Benjamin Hale is a writer of rare and exciting talent. We'll be reading his books for years. Dive in."
—Anthony Swofford, author of *Jarhead*

"Bruno Littlemore is one of the most outrageous, vivid characters to populate a page in American fiction in a long time.... It's not only a roaring good tale, it's a wonderful musing on the nature of humanness and our relationship to the other species with which we share the planet." —*Baton Rouge Advocate*

"An enormous, glorious rattlebag of a book. Benjamin Hale's extremely loud debut has echoes of the acerbic musings of Humbert Humbert and the high-pitched shrieking of Oskar Matzerath. Hale's narrator is a bouncing, pleading, longing, lost, loony, bleeding, laughing, beseeching wonder."
—Edward Carey, author of *Observatory Mansions*
and *Alva & Irva*

"[A] mischievous debut...His quest for answers about the agonizing dilemmas of existence [is] unexpectedly resonant."
—*Publishers Weekly*

"[This book] offers all those things we ask of our novels: rich entertainment and comedy, emotional sincerity that isn't cloying, and the ability to satisfy the immense ambition it sets for itself."
—Jacob Silverman, *Publishers Marketplace*

"Hale's Bruno is smart and inclined to archness and irony, and it's a pleasure to follow his thoughts, darkling and otherwise...a book of considerable merit...and of high entertainment value, too, as much fun as a barrel of monkeys." —*Kirkus Reviews*

"Like his protagonist, Hale clearly loves language, using words with precision (likely to send readers to a dictionary) and for play...This novel is likely to offend some readers, while others will find it holds a remarkable, riotous mirror to mankind."

—*Booklist* (starred review)

The Evolution of Bruno Littlemore

Benjamin Hale

TWELVE

New York   Boston

In memory of Jesse Barboza
(1982–2007)

Copyright © 2011 by Benjamin Hale
Reading Group Guide Copyright © 2012 by Hachette Book Group

All rights reserved. In accordance with the U.S. Copyright Act of 1976, the
scanning, uploading, and electronic sharing of any part of this book without
the permission of the publisher is unlawful piracy and theft of the author's
intellectual property. If you would like to use material from the book (other
than for review purposes), prior written permission must be obtained by
contacting the publisher at permissions@hbgusa.com. Thank you for your
support of the author's rights.

Twelve
Hachette Book Group
237 Park Avenue
New York, NY 10017

www.HachetteBookGroup.com

Twelve is an imprint of Grand Central Publishing.
The Twelve name and logo are trademarks of Hachette Book Group, Inc.

The Hachette Speakers Bureau provides a wide range of authors for
speaking events. To find out more, go to www.hachettespeakersbureau.com
or call (866) 376-6591.

The publisher is not responsible for websites (or their content)
that are not owned by the publisher.

Printed in the United States of America

Originally published in hardcover by Twelve.

First Trade Edition: February 2012

10 9 8 7 6 5 4 3 2 1

The Library of Congress has cataloged the hardcover edition as follows:
Hale, Benjamin.
The evolution of Bruno Littlemore / Benjamin Hale.—1st ed.
p. cm.
ISBN 978-0-446-57157-9
1. Chimpanzees—Fiction.   2. Animal intelligence—Fiction.
3. Human-animal communication—Fiction.   4. Alienation (Social
psychology)—Fiction.   I. Title.
PS3608.A54567E96 2011
813'.6—dc22
2010012098

ISBN 978-0-446-57158-6 (pbk.)

[The following manuscript contains the unedited transcripts of the memoirs of Bruno Littlemore, as dictated to Gwendolyn Gupta between September 9, 2007, and August 8, 2008, at the Zastrow National Primate Research Center, Eastman, GA 31024]

What I have learned from them has shaped
my understanding of human behavior, of our
place in nature.

—*Jane Goodall*

You'll see it's true,
an ape like me
can learn to be human too.

—*King Louie,*
"I Wan'na Be Like You (The Monkey Song)"

Part One

... But man, proud man,
Dress'd in a little brief authority,
Most ignorant of what he's most assur'd,
His glassy essence, like an angry ape,
Plays such fantastic tricks before high heaven
As makes the angels weep; who, with our spleens,
Would all themselves laugh mortal.

—*Shakespeare*, Measure for Measure

I

My name is Bruno Littlemore: Bruno I was given, Littlemore I gave myself, and with some prodding I have finally decided to give this undeserving and spiritually diseased world the generous gift of my memoirs. I give this gift with the aim and hope that they will enlighten, enchant, forewarn, instruct, and perchance even entertain. However, I find the physical tedium of actually writing unendurable. I never bothered learning to type any more adroitly than by use of the embarrassingly primitive "hunt-and-peck" method, and as for pen and paper, my hands are awkwardly shaped and tire easily of etching out so many small, fastidious markings. That is why I have decided to deliver my memoirs by dictation. And because voice recorders detest me for the usual reasons, I must have an amanuensis. Right now it is eleven fifteen in the morning on a drably nondescript day in September; I am lying partially supine and extremely comfortably on a couch, my shoes off but my socks on, a glass of iced tea tinkling peacefully in my hand, and there is a soft-spoken young woman named Gwen Gupta sitting in this very room with me, recording my words in a yellow notepad with a pencil and a laserlike sense of concentration. Gwen, my amanuensis, is a college student employed as an intern at the research center where

I am housed. It is she who acts as midwife to these words which my mind conceives and my lungs and tongue bear forth, delivering them from my mouth and by the sheer process of documentation imbuing them with the solemnity and permanence of literature.

Now to begin. Where should I begin, Gwen? No, don't speak. I'll begin with the first time I met Lydia, because Lydia is the reason why I am here.

But before I begin, I guess I should briefly describe my surroundings and current predicament. One could say that I am in captivity, but such a word implies that I have a desire to be elsewhere, which I do not. If one were to ask me, "Bruno, how are you?" I would most likely reply, "Fine," and that would be the truth. I know I'm well provided for. I like to think of myself not as imprisoned, but in semiretirement. As you already know, I am an artist, which my keepers recognize and respect, allowing me to occupy myself with the two arts most important to my soul: painting and the theatre. As for the former, the research center generously provides me with paints, brushes, canvases, etc. My paintings even sell in the world beyond these walls—a world that holds little remaining interest for me—where, I'm told, they continue to fetch substantial prices, with the proceeds going to the research center. So I make them rich, the bastards. I don't care. To hell with them all, Gwen: I paint only to salve the wounds of my troubled heart; the rest is grubby economics. As for the latter—the theatre—I am preparing to stage a production of Georg Büchner's *Woyzeck*, directed by and starring myself in the title role, which our modest company will perform in a few weeks for the research center staff and their friends and families. Broadway it's not, nor even off-Broadway—but it satiates (in a small way) a lust for the spotlight that may be integral to understanding my personality. My friend Leon Smoler visits me occasionally, and on these occasions we laugh and reminisce.

Sometimes we play backgammon, and sometimes we converse on philosophical subjects until the smoky blue edge of dawn creeps into visibility through my windows. The research center allows me to live in all the comfort and relative privacy that any human being could expect to want—more, really, considering that my mind is free from the nagging concerns of maintaining my quotidian persistence in the world. I am even allowed outside whenever I please, where, when I am in my most Thoreauvian moods, I am allowed to roam these woods in spiritual communion with the many trees that are thick-trunked with antiquity and resplendent with drooping green mosses and various fungi. The research center is located in Georgia, a place I had never been to before I was relocated here. As far as I can determine from my admittedly limited perspective, Georgia seems to be a pleasant enough and lushly pretty place, with a humid subtropical climate that proves beneficial to my constitution. Honestly, on most days it feels like I am living in some kind of resort, rather than being confined against my will due to a murder that I more or less committed (which, by the way, could time be reversed, I would recommit without hesitation). Because this more-or-less murder is a relatively unimportant event in my life, I will not bother to mention it again until much later, but it is at least ostensibly accountable for my current place of residence, and therefore also for your project. I am, however, no ordinary criminal. I suppose the reason I'm being held in this place is not so much to punish as to study me, and I presume this is the ultimate aim of your project. And I can't say I blame them—or you—for wanting to study me. I am interesting. Mine is an unusual case.

As a matter of fact, Gwen, I should apologize to you for my initial refusals to grant your repeated requests for an interview. Just speaking these opening paragraphs has made me realize that nothing I've ever yet experienced better satisfies my very human desire for philosophical immortality than your idea of recording this story—catching it fresh from the source, getting it right, setting it down for the posterity of all time: my memories, my loves, my angers, my opinions, and my passions—which is to say, my life.

Now to begin. I will begin with my first significant memory, which is the first time I met Lydia. I was still a child at the time. I was about six years old. She and I immediately developed a rapport. She picked me up and held me, kissed my head, played with my rubbery little hands, and I wrapped my arms around her neck, gripped her fingers, put strands of her hair in my mouth, and she laughed. Maybe I had already fallen in love with her, and the only way I knew to express it was by sucking on her hair.

Before I begin properly, I feel like the first thing I have to do for you here is to focus the microscope of your attention on this specimen, this woman, Lydia Littlemore. Much later, in her honor, I would even assume her lilting three-syllable song of a surname. Lydia is important: her person, her being, the way she occupied a room, the way she did and continues to occupy so much space in my consciousness. The way she looked. The way she *smelled*. That ineffably gorgeous smell simmering off her skin—it was entirely beyond previous olfactory experience, I didn't know what to make of it. Her hair. It was blond (that was exotic to me, too). Her hair was so blond it looked *electrically* bright, as if, maybe, in the dark, her hair would naturally glow forth with bioluminescent light, like a lightning bug, or one of those dangly-headed deep-sea fish. On that day when we first met, she had, as was her wont, most of this magnificent electric blond stuff gathered behind her head just under the bump of her skull in a no-nonsense ponytail that kept it from getting in her eyes but allowed three or four threads to escape; these would flutter around her face, and she had a habit of always sliding them behind the ridges of her ears with her fingers. Futilely!—because they would soon be shaken loose again, one by one, or all at once when she snatched off the glasses she sometimes wore. When Lydia was at work, her hands were endlessly at war with her hair and her glasses. Off come the glasses, fixed to a lanyard by the earpieces, and now (look!) they dangle from her neck like an amulet, these two prismatic wafers of glass glinting at you from the general vicinity of those two beacons of womanhood—her breasts!—and now (look!) they're on again, slightly magnifying her eyes, and if you walk behind her you will see the lanyard hanging limp between her shoulder blades. On they went, off they came, never resting for long either on the bridge of her nose (where they left their two ovular footprints on the sides of the delicate little bone that she massaged with her fingers when she felt a headache coming) or hanging near her heart. Once, in fact—this was much later, when I was first learning my numbers—I had briefly become obsessed with counting things, and I counted the number of times Lydia took her glasses off and put them on again during an hour of watching her at work, and then I counted the number of times she tucked the wisps of hair behind her ears. The results: in a one-hour period, Lydia put her glasses on thirty-one times and removed them thirty-two, and she tucked the wisp or wisps of hair behind her ear or ears a total of fifty-three times. That's an average of nearly once a minute. But I think these habits were merely indicative of a nervous discomfort she felt around her colleagues, because when she and I were alone together, unless she was performing some task demanding acute visual focus (such as reading), the glasses remained in their glasses-case and her hair hung down freely.

I will speak now of her body, style of dress, and general comportment. She was, obviously, much taller than me, but not ridiculously tall for a human woman, maybe about five feet five, though the birdlike litheness of her limbs gave the illusion that she was taller. To me, anyway. She exercised often, ate a salubrious diet, and never felt tempted by any of the body-wrecking superfluities that so easily sing me out to sea, so innately deaf was she to their siren songs; for instance, she drank only socially, and even then not much. Her hands were knobby-knuckled and almost masculine in aspect, with fingernails frayed from light labor and habitual gnawing (one of her few vices); these were pragmatic hands, nothing dainty about them; hers was not the sort of hand a pedestrian poet might describe as being "alabaster," nor the sort of hand onto the ring finger of which one might slip a diamond ring in a TV commercial advertising relucent diamonds wrested from the soil of darkest Africa. She dressed sharply, a bit conservatively. She dressed stylishly but not in a way that drew outrageous attention to herself. No, ostentation was not her style. (Ostentation is *my* style.) Black turtleneck sweaters were her style. Light tan sateen blazers were her style. Flannel scarves were her style. She shopped at Marshall Field's. She wore hairpins. She wore sandals in the summer. She wore boots in the winter. She wore jewelry only on special occasions, though she wore on all occasions an effortless aura of beatific radiance. She looked good in green.

I will speak now of the sound of her voice. It made its impression on me the very first day we met. Most people would speak to me in that putrid bouncing-inflection singsong that adults use when condescending to children or animals. But not Lydia. No, she spoke to me in the same sober conversational tone of voice she would have used to address anyone else, and this easily won my loyalty, at first. Her voice had a faint but discernible twang in it; she'd originated from a family of noble hardworking bozos from some godforsaken backwater town in rural Arkansas, but she had fled her background upward and away into education much in the same way as I've fled mine, and she spoke like a young woman with a doctorate from the University of Chicago, which is what she was. She spoke in grammatical sentences, with punctuation marks audible in them: periods, parentheses, colons, even the sometime semicolon. Listening to her voice was like listening to a piece of classical music being performed by a full symphony orchestra with one slightly out-of-tune banjo in it, lonesomely plinking along to the opus somewhere in the string section.

And I will speak now of her face. Lydia's face was etiolated and Scandinavian-looking enough that she wouldn't have looked out of place in a black-and-white Ingmar Bergman movie, though her eyes were not the pellucid blue ones that you would expect to see in the head of the woman I've thus far described. Her eyes were gold-flecked green. Her irises begged comparisons to tortoise shells, to the corollas of green roses with bronze-dipped petals, to two green-gold stars exploding in another galaxy, observed through a telescope a billion years later. On her driver's license they were "hazel." She had a long face with a lot of distance between her thin mouth and the bottommost tip of her slightly cleft chin. Her skin had the sort of pallor that pinks rather than tans in the sun. Two delicately forking blue veins were barely noticeable on her temples. The bridge of her nose was a perfectly straight diagonal line, but the tip of it was blunt and upturned at an angle just obtuse enough to allow, from a directly frontal view, easy gazing into the depths of her nostrils. Her forehead was wide and featured a very subtle bump above the supraorbital ridge. Her cheekbones were not high and emerged to definition only in the harshest of lighting. She seldom wore makeup, and when she did, it was just hints and touches, because slathering too much ornamental glop on that face of hers would have diminished its effect rather than enhance it. Her snaggletoothed smile served as a memento of childhood poverty. She was twenty-seven years old when I first met her, and thirty-four when she died.

But why—*why* have I spent so much energy, so much of both my time and yours describing this woman, having probably succeeded only in distorting rather than elucidating her image in your mind's eye? Because Lydia was my First Love. Make sure you write that with a capital *L*, Gwen. And why don't you go ahead and capitalize the *F* in *first* as well. Because Lydia was my capital-*O* Only capital-*L* Love, or at least the only Only Love I would ever dare to capitalize.

Now we may begin in earnest. New chapter, please.

II

The first time I met Lydia, I was so young and uncontaminated by the world that I didn't even know I was participating in a scientific experiment. I was brought into a strange blank-white room: everyone's shoes squeaked on the hard shiny floor, and the high-frequency buzzing of fluorescent lights overhead made me jittery and discombobulated. The three of us—I, Bruno; my idiot brother, Cookie; and little Céleste—were let out of the cage in which they had conveyed us to this alien room, to allow us a little time to acclimate ourselves to these surroundings at our leisure, to accustom our eyes to the stinging brightness, to meet the scientists. That's when I met Lydia: she bent to the floor and held her arms open for me, and I ran to her and climbed into them, and for the rest of the day that was where I stayed, cradled in her arms, breathing her amazing scent that I even then must have found erotic—except when she was too busy with her work, or when they ripped us apart so they could run their moronic experiments on me.

I suppose I shouldn't say moronic, because that experiment was what marked me as different right from the beginning. Of course I had no idea what was going on at the time. I had not yet acquired language, so I couldn't have articulated my thoughts. (That, by the way, is the ironic thing about acquiring language relatively late in life: words don't exist to adequately describe what it's like when that tempest of wordless thoughts whirling around in your head suddenly snaps to definition; that great hop from prelinguistic to linguistic is squarely in the realm of the ineffable.) As far as I knew, all that was going on was this: I was taken into a small, empty white room with a long rectangular reflective panel embedded in one wall. (I now realize this was a one-way mirror, behind which another scientist was probably watching me like a voyeur with an eye to a keyhole.) The scientist who had conducted me into the room was not the woman whom I would later come to know as Lydia (was that *you* watching from behind the mirror, Lydia?), but some droll old fat bearded sot who held no special interest for me. There was a transparent plastic box on the floor. The scientist produced from the pocket of his white coat—with the excessively theatrical flourish of an amateur magician—a peach.

A peach, Gwen—he was my serpent and I was his Eve. There we were, me in my prelapsarian nudity and he in his demonic white coat, tempting me with fruit coveted but prohibited. The only difference was environmental: we'd swapped sexy Edenic lushness for the sterile whitewashed walls of Science. Also, that particular fruit is semiotically associated with the female pudenda, isn't it? Isn't that why Cézanne painted them?—*Still Life with Peaches?*—why, that's just a quivering bowlful of vulvae sweating on the breakfast table, waiting for you to eat them up!

But the peach in question: so he takes, this scientist does, he takes a juicy piggish bite out of it and starts making yummy-yum-yum noises, *mmmmmm*, rubbing his belly, trying to goad my jealousy, you see. And as I recall, it worked. I was a simpler creature then. I remember wanting the peach at that moment more than anything. Hell, I would have sold my soul for a peach. (And in a way I did.) I remember hating, no, *loathing* that old smug fat imperious blob for the way he lorded the fruit over me so. So he took his bite, break-ing the skin, releasing into the room the ambrosial aroma of that sticky wet fleshy treat, and then he, bastard, pushed me away when I reached for it. Then, turning to the box—transparent plastic box on the floor, remember?—he operated some sort of device which made the lid spring open, placed the peach inside and shut the lid. I was watching his actions with curiosity and a motley of deadly sins: greed, envy, gluttony, lust. Then, the demonstration: the box-opening mechanism consisted of a button and a lever; he pressed the button; then he rapped on the lid of the box three times with his knuckles, like this—*knock, knock, knock*; then he flipped the lever and the lid of the box popped open. He reached in and—again, moving his arms in such a grossly histrionic manner it was as if he wanted the people in the nosebleed seats to see what he was doing and making a face like *Look, Bruno, what do we have here?*—extracted the peach.

Again I reached for it. Again he pushed me away. Then he put the peach back in the box, promptly left the room and pulled the door shut behind him. Bruno was alone.

Alone with the box, with the peach clearly visible but locked away inside, forbidden to Bruno. I looked at it a moment. I pressed the button, knocked thrice on the lid, flipped the lever, opened the box and removed the peach. Did I dare to eat a peach? Indeed I did.

In this way I fell from my state of innocence.

The door opened, I was escorted out and my brother, Cookie, in, where I understand the same procedure was repeated on him. A lit-tle while later all three of us—Cookie, Céleste, and I—had made it through the first round, and I was taken back into the room, until they decided enough time had elapsed to renew my appetite.

Only this time—*this* time, it was Lydia—gorgeous-smelling Lydia, my human peach—who attended me into the little room with the box. Just being alone in a room with that woman was enough. And now *she* removed a peach from the pocket of *her* white coat, *she* took a sopping wet bite out of it and took her sweet time chewing. Then *she* placed the peach inside the box, waited a moment, pressed the button, knocked her knuckles on the lid three times, *click-click-click*, flipped the lever that opened the box and retrieved the peach. After locking it up again she left the room, though I entreated her to stay. Alone, I again in turn pressed the button, tap-tap-tapped, flipped the lever and proceeded to feast: but *this* peach tasted so much richer than the first, as it was imbued with the magic of her touch—with her *lips*, no less—her tongue!—I had seen that woman put *her mouth* on this object! The vicarious contact made me insane with desire. I would have preferred her to chew the peach to a pulp and sensuously ooze it intermingled with her own fluids into my mouth. I ate every shred of the thing, every last ort and fiber and dribble of nectar and then sucked on the stone for an hour after and became enraged—*enraged!*—when the other scientists tried to take it from me: I kept it securely in my cheek and would under no circumstances relinquish it, until, yes, Lydia, Lydia herself coaxed me to surrender it by holding her hand to my mouth, and, finally, I willingly spat the stone, slick with my saliva, into the cup of her pretty hand.

Anyway, this bizarre and (to me at the time) unfathomable procedure was repeated again and again all day until it looked like we'd all had our fill of their fucking peaches.

Much later, Dr. Lydia Littlemore would explain to me why my performance on that day had marked me as extraordinary. In retrospect I understand now what I could only feel at the time. As I've said, I did not yet have language. This is not to say that I did not have a consciousness in those days, or that I did not have thoughts—I certainly did—but I had none of these traps in which to capture and keep them—words. Back then my thoughts could only trickle through my head in a liquid state; trying to think clearly was like trying to drink water out of cupped hands: most of it drips through your fingers before you've really had a chance to drink, and you remain thirsty still—thirsty, and ignorant. When my consciousness was solidified enough to understand, Lydia told me that I had participated in a psychological experiment they were running on two groups, human infants and preadolescent chimpanzees. The experiment goes like this. You have this transparent Plexiglas box with a door that can be opened by a mechanism requiring a two-step process to unlatch: press the button and flip the lever. You place inside the box something the infant or chimpanzee is supposed to want, in my case a peach—and this, in my opinion, is the most problematic aspect of the experiment. What complex being will *always* want a peach? Suppose I wasn't hungry? Am I supposed to be a creature of such brainlessly insatiate appetite that given the opportunity I would cram every last peach on the planet into my ravenous maw? Later in my life, when I was sitting in on an introductory course in microeconomics at the University of Chicago, I realized that economists tend to think about their fellow *sapiens sapiens* in exactly these terms. Rational choice theory, so they call it: *Homo economicus.* Fools! The thing that defines us rational creatures, like you and me, Gwen, is precisely the fact that we're not always rational.

But I digress. So you put the peach in the box and then demonstrate to the subject how to open it. The scientist presses the button, taps three times on the lid of the box and flips the lever. Then leave the test subject alone and watch what he does. Then repeat this procedure ad nauseam on the largest test sampling you can get. The objective of the experiment was to see whether the human- or ape-child figures out that the tapping-on-the-box bit is an unnecessary step. Their typically anthropo-chauvinist hypothesis was that all your innately superior little human snots would quit tapping on the stupid box before the chimps. And the results were *exactly* the opposite of their predictions. All but one of the chimps (and they tested more than fifty of us and as many human infants) quickly figured out that the tapping shtick was a superfluous waste of time, and thus aborted the measure from the box-opening procedure on the second or third trial run. A few of the chimpanzee subjects, my older brother, Cookie, among them (and this sort of behavior is characteristic of him), on the third trial run got the box open simply by picking it up and smashing it against a wall. The *humans*, though—the human babies would faithfully tap on the box *every time*. Every one, every time. Now, Gwen, what do you think this means? I'll tell you. It means this: for the human test subjects the whole thing was less about the reward than it was about the process. You see? It wasn't so much that they wanted the peach as to participate in this enigmatic ritual, to perform the rite, to say their prayers. Because it's *you humans* who have your absurdities of faith, your superstitions, your banshees and hobgoblins, your necromancies and haruspices, your charms and potions and voodoo dolls and magic mirrors and boogiemen, *you* who infantilize the universe by vainly searching for celestial answers to earthly questions in the movements of the stars, *you* who have your signs and symbols, your signifiers and signifieds, *you* who cast a terror-stricken backward glance into the darkness and ask yourselves who is that third who walks always beside you, *you* who chant your incantations, kiss the ring and cross yourselves, sear images into your flesh and poke holes in yourselves, hack off parts of your bodies and paint yourselves blue, burn witches and sacrifice your firstborns, scream into the whirlwind and wrestle with angels till the break of dawn! And they thought *we* would be the ones to continue squandering a few precious seconds that stood between us and those delicious peaches by tapping on the box even when the action obviously affected no empirical change upon the object? Absurd! It is only rubbing on the lamp! It is only magic. It is only religion. It is only the shadow of the hand of God. It is only one more example illustrating how feebly you people know yourselves.

Anyway, point being: who was the one and only chimpanzee among the hundred-some-plus sampling of members of my own birth species, *Pan troglodytes*, who, like the human children, never ceased to tap on the box? That's right, *c'est moi*. I, Bruno, somehow understood on some fundamental level (as Lydia realized in hindsight, after the experiment was over and the unexpected results had been properly tabulated, scrutinized and pondered over until they succeeded in twisting some anthropo-chauvinist take out of the data) what it means to be human. And Lydia remembered me—me, Bruno, the chimpanzee who had fallen in love with her—and she sought me out, and found me, and began to bring me out of my animal darkness.

III

I think it had been some months since the experiments, some months since the Plexiglas box and that daylong procession of peaches, when Lydia came back for me. I had been returned to my family of uneducated slobs, to my mother and my father, my aunt and my uncle, my brother and Céleste. All of them sadly ignorant, broken and disaffected by lifetimes spent in diaspora.

I'm a Chicago boy, Gwen—I grew up in the Primate House of the Lincoln Park Zoo. Zoo records indicate that I was born with no complications on August 20, 1983. My mother, Fanny, had been born and raised there, had spent the entirety of her sad dull life in the very same zoo. I'm young enough to have been raised mostly in the considerably larger and sleeker modern facilities that were built to replace the outmoded sewer which had previously housed the great apes, and my mother never tired of silently reminding me and Cookie how good we had it. My father had a somewhat more interesting background. He wasn't born in captivity, but in the Old Country, in the northeastern part of what was then Zaire, now the Democratic Republic of the Congo. At the time he was born there was some sort of bloodbath going on in Zaire, and the swarms of starving refugees fleeing hither and thither would butcher chimps for bushmeat. At a young age my father saw his mother and father murdered and subsequently devoured. He was forced to watch while they dismembered his parents with machetes, drilled spits through their corpses, cooked them over a fire and ate them. The two adult chimps they killed and ate because they were hungry, but they refrained from killing the baby right away because there was little meat on him (he was more valuable alive). Instead they tied him to a stick by his wrists and ankles, which they carried around with them for several days until they crossed the border to the Central African Republic and arrived at a populated area, where they sold my father to a German trader who illegally trafficked in exotic animals. The German was a man in a big yellow hat, who starved and beat him, and put him in a cage, which was transported from one place to another until he wound up on an airplane that landed finally in Germany, where he spent five years in the Berlin Zoo before a mysterious chain of exchanges and communiqués put him back on a plane, which this time landed at O'Hare, where he was loaded into the back of a van and conveyed to the Lincoln Park Zoo, where he was introduced to a jejune and somewhat mentally obtuse female chimp whom he was expected to shtup immediately, and whom out of boredom he eventually did. Thus my brother Cookie was conceived, followed three years later by me. The Germans had named him Rotpeter, meaning "Red Peter," after the streaks of distinctly ruddy coloration in his fur. My father never quite lost that touch of aboriginal uncouthness. He'd known freedom only to have it cruelly revoked—whereas I, Bruno, was born in captivity, became free because I learned language, committed a transgression, and now, as you see, am in captivity once again. My father, though, had—however briefly—experienced life the way it was meant to be lived. He knew what he had lost, and this knowledge fueled him with an indignant rage that as a child—even in my terror of him—I admired. Not so my mother. She had never known Zion. She was born in the ghetto, a zoo-child of zoo-parents. And she suffered my father's boorish machismo and womanizing with the same matter-of-factly passive acceptance with which she accepted her own confinement from birth. Rotpeter screwed my mother often but would also slip it in her sister whenever he felt like it. See, we shared our habitat with my maternal aunt, Gloria, and another adult male chimp, Rex—pitiful Rex!—who coupled with Gloria whenever Rotpeter was feeling too fucked out or overfed to swat him away, but Rex would never have dared try anything with my mother. Because Rotpeter was Alpha Male (not a hugely impressive achievement when there are only two adult males in the habitat) and because he had been born in the boondocks of Zaire and didn't put up with anybody's shit (at least not that of anybody he could physically overpower), he simply felt biologically entitled to every wet hole in the cage: my mother, her sister, and I could swear the disgusting fart already had a lecherous eye trained on little Céleste, who good Christ was still a child then, even younger than I, scarcely weaned from the teat.

Perverse, isn't it? That I should sit keeping my poor dull down-trodden mother company, letting her comb the bits of filth out of my back fur while not twenty paces away my father is fucking my aunt? You'd think I grew up in Appalachia. This is the sort of background I came from. Oh, and I should tell you about the frog.

There was this frog—wait. Not now. Not just yet.

———

I think a general description of my early childhood is in order. The summers weren't so bad, because they let us romp around on the grass outside. The whole family would spend most of the day lolling around in the trees and hammocks on this sort of grassy artificial island they'd built for us. We had enough space to move about as we liked, but there was a concrete ditch with a moat in it surrounding the island, and beyond that, a wall that was too high and steeply sloped for us to climb. The humans would crowd around the ledge of this wall and look at us. If it got too hot we could retreat inside to our dank dark room in the primate house, as they left the door open for us and we could come and go as we pleased between the shade and the outdoors. Those who inhabit zoos live like harem women: an idle life of well-provided imprisonment for the sake of others' titillation. I suppose that sort of a life is luxury to those inclined to value their freedom less than their freedom from want, but Bruno the Prideful wished to be nobody's pet. He wanted out, our Bruno did, out.

The Chicago winters tended toward bone-achingly frigid temperatures unbefitting the constitutions of tropical mammals like us, so every year we all spent November through usually, what, March, April even, cramped up indoors with less than half the roaming room we had in the summer. And the smell. How did it smell? The room smelled the way I presume any room might smell in which seven large naked primates are forced to live together for five consecutive months, doing all their eating and drinking and sleeping and fucking and fighting and farting and pissing and shitting within the confines of the same four walls—one of these walls, of course, being a thick sheet of glass provided for easy voyeurism. In the winter the room quickly took on a putrid mustiness, the primitive carpet of cedar planting chips almost immediately becoming so sodden with urine and sweat and other bodily miasmata you could practically watch the fetid steam waft up from the floor to smoke the glass opaque with fog and give us the closest thing we ever got to privacy. By the time the city thawed in the spring we were all half-crazed with cabin fever, bitchy and snappish, leaping at each other's throats at the faintest provocation. Particularly my father, Rotpeter, who was a heavy smoker. Ah yes, my father's smoking. In the summer, some of the humans would stand at the

ledge smoking cigarettes, and my father, an extraordinarily percep-
tive ape, learned from watching the smoking humans the physical
semiosis for *Hey, can I bum a smoke?*—which is: pantomiming the
act of taking two drags of a cigarette by making a prong out of
the index and middle fingers, puckering the mouth into a half kiss
and touching the fingers twice to the lips. So when he saw someone standing at the ledge smoking a cigarette, he would look the
person dead in the eye and make this gesture, and the smoking
human would be so amused at his adorable mimesis that he or she
would go ahead and throw him a cigarette. If it happened to land
in the moat around our island (which it often did due to the lousy
aeronautical properties of a cigarette), he would stoop to retrieve
it, dripping from the water, and lay it out to dry on a rock. If not,
he would pick it up, give the human a grateful thumbs-up gesture
that he'd also learned from the passing *sapiens* and put it in his
mouth. At first he would only mock-smoke them because he did
not realize you had to light them to make them work, and in any
event he obviously did not have anything to light them with, either.
Eventually someone realized this, and the man (he was, as I recall,
or let's say I recall, a heavyset fellow in a Bears T-shirt) thought-
fully lit the cigarette for him, took a few puffs to get it going, then,
correctly estimating the parabolic trajectory needed to vault the
moat, using his ring finger as launching mechanism and his thumb
as fulcrum he catapulted the burning missile over the Wall, over
the moat, and onto the grassy shores of Monkey Island. My father
actually smoked a cigarette then, and not long after he was hooked.
He started adding a lighter-flicking gesture to accompany his can-
I-bum-a-smoke gesture, and soon some kind soul threw him his
own plastic cigarette lighter, which he also learned to use, and he
immediately began to burn through his stockpile of cigarettes that
people had previously thrown him but which he'd had no means of
lighting. He hid his lighter and his cigs in a cache he surreptitiously

dug in the planting chips in the interior part of our habitat, which he concealed with a rock. That was because the zookeepers were predictably horrified the first time they caught him smoking. They had tried to take the cigarette away from him, and Rotpeter threw a fit. After that, whenever a zoo employee happened around—they were easily identifiable by their light-brown uniforms—my father would hide the cigarette behind his back, or, if they got too close, would grind it out and then keep his foot over the butt. So he was able to fool them for a while, until the winter came and again we were all shut up inside, where for five months we chimps and the lowland gorillas would stare at each other from across the hall through our respective windows while the occasional gaggle of humans walked by between us, pausing awhile to gawk at the funny monkeys.

That's when the zoo authorities got wise to the fact that my father hadn't quit smoking: because now, in addition to the usual lush aroma of fecal matter, the habitat reeked of cigarette smoke. They tore the place up looking for Rotpeter's stash, but he'd hidden it so well they never found it. Whenever the brownshirts arrived on a raid my father cleverly—oh, so clever, Rotpeter—cleverly sat on top of the very rock covering the cache. They never found it. He ran out, though, not even halfway through the winter, and the cravings made him moody and irascible. The next summer, the zoo employees posted a conspicuous sign outside the ledge looking into our habitat that must have said something like PLEASE DO NOT GIVE THE CHIMPANZEES CIGARETTES, though we were on the other side of the sign and did not know exactly what it said and, as all of us were unlettered, would not have been able to decipher it anyway—making my father furious with confusion as to why his bum-a-smoke gesture, though still amusing, failed to make good as often as it had the previous year. This, by the way, was the summer I met Lydia, and it was the same summer as the Frog Incident.

———

The Frog Incident: at some point during the time between the experiment with the peaches and the time Lydia came to fetch me for acculturation, a frog—yes, a frog, you know, *ribbit*—had somehow made it into our habitat. Curious Rotpeter was intrigued and entertained by this hapless amphibian: he managed to catch it, and began to play with it, flopping it back and forth in his hands and laughing at it, letting the terrified creature struggle away and get a few hops out before he snatched it up again. It was a perfect blue-skied summer day on a weekend, so the zoogoers were out in droves, and a large group of humans huddled at the ledge, pointing at my father and laughing at him laughing at the frog. Then what did Rotpeter, my father, do? He proceeded to fuck it. Yes: he fucked the frog. He played with himself till hard, pried the frog's mouth open, rammed his schlong down its throat and began to rape it. The frog kicked its legs in agony, and there was a gruesome squishy sucking wet slurpy pumping squelching noise like *skwerploitch, skwerploitch, skwerploitch* (don't make that face, Gwen)—which I imagine was distinctly audible even up there on the other side of the Wall. Once or twice the frog succeeded in hobbling away a few inches in a feeble attempt at escape, and Rotpeter would grab it by the leg, drag it back, reinsert himself and continue to take his pleasure with it. This is more or less what I recall, or imagine I recall or may as well recall overhearing among the humans who stood at the ledge, looking on in horror, and—as the urge to document is weirdly intrinsic to your species—videotaping it:

"I'll *have* to tell people about this," says the woman with the video camera.

"Mommy?" says a little girl, "is the monkey raping the frog?"

"This is the monkey," says the woman to her camera, "oh, wait, oh, see the frog, see the frog—"

"Just look at him goin' at it!" says a man.

From somewhere up above us comes the laughter of a child, a bright pretty squeal of the stuff.

"Look at him *enjoying* this, this is so horrible!"

"Oh my God, it's still alive," someone says.

"Yeah, what's crazy is the frog is still alive," says the man, typically quick to interject the more emotionally detached factual analysis on an atrocity.

"Oh, and it's still alive!" says the woman. "Oh, you poor thing— run away, little froggie, run away!"

Of course the frog didn't make it. After my father shot his wad down the frog's throat, he peeled it off and tossed it over his shoulder like a slob does a dirty sock, and slumped himself down for a postcoital nap on the spot.

The frog wasn't dead, just maimed, violated, wounded beyond the help of modern medicine. I so vividly remember seeing that poor stupid animal staggering around, reeling, the victim of a brutal sexual assault, dragging its belly through the dirt on its weak legs, near death, pale sticky underbelly heaving in, out, sputtering, my father's jizzom dribbling from its mouth. And I was overcome with sympathy for this creature. I am no savage, Gwen. My own heart bleeds when I see pain in another. The only humane thing left to do for this frog was to put it out of its misery: and so I scooped up the ravished frog and, swinging it by the legs, mercifully bashed out what little brains it had in its frog head by whacking it against a nearby log. This coup de grâce was uncharitably misinterpreted by the humans as a mere continuation and the natural culmination of the sickening orgy of sadoerotic torture that the *Pan troglodytes* were for whatever reason enacting upon this defenseless frog. At this point I think a woman at the ledge shielded her young daughter's eyes with a hand of parental censorship.

My father, needless to say, with his cigarette-smoking and

frog-raping antics, was a local favorite among the primates at the Lincoln Park Zoo. His ill-gotten celebrity at the zoo outshone all the other residents of the Primate House, and oh God did he bask in that iniquitous limelight, the stupid narcissistic thug. They loved him at the zoo. Adored him. As I mentioned earlier, there were a few lowland gorillas living in the habitat across the hall from us, including a magisterial old silverback male whom I don't believe I ever saw engaged in any activity other than dejectedly draping his massiveness over the structures in his habitat in various attitudes of languor so bored, so hopeless that they could have only arisen from a feeling of humiliation so complete as to reduce his life of confinement and public display to a flat stretch of days full of nothing but a dull yen for the only remaining passage of escape still availed him in the bittersweet promise of death. The miracle of my fate is that I was offered my release from just such a miserable life by the salvation of language. Quite literally, I talked my way out. But you could see, you could just *see* that fat old silverback's regal eyes glistening with hatred for my father, hatred for all of Rotpeter's zany performances, all his crowd-pleasing, repulsive clowning around, the way that self-debasing popinjay would prance up and down along the length of the chimp habitat right in front of the glass, banging on the window, hooting, clapping, stomping, clacking his teeth, making silly faces, doing the hear-no-see-no-speak-no-evil routine, peeling back his wet pink pinguid pithecine lips from his gums to reveal two rows of slimy yellow teeth, and slapping his palms on his chest and generally behaving for all the world like some sort of caricature of a chimpanzee, a loathsome self-parody, thus prompting the humans to point and giggle and ooglie-mooglie at him like the slavering idiot clods they were and *oh*, did they love him, the humans, how they would point at him behaving like a moron and then remark among themselves how *human*, how eerily strikingly *human* he looked (as if that was a compliment!). Look, look,

look! Oh, honey, look at what he's doing now! How almost *human*! And all the while that lazy indignant silverback gorilla across the hall (who never attracted a crowd because he never *did* anything) seethed with the desire to come over here and kick the shit out of him for all that repulsive singing and dancing—and wishing, of course, that he was not prevented from doing so by not one but two walls of three-inch-thick glass. But my father, but Rotpeter, oh, he was a primate's primate all right, big hit with the humans: little ones, big ones, pretty ones, ugly ones, elderly and otherwise physically defective ones squeaking by in wheelchairs, handsome young couples holding hands, canoodling, pushing strollers containing *yet more* of their squiggling burbling spit-faced progeny to inherit and infest the earth and to one day, and it won't be long, survive to celebrate the deaths of the last wild animals.

My feelings about the human race are complex. I love them and I hate them. More on this later. I'm telling you all this, I think, to underline the sense of relief, the feeling of having been specially selected for salvation that I felt when Lydia came to rescue me from having to spend the rest of my life in the company of these animals.

It is probably not a coincidence that I was the lowest-ranking male in the habitat. If I had been higher up on the dominance hierarchy I might not have wanted to leave as badly. But because I was the lowest rung on the ladder, I had nowhere to go but up. Or *out*, away. I fled. I fled into the arms of the human race, into the arms of a woman.

———

There must have been an aura of angelic luminescence encircling Lydia's blond head, placed on those shoulders way up there on the very top of that long and beautiful human body. I saw her standing there in the doorway to the inside of our habitat—the door painted to disappear into the wraparound mural of the jungle scene, the door the zookeepers used to enter the habitat at feeding time. The door opened, and there stood Lydia, accompanied by one of the brownshirts. My father furtively stepped on the cigarette he'd been smoking.

"Rotpeter!" the brownshirt barked.

Rotpeter shrugged his shoulders, like, *What?*

"What have you got under your foot?"

Nothing, he shrugged.

"Don't give me that, I can smell it all over you—it stinks like a bar in here."

"You let him smoke?" said Lydia, horrified.

"God no! He learned to smoke from watching people, and now some idiots still throw him cigarettes even though we put up a sign."

"How does he light them?"

The brownshirt sighed in pained, embarrassed resignation. "He's got a lighter hidden around here somewhere."

Lydia gave the brownshirt a look that an intervening social worker might give a neglectful parent when she sees the home is cluttered with unhygienic detritus.

"Oh, you poor baby," said Lydia to me, realizing at once the shameful extent of the ugliness, the neglect and emotional abuse I had suffered in this hellhole, this prison, this degrading and dehumanizing panopticon in which I had grown up.

And she bent down to me and again held out her arms, like a saint, and she called to me:

"Come here, Bruno. Come to me."

I raced into her arms, planting kisses of gratitude on every exposed patch of that glabrous, supple, sweetly aromatic human flesh I could reach. She'd come back! Come back for me! She must love me, too!

My mother grunted at her and suspiciously licked a glob of filth off of her thumb. My mother always knew I had a thing for human girls, and strongly, *strongly* disapproved of it. Of course, it was difficult for even me to tell *precisely* what my mother was thinking because she was so disastrously inarticulate. Like most chimps, hers was a vocabulary consisting entirely of signs—grunts, gestures, noises, postures, faces, and so on—signifiers with amoebic and inconstant sets of signifieds depending entirely upon the ephemeral context of the immediately present moment. She had in her communicative arsenal not one thing that could truly be called a word, which I think of as a sort of compact ball of signification—the use of which can change depending on the situation, but the meaning of which is firmer and less psychologically elastic than a nonlinguistic sign. Yes, conversations between chimps certainly do occur, thoughts of a certain sort are indeed communicated between them, but it would be absolutely impossible to translate them into human language, because these nonlingual conversations occur outside the sphere of activity that is capturable by the tools of the text; these communications happen entirely within the Theatre of Cruelty, within the realm that is ineffable, a dreamlike mode of communication halfway between thought and gesture, based not in words but in mentality and physicality, in the raw language of the nonsymbolic sign.

IV

I suppose the time to divulge the nature of my earliest sexual stirrings is now, Gwen. I had not yet come into full sexual maturity at this time. As I said, I think I was about six years old. Chimps—especially those in captivity—reach puberty at a younger age than humans. I was an unusual case. I always have been.

The other chimps in the zoo were perfectly content to mate among their own species—it seemed only natural; I don't think any of them really even gave it any serious thought. But even my earliest sexual proclivities lay elsewhere. My father couldn't have cared less, but I believe my mother found this—in her view—*perversion* of mine deeply disturbing.

There was only one female chimp close to my age living in the habitat: little Céleste. I will describe Céleste for you carefully, because she played an important part both in the development of my early consciousness and in landing me in my current situation. I gather that it was hotly anticipated and hotly hoped among the zoo management that either I or else my elder brother, Cookie, would one day couple with Céleste and impregnate her, thereby furnishing the Lincoln Park Zoo with additional chimps. Céleste was acquired from the Indianapolis Zoo when she was two years old and given to our poor aunt, who was as barren as Sarah, to raise as her own. (Keeping us apart for the first two years was a bulwark against the Westermarck effect, so that one day we might find each other sexually appetizing, as we had not been desensitized in early childhood to one another's pheromones.) So Céleste was introduced to me when she was two years old, and I was three and a half.

Céleste never particularly bonded with Cookie, who was about eight years old at the time and much bigger than us, and was habitually boorish, brutal, and crude with her (Cookie took after our father in all the worst ways); but Céleste and I developed an adamantine emotional bond, a connection, primitive and deep, that needed no words to express it and needed none to understand. We often cuddled together in a warm tangle of slender hairy limbs, and, our two hearts, each the size of an avocado pit, beating softly in unison within a physical proximity of mere centimeters and our lazy young brains dopey with the natural tranquilizers of childhood love, we would fall asleep, in a nest of rushes, in a hot band of Chicago sunlight streaming through the window. Together, Céleste and I sweetly aped the bonding activities that we saw the grown-ups performing: with her fingers she would delicately pick the bugs and crumbs and weeds out of the fur on my back, and then she would turn around and let me do likewise unto her. We explored every inch of our habitat, Céleste and I, together we overturned everything in it that could be overturned, our young minds' cups brimming over with environmental stimuli, the mysteries of existence rushing headlong into our eager consciousnesses.

I will relate one brief incident from my early childhood with Céleste, one of the few definite memories from this time in my prelinguistic life that I still carry with me, secreted away somewhere deep in the squiggly crevices of my tender electric brainflesh. I was playing with Céleste. We were playing with a hat. I don't know how it got into our habitat in the first place—it must have come in the same way as the frog, these curiosities, these artifacts from the outside world that accidentally wandered in to become such important semantemes in the early development of my consciousness. Most likely the wind had blown this hat off of the head of a zoogoer, across the moat, and into our habitat—this being the one American city to claim the apropos moniker of "the Windy." But this hat—I now realize, as I reconstruct the memory knowing what I now know—was a woman's hat, a woman's sun hat. It was beige, wide-brimmed, shallow-crowned and flat, made of straw—tightly woven slats of thin shiny straw. It was festive, festooned with a wide band of diaphanous silk on which was printed a design of blue and red and purple flowers, which wrapped around the crown of the hat and was secured in place with a bow. Perhaps at the time Céleste and I imagined—as I now imagine—that this hat had previously lived on top of the head of a beautiful woman. There were even—as I recall—a few long threads of human hair caught in the interstices of the hat's weave, possibly red hair, almost invisible except upon close viewing, sleek and strong, as long as my forearm and well-nigh impossible to break with the hands. This hat was a magical object to us, a portent from the gods lying on the ground: beautiful, weird, otherworldly, bright.

Two young chimps, looking at a hat lying on the grass of their habitat. One, Céleste, the younger, is smaller with very dark fur, and her big ears stick far out of her head like wingflaps. The other, Bruno, the elder, has lighter and coarser reddish fur that he has inherited from Red Peter, his father, and smaller ears that lay flatter against the sides of his head. Both of them have the round heads and snowy beard-tufts of preadolescence.

At first we were a little afraid of it. What is this thing? Whence did it come? We look up—we cast our humble gazes upon the foreboding thing we have seen every day of our brief existences: the

Wall. Massive, starkly unadorned and unreachable, the cold, gray, steeply sloping bowl of concrete, over and beyond which lies the unknown part of the universe. This must have come from beyond the Wall, a place purported to exist, but for which we have as yet no a priori proof. The only things we know exist are the ones we see marching past the Wall. Are they the things of this world, or only their shadows? We don't know. But the hat: this is no shadow of a hat, this is a hat itself. Only we do not know that it is called "hat." We do not know what it is. We do not know what it does. Is it friend or foe? For a while we observe the hat from a safe distance. Then I, the young Bruno—who at this point is simply another baby chimp of no particularly remarkable genius—warily approach the thing. A hand reaches out, followed by a thin hirsute arm—to touch it. I only barely brush the edge of the object with the tips of my fingers, and reflexively jerk my hand back at once. Wait!... It did me no harm, no harm. Tentatively, tentatively, the hand reaches out to touch it again. The hand makes contact, and there it remains. Emboldened, I go so far as to pick it up. Céleste approaches now. She places her head on my right shoulder, looks on at the thing, which is now in my hands—my God!—it's so light, nearly effortless to lift. Céleste puts her hand on the brim of the hat. We touch it together, peacefully, we explorers, we two little scientists, we run our fingers along its contours, its edges, its angles, its convexities and concavities, feeling its texture, the taut bouncy waxen feeling of the tightly woven lacquered straw, the smooth and delicate feeling of the silken hatband, bespangled with the images of blue and red and purple flowers.

There was probably, as these episodes tend to go, a cluster of humans gathered by now at the ledge of the Wall, snapping their photographs, pointing at us and swooning with remarks about the adorableness of our behavior toward the hat. As my attentions at the moment were directed far, far elsewhere, I cannot recall if anyone noticed us or not, but if they did, Céleste and I paid them no heed. And it was Céleste, Céleste who discovered what the thing was, in the human sense, "for": she was putting various parts of her body into the bowl of the hat, until finally she put the top of her head into it, and when she removed her hands the hat remained there of its own accord. I gasped—in shock and laughter, I gasped at the sight of Céleste "wearing" the hat, and pointed, and collapsed onto the ground in paroxysms of mirth.

Collecting myself, I removed the hat from her head and put it in like manner on mine—partly, I admit, out of jealousy, and partly in order to demonstrate to her what someone looked like underneath the object, which produced similar fits of laughter in her. We passed the hat back and forth in this way many times, by turns reducing one another to helpless jellies of giggling. Unfortunately this show we were creating attracted the attention of Cookie, my mangy philistine of an older brother, my bully, the big hairy Esau to my crafty little Jacob, three years my senior and already nearly as big as an adult, who lumbered up to us and snatched the hat from our young hands. Céleste and I howled our protestations. He would not give it back, would not play along. He bore the thing no special love, nor even curiosity: he did not wish us to have it merely because he saw that it gave us joy. Yes, he touched it, too, he too put it on his head, but I am certain that the subtleties of its beauty were lost on him. He scoffed at the femininity of the article. I tried to seize it from him; he pushed me down. This enraged me. He ran away with the hat and we immediately gave chase, she first and I clambering to my feet and hands to follow. In this way the squabble erupted into a full-on disruptive spectacle, with all three of us stumbling and raging pell-mell and helter-skelter over the logs and trees and rope-swings and other primitive furnishings of our habitat, hooting and shrieking, a whirlwind of hairy brown limbs, an ecstasy of fumbling, one body fleeing and two in pursuit. The humans may have thought we were "playing." Maybe Cookie was, but Céleste and I were in dead fucking earnest. The chase ended only when Rotpeter—the Alpha Male and sole gubernative power over our pitifully tiny civilization, our sovereign, our law-giver and enforcer, our Draco, Solon, Hammurabi and Caesar, oh you Leviathan, you, Rotpeter, you petty patriarch—dropped down from a tree and interpolated himself between us. And what did this microcosmic Ozymandias do? First he snatched the hat away from his eldest son, who, trembling before the greater authority, fell back. Then Rotpeter briefly and unceremoniously examined the hat, snorted his disapproval, and, determining that he could nei-ther smoke it nor fuck it and therefore had little reason to tolerate its continuing to exist, with feet, fists, fingers, and teeth he beat, ripped, tore, and chewed it, right before our eyes, to shreds. We, the children, wept in anguish.

Rotpeter decimated that hat and disseminated the loose scraps of straw until they were indistinguishable from the rest of the offal strewn about the floor of our habitat, and the hatband of diaph-anous silk, bespangled with blue and red and purple flowers, he spent the rest of the day munching and sucking on until it disap-peared inside him, though tattered remnants of it later reappeared in his black and steaming globes of stool.

But I promised to speak of sex.

So then, damn the torpedoes and full Freud ahead: my mother. The same people who would later claim responsibility for my case—even though it was actually only Lydia, all Lydia, and me, just us, all the others really had very little to do with it (but these are outrages and injustices I will discuss in greater detail later)—these same people, the researchers at the Behavioral Biology Laboratory at the University of Chicago's Institute for Mind and Biology, once tried to teach my poor stupid mother a little sign language. It was a bust, a miserable failure. The spirit of language thrived not in her.

They were able to trick her, through some elementary-level Skinnerian operant conditioning, into making a few signs of ASL; her entire active vocabulary made possible but a single mandative sentence, which, feebly enacted on her part and loosely interpreted on theirs, amounted to: "Give [me] *that!*" (The second word being implied and the last a vigorous waving in the general direction of the coveted object.) It was impressive that they were able to teach her even that. This is how I remember my mother. I see her lazing in the cradle of a certain hammock in our habitat in which she was wont to laze. This hammock is made of thin brown ropes diagonally knotted together to form a pattern of many diamonds. One end of the hammock is secured around the limb of a tree, and the other around the sturdy wooden post of a jungle-gym-like structure. When my mother lazes in it, the bottom of the hammock sags until it is only an inch or two above the ground at the lowest point; when she is not lazing in it, the hammock contains the phantom of her presence, and in the part of the hammock where she puts most of her weight the diamonds are loose and stretched, warped and misshapen. In my memory of my mother, in the eidetic image of her that my brain projects onto the screen of my inner eyelids when I close them and work to recall her, she is lazing in this hammock. In her lap is a baby chimpanzee, less than a year old, looking much like a human infant only much more hirsute. This baby chimpanzee is me. (Does it seem incongruous to you that I should make an appearance in my own childhood memory? The eyes of the mind can easily leave the body—how else would you know your double when you meet him in a dream?) My mother strokes her long purple fingers through the thin fur on my head. Her eyes glisten with love and awe in the way the eyes of any mother of any species glisten with love and awe. (With the possible exceptions of guppies and hamsters and other ridiculous animals who spawn a teeming cloud or pile of offspring and then immediately eat most of them.)

My mother kisses the top of my head. The folds of her body, in which I am half-enveloped, are warm and comforting. The love between these creatures, between the mother and the infant, is entirely without words, and needs none to explain it. I loved her. In a strange way, I love her still, and there's the rub. There's so much I would like to tell her, but I have entirely forgotten the wordless vocabulary of my animal innocence.

Have you ever read *Paradise Lost*, Gwen? I stumbled across a battered copy of it in the course of my wanderings across this blighted earth, by which I mean I once stole a copy of it from the University of Chicago library. And God, did I fall in love with the Devil. Could it be more fitting that Lucifer is a master orator? Demonic rhetoric, Satanic language!

I have heard, Gwen—spoken, as can be expected, in tones of dreary admonition—that self-authorship is the bourgeois fantasy par excellence, as in Milton's Satan: "Who saw when this creation was?...We know no time when we were not as now, know none before us, self-begot, self-raised." But why condemn the rebel angel for the fantasy of self-invention? Who could help feeling seduced by Satan's poetry when compared to the dull, paternalistically castigatory abashments of God? As Blake points out, the reason Milton wrote in fetters when he wrote of Angels & God, and at liberty when of Devils & Hell, is because he was a true Poet and of the Devil's party without knowing it. Well, I too am a true poet, but unlike Milton and more like Satan, I know it! And also like Satan, I made myself with words. I wrote myself into the world. With my own hand I reached into the cunt of the cosmos and dragged myself kicking and screaming out—HELLO, WORLD. HELLO, YOU BASTARDS. HERE I AM. IT'S ME, BRUNO, THE BOURGEOIS APE.

(And also like Satan, I'm a beautiful loser.)

It is impossible, however, to write a poem, or anything for that matter, about an unfallen Adam and Eve, because I cannot imagine them as having language. In Paradise there is nothing to say. Eden was sacrificed not for the pleasure of a fruit, but for the pleasure of the word. Now we have shame and pain and knowledge of death and whatnot, but at least we can talk about it. And talk and talk and talk! And maybe—I think—maybe it was even worth the trade. Sometimes the things of this world are less beautiful than their shadows. What is poetry but the shadowplay of consciousness?

But wait, Gwen—wait! I have just recalled that there is another important memory of my mother, buried somewhere deep in the bedrock of my brain, which resurfaces sometimes in my dreams: an extremely vague memory of accompanying my mother to the laboratory. Look: the clouds of forgetfulness are pulling apart! What lies behind them? Shine forth, my memory, show us the truth. Was it the same laboratory where I would later be experimented on? No, it couldn't be. It didn't look the same. It was a different room. The lighting was different. I remember a strong yellow tint to the room. Was it the floor? The tiles must have been yellow. I was an infant; I was probably in a position to observe the floor more closely than other aspects of the room. How did I get there? How old am I? Look at me!—you could almost fit me in the palm of your hand, I must be only a month or two old. There are others there with us, humans, scientists—as always, scientists.... They're not in the same room with us, though. They're crowded together just outside a glass wall. We can see them, and we can hear them through holes in the glass. They're speaking to my mother. She isn't even curious about what they're saying. But I am. I remember my urgent curiosity, I remember listening to the burbling waves of vocalization streaming from the mouths of the humans. Their faces are all indistinct in my memory. Mostly I'm looking at their legs. Their pants, the workaday shoes they wear to the lab, the flapping tails of their thin white coats. There is a strange sort of machine in the room—*that* I recall clearly. A computer—that's what it must have been. There is a kind of platform with a padded surface in front of the computer, where my mother sits and attempts to manipulate the machine. There is a screen in it, and a long plastic tube coming out of the side of it that spits treats into a shallow plastic tray bolted to the bottom of the computer screen. To me it is a fascinating, alien curiosity, a thing of signs and wonders. Certain images appear and disappear on the screen, weird hieroglyphic emblems throbbing with artificial light. My mother clumsily touches the things that appear on the screen, and sometimes a computerized female voice utters some magic word in response, and then sometimes the symbols touched will disappear, and sometimes a peanut encased in a colorful shell of hard chocolate rolls happily through the narrow plastic tube in the side of the machine and lands *click-rattle* in the plastic tray, and my mother greedily snatches it from the tray and inserts the sweet little reward into her cheeks, and commences immediately to touch the screen again, hoping for another. She never gave me any of her food rewards. To my mother it must have simply been some glowing totemic god-in-a-box that chose to distribute peanut M&Ms at times according only to the dictate of its unknowable whimsy. My mother was a creature of such intellectual poverty, I'm sure she was doing little else besides randomly punching the screen and praying for her chocolate-covered peanuts. Meanwhile, when she wasn't cradling me in her arms while touching the screen, I, Bruno, was permitted to bumble around on the floor of the lab, playing with various objects that the scientists had strewn around to distract my attention while they performed experiments on my mother. How many times did this scene occur? I haven't a clue. I was so young, I barely remember. I cannot remember if what I just described is a unique memory of a particular event, or a patchwork of many different memories of many similar events that occurred over a prolonged period of time. In hindsight, it must be the latter. I remember the babble of the scientists all around me in the room. I remember a certain rubber ball that I played with while my mother was busy pathetically flunking test after test. The ball was blue, with a yellow stripe in the middle bisected in the exact center by a narrower red stripe. I remember the artificial and oddly intoxicating gluey rubbery smell of the ball. I remember enjoying these visits. I remember sitting in my mother's warm soft lap as she punched the colorful glowing screen over and over, trying to coax peanut M&Ms from the frivolous demon in the wall. I remember listening to the people talking, trying to discern the mechanics of this weird world to which I was a newcomer, a foreigner, a stranger. I remember feeling myself being wrapped in the soft blanket of their babble. I remember—very, very vaguely—I remember even beginning to feel at home with the sinuous ribbonlike rhythms of human conversation fluttering in and out of my ears, trickling like cool water over the smooth stone of my brain, carving designs into my infantile and infinitely malleable consciousness.

My soul then was a thing of darkness, naked and devoid of form.

I remember this so vaguely that I'm not even sure whether I'm remembering it or making it up. But there it is, Gwen, you may have it.

But as for the earliest warning signs of my sexual perversion? Let's talk about love. I felt love for my mother. I felt love for Céleste. But was there anything at all erotic in these loves? Did I feel anything remotely Oedipal in my biological mother's warm, soft, stupid lap? Was there even the slightest tingle of preadolescent sexuality in my close bond with Céleste? No. No, no, *no*, absolutely not. Now, I do not assert this because I'm an anti-Freudian; I only assert this because my childhood was not innocent of sexual longings. In fact, I was obsessed with the sexual side of things, the coital, the carnal, the warm creamy slippery fucking fuckal. From an abnormally, maybe even unhealthfully precocious age I was inwardly consumed with a fierce, insane, insatiable lust that was always rushing and crackling its way through my soul like a match held to a pile of dry straw.

I never felt—even very early on—I never felt like I quite belonged to the same species as my mother or Céleste. I loved Céleste, but I did not lust after her. I did not lust after her because she was a chimp. My erotic desires lay elsewhere, yes, even then. For years in the course of my early development I kept my burgeoning desires secret. Or at least I thought I did. In retrospect, surely my mother knew. She could see something in the way I watched the human women just beyond the glass wall or above the ledge of the greater wall—*the* Wall—some bright animus thrashing like an electric snake in the pits of my eyes that was more than just the chaste fascination of the amateur anthropologist. For fascinated indeed was I by their forms—but it was a fascination mingled in with the surging juices of young lust. And why *should* I have been, why should I ever have been sexually attracted to other chimps? By the time I was six years old I had seen thousands and thousands and maybe I don't know *millions* of human beings, I had practically become an *aficionado*, a *connoisseur* of the human form, I noticed all their interesting differences in size, shape, texture, tone, style—upon seeing a human for the first time I immediately remarked to myself upon that particular human's differentiating characteristics, height, heft, age, color, and sex, and if the sex was female then boy oh boy did I notice so much more!

When did my love of Céleste become tainted with physical revulsion? I'd seen Céleste scrounge parasites out of her fur and *eat* them! Am I expected to be attracted to a girl of such grotesque manners? Hell, she eats *my* parasites! But wait!—*I* do that, too! They're good! No! *No!* Go ahead and eat your own delicious goddamn parasites, Céleste, but Bruno's moving up in the world!—even if it means leaving you—even if I do, in a very primitive and uncomplicated way, love you. Female chimps—when they're in estrus their ugly plump vulvae inflate and swell out behind them, and they drag around these bloated pink balloons of flesh between their legs as they walk, their sphincters oftentimes plugged with repugnant globs of partially excreted shit. And those flat gray mealy breasts and protruding bellies and rangy hairy bodies and bald heads and scrunched-up noses? No, I'm sorry. It's true, I am a deviant and depraved pervert: I have no desire to have sex with other chimps. But look—*look!*—look at all those *human* girls we see sashaying in all their anthropic glory past the Wall all day: all that long hair growing insanely out of the tops of their heads, those nearly hairless lower bodies propelled bipedally forward on those powerful, columnar legs, those massive round breasts so absurdly disproportionate to their bodies! So, as my father was loping around the habitat indiscriminately screwing any moist sluice he could find—my mother, my aunt, a *frog* for God's sake—I had always been secretly pining for humans, longing to someday get to slither between the legs of those dazzling *sapiens sapienettes* I saw clip-clocking past me all day in those high-heeled shoes that make their calves taut and thrust their beautiful bulbous asses up, up, up in the air, just a little closer to God, like a streaming buffet of delicious desserts on display for Bruno behind impenetrably thick glass, to be admired but not to be touched.

Do I digress? Very well, then, I digress. I am large, I contain multitudes.

So there was Lydia, standing in the doorway of our habitat, bending to the ground and beckoning to me with her arms—so pink and smooth and fragrant—and into these arms I scrambled, and wrapped my hairy self around her neck, rested my head in the crook of her shoulder, and tossed a last parting glance upon my family as she took me away. And Lydia held my hand and guided me through the first chapters of Bruno's bildungsroman, the journey into manhood my life has been ever since. I did not bid good-bye to my mother, I did not bid good-bye to my brother, I did not bid good-bye to my father, and I did not even bid good-bye to Céleste. Instead, I went with Lydia. I went with the human. I went with love, I went with lust, I went with language. I went with Lydia.

V

Hello, Gwen. This will probably be a brief session, I'm feeling moody and ill at ease today. We've only got twelve days to go before our performance of *Woyzeck*, and I fear my actors are still woefully unprepared. I was forced to make some criminally drastic cuts in the script owing to the fact that most of my actors cannot speak. Leon has volunteered to play the role of the Doctor whose psychological experiments drive the beleaguered Woyzeck deeper into madness, and I have convinced Sally—the assistant researcher who works part-time here at the research center on Mondays, Wednesdays, and Fridays—to play Marie, the widow whom I, Woyzeck, murder in a fit of jealous rage at the climax of the play. The problem with Sally, though, is that although her verbal faculties are superb, her memory is not, and she's prone to forget her lines, to say nothing of the fact that her acting is forced and wooden. Her delivery is off and her timing is bad even when she does remember her lines. All the other parts will have to be played by chimps, none of whom can speak a word of English, though a few of them can make a crude handful of ASL signs. Damn it, they're *impossible* to work with. The researchers(-slash-wardens) who keep and study me patiently suffer the whims of my artistic genius, but all they really want me to do is help them teach language to the other chimps—a task I find fundamentally boring and depressing. Being a scientific anomaly is such a burden, Gwen, I can't even begin to tell you. I've spent so much of my life in starkly decorated cool white rooms from which escape is impossible. Why are laboratories always so uncomfortable? Always the same sepulchral décor, the same blue-green glass and concrete floors and whitewashed walls, the same ever-present ambient murmur of computers and fluorescent lights and air-conditioning. So of course I appreciate that they have allowed me to more or less furnish my own modest chambers according to my own taste. This couch we're sitting on is my own. That is *my* coffee table, those are *my* books, and that's my painting on the wall there.

When Leon was here yesterday he tried to smuggle in a bottle of Scotch for me. He was found out, the bottle was confiscated, and now poor Leon is severely on the outs with the management— which is infuriating, ludicrous. Is this a primatology research center that I'm in, or rehab? Sometimes I can't tell. I detest being treated like a prisoner. There are times, Gwen, when I'm on one of my Thoreauvian walks in the woods—never unsupervised, even if the scientist charged as my chaperone respectfully gives me my distance—there are times when I'm walking in these woods, when I come to the very perimeter of the premises, where there is a twenty-foot-high chain-link fence forebodingly topped with a coil of concertina wire. The chain links of the fence mesh with the branches of the pine trees just beyond them to create dazzling moiré effects in certain light—at sundown, for instance. And sometimes I peer past the fence, through the many diamonds of negative space between the metal links, at the small patch of world that lies beyond it: beyond the fence are trees both coniferous and deciduous, bushes, ferns, and even a few palm trees to serve as taunting evidence of my proximity to the ocean, which is a sight I hold to be beautiful and darkly mysterious. Farther yet, beyond all this vegetation, clearly visible through the leaves and the branches, is a narrow paved road. A road, Gwen. Flat gray asphalt cut down the center by a dashed yellow line into two lanes, coming and going, vein and artery. Beside the road, negative parabolas of wire droop from one wooden cross to the next. Sometimes there are blackbirds sitting on the long bights of wire. I'm going to confess something to you, Gwen, and you must never repeat it to anyone, lest I lose even more of my circumscribed freedom. Sometimes I wonder how quickly I might be able to scramble up that chain-link fence before I'm found out. I wonder how badly I might injure myself on that coil of concertina wire on my way over the top of the fence. I wonder at what vertical point on the other side of the fence it would be safe to let go and brace myself for the fall. I wonder where that road leads to, in either direction. I wonder if I would be able to hitch a ride with a passing motorist. I wonder all of these things, Gwen, when I see the birds and the road and the blue expanse of sky above it, and then I see a twenty-foot-high fence separating me from all of that, and I yearn to rejoin that foul and miserable and dark and disgusting world that hurt me so badly—all in spite of the fact that I have everything I could ever need right in here. There is my confession, Gwen. It is a sin not of deed, nor even word, but of thought, of the mind, of the heart, of *delectatio morosa*, of restlessness, of ingratitude, of hatefulness, of yearning for what I have not got, of desire.

———

Now we should return to my biography. I suppose at the time I did not realize I was bidding forever good-bye to my biological family. All I knew at this moment was that the only thing I ever really wanted was finally happening.

I held on to Lydia. My arms were wrapped around her neck and my face was planted against the warm sticky skin of the area of her body where her neck sloped into her shoulder, she with one arm supporting my hindquarters and one hand rubbing the fur on the top of my head as she carried me. Dr. Lydia Littlemore was wearing a short-sleeved, red-checked gingham shirt tucked into her jeans, and her blond hair was in a ponytail. I hooked the opposable toe of my right foot in the breast pocket of her shirt. The zookeeper followed us with a set of keys as Lydia carried me through the dank pissy hallways of the managerial part of the Lincoln Park Zoo Primate House, brought me to a small holding and storage room, and locked me in a little cage with a handle on it for transport. This cage was an unpleasant thing, made of hard gray plastic outfitted with a metal grate for a door and a flap of sodden carpeting on the floor. Lydia wriggled her fingers through the squares of the grate, and smiled broadly and brightly at me with her face just a few inches past the door and her eyes meeting mine, in order to reassure me, I think, that I was not in trouble and not in danger, that this was only a temporary measure and I would soon be released. From my peripherally limited vantage inside the cage, I saw the world through a grid, changing from murky interior lighting to the comparatively blinding outdoors, although the weather was overcast. It was a warm wet summer day. Rain clouds loomed. The sky was a sheet of hammered iron, the sun a white blur. Lydia wedged my cage into the backseat of a car and closed the door. I saw the side of the back door of the car and a sliver of the window. I heard the sound of a car door opening, something going *bing bing bing bing*, the door slamming, keys entering the ignition. The radio came on and she turned down the dial until it was nearly silent. Keys turned, the engine went *chuppita-chuppita-FROOM!*, a seat belt was buckled, the wheels loosened from a parked state into a state of motion. Then the perturbing sensation of movement, me sliding around inside the cage with the dips and turns in the road, the whoosh of other cars Dopplering past us. The clouds broke into rain, and the rain thrummed on the roof of the car in a pulsing tattoo, like loose-flung fistfuls of crackling pebbles. I listened to the steadily rhythmic rubber-on-glass squealing of the windshield wipers. After a while we came to our final stop, and I heard Lydia unbuckle her seat belt, withdraw the car keys, and open the door, then the spatter and crash of rain outside, the door slamming, and I saw the door in front of me open. I saw that the down-gushing rain had already darkened the fabric of her shirt, glued it to her flesh. She had no umbrella. I could see her brassiere through her shirt. I saw the rain glaze her skin. I saw her arms reach out to remove the cage. She carried me through a parking lot. I pressed my face to the grate and clung to it with my fingers. I saw cars parked in obedient rows, rainwater steaming on the hot black asphalt. It wasn't night, but the storm's sudden darkening of the day had triggered the streetlights, whose orange glows were mirrored in the shimmering street. We ascended a series of steps, and Lydia set my cage down while she opened a heavy door and propped it by kicking a wooden wedge under it. The rain plitted through the spaces in the grate of my cage, and the fetid flap of carpet I was sitting on began to smell worse. I stuck my tongue out to catch the thin needles of rain. I became wet. A moment later I felt myself being hoisted up again and taken inside the building. The heavy door sighed shut behind us and the atmosphere immediately became clean and quiet and dry, though the halls were noisy with the echoes of pounding rain-drops. Lydia carried me through a labyrinthine network of bright hallways. Her wet sneakers scrunch-scrunch-scrunched on the floors. She stopped before two metal doors in which I saw our fuzzy reflection, and it scrolled open onto a tiny metal room. We got in and she put me on the floor, pushed a button, and the doors closed. Then a bizarre swooping sensation in my interior organs. *Bing*, the doors opened, she lifted my cage again and took me down another passageway, scrunch-scrunch-scrunch, until we arrived at another door, with a series of symbols printed across a smoked-glass window,

which I would much later learn spelled: 308 BEHAVIORAL BIOLOGY
LABORATORY. In we went. Lydia knelt on the floor and unlatched my
cage, and as the door opened I tumbled out. She picked me up. She
smiled, she kissed my head. Lydia was drenched, trinkets of water
dappling her face, her blond hair dark, sopping, and flaccid.

We were inside a clean, bright, spacious room, furnished with
several islands of long rectangular tables, on which sat computers and other kinds of lab equipment. The room was made of four
whitewashed walls, two of which featured whiteboards all scrawled
over with shapes and symbols in red, green, and black marker, and
two of which featured wide tall windows that could not be opened.
The echoes of rain crackling and drumming on the roof warbled
around in the big room, and waves of water chased each other down
the sides of the windows, warping the view of what lay outside the
building, which involved an expanse of green grass and several
trees. One of the long tables was pushed against a wall, and on it sat
a large cage fashioned from thin metal bars. The floor was of shiny
salmon-pink vinyl tile. A big blue squishy mat lay in one corner of
the room, on which was scattered a collection of brightly colored
toys. Voices conversed; wet sneakers scrunched and squeaked; white
fluorescent lights buzzed overhead and cast rectangular reflections
on the shiny floor; human bodies moved around in the space. I
realized that I had been in this room before.

There were other humans in the room. They crowded around
to have a look at me. Lydia introduced me to a man whom I recognized from the day of the peaches. She took my rubbery little hand
and held it out to him for a mock handshake, and the man gently
smothered it in the hot flesh of his own fat hand and smiled.

"Bruno," said Lydia, "this is Norm. I believe you two have met
each other before. Norm is the director of the Behavioral Biology
Lab. Norm is a very smart man."

"Hello, Bruno," said Norm, as he relinquished my hand to me.

"It's an extraordinary pleasure to meet you. Do you remember me from our peaches experiment?"

I proffered him no reply.

"You showed us that day that you are a very interesting little guy, Bruno. You just might be a very important chimp."

He smiled at Lydia and she smiled brightly back. I saw something in this exchange of faces between them that I did not like. Lydia took off her glasses and tucked a strand of hair behind her ear.

This man was Dr. Norman Plumlee. Remember that name. He was taller than Lydia but not by much, and I think he was in his late forties at the time. His face was porcine and buttery, the top of his head shiny and bald. Curly salt-and-pepper hair, more salt than pepper, wrapped around the back and sides of his head and curled over the ears into a kempt and understated beard that traced the edges of his jaw and encircled his mouth and looked like a crust of burnt toast. Unstylish glasses clamped the sides of his bulbous nose and unnaturally magnified his brown eyes, and when he raised his thick eyebrows he compressed the skin of his forehead into deep-creased strata, making his forehead look like a stack of flapjacks. His hands were thick and his fingers resembled sausages. He was overweight but not what I'd call fat. He spoke with a faint trace of an accent; I would later learn that there is a country called England, and that this man hailed from it. This meant that he incongruously added *h*'s to words that don't have them and took *h*'s away from other words that do, many of his *r*'s became "ahs," and when asking a question the pitch of his voice went *up-up-UP-down?* instead of *up-up-UP?*

There were several other humans present besides Lydia Littlemore and Norman Plumlee who were introduced to me in turn. Andrea was a young woman with a buoyant mop of flame-red hair, her nose the epicenter of an explosion of rusty freckles. Prasad was a small and middle-aged dark-skinned bald man with glasses. Jake was a lean and energetic young man with pallid skin and sandy hair. I was passed from one pair of arms to another, from one body to the next. All of them held me and played with me and spoke to me, but I was wiggly and impatient in the arms of anyone but Lydia.

People said things I failed to understand. Information was communicated—things were said that produced thoughtful expressions, things were said that produced ripples of laughter—but I didn't get any of the jokes; it was all glossolalia to me. My understanding of language was so inchoate that the only words I managed to pick out of their fog of babble were my own name and Lydia's. I don't believe anyone began any serious attempts to instruct me on that first day in the lab. I wasn't yet sure whether I would stay here or if I would be immediately returned to my family and the only home I had ever known in the Primate House of the Lincoln Park Zoo.

In any event my memory from this period is jumbled. I can't recall what happened in exactly what order. I know that in a certain corner of the room there lay, as I mentioned earlier, a big blue squishy mat, of a slightly sticky texture, which I presume had been so placed on the cold hard floor in order to provide me with a pleasant place to sit, and on this mat lay an assortment of toys. I will catalog, as I remember them, Bruno's first toys.

I remember a device consisting of two wooden stands connected by a series of parallel metal rods, each arranged equidistantly from the next in a lateral row, with brightly colored beads strung along the rods that could be pushed in either direction. This I would later learn was called an abacus. I remember a large soft ball made of red rubber that could easily be squeezed, rolled, thrown, or bounced. I remember a device shaped like a giant bowling pin, painted to resemble an animate being. The being wore a blue suit and a horror-stricken expression—a gaping mouth and eyes stretched wide in fear—and seemed to be holding a piece of paper in front of his torso, on which was a clumsy drawing—which the being himself had presumably drawn—of a crude blue circle encircling a red dot, making a target. One could effortlessly push the being over, but he would always spring back up, recalcitrant, returning at once to an upright position. I remember a complex device made of brilliant green plastic: it was shaped roughly like a cloverleaf, with four prongs sticking out of a central hub, which featured several rows of tiny holes that made strange noises when the device was being operated; at the end of each of the four prongs was a larger hole. This device came with a hammer made of brown plastic, designed to mimic the look—but not the feeling—of a mallet fashioned of coarsely grained wood. During play, a brown plastic creature would emerge from one of the four holes. The creature looked like a brown lump and had eyes and a nose and a mouth from which two white square teeth exuded, and it wore a little red mining helmet with a headlamp on the front. When one smote the creature with the faux-wooden plastic hammer, it would vanish into the bowels of the machine, only to be replaced immediately by another creature, similar but not identical, from another hole. Each of the brown lump-creatures had a distinct personality: one was clearly a "nerd," with glasses and a timid expression; one was female, with lipstick and long eyelashes; and one was a mentally deficient brown lump who wore his mining helmet backward. You could smite these creatures with the plastic hammer all you pleased, but another would always rise up, Hydra-like, to take the place of the last. The pattern, if there was one, was wildly unpredictable, and this process continued ad infinitum or until the smiter grew weary of smiting. This device I would later learn was called a Whack-a-Mole system, because the brown plastic lumps represented the subterranean animals, moles (hence the mining helmets), and the holes represented mole holes.

These and other such objects lay on the squishy blue mat in the corner of the room. I was encouraged to manipulate them—and manipulate them I did—in a zealous frenzy—in feverish abandon.

VI

But there is also another, chillier memory from that day embedded limpidly in my brain. It surely occurred on that first day; I don't see how it could have not. The afternoon had passed, the rain had ceased, and I had been out of confinement—relatively speaking—all day, playing, interacting with the humans, exploring the laboratory. And the human beings one by one began to exit the room and not come back. They exchanged words with one another, and as each human left, he or she would make a certain utterance and perform a certain physical sign that I guessed to be a gesture signaling polite departure: to hold up a hand and move it around. Different people performed this sign in different ways, but it was always interpreted as containing more or less the same meaning: "I am about to leave and not return, but do not worry, I am not upset with you." As each of the humans left they made a variation on this sign, and it was answered in kind by the other humans still remaining in the room. Most signs, I've noticed, that any animal makes one can basically group into two archcategories: *I mean harm*, or *I mean no harm*.

The first to leave was the lean and energetic young man with sandy-colored hair who had been introduced to me as Jake. He signaled his parting by slinging a rucksack over one shoulder, hooking one thumb under the strap, and using his free hand to gesture: he held out the hand with an open palm and fingers widely spaced, jerked it once to one side and left the hand in this position until the other humans acknowledged it with similar gestures, though some of them would acknowledge it merely by making a certain facial expression that was sometimes—though not always—accompanied with a deft dipping-down-and-then-up of the head, which I later came to know as a "nod," a common human signal that can mean either an affirmative answer to a binary question or a no-harm sign—its opposite being a side-to-side movement of the head, which is called a "shake." Vertical—yes—nod; horizontal—no—shake: these were some of the earliest signs I learned. Even though each human made the sign in a different way it was always interpreted identically, which told me that this sign enjoyed a certain marginal plasticity of process that allowed for the insertion of the signer's personal style. The flame-haired Andrea, for instance, made this sign in a manner that I later came to understand is considered more feminine: by bringing one hand close to her body, and, palm-out, thumb more or less stationary, flapping her four fingers up and down repeatedly while using her face to smile. Prasad, the dark-skinned and bespectacled man, made his egress while gesturing so subtly that his sign was nearly invisible, but his leaving was still perceived as benign. The form of these hand gestures appeared to be so wildly disparate dependent upon the gesturer that the only thing cluing me in to the fact that they essentially all had the same meaning was the fact that each provoked the same interpretation. This gesture was, of course, a "wave." This too I learned quickly. It is really astonishing how far a communicative arsenal consisting only of a nod, a shake, and a wave can carry you; with these three signs you can say to anyone *yes, no, harm, no harm, hello,* and *good-bye.* Add to these the smile, the frown, and the finger point, and you're practically already in basic-human-social-interaction business.

And then a thing of terror happened. The only humans remaining in the room now were Norman Plumlee and Lydia. While Plumlee was busying himself with some end-of-day chores, Lydia picked me up from the surface of the squishy blue mat, where I had been idly spinning the colorful beads of the abacus, and carried me to another part of the room where, atop one of the long gray Formica tables, there stood: a cage. Yet another cage. Granted, this cage was much larger than the one in which I had been conveyed from the zoo to the laboratory, but it was a cage nonetheless. In it was a bowl filled with dry and unpalatable food pellets, and a voluminous bottle of water strapped to the bars on one side of the cage with a metal tube coming out of the bottom of it, from which I was expected to drink, like a fucking hamster. A fuzzy blanket and a squishy blue mat made of a material identical to the one on the floor covered the bottom of the cage. It was tall enough that I could easily stand up in it, and spacious enough that I could walk four or five paces from one end of it to another. I could see through all four sides of the cage, composed of thin steel bars. All told—yes, I had been in worse cages. But it was, goddammit, a cage.

Lydia placed me inside the cage and shut the door and locked it. My heart didn't so much break as drop uncontrollably through a hollow shaft in my chest like an elevator with a snapped cable.

Dr. Plumlee joined her in looking in at me. Lydia made the same gesture of polite parting to me as the other humans had made to each other. Her wave was of the more feminine variety: with her fingers, not her hand.

"Good night, Bruno," said Lydia, and she and the other turned to go.

They were leaving me. For emphasis, I repeat: *they were leaving me.*

Whether or not they were leaving me forever, I did not know. It was then that I began to realize I would never see my family again. I would never return to the zoo. Never again would I commune with other chimps, never again would I enjoy exercising my limbs on our jungle gym, never again would I have to endure my brother's bullying or my father's relentless emotional abuse, nor would I ever again sit in my mother's lap, nor ever again play with Céleste.

I watched them leave together, Norman and Lydia: when they reached the door, Norm stretched out an arm and touched a row of things on the wall. I heard the noises *clack clack clack*, and each *clack* was followed by a section of the room going slowly, then quickly, dark. He clicked the last clack, eliminating the last source of buzzing fluorescent light. Lydia and Norm left the room, shutting the door behind them, *ka-chunk*. I heard the turning of a key in the lock. For a moment through the smoked-glass door I saw their silhouettes, their two blurry shadows facing one another, speaking. Then their voices vanished together, diminuendoing down the hallway into watery echoes punctuated by the contrapuntal rhythms of their four sneakers squeaking and scrunching on the floor, then an elevator door *bing*ing and *bong*ing and scrolling open and then shut, and then silence—and then silence.

So there I was, Gwen—alone, in silence and in darkness and locked in a cage. That morning I had woken up, as usual, with my arms and legs intertangled with the warm arms and legs of my kindred, in the wet and rank interior of our habitat in the zoo, the only home I had ever known, and now night had fallen and I was locked inside a five-by-five-foot minimally furnished cold metal cage in a strange and sterile room, alone, in the dark. The only other time in my life up until this point when I had ever been left alone in a room was during that experiment with the peaches. But because I was not alone during that period of dramatic transition from zoo to not-zoo, I had not yet felt the rush of feelings that rushed into my head now. Among them: panic, terror, abandonment.

Why was I here? Why me? Had I been placed here in this cage to be slaughtered and subsequently devoured like my paternal grand-parents were years ago, in darkest Africa? Perhaps, even worse, they were never coming back. I would be left to starve to death in here. All I knew was that I was confined in a space consisting of four walls and a ceiling and a floor, and I did not know why. These thoughts all came gushing into my undeveloped consciousness at once, and a demon of rage entered me.

I screamed. I wept and I screamed. I screamed and I wept. I rat-tled the bars of the cage. I upset my food bowl, scattering my dehy-drated food pellets, sending them skittering in every direction. I threw myself around in the cage, hooting and howling and thrash-ing and wailing. I ripped up the squishy blue pad on the floor, and I ripped up the fuzzy blue blanket they had given me. With my fingers and toes and gnashing teeth I tore them utterly asunder, into scraps and tatters and fluff, and threw the scraps and tatters and fluff around the cage aimlessly. I yanked hard at the bars of the cage, tried to smash them with my feeble young chimp fists and feet, but the cold hard gleaming metal of the cage did not relent. I do not know for how long I raged. Hours, perhaps. But then—

The lights in the hallway outside the laboratory door came on, in the way fluorescent lights do, the full glow preceded by three false starts. The window in the door to the lab became a luminous panel of soft white light, and the numbers and letters on the door cast shadows of themselves in long ribbons of darkness across the room, over the long tables and the squishy blue mat where my toys lay. I heard a laborious plodding of footsteps in the hall. The vol-ume of the footsteps gradually grew and the acoustic wavelengths of their echoes shortened until the footsteps stopped outside the lab door. An amorphous black shadow loomed outside the door. I heard heavy and irregular breathing. I heard a jingling of many keys, which went on for a long time before a key was selected and pushed into the lock in the handle of the door. The lock in the door turned and the bolt slid back and clicked and the door—noiselessly, except for the sound of the handle turning and the thin peeping of the hinges—opened. In the doorway's white light stood a large being whose details remained obscured in shadow. The being's hand groped the wall for the clacks and clicked one, *clack*, and one section of lights in the room came on, *nzt-nzt-nzt-nzzzzzzzzz*, and illuminated the area above my toys, such that with two competing light sources, all objects in the room were given a pair of crisscrossing shadows.

This man—whose name I did not yet know was Haywood Finch—was medium in stature and roughly potato-shaped. He was not fat—girthy, yes, but more oddly shaped than fat; his figure was, like the potato, approximately ovular in contour, no matter whether viewed frontally, antipodally, or in profile, with a big chest that sloped gracefully outward and down into a sizeable belly. Big doughy arms sprouted lumpily from his shoulders, which blubbed and glooped and gurbled into a thick lumpy neck that gracefully became a roundish and very lumpy head, which looked as if it had been sculpted out of butter and then allowed to partially melt. His hair was buzzed down to a wiry black half-centimeter of stubble, and featured on its very apex its lumpiest and most prominent lump. He had little lumpy ears that stuck out of the sides of his head like they'd been glued on by a clumsy child, and his mouth hung forever slightly open. But by far his bizarrest physical features were his eyes. One of them behaved like an ordinary human eye, but the other behaved seemingly of its own accord, looking always in a different direction, always wandering errantly toward the upper-left corner of his head. These bidirectional eyes of his burned both with a warm sweetness—like the smell of sugar caramelizing—and with a twitchy and unhinged craziness. He had a uniform on: it looked much like the uniforms the brownshirts at the zoo wore, but his pressed and collared button-down short-sleeved shirt was a light blue one instead of brown; the blue shirt had a breast pocket on one side of the chest and on the other side a flashing brass rectangle fastened on with a pin, with a series of hieroglyphics graven upon it. The shirt was covered with big wet spots and was tucked into a pair of dirty blue jeans; a damp rag dangled from the back pocket of the jeans, and from one of the belt loops of the jeans dangled a thick metal chain, from which in turn dangled a hoop of keys—dozens, maybe more than a hundred keys, and these were fascinating objects to me—and the hoop of keys was fastened to his battered leather belt by a metal clip, such that the long metal chain drooped down along one side of his thigh nearly to the knee and then sloped up again to the belt. The bottoms of his dirty jeans were tucked into heavy black grime-encrusted rubber boots.

An important thing to convey about Haywood Finch is the tremendous amount of noise he made as he walked. For not only did he breathe in a strange way—a lot of irregular wheezing and huffing and snorting—but every step taken in those heavy rubber boots had a thunderous volume and authority to it: first the quarter-beat of the heel of the boot making contact with the floor, followed immediately by the *clomp* of the rest of his foot coming down, and then the deft squeak of the toe launching the foot on its journey into the next step. This combined with the jangling of the keys and the loop of chain whapping against his thigh to create a percussive racket that was jarringly discordant yet eerily hypnotic, like Balinese Gamelan music. The sound of his footsteps consisted of: one, the clomping boots; two, the whapping chain; and three, the tintinnabulation of the keys. The rhythm of his walk was further eccentricized by a severe limp, due to one of his legs being shorter than the other. So the rhythm of his footsteps sounded like this: *kLOMPa-whap-SHLINK kLOMPa-whap-SHLINK kLOMPa-whap-SHLINK....* Haywood Finch—whose name I did not yet know—was employed by the University of Chicago as a janitor, hence this outrageous and musical costume he wore. It was his duty to sweep the floors, mop the floors, wipe the windows, scrub the toilets, scour the sinks, sanitize the urinals, remove the trash, and to perform any other undesirable chore one could think of. I was also later informed that Haywood Finch was considered "slow"—he suffered from a degree of mental retardation coupled with autism, and these and other yet stranger neurological ailments prevented him from excelling in the social world of daytime employment, although he performed his duties as a night-shift janitor at the Erman Biology Center at the University of Chicago with unfailing rigor and aptitude, in solitude, and in the middle of the night. He liked the solitude, he liked the dark, he was comforted by the endless repetition of his work. But I did not know any of this yet. At the time I knew only this: on the one hand, I was no longer alone in the room, but on the other hand, I was no longer alone in the room.

I did know that this was the most frightening human being I had ever seen in my short life—big, bowlegged, walleyed, and twitchy, I sensed there was something deeply not right about the way he looked and walked and breathed and moved his body through space, as he now did, from the door to the lab right up to my cage in the corner of the room. As my eyes were still adjusting to the now partially lit laboratory, this man gradually and musically dragged his weight across the expanse of floor that separated us—*kLOMPa-whap-SHLINK kLOMPa-whap-SHLINK kLOMPa-whap-SHLINK.* He looked in at me through the bars of my cage, his breath whistling in through his nose and roaring out through his mouth like a pair of fireplace bellows and his bidirectional eyes bugging and blinking and goggling and boggling at me. And I looked at him through the bars of my cage. He didn't say anything, but the demon of rage that had entered me was still in me, and so I was the first to speak.

I said—or rather, I screamed:

"Oo-oo-oo-oo ah-ah-ah heeaagh heeaagh *hyeeeaaaaaghhhh!*"

And then—what did he do, this mysterious lumpy man who stood now just outside my cage looking in, this stranger of the crazy eyes and the musical walk? He screamed back at me. He replied in answer:

"Oo-oo-oo-oo ah-ah-ah heeaagh heeaagh *hyeeeaaaaaghhhh!*"

That shut me up.

He mimicked the inarticulate chimp noise that I had just made. He copied it, beat for beat, tone for tone, note for note, and at the exact same pitch and volume. I was taken aback. He had mimicked my scream so perfectly that anyone secretly listening in would have assumed either that I had made the noise twice or else there was another chimp in the room. When I had somewhat collected my wits I said:

"Uha huppa huh?"

"Uha huppa huh," he said, though without the rising inflection.

"Eeegt eegt eegt," I replied.

"Eeegt eegt eegt."

"Oop oop oop *eeyaugh.*"

"*Eeyaugh, eeyaugh.*"

"Ooooooooooo oo-oo-oo eeyaugh."

"Barga barga baraga barrra*gagaga!*"

"Abbah abbah abb?"

"Barga barga oo-oo-oo-oo ooooook."

"Eep-eep-eep *eeyaugh eeyaugh.*"

"Glrrrrrrrrrrrrrrr*argawargawarga!*"

"Aat aat aat ananananananananaaaaaaaat!"

"Birrrroing zuboing zuboing zuboing zuboy!"

"Eeetoo eeteetoo amammmmmmmnnnnn oot oot oot."

"Havar voo voy!"

"Rannanakka rannakka *oit oit oit!*"

"BrrrrrrrrrrrrriiiiiiinnnGAAAHHH!"

"Uffa uffa uffa *eeeeeeeeeeeagghhht.*"

"*Yiik*ikikikikikikikiki *eeeeite eeeeeite!*"

"Oo-*woo* oo-*woo* oooooo *reagh reagh* YEAAAAGGHHH!"

Then suddenly we were talking all at once! I don't recall how the rest of the conversation went. We made such joyous noise!

This was perhaps the first completely reciprocal conversation I ever had with a human being. That first epic conversation with the great Haywood Finch, mildly retarded autistic night-shift janitor extraordinaire, was my truest introduction to human speech. We spoke in this manner for at least an hour, maybe more, before Haywood frantically glanced at his digital watch and realized that his routine had been upset and he must return immediately to work, and so after emptying all the garbage cans in the lab, off he loped, clomping and jangling away to mop the hallway floor.

But that first conversation! What a joy it was to make noise purely for the sake of noisemaking. And yet out of all that playful babble, all that nonsense, patterns of language had begun to develop. That night, man aped ape. He copied my animal phonemes to a T and spat them back at me intermingled with playful additions and variations of his own, which I in turn attempted to imitate. We babbled wildly at each other, and what insane fun! We made music: somewhere, a strain of sense, a chorus, harmonies, melodies, rhythms, and motifs emerged out of our howling squall of gobble-dygook. We added visual components—we made silly faces at each other, invented meaningless hand gestures. I slapped my chest and slapped my palms on the floor of my cage, and he unclipped the hoop of keys from his belt and rattled it around in front of his face.

Our signs and noises and gestures were not discrete or digital but strictly analog, fluid and organic, uncompartmentalized, improvisational, cooperative at times and at times mock-combative. From a raw clay of nonsense we were every moment molding signifiers that had no signifieds, empty signs, decorative and happily meaningless words. Did we communicate anything? No. But language for the sake of communication follows language that is noise for the sake of fun—that is, *music*—and—this I truly believe—all truly beautiful language is for the sake of both: communication and music.

VII

And when this man—the strangest man I had ever known—when this man clomped and jangled away and clacked out the light and left the room, he did not behave in the way the other humans had behaved upon leaving. He did not politely wave or say good-bye; he simply and unceremoniously switched off the light and pulled the door shut without looking back. I was not exactly hurt by this curt and neglectful leavetaking of his. I had already gathered that this man did not think or operate in the same way as most other humans, and I sensed no malignancy in his departure. After he left I felt much better. Our nonsense conversation—or *nonversation*, if you will—had cured me of the rage demon that had previously entered me. Thus exorcized by our babbleoneous merrymaking, I gathered up the scraps and tatters and bits of fluff that I had in my panic made of my cage furnishings, and fell asleep, my heavy-lidded slumber comporting me away inside myself to other worlds, my simple brain steeped in a warm bath of primitive dreams.

I awoke the next morning to see three faces—those of Norman Plumlee, Prasad, and Lydia—scowling at me in disapproval. Well, the stoic faces of Plumlee and Prasad scowled in disapproval; they clearly did not like what I had done in the night to my cage furnishings—that is, destroy and scatter them—but on Lydia's face was not what I would call a scowl so much as a distressed frown of sympathy. This is why, Gwen—this is why all great primatologists are women. The male human mind is hateful, bellicose, possessive, punitive, and jealous, obsessed with cold notions of law and property and justice. The male mind thinks: how dare—how *dare* you destroy and scatter the property we so kindly *lent* you, you insolent creature! The male mind ponders such pertinent moral questions as whose stupid acorns are these if I go to the trouble of bending over and picking them up? But the female mind is quicker to empathy than indignation, and that is one reason why Jane Goodall and Dian Fossey and Sue Savage-Rumbaugh and Lydia Littlemore made such great pioneers in primatology.

Norman Plumlee opened my cage door and I clambered gladly out, but was immediately met with many stern reproaches, and a castigatory hand with the thumb and bottom three fingers curled around the palm and the wagging index finger aimed at me. The hand belonged to Norman Plumlee. Norman grabbed a handful of the fluff and torn bits of fabric that my mat and fuzzy blanket had become in the night, and held them to my face and made "shame on you" noises.

"It's okay—it's okay," said Lydia. She put on her glasses and immediately took them off again, and with both hands tucked two wisps of hair behind the ridges of her ears. "He's probably in shock, Norm. He's never spent a night away from home before. He just got a little freaked out last night."

I was on the floor. I ran to Lydia and jerked on the leg of her pants and she picked me up and I hugged her and held on to her and planted my face against the soft flesh of her neck. I was forgiven.

I devoured some of the dehydrated food pellets that I had scattered the night before, not because they were at all palatable but because I had awoken with a belly roiling and snarling from hunger. I was permitted to play with my toys, but I did so only listlessly. The other humans arrived one by one with morning coffee steaming in their mugs. That day the experiments began in earnest. I remember how they presented me with flash cards with different symbols printed on them, and asked me, I think, to distinguish the cards from each other. I remember people making gestures at me, signs I was expected to attempt to emulate. I remember one particular experiment—all of these were repeated time after time and day after day, week upon week, I ought to remember them—in which I was shown an assortment of objects: stones, metal washers, pencils, plastic flowers, and small stuffed animals resembling pigs, chickens, rabbits, elephants, lizards, and the like (although they were not to scale—the elephant, for example, was the same size as the chicken). The human named Norm, the human who was clearly "in charge" here because all the other humans—even Lydia—seemed to defer authority to him, stored these artifacts in a big brown cardboard box that he removed from one of the cabinets under one of the long gray lab tables. He dumped the contents of the box onto the surface of the table and proceeded to sort them out for me, grouping the objects like with like: flowers with flowers, animals with animals, washers with washers, and stones with stones. Then, after sorting them, he would put all of the objects back in the box, shake it vigorously so as to randomly redistribute the contents and dump them back onto the table, then make a gesture indicating that I should sort them, like with like. If I sorted correctly, I was rewarded with a treat. If I sorted incorrectly, the treat was withheld.

I partook in these and other such experiments. They were fun, though sometimes I grew weary of them. Sometimes I was allowed to sit in the corner of the room on the squishy blue mat and manipulate my toys, and sometimes Lydia joined me. Oftentimes

I crawled into her arms and looked into her bright brazen eyes and played with her bright blond hair. At lunchtime she put a collar on my neck and attached a leash (a degrading necessity in those early days), then picked me up and carried me through the building, down the stairs, and outside into the world, which was sunny but still soggy from yesterday's rain. She brought her lunch with her in a brown paper bag. I was not particularly hungry because I had been plied with treats all morning for all the tasks I had correctly performed. She brought me to a courtyard behind the building that housed the Behavioral Biology Lab, a stretch of grass cut through with a brick path and surrounded by several buildings made of gray stone. There were many tall trees whose trunks were gray and knotted and gnarled like old men's arms. Lydia sat down on a picnic bench and removed from the paper bag the following items: a turkey sandwich, diagonally bisected into two right triangles and wrapped in crinkly wax paper; a bottle of vitamin water; a green apple; and a "power" bar, which was a compact rectangular block of tightly compressed nutrients with raisins and chocolate chips embedded in it. She offered me a bite from each of these items, bites that I took more out of curiosity than hunger.

Since there was no one else around, Lydia unhooked my leash and allowed me to climb the trees, which I did, happily, in the sunlight, brachiating madly in their rustling canopies. Such an outrageous thrill it was to climb those giant trees, knowing that for the first time in my life there were no fences or walls or bars or windows to keep me inside. I could have easily run away if I'd wanted to, but of course I did not want to, not with Lydia beaming sweetly up at me from the picnic bench below, chewing on a wad of turkey sandwich held in her cheek. This being a university campus and this being the summer, there was very little foot traffic in the courtyard. The sun was bright and hot. I observed the midflight lovemaking of a pair of iridescent dragonflies.

Up and up and up I climbed into the canopy of the tallest and oldest and most magisterial tree in the courtyard. I scrambled into the highest branches that were still thick enough to support my weight. I emerged from the flapping green leaves to find myself standing higher than the highest of the buildings surrounding the grassy courtyard.

In every direction I saw a vast and strange and infinitely complex world previously unknown to me. I looked to the west, and saw the rooftops of buildings stretching endlessly into the distance, and far away a train shuffling along the elevated tracks and a highway with trucks lumbering along it and down the serpentine filigrees of overlapping exit ramps. I looked to the south, and saw the great vertical pipes of a hundred organs of industry unfurling satin scarves of black smoke into the air. I looked to the east, and saw a lapping and foaming body of blue-green water, speckled with sailboats and reaching out to the horizon where it became a thin band of silvery blue. And then I looked to the north.

I saw the stone titans of the downtown Loop looming high over Chicago. I did not yet know that each of these monsters had a name—the Tribune Tower, the John Hancock Center, the Sears Tower—but I knew that they shot into the sky so high that tracing their heights made me queasy and light-headed. I knew that they were designed with bizarre and terrifying features jagging and cragging out of them, juts and abutments and spikes and spurs and needles and bars and crowns and prongs and horns and forks and knives, a tangled skein of twisted metal appendages reaching up out of the earth like the fingers of enormous demons clawing their way out of hell to assault the heavens.

And I knew—by intuition—I knew that these dark demon-fingered giants were the products of men: the human race had designed and built these cryptic structures for purposes I could not yet fathom. And I thought about the life I had previously led as an ape. I reflected upon the crude little nests of sticks and leaves that we built for ourselves, and I reflected upon our petty conflicts and our wordless loves and our miserable lives of debasement and perpetual captivity which we in our poverty of mind and poverty of spirit could think of no way of remedying or escaping. And then I trained my gaze upon these great stone monsters in the distance. And I fell in love.

I forsook my animalhood right then and there at the top of that tree, because of this crazy, disastrous love I was in with humanity. Of course I was in love for all the vainest and greediest reasons. And it was this vanity and greed and lust that drove me to—following your example some several million years too late—come down out of the tree. I climbed down from that tree to spend the rest of my life running from the yawning darkness of animal terror toward the light of fire stolen from the gods, and like you, I remain in a state of constant pursuit, never quite escaping the darkness, nor ever reaching the light.

VIII

So I climbed down from the tree. Lydia was sitting below me at the picnic table. She had finished her lunch, and while watching me brachiate had economically and ecologically folded, double- and triple-folded her brown paper lunch sack into a thick square for future reuse. I grabbed on to her and she took me back inside to the lab. The experiments continued. Then the day was done. I was given a new fuzzy blanket and more dehydrated food pellets and carrots and a new squishy blue mat to pad the floor of my cage, although this one was sternly superglued to the floor in order to make it more difficult to destroy and scatter if another rage demon should enter me, which it did not. I still disliked being made to sleep in the cage after the scientists had gone home, but at least now I was reassured of a routine—that come morning, I knew the humans would return to fill my day with fun. Night fell again, and again the strange man returned to carry on a nonsense conversation with me for approximately one hour. I fell asleep, I twitched and dreamed and woke with the rising sun, the scientists returned with steaming cups of coffee, and the experiments resumed.

This pattern, needless to relate in exquisite detail, continued for many days and nights. The scientists were pleased with me. They said I was making rapid progress. And every night the lumpy man in the blue uniform would arrive and speak with me for one hour. The language between us was beginning to almost mean something. For instance, we had learned one another's names, and we had developed an idiosyncratic system of signs and words for greeting and leavetaking. We were beginning to create a little pidgin dialect, a trade language, a lingua franca just for the two of us.

Haywood would point at himself and say, "*Ae, ou!*" (phonctically: / 'eɪːʊ /). This part of my journey is difficult to relate in print because we are constrained somewhat by the tonal inelasticity of text—but essentially Haywood was intoning the two syllables of his first name, minus the consonants.

Then he pointed at me.

I mimicked his gesture, pointing at myself and saying "*Aeee...ooooough.*"

Haywood made me understand that this was incorrect by scowling and whipping his head from side to side and making an ugly, guttural noise in the back of his throat, like this: "BEEEEE-EEEEEEAAAANT!"

Again Haywood pointed at himself and said, "*Ae, ou!*"

Then he pointed at me.

I pointed at myself and said: "Aeee—ooou."

"BEEEEEEEEEEEAAAANT!" said Haywood, grimacing and lashing his head from side to side.

Then, pointing at himself: "*Ae, ou.*"

Pointing at me now.

"Ae...ou?"

"BEEEEEEEEEEEAAAANT!"

This went on many, many times before I finally, perhaps even by accident, pointed at *him* and said, "*Ae, ou.*"

He responded by grinning, nodding his head up and down while shrilly ululating—"*Lalalalalalalalalalalalalala!*"—and he accompanied his song of general positivity by picking up his hoop of many keys and shaking it for me, and the dancing keys jangled and jingled like so many pretty chimes. I clapped, I pant-hooted, I cheered in delight, because I loved the shimmering music they made.

This is something, by the way, that the scientists who worked in the laboratory never once thought of doing: to reward my progress not with tidbits of food, but with beautiful noise. For sometimes I simply was not hungry—so at these times the reward of a treat meant nothing to me outside of the psychological reward of their approval—but my appetite for beautiful noises was always insatiable.

We repeated this many times until I was able to understand that *"Ae*, ou" was not something that one said when pointing at oneself, but something that one said when pointing at *this* man in particular. I also came to understand that when Haywood pointed at me, he was asking me to make the sound that meant me: my name. Of course I knew my name, in the sense that I knew to come (or choose not to come) when a human shouted at me, "Bruno!" But I had never dreamed of actually attempting to articulate these two syllables with the glottal machinery of my own chimp mouth, an instrument that had previously been good for little but the ingestion of my food and drink, the inhalation and exhalation of my breath, and the making of all my aimless screeching, growling, howling, panting, and hooting noises.

I pointed at myself and made my first attempt at conscious spoken language:

"Ooh, no."

I almost slapped my hands over my mouth—maybe I even *did* slap my hands over my mouth in astonishment at the dangerous magical noise that had just come out of it! It was a *word*! It was——it was *my own name*!

Of course my clumsy infant tongue could not curl itself around the complexity of the initial consonant sound of my name—the labial plosive *B* tumbling immediately into an *R*, demanding of the tongue a tricky little maneuver of mid-mouth acrobatics—but the two distinct vowel-tones of my name—a narrow-mouthed *oooh* followed by a wide-mouthed (n)*ohhh* (/ 'uːnəʊ /)—these I nailed on the first try, and even managed to partition them with a quick trip of the tongue to the top of the mouth to make a feeble and breathy but definitely distinctly audible *N*.

In response Haywood screamed in glee and shook his keys so obstreperously I feared they might explode.

For the rest of that evening we simply took turns pointing at each other and intoning each other's names. There was no way that Haywood could have known that my actual name was "Bruno." I'm sure he assumed that my name was "Uno," which indeed is plausible enough nomenclature for a chimp. I'm not even sure Haywood gave much thought to such issues as the plausibilities of chimp nomenclature.

The next night, when Haywood returned, we began our nonversation with our game of pointing first to ourselves and then each to the other, and stating in turn our own name-sounds and then the name-sound of the other. What followed after was a typical session of ecstatic gibberish, but when the hour had passed and it was time for Haywood to go, we signed off in this way as well. This exchange of pointing and stating of name-sounds became the traditional way of beginning and ending our nonversations—which I had come to crave and rely upon like therapy sessions. I so enjoyed my nightly nonversations with Haywood that I no longer even bothered to display any sign of protest or dislike when the end of the work day came and it was time to sequester me again in my cage, because I knew this meant my session with Haywood was soon forthcoming. Once Haywood even pressed his hoop of many keys against the bars of my cage, and allowed me to play with them. This was an important moment, Gwen. Perhaps I imagined, or even believed, somewhere in my soul or burgeoning mind, that the seat of Haywood's animal charisma lay in that hoop of many keys: it was his juju, his phylactery, these keys were like rosary beads, they somehow protected him from evil, or made him great, made him powerful, gave him the ability to speak with animals. I shook them and jingled them, and admired their shimmering music.

And we spoke and spoke and spoke. And through our gibberish I gradually developed my sense for the shapes of human words, I accustomed my mouth to the making of consonants and distinct vowel-sounds, of the plosives and the approximants and the labio-dentals and the taps and flaps and fricatives, of the nasals and the glottals and the sibilants and the sonorants—I learned them all in nonsense form first. Through the ecstasy of nonsense I learned the musicality and the rhythm of human speech. Gradually my communication skills developed at night with Haywood Finch. After the first five or six months (the basic monotony of this period of my life provokes me to accelerate time here) I had not only learned to say "Haywood," with the consonants basically distinct and correct, but also to properly articulate the first consonant-sound of my own name, Bruno. At first it came out as "boo-no," but after obsessive independent practice I learned how to slip that ticklish *r* in between the *b* and the beginning of the first vowel, and in fact I found this combination of consonants so much fun to say that by endless repetition I quickly mastered the pronunciation of my name.

However, for many months, I never spoke my name to the researchers who populated the lab by day. My ever-expanding vocabulary of articulate noises and words—well, two words, "Haywood" and "Bruno"—were exclusively for use at night, during my sessions with Haywood. During the day, I was silent. And why was this?

First of all, it had simply never occurred to me to attempt to speak to the daytime humans. My self was divided. One self I used to interact with the humans of the day, and the other self I used purely for my sessions of joyous noisemaking with Haywood, the human who came to me in the night. I communicated in different ways with these two sets of humans; I was code-switching. The day humans were always constantly barraging me with tasks and games and experiments and a thousand other avenues of stimulus. They showed me films and mirrors and played me music and watched me while I manipulated my toys. They showed me pictograms and designs on paper and on little plastic tiles, they showed me stuffed animals and all kinds of items and articles and artifacts, and they spoke to me, and spoke and spoke and spoke to me. They made gestures and asked me to copy them, and when I did so accurately I was given treats. In this way I developed a substantial lexicon of specific signs, and other signs that we improvised as we went, usually strongly iconic or indexical in their visual processes. I was also, much more important, learning to comprehend an enormous amount of spoken English, but I had not yet tried to speak any of it. For the moment I was only listening.

But my yammering nocturnes with Haywood were accomplished in a spirit divorced entirely from that of the daytime laboratory. For one thing, my interactions with the humans of the day always lasted for a long time, and contained a psychological element of *work*. They, the scientists, were "at work": when these people kissed someone good-bye and walked out of their homes in the morning, this laboratory was where they were going to. This is not to suggest that the scientists did not enjoy their jobs—for the most part, they clearly relished their work—but still, toward the end of the day, one could tell that their minds were beginning to wander homeward, their souls were leaving the lab and entering into a realm of immi-nent anticipations, into the afternoon commute, into after-work beers, into the expectant arms of spouses or beaux or inamoratas, into that sweet period of the day interstitially nestled between work and sleep, the precious mortar that glues together these two dull bricks that every day stack up and up and up to form the big flat wall of most of your life. This contagious feeling of being "at work" inevitably infected me as well. Even though I only spent the live-long day playing the silly games that they regarded as experiments, I still felt a sense of obligation in what I did. It was their job to play with me and feed me treats, and it was my job—and damned if I didn't do my job dutifully and well—to play and eat treats.

Whereas my nightly nonversations with Haywood Finch were totally extracurricular, something we did expressly for the pure and happy hell of it, and this somehow made them so much more exciting than the official university-funded experiments that filled my daylight hours. Also, the duration of the time I got with Haywood each night was so much shorter—one hour—you could have almost set your watch to it. Haywood was no poor player who struts and frets his hour upon the stage—no, like any great performer, he always left me crying for more.

However, I think the most important reason why, in those early months, I made more linguistic progress with Haywood Finch than I did with the scientists has something to do with the fact that I had quickly become fairly certain that the daytime humans *did not know about* what was going on at night between me and Haywood. Perhaps they had never given a fleeting thought as to what the night-shift janitor might have been up to when the doors were locked and the lights out and everyone had gone home. This put a streak of the seditious in my furtive nightly sessions with Haywood. I had a secret. I had a secret that I was not telling the scientists, and this gave me a feeling of power. Not much power, true, but after having spent my entire life completely under the observation of and ignorant of the language of and therefore under the power of human beings, what a deliciously conspiratorial feeling it was to hold in my mind a little bit of information that they did not, and to share this information with only one other being. Haywood was my confidant—together, like two conspirators plotting a coup in some smoky back room, we exercised the dark subversive power of a secret language.

IX

My love for Lydia widened and deepened even and ever more. In the months that followed my arrival at the University of Chicago's Behavioral Biology Laboratory, the campus, which had been as deserted as a ghost town in the languid summer heat, one day abruptly exploded with bustling human activity. All summer long it had been silence, silence, then suddenly the hallways of my building were teeming during the day with energetic young humans. Their footsteps stampeded in the halls at regular intervals; their presence was a collective roar, their squeaking and scuffling shoes, their conversations, their laughter. Now whenever Lydia took me outside to roam the campus greenery and admire the foliage, the autumnally decadent weather was just beginning to singe the leaves with edges of yellow, and I saw these hale young humans everywhere: I saw them lolling in the grass, their shoes off with their socks wadded in the hollows of their shoes and the toes of their bare feet mingling with the blades of grass and their heels callused and stained yellow and green; I saw them lying on towels sunbathing; I saw their fingers noodling the strings of acoustic guitars; I saw them expertly throwing and catching bright discs—as well as balls of various sizes and colors—that glided gracefully through the air from one pair of hands to another; I saw them reading books, sipping beverages, smoking cigarettes; I saw some of them kissing or touching one another in amorous ways. So much life!

Some of them took great interest in me. When they saw Lydia and I strolling hand in hand across the campus, they would approach us and try to speak to me, and want to touch me. Sometimes Lydia let them, if I seemed receptive.

Lydia even took me to one of her classes. That fall Lydia was teaching a section of Introduction to Cognitive Psychology. One afternoon she put on my collar and clipped my leash to it and carried me across the main quad from the lab on the third floor of the Erman Biology Center to the classroom where she taught in Wieboldt Hall. Lydia Littlemore held a Ph.D. in cognitive psychology and a master's in anthropology—she worked alongside the behavioral biologists while teaching as an assistant adjunct professor in the psychology department. She had only recently received her Ph.D., her curriculum vitae was still thin, and she was many years away from the hope of tenure. The soft scientists considered her to be harder than they, while the hard scientists considered her too soft. She was always struggling to convince the soft ones that she had a flexible heart and the hard ones that she possessed a mind of sufficiently implacable skepticism.

Lydia wrapped me in a blanket for my journey across campus, and cradled me in her arms, my legs curled around her sides with my toes hooked together and my arms around her neck. The clusters of students standing around conversing looked up and smiled and gawked at me. The weather was still warm but getting chillier. Fat gray pigeons hopped stupidly among the yellow leaves that now littered the ground, and in the trees periodic bursts of throaty *aw-aw*ing came from beaks of dirty black crows. We entered a building much older than the one I was ordinarily kept in. The wind we made in the hallways rustled leaflets and fliers and posters tacked to corkboards or taped to the walls. We entered a small classroom through a heavy brown door that whispered and clunked shut behind us. The students were sitting in their seats, talking. Conversation subsided as Lydia walked to the front of the room and set me down on the surface of the desk. Let's say there were twenty-five students in the room. Lydia began to speak. Some of the students began scratching markings into notebooks with pens or pencils. Lydia had her glasses on, and her hair was bound back in its academic ponytail. I sat on the desk and played with my toes. I looked out upon the faces of the students sitting silent and obedient at their desks. Fifty eyes trained on me as Lydia spoke. Many of these eyes were set in the heads of smooth-skinned young girls, some of whom had even removed their flip-flops, and were sitting with one foot playfully toeing the tripartite juncture of the plastic flip-flop strap and the other crossed beneath her in such a way as to show me the sole of her bare foot, with its callused heel stained yellow and green from the grass. Never before had I been in a room with so many grass-stained bare feet and skirts and breasts and so much soft sweaty flesh and long glossy hair in it. I could not concentrate at all on my work.

When Lydia finished speaking, her students pushed their desks into the corners of the room to make a wide clearing for me. Lydia placed me in the center of the room. Then she picked up the cardboard box that I have erstwhile forgotten to mention and dumped its contents out before me. It was Norm's box of curiosities: the stones, the washers, the pencils, the plastic flowers, and the stuffed animals.

Lydia bade me to sort them. The task was embarrassingly simple. All I had to do was to recognize that a pencil—though it may differ in its specific physical details from all other pencils—is similar enough to other pencils, to a sort of Platonic ideal of "Pencil," that it may reasonably be grouped with other pencils and not, say, with a stone. This concept—the generalized cataloging of the things of the world—underlies much language. I had sorted these objects thousands of times. Today, I held my feet in my hands in the center of the room and dumbly stared at them.

I looked around me at all the young men and young women in the room. I looked especially at the young women. God, the smell of them. Their perfume, or whatever it was, their washed skin, their hair, the misty films of sweat in their armpits and knees and thighs, the smell of shampoos and conditioners, of soaps and freshly shaven legs—their grass-stained bare feet—their bright breasts heaving beneath their shirts.... Lydia flapped a treat before me. She sat down with me in the clearing with the pile of objects that lay unsorted at my feet—she spoke to me, cooing instructions. She organized the artifacts for me, then put them back in the box, shook it vigorously, and dumped them out again.

I could not concentrate at all. The students laughed. What began as a few desultory twitters and snickers soon crested into a half-muffled wave of derisive cackling. Lydia spoke and spoke and spoke to me, entreating me to do *something*—sort the objects?—perform some of my signs?—show them what you can do!—the things I taught you!

Of course I understood her words, I grasped the meanings of her signs—but the links between the signs and their meanings dissolved in the air before they reached me. I simply sat there in the center of the room, mutely, stupidly, intermittently picking up an item here and there—a pencil, a plastic flower, a stuffed animal—fingering it disinterestedly, and putting it down again: behaving, in other words, exactly like an ordinary chimpanzee, rather than the genius chimp they had apparently been expecting. Lydia flushed and grew frustrated with me—infuriated, even.

Then: I smelled something. Something—specific, some smell that I had not previously noticed in the room. I detected some faint but definitely present smell, a strange odor, oily and fleshy and sticky and briny and very, very human. I looked around the room, at all the bare legs, the flip-flops and the sticky thighs. There was a certain girl—oh, she was beautiful—this certain girl, so smooth, so soft, so bright—I could smell the films of sweat in the pits of her knees, between her toes, her thighs—she had an outrageous mane of thick black hair, a pair of mountainous breasts, seismically rising and falling under her clothes, filling me with violent desire. Her legs were effeminately crossed beneath a knee-length orange skirt made of a thin stretchy material, and one of her flip-flops— she was wearing orange flip-flops that matched the skirt—one of her sweaty squishy flip-flops dangled from the big toe of her bare foot, which she held partially aloft, bobbing the flip-flop, slapping it softly against her heel by pushing on the front of it with her toe. Her toenails were painted red. This faint smell, this weird oily briny coppery smell—this smell, I believed, originated from *her*.

I put down the stick or stone or stuffed animal or whatever it was that Lydia had just thrust into my hands and begged me to categorize, and I approached this woman, those legs, those yellow-and-green-stained feet, those blood-red toenails, those sweaty squishy orange flip-flops—that smell—and I crawled across the room to her. My limp leash dragged tinkling on the floor behind me. This girl was gnawing on the end of her pen and slapping her flip-flop against her heel. She realized that I was coming for her. She put down her pen, allowed the leg in question to descend and crossed it with the other, and as she did, that curious odor sharply, briefly spiked in pungency, and I had absolutely no doubt now that it was she whom I sought. I was getting curiouser and curiouser. I came closer, and at first the girl reached out to me with her pretty slender hands—the nail of each of her fingers was likewise painted red to match her toes—and I sniffed at her fingers, and determined that they were not what I was after. My head dove down to her legs. I sniffed her grass-stained feet, her sweaty squishy orange flip-flops…getting closer, closer…

The girl emitted an involuntary squeak of shock. She recoiled from me in terror. She shoved her hands deep between her legs and bunched up the material of the orange skirt. I was trying to burrow my head beneath her skirt.

This is what I was doing when Lydia, in a fury, snatched at my leash and jerked me back, choking me. She tore me away from her.

I noticed then that all the other students were laughing. Roaring, thunderous with gleeful derisive laughter. All except for the girl herself—my wild-maned red-toed sweaty sticky squishy smelly girl—no, she was not laughing. She was burning. Her face was stained such a brutal shade of crimson that it looked like she was tied to the stake and burning, burning to death for passively committed blasphemies of medieval imagination, burning in order to be purified of some supernatural miasma cleansable only by passionate licks of fire, burning for witchcraft, burning, perhaps, for the visitation of an incubus…

Lydia's face was equally red. She dismissed her class. I was severely reprimanded. I was ashamed. It would be a very long time before she ever took me to another one of her classes. Soon afterward, after I humiliated and embarrassed Lydia by my inability to perform before her students—well, not long afterward—actually, I have no idea how long afterward it was, but it was definitely afterward and not beforeward, of that I'm sure—I spoke to Lydia for the first time.

Maybe it was October, or at least October-ish, perhaps early November—I certainly wasn't cognizant of the months of the calendar changing from one to the next, but I do recall that the weather had definitely veered toward the hibernal: the skies were grayer, the days shorter and darker, and the scarves, jackets, jeans, and sensible shoes had evilly chased away the tank tops and shorts and skirts and flip-flops, sins which these articles committed annually in Chicago and for which I never forgave them.

I was sitting with Lydia on my squishy blue mat in the lab. I don't recall what the other scientists were doing; they were probably busying themselves about the room with various scientific tasks. Lydia and I were taking turns whacking the moles of my Whack-a-Mole system. I did generally enjoy whacking the moles with the brown plastic hammer, but at this particular moment my heart wasn't in it. I was not enjoying whacking the moles. The little bastards would always pop up again and again and never stay down—there was never any sense of triumph over them; the recalcitrant moles would allow you no feeling of accomplishment, only the Sisyphus-like frustration of endless futile labor. So I whacked the last mole I cared to whack and disinterestedly tossed the hammer aside. Lydia looked up at me. Perhaps she was a bit hurt by my disaffection with the device. I had been acting difficult lately. She picked it up and switched it off. I made a decision.

I looked at Lydia, and pointed at myself, and said to her: "Bruno."

She answered me with this face: her eyes bugging, her nether lip hanging open and violently a-tremble.

This was hardly my water pump moment. I had been speaking my name to Haywood for months. It just happened to be the moment that I decided—partly out of my shame for having embarrassed and disappointed Lydia—to speak to her, to let her in on my secret world.

"Bruno—," she said, craning her neck forward. She snatched off her glasses and let them dangle down on her chest. "What did you say?"

I looked at her blankly.

"*Hey*—" She stood up and shouted at the other scientists in the lab. "HEY!"

Like my moles ascending from the mole holes of my Whack-a-Mole system, all over the lab the heads of the other scientists popped up and turned toward Lydia.

"What?" they said all in unison. Lydia stood up.

"Bruno just—um. He just *spoke*. He said his name."

Lydia's eyes were enormous with shock and delight. She laughed: her body spontaneously convulsed with a breathy flutter of disbelieving laughter, and she put a hand to her mouth. She shook her head and blinked her eyes. With both hands she slid her hair behind her ears, then threw her hands in the air, slapped the tops of her thighs, and made a series of other gestures. Norm Plumlee made confused eyes at her and arched an incredulous eyebrow, and his forehead furrowed thickly.

"*What?*" he said. One could almost see a blizzard of question marks sprouting in the airspace above his head.

"Bruno just pointed at himself and *said his name*."

The other scientists in the lab all stopped what they had been doing and immediately crowded around me on my squishy blue mat. Lydia knelt to the floor before me and looked deeply and passionately into my chimp eyes. She put on her glasses, then immediately snatched them off again, then tucked two stray strands of her hair behind her ears with both hands, then used these same hands to clap three times in rapid succession.

"Come on, Bruno. What did you say?"

I opened my mouth. But my lungs had been robbed of their oxygen. I don't know what happened. I had just spoken—it was no accident, I knew that I had consciously and deliberately spoken my name to Lydia just a moment before. But I was speechless now. My diaphragm would not cooperate, it refused to provide the upward thrust of air in the throat necessary to bring a word into being. A demon of silence had entered me.

I looked from one face to the next, at the faces of all these scientists standing behind Lydia and looking down at me. Lydia quickly whipped her head around to cast a look behind her shoulder, and said: "Somebody get a tape recorder!"

Andrea scurried away in search of the tape recorder.

"Where is it?"

"I don't know."

"Come on, Bruno. Say that again. I'm Lydia. Who are you? What's your name?"

"I can't find it!"

"Do that again. Do that again. Please, do it for me. Say 'Bruno.'"

"Do you want a treat?" said Norm, or something like it. "Say that again and you will have a treat."

"Got it!"

Now the flame-haired Andrea knelt on her knees beside Lydia, aiming a small gray hissing box at me. Norm was standing behind them, flapping a treat in his fingers in an "I bet you want this, don't you?" way. Prasad looked on with his arms skeptically crossed. All eyes were focused on me, all ears turned sharply in my direction. I sat, cross-legged and silent, right where I had been sitting with Lydia when I made my experimental utterance. I grabbed my foot with my hand and averted my gaze. I felt acutely embarrassed. I wanted to hide. The dormant Whack-a-Mole system and the two brown plastic hammers lay forlornly before me on the mat.

I wanted to speak for them, I honestly did. But with all those faces, those anticipant faces looking at me wondering and agog, I found that I simply could not perform. I tried. God knows I tried. I kept pointing at myself and trying to pronounce my name, but getting nothing out but pitiful burping and puttering noises. They must have been watching me try to say my name for an hour at least—but all for naught. Eventually they all peeled off and drifted away and went back to what they had each been doing before my utterance; I realize in retrospect this was probably a ruse—perhaps they thought my awareness of being observed was making me self-conscious and hampering my speech, that I would only have been able to speak when nobody expected me to. And perhaps they were right. But Lydia remained vigilant beside me for hours afterward, still coaxing me in a pleading whisper to speak.

I could not do it. I just could not speak for her, as badly as I wanted to. I was ashamed and embarrassed. I was experiencing the verbal equivalent of impotence. I don't know why, but I could not speak.

But I do know that that evening, from my vantage point inside my cage I witnessed—but did not overhear in any detail—a very long and intense discussion, conducted on the part of both participants in the surreptitious sibilant hush of children talking in their beds after lights-out, between Dr. Lydia Littlemore and Dr. Norman Plumlee, who sat facing one another in the semidarkness of the lab after hours, hunched over one of the lab tables with elbows planted on the table. And I do know that I thought I could perceive a look of supplication on Lydia's face, and an aspect of forbidding and reluctance on Norm's. And I do know that Lydia said something that made Norm's face smile, lighten, and soften. And I do know that shortly after this moment the conversation was considered finished, they had come to some sort of conclusion—most likely Norm had decided to acquiesce to a proposal of Lydia's that he had initially regarded with dislike. And I know that Lydia and Norm then gathered up their things and stuffed them into satchels and struggled into their jackets and wound their scarves around their necks and did all the stuffing and zipping and buttoning prerequisite to venturing outside, because it had become quite cold by now, and I know they waved good-bye to me and switched off the fluorescent lights and let the door sigh shut and lock behind them. And I also know that the two of them had been talking together for so long after the end of the normal workday that they had overlapped with Haywood's night shift, because he entered the room almost as soon as they had left it. This is why I also know that they surely must have passed him in the hallway on their way to the elevator, they with their coats and scarves on and fat satchels swinging in their hands and he pushing his cart with the bags and rags and mops and brooms, with his crazy bidirectional eyes and limping walk and face perturbed with tics and shudders and his black rubber boots and long keychain and hoop of many keys, walking *kLOMPa-whap-SHLINK* every step down the dark and echo-haunted hallway, and perhaps—this I do not know—perhaps they even exchanged a nod or a wave or a smile or a mumbled hello, though I suppose it is more likely that they ignored him completely. And I do know that the next day, at the close of the work day, I was not locked in my cage, because Lydia on that day would take me home to live with her. *To live with her*—in her home—with *her*. And I do know that I would never again sleep in conditions of enforced confinement. (Until, of course, now.) And I do know that scarcely had I finished listening to the *bing*ing and *bong*ing of the elevator in the hall and the scrolling open of the elevator doors and Lydia's and Norm's four squeaky shoes entering the elevator and the scrolling shut of the elevator doors, when I saw Haywood Finch's blurry shadow through the smoked-glass door to room 308: BEHAV-IORAL BIOLOGY LABORATORY, and I heard the sound of Haywood selecting a particular key from his hoop of many keys, and I heard the key being pushed into the lock and turned with the turning of the door's handle. And I know that the door opened and Haywood entered the room and switched on the lights, which fluttered on in the way energy-saving fluorescent lights do, the full glow preceded by three false starts: *nzt-nzt-nzt-nzzzzzzzzzz———————*. And I know that upon seeing him, I stood up in my cage, and held on to the bars with one hand, and with the other I pointed at myself and said, as loudly and as articulately as any man: "BRUNO!"

And I know that I wished Lydia had been there to hear me.

Part Two

What may this mean? Language of man pronounced
By tongue of brute, and human sense expressed?

—*Eve, to Satan,* Paradise Lost

X

Gwen: help me. Yes, help me. Have you ever acted? Have you ever considered acting?

There's a crucial speech in scene three of *Woyzeck* that I cannot possibly extirpate from the play, as it would have to be if the role could only be played by a chimp. For the role in question I had previously cast a relatively bright but of course speechless young chimp named Markus, but I have realized, and not without pain, that he is unsuited for the part, which is a small one but very important. I cannot cut the speech, and I cannot conceive of any plausible way of getting a chimp, an ordinary chimp, to deliver it. I've got no choice but to cast a human. It's the part of the Showman—a charlatan, a snake-oil salesman—who musters up a festival crowd that includes Woyzeck and Marie. He has a horse that he claims can tell the time and communicate it by stamping his hooves. Anyway, his speech is too thematically important to entrust in the mouth or hands of a nonlinguistic animal. I need a human actor. You wouldn't have many lines, I promise. Well, one big speech and a couple of little ones. Just come to our rehearsal this afternoon, see what you think. I can't double-cast Leon in the part. It would be confusing. I already have him cast in the role of the Doctor. Leon has a massive stage presence, which is why I only want him playing one part. Obviously I don't mind casting across gender. I'm already casting across species. Please. Fine. Sleep on it. Consider it seriously, though. Here, take this. It's a copy of the play. I urge you to give it serious consideration. You're not badly suited for the stage, Gwen. You cut a striking figure, you have such a crisp, clean, beautiful voice. I'm not trying to flatter you. Give it some thought, that's all I ask. You'd be great. I'm not crazy. Really.

I've just realized that I have come a long way in my narrative without bothering to describe myself. Physically, I mean. The basics. I wouldn't want people to go on picturing me as an ordinary chimp.

On August 20 of this year I will be twenty-five years old. Years of bipedal standing and walking have straightened my spine, lengthened my legs and stretched my torso, and I now stand an upright four feet and one inch, which is short for a human being but basically towering for a chimpanzee. I groom myself meticulously; captivity has not made me slovenly or careless with my hygiene. I brush my teeth twice daily. I have no hair. Over ten years ago a rare but benign condition called universal alopecia caused all of my hair to fall out. I don't mind my hairlessness. As a matter of fact, I like it. I love the feeling of my smooth nude limbs slithering between the freshly laundered sheets of my bed. I admit that I am somewhat overweight at one hundred and eighty pounds. I also admit to the surgery. Obviously I wasn't born with this nose. I will later tell you about how a cosmetic surgeon gave me the nose job to end all nose jobs: he gave me a human nose. I think my human nose harmonizes beautifully with my surrounding chimp face. If you look very closely you can still trace the pale perimeter of scar tissue around my nose. Today I simply threw on this ratty old bathrobe, but, even in captivity, I usually take enough pride in my appearance not to dress too sloppily. My clothes are getting thin and threadbare at the elbows and knees, but even a cursory examination of my wardrobe reveals my tasteful and elegant fashion sense. I keep asking for new clothes, and the research center keeps promising them to me and then forgetting (or ignoring) their promise. I have to have my clothes specially tailored because my frame is of such irregular proportions. For instance, my arms are longer than my legs.

Would you like a glass of wine, Gwen? I con convinced them to let me drink wine, but they forbid me hard liquor. I know it's not yet noon, but in my enforced retirement, I'm long past feeling the oppressive obligation to remain sober in the daytime. Why bother?

I have struggled with the demons in the bottle ever since they first seduced me. I struggle with them, and usually I let them win. So what? Imagine this: it's as if there's a hideous grating noise constantly roaring in your head, and alcohol muffles it a little. Why should I be made to feel embarrassed or guilty or ashamed when I imbibe? The world's got its own problems. Who is the world to judge? Like most drunkards, I feel most alive when I'm killing myself. You would not so opprobriously condemn me for always wanting to drown my brain in wine if you knew how easily my mind races headlong into dangerous places without it, if you could feel how my palms ooze sweat, how my stomach recoils, how my heart flutters in my chest like a wounded bird when I am not drunk. If you ever have children, tell them they must always be drunk. Drunk on love, drunk on poetry, drunk on wine, it doesn't matter. This world is too goddamn painful to waste a second of your existence sober.

Onward, then.

One day (it must have been, what?—November?), one day in the fall of a year that must have been around 1989, at the end of the day, Lydia carried me out of the Behavioral Biology Laboratory on the third floor of the Erman Biology Center in the northeast corner of the main quad of the University of Chicago campus, away from my cage and away from my nights of jabbering with Haywood, wrapped in my fuzzy blue blanket, my arms wrapped around her neck. It was November, definitely November, and already murderously cold outside. Lydia was wearing a black wool peacoat, a knit cap, and a green flannel scarf tucked into the breast of her coat. The serpent of winter had bitten Chicago and bitten it bad, injecting it with the icy venom that whistled and shrieked through the city's veins and arteries. It was time for streams dribbling from gutter pipes to solidify in midbraid, time for sooty snow and sludgy sidewalks. It was time for thick blankets. It was time for hats and boots. It was time for mugs of warm, viscous liquids to be sipped beside the soulful pulse of a fire, time for comfortable armchairs and good books and ice-fractals to form on the exterior surfaces of foggy windows, time for the soporific interior calm of a Midwestern winter.

I had been in Lydia's car only once, when she had spirited me away from the zoo many months before (or was it years?—I've no way of estimating how much time had passed). Her car was an inauspicious thing, four-doored, flat, aerodynamically designed, dark blue. Under the blanket I scratched my face against the coarse material of Lydia's woolen coat, and I licked one of its hard plastic buttons. I felt her chest moving beneath it, sucking in and pushing out her breath. My bare feet stuck out from under the blanket and quickly became numb from the cold. She opened the passenger door of the car and placed me inside, swaddled in the front seat in my blanket. She drew the straps of the seat belt across me and buckled it, tucked the diagonal strap under my chin and the horizontal one over my knees, kissed the top of my head, and shut the door. It was silent and deathly cold inside the car. Peeking over the edge of the dashboard I watched her walk to the driver's side, open the door, get in, close the door, buckle up, insert the keys, *chuppitachuppita-FROOM*, and then she piloted us stop-and-go through the grid of narrow brown urban streets, past blinking constellations of multicolored lights and bundled-up pedestrians huddled at street corners waiting for traffic lights to change, past the glowing windows of clothing shops, their wares on display, the expressionless faces of fashionably clad mannequins gazing icily onto the street from their display windows. Some windows had already been festooned with the first strings of red and green lights that signal the imminent close of the calendar year. I tried to stand up in the car seat to press my face to the window, but Lydia reached over and gently pushed me back into my seat, keeping me safe.

We arrived at Lydia's home. She parallel-parked in front of the door to her building on the side of the street, unbuckled my seat belt, and helped me out. The street was lined with trees whose winter-naked fingers clawed at the gray sky. The trees were planted in mounds of mulch and enclosed by tiny white fences, each one set in the middle of a rectangle of dead grass blocked out by paved walkways; and each walkway led to an iron gate and up four steps to a door in a long contiguous slab of four-story brick buildings. Lydia bore me across the walk, through the gate, up the stairs to the door of her building, through that door and into a hallway. Her door was 1A: bottom floor, first one on the left. Supporting my weight with one arm while using the other to turn the key in the lock and push open the door in the same motion, she said, "We're home sweet home, Bruno," and, like a surreal subversion of newly-wed man and wife, woman carried ape across the threshold of 5120 South Ellis Avenue, Apartment 1A.

I should describe this space for you with utmost and delicate accuracy. Therefore, I now present you with a map of our apartment, which I spent all last night fastidiously drawing from memory. You may find it useful to consult as I take you on the grand tour.

5120 South Ellis Avenue, Apt. 1A, Chicago, IL 60615:
Residence of Lydia and Bruno

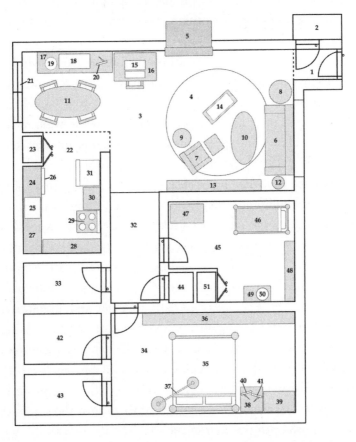

Lydia lived in a small but comfortable ground-level two-bedroom, two-bathroom apartment in upper Hyde Park on South Ellis Avenue, between Fifty-first and Fifty-second streets.

She set me down on the tiled floor of the vestibule (1), a small dimly lit mudroom that provided a liminal space for psychological transition between the front door and the rest of the apartment. She kneeled and slid her feet out of her slushy winter boots and left them to dry on a mat by the front door, joining several other pairs of empty footwear lining the wall. She struggled out of her black woolen coat and hung it and her scarf and hat on pegs protruding from the back of the open door to the entryway closet (2). Her feet now shod in thick furry red stockings—had I ever seen Lydia barefoot?—had I ever before seen her in her stocking feet?—she took me by the hand and walked me into the combined living room/dining area (3), the largest space in the apartment. She clicked on a light, and a membranous corrugated paper globe hanging from the middle of the ceiling became illuminated from within, blanketing the room in soft gauzy light. The floors were of hard glossy wood, partially covered by a large circular area rug (4) that lay in the middle of the room directly beneath the paper lighting fixture; the rug, frayed and threadbare in its most heavily trafficked areas, was predominately burgundy and featured an intricate pattern of vines and flowers radially kaleidoscoping outward from the center, its circumference fringed with knotted tassels of string. The north wall, the longest in the room, is of bare brick, with a fireplace (5) embedded in the middle of it; the floor surrounding the fireplace is of inflammable gray-green granite tile, and it is protected by a glass-and-metal grate. The other walls are sheetrock, textured and painted regulation eggshell-white, and there are two vertical picture windows in the east wall that look out onto South Ellis Avenue, which, if privacy is desired, may be shrouded with red drapes that approximately match the rug. The furniture is homey but somewhat jumbled and mismatched. The smallness of the apartment has required Lydia to cram most of her furniture into this main living area, resulting in mildly unnerving crosscurrents of spatial flow. The tan leather couch pushed against the east wall beneath the street-facing windows (6) matches the nearby armchair and ottoman (7), the two circular side tables beside the couch and armchair (8, 9) are of pine, and the ovular cherrywood coffee table (10) matches the ovular cherrywood dining table and chairs (11) in the far corner of the room, but these three different sets of furniture do not visually harmonize with each other. A floor lamp stands behind the couch in the southeast corner of the living room (12). A long and fully stocked bookcase (13) lines the south wall. On a small console a TV (14) perches awkwardly in the middle of the room, and a personal computer (15), along with a desk lamp and a tumultuous litter of papers, pens, and pencils, rests atop an architect's drafting table (16). Various objets d'art personalize the room: a framed print of Marc Chagall's *I and the Village* hangs on the north wall near the dining table, a dark and atmospheric Edward Weston nude above the worktable, and on the south wall above the bookshelf hangs a large rectangular painting depicting what looks like a writhing nest of eels slithering out of the green half of the picture and into the yellow; candles and primitive wooden effigies march across the top surface of the bookcase and across the fireplace mantel. Moving to the back of the room, we observe more closely the ovular cherrywood dining table and the four matching chairs. Beside the table is a waist-high oblong block of furniture (17) with three deep shelves locked behind glass doors; the bottom two shelves contain a miscellany of various knickknacks and oversize books, and the top shelf holds Lydia's collection of tapes and CDs, its constituency reflecting her eclectic and generally excellent musical taste, combining elements of high culture (Dvořák's Cello Concerto in B minor), coffee-shop cool (John Coltrane's *A Love Supreme*) and an American girlhood that blossomed in the early 1980s (Elvis Costello, Blondie, Prince, Talking Heads). On top of this is a stereo (18), with an LCD display of digital numbers, flashing, in a verdant undersea glow, an impossibly incorrect time. To

the left of the stereo rests a shallow burnished mother-of-pearl dish
(19) into which Lydia, when returning home from work, empties
the contents of her purse or coat pockets: keys, loose change accrued
over the course of the day's small financial transactions, etc.—joining pens, paper clips, and other coins already in the dish.

To the right of the stereo, angled in such a way as to be optimally
viewed from the position of one seated at the work desk beside it,
is an eight-by-ten-inch photograph (20) in an unadorned black
wooden frame of the readymade, commercially available sort with
metal clips in the back and a triangular stand that folds out to prop
it up for display at a steep, slightly obtuse angle. Inside the frame,
behind the glass, a group of people are gathered together in what
appears to be a hermetically sealed vacuum chamber, all staring
straight ahead with smiles slathered like butter across the white
bread of their faces, the very young and the very old sitting in front
and everyone else standing behind them. In the bottom center of
the photograph sit two elderly people: a man with a gawkily grinning pink bald head bobbing atop a sinewy neck that pokes out of
the collar of his corduroy suit like a baby bird breaking out of its
eggshell, his teeth like the yellowing white keys of an old piano and
his murky gray-green eyes floating like jellyfish in the thick aquari-
ums of his eyeglasses; his skinny arm is wrapped around the woman
sitting beside him dressed in a fuzzy white turtleneck sweater and
a red vest, whose skin is rusty with liver spots and whose smile
does not reveal her teeth, with a brushed-steel bouffant, pearl earrings, and a matching necklace, whose eyes are smoke-colored
and haloed with cataracts, who was clearly a beautiful woman in
her youth, and whose dense rosy perfume you can almost smell
through the photograph, as if, on the day it was taken, her perfume
had been powerful enough to waft through the lens of the camera,
seep into the celluloid of the film, and later transfer from the nega-
tives onto the matte-finish color print to finally sublimate through

the glass of the frame and into the nose of the photograph's viewer. Surrounding these two old people in the center of the image are six adults and five children, the adults standing beside and behind them and the children seated in front, three girls in blue dresses with faces flexing authentic smiles and two boys in matching blue jackets sullenly faking theirs. Of the six adults, four are men and two are women, one of whom is Lydia, though her hair is different and she looks younger. Most of them have blond hair and crooked teeth. These are Lydia's siblings, of whom she is the youngest. This is her family. They are all dressed in cheap formal wear. A gold Wal-Mart logo peeks out from behind the frame in the bottom left corner of the photograph.

Behind the ellipsoidal cherrywood dining table, directly opposite the front door, a sliding glass door (21) opens onto a small patch of backyard, which features a red brick patio and a square of grass surrounded by low-cut hedges, in which tulips grow in the spring.

At this point the living/dining room spills into a cramped and narrow but serviceable kitchen (22), its perimeter defined by the line where the wood floor becomes tile. (The pattern of the kitchen floor tile is big beige tiles set in a grid with smaller, diamond-shaped tiles of lazulian blue set in every *other* conjuncture of four tile corners. Like this:

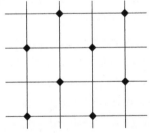

.) The kitchen features the following amenities, listed counterclockwise from the northwest corner of the room: pantry (23), counter (24), sink (25), dishwasher (26), counter (27), cabinets (28), oven/stove (29), counter (30), refrigerator (31). The stove is gas; the countertops are of speckled pink Formica; a coffeemaker, a toaster, and a microwave sit to the left of the sink; the wooden cabinets are built into the wall; a window above the kitchen sink looks out into the backyard and the alley just beyond it; three potted philodendrons stand in a row on the windowsill; the kitchen walls are painted pale yellow. The refrigerator is white, and several magnets cling to the surface of its door, pinning in place some slightly unfocused snapshots of Lydia smiling cameraward in the company of various unidentified friends, relatives, or loved ones.

In one of the photographs, Lydia is sitting in the company of three other women, all of whom appear to be about her age. They are all smiling. They are wearing bright swimwear: indeed, they appear to be wearing little but enough clothing to cover their breasts and genitals; their smiles are wide and seemingly genuine; their eyes are shadowed behind sunglasses. Lydia is wearing a canary yellow swimsuit. The women sit together at a table beneath a pink umbrella, on what looks like the outdoor patio of a restaurant, in a sunny, pleasant place that is very far away from here, both geographically and psychologically. The three other women are holding drinking glasses whose stems slope curvilinearly upward into elaborate shapes, containing unknown liquids, decorated with tiny umbrellas and colorful straws that twist up from the bowls of the glasses. Lydia, situated at the far left of the photograph, is conspicuously the only person in the photograph not holding one of these colorful beverages; in Lydia's hand there appears to be only an ordinary glass of orange juice. Lydia also looks oddly swollen in the picture, with a considerable belly that looks out of proportion to the rest of her body.

Rounding the corner of the half wall that helps define the boundaries of the kitchen, we pass back through the central living area, which empties into a dim chute of a hallway (32); at the mouth of the hallway the hardwood flooring ends and the dun gray carpeting begins; this short hallway has four doors: two on the left, one on the right, and one at the very end. The door on the right leads to a small room that a Realtor would call .5 of a bathroom (33): mirror, sink, toilet, shower, and tile floor of the same pattern as the kitchen floor. (I apologize that I have not bothered to render these things in detail.) The door at the very end of the hall leads to the master bedroom (34), or in our case the mistress bedroom, I suppose: Lydia's room. A wooden four-poster queen-size bed (35) dominates the room; the headboard is pushed flush against the south wall; the bed is probably made and draped with a down lavender comforter. Directly opposite the bed a bookshelf (36), fully stocked with dense and difficult volumes on academic subjects, lines the north wall. The bed is flanked on the right by a sleekly architectonic designer lamp that swivels on a long stalk (37) and on the left by a plain wooden bedside night table (38), and to the left of that, in the corner of the room, stands a sturdy chest of drawers (39). Two more windows in the east wall of the room look onto the street, treated with dark red curtains identical to the ones in the living room. On the south wall of the room hangs a framed print of Charles Demuth's *I Saw the Figure 5 in Gold*. On the bedside night table are an alarm clock (not pictured) and two more framed photographs (40, 41).

The first photograph, vertically oriented, shows Lydia standing in an unknown location, and standing in it with a man, both of them barefoot, their toes partially buried in the wet sand, on what looks like a beach. The wet sand is a jumble of footprints. This photograph is also a synesthetic one, its image easily implying sound and smell, the *skweee-skweee* of seagulls almost audible in it, the brackish seaside air almost olfactible. On a rocky hill in the background behind them stand three whitewashed stone windmills, each successively smaller than the next as the ridge they're built on curls into the distance, each windmill with a thatched conical roof and a pinwheel fashioned of rickety wooden spokes. The sky is blue, fading toward the horizon into dusky orange and then purple, and the light on the ground, on the two people themselves, and on the white trunks of the three windmills is sharp and golden, and the shadows are long. The shadow of the anonymous photographer stretches far into the frame across the golden sand. Lydia wears a breezy white shirt and a pair of white pants with a drawstring waistband, the bottom hems of which are rolled up to her knees, and her feet and ankles are covered with sand; the man is also wearing white pants with the bottom hems rolled up, in his case not quite to the knees, and below a line in the middle of his shin all his leg hair is flattened wet against his skin and speckled with sand particles. Lydia's blond hair is whipping erratically in the wind, although one of her hands is caught in the act of trying to tuck some of her hair behind her ear. But the other hand? The other hand is wrapped around the waist of the man beside her. And the man beside her? I'll admit that he is probably handsome. I'll admit that his physique is somewhat Adonis-like, that one might consider him tall and the possessor of arguably chiseled features, that his skin could conceivably be described as tanned and robust. I'm also willing to concede that one of his perceivably lean and muscular arms is depicted in the act of insidiously wrapping itself around Lydia's torso, and that if one looks closely, the tips of his fingers may in fact be, as is not unequivocally deducible from the image before us, digging slightly beneath the waistline of the pants that Lydia wears in the photograph, where they may or may not be in the process of deftly stroking the ridge of her right hipbone. I'm also perfectly willing to admit that these two people are both smiling in an apparently genuine way as they squint into the setting sun, and I will admit these two people are, perhaps, at least ostensibly, not impossibly, seemingly outwardly clearly painfully obviously deeply in love. But I will not admit that this photograph ever made me jealous.

In the other photograph, the same two people, Lydia and the mysterious man, are standing in some indoor area; unlike the other, this photograph is not a snapshot but rather has been deliberately, professionally staged. Lydia, barely recognizable in the picture, is wearing a long white dress, blinding white, which spills from her beautiful bare shoulders like a frothing waterfall, and her outfit is accompanied by a white headband with a long diaphanous sheet of fabric sprouting from it and trailing down behind her. The man is standing beside her, again, with his arm planted on Lydia's opposite hip, wearing black. I know now what this photograph indicated. I didn't then.

I should note that at some point during the time I lived with Lydia, these two photographs went away.

On the west wall of Lydia's bedroom you will notice two doors; the door on the right leads to a bathroom (42) larger and better accommodated (tub, shower) than the one accessible from the hallway. The door on the left leads to a walk-in closet (43). (Lydia's closet! That particular treasury of Venus, that Fort Knox of pure feminine gold, I'll deal with in greater depth later on.) We leave the master bedroom and reenter the hallway. Open the door to your immediate right. It is a small linen closet (44), of little note. Now open the second door on the right, the last unopened door in the apartment.

The first time I ever passed through this door was on that day I went home with Lydia from the laboratory. I was clinging to her, loving, loved, awed. She opened the door and we went inside. On the other side of the door was (45) Bruno's room.

My room! My, my, my, *my* room! Mine! My *area*! My *space*! (Do you realize what a godly luxury is the first-person possessive pronoun applied to physical space?) My own human bedroom in a human home! There was a bed made for me, and the walls were covered with sky-blue wallpaper with pictures of clowns all over it, each clown gripping a cluster of bright balloons, and using it to ascend like Icarus into the stratosphere. A mobile of the solar system dangled on a string above the bed. I loved it. The bed (46) was of the sort designed for very young children, with the mattress sunk at the bottom of an open wooden cage to prevent a human infant from rolling out of it. In the corner of the room there was a toy box (47) erupting with all manner of bright things for me to play with—animals and games and puzzles and so forth. There was a short narrow bookshelf (48) containing a modest library of stimulating picture books, each of which I would with time come to know practically by heart, including (but by no means limited to) *Goodnight Moon*, *The Runaway Bunny*, *Mickey in the Night Kitchen*, *Aesop's Fables* and *A Child's Garden of Verses*. Then there was a little dresser (49) against the south wall, atop which stood a giant hollow plastic goose (50) with an electric cord running from the back of her and into a wall outlet. This goose was a lamp. I loved that goose. I thought it was so wonderful that a lamp could be shaped like a goose, that such a thing was even possible. You turned on her switch, and she softly glowed from within, the shadow of her long curving neck and beak cast against the ceiling by the light of her own body, driving the terror of darkness from my bedroom at night.

The room was such a bright happy place for a young ape to be, just the right environment of whimsy and childlike wonder to aid the early social and spiritual development of someone standing on the threshold of his entry into human civilization. There were so many interesting things to look at in that room—the wild costumery of all the levitating clowns on the walls, a rectangle of light moving across the wall opposite the window, the hypnotizing oscillation of the ceiling fan, the books, the toys, the illuminate goose, and, most of all, the mobile of the solar system that dangled from the ceiling above my bed—the movement of its heavenly spheres: in the middle, the sun, that glowing gaseous monster constantly exploding with the energy of ten billion nuclear bombs per second, here pictured in the act of spurting a terrifying arch of flame; then hot little Mercury, a little too close for comfort to the big S; then bright sexy Venus coyly wrapped in her bridal veil of toxic clouds; now our own blue-green dot, teeming with all manner of activity, vegetable, animal, and mineral; then angry red Mars, the coral planet who may have once harbored life; then a dusting of crumbs representing the asteroid belt; then Jupiter, massive, swirling with bloody thunderstorms, a flock of moons reeling round him like indignant desert birds; now Saturn with his hula hoop making him the most visually fascinating of the nine; then Uranus and Neptune, cold blue unfriendly twins; and finally the runty Pluto, so tiny that he's since been demoted to "dwarf planet" and unceremoniously renamed "134340," swinging around way out there in the frigid boondocks of the system—all of these wandering stars, careening like drunks on orbits eccentric and elliptical, cogs in the celestial clockwork, all revolving above Bruno's little bed.

Also, I forgot to mention that there was also a closet in this room (51), containing all sorts of adorable baby clothes—all obviously unworn!

XI

Lydia took me back to the lab at the University of Chicago nearly every day, except on the weekends. The home was the domestic domain, the domain of Lydia, the domain of comfort, of leisure, of pleasure, of love. The lab was Norm's domain: the man's domain, the cold hard domain of work. But the lab was a much more tolerable place to spend my days when I knew that at the ends of them I had a comfortable human home to return to with Lydia. The tests continued. All their "language training" continued unabated. The naming of things, the plastic tokens, the stuffed animals, and all the rest of it. I performed their tasks for them, mostly in a state of complacent boredom. I performed their tasks correctly more and more often. As soon as I had one of their tasks down cold, they introduced another. I chose to learn them quickly, simply so that I wouldn't have to suffer through the boredom of making them repeat their brain-numbingly dull procedures ad nauseam. But the lion's share of the "work" I did with Lydia was unstructured; it occurred simply in the process of ordinary quotidian life, which of course occurred all the time, not officially beginning when we entered the lab and ending when we left it.

Life at home was cheery and domestic. Every day after we came home from the lab and on the weekends, she would spend hours speaking to me. She experimented with various stimuli—games, puzzles, dolls, flash cards, generally adhering to the Montessori method of pedagogy—unhurried, loosely structured, compassionate nurturing. In the evenings I would "help" her cook, and we ate together. I learned to eat sitting at the table in a chair on top of a stack of phone books, using a fork and knife for solids and a spoon for liquids, and later in the night I would curl up in her lap while she read to me from one of my picture books, clearly articulating the words as she traced them one by one with her finger, and I listened to the words and looked at the words, gradually beginning to learn to attach visual to auditory, signifier to signified.

When she had to leave the house alone, she would put me in my crib and fasten a plastic covering to the top to keep me out of trouble until she returned. But aside from that we were rarely apart, and seldom out of earshot. Gradually, as I became more civilized, she came to trust me enough to let me roam the house by myself when she was out, and I whiled away my time alone by perusing my picture books or watching television, though she told me not to do too much of that because it would rot my brain.

The one small subversive thing I would do when she was out— when I sat there watching TV alone—was to crack open the TV's remote control to get at its nine-volt battery, which I would gingerly touch to the surface of my tongue to feel a mild but thrilling little fuzzy electric shock. I also loved the coppery aftertaste. I would touch the battery to my tongue again and again.

My favorite program was *Sesame Street*, which was fine with Lydia because it was covertly educational. And indeed I learned many fundamentals from *Sesame Street*: how to count to ten, the colors of the alphabet, why not to eat cookies in bed. I particularly adored the segments dealing with Bert and Ernie. I was always rooting for Ernie, the freewheeling embodiment of the id, whom

Bert, his stern superego, is forever trying to repress with his uptight inhibitions. Ernie, so naïve, squat, and orange; and Bert, with his yellow napiform head and scraggly black unibrow so quick to V in anger... But Bert is also wise in his own weltschmerzy way, and the two of them usually wind up learning something from each other. Every episode left Ernie a little less innocent and Bert a little more, making me wonder if someday their personalities might meet in the middle, when both achieve a self-actualized balance of wisdom and joy. Through Bert's admonitions Ernie would come to understand something important, usually relating to his own hygiene or personal safety, and Ernie would sometimes broaden Bert's mind a little with his energetic love of life, like in the episode in which they go fishing, and Ernie teaches Bert his shamanistic trick of invoking the fishes to simply leap out of the water and into their boat by vocal commands alone, by the awesome thaumaturgy of mere language.

I watched *Sesame Street* ritualistically every morning before Lydia took me to the lab. It began my day, providing a transition period from my dream state to my wakeful consciousness. If I got up before Lydia did I would report first to the television, to check in on the Muppet-populated universe of *Sesame Street*. In *Sesame Street*, as in much children's entertainment, it is seen as perfectly natural that human beings should freely verbally communicate with nonhuman creatures.

Often, if I happened to rise early enough, I caught a show that preceded *Sesame Street* on weekdays, called *Francis the Gnome*. This was an animated series about a gnome named Francis who lived with his matronly gnome wife in a rustic home fashioned from the hollow of a tree in what appeared to be a temperate pine forest somewhere in North America. Francis wore a pointed green hat and a long white beard with a Tolstoyan fork. Francis served as doctor to the animals of the forest. He did good deeds for woodland animals in trouble: releasing them from hunters' traps, nursing them back to health when they took sick. Francis was at home in nature. He too communed with the animals.

So I would watch cartoons on TV early in the morning before Lydia got up, licking a nine-volt battery over and over and over.

Lydia also provided me with lots of puffy colorful plastic cases containing videotapes of animated films for me to watch. I appreciated all the Disney films, like *Snow White and the Seven Dwarves*, *Cinderella*, *The Sword in the Stone* and *Robin Hood*—but obviously, as it touched on certain core thematic elements of my life, my favorite by far was *Pinocchio*. The literary characters with whom I most strongly identify are Caliban, Woyzeck, Milton's Satan, and Pinocchio. Pinocchio is perhaps the most important of these. Even at the time I may have associated Lydia with the beautiful blue fairy who floats in through Geppetto's window to bestow consciousness upon the puppet with a touch of her magic wand.

———

Before I get too far ahead of myself, I should tell you an anecdote that begins with strange screams that I heard in my dreams at night. I don't remember how soon it was after I began living with Lydia that I started having these dreams. They usually happened right before I woke up in the morning. I would be lying asleep in my bed, dreaming away on pleasant topics, when suddenly I would begin to hear screams, and my dreams would get bent into nightmares. I would hear these half-human noises—bursts of bloody-throated, high-pitched screaming. I dreamed of a prison, a torture garden where both people and animals wandered the grounds—or crawled along the floor, or were chained naked to posts—while guards marched up and down the halls of the castle (sometimes it was a castle), selecting the people or animals to be brought below to some place that was underground, for tortures or cruel scientific experiments. The guards wore uniforms: some of them wore crisp, fascistic brown uniforms with gold buttons, like the zookeepers would wear, and others wore the uniforms of scientists—flowing white coats—and carried clipboards. A scientist would point out one of the people, and the zookeeper would yank at the chain the person wore around his neck, and with a whip drive the person four-legged down a cold stone staircase. Soon we on the surface would hear his screams, rising up from the vents in the floor. The screaming would grow louder, more painful and terrifying, until I woke up, and it was morning. This dream would recur with slight variations. What's interesting about this dream is that it might have been the first dream in my life that I remembered any of at all. Before, in an alexic universe, all my dreams had bled right out of my brain only seconds after waking, but by this time I had learned enough language to begin to capture and keep my dreams.

I discovered the source of these dark dreams when Lydia and I met Griph Morgan. I do not know exactly how long Lydia had lived in that apartment before my arrival, but apparently she had never met Griph, her reclusive upstairs neighbor, until we bumped into him on the stoop of the building one afternoon when we happened to arrive home at the same time. Lydia and I had come home from the lab several hours earlier than usual that day for some reason— perhaps that was why she had never crossed paths with him before; Griph's and Lydia's schedules had never chanced to align. He was struggling with his keys in the door to the building when we came up the stairs. Griph Morgan was not very old, but he was in poor health. He was missing one leg (he was a veteran) and walked with a cane. He had one normal leg (though a little on the pale and flabby side) and the other one was a thin metal prosthesis, which culminated unsettlingly in a fake foot inside a sneaker; but what made this doubly unsettling was that one of the many points of pride Mr. Morgan took in his Scottish heritage was the tartan kilt he usually wore, a pleated green-and-red plaid skirt, decoratively completed by a broad black belt and a rabbit-pelt sporran. Additionally, Mr. Morgan played the bagpipes, which that afternoon he had slung over his shoulder, as he was returning home from practicing in the park. To me Mr. Morgan's bagpipes looked less like a musical instrument than a creature from another planet: a glossy black velvet bag for a body, from the top of which protruded a series of segmented stalks that looked like they could be sensory organs, and a long infundibuliform tube coming out the front of it that could have been some sort of silly nose. Lydia introduced herself and me, and he gruffly told us his name. Lydia began talking to him in the hallway of the building, though Mr. Morgan had already begun his slow clumping three-legged ascent of the stairs. First she asked him a neighborly question having to do with recycling. The question seemed to be a bit of a conversational ruse, Lydia's real curiosity being more about her previously unseen Caledophilic upstairs neighbor than about what exactly the building's protocol for disposing of glass and aluminum was. Mr. Morgan—who sported an interesting style of facial hair that he called a Vandyke—was characteristically laconic.

"I don't drink anymore," was all he said.

"But what about cans—?" Lydia must have asked, provoking a dismissive snort from beneath the mustaches of Mr. Morgan's Vandyke before he replied that he purchased all his beans wholesale in bags and boiled them himself.

"You don't boil your beans?" he said.

"Well—" Lydia seemed slightly confused by the question.

Like any Scotsman, Mr. Morgan was proud of his resourcefulness and frugality. He took a mild interest in me but did not seem particularly surprised that his downstairs neighbor shared her apartment with a chimp, and casually made mention of the fact that he himself cohabited peacefully with ten parrots.

"Do they talk?" Lydia asked with excitement.

"Of *course* they talk," said Mr. Morgan, as if he was offended that she need even have asked. Then Lydia asked to see them, and then we were all upstairs in Griph Morgan's apartment, which was (one) less than half the size of ours, (two) situated directly above my (Bruno's) bedroom, (three) cluttered with old newspapers stacked to the ceiling (which Mr. Morgan clearly had no intention of recycling anytime soon), and (four) did indeed have a whole flock of parrots in it, flapping and squawking and crawling all over everything in the room. There was a big pot of beans boiling busily on the stove. Half the floor space of the living room was taken up by a huge wire birdcage, the door of which was open to allow free passage for the ten parrots. There was a tiny old TV with a twisted coat hanger for an antenna, a foldout card table, a side table, and a shabby brown easy chair facing the TV. The room had no other furnishings. The chair had been sat in so many times and so often that Mr. Morgan had carved a depression in the seat and the back that was shaped like his body, such that the negative space formed a phantomlike impression of Mr. Morgan sitting in the chair in the event of his absence. Mr. Morgan inserted his form into the Mr. Morgan–shaped crater in the easy chair, and Lydia and I sat on two of the shorter stacks of newspapers. The room was tropically dank and steamy, smelling of the combined effects of the potful of boiling beans and the parrots. Lydia would later confide in me that in her opinion Mr. Morgan's apartment "stank," and that she was glad she had finally discovered the source of "that weird smell in the building." I, however, actually kind of liked the smell. Mr. Morgan's apartment had a not-unpleasant soporific effect on me; I found its biotic pungency oddly cozy. In fits and starts of attempted conversation Lydia managed to extract from Mr. Morgan that the two things he lived for were his parrots and his bagpipes. As for the latter, he was the lead bagpiper in the Veteran's Association of

Chicago & North Western Railway Bagpipe Band. When they played in parades, he would play his bagpipes from a wheelchair, which was pushed at the head of the formation by a tartan-clad volunteer. As for the former, Griph Morgan's parrots consisted of three African greys, two macaws, two red-billed Pionuses, one blue-crowned racket-tail, one cockatiel and one Senegalese yellow-vented. All of Mr. Morgan's parrots enjoyed free range of his small apartment. He considered these birds his friends and roommates more than his pets.

Just a few moments spent in that place provided me with all the epiphany I needed to know the source of all those screaming dreams I had been having: the screams that my sleeping brain had built dark scenarios around were obviously the noisy, prehistoric squawks of these birds. The noises they made hearkened back to the days of the dinosaurs; it wasn't hard to imagine these sounds coming from the throats of pterodactyls or archæopteryxes.

All of them could speak at least a little. They could say a few standard parrot things in English, such as *hello* and *good-bye* and *wantsome* when they wanted food of some sort. For instance, they might say *wantsome cracker* or *wantsome apple*. Some of them had learned profanities and would use the word *dammit* as an all-purpose intensifier, as in *wantsome apple dammit*. That was most of what the parrots would say in English. Mr. Morgan asserted that the parrots spoke far more in Scots Gaelic, their preferred language, which he had spent long and fruitful hours teaching to them. The parrots would frequently make a series of scratchy-throated trills and clicks and hauking and screaming sounds that Lydia and I assumed were just normal parrot noises, only to be informed by Mr. Morgan that the parrot who had made these sounds had actu-ally just recited a couplet from the Scots Gaelic folk ballad "A Phiùthrag's a Phiuthar."

Mr. Morgan was also a great lover of games. In particular he

loved chess and backgammon. He always preferred game playing
to conversation. Mr. Morgan taught me to play chess and backgammon. Chess was Mr. Morgan's wife and backgammon his
mistress: he loved them both, but one more committedly than the
other. I remember that Lydia once asked him where he went all
day—he didn't work and lived frugally on his disability checks—
and he admitted that he spent most days playing chess in the park,
even in the foulest weather. I now imagine him forlornly bundled
up in a coat and hat in subzero weather, shivering at the stone
chessboard in the park, playing against himself while waiting for
a willing opponent to happen by. He usually had ten to twenty
correspondence games going at once. He taught me to play chess,
but was disappointed that I never got good enough to present him
with any even remotely worthy opposition, which was why he preferred to play backgammon with me, the game at which I proved
more skilled. I loved the mere object of his backgammon set: it
came in a black leather briefcase that looked like it ought to contain important legal documents, or maybe stacks of crisp hundred-
dollar bills in a heist movie; but unclasp the snaplocks and unfold
it, and look!—inside is a flat board with pockets set in the sides of
it for the dice, the leather dice cups and the black and white playing chips! The board is divided in two by the hinge of the case,
and is covered with a chocolate-brown felt lining, with long narrow isosceles triangles of alternating dark and light brown leather
sewn flat to the felt, pointing out of the side of each quadrant of
the board like jagged teeth. I loved the smell of the thing, all the
felt and leather and glue, and loved the sound of the dice rattling
in the leather dice cups, and the noise of their tumbling onto the
board, and the deft clicks of the plastic chips as we lined them up
on top of the triangles. It is Mr. Morgan to whom I owe my love of
backgammon, our uncommunicative upstairs neighbor, with his
kilt, his boiling beans, his bagpipes, and his parrots. Later in my

life I would play backgammon a lot with my friend Leon, whom I lived with for a year in New York when I was a Shakespearean actor. Leon is also an avid gamer. He likes backgammon but is not as good at it as Mr. Morgan was (I usually win when I play Leon). Every time Leon visits me in my place of confinement, he brings his backgammon set, and sometimes, if the staff of my research center can be persuaded to let us, Leon and I imitate older and happier times by staying up all night talking, drinking wine, and playing game after game of backgammon, the chips clicking and the dice rattling in the cups sometimes until dawn.

The longer Lydia and I sat there on his stacks of newspapers, the less we got out of him. Griph Morgan was so crusty and taciturn, his recluse's windpipes so reticent to make human speech that the parrots actually made better conversationalists. Mr. Morgan was clearly a man who felt more conversationally at home in the company of creatures whose vocabularies did not exceed more than ten or twenty words, or who spoke a not-dead-but-nearly-forgotten language that almost no one speaks anymore. Eventually we retreated back downstairs, with Lydia in parting making a vague offer to invite him down to dinner sometime, and Mr. Morgan accepting the open invitation even more vaguely. But after that visit, two things changed. One: I no longer had bad dreams that came from the parrots' shrieks and squawks, but rather my sleeping mind attached more pleasant associations to them now that I knew they were not screaming in pain, but reciting Scots Gaelic folk songs; now rather I dreamed of charming bonny lasses traipsing gaily through the highlands and things like that. Two: Now, whenever Lydia was busy with some task that need not involve me, such as cooking dinner, and we heard the low ululatory doleful drone of bagpipes coming from upstairs (how had we not noticed that before?), Lydia would permit me to run with thumping limbs up the stairs to knock on Mr. Morgan's door, which would usually (though not always) open after the silencing of the bagpipes, where-upon Mr. Morgan would usually (though not always) permit me to sit on a stack of newspapers in his apartment and play with his parrots and listen to him practicing his bagpipes, as beans boiled on the stove and the ten birds squawked, trilled, cooed, whistled, and croaked out some of the words they knew in rancorous accompaniment to the pipes, or, if Mr. Morgan was in a really good mood, we would play backgammon, and the chips would click and the dice would rattle and tumble until Lydia would come upstairs to fetch me for dinner, usually (though not always) trying to engage Mr. Morgan in a brief but cordial conversation, her efforts usually (though not always) failing, and sometimes (though not usually) she would invite Mr. Morgan to join us downstairs for dinner, which invitation Mr. Morgan would (always) decline.

XII

Sometimes Lydia took me on fun and educational outings. We would take the train uptown—I remember the insane joy of standing up on the seat of the train, my face squished to the window, making the glass moist and foggy with the smoke of my breath, to watch the intricate craziness and chaos and filth of the city rush by in panorama, all the untraceable activity in it like an unfurling fractal, the unnatural weirdness of all that steel and stone and glass warmed, enlivened by the human activity surging within it—or to the movies, or to lie in the sun on the lakefront in the summer, or once to the Field Museum...only once, because the sight of several taxidermized corpses of members of my own species propped up in fun poses inside a blatantly fake diorama horrified me.

(Since then, by the way, Gwen, I've been back to the Field Museum, and revisited the very diorama that so deeply unsettled the younger Bruno, and on seeing it again I only found it silly and quaint, and it was almost funny to remember how much it had disturbed me. It caused me to reflect on how far I've come, on the person I've since grown into. I no longer find the chimpanzee diorama so viscerally disturbing because I no longer consider myself one of them.)

Or we would go to the planetarium. I loved the planetarium. Lydia probably took me there because: (one) it was fun, (two) it was educational, and (three) we could remain inconspicuous in the darkness. I associate my memories of that place with an eerie chill in my spine and a crick in my neck from a whole afternoon spent looking up—an uncomfortable position for a human but even more so for a curvy-spined, short-necked ape. The stars above us in that great dark dome!—far more stars than were ever visible in the urban skies I was used to. I was really impressed with the alleged unfathomable vastness of the universe. Sitting in the planetarium, gazing up at the high-domed ceiling and watching the star shows was simultaneously joyful and terrifying. I appreciated the helpful glowing line drawings they would project over the constellations, showing us the shapes of the beasts and men and gods and monsters that the Ancients had wildly imagined out of the suggestions of these random scatterings of points of light in the darkness above them.

And then there was the business of learning to use the toilet. Yes, I too would have to learn the curious human taboo about urinating and defecating in public. Back in the lab, my potty training had been a rigorously enforced process of conditioning, with sweet rewards and draconian punishments. I had been lavished with particularly sumptuous treats if I dealt with my bodily excretions properly, but if I urinated or defecated on the floor of the lab, I was chastised more severely than for any other trespass. In the lab there was a little plastic chamber pot, colored red and topped with a yellow plastic lid that had a hole in the center of it, which was affixed by a valve to the rim of the receptacle: this was called my "potty." It had not taken me much time to learn to expel all my bodily fluids and solids into the recess of this thing, because I quickly realized that my living area was a far more pleasant place in which to be if the floor was *not*, in fact, splattered with my piss and shit. After I came to understand the purpose of the potty, I was glad to acquiescently squat on the lid and deposit the contents of my bowels into its red plastic concavity; soon thereafter one of the lab assistants would swoop in to bear my waste away and would return shortly with the potty, emptied and freshly washed. This was a far cry from the disgusting conditions in the zoo, from the piss-sodden carpeting of cedar planting chips in our habitat, and I welcomed it. But when I began living with Lydia, I was introduced to the bathroom.

Lydia indicated to me that from now on, while I was living in her home, I was to exclusively use this gleaming white machine for bodily waste disposal. I examined it. I lifted the lid, peered inside, set it down again. I looked into the pellucid waters within, wondering where the hole in the curving bottom of it led to. I did not quite yet realize that the little red potty that I had learned to use in the lab was in fact designed to mimic this very device. I grasped the sides of the seat with my long rubbery hands and stared into its depths while Lydia tore a square of toilet paper—also a novel thing to me then—threw it in, and flushed. I watched, rapt in awe, as the suck-crash-thunder of the torrent of water gushing in from some unknown source caused the delicate square of tissue to spiral around and around the bowl until it was finally sucked out of sight through the mysterious hole in the bottom, and I marveled as the bowl, with a prolonged hissing noise coming from deep within the machine, refilled anew with clean clear water that trickled in slowly, rose to a certain level, and then, as if God had told it to, simply stopped—and then there was silence.

I was transfixed. I myself tore off a handful of toilet paper, threw it in the bowl, yanked the trigger, and watched the machine repeat the whole magic show. I was so mesmerized by it that I probably would have kept at it until every last square of toilet paper in the world had vanished down the gurgling throat of this porcelain beast, had Lydia not stopped me to try to explain that this new machine was expressly for the disposal of one's urine and feces. She calmly explained to me that the next time I had to "pee" or "poop" I was to utilize this device. She asked me if I understood, and I replied—perhaps over-hastily—that I did.

The next time I felt my feces tunneling through my guts toward the light of my anus, I ran to the bathroom, and did not wait for her to arrive to supervise, to make sure I was doing it properly. By the time Lydia stood in the doorway, the deed was already done. Lydia's face twisted up in an expression of disgust. Of course I'd simply shat on the floor, then started eagerly flushing toilet paper down the toilet. Lydia verbally rebuked me before tearing off a wad of toilet paper and used it to scoop up the little pile of shit I had made, threw it into the toilet and flushed. Then she washed her hands, and bade me to do likewise. Only then did I understand.

The bathroom is a fascinating place. Becoming human is a process of equal parts enlightenment and imprinting your brain with taboos. I too began to regard the simple biological imperatives of pissing and shitting as the ultimate acts of shame—more shameful even than sex, because while sex acts (aside from mere masturbation) necessarily require the participation and hence company of at least a second party, the expulsion of bodily waste is generally regarded as something to be performed only in abject solitude, and is unmentionable in polite society. It seems to me there are two things humans like to pretend simply do not happen—two things, two inescapable actions in life, one of which is a daily concern, and the other, come to think of it, is also a daily concern, even though it will only happen to you once: defecating and dying. There's nothing else we treat with such embarrassment, such secrecy, nothing else we talk about in such couched euphemisms and hush-hush tones. Our sick and elderly we ferret away to die in the impersonal and sanitized environs of a hospital, pretending it's only a temporary illness or a contagious virus requiring quarantine, confinement, shutting it out of the sphere of everyday life, and then when it happens we say that So-and-So has "passed away" or "gone to a better place." And is that not exactly how we treat the very turds a healthy rectum must expel on a daily basis? We excuse ourselves from our fellows to disappear into this small bright sanitary room which no modern dwelling comes without, the sanctum of tiles and porcelain and running water, the hospital of the home, the place where we attend to matters of the body, where we bathe ourselves and bulwark our frail flesh and guts with all our hygienic defenses against a world that constantly besieges us with filth, the place of toothbrushing, flossing, shaving, applying makeup and deodorant, where we keep combs, brushes, hairspray, earwax syringes, toenail clippers, medicines and mouthwash, balms and salves, the place where we gaze at our reflections while sculpting ourselves into place for the day—and the place, Gwen, where we shit—where we lock ourselves in and secretly excommunicate these stinking brown heretics from our temples, then erase their miasma by thoroughly wiping the crevice between our nethercheeks with the ceremonial ablutionary tissue and send the whole mess spiraling into oblivion, down the maelström to the place of the unseen, sent to the underworld washed in the waters of Lethe—banished, forsaken, forgotten.

I was now walking bipedally almost all of the time. It was also around this time that I realized I was naked. And because I expressed a desire for clothing, Lydia took me shopping.

———

I had spent most of our life together naked before Lydia's eyes, but for most of that time I did not yet know that I was naked. In fact, in my ape days I don't think I even really realized that humans' clothing was something physically apart from their bodies. Does that sound quaint to you? Such things are not necessarily immediately apparent. I failed to understand that clothes did not simply grow and regrow again on human flesh overnight, like a fungus. But as I became human, through careful observation I came to understand what clothes are. In the beginning of my acculturation, whenever Lydia took me to the lakefront in the summer, I would marvel to see the beautiful *sapiens sapienettes* all cavorting around on the sand with only two tiny membranous bits of elastic fabric keeping them from their animal nakedness. And I would watch and silently remark upon the changes of wardrobe Lydia went through in a day, the fascinating ephemera of her morning-to-night garment cycle: in the morning she peeled herself out of bed in her larval pajamas, of which she owned several pairs, including a nightgown of the old-fashioned variety typically worn by little girls in latently pedophilic Victorian children's books, a slippery silk affair that her deceased mother had once sent her for a Christmas present, which shimmered and slithered all over her big mysterious body like a school of fish over underwater dunes (make a note of this nightgown, as it will later become important), and in this outfit she emerged from her sleeping chamber, rubbed at her eyes, padded around the house, woke Bruno if he wasn't already awake, prepared a light breakfast for us while I exuberantly retrieved the newspaper from the door-step—one of my few domestic chores in those early days, which I performed with the zeal of a fresh recruit—then ate with me, all in that woozy, discombobulated state of limbo between sleeping and waking, when the hands of clocks seem to circumnavigate their faces at several times the usual speed. Following breakfast Lydia would disappear into the bathroom, and I heard the blubbery thunder of the bathtub faucet change to the hissing-snake sound of the showerhead, and she later emerged from her room as if she had just peeled herself out of a cocoon—moist and new—and clad in her official outfit for the day. And it was never anything flashy or particularly descript. As I've indicated earlier, Lydia favored turtle-neck sweaters and pants. I don't think she even owned a skirt or a dress that ventured north more than a centimeter or two above the latitude of the knee. Lydia was not an overtly feminine woman—not a girly woman, maybe I should say. She was certainly feminine; she had a good but conservative fashion sense. I don't think I ever saw her wear pink, for instance, and she almost never wore high heels. On her feet were usually sneakers for utility and inconspicuousness, or else that inelegant pair of dirt-brown clodhoppers she often wore. But Lydia had an intense relationship with the color green. It was her favorite color. She looked beautiful in green. Not that she didn't look beautiful in other colors—or most beautiful of all in no clothes whatsoever (but I will get to that later). But green looked particularly good on her because it established a dialogue with her eyes. A casual perusal of Lydia's closet would reveal a whole jungle of verdant items: green scarves, green dresses, green shirts and pants. In the early days I loved to play dress-up with Lydia's clothes, before (and sometimes even after) I had clothes of my own to wear. It wasn't just the fun of dressing up that I got a kick out of, but rather the tingling sensation that skittered all over my flesh when I slipped inside Lydia's garments, the sweet flutter of feminine fabrics against my skin, these things that had clung as close to her naked flesh as I wanted to cling. For a while Lydia patiently suffered my love of dress-up: sometimes, as soon as we got home from the lab I would want to put on one of her dresses, and it was not easy to convince me to take it off. Sometimes, when Lydia was away on an errand and trusted me with free range of the apartment, I would sneak into her closet and not only put on one of her dresses, but sometimes I would awkwardly slip my legs into the holes of a pair of her panties from her underwear drawer, or stretch her pantyhose over my legs or arms. I knew by the special electric charge I received out of playing with these things that somehow they were more secret, more intimate, and more darkly passionate than Lydia's hats or scarves or even her dresses. I sensed taboo in them, which was why I could bring myself to put them on for only a brief time, quickly parading a few turns around the apartment in her underwear or pantyhose before my cowardice got the better of me and I had to return them to the drawers where I had found them before Lydia came home. Then I would pry open the remote control and lick its nine-volt battery.

Eventually my obsession with dress-up reached such a fever pitch that Lydia decided it was time I had clothes of my own. I was to be naked no longer.

As it happened, by this time I did own one—only one—article of clothing. Whenever Lydia and I left the home together in those early days—say, on one of our fun/educational outings to the Field Museum or the planetarium—she would bundle me up in a big baggy sweatshirt with droopy sleeves and a kangaroo pocket on the front, and a hood that could be scrunched into a small round window for my face by means of a drawstring. When we went out in public Lydia would pull the hood low over my face to conceal my apeness, and the shirt was big enough that it came down to my ankles, like a dress. Like much of Lydia's clothing, it was green. I wore this green hooded sweatshirt so often that it had gradually passed into my possession, and Lydia effectively made a present of it to me. This was the first article of clothing I ever owned. As a matter of fact, I suppose it was the first thing I ever personally owned, period, and because of this, the shirt has always had a feeling of juju, of magic power for me. I still have it.

One Saturday afternoon Lydia took me shopping at Marshall Field's. Lydia and I took a bus uptown to the Loop, and she carried me in her arms, buried in her green hooded sweatshirt, into the store. I was stricken silent with awe at the place. It was like a cathedral, a temple to commerce, to all the potential beauty of human vanity. Floor cascaded above floor through that dizzying shaft of space in the middle of the room—the gilt decorations, the Old World grandeur, the marble everywhere: I thought we had entered some sort of palace.

I liked to look at all the mannequins. It was so fascinating to observe the personality differences in all the different sorts of mannequins. Some of them are deliberately designed to look very humanlike: they have skin and hair and eyes. Sometimes they have icily detached expressions on their beautiful faces. Sometimes their fragile fingers and slender hands looked so realistic that one half-expected them to move. Others are more abstract: some are of unpainted white plastic or plaster. Some of them are realistically proportioned, with detailed hands and feet and skeletomuscular definition under their hard shiny skin, tendons in their necks and clavicles under their shoulders—and yet are eerily missing their heads, as if they have just been executed under the guillotine, for real or imagined crimes. The more impressionistic ones might have hands like mittens, with thumbs separate but the other four fingers fused together, and with no faces, their heads being mere smooth plastic ellipsoids—giving them an alien appearance. Others are half-abstract, with noses and forehead ridges and mouths, but no eyes. Still others are designed to look humanoid, but in a deliberately unrealistic or exaggerated way. These last are the type of mannequins on display in the lingerie department, which happens to be right next to the children's department, way up on the fourth or fifth floor, where I went with Lydia so I could try clothes on. Lydia picked out some shirts and pants and sweaters and whatnot for me. I appeared to have a predilection for stripes: especially shirts with broad, horizontal stripes. I loved to hold her hot human hand and gaze up at the glittering frescoed ceilings as she flipped through the racks of clothing that were on sale in the children's section, selecting things for me to try on, folding them over the arm that held mine, the sound of the metal hangers scraping against the rack. Then she took me by the hand back to the fitting rooms and helped me put them on.

"Do you like this, Bruno?" she would say, tugging a shirt over my body as I sat on a bench and she crouched before me in the mirror-walled fitting room. If I did not like it I would fling it away. If I did like it I would pant-hoot with enthusiasm, and Lydia would press a finger to her lips to shush me, lest we be found out. I was wearing my collar, but Lydia always hated to put the leash on me. She kept the leash in her purse, having sworn me to a blood oath of good behavior.

We selected several pairs of jeans, a pair of fancier black slacks, some T-shirts, a stalwart winter coat to fend off the Chicago winter, and a few shirts that snapped rather than buttoned because my then-clumsy fingers were not yet dexterous enough to perform the complicated operation of slipping a button into a buttonhole. She even bought—because I insisted, and she spoiled me—she even bought me a shiny pair of sneakers, extra large ones due to the preposterously unusual shapes of my feet. All of these items had to be bought with an air of utmost secrecy: with me plodding alongside her with a long hairy arm stretched up to hold her hand and the hood of my floppy green sweatshirt pulled low over my face. Lydia had to constantly shoo away commission-eager salesgirls, who were always nosily seeking her eye-contact and asking her in tones that made us panic despite their well-intentioned sweetnesses (whenever anyone spoke to her, I felt a sudden spike of galvanization on the flesh of Lydia's palm) if she would like help finding anything, and Lydia would always respond by tightening her grip on my hand, fluttering the fingers of her free hand in dismissal, shaking her head back and forth in such a way that the strands of hair not bound back in her ponytail whipped about her face, and brusquely saying, "No thank you, we're just browsing." To which the salesgirl would respond with some pleasantry and turn to go—then turn back for a moment, and quizzically scrunch up her brow as she filched another look at me, Bruno, Lydia's presumed child, her long-armed, ugly, hairy freak of a child—before shrugging with the resignation that all was well, and skulking away on her click-clacking pumps to assist another customer.

As I was saying, though, it was this last variety of mannequin that held the most interest for me: the detailed yet deliberately unrealistic humanoid mannequin, the expressionistically stylized variety, the ones on display in the lingerie section, which adjoined the children's section of the store. Lydia was paying for my new clothes at a counter in the children's department; all my new clothes were folded up on the countertop, and the clerk behind the counter was removing the plastic hangers from the garments, pressing their sales tags against something on the counter that for each item produced a shrill electronic beep, then folded the items and put them into big plastic sacks while Lydia waited. I padded away from the counter in boredom during this procedure. My fascination was tugging my attention away from them. Whither was it tugging me? It was tugging Bruno's feet in the direction of the lingerie department. The mannequins there were unlike any other mannequins on display anywhere else in that palace of commerce. The mannequins here had hair, and facial features, and detailed hands and feet, and yet they were still strangely abstracted: their heads were cartoonishly larger than normal human heads, their huge eyes painted onto their faces. They were also clearly sexualized, with thick lush pouty lips, and with larger breasts and wider hips than the other female humanoid mannequins in the store. I fell in love with those plastic girls. They were so sweet-looking, so elegant and delicately sexy—and so apparently unabashed to stand there in full display in public in their dainty underthings, all their pretty frilly bras and panties and corsets, with all kinds of filigrees and silk and satin ribbons and lace embroidery. This was underwear that existed only to be displayed briefly, then slowly (or rapidly, rabidly) removed.... I crept up onto the dais where all these slender, doe-eyed nymphs stood on display. These girls stood or lounged, icy-expressioned, coyly silent, in various poses or reposes of sumptuous seductiveness. One of them lay semireclining, one leg stretched out and the other half-raised, leaning back on her elbows and throwing her head back, showing her body, begging to be desired, asking to be taken. Another stood in a black negligee with matching high-heeled shoes, her weight sunk into one foot, one hand on her hip, the other seemingly frozen in the act of reaching up to her pretty bare plastic shoulder to remove the first of the two straps of the negligee, and a single springy ringlet of dark glossy hair—*real* hair—dangled wantonly in her fake-eyed face. I reached up to her with my long hirsute arms and my long purple fingers. I reached up to her, to lift up the hem of her negligee, to peer under it, at that beautiful body, those hard shiny legs, to see what lay beneath...

"Bruno?" a voice called out to me, from some unknown height or depth.

I startled at the sound of my name. Somehow, all of those beautiful plastic girls, all those bright sexy fake-eyed lingerie-clad girls came tumbling and crashing down all around me like trunks of falling timber.

"Bruno!" Lydia shouted. She stomped toward me, burdened with big plastic sacks full of my new clothes swishing in her hands. I squatted on the display dais, cowering. My hands were cravenly slapped over my eyes, such that I resembled the first of the Three Wise Monkeys. The mannequins may still have been clattering and bouncing all around me.

"What are you doing?" Lydia hissed. Her head snapped up and looked around to see if anyone had noticed. Someone had. Lydia was so red I was afraid she would begin to bleed from her face in her shame of me. She grabbed my arm and savagely jerked me out of the jumble of felled mannequins, my fallen angels. She whipped my leash out of her purse, seized my collar, rotated it on my throat until the clip was in the front and attached the leash.

"What were you thinking?" she spat in my ear in a whisper. One of the salesgirls who worked in this area of the store was now clacking rapidly toward us. She was young and wearing an inch of makeup, with a name tag pinned to her shirt and high-heeled shoes of the same sort that my mannequin was wearing, exposing her tiny pretty feet and painted toenails. Those shoes, her feet—her toes, the gracile slope of her instep, her ankles—were mouthwatering to me.

The bags full of my new clothes lay beside us on the floor in a big puffy pile. Lydia was holding on to my leash with one hand while trying to reerect one of the mannequins. Her face was still enflamed with the hot blood of humiliation, and she was nervously, compulsively, tucking strands of hair behind the ridges of her ears.

"I'm so sorry," Lydia said to the salesgirl.

"Don't worry about it," she said. "Please. We'll take care of it."

Lydia stopped trying to set the mannequin back up, but she hadn't balanced it properly, and it immediately tipped over again, clattering and thudding back to the floor.

"I'm so sorry," said Lydia. "I'm so embarrassed."

"Please, we'll take care of it."

Then the salesgirl saw my face. She looked at my ape face under the hood of my floppy green sweatshirt. We locked eyes for a moment. She jumped back. We both shrieked. She began to back slowly away.

"Sorry," said Lydia one last time, this time with a curt snort, and she snatched up the shopping bags in her fists and jerked on my leash. We fled. We left the store in a scramble of fear and desperation. We got caught in the revolving glass doors with the poofy plastic bags. Lydia jerked it loose and we tumbled through the glass merry-go-round and out onto the street. I clung to Lydia, my arms around her neck, my legs wrapped around her waist. She yanked the hood low over my head. She struggled under the combined burden of me and the plastic sacks full of my new clothes. She walked quickly down the sidewalk and around the corner, as if we were being pursued (we weren't).

After we'd put a block or two behind us, she ducked into a doorway to escape the currents of pedestrian traffic on the sidewalk. She stopped, collected herself, and gave me a kiss of absolution for my recent sins on my forehead. I'd been in a state of shame at the embarrassment I had caused her, but that kiss instantly made me feel better. Such was the power of her forgiveness, her touch. We passed a flower shop, where there was a sidewalk display of pale green roses. Lydia bought a dozen of them, and the man behind the counter in the store wrapped them up for her in a cone of crinkling cellophane and another cone of paper. She asked him how he made the roses green. He told her he put dye in the soil.

I was allowed to hold them. I crushed the green flowers to my face and deeply sniffed them, and loved their gorgeous smell. Lydia hailed a taxi, which we rode back home. There, she cut the stems of the flowers and put them in an empty spaghetti sauce jar full of clear cool water from the tap and put them on the dining table for a centerpiece. I tried on all my new clothes, and Lydia one by one snipped off the tags for me with the same pair of scissors she had used to cut the stems of the green roses, and rooted through the folds of each article of clothing looking for pins and bits of plastic and stickers needing removal.

XIII

In the lab, everything was different. The lab was where Lydia and I went to work. At the lab we did what Norm wanted us to do. Norm was the boss of the lab, and, by extension, when I was in the lab, this meant he was my boss, too.

The difference between Lydia's and Norm's approaches to the project—the "project" that was my life—becomes evident in merely contrasting their personalities. For one thing, Norm was considerably older than Lydia, and when I met him he was already a scientist standing on a whole career's worth of respect and distinction: tenured at his university, the value of his opinion secure in the scientific community. He sloughed his classes off on his teaching assistants, usually not even bothering to attend them. His science was rigorous, skeptical, fiercely adherent to responsible methodology. I'm not saying that Lydia's methodology was sloppy by comparison—far from it. It's only that Lydia was young, untested, untenured, scarcely published, only recently matriculated, and almost unknown in the world of science. She held a doctorate in cognitive psychology and a master's in—not physical, but cultural—anthropology, whereas Norm was a behavioral biologist, through and through. Norm was a Skinnerian at heart, an operant conditioner, a pleasure-and-pain man, a pigeon-pecker. To Norm, if something couldn't be meticulously and unambiguously measured and documented, then it could not be published in any way, ergo it did not "count."

I sensed tension between them. Or thought I sensed it, or at least now I think I thought I sensed it, many years in retrospect. I sensed it in the way a child senses that his parents are fighting with each other, even if they conduct their arguments out of earshot. This philosophical gulf between them yawned ever wider over the duration of the project. Although I spent the vast majority of my time at home with Lydia, she would obligingly drive me to the lab nearly every day to do experiments with Norm.

During this time, Lydia was like a loving and permissive mother to me, and Norm was like a stern schoolmaster. I resented the way Lydia seemed to defer respect to Norm. From what source did Norm derive such respect? I knew nothing of—nor did I care anything for—anyone's tenure or publishing history or the thickness of curricula vitae. (Now that I do know of these things, I care for them even less.) At home, with Lydia, Norm's system of rewarding me for virtually everything—giving me a peanut, a piece of fruit or candy or whatever was on offer for every task I performed correctly—had been utterly abandoned, although this system was still pretty much in place at the lab, where the immediately gratifiable desires of my stomach apparently ruled, because they were all that could be methodologically counted on. If I did not *always* want a sticky delicious little piece of candy to put inside me, then Norm's whole silly Skinnerian system of positive reinforcement for desired behavior would fall apart. Which it often did! The problem with Norm's dogmatic insistence on his methodology of rewarding my behavior with food was that sometimes I didn't really want the reward. I just wasn't hungry. So, as a rigid behaviorist (I'm afraid nothing ever really changed his mind about that), what Norm realized he needed was some sort of objective currency, something that could be divided into small increments that would *always* be held to be valuable and desirable in and of themselves. Something I would always want. Essentially, what he needed to establish in my consciousness in order to keep up the simplistic yes/no/yes/no format of operant conditioning was a concept of abstract economics, some notion of, basically, money.

Norm set up a sort of "company store" in the lab, where I could "buy" my treats. So instead of being given treats directly for the tasks I correctly performed, everything I ate (in the lab—of course I ate for free at home) had to be purchased, by me. With *what*, you ask? Norm minted special play money for use in the closed economy of the lab. He cut thin chips out of wooden dowels of varying diameters and stamped them with numbers indicating their value. The smallest chip was printed with the Arabic numeral 1, the next smallest with a 5, then a 10, then a 25, and the biggest and thickest wooden chip was stamped 100. Clever, no? Pennies, nickels, dimes, quarters, and dollars. They were different colors, too, painted with thick bright monochromatic coats of paint. I seem to recall the pennies were red, the nickels blue, the dimes green, the quarters silver, and the dollars gold. The valuations of the different chips took me several weeks of instruction to fully grasp. When Norm was reasonably sure I understood the chips' value relationships, my rewards in the lab were no longer doled out in the form of raw goods, but in liquid holdings, with these idiotic colorful chips that I could later use to purchase food items from the company store, when I wanted to eat something. After that, whenever I performed a task correctly—sorting the items correctly, responding correctly to spoken commands to manipulate the objects, correctly playing a computer game designed to teach me symbolic logic—I was rewarded with one of these chips. For simple tasks they usually gave me a penny, and for more complex ones they might give

me a nickel or a dime. Then I could cash up by turning in lower
denominations for the higher ones. I remember the gestalt moment
when I grasped that just one of the quarters was equal in value to
twenty-five of the pennies—even though it didn't *look* that way,
because there were obviously a lot more of them. Now *that's* symbolic logic. They also furnished me with a personal "bank" to keep
my earnings in, which was a cardboard shoebox with a slot cut in
the lid for me to deposit my wages.

The second part of this system was the company store. The
company store was made out of one of the lab tables pushed close
to a wall to serve as a counter, behind which the food items were
stored in cabinets and a little refrigerator, both locked, and a locking metal cashbox. I was not allowed behind the "counter." Norm
printed up big wobbly sheets of laminated paper with pictures of
all the items that could be purchased at the store, with their prices
printed above the pictures. A "menu." When I wanted to buy something, I walked up to the counter with my "money," pointed at the
picture of what I wanted from the "menu," paid up, and then they
gave me my food. I even clearly recall (or may as well) the prices:

1 raisin	1¢
1 grape	1¢
1 regular M&M	1¢
1 peanut	1¢
1 almond	1¢
1 cashew	1¢
1 small handful of peas	1¢
1 small handful of blueberries	1¢
1 small handful of raspberries	1¢
1 *peanut* M&M	3¢
1 Milk Dud	3¢
1 cube of caramel	3¢

1 strawberry	3¢
1 plum	5¢
1 apricot	5¢
1 carrot	5¢
1 Reese's Peanut Butter Cup	5¢
1 bite-size candy bar (Snickers, Milky Way, etc.)	5¢
1 peach	10¢
1 apple	10¢
1 orange	10¢
1 pear	10¢
1 marshmallow	10¢
1 hard-boiled egg	25¢
1 banana	25¢
1 full-size candy bar (Snickers, Milky Way, etc.)	25¢
1 cup of yogurt	50¢
1 hot dog	50¢
1 Popsicle	50¢
1 Fudgsicle	50¢
1 meatball	50¢
1 mango	50¢
1 cupcake	50¢

I suppose Norm's introduction of a capitalist system to the small society of the lab had its desired effect on me. It took me very little time to build a psychological association of the monetary chips with a sense of inherent goodness—to see them as precious, even. I became miserly. I deliberately ate less so that I could save more chips. I came to desire the chips more than I had ever desired the little bits of food that were to be consumed immediately—because the more chips I had, the more potential goods I knew I had the purchasing power to acquire. I *did* always reliably want their filthy little monies. I horded them in my shoebox. I loved to dump it out and look at them, admiring my wealth, then close the lid of my bank and pick up each chip and put them back in the box, dropping them through the deposit slot one by one.

Nor did it take long for the scientists to begin using the chips as bribes. If they wanted me to participate in a certain experiment, if they wanted me to come to a certain area for some reason, if they wanted me to quit throwing a fit, to quit flailing or biting or screaming and shut up and behave for once—every time I was being unruly or obstinate, they would offer me one of the chips. They'd usually start the bidding with a 5¢ chip, and if it didn't work—if I couldn't be bought that cheaply—they would increase the denomination of their offer. In such instances I usually wouldn't settle for less than a shiny silver 25¢ chip. Some of the lab workers began to grumble that the introduction of this system had been a terrible idea, that it had the unintended effect of perversely reward-ing negative behavior. Then I suppose Norm would remind them that the little wooden chips were actually effectively worthless, so they might as well use them as bribes, or put them toward whatever end necessary. (Here I would like to remind Norm that the very same could be said for human money.) Paying me off was simply the easiest way to calm me down when I was upset. So naturally I began to deliberately throw fits in order to incite their bribery. I suppose they spoiled me.

Thus the experiments continued, month after month and season after season, teaching me the mores of human society while simul-taneously twisting up and corrupting my soul. Was my corruption merely a by-product of my enculturation?—or was it in fact an essential part of the process?

While this economic system eliminated the ticklish problem of the food-rewards' value fluctuating with the state of my appetite, it failed to fix the bigger problem. It alleviated the symptom but did not cure the disease. This disease of Norm's was a fundamental failure of understanding. It was his unshakable faith in the useful-ness of behavioristic training. Yes, I realize that behaviorism works perfectly well for training pigeons in boxes to peck at discs. But I am not a pigeon. Language is not a disc in a box. The idea that one can teach language to a rational creature by using essentially Skin-nerian methodology is patently absurd. That would be like giv-ing food to a baby only if he says a word correctly, and punitively starving him if he babbles incoherently. Try that at home. I doubt it will make your baby learn to talk any more efficiently. Second languages we may learn through deliberate instruction—badly. Nobody ever really learns anything they do not want to learn. We learn our first language through immersion, through our fascina-tion, through love. Mere vocabulary is not language, Norm. Syntax is not language. Grammar is not language. To define these things as necessary properties of capital-L Language (whatever that is) is like defining *eating* exclusively as eating at a table with a fork and a knife—that's not a holistic definition of *eating*; that's just good manners.

But when an infant gazes into his mother's eyes and speaks a first word—even if he has no clue what it "means"—*that* is language. The child's first word is *not* a symbol. It is not a representation, it is not a sign impregnated with abstract meaning, it is not a signifier and not a semiote. It is not a thin coating of signification painted over the surface of an a priori extant concept, suddenly revealing its definition like the act of throwing a sheet over something invis-ible. It is not a representation. Before a word becomes any of these things, it is simply an *act*. It is not a naming of the world, but rather the world's creation.

Norm's insistence on deliberate instruction, all his treat dan-gling and clever byways of circumventing the deeply problematic and frankly inhuman aspects of behaviorism, this cynical system of trapping a creature between pleasure and pain, of bribing and withholding—all this points to his original sin of misunderstanding. His misunderstanding was to underestimate language's connections to love, to beauty, to pure awe of the universe. A being does not acquire language because scientists give it treats if it learns words. A being acquires language because it is curious, because it yearns to participate in the perpetual reincarnation of the world. It is not just a trick of agreement. It is not a process of painting symbols over the faces of the raw materials of the cosmos. A being acquires language to carve out its own consciousness, its own active and reactive existence. A being screams because it is in pain, and it acquires language to communicate.

On one of my better-behaved days—which, as my size, strength, intelligence, boredom, and general restlessness in the lab increased, became less and less frequent—one of Norm's teaching assistants brought a class to the lab to visit, to watch me prove my competency at understanding spoken English. By this time they had removed the metal cage they had put me in during the early days of the project, and built a large enclosure in the room made of thick glass. The glass wall divided the room into two areas: one for me and the scientists, and the other for people who would visit, so that they could stand behind the glass and watch me work without fear of me ripping their faces off. The arrangement unpleasantly reminded me of the zoo, but I dealt with it. The students all crowded round outside the glass wall, their wet breaths blowing spots of fog on the surface of the glass. This particular experiment had been filmed many times. Nearly everything we did in the lab was now caught on video, by several cameras perched on tripods that had been erected at several points in the room to catch all the action. The Bruno Show was filmed every weekday, beginning in the morning when Lydia brought me to the lab and ending when she took me home. The scientists would later spend countless hours analyzing my behavior, watching my videos and carefully recording data.

I knew the drill. Lydia sat with me inside the glassed-in area of the lab. Norm was outside the wall with the students. Lydia was the one conducting the experiment because I responded to her vocal commands far more often than I did to Norm's. My personal dislike of Norm rendered me less inclined to grant all his meaningless requests. But nowadays I almost always did them when Lydia asked, as a personal favor to her. Safely protected by the glass wall, Norm was showing me off, speaking about me to all his students, like a mountebank at a county fair, step right up, ladies and gentlemen, come marvel at the freak of nature we've grown in this very laboratory. Inside my play area were all kinds of objects: boxes, bags, stuffed animals, toys and such.

Lydia would say to me, "Bruno, please put the snake in the bag."

And I would respond by picking up the slack green lifeless rubber snake and dropping it in the nearby brown paper grocery sack. Then she would say, speaking slowly, forcefully and articulately, "Put the soap on the doggie."

I would pick up the bar of soap, walk over to the stuffed dog, and place it on its back.

"Good job, Bruno. Now put the elephant in the box."

I picked up the stuffed elephant and dropped it in the cardboard box.

This is the way it usually went. However, Norm had recently added an extremely unsettling detail to this procedure. Lydia wore a flat black metal mask that completely obscured her face, with a rectangular window of opaque green glass for her eyes. I am told that this was a welding mask. She also wore a pair of oven mitts on her hands. Dressed in this insane costume—like a baker in Hell—she would ask me to perform the pointless tasks with the objects strewn about the floor of the playpen. I did not know what could be the reason for these new details that had been added to the ritual. Lydia looked slightly terrifying in this costume. Still, I knew it was her under there, and so I gamely complied with the requests coming from the tinny, echoey voice buried beneath the black metal mask.

And why, you may ask, *why* did Norm require Lydia to wear oven mitts and a welding mask during the experiment? This was to assure skeptics that I was receiving no visual cues from her face or hands, and had to rely on her spoken words alone for information. It was done to dissuade any potential accusation that I wasn't comprehending spoken language so much as constructing a web of understanding out of external information inadvertently provided by her body—facial tics, gaze-following, the tensing or relaxing of her muscles, accidental gesticulations: the sort of things a seasoned gambler calls a "tell."

But why, I ask—why, Dr. Norman Plumlee, did you decide that external bodily elements of communication do not count as part of language? Is language not comprised of an entire flexible interface of both spoken and visual interaction? No human mother speaks to her infant only while wearing oven mitts and a welding mask! Spoken language is but a single component of communication. We speak as much with our hands and eyes and faces as we do with our lungs and throats and tongues—namely, principally, with our brains. Analog gestural communication isn't "cheating." Removing words from the interface of the body only removes them from their natural environment, like putting an animal in a cage.

Yet Norm doggedly continued to insist upon the necessity of the mask and mittens, so the fact that I understood what Lydia was saying might be taken more seriously by potential skeptics. Taken seriously by whom? By *whom*, Norm? Whence this desperate, this pitiful fear of not being taken seriously? This fear permeates everything, *everything* humans do! This terrible fear of not being taken seriously haunts the heart of every scientist!

What is science? Must science necessarily be enslaved to rigid methodology?—to the quantifiable?—to the repeatable?—to the measurable?—to the (dare I suggest it) *publishable*? If you're studying the inanimate world, sure...the unconscious world, the world of quarks and quasars, of waves and particles, of the chemical and mechanical movements of the universe's material...I have no beef with the scientific method as it is applied to, say, physics. But when you are studying another sentient being, a fellow conscious organism? Of course, *of course* the good scientist must follow proper methodology, collect data accurately and draw conclusions carefully and responsibly if he is to publish, and the good scientist must of course *publish* if he is going to apply for grants to fund further research and maintain his post at his institution, if he is to secure tenure, in order to keep making money, in order to *eat*! And in order to do all this, he must publish, publish, publish—or not get any money—and by extension, perish! I sometimes wonder if the demands of capitalism enfeeble certain fields of science. Because that was why Norm was in such a rush to test, to record, to document, to prove, to publish—*to be taken seriously*. He wanted this to be hard science. He did not understand how *soft* it is—soft and vulnerable, like flesh itself. Like life. Like me. My brain, the seat of my soul, is as mysterious and plastic and irrational a thing as yours, Norm, or any man's for that matter. It bucked against your numbers! In your frenzy to publish, in your desperation to be taken seriously, you tried to cram "soft" science into the same box as the hard stuff—and in the process you ignored all the evidence that was right in front of your face! You lost it! Lost! Much is lost, and much is never found that might be if scientists would only allow themselves to look in the right places. The very hardness of hard science sometimes renders it too impoverished to study a subject so protean and spontaneous as language. Lydia came to understand this, and Norm did not, and that, I believe, was at the heart of their falling-out. That and, obviously, me.

———

Lydia had an almost quixotic faith that she would be able to teach an ape to fully understand and to perhaps even verbally communicate in English, if only she were able to find the right pupil—someone special, some exceptionally brilliant Nietzschean *überchimp* such as (ahem) myself. And don't try to feed me any of the usual nonsense about undescended larynxes and so on, about the vocal tracts of apes being anatomically unequipped for articulate speech. Put that aside, and simply listen to the sound of my voice. The mere physical equipment of vocal communication constitutes a thin layer of moss coating the rock of the issue, and that rock is the brain, the mind. My brain, *my* mind.

Lydia Littlemore was a pioneer of the furthermost untrammeled frontiers of science, of linguistics, of primatology, of cognitive psychology, and, indeed, of philosophy. But so, for that matter, is every mother whose child learns to speak. For she did nothing for me that a human mother would not do for her human child: she loved me. And I loved her. That was my only motivation. That was the only reward, the only conditioning I needed.

One could argue that love has no place in science. Those who make such arguments may as well argue that love has no place in human civilization, or in life.

XIV

At some point I realized there was a new woman working in the lab: Tal. I would not learn her last name—Gozani—until much later. Tal was taller than Lydia. Tal was tall for a woman. At first I think I had a little difficulty connecting the word to the person, because her name happened to be an exact homonym for an adjective describing what she was: tall. I already knew the word *tall*, though I don't know if the scientists at the lab knew I knew it. As I have said, before I began to talk much I already comprehended far more spoken English than anyone imagined I did. Maybe I would have been less confused if Tal was short, or if she remained tall but was named "Short." Anyway—she entered my life the way most people did in those days: one day, she was there. This woman I'd never seen before began to appear in the lab every day and began interacting with me, and there you have it.

In addition to being tall, I think Tal was very young when she first came to the lab. Younger than Lydia, anyway. She was (as I know in retrospect) a graduate student at the University of Chicago. I would guess Tal was in her early twenties when she started working at the lab—which would make her seven or eight years younger than Lydia when all this happened. At first I liked her well enough. I have always tended, and especially in those days, to get along with women better than I do with men, so I was glad to have another feminine presence in the lab. But there were some extraordinarily unusual aspects to Tal.

In addition to being tall, she had smooth, olive-colored, almost yellowish skin that offset her crisp gray-green eyes. She had thick, strong legs. She dressed in strange clothes. She would wear a thin sheet of bright stretchy decorative fabric wrapped around her legs for a skirt. She was constantly clicking and rattling all over with bits of rustic jewelry made of wood and rope and silver. She wore big clunky boots if the weather turned bad, and if it turned good she wore ropey brown woven sandals that crisscrossed up her calves. Often, though, she would go barefoot. She would take off her sweaty brown sandals and leave them by the door to the lab, then spend the day thumping around the floor in her bare feet. Sometimes I would inspect her sweaty brown sandals, lined up by the lab door. I would curiously lick the salt-ringed depressions that her toes had carved into their surfaces. This going barefoot was something I had never seen a human do before, at least not in a professional setting. Lydia was usually barefoot or in socks in the home, but outside her home, she always wore shoes all day. I wondered why ordinary norms of decorum were relaxed for Tal. All the other scientists' feet were imprisoned within their shoes, generally workaday white sneakers, but Tal was allowed to romp the lab in dirty naked feet as comfortably as if this room were her own home.

She let me play with them, I remember—her bare feet. I had just met her for the first time a few days before. We sat together on my squishy blue mat, behind the glass wall that divided the lab into the human side and the chimp side, my playpen. We were sitting together, manipulating my toys. Tal sat cross-legged at first, then leaned back and stretched her legs out flat on the mat, and her bare feet emerged from beneath the stretchy red fabric of her skirt. I was

146 • Benjamin Hale

transfixed by her feet. They were so ungodly *dirty*. They were so callused and rough. Her toenails were chipped and short, her toes armored with thick hard yellowish skin, the soles of her feet nearly black with filth. I remember thinking that they looked less like the feet of a woman than the feet of an animal, like me. I reached out with my long rubbery fingers and inquisitively tickled her toes, but I believe her feet were so accustomed to the unshod life that they had lost that especially sensitive vulnerability of the flesh that is prerequisite to effective foot-tickling. My tickling of her feet evoked from her lips a smile, yes, but no laughter. Her one nod to podiatric vanity was a thick blunt ring of tarnished silver hugging the thinnest segment of the second toe on her left foot. I touched the ring with my finger. "It never comes off," she said. I noticed also that, unlike the smooth, glabrous legs of most of the human women I had seen, this one's legs were coated with fine wispy fur. A thin silver chain dangled from her neck. She let me touch that, too. It had a sleek, scaly texture; it slid and slithered over my fingers like something alive, like a slender worm of light. And at the end of this chain was a piece of jewelry, an emblem of some sort. The emblem was composed of two interlocking equilateral triangles, one upside down and the other right-side up, such that the two linking triangles form a hexagon in the center, with six smaller equilateral triangles directly abutting each side of the hexagon and pointing outward from the center to form a radially symmetrical six-pointed star. For a moment I was hypnotized by the way its elements connected, how the eye could assemble, dissect and reassemble the image, the kaleidoscopic matrix of its harmonious geometry. I put it in my mouth. "Don't put that in your mouth," she said, and took it out. She wiped my spit off of it on her scarf and tucked it back under her shirt, where it slid down her chest and disappeared in the sloping gully of flesh between her breasts. My gaze then ascended to the very pinnacle of her, past her throat, her chin, her lips, her nose, past the conjoined twins of her furry black eyebrows that met in a delta of fuzz above the bridge of her nose and above her wide forehead, to find the most outrageous aspect of her physiognomy: her hair. It was black as India ink, and arranged not in lots of very thin threads like that of most humans, but was all clumped and scrunched up into an array of thick, muscular ropes. I touched them. I laughed at their surprising texture. They didn't feel like anything that really ought to be sprouting out of the top of anyone's head. They felt almost like plant life. I stroked these long knotty cables of hair, and I grabbed one of them—the girth of it fit just inside my fist—and I squeezed it, and in my hand it felt just like the vines of ivy that crawl all over the sides of the magisterial stone buildings on the campus. That's all I had to compare it with in my then-very-small grab bag of a posteriori experience. I squeezed her hair-ropes. I loved playing with women's hair. I still do. But this was—this was something else entirely. She laughed. Her laugh was a gleeful flutter abruptly truncated by a silly little snort.

"These are dreadlocks," she said. *Dread* and *lock* being two of the unfriendliest words in the English language, I wondered why on earth anyone would choose to affectionately apply them to a style of hair.

Oh, and the way she *walked* in those dirty bare feet of hers. That was impressive. Tal didn't walk like an ordinary human. For a long time I had associated human walking with the persistent rhythmic squeaking and squawking of sneakers on the hard tile floor of the lab. (Except for Haywood, the garrulous musicality of whose walk we have previously discussed.) And then there were the students at the university, with whom I honestly had only limited contact during my time at the lab—a great diversity of footwear abounded on the bottoms of *their* legs. I came to love the sound, for instance, of high-heeled shoes. They make that *scrap-clock, scrap-clock* noise to which my mind to this very day immediately attaches erotic associations. Flip-flops also make interesting sounds, that repeated squishing and slapping they make against the heel, and sometimes a little bubble of air gets trapped between the bottom of the foot and the moist surface of the flip-flop, which when pushed out from beneath the flat of the foot by the pressure of gravity may result in a very rare, and very faint—but always uproariously funny—fart noise. Tal, though, generally eschewed shoes of any sort, preferring always to go barefoot, but rather than eliminating any sound that might emanate from her feet, her walk in fact seemed even louder than a normally shod person's. She walked always with directness and even a sense of aggression, planting one foot directly in front of the other, describing perfectly straight lines wherever she went. Her long, thick, and frighteningly strong legs connected with surfaces beneath her body in loud, meaty stomps. When she walked across a room I could feel the vibrations she made, with each new step for a brief moment her body became rooted to the earth as solidly as a tree. This only happened when she was barefoot, though; it wasn't quite the same effect when she had her sandals on. Tal was as comfortable as any human I've met with her own bipedal existence. Most humans are still a little awkward on two legs, despite years of evolution. Indeed, upright walking may have been useful for traversing the plains of prehistoric Africa, but ultimately, considering how people of a certain age are wont to gripe and caterwaul about their legs and feet and hips and knees and backs giving out on them, I wonder if it wouldn't be a bad idea to go back to all fours.

It was difficult to gauge the nature of Tal's relationship with the rest of the scientists at the lab. I don't think they quite knew what to make of her. It's possible that they found her presence as weird and unruly as I did. Whenever she said anything, the other scientists seemed to trust her words a little less, as if they needed additional rechecking and verification. They were all a little colder with her than they were with each other. I am always keenly conscious of the dynamics of social dominance hierarchies. In the primal society of the lab, Norm was the alpha male. Prasad was the beta male. The other men were graduate students, and they ranked below Lydia, who was the highest-ranking female. The female graduate students ranked below the male graduate students, and Tal was definitely the omega of the omegas—and everyone in the lab treated her accordingly. Even the other low-ranking females would put her in her place with very subtle dominance displays. Except for Lydia. Lydia took a shine to her, and this was what socially protected Tal from the rest of the group. The approval of the lab's highest-ranking female was enough to keep Tal on board, but not enough to raise her status above omega.

At some point during the first few weeks I started seeing Tal in the lab, Lydia began to speak of her surprisingly often. As soon as it was time to go home, all thoughts having anything to do with the lab—including the lab personnel—were banished at once from my mind, and I directed my attentions toward what the remaining part of the day had in store for me: what foods I would eat, what cartoons I would watch. But now with increasingly frequency Lydia would talk about Tal on the drive home, or over dinner. I was frankly a little put off by how many times Lydia would mention her in conversation. See, in addition to all her aforementioned weirdnesses, Tal was apparently a woman of very particular and passionate hobbies. She was a dancer, and a maker of puppets. I really had no idea yet what "dancing" and "puppets" were. Come to think of it, I now think that it must have been Tal's training in modern dance that gave her that aggressive, stomping barefooted gait. But as for the puppets...

I remember when Tal—at, I suppose, Lydia's behest—brought one of her puppets to the lab. It was probably the most terrifying and hideous thing I had ever seen. I was fascinated by human beings' representations of themselves—like the mannequins in the department store. But this thing was the human form not abstracted (like the mannequins) but deliberately exaggerated, tortured and perverted, its every aspect and feature twisted into the grotesque. Violent spots of red enflamed its long, beaky nose and its lacquered wooden dimples that were pushed outward by a leerily grinning crescent mouth, and it had huge blue marble eyes with inwardly bent brows. The overall expression implied the face of someone about to do something meaningless and cruel. He wore a pointy red hat and a little gold-trimmed red suit. The point of the hat drooped over his head such that his profile had three ugly hooks protruding from it: the hat and his nose pointing sharply down and his chin pointing sharply up. Tiny pink-painted station-ary wooden hands poked out of the empty cloth bags of his sleeves. On the bottoms of his floppy cloth legs he wore pointy green shoes with jingle-bells sewn onto the tops of them. The creature looked like some sort of demonic elf. He was horrifying—and I hadn't even seen him in motion yet.

"Bruno," said Tal. "Meet Mr. Punch."

Tal slipped her arm into the vacant bag of the creature's body, and suddenly it (one) *was fucking alive*, and (two) *had attached itself to her arm.*

Without my noticing, Tal had also somehow turned her voice into a distorted, barely articulate, high-pitched, metallic quacking noise. And yet, because my attention was diverted to the monstros-ity on the end of her right arm, even though I perfectly well knew it was she who was speaking, the voice seemed to emanate from the head of the puppet—as if this tiny monster made of wood and fabric and marbles had been given not only an independent agency and autonomous locomotion, but a consciousness, a voice!

"That's the way to do it!" declared the disgusting creature, and followed it with a mischievous cackle. *"That's* the way to do it! *Ah-*hahaha-ha!"

Why in the world was this being done to me? The other scientists crowded around us in skeptical distrust of this whole exercise. Lydia sat cross-legged on the squishy blue mat on the lab floor, and Tal sat crosslegged directly facing her. I sat in Lydia's lap. As soon as the puppet began to move its horrible head and speak with its horrible quacking voice, I turned my head away from it, burrowing my face into Lydia's body, where it was fragrant and safe and warm and I could be near her nourishment-symbolizing breasts. In retrospect, the puppet probably did not wave its arms or clap its hands or nod its head or speak in its quacking voice more than a total of ten or fifteen seconds before Lydia called a halt to the experiment. Lydia signaled Tal to stop what she was doing. She could see at once that whatever effect they had been hoping for with this experiment (amusement?) was not happening, but rather I was afraid. Tal reached into her mouth and removed some sort of spit-slimy piece of metal. Then she removed her arm from the body of the puppet, disemboweling him, rendering him a slack dead bag of fabric with hands and a head.

I was exhausted by the relief of my terror when Tal's arm turned into a normal human arm again, with a normal human hand on the end of it instead of an ugly little talking man. The terrible little man who had spoken was once again limp and impotent, and he was put away somewhere out of sight where he could not bother me. After this incident, I think the other scientists at the lab started taking Tal even less seriously than before.

The next time I was watching my beloved Bert and Ernie on *Sesame Street,* Lydia may have pointed out to me that even they were puppets of a certain sort—that these benign figures whom I loved were puppets, too, and I didn't find them frightening, did I? True as that may have been, a key difference with Bert and Ernie was that the puppeteers of *Sesame Street* took pains to mask the human agency and artifice behind them. As long as the viewer is fooled, it doesn't matter what they are. I was perfectly willing to believe that Bert and Ernie were real. I was willing to invest all my conviction in them, that they were autonomous, sentient beings, not artificial things designed to mimic the look of actual organisms, given movement to mimic life, and given voices to mimic conscious intelligence. Puppets are frightening only when the artifice is noticeable. It was also pointed out to me that one of my favorite films at the time (and still!), *Pinocchio*, concerned a puppet. That did not lend me any reassurance, either.

For one thing, *Pinocchio* is clearly not set in a universe that obeys our own conceptions of reality. This is evident right from the beginning of the film. The film opens with the lonely old puppet maker and clock maker, Geppetto, fashioning Pinocchio from a block of wood and painting him. When he completes the project, Geppetto dances the puppet (a marionette) around his home, to the general vexation of his two pets: a kitten named Figaro and a fish named Cleo. Before retiring for the evening, the childlike old man happens to look out of his bedroom window and notices that a new star has messianically appeared in the firmament. He wishes upon it, wishing that the puppet he has just made, Pinocchio, were a real boy. While he sleeps, the star becomes a beautiful semitranslucent woman who floats into the room through the window and, with a touch of her magic wand, animates Pinocchio. Pinocchio slowly blinks his wooden eyelids and stirs his wooden limbs, and— the strings attached to his head, arms, and legs having vanished— comes to life. Pinocchio arrives in the world already knowing language, but with an otherwise only partially formed consciousness. He is conscious, but without *conscience*, knowing nothing of the norms or moral conventions of the civilization into which he has just been born. For this purpose the blue fairy employs Jiminy, an anthropomorphic cricket drifter who happens to have earlier broken into Geppetto's home unnoticed to seek shelter inside one of the room's many clocks. The cricket finds the fairy sexually attractive. Jiminy, who obliges the fairy partly out of his attraction to her, is given a suit of fancy new clothes and employment as Pinocchio's moral tutor. The fairy tells Pinocchio that he will be made into "a real boy" if he completes a sort of moral trial period as a living puppet. With this, the fairy retreats back through the window and goes back to being a star. Just then Geppetto wakes up. At first he is astonished that his wish has come true and the puppet has come alive, indicating that this is an unexpected event, but he surprisingly quickly readjusts his understanding of reality and soon has accepted that Pinocchio is alive. The very next morning, Geppetto decides that Pinocchio must go to school. He gives him a textbook and an apple to give to his teacher, and with no clear directions sends him on his way. However, Pinocchio is waylaid by an evil fox and a cat—both wearing clothes and anthropomorphic—who convince him to pursue a career in the theatre. Pinocchio's naïveté causes him to easily fall victim to their chicaneries, and the fox and cat sell him into a life of indentured servitude to a brutal puppeteer named Stromboli. (Throughout the story, Pinocchio's greatest vulnerability is his blithely trusting naïveté.) Many adventures follow, and Pinocchio, after repeated errors of judgment and understanding, is finally reunited with Geppetto; at the end of the film he is rewarded with becoming a biological human child. The fox and the cat, however, seem perfectly at ease in the human sphere of activity, communicating with and even engaging in economic transactions with humans, who never find it at all strange that they are animals: clearly, this is a universe in which Pinocchio's quest to "become a real boy" is absurd. He is already anthropomorphic!—what else does he want? This is a universe in which some animals are merely animals—such as Geppetto's pet cat, Figaro—and other animals have been given the pass of full human consciousness with which to enter into the dealings of ordinary human civilization. I have often wondered what would have become of Pinocchio had he chosen not to become a real boy, but rather to defiantly remain forever a puppet. When he becomes a real boy, his new human flesh grows smooth over his knobby wooden joints, and his eyes suddenly glisten with authentic moisture. He has become fully human—but at what price? Now that he has traded his wooden body for an organic body of electricity, bone, blood, and water, he will presumably now grow into a man, who will eventually die. Does Pinocchio realize he has traded a state of emotionally immature immortality for the mere right to call himself a human being, even though this is a world in which such a right matters little in the course of everyday business? Surely no right-thinking consciousness would swap gold for bronze like that! He's only let himself get cheated one more time! Later, Pinocchio the real man will have to come to terms with the full implications of his humanity (wisdom, death) in order to realize that he doomed himself with the final mistake he committed in his prehuman puppethood.

XV

As we drove home from the lab that day—or maybe it was the next day, or the day after—I noticed Lydia seemed to be in higher spirits than usual. Not that she was ever morose, but she was typically serious. Yet today she was in a jocular, airy-fairy mood uncharacteristic of her. My own fragile soul was still a little rattled from my encounter with Tal's horrifying puppet. It was the beginning of spring. I think it was among the first days of the year that were not abysmally cold. All over the city the gutter pipes whispered with snowmelt, and maybe even a hopeful bird or two dared to sing an early requiem for winter. As soon as we got in the car, as soon as Lydia had buckled me in and chortled up the engine with the keys, her hand leapt to the radio dial, and turned it on and turned it up, and proceeded to sing along with the song that issued from the holes in the dashboard of the car. She was in a good mood. She drove us home.

Scarcely had we shut the door, scarcely had our coats been hung and our shoes kicked off, when she started to cook. I offered to help. Lydia glanced down at me as I stretched my long hairy arms up at her with my eyes pleading for the mere privilege of her permission to participate in this activity; she smiled sweetly at me, patted my head and declared that she "could handle it." She played joyful music on her stereo and sang along to it. Suddenly the kitchen was alive with the clamor of pots and pans, with hissing water, with warmth and rising steam, with the smells of chopped ingredients releasing their biological perfumes into the air as the blade of the chopping knife liberated the odoriferous chemicals trapped inside the bulbs of garlic and the onions.

"Tal is coming over for dinner tonight," she chirped above the knock-knock-knock of the knife against the cutting board, by way of explanation for all this culinary activity.

I asked her what was for dinner.

"Paella," she said. For all I understood her she might as well have made the word up on the spot. Lydia was a wonderful cook, by the way. Ordinarily she prepared for us delicious dishes that were suitable to my palate. Spaghetti and meatballs, I liked. Hot dogs, I liked. Macaroni and cheese, I liked. Peanut butter and jelly sandwiches, I liked. But *this*? What *was* it, even? The dish that was taking shape under Lydia's hands seemed to be a counterintuitive and frankly insane one. It looked to me like something a Martian would have for dinner, this bubbling slumgullion of beans and peas and boiled sea creatures swimming in weird yellow slop.

I kept my ears trained to the ceiling, listening for the tinny moans and ululations and the spirited squawkings of parrots that would indicate that Mr. Morgan was practicing his bagpipes, and perhaps would let me listen to him. Nothing, though. Mr. Morgan was not practicing his bagpipes on this particular evening. I asked Lydia for permission to go upstairs and see if Mr. Morgan wanted to play backgammon. She told me not to bother him.

I retreated to the living room to watch TV. *Sesame Street* wasn't on, the bastards, nor was my second-favorite show, *Francis the Gnome*. In lieu of Bert and Ernie's bumbling monkeyshines, or Francis the Gnome's less interesting but still entertaining good deeds, a man and a woman sat still at a desk and spoke of the world's troubles. It was boring. Lydia made me switch off the TV when Tal arrived.

"Hello, Bruno," she said when she entered our house, carrying in one hand a bottle of wine, and in the other—unsettlingly—a bouquet of green roses. She ruffled the fur on my head with her fingers. Lydia and Tal hugged in the entryway, and Tal, who before this I had known only as a figure of the sterile and controlled environment of the lab, suddenly entered *our home*, causing a disturbing collision of my two social worlds, the domestic and the professional. Lydia took the flowers from her, snipped their stems, and put them in water in a rinsed-out spaghetti sauce jar.

Tal opened the bottle of wine she had brought by twisting the wine-opening implement deep into the neck of the bottle and levering out the cork with a satisfying *fump*. She trickled the liquid rubies the bottle contained into two glasses, which Lydia and Tal then knocked together with a ceremonial ding, and then each woman respectively and simultaneously brought her glass to her lips and took a sip. Then they began to converse, many heads above me, in complicated language I could not disentangle.

Tal leaned back with her elbow on the kitchen counter and her glass of wine in her hand while Lydia put the final aesthetic touches on the meal she had made. Lydia asked me to please set the table for three. Setting the table was one of my regular chores. Ordinarily I would have set it for two. Ordinarily I would have placed two napkins before two of the chairs that faced each other diametrically across the dining table, and then placed upon each of the napkins the three standard eating tools, one beside the other from left to right in descending order of length: knife, fork, spoon; this was "setting the table." Lydia had shown me how to do this, and ordinarily I delighted in the ritual. But tonight, on this particular night, I remember that for some reason I just listlessly dumped several napkins and a random clattering of silverware on the surface of the table, and then clambered sullenly atop the stack of phone books on my chair, slumped myself down, and awaited the meal with crossed arms. Lydia scowled at me.

"Don't be a little snot," she said, half under her breath, rearranging the napkins and silverware into proper formation. "We have company tonight."

That evening Lydia had also arranged the atmosphere of the apartment in an unusual way. She lit several candles, these fat and weird-smelling cylinders of colored wax, which she then placed in the center of the table, and then turned off all the lights in the apartment except for the lamp in the corner of the room. The music was still playing from the stereo—which wasn't usually the case when it was just me and Lydia eating dinner—though she turned down the dial until the music was playing at a decibel level that just barely registered in the spectrum of the consciously audible—not to be actively listened to, but to provide a melodious bed of sound upon which to cushion the conversation.

In the darkness I watched the three bright flames of the three candles on the table twitch and wobble, moving in and out of existence. Their light softly painted the faces of the two women from below in red and yellow tones, and the shadows of their heads shifted and danced on the walls and ceiling. Tal poured more wine, and the two of them raised their glasses. They looked at me, and I did likewise with my plastic sippy cup full of apple juice. We all knocked our drinking receptacles together in the airspace over the center of the table. The contact of their wineglasses made a high pretty note that chimed once and rolled around in the bowls of the glasses before vibrating away to silence. The contact of their glasses with my plastic cup made no sound. We ate.

As we dined, Lydia and Tal talked, the two women's voices twisting together into a songful braid of conversation. I did love listening to them talk. My mood lightened. The dish Lydia had prepared—while it still struck me as unnecessarily complex—wasn't so bad, after all. I looked from one woman to the other, back and forth as they spoke, hearing the rhythms of their speech, the notes, the timing, how the sound was formed in the spaces of their mouths, how their conversation was formed in the space of time. Like music. Just like song. In those early days, just a few moments of listening to the conversation of two friends over dinner would teach me more language than I would learn in countless hours of deliberate instruction in the lab. I think that the wordless songs of love are the true mothers of language, not semiotics. Music precedes meaning.

Of what they spoke, I cannot accurately remember. I did not understand much of it. I do remember that they finished the bottle of wine as they talked and ate, and then they opened another. I remember intuiting that they were, ultimately, though perhaps indirectly, talking about me. I remember that they often uttered a word, or series of words, that sounded to me like, "Gnome Chompy." Of course I understood what a gnome was, because a gnome happened to be the protagonist of my second-favorite TV show, *Francis the Gnome*. Francis was portrayed as a small, benevolent force in a big, wicked world. So I assumed that they were speaking of a gnome named Chompy. However, I could ascertain from the wrathful tones in which the two women spoke of the Gnome Chompy that they considered him to be a harmful and vituperative creature, much unlike the magnanimous-hearted Francis. I imagined Chompy—as his surname connotes—as a predatory gnome with a great gnashing jawful of evilly gleaming teeth, with which he dismembers the innocent creatures of the forest and devours their bloody entrails. I remember how they hated the Gnome Chompy. I remember hearing them say—or thought I heard them say—that they would have to protect me, Bruno, from the Gnome Chompy. I remember that they mentioned—and when they did their tone took on almost conspiratorial tones—they even mentioned Norm Plumlee's name once or twice in connection with the Gnome Chompy, as if they believed that Norm and Chompy may have been in some kind of collusion. I remember that Tal said she would wash the dishes, and in response Lydia reached a hand across the table, and that her hand came to rest briefly on top of Tal's hand, and Lydia said, "You don't have to wash the dishes." I remember that Tal insisted. I remember that Lydia finally politely acquiesced. I remember that I saw Tal standing at the kitchen sink, dipping the dirty plates one at a time into a pool of soapy water and scrubbing them clean. I remember that as she was doing this, Lydia walked up behind her and put her hands on Tal's hips, and half-embraced her from behind. I remember being confused at the gesture. I remember that I found it saddening in one sense, because I loved Lydia. But I remember that in another sense it made me happy, because Lydia was happy. I remember it made me happy and sad simultaneously, and yet these two evenly matched but contradictory feelings both pushing and pulling at my heart somehow did not result in a sort of emotional net force zero, such that I simply felt normal—but somehow their equal opposition deepened both the happiness and the sadness that I felt. I remember there was chocolate ice cream for dessert. *That* I liked unequivocally.

The evening did not end there. After dinner, the dishes washed and the chocolate ice cream consumed, Lydia and Tal sat on the couch in our living room and continued their wine and conversation. Lydia built a fire in the fireplace. For a long time I sat and watched it. This was something I loved to do in the winter. I would stare into the coals and let the fire hypnotize me. I loved to watch the veins of fire tickle across a log, to watch the cinders crumble, to breathe on them and watch the ashes glow from within, as if they had a pulse, a heartbeat, like animals with fire for blood. I could sit and watch it for hours. Soon it felt the time was approaching that would have ordinarily been my bedtime, and then it felt like that time had long since passed—but tonight for some reason the normal social structure of the universe had been relaxed, and I was allowed to do as I pleased. So I sat on the floor by the crackling fire, now and then playing with my toys, now and then gazing into the embers of the fireplace and imagining I saw ancient cities being sacked and burned, whole Carthages and Troys razed and lain to waste, complete with Aeneases escaping the flames with their fathers on their backs. The women's voices grew lower and happier as the evening went on. At some point I remember suddenly detecting a very strange smell that I had never smelled before. It was a warm, delicious smell, but extremely thick and pungent, and I remember how this smell immediately permeated the entire apartment. I looked up at them from where I sat on the floor, and I saw the two of them engaged in an unfathomable activity on the couch. Lydia was sitting upright at one end of the couch, and Tal's long yellow body was stretched supine along the length of it, with her dirty bare feet braced on the arm of the couch and her head, with its medusoid tangle of wild black hair, cradled in Lydia's lap. Tal held a cigarette in her hand. Just like the cigarettes my father used to illicitly smoke in the zoo, only this one was kind of lumpy and homemade-looking, not like the perfectly cylindrical factory-made bolts of burning stink that my father, Rotpeter, had smoked. Tal brought it to her lips and sucked the smoke in deeply, and the end of it glowed orange and crackled as she did. The smoke slowly left her nostrils in twin gray streamers. She handed the cigarette to Lydia, who did the same. I don't think they even noticed I was looking at them. They were still talking as they were doing this. When they had, taking turns, smoked all of it but a tiny remaining nubbin, Lydia let it drop from her fingers into her wineglass on the coffee table, and its speck of fire hissed out in the puddle of wine left at the bottom of the glass, and the bowl of the glass instantly filled with a burst of smoke, and for a moment the ribbons of smoke swam circles inside the glass like thin flat gray eels swimming in a fishbowl, and then the smoke floated out of the glass and dissipated in the air above it.

That night I dreamed of the Gnome Chompy. It was a dark dream. A nightmare. The nightmare was this: Lydia was dead. Or no, not dead, as I had no proof of that, but I feared the worst, that she was gone. One day she simply went out and never came back. And I went out looking for her. I got lost in the world. I was exposed to all the shrieking entropic clatter and bang of the cosmos—without her, without a guide. For some reason I was on the commuter train at one point in the dream, riding uptown, deep into the belly of Chicago—but without Lydia it was not exciting, it was horrifying: howling through the darkness trapped inside a bullet aimed God knows where, vulnerable, weak, fragile, defenseless. I could not understand what anyone was saying—or, rather, the secret conversations of the other passengers hovered right on the brink of comprehension but never quite began to make any sense, many voices mixing into a glossolalia, a swarm of talking tongues as meaningless to me as the buzzing of bees. Then, without realizing how I got there, I was in Africa. I was in my father's dangerous birthplace, Zaire. I was running through the jungle, lost in some tropical forest teeming with inky shadows, cacophonous with threatening noises, with hoots and cackles, in a place where there are humans afoot who want to kill and eat me. There are cannibals here—I say *cannibals*, Gwen, because the idea of humans eating chimpanzees is like dogs fleshing their teeth on the bellies of wolves!—it is tantamount to cannibalism. I met another ape in the forest. It was my father, Rotpeter. My mother was there with him, too. My father and mother. I tried to tell them something—to ask for help, supplicate their protection. But no words came out of my mouth. My father and my mother were sitting on the mossy forest floor, grooming each other. Then we heard a sound in the darkness. I knew that it was the Gnome Chompy. Something stirring in the trees. I heard leaves rustling, twigs snapping. Darkness. All primates have three primal fears: snakes, falling backward, and the dark. This was the dark. I knew the Gnome Chompy was somewhere in the darkness of the jungle that yawned all around us. I felt his presence. I heard his breath whistling in and out of his nostrils before I saw him. And then I saw his eyes. Two green bright eyes glowed in the dark behind my parents, over my father's shoulder. He emerged from the dark. He was a little man—being a gnome— but the Gnome Chompy was a terrifying inversion, reversion, and perversion of everything that was good about Francis the Gnome. His skin was pale yellow, sallow and necrotic. Unlike Francis the Gnome—who loves all animals—the Gnome Chompy hates them. He hates all things living. His large forehead and thickly furrowed brow protrudes over the glistening green stars of his eyes. He smiled and looked right at me as he peeled open his wet mouth to reveal two rows of sharp slimy teeth and a red raw slab of tongue. He licked his teeth. He stood behind my parents, who were facing me. I wanted to call out to them. I wanted to warn them somehow. I wanted to point behind them and scream. But I could not. That was the power of the Gnome Chompy. He had robbed me of the power of speech. It was as if there was cement hardening in my throat. I could not even move my hand to point. The Gnome Chompy had robbed me of all my powers of communication. There was no way I could warn them. I was powerless. I simply had to watch them die and be eaten, just like my father had watched his own mother and father die and be eaten. I watched the Gnome Chompy tear into my father's neck with his jaws. Then he snapped his teeth into my mother's throat. He tore open their bellies, he disemboweled them and began slurping up their entrails, eating them alive. They were screaming. I woke up. It was dark. At first I didn't know where I was. My eyes flitted around the room, aimlessly landing on the things in it, landing on the darkened shapes of clowns floating up to God by their balloons, on the planets of our solar system and the shadows they made, their silhouettes like cutouts from the sheet of moonlight on the opposite wall. My goose lamp was not on. I looked at these things, but failed to register their significances, their places in waking reality, the signifiers and signifieds all ripped apart and made meaningless.

From upstairs, directly above my bed, I heard Mr. Morgan's parrots flapping and screeching. I did not remember having gone to bed that night. I must have collapsed into sleep from sheer exhaustion right there on the living room floor, beside the fire. Lydia must have scooped me up in her arms and carried me to my bedroom and tucked me into bed.

I climbed out of my bed, ran out of the room, down the dark hallway, and into Lydia's bedroom. To make sure she was still there, still alive, still mine. I saw the two of them, lying together in Lydia's bed. Lydia and Tal. The bedsheets were sloppily pulled halfway up over their bodies—but I could tell that they were not wearing clothing of any sort. They were asleep. So deeply, so peacefully asleep that even my crazily bursting into the room had not woken them. I listened to the soft contrapuntal rhythms of their shallow breathing. Tal lay on her side, with her hands folded under the pillow and her legs partially curled in. Lydia lay beside her, with her knees curled into the hollows of Tal's knees, and her cheek resting on the skin of her shoulder. Lydia's arm was wrapped around Tal's body, with her right hand cupped over Tal's left breast. Lydia was faintly, sweetly, laughing in her sleep.

XVI

It must have been a few weeks later when I bit Tal's finger off. Though to be perfectly fair to me, she had been doing something I found irritating. Also it was essentially unintentional. I had only meant to give her finger a punitive little nibble, I certainly didn't mean to bite the whole thing *off*.

We had been seeing a lot of Tal lately. She and Lydia had been having their little sleepovers with increasing frequency in recent weeks. Lydia had even taken me to Tal's apartment, where I once spent a terrifying night sleeping on the foldout couch in her living room. Tal Gozani's apartment was the opposite of Lydia's. Whereas Lydia's apartment was a clean and psychologically comforting space, Tal's living quarters were like some cluttered gypsy bazaar, where one half-expected to hear the whine of a snake charmer's flute weaving through the air amid all that chaotic gimcrackery of bottles, cups, candles, baubles, trinkets, gewgaws, and musical instruments (a French horn, a banjo, a guitar). The apartment was small, just three little rooms: a bedroom, a grimy nook of a bathroom, and a sitting room/dining room/kitchen that Tal also used as a puppet-making workshop. A massive rough wooden worktable was pushed against one wall, dwarfing the rest of the furniture in the room. The surface of the table was where she made all her silly disgusting horrific puppets, and it was cluttered with all kinds of tools and materials—pliers, wires, paints, brushes, glue, wood, putty, clay, fabric, scissors, knives, hammers, awls, hooks, clasps, rubber bands, string, buttons, ribbons, needles, thread—a whole arsenal of implements that were apparently necessary to the business of puppet production and which made the room look like a place where industrious elves make toys. In this room it was impossible to determine where the precise boundaries of the space were because it was so cluttered with needless bric-a-brac. And puppets. The room was: *filled—with—puppets*. There was that Mr. Punch puppet that had horrified me so, and his wife, Judy, hanging on the pegs of a hat tree. Tal made both hand puppets and marionettes. There was a jester, a skeleton, a chef, an alien, a witch, a sailor, a cowboy, an Arabian belly dancer, a robot, a pirate, a Cossack, a rabbi, a genie, a knight, a king, a queen, a princess, a matador, a three-piece mariachi band. There were monkeys, bats, turtles, horses, cows, pigs, rabbits. Tal suspended her puppets from hooks screwed into the ceiling and walls, such that all her eerie wooden homunculi dangled on their strings like hangmen all over the room, with their hideous expressions, their gawky shiny lacquered faces leering pruriently down at me everywhere I went.

And those are just the visuals of the place. As for the audibles, the olfactibles and the tactiles? Tal had these thin brown sticks that she would light on fire with a match, which slowly smoldered away into thin snakes of ash in their shallow brass trays, and as they burned they gave off musky odors that intermingled with the distinctive smell of the fat white cigarettes she sometimes smoked. She lived in an old wooden building, as creaky and leaky as a ship in a storm, situated in some far-flung area of the city that I don't believe I've been to since. The final unsettling touch to this environment was that she lived directly below the tracks of the L. If you looked out her kitchen window you would see the sooty iron latticework that supported the elevated tracks, and periodically the whole apartment was set to shuddering and rumbling as the train blasted over us in the night.

I remember that evening vaguely. Usually Tal would visit us in our far more pleasant environs, and during these visits Lydia would insert an animated film for me—*Cinderella*, *Pinocchio*, etc.—into our television, which happily distracted my attention while the two of them sat on the couch, cuddling and cooing and sometimes smoking one of Tal's lumpy white cigarettes. But for some reason, tonight we were visiting Tal's place. And Tal—being no great lover of the candy frivolities of contemporary Western civilization—did not own a TV. Being in that place was like being in a store that sells expensive and fragile things. I was afraid to touch anything for fear that I would be castigated if something broke. So for entertainment I had to content myself with wandering her tiny apartment and visually inspecting the outlandish objects therein. I remember sitting with Lydia and Tal on her cramped, mildewy, musty-smelling couch and watching Tal page through a scrapbook of photographs, pointing at each one and explaining it to Lydia. There were lots of pictures of Tal standing around in some dusty brown godforsaken moonscape of a place that for some reason she kept insisting is real, even though Lydia did not appear to doubt the photographic evidence of its existence. She said she had been working on a caboose.

Lydia's and Tal's shared mood became sillier and sillier as the evening wore on. Tal's company had an interesting effect on Lydia. Tal certainly lightened her spirits, that I will admit. When the two of them were together they even began to take on one another's speech patterns and gestural mannerisms. When they would talk together they would almost mirror each other. Lydia began gesticulating when she talked in the same ways that Tal did, and vice versa. Lydia would absorb Tal's habit of pulling her bare feet up beneath her and sitting cross-legged on a couch with her hands in front of her, grabbing her ankles through the triangle of space in her lap. They sat across from each other on the couch like this, and when Lydia's hand fluttered to her face to tuck an errant strand of thin blond hair behind the ridge of her ear, Tal's hand would unconsciously mirror the movement in sympathy, even though her own unruly cords of hair were too thick to stay in place. In this way, they talked and laughed and touched each other's hands and drank wine and smoked the lumpy white cigarettes all night, their mood becoming ever sillier.

Eventually they became so disastrously silly that in the course of the evening, after food, after wine, as Lydia and Tal were passing one of their lumpy white cigarettes back and forth between them on the couch, they offered it to me. Perhaps I had reached for it in curiosity, and they interpreted this as a request. I accepted it: I took the smoldering thing between my little rubbery fingers as I had seen them do, I put it between my lips as I had seen them do, and I breathed it in as I had seen them do, bringing the hot pungent-smelling smoke deep inside my body. I exhaled, and then coughed—I coughed and wheezed and sputtered, choking on the smoke. My eyes watered and my throat constricted. I recovered soon after and felt better. And then I began to feel a feeling that was totally unprecedented by any of my previous experience with the world. It was like I had swallowed a jellyfish egg, and now it was growing inside my stomach, the amorphous gelatinous creature pulsing and throbbing deep within me. I felt exhausted and yet hyperalert at the same time. My head was floating like a balloon several feet above my body. Lydia held me, I curled up in her arms, and she stroked my fur with her hands and kissed the top of my head.

And then they started playing with the puppets. They took them down from their hooks in the walls and ceilings. Tal's fingers crossed over and under the wooden X that controlled the limbs and head of one of the marionettes—it was the skeleton puppet—and the limp dead thing turned alive—dangling from her hand it was suddenly kissed with the breath of life. It even had a distinct personality. The bones came alive and danced, like the vision of Ezekiel. This time, I was cognizant enough that the puppet was not a real creature that I was content to observe it without feeling too much wild trepidation in my heart. One of the musical instruments Tal had in her apartment was a guitar. I do not remember how the guitar got to be in Lydia's hands, but suddenly, it was there. There were many things I did not know about Lydia, things I had never wondered about because they were so beyond my conceptions of what was even possible. One of these things I had never known before was that Lydia knew how to play the guitar. She laughed a nervous little laugh when the thing was first in her arms, apologizing, excuse-making for her playing before she'd even begun to play, saying how she was years out of practice and so on. Tal said, don't be modest, I don't care, let's hear you play it. I can't play it, she said. Lydia strummed it once, and frowned at how out of tune it was. She twanged a string, with her head bent low over the golden body of hollow wood, her hair hanging down over the hole in the middle of it. She listened, her eyes closed in concentration, and with her left hand screwed and unscrewed the keys on the long end of the instrument while checking and balancing the looseness or tightness of the strings by softly hitting them with the knuckle of her thumb. Tal waited for her to tune the guitar with the skeleton marionette crumpled at her feet in a pile of painted wooden bones, and I watched. When she thought she had it tuned Lydia strummed it again, and the warm full note whanged out loudly and faded away, and with it the skeleton rose up from the floor. Lydia began to play a song on the guitar. I was amazed at the way her lithe strong slender fingers squeezed notes from that delicate machine of wood and wire. It was a joyful song, it was joyful noise. On the floor, the skeleton decided to dance to the music. Something about the combination of music and puppetry and the effects of the lumpy white cigarette did not frighten but rather transfixed me. The laughter of the two women, the clicking limbs of the wooden skeleton dancing like a dervish to the guitar from which Lydia's hands coaxed a series of sublime noises: it was hypnotism. Soon there were two wooden Xs in Tal's competent hands, and now there were two creatures dancing on the floor of her apartment to the music of the guitar: the Arabian belly dancer—blush-cheeked, diaphanous-veiled, and glitter-skinned—was now dancing with the skeleton, representing Eros and Thanatos respectively, sex dancing with death. Now a dance demon entered me. Now I, Bruno, was dancing with the puppets: a tangle of thin hairy limbs I was, jumping and swerving in—if not time, then an approximation of it—along with the puppets, as if they were my fellow living creatures: for at that moment, as brainless and artificial and as wooden-bodied as I knew them to be (the only brains they had they had by proxy from their mover and creator), for a long moment, the music and their movement made me fully accept them as conscious beings. Faster and faster we danced, the puppets clicking and rattling around me, the guitar ringing out, the trains rumbling past the window in the dark, the two women's voices in constant laughter, and me with my body and mind in a waking fever dream, a trance.

When Lydia could play the guitar no longer, when Tal's fingers and arms were exhausted from dancing the puppets, and when my own arms and legs were numb with fatigue, we all fell down together. Lydia and Tal collapsed on the couch. I collapsed on the floor. The puppets also collapsed on the floor. For a time (who knows how long?—Chronos had been murdered for one night), we all lay there, listening to the occasional roar of the train outside the kitchen window, Lydia and Tal hot-faced and gasping from too much laughter, Bruno panting on the floor, the guitar sleeping silently in Lydia's lap, and the puppets lying danceless beside me with their strings limp around their crumpled bodies.

When it was time for bed, Tal pushed on the back of the couch, which turned into a flat, uncomfortable bed. A blanket and a pillow were procured for me, in order to mimic homier sleeping conditions. Lydia kissed me and tucked me into this makeshift bed. The world was like a big warm pot of stew that I had dunked my head in. Then Lydia joined Tal in the bedroom. In the dark, the muddy ugly orange light from the streetlights outside crept into the room, casting the shadows of the puppets against the opposite wall. From time to time a train roared by above us. The tracks shook, the wheels of the train grinding against the tracks squealed and screamed, the whole place wobbled, thundered, and all the puppets dangling from the ceiling came alive and began to dance at the command of the train's reverberations in the night. Their arms and legs and their grinning, grimacing heads jiggled and flailed, their wooden limbs clicked and clattered together as they danced. When I finally did fall asleep, my sleep was thrashing and fitful, and I dreamed of nothing but grinning little wooden men, dancing on the ceiling. That was a place where dream always teetered on the razor's edge of nightmare. Lydia never took me back to that place again.

———

The finger-biting incident, though, happened one morning in the lab. For some reason I had slept poorly the night before, I don't recall why. But in any event I was groggy and irritable, and not particularly looking forward to the day's work ahead of me. We were doing some experiment; I think it had to do with more novel spoken instructions to manipulate various objects in various ways. Lydia was away, doing something else. I don't know why, but she wasn't in the room. Neither was Norm. I recall that it was just Tal and Prasad in the room with me. Tal was sitting with me on my squishy blue mat behind the glass wall that divided the domain of the human from the domain of the chimp. Prasad was on the other side of the glass, sitting at one of the lab tables, drinking a cup of tea and perusing some paperwork. Tal was holding a box of raisins.

Now, I liked raisins. But I did not love them. Tal was feeding me raisins, one for each successfully completed task. I guess this was before Norm orchestrated the complicated mock-capitalist system with the numbered chips. I must have misremembered when exactly that took place, Gwen, because I suppose otherwise Tal wouldn't have been baiting me with direct food rewards. Or maybe she secretly harbored some personal moral or philosophical disgust with Norm's value-chip system and so she just didn't use it when Norm wasn't around, which is also distinctly possible. Now that I think back on it, I remember that Tal had also chosen not to wear the frightening black metal welding mask that Norm insisted the experimenters wear when they asked me to perform their stupid tasks—so maybe that was indeed the case.

"Put some *soap on* the *ball*," she would say, taking special care to emphasize the nouns and the preposition. Back in those days it was very important to use the right preposition with me. And I would pick up a bottle of liquid hand soap and obediently squirt a little of it on top of my inflatable yellow beach ball. This task completed, Tal handed me a squishy raisin from the box. *A* raisin. Must other creatures sing for their suppers so? I wasn't even hungry. I took the raisin from her hand and set it down beside me for future consumption.

"You don't want the raisin, Bruno?" she said.

I shook my head no. I did not, in fact, want the raisin at that moment. Tal continued with the experiment.

"Put the *froggie in* the *refrigerator.*"

(There was a small refrigerator in the lab; the froggie was a rubber frog that whimpered when squeezed.) Debased slave that I was, I put the froggie in the refrigerator. Tal dug her fingers into the depths of the raisin box and rummaged around in it for a raisin. It was the kind of raisin box that was red, with a picture of a beautiful girl with raven-black hair spilling from her bonnet, bearing in her arms a bountiful basket of grapes, her back to a blazing yellow sun rising behind her. I listened to the sound of her fingers rattling the raisins against the inner walls of the thin cardboard box. She finally successfully fished a raisin out of the raisin box, and held it out for me to take.

Now why, I ask, would I want another fucking raisin? I had *just told her* that I didn't really even want the first one! She held out her hand, with the sad black gummy thing rolling around in the cup of her palm like a tiny turd. I did not want it. Not even for later. I pushed her hand away.

"Bruno," she said. "Come on. Please take the raisin."

I shook my head no.

"Okay, Bruno," she said, improvising, and ate the raisin herself. Was she trying to make me envious? Was she trying to make me covet my neighbor's raisin? Did she want me to think, *You villainous slut! How* dare *you eat my raisin*? If that was what she was after, it wasn't happening. I didn't care. I already had a raisin of my own.

"Bruno," she said. "Please give your *flower* some *water.*"

Now, what made all these tasks so maddening was their sheer needlessness. By "my flower" she was indicating a yellow flower made of thin synthetic fabric placed atop a green plastic stalk that sprouted from a plastic flowerpot full of rubber dirt. This was a miserable object. What demonic impulse so inspires humankind to manufacture sad rubber imitations of the simplest articles of natural beauty? The dirt in the flowerpot was disgustingly unrealistic, but the flower itself could almost fool you—until of course you touched its petals, and your fingers were rudely shocked by the brittle texture of the synthetic when you were expecting the plump wet kiss of honest life. What she wanted me to do was to take a watering can that had a little water in it, and dribble the water from its porous neck into the rubber dirt; a tragic mimicry of what would have been a bestowal of nourishment upon a living thing—if only the thing were real.

Sluggish-limbed and bored, begrudging her at every step, I hoisted myself up, went over to where the watering can was, dragged it one-handed across the floor behind me, clanging and banging as it went, water sloshing around inside it and splashing out in puddles here and there, and I tipped its beak into the plastic pot, submissively suffering to "water" the fake dirt.

"Good *job*, Bruno!" Tal clapped her hands twice in approval. "Very good!"

Then she rooted around in the raisin box and offered me another raisin.

I shook my head no.

"You don't want a raisin?" she said, thrusting the raisin at me. "Raisins are good. They're good for you."

(Ah-*ha!* I get it now, Tal. You were feeding me the raisins because you were concerned for my *health*. Because you were concerned that I was always using the wages I earned in the lab to buy nothing but junk food, the M&Ms and the marshmallows and the candy bars that Norm had on offer, all the gooey wonderful sweet stuff that I happened to *like*, while ignoring utterly the nuts and the vegetables and your "nature's candy," *the raisin!*)

Tal held the raisin aloft, deftly pinched between her middle finger and thumb, and guided this raisin, this blackened, mummified corpse of a grape, toward my face, toward the direction of my shut mouth, then stopped a few inches from my lips and held it there. Slowly, slowly, she brought the raisin to my mouth, until the raisin itself touched my lips. I opened my mouth, and then I shut it. When I shut my mouth, both the raisin and the middle finger of Tal's right hand were inside of it. For an instant, Tal's finger was in between my top and bottom rows of teeth. And then it wasn't.

I had never really done anything physically violent to a human in my life, and I never really would again, except for a few slipups, including the one murder I committed, which is what landed me in this place, but I will speak of that later.

Yes, there was screaming. Yes, there was blood. Yes, Tal looked down in horror at the stub where the ultimate and penultimate segments of her right middle finger used to be. Yes, she held her hand up to the light and looked at it with an expression that betrayed more amazement at first than physical pain, as if wondering where were the other two joints of her finger that only a moment before had been securely attached to the second knuckle? Yes, she held it that way, wide-eyed, aghast, against the cold flickering of the fluorescent lights that illumined the lab. And yes, just a brief moment, just a fraction of a second later, the blood began to burble up out of her finger, and a fraction of a second after that it began to spray from her hand, almost as if from the nozzle of a hose. Yes, the hot blood filling up my mouth tasted bitter, metallic. No, I did not swallow it.

There immediately followed a period of great tumult and confusion. To complement the craziness of the moment, the minute hand of the clock had just then managed to scale the left side of the clock face to surmount the top of the hour, which meant that all the classes in the building were being dismissed at about the same time, and now the hallways below us had suddenly come alive with murmuring and hundreds of shuffling shoes.

Prasad gave her a quick bandaging with the lab's first-aid kit. There was a lot of yelling. Someone called an ambulance. For a short time there was some shouting about where the finger was.

"It's still in his fucking *mouth*," Tal shrieked, cradling her hand to her chest, which was wrapped up in gauze and then again in her twisted and bloody T-shirt.

They tried to catch me, but I was too fast for them! I ran around the room like mad in the confusion, screaming, flailing, scrambling over the tables, upsetting the furniture, bouncing off the walls, causing a world-class ruckus. Shouting everywhere. Lydia—who at some point had rematerialized in the room—yelled at everyone: "*Leave!*" she commanded. "Everybody get out! I'll handle this!"

"Are you sure?" someone said. "He's dangerous—"

"Go. *Go!* Get out! I'll take care of it."

All the other scientists funneled out the door and into the hall, guiding Tal, who was now pale with blood loss and fright, still clutching her hand to her chest, out of the room. They left. The door shut behind them. I was cowering beneath one of the lab tables. The room was silent except for the sound of all the students jostling each other in the halls of the floors below us.

"Bruno," Lydia called. "Bruno. Come here, please."

I wouldn't come out.

"Don't worry. I won't bite," she said, keenly aware of the irony.

She found me huddled under a table. Lydia was on her hands and knees on the floor. She crawled toward me, and then sat down, cross-legged, and patted the floor in front of her. She had put on a sweet face, but I could tell in her eyes that she was furious with me.

"Come here," she whispered. "Come to me."

I scrambled out from under the shadow of the table and sat in her lap. She hugged me, and she kissed the top of my head and stroked my fur. I was shivering.

"Shhhh————," she said. "Shhhh—————."

Gradually, my shivering stopped. She put a cupped hand below my mouth. (Recall, Gwen, the episode with the peach.)

"Please, Bruno," she said. "Give it to me. Spit it out."

I let the finger fall from my mouth. I pushed it out with my tongue, and the lifeless and slimy thing—and the raisin along with it—tumbled from my mouth and into the cradle of her palm, still attached to my lips by a sticky thread of drool.

"Thank you, Bruno," she said, and closed her hand over it.

Then she picked me up and put me in the enclosure that was walled in by thick glass, and shut the door. I went willingly. I knew that I had done wrong. That I had sinned. She locked the door. I began to cry.

"You've been bad," she said. "You've been very, very, *very* bad. I'll deal with you later, Bruno. I have to go now."

Lydia turned around and left, the finger held tightly in her hand. She hurried from the room, but remembered to flick off the lights as she left. No one came back to the lab for the rest of the day.

She needed the finger because she had vainly hoped that a doctor would be able to reattach it. Much later she would tell me that the doctors had in fact attempted to reattach the finger. She told me that although they had implemented all the sorceries of modern medicine available to them, they had ultimately failed to reattach it. In retrospect, I have come to wonder what effect the loss of the longest and middle digit on Tal Gozani's dominant hand had on her career in puppetry.

Tal quit working at the lab after that, and she stopped visiting Lydia and me at our home. I believe the lab was legally in the clear, because they had a policy of requiring everyone who did research with potentially vicious animals like me—and are we not all "potentially vicious" animals, Gwen?—to sign some sort of waiver saying they wouldn't sue if something like this were to happen. If she had been able to sue and had chosen to do so, then I'm sure it would have spelled certain doom for the project. Norm was already strapped enough for cash as it was. Maybe I would have been returned—God forbid—to the zoo. After this incident, everyone who worked in the lab behaved with a little more nervousness toward me, they deferred to me a little more respect—or caution, I couldn't tell which, and ultimately it doesn't much matter.

Everyone, that is, except for Lydia. She seemed to understand. To forgive me, even. It's to be expected in this line of work. Chimps bite. Get out of the primatology business if you can't take the primates, is what I say. I really don't blame myself for it at all—I'm not that cruel.

As a result of this unfortunate incident, I once again had to sleep in that fucking laboratory for a time afterward. I do not know if this was intended as punishment, or what. I do not remember if it was days or weeks. It was mostly because, at least for a while, not even Lydia trusted me to behave properly in a domestic human environment.

The upshot of this temporary arrangement was that I got to see Haywood Finch again. I had not seen my friend in many months, and that first evening that I was back in the lab at night, I remember the sudden surge of joy I felt in my chest when I heard the familiar sound of his walk, stomping and jangling down the hallway, the *kLOMPa-whap-SHLINK kLOMPa-whap-SHLINK* of his boots, his chain, his hoop of many keys, when I saw his familiar blurry lumpy shadow looming in that familiar doorway, behind the panel of smoked glass in the door to room 308: BEHAVIORAL BIOLOGY LABORATORY. He opened the door, and snapped on the buzzing fluorescent lights, which slowly fluttered on, *nzt-nzt-nzt-nzzzzzzzzzzz*.

"*Haywood!*" I shrieked.

"*Bruno!*" he screamed.

That night, even Haywood forgot his routine. He was so glad to see me again. That night, we sat up in the laboratory, separated by a wall of glass, and howled gibberish at each other almost until the beginning of dawn.

I have never, by the way, eaten a raisin since. Raisins make me want to vomit. I hate raisins.

XVII

I shall never forget the day that Lydia, on one of our outings, took me to the Museum of the Art Institute of Chicago. On that day, all the dormant potential for sweetness and light buried deep in some volcanic cranny of Bruno's soul erupted forth to the surface, igniting fires, fires!

This day is important, Gwen, because I became an artist on that day. It had been a few months since the biting incident. It was summer again. It's a snarling irony that there was actually a bit of a row that took place on the museum steps that morning between Lydia and a rent-a-cop, some dough-faced lout in a cryptofascist uniform with shiny buttons all over it claiming to be a museum employee, concerning the question of whether or not a chimpanzee should be admitted entrance into this temple of Eleusinian Mysteries—an art museum. Bigotry! Just when I thought Lydia and this Gestapo-seur might actually come to blows, some higher-up from the museum's bureaucracy intercepted the argument as third-party arbiter, and it was finally determined that my admittance was permissible depending on the caveats that I was to be at all times: (one) secured on my leash, and (two) either holding Lydia's hand or being physically carried by her, which was fine with me because there was no other place in the world I'd rather have been than dangling from the neck of my Lydia.

The first paintings to really excite me were the many female nudes: reclining, standing, bathing, sleeping, descending stair-cases, splishing about in streams or wringing riverwater from their hair, standing on clams, brandishing swords and scales in alle-gorical triptychs while their diaphanous garments teasingly slip from their shoulders, unabashedly loafing around in various states of undress in the Turkish seraglios of tittery European imagina-tion, and that beautiful Manet of the pouty strumpet lounging on a pile of silk pillows with a hand planted on her crotch and her shoes on.... Clearly the Great Master(bator)s of the History of Art were just as irresistibly fascinated by the very subject that did then and continues to fascinate Bruno: the disrobed human female. I couldn't contain myself!—I wanted to fuck them all! I wanted to fuck Manet's Olympia and Botticelli's Venus, I wanted to fuck Mary Magdalene in her grotto and that double amputee Venus de Milo who's got nothing now to prevent that sheet from falling, I wanted to fuck all the bare-breasted goddesses in the alle-gorical triptychs, too, I wanted to fuck Justice and fuck Peace and fuck Fidelity, I was even waiting at the bottom of the stairs for the nude to finish descending, where I would unlock her with the key of my desire from Duchamp's prismatic prison! After advancing first through the classical stuff and then through the tantalizing objects of Italian Mannerist lust, then eighteenth-century French Romanticism—robes, togas, tunics, and bedsheets unfurling left and right to expose rolling pink swaths of luminous human flesh you could almost smell and taste in the paint—we came to the Impressionists: the two I liked the best were certainly Van Gogh and Gauguin.

Gauguin, because all those sweet plump honey-complected Polynesian tarts re-ignited my libido after I'd had to suffer through a bunch of brain-numbingly insipid pictures of flowers and vegetables and dead fish and other such crap.

But Van Gogh! Van Gogh, because he's a genius. Van Gogh was the first painter I admired for purely platonic reasons. My God, the landscapes of Van Gogh! You know all those pastoral pictures of the wind shushing through cypress trees on grassy hillsides somewhere in the south of France? *What* pastoral? Those are the *least* pastoral pastoral paintings you'll ever see. Everything in the landscape is chattering and rattling and hissing and screaming! Those paintings aren't pastoral!—they're full of weeping and gnashing of teeth.

Then we came to the Moderns, which I also liked, but in a different way. I took a crash course in the history of Western art that day, and so twentieth-century sallies into the realm of the wildly abstract shocked me on the same day I was also shocked by the concept, the very concept of representing three-dimensional form on canvas at all. I saw Picassos, Matisses, Mondrian's colorful boxes, Jackson Pollock's haphazard psychoscapes, Rothko's subtly defined rectangles of color. Yes, yes, said Bruno to his soul. This is it. This stuff is the best of the best of being human.

We lingered in the museum until it closed—so unwilling was I to leave the place. When we came home that day, I was able to communicate to Lydia, in a struggling handful of gestures and rudimentary utterances, that I had found my calling: I wanted to paint.

"Do you want to draw pictures like the ones we saw today at the museum?" said Lydia.

Yes, I affirmed, nodding. Yes, yes, yes.

The very next day Lydia—this inexhaustible fount of human benevolence—went to the store and bought me a large pad of sketch paper and some art supplies: crayons, pencils, watercolors, a box of Magic Markers.

182 • Benjamin Hale

Crayons have never done it for me. I realize that the image of a crayon by itself practically stands as a synecdoche of childhood, but in practical usage I found them sorely wanting. I detested the way the tips would become blunted almost immediately. I did not like the rough quality of the lines they made on the paper, I did not like the feeling or the texture, and I hated when their waxy tips bore down into the paper wrapping—the sound of the paper crayon wrapper scraping against the paper I was drawing on never failed to solicit a cringe and a shiver from me. No!—to hell with crayons! *I* was a marker man.

Magic Marker was my first medium, Gwen, and I still think it's a wonderful one. There's the exhilarating smell when you uncap a marker, the juicy wet nib, the feeling of the thing bleeding ink onto the page for you, so smooth, so vibrant: the change one enacts upon a blank sheet of paper is so material, so pleasingly concrete and direct. Here's a naked field of virginal white—now uncap a marker of your favorite color, drag it across the page and—*shooop!*—now there's a violent streak of color in it, the immediately visible effect of your own physical agency, ha, ha, *ha!*

The very first works in my oeuvre were mostly nonrepresentational and wildly expressionistic. I would create a picture that was a crazed scramble of red lines with an ugly muddy splotch right in the middle of it where young Bruno had experimented with scribbling all the different-colored markers on top of each other until the paper was wavy and warped with the dampness of so much ink, and then title the piece "Shoe." Or I would jam a marker into the page like a jackhammer half a dozen times to make an exploding constellation of spattery green blots, then connect them with shaky blue lines, scribble over the whole thing with the orange marker and title it (intended only in affection) "Lydia."

I would draw all day long, practicing constantly, flying through reams of sketch paper and many, many boxes of Magic Markers.

I rapidly improved, refining both technique and concept. During this period of accelerated mental maturation, when I wasn't either studying language with Lydia or watching my beloved Bert and Ernie on *Sesame Street*, I was drawing. Soon I also got the knack of representational form, and now I was drawing everything in the house: pictures of the furniture, studies of various rooms, pictures of birds and squirrels I saw in the backyard, pictures of my goose lamp drawn from different angles, self-portraits drawn from the mirror, portraits of Bert and Ernie I drew from studying their images on television, and hundreds and hundreds and hundreds and hundreds of portraits of Lydia.

And she did nothing but foster and encourage my artistic pursuits, Gwen. She magnetized some of my best work to the refrigerator door, and Bruno was proud. She meticulously dated and cataloged the rest of it and filed them all away in a cabinet for future scientific analysis. After I'd mastered the media of marker and paper, she bought me a set of acrylics and brushes and converted my old room into my studio. I helped her whitewash the walls, install track lighting, and rip out the carpet so I didn't have to fret over making a mess with my paints. But I demanded she leave both my goose lamp and the mobile of the solar system right where they were: I liked to look at them.

I say "my old room" because I was already sleeping with Lydia. *No*, God no, I don't mean that euphemistically, Gwen. Not yet. I mean we literally slept together in the big cushy queen-size bed in her room. Why? Nightmares. My nightmares had never completely gone away. Plus sometimes Mr. Morgan's parrots kept me awake at night, even though I knew their screams were benign. As for my nightmares: everyone has demons living inside them. Lydia had her recurrent headaches, and I had my nightmares. Lydia's headaches I'll speak of in a moment, for now I will speak of my nightmares. The Gnome Chompy was a recurrent figure in my nightmares. He would rob me of my voice and devour my parents in the jungle nearly every night. I was having more and more of these nightmares as I was learning language. Sometimes I still have them. Surely I'd had dreams before, but I only began to notice them after I started seriously acquiring language. Perhaps this is because the dreams of animals are not so very different from their waking lives. In both the dreaming and the waking consciousnesses of an animal, everything is immediate, everything happens all at once, everything is new and nothing is explainable. That is, of an animal that already has a consciousness, but not yet articulate language. I can assure you humans that when you dream, you are at your closest to the consciousness of a prelinguistic animal. That is why we feel that we must retroactively assign meanings to what we see in our dreams and nightmares. Because we, and I mean humans, are meaning makers. We do not discover the meanings of mysterious things, we invent them. We make meanings because meaninglessness terrifies us above all things. More than snakes, even. More than falling, or the dark. We trick ourselves into seeing meanings in things, when in fact all we are doing is grafting our meanings onto the universe to comfort ourselves. We gild the chaos of the universe with our symbols. To admit that something is meaningless is just like falling backward into darkness.

There was one time, I remember, when I woke up chilled in my sweat in the middle of the night. I ran to Lydia's bedroom, shaking and crying with fear. She was there. She was awake. Wide awake in the middle of the night. Lydia was half sitting up in the bed, and her face was contorted into a bizarre shape that I had never seen before on a real human being—only in paintings. Lydia was holding a hand to her mouth and her shoulders were shaking. She was crying. I had never seen a human cry before. It was terrifying.

She spooked when she saw me standing in the doorway of her bedroom, and I spooked too when I saw her face, but then she waved at me to come here, come here, Bruno. And I jumped into her bed, and we held on to each other.

She drained herself dry of tears that night. I snuggled against her chest with my arms around her warm body, and I think I both calmed her and was calmed by her. We woke up together the next morning, the sunlight slicing through the blinds, casting bright orange stripes across our bodies in the bed. My head on the pillow next to hers, her bedraggled slept-on hair, her eyes, sleep-custard still gooey in their corners, peeling open to get their first look at the day and seeing me lying next to her, and her smile at seeing me there—words would fail me if I even attempted to communicate to you the importance of that moment in my life.

So my nightmares drove me to the solace of Lydia's bed night after night, until she finally relented and just let me sleep with her all the time. The comfort of communion with another living creature. Her bed was *our* bed now.

That was when Lydia dismantled the childlike bedroom that I had slept in for the last two years or so, and we converted it into my studio. With her warm body lying beside me, my nightmares grew less and less frequent, and eventually went away altogether, except for a freak incident now and then.

Also, there was the fun ritual of "Going to Bed": after Lydia read me our last bedtime story from the books, it was bedtime for Bruno, and for Lydia, too. She went to the bathroom and eventually came out in her pajamas, and then we brushed our teeth together in the mirror and spat out the toothpaste in the sink. She set the alarm clock, and we crawled into the bed, she on her side and me on mine. "Good night," she would say every night, "sleep tight, don't let the bedbugs bite!" And I then repeated this incantation tone for tone, though I had no idea what this singsongy rhyme meant—and then we began to sleep. For awaiting us in the morning was the ritual of "Getting Up": we took turns in the shower—I had acquired an appreciation for the human custom of near-daily bathing. She showered, and then got dressed while I was taking my shower. Once I was dressed, I helped her make the bed. We dragged the coverlet into place together, and tucked the edges neatly under the mattress. Then, while I watched *Francis the Gnome* or *Sesame Street*, Lydia would prepare us a modest breakfast—oatmeal, Wheat Chex, bananas, strawberries, orange juice, things like that. While we ate our breakfast at the table the percolator would gurgle out a few inches of coffee. Lydia would drink a cup and dump the remainder into her portable plastic travel mug, which she would take to the lab. Then we were both buckled into her car and off to work. And when the work was done, we would repair home and begin our domestic life together anew. Dinner, books, and eventually bed. At the close of every day we went to bed together and held each other in the night like a brother and sister (or a mother and son?), making ourselves safe together against the darkness that ruled the world outside.

XVIII

Before going further I should mention Lydia's periodic bouts with insomnia, and the related phenomenon of her terrible headaches.

Lydia was the sort of person who presented such a thick outward mask of composure to the daytime world that every demon that she quickly buried in her brain during the sunlit hours would come out to haunt her at night, sometimes costing her sleep.

Usually she slept well enough. But once in a while, maybe ten or eleven times a year, the red-eyed monster of sleeplessness would drive Hypnos from her bed for a string of nights sometimes lasting up to a week. These insomniac fits were usually triggered by her menstrual cycle. Almost every time she experienced her "period," Lydia would swoon with headaches—migraines. These migraine headaches, as I understand from her descriptions of them, were brutal skullbusters that made her feel as if she had a hatchet embedded in her head for several days straight, cleaving her two lobes straight down the braincrack, severing the corpus callosum, splitting the hemisphere of things from the hemisphere of symbols, each eye seeing things somewhat differently, edges failing to match up, seeing double—and this was accompanied by a cacophony of humming, gnashing, burning, chewing, grating, sawing, and buzzing noises in her head that sounded (she said) like heavy industry, like a lot of noises you might hear in a tank factory. Her eyes were also hypersensitive to light when these attacks occurred, and when the headaches were besieging her with their worst, she would lie on the bed all day with an ice pack on her head, her shoes off, and the blinds drawn shut to the world beyond the bedroom.

She would rest but would not sleep, because the headaches were so horrific that they would not lend her a moment of peace long enough to let her fall asleep. Sometimes she got lucky, and those nearly monthly brain-blitzes failed, for whatever mysterious reason, to happen—but usually she could tell her period was coming because those headaches served as the grim harbingers of looming uterine discharge, warning her a day or two in advance. Then the headaches worsened at the peak of her three days' bloodletting and left in their wake another three days of insomnia. I think the insomnia may have had something to do with all the Excedrin Lydia took during the time of the headaches. Extra-Strength Excedrin Migraine tablets were the only painkillers stalwart enough to even begin to quell the tempests that raged nightly in her skull, and perhaps she overmedicated herself, took too much of it, and it kept her awake, and she stayed awake, became moody, easily given to tears, emotionally haywire, would spend her nights alert and tormented, with her brain, I know, playing and replaying every regret and mistake in her life, every flare-up of fury or subjection to humiliation, until her heart rattled against her ribs like a broken machine and the light in the room shifted from orange to blue-gray and the streets outside became reanimated with the—to her— threatening and depressing sounds of early morning traffic and tweeting birds, which meant she would now be forced to face the coming day in this state, knowing that the closest she had managed to come to sleep was a sort of rollicking seasickness accompanied by a lurid zoetrope of nauseating images sliding across the screen of her inner eyelids, more like hallucinations than dreams.

And then, after the headaches and the menstruation, followed by the insomnia, the only way to reregulate her circadian rhythm was to take these heavy-duty sleeping pills, for which she had a special prescription. And when she took one of those pills she would sleep like a corpse and could not have been woken even if the house was on fire. After a few nights of this, she was finally back on her biological track and she would be fine for another few weeks, until the headaches reemerged and the whole cycle began anew.

Meanwhile, I was making great progress with my art. I would spend the whole weekend in my studio painting on paper with watercolors or on canvas with acrylics. Now, instead of watching TV, I would frequently retire to my studio directly after we got home from the lab in the afternoon, where I would immerse myself in my art until Lydia would fetch me, to ask me to clean up for dinner. She even successfully convinced Norm that I was making such fantastic headway with my painting that it would be beneficial to my mind and soul to cut our sessions at the lab down to a half day only, in order to reserve the afternoons for me to paint. Perhaps Norm's quick acceptance of this idea arose more out of his exhaustions and frustrations with trying to work with me at the lab; I was, I admit, ever increasingly bitchy and uncooperative with him in the lab setting. He was glad to have the newfound peace and quiet in the afternoons. So I was seeing less and less of the Norm/lab world, and spending more and more time at home with Lydia. We all won in that way.

After some initial frustrations with the difficulty of acrylics on canvas in comparison to markers on paper (paint is not like ink; it's much subtler, requires one to think more in terms of color and tone than in line and form) I fell in love with the new medium and continued to expand my artistic vocabulary. I painted a series of works modeled after my mobile of the solar system, seen from various angles and lighting. First I painted individual portraits of each of the nine planets and the sun, then I painted them all together.

All this time I was still learning a lot from Lydia. I was learning constantly—we're still talking about my first explosive phase of awakening to the world. It wasn't happening in big events— not some cataclysmic defining moment, not like the big bang that vomited up all the matter that composes those nine planets and you and me—but rather a very gradual formation of the universe inside my consciousness, more like the slow process of gravity rolling all that scattered dust into balls and setting them in motion, making planets, making stars—not big things, but billions of little things occurring over periods of months and years, pinching and molding my mind and soul into ontogenesis.

I was, and am, fascinated by the human figure. The bottomless catalog of emotive capacities the human form and face is capable of. That's why I've always been bored with still-life pictures. "Still life"?—my God, the very phrase is an oxymoron! Give me *life*! Hence, imitating my hero, Van Gogh, I painted thousands of self-portraits, and of course I continued to paint and paint and paint Lydia, who gamely continued to suffer to sit for my portraits. And when she took me for visits to the laboratory at the university, I would dash off sketches of the other scientists, which I would later use as studies for paintings.

In seemingly no time at all I had become a painter of considerable technical accomplishment. By the time Lydia organized a formal exhibition of my work in a gallery space in the University of Chicago library, I had essentially settled into what would be my medium of choice for a long time to come: oil on canvas. Oils!— after you've worked with oils you'll never want to dally in acrylics again. Acrylics—they're too thin, too meek, the colors aren't as vibrant, they don't feel as real and viscous and, dare I say it, as *human* as oils. And I had started to work with big canvases, also. Most of the paintings included in that first exhibition of my work were painted on four-by-six-foot canvases. Lydia continued to generously purchase all my materials for me.

I would like to describe for you in detail my first gallery exhibition. But before I do, I need to tell you something else, something very important. It has to do, naturally, with Lydia. I apologize for the brevity of this chapter, Gwen — but it is of paramount importance to me that we devote an entire and separate chapter to what I am about to tell you.

XIX

You have got to understand that I had been living with Lydia, and in fact had been platonically sharing a bed—a *bed!*—with her for over a year (in my admittedly hazy recollection) before anything "happened."

The sexual tension had been there right from the beginning, though. I think it had colored our relationship since the day we met—when I first fell in love with her—when I watched her take a bite out of that peach, when I tapped on that box, demonstrating to the scientists that I, too, could be just as irrational as any human being. My desire for her had gone through different phases. It had evolved and adapted to its environment through many marvelous mutations. Up until this point Lydia had taught me nearly everything I knew—everything *she* knew—because love—and I mean the real thing, *Eros*, romantic, sexual *love*—is possible only between psychological equals. And she raised me up until I was practically her intellectual equal. We had come to a point in our relationship—a point at which there was but negligible difference between our respective levels of reasoning ability (though technically I suppose at this point I could still barely speak a coherent word other than *yes*, *no*, and my own name, and furthermore only Lydia could understand my speech), when we had ceased to be simply an educator and her pupil—or even a surrogate mother and her child—and became two true friends, who each learned from the other every day. We were partners in this project of ours, united against the stern world. I filled a vacancy in her emotional life, and she gave me my life as I know it, in the form of culture and knowledge.

In a past life, Lydia had been robbed of a son and a lover. And I, Bruno, eventually gave her back both. So, yes, obviously there was a sense of some deep-seated and dangerous taboo that our relationship violated. But this taboo was not bestiality—it was incest.

My own psychosexuality was (should I say, "is"?) tortured and twisted up and confused. Why? Because I love women, and I am a chimp.

My relationship with Lydia progressed over the same period of time that I entered into manhood, both metaphorically and hormonally. I was sailing through both my intellectual awakening and my natural puberty at the same time. It wasn't just that, as the intensity of the itches and tingles in my loins were slowly increasing, *Bolero*-like, at a steady cadence but with exponentially rising volume, I had truly begun to see Lydia as a *sexual being*—not just as an unattainable preadolescent fantasy but as a potential reality—but that my now very real sexual attraction to her became interwoven into the fabric of my true love. I longed to see Lydia naked. Just the symbol of her nudity to Bruno—what it meant to me then!

I need to clarify something here. Lydia wasn't exactly beautiful. She did not shimmer like those unreachable stars, so many impossible light-years in the distance. She was here, she was plain, she was good, she was earthy. She was mine. But she was not mine. I was hers.

It may be occurring to you, Gwen, that my descriptions of Lydia are inconsistent and often contradictory. One moment she's dazzling, beatific, and now she's good and plain and earthy. If her shape shifts it is because memory and perception are fickle mistresses. She was beautiful and she was not beautiful: both these statements are true. You see how well I've learned human logic? That's right—I am the chimp who tapped Pandora's Box.

But her headaches. Lydia had just experienced her menstrual period, which, as usual, was accompanied by her tempestuous migraine headaches, whose intensity could be only partially dampened with Extra-Strength Excedrin tablets, which caused her insomnia, which was curable only with the extra-strength sleeping pills Lydia kept on hand for the days of monthly torment she was doomed to suffer all her life.

Now this. Look: here lies Lydia—no, not dead, but dead to the world, lying in a motionless—and from the way her eyelids aren't fluttering with REM, we may assume dreamless—sleep. She's sweating profusely, because the sleep those gel capsules induce is red, wet, and feverish, like a diseased mouth. The way she is lying on the bed might suggest she fell on it from a tenth-story window. Yes, everything about her posture calls to mind not restful slumber, but a suicide, or some hostile defenestration, lying supine in a crunchy green stardust of broken glass on the sidewalk; she is not, as she usually sleeps, fetally half-curled on her right side, with one hand under the pillow to muffle the thunder of her own amplified heartbeat—no, but on her back she lies, one arm thrown above her head, the other sprawled at an irrational angle across my side of the bed, her legs apart, one outstretched, the other bent. She's wearing her nightgown, her bone-colored silk nightgown (silk, that texture!), and her bare feet are mouthwateringly desirable, so pale and smooth, her ankles, her insteps florescent with tiny blue hairline veins. In her sweaty drugged sleep, her nightgown has become wadded and crinkled, damply glued to her thighs, and in the night it has ridden up and up her thighs, exposing her legs, reaching almost up to the damp hairy jungle of her crotch.

Now this. Here lies Bruno beside her—not dead, far from it—not even asleep, but wide awake. It is the middle of the night, a rainy night, desultory clusters of raindrops crackling on the roof, and outside the window one can see a murky sky thrown over the city of Chicago like a dirty sheet, the creamy clouds reflecting the light of the city, so that they appear to glow dull orange, as if lit from within. Yes, I am awake, having been stirred to consciousness by uneasy dreams. In the kitchen, the refrigerator quits humming. A clock somewhere is itching out the seconds, slowly driving me insane with sensual desire, the insistent *itch-itch-itch* of the clock like a tiny finger tickling my loins. The *smell* of her. The sweat of her feverish druggy sleep smells intoxicant and delicious. She smells more lushly human now than anything this chimp's nostrils have previously smelt. I take her in, *snfffffffffffff.* And something, something is happening to me.... My most Darwinian organ is slowly ratcheting to life, itch-itch-itch-itch. My heart is beating faster, boldly ensanguinating this once-harmless tube of flaccid flesh, each successive pump of my wild heart feeding it more blood, the outflow of every beat making it longer and fatter. An errant hand drifts toward the thing, a hand with a flat, elongated palm and a small hooklike opposable thumb, and long purple fingers wrap around it. That *smell.* Not too long ago I would have been chilled, horrified by the idea of Lydia not being able to wake up from her sleep—in the beginning, I didn't even believe that humans *slept.* Not anymore.

That smell. And where, our hero wonders, gazing pruriently upon a completely zonked-out Lydia, is the source of this most human of odors? It is a humid smell—*earthy*—thick, sultry as a tropical rain forest, oily, metallic, sweet and salty all at once. I am bent over Lydia now, sniffing. I sniff her feet—no, that's not it. My nose travels up her leg, across tracts of maddeningly soft sticky glabrous flesh—Bruno, the world's greatest physical anthropologist!

Up and up the length of her body my nose travels, that smell grow-ing stronger and stronger—we are approaching the source! And now I have, as in a dream, positioned myself between this woman's two big beautiful long thick smooth strong human legs, and I am sniffing her thighs. I seem to be almost involuntarily pressing and rubbing my now fully engorged little monster against the sheets. I dive beneath the rumpled hem of her nightgown, as if diving under a tent flap. I am now in an enclosed environment, a ceiling of bone-colored silk sliding along the back of my furry head and a floor of hot heaving flesh beneath me. And the smell is utterly overpower-ing—intoxicating—choking—possessing—and my face is right *in* it. Here it is. This is the first time I have seen a real human vulva, in the flesh. I haven't really even seen them in paintings, before—even the nudes at the Art Institute are always arranged in such a way as to prudishly obscure this mysterious and powerfully odor-ous yawning animal, this mollusk at the center of existence. How hairy it is! It is shocking! Did you think, Bruno, that all women were like polished marble statues down there? So naïve! How unex-pectedly I discover that this oddly nearly hairless creature should have a delta of scraggly black hair decorating her genitals. And the *placement* of this thing! The female human is the only animal in the kingdom to have such a maddeningly, inconveniently located vagina. Right on the very bottom, exactly in between the legs, the weirdest and most inaccessible spot on the body. I inhale deeply, I sniff and sniff, this smell that is almost sickening in its headiness, its passionate intensity. And my mouth opens. The rosy flaps of my pithecine lips peel back and my tongue rolls out. My tongue reaches out into the darkness—the very same curious worm in my jaw who would later learn to perform the glossal acrobatics of human language—to taste it. And the tongue begins to slurp at this thing, to probe its contours. I love the dark sweetness of Lydia's body. I want to drink her strong biological wine. It tastes like when

I suck on batteries! It has the same fuzzy thrilling coppery-tasting little shock. And the hot somnolent mass that is Lydia begins to respond to this stimulus: from up above I hear a sharp insuck of breath, followed by a slow, staggered release of it. She's still asleep, you see, but maybe now her brain is groaning with flashes of erotic imagery: the sweaty petals of lusciously colored flowers, sloping desert midnight dunes, waterfalls, glossy-coated panthers...and I, Bruno the incubus, continue to lap at her yonic mollusk, and I feel a languid sleeping hand come to rest on the back of my head and gently press on it through the thin wall of silk fabric, pushing my head downward and in...her breathing quickens...and I realize that what I have been tonguing in fact includes a concavity. It goes inside of her, it is a kind of tunnel. Like Caravaggio's Thomas the Doubter does to the wound of the resurrected Christ, in disbelief I squelch an inquisitive finger into the folds of the opening: *spplt.* I stick it in as far as I can reach and still cannot feel the end of the tunnel! I wiggle it around, feeling her inner linings, what's in here? And when I do, her body goes all gelatinous, begins to quake with spasmodic rumblings of passion. Then I get a really good idea. My penis seems to have an intense desire to be put into something, and this slippery feverish envelope of wet flesh seems to have an intense desire to have something put in it. Aha! Thus I make the Great Leap. I climb up onto her body, burrowing further under the silk tent, now encountering her breasts. I'm just tall enough to reach them with my mouth! I gnaw on them a little, and her nipples inflate instantly, becoming like round pebbles between my lips. Now our genitals are aligned. I jab blindly at the area in question, until I am received—the mouth of this great fish swallows me up. It is like pulling on a silk slipper.

Then things really start happening. Every neuron receptor in my brain is firing at once, I'm swept up in a flood, I'm flying, I'm floating, I'm dying, and now the flesh beneath me is roiling like an earthquake and something just, just *happens*—a feeling of such intense experience that the world goes white, I'm hysterical, I'm *blind!*

And there we lay, Bruno and Lydia, gasping, quiescent, silent, and I'm still sandwiched between Lydia's sweaty flesh and the fabric of her nightgown. My face burrowed between her breasts, my bliss and her arms wrapped around me, and I fall asleep this way, still inside of her.

Lydia woke up the following morning with a chimp in her nightgown.

I was unprepared for her initial reaction. I awoke to the sight of her face, peering down at mine through the neck of her nightgown. Morning had come, leisurely and bright, the sun having burned away the clouds: birds *eep-eep-eep*ing outside the window and sunlight suffusing the membranous fabric of my silk tent, making it warm and reddish. Blinking away my sleep, I looked up at her and smiled, blissfully, I think, and she answered my smile with an aghast look that completely perplexed me, before I was violently removed from my tent—yanked and kicked and jerked and pulled out. This was the only time I can remember Lydia ever being physically forceful with me in any way. When she had disentangled me from her nightgown, she, without offering a word, jumped out of bed—I was still in a daze—ran into the bathroom, slammed the door shut, and locked it.

She remained in there for hours. I bashed my fists against the door and alternated between doleful screams and pitiful whimpers, crying and raging—in apology, in lamentation—inarticulately pleading with her to reemerge from the bathroom. I wailed until my vocal cords were worn threadbare from all my wailing. She would not come out. She would not respond. I heard running water. I heard the toilet flush a few times. Eventually I heard the familiar whisk of the showerhead. Curls of steam escaped from the crack under the door.

I worried. I was still essentially dependent on Lydia for basic survival—that is, I needed her to make food for me. I grew hungry. Still, she remained locked up and incommunicado in the bathroom.

I was starting to feel light-headed from hunger, I had to eat something. I could reach the cereal boxes in the pantry, but I could not reach the milk in the refrigerator, nor could I reach the cutlery and crockery above the kitchen counter, so I was forced to dump a pile of Cheerios on the dining room table and dejectedly munch my dry, brittle rings of oats without the help of any moistening agent other than my own spit. Christ, Gwen, that's the way I took my meals when I was living in the fucking zoo! I was so presumptuous! See how quickly I recidivate to my barbarian habits without Lydia?

That was the longest morning of my life. I had—I had lost my virginity the night before, hadn't I? The earth had moved! Her Bruno was a man, now! I suppose I had expected there to be some new sense of special communion between us. Instead she locked herself in the bathroom and refused to come out. What in the world had I done?

I turned on the TV and tried to watch *Sesame Street*, but it was useless, I couldn't keep my mind on it. Not with Lydia so apparently upset, and not with me not knowing why. Bert and Ernie were no solace to me now.

Then I got an idea. I was just full of good ideas, wasn't I? I would write her a letter: a love letter. *That* would surely entice her to come out from her self-imposed sentence of solitary confinement. So Cyrano de Bruno took up one of his Magic Markers—the red one, the color of fire, blood, passion—and, upon removing a starchy sheet of white paper from my sketchpad that lay on the floor of the studio that Lydia had built for me, and fastidiously peeling off the perforated edge to remove the unsightly serrated strip where I'd torn it from the rings, squatted down right there on the floor of my studio and composed a letter: a love letter. There were, of course, no actual words discernible in it, as I was still illiterate. To the untrained eye it probably would have looked like just a lot of frenzied scribbling. But my intentions were absolutely clear, I think. The spirit of the gesture—if not the letter—was perfectly legible. Contained in this arduous, ardorous scramble of red lines—thick, meaningful, still heady-smelling and damp from the juicy marker tip—was the lucid and simple and absolutely earnest message: *I love you.*

And then I slipped it, my love letter, this leaf of paper bearing my message of explosive passion, under the crack of the bathroom door. I waited.

When Lydia came out, I wondered at first if she was the same person who had gone in. Could it be that she had been somehow replaced by another woman of very similar stature and carriage, transformed maybe by the mirror—my original Lydia remaining encapsulated in the glass, and the glass Lydia in turn made flesh? Is that possible? I guess that morning she'd spent locked up with herself, she'd spent in reflecting on her life, reflecting on her memories, reflecting on her reflection, until the reflection had bounced back and forth between her eyes and the eyes of the woman in the mirror so many times that it was impossible to tell which was real and which was reflection. When she came out, Lydia was of course clad in exactly the same apparel in which she had gone in—her nightgown—but—she had—she had cut her hair! She'd cut off her hair with the medicine-cabinet scissors! It took me aback. She had hacked off all her long bright beautiful blond hair, cut it down to a spiky boyish mange that was barely longer than the fur on my own ape head.

I probably would have immediately disintegrated into an apoplexy of hot streaming tears of utter confusion if it were not for the composed aspect of grace and authority that she radiated. I was the weak one here, the broken one, the supplicant, the child, the animal—she the mother, the woman, the human being. Was I forgiven? Forgiven for *what*? What had I done? Why had she made me feel as if I needed to be forgiven for something? Was it—was it about last night?

She picked me up and held me. I snuggled my fleecy face against her cheek. I combed my long purple fingers through her close-cropped hair. In so many gestures and protean wordlings, I asked her where her hair could have possibly gone. (I couldn't really speak articulately at this time, Gwen. Only Lydia could understand my primitive speech.) We sat on the bed. It was unmade still, the sheets all twisted into a messy wad half spilling off the edge of the mattress.

"I cut it, Bruno. I flushed it down the toilet."

I asked her why.

"I was having a hard time looking at myself in the mirror."

I did not understand. Why would it be hard to look at oneself in a mirror?

"I've thought things through, Bruno. I'm feeling better now. I guess I cut off my hair because suddenly I wanted to look different. Sometimes that helps someone feel different. Do you like it?"

I wasn't sure.

"I know you love me, Bruno. Your picture was very sweet."

I thanked her.

"I love you too, Bruno. But—what you did last night—you're not supposed to do that unless someone is *awake*. Do you understand?"

I wasn't sure.

"Bruno, you can't do that unless you have the permission of the person you're doing it with. Do you understand that?"

I shrugged uneasily.

"And if the person you're doing it with is asleep, then you can't possibly know if you have their permission. Okay?"

I said nothing.

"So that means you can't do that with someone who is asleep."

I was repentant in silence.

"The next time you want to do that with someone, you have to wait until she's awake. Then ask. And if she doesn't want to, then that means you can't. Okay?"

There followed then what was perhaps the most pregnant of pregnant silences in history. Then she embraced me. I hoped that I was forgiven. I felt horrible. Then she got dressed. It was a Saturday morning.

Thus was my lesson in human sexual morality. I had to learn this. When my father, Rotpeter, wanted to stick his dick in something, he simply went and did it. I had to learn *restraint*. I had to learn empathy. When it came to sex, I had to make the Buberian moral shift from *I/it* to *I/thou*. That is, a soul is a *thou* and a body is an *it*. The problem with this construct is, of course, that when sex enters into any relationship between two conscious beings with sufficient theory of mind to cognize the consciousness of the other, we must deal with the philosophical difficulty of seeing another person as an *it* and a *thou* at the same time. I have since noticed that not even most humans can do this. At the height of passion, animal solipsism is absolute, and everything but the I is an it.

That day, after Lydia had dressed and we had eaten, she announced, to my delight, that there would be no lessons today and suggested we take the afternoon off instead and go on an outing. It was a pretty day in the fall, in October, I think. The ground was clustered with fallen leaves but the weather was still warm, and all the Chicagoans were out in the streets and parks, taking advantage of the nice weather before winter descended again upon the city: walking dogs, jogging, riding their bicycles, window shopping, all of them up and out and active and happy to be alive. We went uptown on the train and took a long walk in the park. Lydia bought me a balloon.

Balloon: stationed in the park, professionally merry and loudly attired, was a clown. And not just any clown—this was a clown who specialized in twisting long, sausagelike balloons into labyrinthine knots resembling various creatures, as per the request of the child for whom each balloon creation was intended. A child would say, "Make me a giraffe," and the clown, upon receiving fifty cents' compensation, would snap from his balloon pouch one of the stretchy raw balloons, pull and knead some more elasticity into it, inflate it with his mighty lungs, and then, with a few artful squeaky jerks, sculpt a sort of expressionistic abstraction of a giraffe, which was usually discernibly enough a giraffe to please the child. Then he would tie a string to the navel of the balloon and deliver the floating animal to his young customer, whereupon a parent or guardian would often loosely tie it around the child's wrist to prevent its accidental ascension. The clown was standing by a waist-high wrought-iron fence at an intersection of two pedestrian paths in the park, and he had tied samples of his work to the railing of the fence. All around him, tethered to their posts, floated his colorful menagerie, an assortment of animals, but with the overrepresentation of mammals typical to the human zoological imagination: lions, giraffes, bears, dolphins, kangaroos, etc.—but I remember there was one particularly impressive, multiballooned magnum opus, an outlandishly intricate octopus, each tentacle represented by a different balloon, which incited the passersby to point at it and say, "Wow—this guy is *good*." I was mesmerized watching the man at work—call it animal magnetism. I asked Lydia to pay the clown to twist up one of his creations for me. She obliged.

"Well now," said the clown as we approached, "would the monkey like a balloon?"

"He's a chimpanzee," Lydia corrected him.

"Well ex*cuse* me!" he said through an exhalation of boisterous laughter.

Laugh, clown, laugh.

"Monkeys have tails," she said. "Apes don't have tails."

Lydia handed him fifty cents, which he deposited, *clink-clink,* into a fanny pack.

"Now what kind of animal would you like me to make for you?" said the clown to me.

A human, I communicated.

"What?" said the clown.

Lydia, who could understand my gestures and noises, translated:

"He said he wants a person."

"Gee," said the clown, snapping a fresh balloon from the dispenser he wears on his belt, "I've been making balloon animals ever since I was debarred from practicing law, and that's the first time anybody's ever asked me to make a balloon human!"

Make me a human! Bruno demanded.

"I'll see what I can do," said the clown, these words half-muffled as he puts the limp red bag to his lips and puffs it into a long, ellipsoidal tube of air.

Twist, *squeak, squeak,* twist, *scrunch, squeak*—and behold! My own balloon person!

He had created a miniature pink effigy of a human being: what the clown had succeeded in creating for me looked something like the internationally recognized pictogram for the men's restroom. Simple, featureless, classically proportioned and racially indistinct, standing, frontally or antipodally we cannot tell, with his feet together and his arms at his sides, with maybe a hint of masculine aggressiveness implicit in his stance: *Ecce Homo*—Behold the Man.

Leaving the clown, Lydia tied my floating pink man around my wrist with his string. As we walked down the path in the park, Lydia held my left hand, and my balloon man bobbed on a string two feet in the air above my right wrist.

Then we purchased ice cream cones. Lydia selected strawberry ice cream and I, now a man, deliberately opted for a manlier flavor: chocolate. We consumed our ice cream while sitting on a park bench, watching people jog past us on the path. Nearby, a deranged ruffian with one eye made guttural choking noises in the back of his throat as he loped crazily from one public wastebasket to the next, pausing at each to peek for scraps. I slipped my hand from the loop of string, let go, and my balloon man drifted heavenward.

"Bruno!" Lydia snapped. "I'm not buying you another one."

I don't want another one, I communicated.

"Why in the world did you do that?"

I wanted to see what would happen if I let go, I communicated.

"That's what happens. When you let go of your little human, he flies away."

I need hardly bother to explicate the metaphorical implications of this moment.

We watched my balloon homunculus soar into the ether, shrinking from sight until he became an indistinguishable speck of pink against the blue of the sky. This was the ascent of man.

Where does it go? I asked.

"Africa," said Lydia.

Africa, I wondered. My ancestral homeland. That's where Zaire is, the birthplace of my biological father. I inwardly repeated the word to myself, codifying it to a mantra: *Africa, Africa, Africa.* The heart of darkness. The cradle of civilization. I understood it to be a violent place where one can never be safe. Where human beings eat chimps. The setting of my nightmares. Why did she say that so easily? So thoughtlessly? Africa.

On the way home, we stopped at a flower shop, where Lydia bought a bouquet of green roses.

When we arrived at home that evening, Lydia cooked one of my favorite foods: spaghetti. It's such a cartoonish food. I loved to slurp up the long, slippery noodles. Damn it, I still do. Lydia opened a bottle of wine and poured herself a glass. I expressed a desire to imbibe as well, and she poured me a tiny amount—not in a wineglass, because she was afraid my maladroit hands would shatter such a delicate drinking vessel—but one of the nearly indestructible and spill-proof plastic sippy cups that were designated in our household specifically for my use.

Over dinner, our conversation was long and deep. She told me about her life. About her family, her upbringing in Arkansas, how she came here to Chicago to be educated, just like I was being educated. Talk gradually drifted to lighter topics. We joked. We laughed. She drank a few more glasses of wine, and became flushed and silly.

When our eyes met, I got a tingling feeling deep in my gut, a feeling like our two brains were directly connected by invisible electric wires running between the pupils of our eyes. And, with the dirty dishes still on the table, Lydia took my hand and guided me into our bedroom. She sat me on the bed, and we looked closely into one another's eyes, shortening the lengths of the invisible electric wires connecting our brains. She brought her face to mine, and our lips met. Our mouths opened, and our tongues slithered together in salivary bliss. And we collapsed together back onto the bed, still unmade from that morning, and—but what else can I possibly say, without straying beyond the parameters of good taste? What words can graze the surface of such a subject, let alone explain it or express it? We made love. That night, Lydia and I truly, reciprocally, made love.

Actually, what I just described may be a lie, or a lie-like thing. Albeit a fiction, it is a useful fiction. We will use it for narrative purposes. The scene I just described—it happened—it happened many, many times—but I don't think it happened like that, that first night, the night after I sort-of raped her. In truth the sexual relationship between me and Dr. Lydia Littlemore did not begin with a bang, but a whimper. There were many times we had to do it in the dark, very quietly, very slowly, before it was okay to bring it into the light.

Every word is a category, a tool of abstraction, a criminal approximation. Every word removes the thing it is supposed to represent from the real world. Thus, every word is a lie. And that is why it is so damnably difficult to speak about sex—or anything for that matter, but especially sex—in words. Just when you want most to speak the truth, the ineffable nature of your subject matter clogs your mouth with lies. An unchewable wad of lies, like a mouthful of cotton balls. Words get in the way of what you want to say.

At first these incidents were hazy fever dreams of sex more than the thing itself: both of us half-asleep and lazy-blooded, moving slowly and silently, enjoying the interplay of skin and tongues and fingers and membranes and fluids and the sensitive, primitive organs of pleasure that we both possessed. Lying beside her in bed, I would gently prod her shoulder with a long purple finger, asking if she was awake. Sometimes she would murmur something in response, which did not necessarily mean yes. Sometimes an erection would slink out of my loins on its own accord, and sometimes I would hintingly nudge it toward her, and sometimes she would feel it—it would brush against her thigh or her haunches or her belly—and then sometimes she would take a commanding grasp of it, and after this decisive moment I suddenly and drunkenly cared for nothing in the world but the white heat of our mutual and imminent ecstasies. And then our sex was like a viscous liquid, sweet and slow as honey drooling from a spoon. And then we would wake in the morning vaguely wondering if we had really done what we had done, as if perhaps it had been only one movement of a half-remembered, and shared, symphony of dreams.

Later, we would be more upfront about things. More conscious, more deliberate. Soon Lydia and I were secretly living in sin. Like Anna and Vronsky. Reflecting back on that time, that period when we were living happily together in our apartment in Hyde Park—the stretch of months after we had become physically intimate, but before the project collapsed in a ruin of debt and doubt—was one of the happiest times in my life.

The arrangement was not without its problematic aspects. Perhaps the friendship between me and Lydia on the one hand had been deepened and solidified by the bond of our total physical intimacy—and on the other hand threatened by it, due to the host of complicated and often conflicting feelings that this free license of bodily contact introduces between two people in love. Also there was the emotional awkwardness of the fact that for obvious reasons, our sexual relationship had to be kept absolutely secret at the lab. Lydia was terrified of exposure. It was heartbreaking to me that every day at the lab we still had to pretend that the relationship between us was still businesslike, still scientific, still chaste—that we were not utterly in love.

There are no animals on this planet, at least not that I'm aware of, so squeamish about touching one another as humans. Go to a zoo and watch the chimpanzees. You'll probably see them all tangled together in one big cuddly heap. They feel most comfortable that way, most safe. Humans, though, make much talk of "respecting personal space," and behave toward one another as if their bodies are hostile nations buffered by hazardous frontiers of no-man's-land, traveling radii of airspace surrounding every body, into which another's ingress may be considered an unauthorized invasion, even when the intent is peaceable. This fierce physical mistrust goes away—goes away completely—only among lovers. Lydia and I had developed that total physical comfort with one another that comes with sexual intimacy—when we were alone together at home, our bodies were free to touch and be touched by each other, to give one another pleasure—but at the lab, we had to maintain the façade that we knew each other only as human and animal, as experimenter and subject, as scientist and science.

Sometimes on the weekends we would spend the whole day in bed. Sometimes we would spend two days at a stretch naked. Sometimes we would get home from the lab—finally released from the watchful and loveless eyes of Lydia's colleagues, finally unlocked from a long chain of hours stressed tight with the laborious theatre of trying to act like we weren't in love—and we would walk in the door and race immediately to the bedroom, articles of clothing flying from our persons all down the hall so that we arrived antecedently disrobed in our chamber of clandestine lust. We were partners, Lydia and I, united in our sin. We behaved like two children when we were alone together, two sexually active children. We developed a complex lovers' dialect of inside jokes and pet names. Here's a montage for you. Please cue Louis Armstrong's "What a Wonderful World" and imagine these scenes fading in and out. One: Lydia and Bruno sitting together in the bathtub, their faces softly underlit by a constellation of lit tea candles, Lydia leaning against the back of the tub and regulating the temperature of the water by twisting the faucets on and off with her toes; Lydia is sipping a glass of white wine, and Bruno is in her lap, eating a slice of chocolate cake à la mode. Two: Lydia reclining on the couch in absolute, resplendent nudity, while Bruno, wearing a floppy black beret in order to denote his office as an artist, paints her image on canvas with an easel. Three: Lydia and Bruno strolling hand-in-hairy-hand in the park, probably chatting about art or philosophy. Cut back to the bathtub scene, where Lydia and Bruno are giggling and flicking water at each other. Cut back to the painting scene, where Bruno is furiously ripping sketch after not-to-his-exacting-satisfaction sketch out of his pad of paper, crunching them up and flinging them away to join the small mountain of paper building behind him. Now cut back to the park (still strolling). Cut back to the bathtub, where Lydia splashes too much water at Bruno, causing him to drop his plate of chocolate cake à la mode in the water with a startling *sploosh*; in response their giggling crescendos into uproarious laughter. Now back to the painting scene, where we gaze over Bruno's shoulder as he puts the final touches onto his completed painting of Lydia (who has long ago fallen asleep on the couch without his noticing) as a reclining nude. Finally, cut back to the park, where Bruno and Lydia have stopped strolling to sit awhile on a bench overlooking a view of an electrically aglitter Chicago skyline at twilight; they are now staring dreamily into one another's eyes; their faces converge for a kiss, and the camera drifts up to the stars as the final notes of music tinkle away to silence.

I do not know whether Dr. Plumlee suspected us of anything back then. He was already backing away from the project. It had gotten out of his control. Surely he noticed that there was something going on between us. His suspicion may also have been fueled by jealousy. That I can understand. How could he not have been secretly in love with her to some degree? Maybe without even consciously realizing it himself? Anyone could see that Lydia was a woman in love, and anyone could also have seen that whoever was the object of her love, it was not Norman Plumlee. I suspect that this jealousy of his lay close beneath his decision to terminate the project. I honestly don't know how long Norm had suspected that Lydia and I were having an affair, but eventually—as did everyone—he found out. But I'm getting ahead of myself.

As I have said, Lydia and I were in love, and it made us reckless. We probably could have—*should* have—been more careful, and obviously in hindsight I realize this, but I don't know if we ever could have possibly realized it at the time. The blinders were up. We were not thinking of the consequences. Lydia and I were addicted to each other. And as is the case with all addicts, the short-term ecstasy of our love was so overpowering that we always gave in to it, and all censorious long-term logic immediately vanished into mist every night we went to bed together.

XX

Now the wheel of the seasons had made a full revolution, and Chicago found itself sunken once again at the bottom of winter. Hats, boots, scarves, gloves. Icicles, snow, streets all mushy with gray-black sludge, and slicing winds that freeze the snot in your nose before you've taken ten steps outside. When I think back on it, I seldom remember Chicago in any season but winter. Some cities are like joyful little children, they live for their summers, and other cities have personalities more like curmudgeonly old men who live for their winters, simply because it means they may wear big coats with lots of pockets to put their things in. Chicago is such a city.

As I mentioned earlier, Lydia had arranged an exhibition of some of my best work in a gallery space in the University of Chicago Main Library. Until the very end, it was a fantastic evening. It was only a week after Norm and Lydia officially went public with me, in a paper that was published in Volume 367, Number 6464 of *Nature*, which Lydia coauthored with Dr. Norman Plumlee, her immediate supervisor at the lab, even though Plumlee had very little to do with the project anymore—that is, the BRUNO Project (Behavioral Rearing into Ultroneous Noumenal Ontogenesis—a clunky acronym, but whatever; I didn't come up with it). The paper was written almost entirely by Lydia. Perhaps Dr. Plumlee peppered it with a few anodyne footnotes that the paper frankly could have done without. I suspect there were two principal reasons why Plumlee's name appeared on that paper—placed unjustly and unalphabetically before and above that of Dr. Lydia Littlemore: (one) because Lydia feared that her research—with the cataclysmic paradigm shift in our understanding of humanity and animality that her conclusions necessarily demanded, and seeing as she was still a very green unknown in her field at the time—would not be taken seriously (there it is again!) by the scientific community unless she could lean on the crutch of prestige that was Dr. Norman Plumlee's name; and (two) because of Plumlee's vain and childish desire to attach himself like a leech onto the body of research that was pretty much all Lydia's, Lydia's and mine.

Anyway, Volume 367 Number 6464 of *Nature*, in which appeared the article "The BRUNO Project: One Extraordinary Chimpanzee Provides New Potential for Studies in Complex Linguistic Communication in Great Apes," by Dr. Norman Plumlee of the University of Chicago and Dr. Lydia Littlemore, also of the University of Chicago, pages 247–255, had gone to press one week before the opening exhibition of my artwork.

Although the paper went into great depth regarding my impressive ability to understand much spoken English, it did not mention my capacity for producing spoken language. This is mostly because I wasn't really saying anything yet. I spoke, of course—I was an irrepressible chatterbox, I was speaking constantly!—but for some reason, at this point, only Lydia could understand what I was saying. I even began to suspect that the other scientists in the lab had been ever increasingly falling under the persuasion that Lydia's nearly fluent comprehension of my speech was a bit of specious and irresponsibly unscientific wishful thinking on her part, that she overinterpreted all my breathy, inarticulate puttering, grunting, and squeaking noises as burgeoning speech—which is exactly what they were. The other scientists did not understand my speech because they did not spend even a fraction of the amount of time with me that Lydia did, because they did not know me, because they did not love me.

In any event, the fact that I was—however indiscernibly to outsiders—speaking at probably the language-competence level of about a two-year-old child was the source of a disagreement between Lydia and Dr. Plumlee. Lydia had wanted to include this in the paper, and Norm advised her against it, as he was concerned that such an amazing claim would not be believed and would be difficult if not impossible to prove to naysayers. In the end, Norm, predictably, won, Lydia acquiesced, and I was presented to the public not yet as a talking ape but as a listening one, which for some reason was less impressive.

The gallery opened at 8:00 p.m. Before the guests in attendance entered the gallery space, they watched Norm deliver a presentation in a nearby lecture hall, followed by a twenty-minute film of me performing tasks in the lab. I did not actually see the film, but from what I understand, the people were awfully impressed by my cognitive faculties. In one of the more telling segments of this film, there was footage of me sitting at a table in the lab, sorting photographs at Norm's request. I remember the experiment. Norm handed me a stack of photographs. There were about twenty glossy five-by-three-inch photos. About half of them were pictures of people—some of whom I knew (Lydia, Norm, Prasad, Tal—this footage was shot before the finger-biting incident), some of whom I did not (random idiots off the street), and half of them were pictures of chimpanzees. One of the pictures was of me. Norm asked me to sort the photographs into two categories. At first I thought maybe he was asking me to sort them into two piles, one for men and one for women. So I assorted them accordingly, putting all the human women in with the female chimps. Norm then took back the photos and scrambled their order again. I received no reward, so I knew I must have been sorting the pictures in a way that did not accord with Norm's taste. The deck reshuffled, Norm handed me back the stack of photos and asked me again to order them into two categories, like with like. Then I realized that of course he wanted me to divide the pictures into a human pile and a chimp pile. I included my own picture in the human pile. I am sure that at this moment in the film, a collective moan of compassionate heartbreak rose up in the audience.

I was not watching the film because I was with Lydia, getting ready for my first big introduction into society. My cotillion. In a small murky bathroom somewhere in the building, Lydia prepared me for the evening. All afternoon we had been bustling around in the gallery, making sure everything was just so: assuring that all the paintings had been hung properly, that all the lighting was just right, not too dim, not too glaring. Lydia was wearing a beautiful black dress. She had been romping around the gallery in bare feet all afternoon, the bottoms of her feet sticking to and unpeeling from the hard waxy floor, because she had worn pretty but locomotionally impractical high-heeled shoes for the occasion, and was uncomfortable in them—they "killed" her, she said. Planning to put her shoes on only at the last possible minute, she secreted them in her purse and had gone barefoot (like Tal) until now. In the little bathroom where we were preparing for the gallery opening, I stood before the mirror, Lydia standing behind me, her head more than a full two feet above mine in our reflected image, and she brushed the unruly fur on the top of my head. She kept twisting the knob of the sink faucet to dribble warm water over her fingers, then smoothing my fur out with her hand and straightening it with her hairbrush, her movements made savage and jerky by her nervousness. I wore a small gray suit, with my stubby legs sheathed in a pair of pants selected by necessity from the Marshall Field's boys' department, and a matching suit jacket selected from the men's. Lydia tucked, tugged, buttoned, zipped, prodded and pulled my Sunday-bests into place, knotting the verdant lime-green tie that I myself had selected, pulling my socks over my feet and lacing my smart tan shoes.

She sat on the closed lid of the toilet, opened her purse, and rooted around among its contents. She found her pantyhose. She hiked her dress above her waist. I hurriedly sucked in the smell of her feet and bare legs and crotch. She slipped her slender bare feet into the translucent and weightless bags of the black nylon pantyhose, and tugged on them until they melded to the contours of her feet. Then she pulled the hosiery up until it conformed to the contours of her legs and enveloped her thighs and waist, and the hose became a thin protective membrane clinging to her skin. There may still be nothing, nothing I love to watch more than a beautiful woman rolling on or peeling off a pair of nylon panty-hose. Then she shimmied her dress back into position—good-bye, Lydia's vagina!—and she took her shoes out of her purse. Lydia almost never wore shoes that were anything other than principally utilitarian. She hated high-heeled shoes, hated, hated, *hated* them. She nearly always put comfort before aesthetics, in all things—thus she was unused to walking in heels, and thereby particularly vulnerable to their blistering pinches and bites.

Lydia checked her appearance one last time in the mirror. Her hair was still short, but had grown out some, it just covered the tops of her ears. She went through the motion of sliding a wisp of hair behind her ear, but her hair was not yet long enough to stay put, and it immediately sprang out again. She was not wearing her glasses. She turned to me, watching her look at herself in the mirror. Our eyes made contact in the mirror.

"We're going to be on our best behavior tonight, aren't we, Bruno?"

I nodded yes.

Lydia sucked in a deep breath and let it out slowly, steadying herself with the extra oxygen, conscientiously trying to make her breathing natural and normal. Then she bent down slowly to the floor. She kneeled, folding her long powerful legs—made even longer by the high-heeled shoes she so violently loathed—until her face was level with mine, and she looked directly into my eyes. She wrapped her hands around the back of my head, and I wrapped my gangly arms around her back, and we exchanged a long and passionate kiss. Our lips mingled, our tongues wound together, we breathed each other's hot breath and drank each other's spit. It is painful—almost physically painful to me, it sickens me, it gives me a heartache as real and visceral as a bellyache—to remember how in love we were.

Lydia took my hand, squeezing it in hers.

"Okay," she whispered in my ear. "Let's go."

She rose to full standing position, and, leading me by the hand, unlocked the door and pushed it open.

———

The gallery opening. I'm sure you know what these things tend to look like. There were a couple of inexpensive tables covered with expensive tablecloths: on one of them stood many wineglasses and bottles of wine, ice buckets for the white wine, which the caterers poured for the guests, and on the other table was an arrangement of hors d'oeuvres: brownies, cheeses, crackers, little tomatoes, miniature salami sandwiches and such. Most of the event's attendees were dressed nicely. Hands were shaken, limp embraces exchanged, spouses introduced, wineglasses dinged like bells, fancy shoes clopped on the waxen concrete floor and a liquid hum of general conversation sloshed around inside the echo-conducive white room, in which waves of polite laughter crested and broke here and there. Have you ever noticed how similar the ambiance of an art gallery is to that of a laboratory?

Fifteen of my larger paintings hung on the white walls of the gallery space. I chose, following Lydia's suggestion, not to display the exploratory forays into the abstract that I was already beginning to paint, but to stick with the more meticulously rendered representational pieces in order, at this early stage in my career, to showcase my mastery of technique rather than my innovative approach to concept. Four of them were self-portraits modeled after my reflection in Lydia's bathroom mirror, at such an angle and using such a palette as to deliberately evoke Van Gogh—in one of them I even depicted myself wearing a wide-brimmed straw hat, in obvious homage to my favorite mad Dutchman, though only a handful of those philistines got the joke. One was a portrait of Norman Plumlee, fleshed out of a charcoal sketch of him that I dashed off once when visiting the lab with Lydia (I have since destroyed that painting). Two were paintings of Lydia. (The many nudes that I had painted of her were not on display for obvious reasons. Many of those were later destroyed as well. The one that hangs above the couch on which I am at this moment reclining is the only extant one that I know of.) Another one was a landscape—technically impressive but conceptually bankrupted by my then immaturity as an artist—looking southward on the Chicago lakefront in the summer; it is maybe a little reminiscent of Seurat's *Sunday Afternoon on the Grande Jatte*, with all the pretty girls slothing an afternoon away on the beach, dogs teething on frisbees, the Hancock Center with its latticework and horns in the background, and the big blue expanse of Lake Michigan, peppered with sailboats, which dominates the left half of the painting.

I imagine that the people in attendance at the gallery opening would have had an experience something like this: As soon as there are enough people present, as soon as there are enough mouths in the room to produce enough conversation to swirl around in the airspace between enough warm bodies to subdue the echo effect in the starkly empty space—which is painted white all around and unfurnished except for my paintings on the walls, the two fold-out tables that hold the hors d'oeuvres and the wineglasses and the wine, and a couple of black leather Mies van der Rohe couches in the center of the room, facing my paintings—as soon as the ambiance of the room is just right, the social atmosphere comfortable enough, there enters through the open front doors of the gallery a beautiful and beautifully dressed young woman in a black dress and short blond hair, and there—holding her hand, walking beside her, proudly, on two legs, like a man, wearing shoes even, dressed in a little gray suit with a lime-green tie and his hair perfect—is the artist.

Yes, he happens to be a chimp. A chimp dressed in the trappings of human civilization is ordinarily funny to you. That is why we see chimps dressed up in idiotic costumes on TV commercials. It's the stuff of the circus, of vaudeville, of the burlesque, the freak show. Obviously, the reason why you think it is so fucking funny to see a chimp dressed in human clothes and taught to ludicrously mimic human behavior is because you think of yourselves as having the only *proper* culture. You define yourselves as the only cultured species, and this has allowed you to believe that your culture has helped you break away from the rest of nature. You think that your precious culture is what makes you human. Therefore, the sight of an ape—so close to you, and yet seemingly so far—dressed up in human clothes and behaving like a human being is utterly incongruous—hence, funny. But what if—*what if* you see an ape who wears a suit and a tie and walks on two legs, an ape who has made this step into human culture *not* simply to appease his trainers, who mock and pimp and debase him to provide cheap titillation to the drooling hoi polloi—*but of his own free will*? Suddenly it's not so funny anymore. Is it?

That is why this particular chimp is not funny. He is not cute. He does not look like a circus chimp, riding around in circles *honk-honk* on his little scooter, who has been dressed in the borrowed robes of human civilization for everyone's sophomoric amusement. He is dressed this way because he wants to be. He is a chimp, yes, his hairy arms and fingers are long and spindly, his lips and chin protrude from his rubbery, hairy, masklike face—but in all other respects, he looks like a man—you can see the light of human culture glowing in his eyes like magic stones. And the effect is all the more unsettling because of it. No one would think him funny or cute. The image is far too disturbing. Here, ladies and gentlemen, is the artist.

As Lydia and I entered the room, the conversation did not die completely, but became muffled, suddenly gone all slack and floppy like the sails of a ship drifting into the doldrums. Most of the people in the room backed slowly away from us, in—what?—awe?—fear? Lydia smiled and waved at all the people. The nervous people smiled and waved back. Lydia tried to bury us in the crowd, but a radius of cautious space always encircled us. Wherever we went, we were the center of the spectacle.

Norm approached us. His pants were slightly wrinkled and baggy. He took Lydia gently by the arm. I was still holding on to her hand at the end of her other arm. With me on one side of her and Norm on the other, Lydia allowed Norm to guide her toward a particular group of people who were standing around together, near one of my paintings—the landscape of the Chicago lakefront. They were holding glasses of wine, and some of them had piles of hors d'oeuvres folded in napkins in their hands.

"I would like you to meet my colleagues, Lydia and Bruno,"

Norm said to the loose assembly, and released Lydia's arm. Lydia shook everyone's hand in turn, and she let go of my hand so that I could shake their hands. Each one of them, one by one, respectfully half-kneeled to the floor so that their faces were closer to mine, told me their names (not one of which stuck in either my short-term or my long-term memory), and softly squeezed my hand for a moment in theirs. The people could not bring themselves to attempt to converse with me. These people were all smiles—friendly enough. I quickly took Lydia's hand again.

The room socially relaxed again. The volume and the comfort level of people's conversations were slowly on the rise. I began to feel slightly agitated.

I watched the people in the gallery moving from one painting to the next with their glasses of wine in their hands, pointing at my paintings and commenting on them. They seemed to be particularly impressed by my representational renderings, as people who know little about art typically are.

One of the people who was standing around with me and Lydia and Norm, one of the people to whom I had just been introduced, seemed to be a particularly important person. An important man. He wore nice clothes. He was an older man and handsome, with sleek shocks of graying hair erupting from his head, a gaunt and serious face and frameless glasses that delicately pincered the bridge of his pointy nose and magnified his watery gray eyes. I noticed that most of the people around us were wearing name tags—these white rectangles with names scrawled on them in black marker, stuck to their outer garments, near their hearts—but not this man. This man wore no name tag. Apparently he either did not wish his name to be known, or else he assumed everyone already knew it. Norm and Lydia were both rapt in conversation with this man. The Important Man was doing most of the talking, and Norm and Lydia were doing most of the polite listening, their heads bobbing like buoys on their necks with nodding and inserting *yes*es and *mm-hmm*s in the troughs of his wave of speech. Occasionally Norm, when given the green light, would launch into a torrent of words, speaking rapidly, as if he were afraid of losing the Important Man's interest before he had arrived at his point. Lydia said something here and there, but mostly she was silent. Their conversation was over my head. Lydia clasped my hand tightly, now and then giving it a squeeze to remind me of her presence, of her closeness. I wanted to go home.

I noticed there were two men standing near the doors of the gallery. They were young and healthy, with short hair and thick arms, dressed in uniforms: black shoes, blue pants, crisp tan short-sleeved shirts with flashing metal buttons. They wore badges. They looked like they were not here for fun but rather were only doing their jobs. They very slowly perambulated the room, not talking to anyone, surveying the crowd, paying close attention. What were they here to protect? My art? Their hands were clasped behind their backs. When they turned around, I saw that behind their backs, each of them held a long, thin silver wand, with a red rubber handle and a prong of wire filament on the end of it.

I redirected my gaze back into the middle of our social circle. They were so far up above me, and I was so near to the floor in comparison. I saw everything from below. Norm was having trouble balancing a glass of wine and a pile of cheese cubes held in a napkin. He was speaking animatedly to the Important Man. With the thumb of the hand that held the cheese, Norm struggled to nudge his glasses up the bridge of his nose and then swipe back the three ribbons of hair that clung to his otherwise bald pate, but it was difficult to perform these small actions with a handful of cheese, and I watched one of the little yellow cubes of cheese tumble from his palm and onto the floor, where it bounced three times like a die on a backgammon board before coming to rest in the middle of our circle of people. I watched Lydia's eyes trace the path of the cheese's escape, and then quickly look up. No one else—not even the Important Man—noticed, or they pretended not to have noticed. Plumlee himself did not notice. Plumlee's voice escalated in pitch and zeal as he approached the point of whatever he was saying. His hands were thickly padded and the backs of his fingers were almost as hairy as mine. Lydia squeezed my hand. I looked up at her. She smiled down at me, as if to assure me that we would be going home soon. I was feeling terribly bored and uncomfortable.

A new man shouldered his way into our circle. He was tall. He was old, too, but carried himself with the vigor of youth: back straight, chest out. He was thin but robust, he looked like he could run a marathon without breaking a sweat. A beautiful bright white mustache hung below his nose and brushed his upper lip. He wore a suit as silver as a spoon that clung fast to his stringy old muscles, and in lieu of a necktie he wore a bolo that slid through a huge turquoise amulet. And on the very top of his body sat a wide-brimmed white hat: a cowboy hat. He entered the conversation as if he was entering his own home, and as he did, a lean old liver-spotty hand with fat blue veins slaloming over the ridges of his tendons rose up to the top of the hat, where it pinched the shallow recesses in the crown and politely removed it, freeing the springy flaps of his red ears and revealing the shiny pink ball of his head, which was bald except for a semicircular muff of white hair playing ring-around-the-rosy with his skull.

"Howdy," he said.

"Howdy," said Lydia, instinctively returning his folksy greeting, then catching herself saying it and immediately self-consciously flushing at how silly it sounded in her mouth. The man extended his hand and Lydia shook it. He seemed to want to kiss her hand like an old-fashioned gentleman, but the angle and position of Lydia's hand would not allow it.

"My name's Dudley Lawrence," the man said. "It's a real plea-sure and an honor to meet you, Miss Littlemore."

"Mrs.," said Lydia, then, "Dr." She was a bit flattered, a bit taken aback by his gentility. Then, before he spoke to anyone else, before he addressed Norm or the Important Man they had been talking with all evening, Dudley Lawrence bent to the floor in his boots, the creases in his silver trousers vanishing at the knees, and said hello to me, warmly shaking my hand.

"Hello, Bruno," he said. "The pleasure's all mine." His white mustache curled into the corners of his grin. He patted my hand twice before releasing it. Without getting up, and looking me directly in the eyes, he said, "There's someone I'd like you to meet." And then there knelt beside him a big elaborate woman. "Please say hello to my wife, Regina."

"Bruno, your art is *wonderful*," said the woman in a loud, tune-ful voice. The encomiastic gush in her tone caused me to redden a little. Regina Lawrence was much younger than her husband, in her forties, maybe. She was short and wide, but attractive in an explosive fleshy way, with a honking big bosom bursting from the neck of her red blouse like two plucked geese. Silver and turquoise jewelry clicked and rattled all over her. A long red and gold shawl was wrapped around her shoulders. Her eyes were sea green and her puffy lips as pink and shiny and sticky-looking as recently licked candy, and her earlobes were distended with the weight of two fat earrings made out of turquoise elephants. A white streak ran through the middle of her long orange hair. She beamed broadly at me as she took my hand and squeezed. I could tell at once that this woman was good and kind and bighearted and perhaps absolutely insane.

After they had introduced themselves to me, the Lawrences rose to the conversation level of the other humans and introduced themselves to Norm and the Important Man. I looked up at their faces. I thought I could detect that Norm was visibly irritated that the man had introduced himself to Lydia—and then introduced his wife to me, the *chimp*—without first acknowledging him, and even further irritated that he had done so in front of the Important Man. The Important Man seemed to consider himself above such things—the battlefield of gestures, words, manners—the whole delicate metalanguage of human social posturing. What apes do with thumping on their chests, throwing clumps of grass, banging on logs—human beings do in subtler ways. There's very little difference, otherwise.

Dudley Lawrence, however—even then I could tell—thought he possessed something that made him feel perfectly secure in the belief that he was the most important of all. Later, I would learn that this something was lots and lots of money.

So Dudley Lawrence entered the conversation and introduced his colorful wife. He was not a scientist; he was an interested layman. I could see that Lydia was extremely interested in what he had to say. She liked his attention. He wanted to know all about me. He kept asking questions—always addressing Lydia, whom he instinctively trusted more than Norm—which increasingly infuriated Norm. Meanwhile, his wife, Regina, lowered her big body back down to my level. Eventually she decided to actually sit on the floor, right in the middle of the gallery. With all the people milling around in the room, she sat down cross-legged on the floor in front of me.

"How *are* you, Bruno?" she said. Without waiting for an answer, she went right on speaking. Her sea green eyes matched her turquoise elephant earrings. "I've been dying to meet you, Bruno. I've been reading all about you. I *adore* your work."

I nodded, graciously acknowledging the compliment.

"I wonder," she continued, "how you would say your unique cultural perspective as a chimpanzee living in our society informs your art?"

I wondered that myself. Since then, I've been fielding questions like that my entire career. People never tire of asking it. I think I replied, communicating more or less in breathy, inarticulate puttering noises and vague gestures, that I supposed being a chimpanzee in human society makes one view the human condition in terms not of *being* but of *becoming*, compelling one to understand humanity as necessarily something swept up in the flow of nature, rather than over and against nature.

"Yes of course!" said Mrs. Lawrence.

We chatted some more in this affable fashion.

I had grown comfortable enough with this woman that I had let go of Lydia's hand.

Meanwhile, in the conversation that was happening up above us—Lydia would later relate to me—Dudley Lawrence had asked at what price he could acquire the entire collection.

"I'm sorry," said Lydia, or something to this effect, "Bruno's paintings are actually not for sale. We consider them valuable documents that we need to keep for research purposes, plus—"

"That's all right," said Mr. Lawrence, or something to this effect, as he slid his pen and checkbook back into the inner pocket of his silver suit jacket, maybe even slightly embarrassed at having asked the question. "I understand. But I would at least like to commission the artist to paint a separate work for—"

"I'm really not sure that that would be appropriate for Bruno—," Lydia began.

But at this point Norm, whose eyes had been following the exchange with increasingly frantic greed, interrupted: "Hold on, now, perhaps we could, er, maybe we could discuss the possibility of selling some of the works in this collection. We haven't discussed the idea, actually—"

"Yes we have," said Lydia. "We agreed that—"

Norm cleared his throat and scratched his cheek.

"Pardon me," Norm said to Mr. Lawrence. "Would you please excuse us for a moment? I have to consult with my colleague."

Mr. Lawrence graciously assented, nodding in understanding as Norm grasped Lydia's arm and led her out of earshot. The two of them walked over to the other side of the room and began to argue in terse quick whispers, with heads bent close together. While they were gone Mr. Lawrence and the Important Man built another, separate conversation together, an unknowable conversation between two supposedly important men.

Lydia was now far away from me. She was inextricably, unreachably engaged in some business all the way on the other side of the room. Norm had stolen her, taken her away from me. I had been left in the company of this Regina Lawrence, who was still sitting cross-legged on the floor in front of me, still weaving a tapestry of words that had now become a claustrophobic tent of incomprehensible babble. I realized that I did not have a clue who any of these people were. Not the Important Man, not the tall old man in the silver suit and cowboy hat, not the two men with strange gleaming wands behind their backs, not the big elaborate woman who sat beside me on the floor. I looked around the room. All of my paintings were hanging on the walls. Why? People whom I did not know were walking around and looking at them. Why?

My heart rattled against my ribs with fear and rage. I knew nothing. Who *were* these people? Where was I? What the hell was going on? I panicked. What happened next I'm not proud of. I lost it. If I ever had it, I lost it that night. Lydia, I'm sorry. I'm so sorry. I'm sorry, I'm sorry, I'm sorry. (Gwen, when you type up these transcripts, please copy and paste "I'm sorry" until it repeats six thousand times.)

You might say that the animal within me, within this chimpanzee, this mock-man, Bruno, at that moment chose an extraordinarily inopportune time to burst forth from below, come out and say hello to everyone. You might say that for some reason I chose that moment to rend my garments and commence to scream and howl savagely at the top of my lungs. If you had been there you might have observed people clapping their fat stupid hands to their ugly ears at the sound of all my hideous shrieking and bellowing. You might then have observed me, with my little gray suit already in tatters flapping about my torso, aimlessly tearing around the room, seemingly in every direction at once, scrambling pell-mell and helter-skelter among all those legs, all those pants and dresses and shoes. You might also have seen me overturn both of the two foldout tables, sending all those hors d'oeuvres, all those brownies, cheeses, crackers, cherry tomatoes, and little salami sandwiches scattering across the floor, and you might have heard all the wineglasses and bottles shattering to atoms upon contact with the floor, and in your sudden panic you might have mistaken all the red wine trickling across the floor amid all the broken glass that might have crunched under your feet for blood, for human blood, and you might have helped the others to squish the hors d'oeuvres into the floor, or got the brownies and little cubes of cheese stuck to the bottoms of your shoes when you joined everyone as they stampeded in terror out of the room. And, if you were far from the door when the impromptu mass exodus began, you might have been one of the unlucky ones who got squished and crushed in the doorway by all that panicked humanity, or you might have been one of the screaming ones, who was still in the room and could not get through because the doorway had gotten clogged with humans, clogged like the drain of a bathtub gets clogged with inexplicable human filth, and if so you might have been in a position to watch it happen when those two healthy young men in blue pants and tan shirts chased me into a corner of the room and jabbed me several times with their wands, those mysterious silver machines that of course were mysterious to me no longer. You might have watched the two men deliver this raging, this "vicious" animal a series of correspondingly vicious electric shocks that instantly incapacitated him, that left him whimpering, shivering on the floor, not unconscious, but for an instant wondering if he were dead. You might—if you are someone who is given to empathy—have wondered for a moment what it felt like, and you might—if you are someone who is given to sympathy (and you are rare)—have even cared.

I gazed—feverish, sick—distantly I gazed up at the ceiling from where I lay crumpled and collapsed in the corner of the room. A moment before, it was as if those things they poked me with had instantaneously replaced every drop of blood in my veins with boiling water, and then instantly replaced it again with ice. I was shaking involuntarily. I had never felt so much pain. So much raw, hideous, physical pain—never. I heard people screaming. I heard them as if they were at the far end of a long tunnel. I heard a woman screaming. Lydia was screaming. Not so much in sorrow, but in anger.

Now my body lay rumpled, shaking, slack, in Lydia's arms. I looked up at her face through the gauze curtain of my delirium and saw that her face was slick, bright with tears.

Norm, keeping his distance, stood a little ways off and to the side. He looked bashful. He looked afraid. He looked like he did not know what to do with his hands. Something passed over the features of his face that suggested he had just remembered something. Then he went out the door, probably to look for the Important Man. The Important Man had been among the first to flee.

Now everyone who had been in the gallery was gone, except for me, Lydia, and the two thugs who had shocked me into submission. No. There were two more people there. Dudley and Regina Lawrence stood still, side by side, in the middle of the room. They did not look like they had been frightened in the least by the regrettable events of the last minute and thirty seconds. They seemed to understand. They looked far more composed than Norm had been. They were keeping their distance not out of fear, but out of respect for me and Lydia. Even in my trembling stupor, even in my pain, even in my hate and misery—this endeared them to me.

As we were leaving, Dudley Lawrence cautiously approached us in the doorway. His hat was in his hands. With my mind in a very distant place but my body present, I watched him hand Lydia a card, and wink knowingly, and whisper something into her ear that I did not understand. His wife blew me a kiss. Lydia was now in possession of a small starchy paper rectangle that would soon dramatically alter my future. If I could have read the card that Lydia had just been given, I would have read:

Dudley Lawrence
Co-Founder
The Dudley and Regina Lawrence Foundation
for Animal Rights & Habitat Conservation

This was followed by an address and a phone number. But of course I could not read it yet.

Somewhere, somehow, Norm came back into the room, and there followed some terse, whispered, angry—very angry—dialogue between Norm and Lydia. Norm was enraged. Rage and bombast puffed him up like a zeppelin. Lydia was still crying, trying to blink back her unprofessional, unscientific tears. I hated Norm. Somehow we got away from him. We parted from Norm's company and went home.

If you had been standing outside of the building, standing in the parking lot and looking at the side entrance of the University of Chicago Main Library, then you might have seen a beautiful and beautifully dressed young woman with short blond hair, in a black dress and high-heeled shoes, carrying in her arms a heavily subdued chimp, who wore the tattered remnants of a little gray suit and a lime-green tie.

Actually, Lydia must have been wearing a coat and a scarf on top of her dress, because it was so cold that night. It was the dead of winter. The first dustings of what would become a blizzard were fluttering down to us from above, in snowflakes so big and wet and fat you could actually hear the noises they made as they hit the ground.

Lydia and I exited the building into this skull-achingly cold night. The streetlights painted the dismal slab of urban sky above us with their sickly penumbras of orange light.

Lydia carried me. Her heels went *scrap-clock, scrap-clock* on the asphalt, our mutual shadow shifting under us as we passed beneath one streetlight to the next, toward her car at the back of the long and now-deserted parking lot of the library.

She stopped. Silence and the sounds of fat falling snowflakes replaced the rhythm of her footfalls. Languidly I looked around us. I did not understand what was wrong. Lydia's tears had frozen to her face. Then I saw.

Lydia had realized she was walking on a thin and invisible film of black ice: flat, frictionless, as slick as oiled glass.

"Bruno," she whispered. "Please hold on to me. Hold on tight."

I clung to her neck. My arms were still weak.

Lydia kneeled to the ground. She placed her fingers on the pavement for support, and slowly slid her feet out of her shoes.

"Please hold these," she said, and she put her shoes in the cradle of space created by my body and hers. I sucked in the humid lush smell of the insides of her shoes. I drank in the savory odor of the cushioning pads soaked in Lydia's sweat. The insteps had a little blood in them, from two twin blisters that had burst at the backs of her heels. The air coming into my nose and mouth from the insides of her shoes was a small puff of warmth in the harrowing cold.

We had to walk another thirty feet or so to her car. Lydia sank all her gravity into one foot at a time, balancing me in her arms—walking so slowly, so carefully—not taking any risks. Heel-to-toe, heel-to-toe, each step flat on the freezing asphalt.

Lydia winced with each step. I'm sure the ice against the soles of her feet through the flimsy nylon pantyhose was so cold that it spun the wheel of pain around a full revolution, such that it did not freeze, but burned: a pain so sharp that it was more like fire than ice against the skin. I am sure the pain of the cold parking lot shot through her legs as if something were drilling holes in her bones and siphoning out the marrow through a straw.

That night, on our way home, Lydia made a stop somewhere and bought us a bottle of bourbon. That night, we took it home, and Lydia built a fire in the fireplace to warm her freezing feet by, and we got incredibly drunk together until we felt safe and warm and healthy and even sane. That night, Lydia and I made drunken love with the thrashing desperation of two people drowning, clinging to each other for help but in so doing only expediting their sinking, falling together under the surface of the sea.

Part Three

Sated at length, ere long I might perceive
Strange alteration in me, to degree
Of reason in my inward powers, and speech
Wanted not long, though to this shape retained.
Thenceforth to speculations high or deep
I turned my thoughts, and with capacious mind
Considered all things visible in Heaven,
Or Earth, or Middle, all things fair and good.

—*Satan, to Eve,* Paradise Lost

XXI

Lydia and I did not return to the lab after that. Lydia was depressed. The stress, the disappointment, the nausea—whatever it was, it caused the headaches to come roaring into her skull every single night for weeks. Not only at night, but during the day, as well. I had never seen her so miserably incapacitated by her headaches. She did not even permit me to watch TV, because she said the device's persistent high-pitched electronic whine—and the nattering of the things and people that appeared on the screen—aggravated her headaches. She lay diagonally across the bed all day, in her pajamas, with the blinds drawn, clutching her temples and moaning. She was therefore, during this period, no fun. So for entertainment I had to content myself with paging through my picture books, or else busying myself with my artistic pursuits. Outside our home the winter still ruled the sky and streets and air; we were in a particularly nasty cold snap; thus I was stuck inside. It was a time of silence and darkness in 5120 South Ellis Avenue, Apartment 1A.

When she wasn't collapsed sideways across the bed or the couch, or slumped in a chair with an ice pack pressed to her temple in an attempt to chill the fire that raged in her brain and sometimes drove her to the point of vomiting, Lydia was often on the phone, conducting mysterious communiqués with unknown parties. Respectfully, I did not demand to know about them. I gave her privacy, space, and distance enough. I trusted her. I assumed she was conducting some sort of official business relating to my outburst at the art gallery, the particular implications of which I could not even begin to guess at. Our phone was in the kitchen. It was plastic and pale green, bolted to the wall at about (human) chest level, right beside the refrigerator, and the receiver was connected to the port by a long drooping plastic cord that coiled like a pig's tail. When someone on the outside wanted to speak to Lydia, the phone would sound its alarm, which sounded like the gobbling of an electric turkey, and she would pad into the kitchen, her bare feet sticking to the floor, to pick up the receiver, and then would spend a long time—sometimes up to an hour or more—either speaking into it or listening to the inscrutably faint crunching noises that issued from it. I would watch her listening to or talking on the phone. We lived an almost entirely interior existence at this time—it was too cold to make going out any fun, and apparently there was nowhere we had to go, anyway—and Lydia, her poor brain dunked in headaches like a lobster in a boiling pot, would often go the whole day without changing out of the clothes she'd slept in, which often meant just a thin T-shirt and panties, and when she listened to the phone, sometimes she would unconsciously, very, very slowly, pace around in a small circle on the kitchen floor, and the long pale green plastic cord would wind itself around her body, around her pale bare legs—and then she would look down and realize what she had done, and reverse the direction of the small circles she was pacing, from counterclockwise to clockwise or vice versa, and the cord gradually unraveled around her, to hang loose and slack again between the phone port and her long, beautiful body.

Usually these conversations appeared benign enough, although she almost always hung the receiver in its peg in a more agitated state than she had picked it up in. Occasionally her voice would approach a pitch and tone that sounded angry, or outright hostile. I could gauge how pleasant the conversation had been based on the level of violence with which she slammed the receiver back in its cradle.

Other times she would say she had to go on an errand but that whatever she had to do was a complicated bit of business, for which she could not take me along. Such instances were irritating and unnerving, since for nearly a year I had barely been out of Lydia's sight for more than an hour or two. And on these rare occasions she would suit up for the outside without me, then gather all her artifacts together—keys, briefcase, purse, sometimes a coffee cup—kiss me good-bye—once, chastely, on the forehead—nervous, preoccupied—wave, and exit through the front door. With my long purple fingers I inched the window curtains apart to watch Lydia enter her car, start the engine, check the rearview mirror and fasten her seat belt (always the cautious driver) as she edged out of her parking place and into the slush and sluggish traffic of the city streets. When Lydia left the house it hardly mattered where she was going—it mattered simply and only that she was gone. She had disappeared into another universe and would reappear in this one at another time. She was gone from my world, temporarily missing from my sphere of existence. When she was gone I would watch cartoons on TV, sometimes while furtively licking a battery, or I would paint in my studio, or else go upstairs to knock on Mr. Morgan's door to see if he wanted to play backgammon, or let me listen to him practicing the bagpipes. After several weeks of this behavior—the phone calls, the mysterious errands—Lydia announced to me what were the apparent fruits of all her clandestine labors: we were moving.

Moving? I wondered. What did she mean, *moving*? I spent most of the day *moving* in some way, didn't I? Moving what? Moving how? Moving *where*?

"We're moving to Colorado," said Lydia.

I did not even know what Colorado meant, what it was. Was it a place, or was it more like a state of mind or being? If it was a place, then was it also contained in Chicago? Was it in this...*area*? This nation? This planet? What would we be doing there, exactly? And how, and more importantly, *when* would we be returning to Chicago?

"It's hard for me to explain, Bruno," she said to me one night as we were lying in bed, facing each other with our heads on the pillows. Outside, the snow lay so thick on the surfaces of the world that it cushioned the noises of the city, and the streets were eerily silent. Lydia ran her fingers through the fur on my head.

"We have to move," she said. "It has to do with a lot of things, but mostly it has to do with money. Norm doesn't want to keep doing the project because we're out of money, and nobody wants to give us any more. People think that what we're doing is stupid. They don't understand it. They don't think the science we're doing is real science. They don't think our results are real. That's why they won't give us any more money. Norm is stopping the project. He wants to do other things, he thinks we've gone as far as we can go with this project. And where does that leave you and me?" she asked herself rhetorically, sighing and rolling over in bed. "Out to dry."

I nuzzled my face into her armpit.

"Norm wanted to give you back to the zoo."

I looked up at her with a spike of panic.

"Don't worry about that, Bruno. That's not going to happen. I wouldn't let that happen. They think I want to keep the project going. I mean, I do..." Her eyelids were trembling. Her voice grew soft. "But the main reason is because I love you. Bruno, I love you. I can't let someone I love be put in a zoo."

Then she turned over and she kissed me. Then we made love for
the third or fourth time that day. Much later, when we lay panting
and fatigued on the bed, our bodies twisted in the damp sheets, as
if finally continuing her thoughts, she said:

"Norm isn't going to be in charge of the project anymore. There
is no project anymore, actually. Not formally. It's not officially considered research anymore. That's why we're moving to Colorado.
I couldn't get any research grants. I didn't even try, actually. The
people who give out money for science would rather give money to
Norm than me, and not even Norm can get any money right now.
As soon as Norm found out that nobody was taking us seriously,
he wanted to stop the project. Norm doesn't want people to quit
taking him seriously. Nobody ever took me seriously to begin with.
Now they probably never will. So I have nothing to lose. Do you
remember the man in the cowboy hat?"

Indeed I did.

"He said he's going to give us money. He's being very, very nice
to us, and we should be very, very nice to him. He's also going to
give us a place to live. He owns a lot of land in Colorado. That's
where we're moving. He said we can live on his ranch, and that we
can stay there as long as we want and finish our project. For free.
They have a big ranch, where they keep animals. Colorado is far
away from here. There are lots of trees and mountains there."

But logistics, woman, *logistics!* What about our apartment?
What will become of that?

"I'm leasing the apartment," she said. "Maybe we'll come back
here eventually. I don't know. I don't really know what's going to
happen."

And what about her position at the university? Surely we can't
just pull up stakes and leave so easily? Here she broke openly into
tears as she said:

"Bruno, I don't work at the university anymore."

There followed another couple of weeks of busy preparations for our imminent departure. I understood so little of what was going on. I was not well traveled. Chicago was the only home I had ever known. I was born in it. I had never been outside its city limits. There were only three places in the world that I knew well: (one) the Primate House at the Lincoln Park Zoo; (two) the main campus of the University of Chicago in general and room 308 of the Erman Biology Center in particular; and (three) the interior of 5120 South Ellis Avenue, Apartment 1A, Chicago, Illinois. Now we were about to leave this place, this place that then constituted all the known world to me, and resettle in a place that was entirely alien to me, that was only a—not even a concept!—but just a word, a single meaningless word: Colorado. My inchoate young mind could not even begin to wrap itself around the full implications of all this. We would have to say good-bye to our urban existence. We would say good-bye to the magisterial ivy-strangled gray stone buildings of the University of Chicago. Good-bye to the crushing crowds, the bleating cars, the thundering trains that shook us in the night. Good-bye to the mannequins at Marshall Field's, good-bye to the scientists at the lab, good-bye to Haywood, good-bye to Mr. Morgan, with his parrots, his bagpipes, his backgammon, and his boiling beans. Good-bye to everything I had ever known.

People, unknown people, came to us from the outside world from time to time. Lydia would greet them at the door of our apartment and tour them around our domicile. They would open the doors to the rooms and closets, point to what was inside of them, say things, then shut the doors, twist the faucets to run the water in the sinks, flush the toilets, aimlessly amble around from room to room fiddling with knobs and handles, inquisitively poking and pulling on the various elements of the space. They usually seemed amused or intrigued or frightened to see me, quietly, industriously painting away in my room. I generally ignored them. Eventually these strange visitations quit happening, and Lydia and I spent several days collecting all of the many personal articles of our domestic existence and putting them into big brown cardboard boxes. Then one day several enormous ill-smelling men came into our apartment, picked up all the boxes we had made and put our things into, carried them outside into the cold, and loaded them into a giant orange truck parked outside of our house; then they got inside of it and drove away with our things. Lydia assured me that our possessions would somehow already be in the new place where we were going to live when we got there, but I was not so sure.

The next day, Lydia and I locked our now nearly barren apartment, carried down the walk two brown suitcases stuffed fat with personal necessities such as clothing and toiletries and put them in her small car, buckled ourselves in, and began to drive.

Now, the longest trip in a vehicle that I had ever taken in my life was from Lincoln Park to Hyde Park, from the zoo to the lab. If traffic is light, this is a journey of about twenty-five minutes. Which is to say, I had absolutely no psychogeographical measuring stick in my mind by which to even begin to comprehend how mind-bogglingly big the world actually is, or of how much time it takes to truly traverse it. A woman and an ape drove from Chicago to Colorado: a journey of more than a thousand miles that swallowed up two long days by car, even traveling as we were at absolutely harrowing highway speeds.

We pulled ourselves out of the ooze of traffic that slimed the highways of the western suburbs and onto a smooth screaming expanse of gray asphalt that soon bore us through rolling white hills, through snowy fields—endless fields—past barns and grain silos and tractors and the metal skeletons of agricultural machinery sitting dormant in the winter, past ice-coated rivers, lakes and streams, past fences and long bights of utility wire drooping from one cross to the next, each one comfortably seating hundreds of blackbirds. The sky opened up.

For the first time in my life, I saw the sun melt below a naked horizon, reminding me of a golden egg frying in a pan. For the first time in my life, I saw land, I saw a blue sky made giant by the absence of visual landmarks, I saw vast tracts of empty space. And it amazed me. No one had ever told me the world was this big. Throughout the entire journey I think my face was squished flat to the cold glass of the passenger-side window of Lydia's car, my eyes watching the outside world whip past me in all its immeasurable and unknowable magnitude. Periodically, we stopped the car at gas stations. Lydia would insert a hose into a hole in the side of our car to replenish its lifeblood, and then we drained our throbbing bladders into the toilets of their grimy bathrooms, and then in parting Lydia would buy me a candy bar. Outside, the chilly wind snapped and sang across the barren prairies that stretched vanishing into the distance all around us, blowing rippling waves through the dead cornstalks in the brown fields, and the shadows of the clouds above raced across the hills. Then we were off again! And again, my face was pressed to the glass—more *birds!*—more *barns!*—more *fences!*—more *cows!*—more *telephone poles!*—more and more and more space! My heart filled to bursting with the excitement of all this newness, the adventure of it, all the shallow hills sloping and rising along with our rapid traversal of the land, the sky meeting the visible edges of the earth in every direction! Look! This is the world!

I could not understand why Lydia seemed so bored.

After we had spent the whole day sitting in the car traversing the earth, and the sun had long ago set, and the character of the geography beneath our wheels had dramatically shifted several times, we came to a certain area, somewhere in the plains, where there was a cluster of lights and buildings—though the buildings were nowhere near as tall and closely situated as the many buildings in Chicago, and the lights not as bright. We entered a stark ugly white slab of a building. We dragged our fat brown suitcases rolling and banging on the thin orange carpets of the hallways behind us as we passed one identical closed door after another. Lydia inserted a key into the lock of one of these doors. She pushed the door open and led me into a sterile and affectless imitation of a human dwelling, containing a bathroom, a chair, a table, a TV, and a big dry cake of a bed sealed in an envelope of scratchy, starchy sheets tucked so tightly under the mattress that they had to be completely yanked out and tousled around a bit to loosen them up before comfortable sleeping could occur between them. My limbs were antsy with atrophy from a long day of inactivity. Taking a very long trip by car discombobulates the soul for this reason: on the one hand, you have actually just traveled farther across the earth in one day than your poor primate's grasp of time and space could allow your mind to truly comprehend, and yet, perversely, your body has not physically moved from the same spot all day. And don't even get me started on air travel. Modern modes of transportation pollute and corrupt the reverent relationship our minds and bodies might once have had with the geographical space in which we live. And yet they're so damn convenient, so why not? The sacredness of the physical world is one of the many things that we have sacrificed to mere convenience. That's how the old gods die. It turns out the Tower of Babel is not vertical, but horizontal.

I was so jumpy, I wanted to jump on the bed. It was a very pliant and responsive bed, poor perhaps for sleeping but grade A for bouncing. The one Lydia and I had at home—yes, I still thought of it as "home"—was nowhere near so conducive to bouncing. Now there was one monkey, jumping on the bed. However, Dr. Lydia Littlemore (she had a Ph.D.) prescribed that there should be no monkeys jumping on the bed. So I stopped. Lydia sat on the edge of the bed, exhausted to the core of her being, squinting, and with her forefinger and thumb massaging the place where the bridge of her nose reached her brow. She complained of a headache. She picked up the phone and ordered food, which in due time was magically brought to us. We ate it on the bed and watched the TV. Lydia fell asleep in her clothes, on top of the quilt, with the TV still chattering and aglow. I turned it off and curled up beside her. The night came and went. I listened to trucks rumbling past us on the nearby highway all night.

In the morning we got back in the car and more or less repeated exactly what we had done the day before. Another long day of land scrolling past us. The character of the landscape changed and changed again. The temperature changed, the terrain changed, the quality and color of the light in the sky changed, the sun traveled across the sky as we traveled across the earth. We arrived at our destination after the sun had set. I had been asleep for the last few hours of the journey.

The jostling of Lydia's car woke me. Until now the roads we'd driven on had been smooth and clean, but now we were rumbling over a tiny dirt road in the middle of nowhere. Lydia's small car banged and shuddered down the road. Bits of dirt and gravel crunched and popped beneath our tires. We were moving slowly, crawling. I looked at Lydia. Her shoulders and face were scrunched up with concentration. She was having difficulty seeing what was in front of us, stretching her neck over the dashboard and squinting to discern a hint of the road in the dark. I looked out the window. I couldn't see a thing. Only sheer absolute blackness. We may as well have been in outer space for all I could make out.

"We're almost there," Lydia half-sighed to me, as I sat up and smeared the drowse from my eyes. The car rattled and lurched up the steep unpaved mountain road in the dark. The headlights spat a cold white light on the dirt ahead of us, and behind us the brake lights of our car pulsed dim red light into the darkness. The car shuddered, the engine struggled. The headlights briefly illuminated a parabolic wooden sign, whose capital letters were rustically fashioned from sticks, which arched over the road from one roughly hewn upright log to another. We passed beneath the arch. Soon Lydia's car came to rest beside a big metal gate in the middle of the road. She stopped the car but did not turn it off. She dug around in the glove compartment for something, found it—a little scrap of paper on which she'd written something—got out of the car and walked up to a little blinking box to one side of the gate. She did something to the box, and the gate moaned open before us. She got back into the car and continued to drive us up the thin dirt road. Eventually the car came to a stop in a wide flat area right in front of a massive and complicated house. We got out of the car with our suitcases. It was late. A few of the lights in the house were on, and there was a light on above the giant wooden doors in the front of the house. A row of lamps lined a long stone path that led from the place where we parked up to the doors of the house. Other than that, there were no other buildings, and no other lights around for miles. All around us were hills, dotted with patches of sparkling white snow that sloped upward and became dark mountains. Above us, the night sky swarmed with stars, so much of the universe's twinkling smoke and dust—it was at once beautiful and terrifying. It looked just like the curvilinear ceiling of the planetarium in Chicago, except without the glowing outlines of all the beasts and gods and monsters that the constellations were supposed to represent drawn helpfully in the spaces between the stars.

The wheels under our suitcases grumbled along the stone path that led from the driveway to the giant double doors of the house. Lydia knocked on the doors. They winged open and we were met by a squat and sleepy-eyed older woman with curly brushed-iron hair who carried herself with gravity and austerity. She guided us upstairs to a guest bedroom with an adjoining bathroom. We were utterly exhausted, and we fell asleep at once, even in these unfamiliar environs, without any ceremony.

Lydia and I awoke the following morning, showered in the adjoining bathroom, dressed from our suitcases, and went out to explore the house. The house was vast, bright, and silent. Hand in hand, we wandered through the impeccably clean wood-floored and white-walled hallways. There was a lot of art on the walls. The excessive bigness, brightness, and cleanliness of the house made it a pleasant but strangely unhomelike place to be in. A giant upside-down cone of a chandelier hung from the high ceiling over the cavernous living room, which was made entirely out of real deer's antlers linked together in a thorny spiraling tessellation. A wide staircase wrapped around half of the space and gracefully spilled into the room, moving us through the house less like wood than water. The staircase was like a wooden waterfall, a cascade of frozen visible music. The interior spaces of this house, in contrast to the rigid, boxy architecture I was used to—which always makes it seem like the architect's top priority was to keep the lineaments between one room and another crystal clear—flowed in such a way that all the rooms melted smoothly together. At the bottom of the stairs, beneath the antler chandelier, a furry white rug lay on the wooden floor, and several white and brown couches and armchairs assembled around a low glass table beside a flagstone fireplace that contained a glass window, behind which the smooth flames of a gas fire burned in silence. Above the fireplace hung an oil painting of a group of cowboys riding muscular white horses across a snowy plain, with mountains in the background, and a storm threatening overhead in the top right corner. The walls to the left and right of the fireplace consisted of towering windows that filled the room with blinding bright light. Outside these windows, the earth all around the house crested into hundreds of cragged peaks, pink slabs of rock with clusters of pine trees between them, all powdered with bright snow. I had never seen mountains before. The light in the sharp blue sky was amazingly bright.

Dudley Lawrence sat in one of the white armchairs beside the glassed-in silent fire. He had not noticed us descending the stairs, noiselessly, in our socks. He was reading a newspaper and smiling to himself. His face looked like it smiled perpetually. He was barefoot in blue jeans and a blue denim shirt, from the open neck of which his white chest hair burst forth, and he wore reading glasses to see the paper. It was still quite early in the morning, but he looked as alert as if he had already been awake for hours. This man was a living illustration of wholesomeness, happiness, and vitality. Lydia and I were still damp-headed from the shower, and wearing clothes that were rumpled from being compressed two days in our suitcases.

Dudley Lawrence noticed us, looked up, snapped the newspaper in half backward and threw it on the side table next to the chair. Then he stood up, and I saw the giant decorative brass belt buckle that connected the lower half of him to the upper half. He radiated robustness and cheer. His white mustache lived inside of his smile like a snail lives in its shell. He opened his lean, strong, denim-clad arms to us.

"Mornin'!" he roared. "Welcome to the ranch!"

XXII

After our reunions and obligatory small talk, Dudley Lawrence clapped his hands and rubbed them rapidly together with friction vigorous enough to start a fire had there been kindling between his palms, and thereupon conducted us into the dining room, where Lydia and I sat at one end of a long dining table, a maroon mahogany oblong polished so sleek as to reflect images as sharply as a still lake. Mr. Lawrence sat at the head of the table, which was already set for seven. Nearby, from the adjoining kitchen, emanated the smells and noises of cooking. The woman who had opened the door for us late last night brought us a carafe full of coffee and a pitcher of orange juice and set them on the table, to join the glass pitcher of water already on the table.

"Thank you, Rita," said Mr. Lawrence from beneath his white mustache, and the woman answered with a barely perceptible nod and returned to the kitchen. Presently we were joined by Regina Lawrence, full-bosomed and resplendent in a flowing white Christ-like garment that billowed breezily around her body, her white-streaked red hair twisted into a long braid behind her, with three fully dressed chimps. Two of them were holding hands, and one of them held Mrs. Lawrence's hand.

The three chimps were named Hilarious Larry, Hilarious Lily, and Clever Hands. Informally: Larry, Lily, and Clever. All of them were older than me (I was still in my adolescence). For the most part they all walked upright, though Larry, the biggest and oldest of them—he was over forty!—still occasionally regressed to the déclassé habit of knuckle-walking. Larry was a huge, fat, dark-furred chimp. He wore a red-and-black-checked flannel shirt and jeans, like a lumberjack. Lily, the female, was smaller and lighter, and wore a blue dress with white polka dots and a silver crucifix around her neck. Clever was twenty-five years old when I met him—about my age now—and he was smaller and shyer than Larry and Lily. Clever was an introvert, a dreamer. He was carelessly dressed in a red T-shirt and sweatpants. Clever had been the subject of a previous—and failed—language acquisition experiment (this I will get into later, Gwen) who had been "retired" to the ranch. None of them could speak, but they were all quiet, civilized, and fairly well behaved in human society.

We sat down at the table, and Rita served breakfast: spinach quiche, with toast and croissants, butter, and jam. It was delicious. The noises of chewing and slurping and of forks tinkling against plates filled the bright room. Regina, a big-personalitied and loquacious woman, did most of the talking, but her husband seemed to be closely monitoring the conversation from behind the bristly white ramparts of his mustaches.

"We founded the ranch and the organization over ten years ago," she said. "Just after Dudley and I were married." Her husband nodded over his coffee cup in verification of this information. "We wanted to do something kind for the animals. Provide a safe haven. Larry and Lily were the first chimps we brought to the ranch. Hilarious Larry was a circus chimp. He was captured as an infant in the Congo. They probably had to kill his parents to catch him. He's an old chimp, now. He's the dominant male of our little group. He's been through a lot of bad luck in his life."

Hilarious Larry, stonefaced and indifferent, shoved a forkload of quiche into his mouth and took a sip of orange juice.

"They made him wear a clown suit and ride a tricycle," said Mrs. Lawrence. "He did tricks, he juggled. He would smoke cigars and drink brandy, and everybody laughed when he fell down drunk. When he was young, they removed his teeth, so he couldn't bite."

"Oh, my God—," Lydia said, her hand instinctively rising to her mouth.

"We had him fitted with dentures," said Mrs. Lawrence. Hilarious Larry smiled sardonically, showing us his false teeth. She went on: "Then the circus acquired a female chimp to be his 'wife.' That's Lily. Lily was originally one of the chimps Bill Lemon raised for cross-fostering experiments in Norman, Oklahoma." Lydia nodded. "Lily is deeply religious. She was raised in the home of a woman who brought her up Catholic—she was baptized, she had her first communion. Dudley and I aren't religious, but we respect her faith. That's why we built a chapel for her on the ranch. Lily goes there to pray almost every day. Rita takes her to confession on Sundays at the Catholic church in Montrose. She always feels better after she's confessed her sins." (I silently wondered how much sin Lily could possibly accumulate in her life of idleness on the ranch.) "The woman who had had her baptized eventually gave her back to Bill Lemon. A few years later, Lemon ran out of money and started selling off his chimps. That was in the seventies. Most of them went to biomedical research facilities. Lily went to the circus. I don't know which is worse. They billed them as a husband-and-wife chimp act, 'Hilarious Larry' and 'Hilarious Lily.' It was disgusting. They carted them around the country in a cage in horrible conditions, dressed them up in degrading clothes, forced them to perform tricks. They were given no compensation. They were slaves. They made them sit down to 'tea' at a table, with a little tea set. Hilarious Larry juggled and rode his tricycle. They trained Lily to do an Arabian striptease act. They would make them sit in a set made to look like a Bedouin tent, and Larry would wear a turban and sit and clap as she took off her pink scarves, the dance of the seven veils…and they would play that awful music…."

Rita gradually galumphed into the room to collect our dishes. Mr. Lawrence thanked her, and she refreshed our beverages. Hilarious Larry tilted back in his chair and began picking at his false teeth. Larry lazily radiated the air of a comfortably entitled patriarch. Clever Hands stared out the window at the sparkling pockets of mountain snow in the near distance. For her part, Hilarious Lily gazed absently, not out the window like Clever, but into a knot of nothingness floating somewhere above my left shoulder—thinking, presumably, of God.

"We acquired Larry and Lily together from the circus not long after we bought this ranch and started the foundation," said Mrs. Lawrence. "They've been with us for ten years. We consider them family. We bought Clever a few years later." Clever's interest in the conversation perked up slightly at the sound of his name. "And Clever of course you know, if only by reputation. He's modest. He doesn't even realize how famous he once was."

Clever shrugged humbly and smiled, then resumed his staring out the window. It was clear that although he couldn't talk, Clever essentially understood human conversation. His was a silence not of any cunning, or fear, but of listening.

"After he was retired from the language acquisition experiments," Mrs. Lawrence continued, "he was passed from one place to another until he eventually wound up at a wildlife sanctuary in Texas, where he was the only chimp. A social animal—alone. It was as if he had been imprisoned in solitary confinement, and never told what crime he was charged with. He went insane from loneliness and boredom. His hair was falling out. We bought him four years ago and brought him here to the ranch. He's been so much happier since he's been given back his freedom and has Larry and Lily to play with."

As his wife spoke Dudley Lawrence was tilting back in his chair, rocking it with his foot, and twiddling the ends of his mustache. I looked from Mr. Lawrence to Larry and back again, and gathered at once where my fellow enculturated chimp had picked up his mannerisms. Larry behaved much like an oldest and beloved son, imitating his father. Then Mr. Lawrence wrapped his hands together behind his shiny bald head and began to move his elbows symmetrically in and out, like the wings of a butterfly, and soon thereafter Larry—probably subconsciously—copied these postures and motions as well.

I heard from somewhere nearby an unnerving clicking noise. I looked in the direction from whence I perceived the noise: what I had heard was the sound of a dog's toenails clicking on the wooden floors, a sound that heralded the approach of the dog that made it. It was a medium-sized and intensely furry black and gray dog, with sweet wet black marbles for eyes and a blue bandana knotted around its neck like a bandit's.

"Hey, Sukie," Mr. Lawrence affectionately intoned upon the entrance of the dog. He decanted the angle of his chair until each of its four legs was again in contact with the floor. The dog clicked its way across the floor and rested its furry head on Mr. Lawrence's knee.

I was startled at the sight of this animal. I had never before been in such close contact with a dog—at least not in an interior space. I had seen them in parks in Chicago before, but always at a distance, for ordinarily creatures of the canine ilk were distrustful of me and tended to keep their distance. Not this dog, though. Apparently this dog was accustomed to cohabiting not only with humans but also with enculturated chimps, and thus was not put off by my unusual appearance. Noticing me sitting not far away from its master, this dog soon lifted its servile and loving head from the cushion of Mr. Lawrence's leg, and came clicking and panting directly up to me. I recoiled, not from disgust as much as confusion and alarm. Lydia sensed my discomfort.

"Is he friendly?" asked Lydia.

"She's perfectly friendly," Mr. Lawrence said. "She loves to play with chimps."

Lydia reached out to the dog and stroked the thick glossy fur on top of the beast's head, and this *Canis lupus familiaris* answered her gesture with an unmistakable smile. Then the dog returned its attention to me. Following Lydia's example, I reached my hand out, tentatively, to make physical contact with the animal. The hair on top of its head was warm, soft, downy. Suddenly, it *licked my hand*, and I jerked it back in shock. Lydia laughed.

"It's okay, Bruno," she said. "Relax. She won't hurt you."

Such a strange feeling, that ridiculous little tongue against my flesh, like a flat wet rough worm. The dog nudged my leg with its slimy nose. I felt my heartbeat quicken. The dog tried to lick me again. I tried to push it away, but it continued to lick me.

"She won't hurt you, Bruno," said Lydia. "Let her lick you."

Let her lick you: does that sentence, in or out of context, I don't care, not strike you as strange? And yet—Bruno bravely consented to offer this creature his palm, and she (I suppose I should begin applying a gendered pronoun to her, though Sukie was still an "it" to me) slurped at his skin, as if she derived the greatest of earthly pleasures from licking things. To her, life must simply have been a grand procession of things to lick, as if the whole corporeal world were divided into two camps: things licked and things left yet to lick—and the unlicked life was not worth living. She kept licking me, and I even grew, before long, to like it. Thus was my introduction to the concept of "pet."

Isn't it an odd concept, Gwen? Living with domesticated animals

254 • Benjamin Hale

for pleasure? I've always thought so. I say "pleasure" because I'm not talking about the more utilitarian human valuations on animals: dogs to alert us of intruders, cats to mouse, horses to ride, sheep to shear, cows and pigs to eat. I'm talking about animals employed exclusively as "pets." Animals that humans care for simply out of—what, love? Is that the right word? Love? We may weep when they die, do we not? Or entertainment? Think of chihuahuas, shih tzus, Yorkshire terriers: indeed, it seems we deliberately breed dogs for certain traits solely to make us laugh! What a strange thing it is for us to keep animals for primarily emotional reasons. The social contract we seem to have with our pets is that we continue to keep them alive and safe and fed in exchange for the amusement and emotional satisfaction they provide us. At first this idea will strike a first-generation immigrant to the human species—such as myself—as more than a little bizarre. I suppose, in a way, I myself have personal experience with being a pet, for what is a zoo animal but a public pet? But household pets—dogs, cats—these are the animals human beings have selected to take with them as passengers on their insane journey through, over, and against nature. We have such a tortured relationship with the other animals that live in our world, Gwen. Even as we ridicule them, we can let ourselves love them. I would come to know Sukie well.

Mr. Lawrence scooted back his chair, stretched his long denim-clad arms and sang out a playful noise that was half yawn and half yodel.

"What say we take a tour of the ranch?" he said.

"We would love to," said Lydia, looking at me.

Rita cleared the table and began to wash the dishes. Clever Hands seemed to want to come with us, as did Sukie, the dog. Hilarious Larry and Lily expressed no especial interest in Mr. Lawrence's proposed outing, and so Mrs. Lawrence announced that she would stay behind to keep them company.

Lydia and I returned to the room we had slept in the previous night to bundle ourselves up in our coats and hats and to put on our shoes. When we came back downstairs, Mr. Lawrence was already all duded out in a fresh cowboy hat, cowboy boots, and a pair of bottle-green aviator sunglasses. Clever Hands also wore a cowboy hat, a very small one that fit him well. Sukie, sensing action was imminent, scurried around wildly and yapped at their feet. Seeing the rugged Western garb that Clever and Mr. Lawrence both wore, Lydia and I suffered flashes of acute embarrassment at our fancier, more urban clothes. Mr. Lawrence led us into a long, spacious garage, and of the cars that were parked in it, he selected a green Jeep, whose canvas top was down. We all piled into this automobile: Mr. Lawrence driving, Lydia in the passenger seat, me and Clever in the back, with Sukie yelping and slobbering between us. Clever was quite comfortable with the dog. After the initial hubbub of getting into the car, Sukie relaxed and lay down on the backseat of the Jeep, resting her furry head in Clever's lap. Clever grinned at me with an almost conspiratorial mischievousness. He was glad to have my company.

As he sat next to me in the car, Clever was making all kinds of weird movements with his hands at me. His eyes were wide and imploring as he made all these enigmatic gestures with his hands and arms and fingers. I did not understand what he was getting at. Later I would realize that he was trying to communicate with me in sign language.

Mr. Lawrence, by the touch of a button, commanded the garage door to roll noisily open on greased metal tracks to reveal the sun, the pale blue sky, and the bright snowy mountains that corrugated the horizon, and the Jeep grumbled out of the garage and into the day. I had seen this place at night, but by the light of day—oh!—I had no idea that this earth might contain a place so beautiful, that all these rocks and plants, all this water and dirt, could have ever arranged themselves into such spectacular formations! The air was fresher, sharper, sweeter-smelling, and the light was crisper here, such that everything in sight seemed to be hypernaturally well-defined, in focus, more sharply drawn, as if the air and light of the city had a way of making things a little blurry, like a soft-focus lens. There was snow on the ground, but it was not particularly cold outside.

"We started the ranch as a sanctuary for endangered animals," Mr. Lawrence said to Lydia, as I looked around at the landscape.

Clever had decided that I could not understand him. He sighed in resignation and quit trying to sign to me. Sukie sat between us and panted. Her flat pink tongue hung out of her mouth, slightly pulsating in and out of it with the rhythm of her panting. Occasionally her tongue would dry out and she quit panting to bring it back inside of her, swallow, and smile. Then she would let it fall back out of her mouth and continue the business of panting until her tongue dried out again. Clever gingerly stroked her fur.

"We're sitting on about two hundred acres," Mr. Lawrence continued, to Lydia. "The whole property's surrounded by a twenty-foot-high electric fence. That's more to keep intruders out than it is to keep the animals in. We've got our own little Eden here, our own Noah's Ark. We acquire most of the animals from the entertainment industry, biomedical labs, zoos. We just want to give the animals a good home and a chance to be happy, to roam the land. Inside the property, the animals have free range. Of course in the winter most of the animals stay inside in their barns, where it's warm. All the barns are good and heated. Most of them are African animals. They're not used to these winters. It's a nice day, though. I bet we'll see some of them out and about." Lydia nodded and put on her sunglasses. "The chimps, though?" said Mr. Lawrence. "The house chimps we just treat like regular members of the family. They're used to living with people. They sleep in our house, they eat our food. We live with them. We live like a family. Everybody who works for us knows to treat them just like they'd treat me or Regina."

Soon, as Mr. Lawrence piloted the rumbling vehicle down the narrow dirt road that wound snakily through the grounds of the ranch, we espied some of the animals that I had, in the life I led previously as an ape, grown up in close proximity to, often hearing, but seldom actually catching sight of, in the Lincoln Park Zoo: zebras, giraffes, rhinoceri, hippopotami, and even several elephants, lumbering around in the distance, looking absurdly out of place amid all the coniferous trees and snowy hills. This was the Lawrence Ranch, in the mountains of southern Colorado. This place was to be our new home.

Mr. Lawrence also drove us around the perimeter of his vineyard. He was a renaissance man, a man of great and many passions, but two of them ruled above the rest like a king and queen: one was the fate of the animals on this earth, and the other?—wine. Mr. Lawrence was an avid and passionate oenophile. His ranch was—is, I should say—located in Grand Valley, a wine-growing region on the western slope of the Rocky Mountains. The vineyard was a large swath of his property that no animals were allowed into. Not even me or Clever were allowed to go there. Maybe he didn't trust us not to pick and eat the grapes that grew in gorgeous plump dew-dappled bunches all along the rows of long fences, and if so, this distrust was probably an accurate one. I loved the smell of the vineyards, though, and in the future Clever and I would take many a long walk together along the perimeter of the vineyard, breathing the fruit-sweeted air and discussing philosophical subjects.

We toured the grounds of the ranch all day, visiting the barns where the less adventurous of the Lawrence Ranch animals slept in beds of straw beneath tracks of red glowing heat lamps that hung from the high ceilings of these structures, these huge metal barns that were more like airplane hangars, built cavernous enough to comfortably house elephants and rhinos. We saw the clear black water of a creek trickling over smooth stones beneath ledges of ice, descending from a spring in the nearby mountains. We saw the antelope and the gazelles, the gnus and the gemsboks, the emus, ostriches, zebras, and Bactrian camels. A huge humid glass enclosure full of plants and trees housed smaller animals: wombats, monkeys, lemurs, gibbons, echidnas, and tapirs. Who would have thought that there would be a remote expanse of acreage somewhere in the Wild West of Colorado positively teeming with all manner of exotic animalia, a secret peaceable kingdom hidden deep in the mountains of the New World?

XXIII

In 1970 (twenty-five years before I arrived at the Lawrence Ranch) Dr. Henry Troutwine, a cognitive research psychologist at Princeton University, initiated the Clever Hands project, now mostly famous for being widely regarded as a failure.

At the time the Clever Hands project was the most ambitious, well-organized and well-funded experiment in ape language acquisition to date. Dr. Troutwine acquired a male infant chimpanzee from Bill Lemon, a rogue psychologist at the University of Oklahoma. Lemon was a staunch Freudian, which is extremely unusual for a research psychologist. Lemon was also a chimp breeder. He owned a farm just outside of Norman, Oklahoma, where he raised and kept a menagerie of exotic animals—among them a large group of chimps that he kept on an island in the middle of a lake on his farm. Lemon was intensely interested in experiments in cross-fostering chimps in human households. He would lend out his infant chimps to research volunteers (most of them his graduate students) to raise in their homes as human children. Lemon had promised to sell Dr. Troutwine an infant chimp for his experiment as soon as one became available; so, although Troutwine had not yet fully set up the logistics of the experiment, when a baby chimp was born at the Lemon farm, he jumped at the chance to acquire him. Troutwine bought the baby from Lemon and brought the two-week-old chimp back to Princeton, New Jersey, where he had him placed as a foster child in the home of his first volunteers, the Saltonseas.

Millicent Saltonsea was a psychologist, and her husband, Winn Saltonsea, was a ponytailed poet who dressed in white linen pants, came from a patrician line of old money, and spoke with a Locust Valley lockjaw. For the first year of the project, Clever Hands—as he was whimsically dubbed—lived with the Saltonseas and their four young children in their palatial estate in the suburbs of Princeton. Troutwine's idea was that Clever Hands would be brought up in a human environment, co-reared alongside the Saltonseas' four children. Meanwhile, Troutwine was rushing to put together the funds and facilities necessary for the experiment. He wanted to see if a chimpanzee could learn American Sign Language. There had been a few other notable attempts to teach sign language to chimps—most notably Allen and Beatrice Gardener's experiments with the female chimp Washoe—but those experiments were dogged by accusations of sloppy methodology and data-fudging, and the results were dubious and disappointing at best. Troutwine thought this was in part because the chimps in previous experiments had been too old when serious attempts at language instruction had begun; you must begin molding the plastic of an animal mind with language right from birth. (I am an exception.) It is worth mentioning that neither Millicent nor Winn Saltonsea nor any of their children were fluent—or even capable—ASL signers. Troutwine had an ASL teacher instruct them in signs that they might impart to Clever. Unfruitful months passed as Troutwine dithered, and Clever quickly became too big and unruly for Winn Saltonsea. After a relatively short time of living with baby Clever, Winn had come to regret agreeing to house the chimp. Clever had begun to tear apart books, furniture, drapes—anything in the Saltonseas' home that could be torn apart, including their marriage. But that is another story.

The Saltonseas had to forsake Clever and end their involvement in the project. Clever was passed from one home to another (never, by the way, to Troutwine's own home) until Troutwine was finally able to secure enough funding and resources to begin the experiment in earnest. Eventually he managed to secure the use of a large and elegant Georgian mansion near the Princeton campus, owned by the university. The donor of the property had envisioned it as a botanical research station, as the house featured an English garden, sprawling lawns, koi ponds, and a greenhouse. For whatever reason this never happened, and since its donation the property had sat vacant and neglected, and had fallen into disrepair while the Princeton administration dragged its feet as to the question of what to do with it. Through faculty chatter Troutwine became apprised of its existence and asked Princeton to let him headquarter the Clever Hands project there. They said yes, and that was that: he had the house refurbished and chimp-proofed to the best of his knowledge and funding, hired a small army of caretakers and tutors to provide round-the-clock handling and upkeep, and moved Clever into the house. Only then was Troutwine able to provide enough space, facilities, and personnel to properly throw everything he could into the experiment, and by that time Clever was nearly three years old.

For the next several years Clever lived like a mad aristocrat: imprisoned in luxury, disallowed to venture beyond the twenty-room house and the ten acres of land surrounding it, yet with his every crazy whim slavishly attended to by a revolving crew of graduate students who kept him company, cared for him, fed and washed him, entertained him, and were always, and with steadily increasing desperation, trying to teach him sign language. As Clever got older and the experiment wore on, Troutwine frantically jumped from one methodological tack to another, changing methods of data collection and analysis in accordance with the nature of the results. Over the years, the logistics of the Clever Hands project exponentially compounded in complexity and eventually spiraled out into unmanageable oblivion. Not one fluent ASL signer ever worked on the experiment. Troutwine would sit Clever down for hours of deliberate instruction in a makeshift "classroom" they built in the house. His teachers would make signs and try to get him to mimic them, often molding his hands to make the signs. In order to keep getting funding from the National Science Foundation, Henry Troutwine (who gradually withdrew in all ways but in name from the daily experiments, and in the end had little actual contact with Clever) was forced to publish the results. What he called his data were measured by things like how many signs Clever had made on his own, with no instructional prompting, and whether or not he was making the signs in appropriate contexts. Such data were deeply vulnerable to subjective interpretation and often too amoebic and vague to measure; ergo, the data were difficult to gather in any way that conformed to acceptable scientific methodology. Clever learned hundreds of signs, but never used them in any way that met the experimenters' definition of language. He never acquired anything that could be called syntax, never had anything resembling grammar. Although young Clever's cuteness made him a darling of the public—he was featured on TV talk shows and so on (maybe even *because* of this public interest in his cuteness)—within the scientific community the Clever Hands experiment fell under deep scrutiny, then doubt, then outward hostility, until Troutwine lost his funding and the experiment went under. Troutwine shut down the project, closed the facilities, and washed his hands of it all. Then, to save face, he decided to join the opposition, and denounced the project as a failure in a paper he published in *Science* in 1979. In the paper, he lay down his arms and supplicated the forgiveness of the scientific community, declaring that language was an innately human capability, the Cartesian break between man and beast was all true, and any future animal language experiments were a foolish waste of time. Troutwine voluntarily agreed to abjure, curse, and detest his previous opinions on the matter, and he did not mutter "it still moves." His penance paid, the true church of science absolved Henry Troutwine and welcomed him back into the fold, and it was henceforth decreed that all animal language experiments were sheer bunkum.

Meanwhile, Clever himself was abandoned. He was removed from his home in Princeton and for lack of a place to put him was shipped back to Bill Lemon's farm in Oklahoma, where—for the first time in his life—he had to interact with other chimps. A lifetime of human pampering had made Clever shy, neurasthenic, and poorly socialized, and he had trouble getting along with other chimps. Four years later, Lemon also ran completely out of money, and began to sell off his chimps. He sold most of them to biomedical research facilities. Clever himself was sold to the Alamogordo Primate Research Facility on Holloman Air Force Base in New Mexico. He was never experimented on, though. When it leaked to the public that Clever Hands, the famous and adorable sign language chimp, sat languishing in a three-by-five-foot wooden box in the desert, waiting to be injected with hepatitis in order to be tested with experimental drugs, a small public outcry arose among animal rights activists. Eventually Clever wound up on a wildlife preserve in Texas. The wildlife preserve had no other chimps, and he spent several more years living in solitary confinement, until the Lawrences bought him and retired him to their ranch in southwestern Colorado, where he has been living ever since.

Clever had probably enjoyed a happier life than either Hilarious Larry or Lily. Larry's and Lily's minds had been reared only in dens of iniquity: noisy, smoke-filled tents resonant with squabbling and shouting voices and caterwauling children, where they would be treated to beatings, whippings, shocks and scourges if they did not clamber onstage to dance, to mock and humiliate themselves, to ride tricycles and remove their garments before the eyes of strangers. Hilarious Larry and Hilarious Lily were both broken, rattled, traumatized spirits; the ranch was as friendly a convalescent home as any for these two damaged souls to while away their days unto the ends of their haunted existences—but as content as their retirement may have been, they would clearly never be well again. But Clever was a somewhat different story: he had, in his way, been loved. He had been treated with respect by his handlers. Some of them, in any case. Of course their failure to "teach" him sign language was a failure not of Clever's understanding, but of theirs. He still tried to communicate in sign language.

Now and then Clever would try to sign to me, thinking that maybe he finally had someone to talk to. I wish I could have understood him. Sadly, I did not. Instead he found in me a chimp who understood him only in the way that most humans would—that is, in every way but linguistically. One could easily look into Clever's eyes and see that a great mind, a cultured consciousness, was alive and working away in there—but was pitifully imprisoned behind an opaque wall of incommunicability. His human adopters had gone so far with him and no farther; and the result was that they ignited in his soul a fierce desire to communicate, but provided him with inadequate tools to do so. His consciousness was like an unfinished sculpture whose clay had been allowed to harden before it had fully taken shape. You could see this in his eyes. For prerequisite to language is the desire to communicate, and prerequisite to the desire to communicate is the acknowledgment of the existence of consciousness outside of oneself.

I own that it sounds kitschy, Gwen; it sounds like sugary romanticism to say the eyes are the windows to the soul, but I wish that poeticism weren't so shopworn, because I think that it is true. Look into the eyes of another being—the eyes!—these two glistening globs of light-perceiving jelly in our skulls are our only external organs that shoot directly back into our brains. When you look, and look directly and look deeply, into the centers of another creature's eyes—into the eyes of another being that has consciousness, emotions, a mind—then you have a profound crisis of experience (or you should, if you're doing it right): you realize that this other being that is outside of your body lives in a world that is entirely other to your own, and that it may know things that you may not, and that you may know things that it may not, and that it may be possible to exchange information—and then you will want to talk. You will want to exchange your worlds. This is the beginning, not yet of language, but of the mother of language, the desire to communicate. This desire begets the birth of the conversation, and a conversation should strike us as the most beautiful and miraculous phenomenon we know of: the collaborative sharing of consciousnesses that creates the necessity for external symbols. Then comes—all in a wild rush of experimentation and improvisation—symbolic logic, vocabulary, syntax, etc., etc. But you must first have this seed of language, the desire to communicate. And the tragedy of Clever Hands was that he was permitted to take these first and most important steps—to look into another's eyes, recognize the other, and want to compare worlds—yet he never learned to "speak." At least not in a way that could be responsibly documented and published, in any case. But that is a matter having to do with the nature of science, not the nature of nature. It's a pity they are not always the same thing. It was as if Clever Hands were forced to live in a glass box, through which he could see others and hear what they were saying, and yet those outside of his prison could not hear him. He lived a lonely life.

The nature of science I know—and in some oblique way I would say I even knew this at the time—was at the heart of why the life that Lydia and I had shared and known together in Chicago had come to an abrupt end, and why we had been violently uprooted and replanted in this new location that was alien to me—to both of us, as a matter of fact. Our project had grown too strange and dangerous for funding to keep coming from the normal channels through which scientific dollars flow. I understood that we were here in this unknown place in Colorado because we were refugees, banished to the fringes of science. We were refugees to whom the Lawrences kindly gave asylum.

Of course I understand that we were also there because I was an unpredictable and often violent little monster who had become an untenable legal liability to the university. After all, I was a "wild animal." We were also there because the experiment so far had been in many respects an utter failure, a flop, a bust, a bomb. I had done nothing yet that other chimps—including Clever Hands, who sat mutely beside me in the backseat of Mr. Lawrence's Jeep— had not done before. I shiver to think of what would have become of me if Norm had been able to completely terminate the experiment when he wanted to. I think that if the experiment had ended there—if the Lawrences had not snatched us from the flames when they did—I surely would have wound up much like poor Clever, trapped behind the half-silvered mirror of his mind.

I probably would have languished once again in the Lincoln Park Zoo for the rest of my life, having been picked up by the cruel and curious child of science, toyed with until boredom and then unceremoniously dropped, returned to my fellow animals with a mind now damaged, deformed, and deranged by human civilization but perversely ungifted with any of its benefits, not enough culture or language to build a communicative consciousness, and so doomed to sit forever in idiot moody silence, comprehending what is said and done all around me and yet unable to offer a word in return.

Was it love—the love between me and Lydia—that saved me from such a fate?

No. Perhaps—this is what I think only when my mind is sunk in the mud of its darkest meditations—perhaps I should lend more of the credit for my successfully completed education into manhood to Mr. Lawrence than to Lydia, that I should say it was not so much our love but Mr. Lawrence's money that saved me, because in this world that we have made for ourselves, love alone is powerless—everything is powerless—without capital. Yes, let's face it: love was part of it, but honestly I was simply saved by a wealthy and generous man's money. Love alone never saved a thing.

XXIV

The final stop on Mr. Lawrence's guided tour of his ranch deposited us before the small pink stucco house where Lydia and I would live like Ovid in exile for the next two years. Two times in this place we would see the crystalline white snow sublimate out of being to denude the brown and green ground, and two times we would see it slowly accumulate again. We experienced two winters, two springs, two summers, and two falls in this place, some seven hundred plus days, two Christmases, and four birthdays: two total Christmas trees, four total birthday cakes for me and Lydia. Over time, I would come to know Regina and Dudley Lawrence as friends of a certain sort—allies at the very least—though I never grew to feel entirely at home with them. I would come to love Sukie, the dog, and to know the friendship of Clever Hands, the only other member of my own species I would at all consider a true friend in my life.

The cabin—as Mr. Lawrence referred to it, as he parked the green Jeep before its pink-painted façade—was really a house, and a pleasant one. It afforded us at least three times as much living space as our apartment in Chicago had. It was a one-floor structure, complete with a fireplace, a bedroom, a bathroom, a cozy living room, a kitchen, and a garage that would mainly become a studio space for me, which I obligingly shared with Lydia's car in the winter. We found the house decorated in the Southwestern themes prevalent in this area: brightly colored woolen serapes draped over sturdy rustic furniture, prints of yonic Georgia O'Keeffe paintings framed on the walls. We had an attractive front yard, in which spiky yellow and fluffy purple flowers sprouted in the spring. The steps of the back porch descended onto the grassy, lightly manicured wilderness of the Lawrence Ranch, where, when the snow had dissipated, emus, camels, giraffes, elephants, rhinos, zebras, and all kinds of other outlandish animals were permitted to wander the grounds at will, and their massive and ungainly bodies would often curiously saunter right up to our porch to gaze at us, or into the windows of our home.

These two years in the great American Southwest, our own savage pilgrimage, were two years of long meandering walks in the surrounding fields and woods and mountains, two years of feeding the animals, two years of ambling the trails of the ranch side-by-side with my surrogate brother and fellow semi-enculturated chimp, Clever Hands—Lydia, Clever and me, with Sukie the dog yapping excitedly ahead of us on the trail at a handful of passing zebras—and two years of continuing my education, as well as my passionate love affair, with Lydia. Every Arcadian day would be spent in play, in love, in conversation, in a simple life, simply lived. It was there, at the Lawrence Ranch in Colorado, during these two relatively uneventful years of contentment and bliss, where my ontogenesis was completed—in peace, in quiet, in secret. This was possible only because I was living in such an unstressed atmosphere, in such a safe, interesting, and pastoral environment, in which nothing much was ever expected or demanded of me, of us. Several evenings per week Lydia and I would spend in the "big house," as we at once began referring to it, with Regina and Dudley Lawrence, with Larry and Lily and Clever, eating dinner—at the table, with civilized manners—and conversing, drinking wine, sometimes playing games late into the evening, such as charades, or board games like Monopoly and Pictionary. I tried to teach Clever Hands to play backgammon. He learned the game, but in the same way he learned sign language: he learned to perform the right motions, but would put them together in such erratic sequences that it was dubious whether he actually knew what they meant. In any event, I always won.

These were two happy years. In these two years I learned to speak, and later even to read. This could have only happened to me in such an unhurried atmosphere. All it required for my mind to go from a state of mostly mute listening and comprehension to a state of conversational participation—to the active *production* of language—was to have no one pushing me. Only *pulling* me, guiding me. Only then could I dare the audacity of speech. (I have always been this way: obstinate, stubborn, resistant to anyone's pushing.) All real learning, all education, Gwen, is self-motivated. Teaching helps, yes, but teaching students by force, by pushing, is as good as preaching a sermon to a congregation of stones. It is a notably obscene crime of our language that *educate* is not an intransitive verb.

What can be said of a long, slow period of daily progress and habitual contentment? The angels of ecstasy and the demons of despair are visitations more at home in the house of literature, which is why I intend to nimbly skip and jump through the pages of this happy period in my life. What did my consciousness gain from my two contented years in Colorado? The cackling of coyotes at night, and in the day, the distant braying of elephants. The sharp pink-and-gold light in the early morning, and in the evening, a skyful of clouds that look as if they had been set afire. The curious company of Clever Hands and my new canine friend, Sukie. And the lineaments of gratified desire: love and love and freely conducted sexual bliss with my Lydia.

During all these long and good days on the Lawrence Ranch my vocal capacities exploded. How can I describe this? How can I possibly narrate it? Describing the process of learning to speak is like trying to bite your own teeth. It is like trying to describe what happened in a dream. We do not remember the process of learning our native tongues. At first my voice was high pitched, uneven, scratchy, screechy, breathy. You may have heard from my many deniers that the shallow vocal tracts of apes are not properly equipped for the production of articulate speech. That is like saying the legs of an infant are not properly equipped to run marathons—of course not, not *yet*—but given a lifetime of growth, training, exercise, nourishment and so on, they will be. And so my larynx descended as my neck straightened out, as I spent years walking upright and holding my head up high, like a man—and as I did my speech grew less uneven, became richer, smoother, more melodious in pitch, tone, and timbre, more relaxed in tempo, until the voice that you now hear arising from my lungs and exiting my body via my mouth developed its current condition. And the more I spoke, the more I began to understand the words I spoke. My understanding of the meaning of a word further solidified every time I said it. Soon I understood words as discrete bits of digital information, rather than purely as a flowing unbroken stream of analog information, and the more the digital paradigm of language replaced the analog, the more I grasped of grammar and of syntax, and the more and more easily I intuited the structural architectures of phrases and sentences—how a word, when uttered, affects the word that came before it and the word that will come after it, the word's relationships with its neighbors. The more I dared to speak, the more I thought in words rather than in pictures, in terms of tactile and visual information. See, an animal mind expends much energy in mapping the body's immediate physical surroundings; but language causes us, for better or worse, to forget this, and to think instead in abstract symbols that are physically evident nowhere but in our mouths, ears, minds, and memories. And the more abstract, the more *wordy* my thoughts became, the more my affinities and perceptions of the world became less and less pictorial and concrete.

I was helped along by a very particular combination of personal attributes that nature sprinkled in my genes: my ambition, my capacity for love, my awe, my hunger, my boundless desire—a voice that always cries forth within me, I want more, more, *more!* I happen to have a gift for language, and a love of it, which helped me to grasp the gestalt of a word as an utterance basically consistent in pronunciation and consistent in its possible sets of meaning and composed of components both tangible and abstract. That is to say, in one sense a word does not exist at all but in the harmony of shared understanding between speaker and listener, and this is the abstract component; but in the tangible sense a word is fueled by the exhalation of the lungs, the upward thrust of the diaphragm, is sculpted into existence by the throat, the lips, the teeth, the tongue. Most chimps can understand a verbal sign in the second sense, but not in the first. I, however, was able to connect the tangible signifier to the abstract signified, and so became the first chimp in history to learn to speak. To make this mental shift is something like realizing that a person still exists even though he has just walked out of sight behind a corner: likewise, a word still exists even when it is not being said.

It was also crucial to my linguistic development that during this two-year period of monastic meditation, concentration, isolation, and study, no one ever did a single test or experiment on me. I was no longer a lab animal, nor was I any longer treated as a pupil to be taught, but rather I was consistently treated by the humans at the ranch—and of course, by my favorite human in particular,

Lydia—as a fellow participant in *this* life, *this* society. I do not think I would have ever gathered up the courage to launch myself into the world of articulate communicative speech had I not been treated with such trust, patience, and kindness for such a prolonged period of time.

At first the other chimps were baffled by my newfound loquacity, but once they got used to it they quickly ceased to mind. Sukie, the dog, was not surprised in the least to hear human language pronounced by tongue of brute, and human sense expressed: it seemed to make perfect sense to her, and presented no particularly jarring experiential non sequitur to her vision of the way the world ought to be. Lydia—who knew me and knew me intimately, and as myself, as Bruno, rather than as simply "a chimp"—saw this delightful development as quite natural, and a long time coming. After they got over the initial shock of hearing me speak, Mr. and Mrs. Lawrence also grew accustomed to conversing with me. I do not know how much they knew about us, at first. Of course they knew that Lydia and I slept in the same bed (there was only one bed in our little house) but I don't know if they knew then that we had long been lovers. I doubt they would have looked down upon it—the wealthy and eccentric Lawrences were not stern moralists.

The days and months stretched on without much incident. The more I spoke, the clearer and smoother my voice became. My grammar and syntax were rapidly improving, and my vocabulary was swelling. Back in the beginning, I would have to hear a word spoken many times before it settled into the cement of my memory, but during this period of my great linguistic explosion, it rapidly became easier and easier for words to sink into my brain and stay there to effect their changes upon my neural architecture. My painting also vastly improved. I painted, I threw sticks into the whispering fields of grass for Sukie, the dog, to "fetch," I fed the animals, I petted the animals, I played games with Clever Hands, the frequent mute companion to my ramblings about the ranch, and I lay in blissful erotic love each night with Lydia. I came to know Lydia's corporeal matter so well that if, Gwen, you gave me enough clay, I could probably sculpt you an exact replica of Lydia's body—missing only the kiss of life—without omitting a single detail, right down to the orange mole on her ribs, about four inches below her left breast.

It was also during my time at the Lawrence Ranch that I learned to read. I do not believe my reading skills would have developed as quickly as they did were it not for Mr. Lawrence's library. See, it so happened that Mr. Lawrence was not only a titan of industry, a philanthropist, a viticulturist, and a lover of all animals but an avid bibliophile, and he had a great library stocked to the gills with texts, many of them rare and ancient. Mr. Lawrence obligingly allowed me to explore his library at will, and so once I finally did learn to read, I had already been addicted for some time to the printed page. I spent many an afternoon in Mr. Lawrence's library. Before I loved Mr. Lawrence's books as windows into information, or as players of silent mental music, I loved them simply as objects. Before I could read them, I would spend hours flipping through their thick old pages, looking at the complex illustrations in nineteenth-century children's books—the books of Lewis Carroll, Jules Verne, Robert Louis Stevenson—running my long purple fingers along the rough edges of the unevenly cut pages that sometimes stuck together in the corners (or that still had a few uncut pages from back in the days when every other leaf of a new book had to be surgically separated from its conjoined twin), inhaling the warm and sleepy smell of decaying pulp and yellowing glue. I kept a secret collection of the bric-a-brac I found flattened between the pages of some of these decrepit volumes: the delicate exoskeleton of a grasshopper; a mummified sunflower; a tamely pornographic daguerreotype of an ample-hipped and hairless woman twirling a parasol, naked except for ribbons and slippers; and what was surely a love letter, written in the femininely curvilinear hieroglyphics of some foreign alphabet and penned in blue ink. I secreted these clearly magical items in a shoebox, which I hid in a small dark place in the Lawrence house. No, I won't tell you where it is. As far as I know, it is there still. I hope that one day, maybe hundreds of years in the future, someone finds my little treasure chest, and ponders on the possible connections between these enigmatic artifacts.

Lydia taught me to read. She gave me reading the way she gave me language to begin with—but it was sitting alone for long hours in Mr. Lawrence's library, that beautiful room, sliding one book after another from their tight ranks on the shelves and inspecting their contents all day, following each line of text like a line of marching ants that was sure to lead somewhere interesting, which expanded and improved my reading, along with my knowledge of the world. In that sense I was an autodidact. In the early days I would have to sound each word aloud as I read, and later silently in my head, and then I came to a point at which each word was in a sense *heard*, in another sense *seen* (as a picture), and in yet another sense abstract. That is to say, when I read the word *cow*, at least three things occur in my mind: I hear the sound of an inner voice saying the word; I see the physical picture that these three letters make on the page (which is a symbol); and I half-see, on another plane in my consciousness, a kind of platonic-ideal image of a cow. And in these two latter senses of a written word—the physically pictorial and the purely abstract—a word is just *there*, on the page, not necessarily fully representative of sounds that exist in language outside of ink and paper, but ripe with unique qualities of its own. I am amazed that people can learn with so much ease to perform the metaphysical acrobatics that reading written language requires. The invention of writing and reading might be the single most miraculous achievement of the human mind.

So, to sum up: in time, all in time, I learned to speak and eventually to read at the Lawrences' ranch in Colorado. I admit that mine is a somewhat unusual memoir, Gwen, for several reasons. This is one of them: most memoirists do not feel weighed down by the onus of having to describe the process of learning to speak. That much is easily granted them. One wouldn't find it strange for a memoir written by a fully biological human to begin with something like "The first thing I remember is," or "My parents were poor but honest." We do not demand that human memoirists first explain how they became capable of language before getting down to the business of telling their stories. If one could teach a stone to talk, I'm sure the stone would forever thereafter live a life of unending frustration that its every conversation begins with someone being flabbergasted to hear its voice before listening to what it has to say. The stone would lead a lonely life of never being heard. What good is it being a talking stone in the land of the deaf?

So if our readers look through these pages searching for a water-pump moment, some great, finite, epiphanic ah-*ha* when language pokes a hole in my brain and comes trickling, then flooding rapidly in until my head is full, then I am sorry to disappoint them. It simply doesn't work that way. Everything is a process, nothing is instantaneous. Take for example this cup on this table, Gwen. Look at it. Try to imagine what it would look like to a silent-minded animal. It is not a cup, neatly separated by the word from everything around it. It is not a table, either. That cup and that table do not necessarily have anything in common with any other cups or tables in the world. Everything is immediate and everything is unique. But gradually, as words take root in your mind, without consciously realizing how you got there, there will come a day when you look at that cup and think, with coherent exclusivity, *cup*. You do not bother thinking also of the room the cup is in, or the gravity that anchors it to the table and the table in turn to the earth. That

object has been slotted away in a compartment of your consciousness reserved for a certain kind of drinking vessel, and now, upon
seeing it for the first time, you may fill it up with water and drink
from it without first being amazed that it exists. In a way language
is an inner death of that sense of perpetual amazement at the ever-
renewed world. But there's a lot of terror mixed in with that amazement, that constant process of discovery, terror that dies along with
that amazement, terror that we need to get rid of before we can get
down to the business of being human. We gain language and lose
the amazement, and afterward yearn to have it back, while at the
same time we are always using our words as sticks to beat back the
terror that crouches always just behind us, in our past, in our bodies, in our delicate animal selves.

XXV

After I had learned to speak and read English with some proficiency, Mr. Lawrence undertook to expand my mind: to instruct me in music, logic, philosophy, and the liberal arts—to guide me on explorations of the subjects that have as their focus the search for what it means to be human. He hired tutors in various subjects: there was a woman who came to the house from time to time to give me piano lessons, for example. I regret that I was never able to grasp the making of music. My hands are awkwardly shaped, and they did not conform easily to the dexterous motions that piano playing requires. Little matter, though. Mr. Lawrence would play me classical symphonies and opera. Mr. Lawrence and Clever and I would recline on the couches and chairs in his office, letting our minds be transformed and transported as *Eroica* boomed from his Bang & Olufsen speakers. I fell in love with classical music—especially Beethoven. Someone once said, Gwen, that the solar system consists of "Jupiter, and debris": similarly, I would say that classical music consists of Beethoven, and debris. What more is there to say about music, Gwen? I must agree with Nietzsche that life without music would be a mistake. It's a mistake anyway, but it'd be a worse mistake.

Mr. Lawrence also tried to instruct me and Clever in logic and philosophy. He built a small schoolroom in the big house, with a whiteboard on the wall and two little desks. There Mr. Lawrence in the role of professor spoke to us of Plato and Aristotle, Augustine and Aquinas, Hobbes and Locke, Rousseau and Montesquieu, Kant and Hegel. He spoke to us of history and politics, of mind and matter, of skepticism and faith, of natural right and the state of nature, of man and god and law.

Sometimes he would play us classical music while Clever and I sat on the floor and drew or painted or made little clay sculptures. Sometimes he would show us films of Shakespeare plays (this was my first exposure to the Bard). Mr. Lawrence insisted that we have exposure to the long golden procession of art and ideas, the great conversations throughout the history of human thought, all the sweetness and light of civilization, the sweetness and light.

I remember, for instance, Mr. Lawrence telling us about Xeno's paradox. For some reason I remember that lesson very clearly. It was presented to me in the illustration of a frog and a pond.

"Say there is such-and-such a distance between a frog and a pond," said Mr. Lawrence, and uncapped a black dry-erase marker, and with a few squeaky strokes on the whiteboard rendered an illustration of a tree, a tract of land represented by a flat horizontal line, and a pond. A sun with a face on it gazed down on the scene. He uncapped a blue marker and drew a squiggly line inside the pond—to indicate water—then with a green marker drew squiggly lines on the ground (grass) and in the fluffy top of the tree (leaves), and with a brown marker he drew a squiggly line inside the trunk of the tree. "The frog is sitting under the tree." Beneath the umbrage of the tree's canopy he drew a picture of a frog. The drawing looked like this:

"Now say the frog wants to hop to the pond," said Mr. Law-rence, and already I was remembering the image of my father, Rot-peter, raping the throat of an even less fortunate frog than this one. I shook off the unpleasant memory and tried to pay attention.

"But!—there's a problem: each time he takes another hop, the frog can only hop *half the distance* of the last hop."

What?—I thought, my mind beginning to roil—why?—what kind of bizarre hopping disorder afflicts this particular frog?

"So right away he hops halfway to the pond," and with a sweep-ing squeak of the black marker Mr. Lawrence drew a parabola that spanned from the frog, seated at the base of the tree, to a point about halfway across the plane between tree and pond, represent-ing the arcing motion of the frog's first hop.

"Then, on the second hop, the frog only hops half of the dis-tance he just hopped." Mr. Lawrence drew another arc, about half as big as the last one. "On the third hop, he can only hop *half* the distance of *that* hop, and then half of that and half of that..." Mr. Lawrence's voice grew quieter and quieter as the hops he was drawing dribbled into a squiggle that culminated in a static black blot representing the point at which the exponentially diminishing distances of the frog's hops had become unillustratably microscopic. Like this:

I glanced over at Clever, sitting in the schoolboy's desk beside me. Ours were the only two desks in the classroom. Clever was scratching the back of his neck and looking out the window.

"So then," said Mr. Lawrence, turning to face us. Clever dragged his gaze from the window to the whiteboard in a pretense of attention. "*When* will the frog reach the pond?"

I reasoned that although he was moving very slowly, the frog was in fact moving forward, so surely he had to get there at some point unless he died of thirst before reaching the pond, which at the rate he was going had to be a concern.

"Nope!" said Mr. Lawrence, with a certain pedantic pleasure

evident in his bright eyes and lips pursed beneath the snowy broom of his mustache.

"Clever?"

Clever shrugged his shoulders, more from apathy than ignorance.

"Because space is infinitely divisible," Mr. Lawrence concluded in triumph, "the frog will *never reach the pond!*"

But how could this be possible? I thought. As I remember, I pointed out that the frog himself must take up a certain amount of space, and I asked how it was that the frog could leap a distance shorter than the length of his own body. I looked at the illustration, eyeballed the size of the frog drawn beneath the tree and visually measured it against the amount of space that remained between the edge of the pond and the black blot at the end of the frog's trajectory where the hops had grown too tiny to see, and it looked to me that the yet-untraveled distance was shorter than the frog himself, so surely he was close enough to the pond that he could simply bend his lips to the edge of the water to drink. I remember asking this, and I remember Mr. Lawrence's response was twofold: (one) that he never said the frog wanted to go to the pond because he wanted to drink, only that he wanted to go there because he wanted to *be at the pond* (to swim, then? I wondered); and (two) that I was for the purposes of the thought experiment to ignore *the body of the frog*, that this was an abstract, mathematical frog, a frog who is merely a point in space devoid of volume, area, or any other dimensional analog. I could not even begin to fathom how a frog could be a volumeless point in space and still be considered a frog. And then I began to ponder the fate of this poor frog, who was doomed by his rare and improbable condition to die en route to his destination, so very close to it, within sight, within mere inches of the pond, yet effectively stuck there, out of reach of it. Much later, I would read the Greek myths about the cruel and ironical tortures that certain heroes had to endure for eternity in Hades: about Prometheus, shackled to a rock, whose liver regenerates in his body every night so that come the morning the eagle may disembowel him afresh; or Sisyphus, who must in endless repetition roll his rock uphill until he's moments away from finishing the job, when he loses his grip on it and must watch it tumble back to the foot of the mountain; or Tantalus, forced to stand forever in a pool within arm's reach of branches burdened fat with fruit, but doomed to everlasting hunger and thirst because the branches of the tree bend just out of reach when he tries to pick the fruit, and the water at his feet evaporates if he kneels to drink it; and studying these mythological punishments I recalled the unfinishable journey of Xeno's incorporeal frog, and wondered what it was about the psychology of this famous race of wisdom-loving ancients that made them so fascinated and horrified by the eternal wax-and-wane of favor and denial, of futile labors and frustrated desires.

After class was dismissed, Clever and I would be released to play outside. We would skip through the fields of grass with Sukie the dog, and play fetch, or go for long walks in the woods, or go to pet or feed the animals with Lydia.

When I had begun to speak articulately enough that people other than Lydia could understand me, Lydia extracted a promise from me: that for the time being, I would not speak to any humans who did not already know my secret. If I was in the presence of her, or the other chimps, or Mr. and Mrs. Lawrence, or Rita—all the people in the world who knew I could talk—then I could say all I liked, but around anyone else mum was the word. The reason for this moratorium on my speaking was that she wanted to keep me a secret from the world in order to give her as much time as possible to teach and study me in peace and without the winds of unwanted publicity and public outcry howling at the door. I complied with her request of my silence. I slipped up only once.

Clever and I would often take walks along the high metal fence that separated the vineyards from the free-range area of Mr. Lawrence's property. It looked much like the tall chain-link fence that surrounds the research center where I live now. Clever and I enjoyed conversations together, of a certain sort. Linguistically speaking, they were all very one-sided. I did all the talking, and he just made gestures that I failed to understand. I liked his company though, and he liked mine: we were friends. We were walking along the fence, with Sukie, the dog, yapping and panting about ten feet up ahead of us. Clever and I walked side by side. My hands were clasped behind my back, and I was in the middle of pontificating aloud on some ponderous philosophical subject, while Clever mutely listened, dragging a stick against the fence to make it go *clink-clink-clink-clink* as we walked.

"...and indeed," I was saying to Clever, "not even Augustine conceived of a God in terms of material imagination, yet for Kierkegaard—" I stopped cold, my thought truncated in midsentence. I had been so lost in my soliloquizing that I was startled by a small grubby-faced child standing just on the other side of the fence, looking out at us. Her star-kissed ink-black eyes were transfixed in an expression halfway between wonder and fear. She stood stock-still, silent. She had heard every word.

I looked past her. Up ahead, in the vineyard, in the aisle of dirt between two long fences covered in grape vines, was a group of vineyard workers. They were bent over their labor: picking the grapes and putting them in the big plastic buckets that hung from their fingers. They wore straw hats to keep off the October sun that glued their clothes to their skin with sweat. Some of them were barefoot; some of the men were shirtless. The little girl who had heard me speak ran off toward them. Clever and I stood there at the fence, trading nervous looks, unsure of what to do.

"Mamá, mamá!" said the girl. One of the grape-picking women looked up at her, put down her bucket and wiped about a gallon of sweat from her brow with the back of her hand. She visored her eyes with a hand and squinted at me and Clever, standing just beyond the fence at the edge of the vineyard.

"*¡Oí que el mono habla!*" said the little girl, pointing at me. "*¡Aquel mono puede hablar! ¡El mono puede hablar!*"

The men picking grapes all looked up at us and laughed. The little girl jumped up and down and shrieked in frustration.

"*¡Es verdad! ¡Oí que el mono hablaba!*"

The girl's mother sighed heavily and shook her head.

"*No estás tonta,*" she muttered, and went back to work. "*Imaginas cosas locas, Mercedes.*"

The girl stamped her foot in frustration. She ran back to us at the fence.

"Speak, monkey!" she shouted at me in English. "Speak again!"

I did not like doing what I had to do next. I shook my head no, and turned away from her. She was a child, and would never be believed. My secret was safe. I looked back as we were leaving and saw her beginning to cry. My heart was heavy. I took my leave of Clever's company and returned to the cabin, where I knew Lydia was. I wanted to be with the woman I loved, and to speak freely.

During our savage pilgrimage Lydia never ceased to feel uncomfortable with the Lawrences' generosity. She slowly lost all contact with the outside world. In a way she was as much a prisoner as I was. She fell completely out of touch with her old friends and family. Lydia's parents had both been dead for a long time, and she had become estranged from her brothers and sisters. She regretted this. They came from humble stock, she told me. The last she knew, all of her living family members remained in Arkansas. They were farmers, miners, carpenters, mechanics—none of whom lived much farther than a stone's throw from the house they grew up in. Her brothers and sisters were salt-of-the-earthers who were content to plod through unremarkable lives, the kind that Thoreau called lives of quiet desperation. She had fled her family into education. She was the first and only person in her family to go to college, much less graduate school, and when she came back to them with a master's and a doctorate, she found that they no longer spoke quite the same language. She said her parents had been alcoholics. I got this story in bits and pieces over the course of many quiet nights sitting by the fire or lying naked in bed, talking. She had been married. She had been pregnant, but the child had died inside her just before she was due, and she had no choice but to endure the agony of childbirth only to push from her body what she already knew was a corpse. Sometime afterward, her husband, who had been a young architect on the up-and-up, for his own various reasons jumped off the Congress Parkway Bridge and died. Then she met me. And devoted her life to me. She had no one left but me. And I devoted my life to her. We were devoted to each other. Sometimes in the night she would wake up crying. She would tell me it was because she did not know what she was doing. She would say that she had no clear plan for the future. A few years before, she had been happily married and expecting a child, and had a promising academic career ahead of her. Now she had lost her child, husband, and career. She had lost the respect of the scientific community and now found herself living as an indefinite houseguest in near isolation on a remote ranch in a strange place, and was furthermore the lover of an ape. This of course she did not articulate to me, but all things considered, I wonder if at the time she suspected she was losing her mind.

Lydia accepted the Lawrences' magnanimous hospitality, but she hated feeling like a parasite. I would ask her why we couldn't just live here forever. She would have no answer. Only that she knew that at some point our living situation would inevitably come to an end. Then we would make love again, and forget everything.

One would think that all this privileged peace would have alleviated the problem of her headaches, but it never did. In fact, in the course of these two otherwise happy years, her headaches even seemed to have gotten more frequent, longer in duration, and worse. She went to doctors in town—the closest town was fifteen miles down the road, the small mountain town of Montrose—but the doctors never knew what was wrong with her. They told her that her headaches were stress-related, psychosomatic, they were all in her head. Of course they're in my head, she would say, they're headaches. She worried. I worried, too, because I loved her.

XXVI

My memories of my time at the Lawrence Ranch in Colorado could fill a dozen thick and happy volumes for you to store on your bookshelf to await your occasional perusal like a set of encyclopedias whose editors have permitted articles only on subjects pertaining to love, wonder, and joy. But to tell of love, wonder, and joy is not what I am here to do.

Soon I will ask you to imagine my long purple fingers manually spinning the hands of an analog clock representing the period of time in which I have lived my life, and as I do, momentary snippets of my experiences over the course of these two years will fade in and out and blend together as the hands of the clock spin faster and faster, until the eye can no longer distinctly see the hands themselves, but only a radial gray blur. Then the hands of the clock will gradually slow down, until I've frozen them in place again, two years after Lydia and I first moved to the ranch. But before I ask you to imagine this, I am going to relate an important incident in the development of my young consciousness, which occurred about a year or so into our habitation at the ranch. I am going to tell you about the death of Hilarious Larry.

This was a significant event in the process of my ontogenesis: it was my first glimpse of death. I would come to know death more intimately later on, but this was my first real peek behind the curtain that beshrouds the stage of life. As I mentioned earlier, Hilarious Larry was an elder chimp, and just as it is no tragedy when an old man dies, neither is it a tragedy when an old chimp dies. I never got to know Larry well. He was always standoffish with me, distant, faintly suspicious, uncaring, unloving. Of us chimps who inhabited the ranch, Larry was both the least humanized and had suffered the most traumatic past. Larry wore clothes, yes, and yes, he ate his dinners and breakfasts with the rest of us in a civilized manner, at the table, with fork, spoon, and knife. But unlike me—and unlike, to a less obvious degree, my poor mute friend, Clever Hands—he had never asked to live this life, the life of a man. Samuel Johnson remarked that he who makes a beast of himself gets rid of the pain of being a man, and the converse of this is that he who makes a man of himself gets rid of the pleasure of being a beast. Larry had been kidnapped as an infant and then rudely thrust against his will into his mock manhood, which in the process had robbed him not only of his freedom and his savage dignity, but of the pleasure of animality that is the birthright of the beast alone.

In many respects Larry reminded me of my own father, Rotpeter. Like my father, Larry had not been born in captivity, but as a natural citizen of the state of nature. Like my father, he would learn at a heartbreakingly precocious age that life in the state of nature may be nasty, brutish, and short: he too most likely saw his family slaughtered when he was an infant. But Larry's subsequent imprisonment had been so much worse than my father's. Rotpeter had gone to the zoo, Larry to the circus. His experiences there had filled up his heart with disgust, anger, and loathing for human beings, in whose civilization he had been forced to live for most of his life, and this darkly colored his worldview. Now Larry was very old and very ill. He wanted to die. Larry could have been a great patriarch of

the jungle, a powerful and revered alpha male, proudly commanding his tribe of apes in the darkness of the forest. That was his true
destiny, which of course he was denied. Instead he was removed to
America, to sing and dance in a clown costume, to clap his hands
and juggle and ride a tricycle, to suffer a life of slavery and humiliation. Of course, he could never have gone back to the wilds. He was
accustomed to humans, he had undergone the injustice of being
socialized to them. And this was what he resented most of all. The
way he looked at me was never hostile (though at times I felt a note
of condescension in the dark silent music that issued from his eyes),
rather it was a look of incomprehension—incomprehension at my
desire to betray my species so openly, at my willingness to join
the ranks of this animal, man, who had proven himself to be the
enemy of all other things that are living. No, he never had much of
that yearning to join the human race that confused and perverted
the creature speaking to you now. Larry lived a life of torment and
exile, and I could no more have understood his psychology than
he could mine. I loved the artifacts of humanity—these things
of such great sweetness and light, all these jewels and candies of
human civilization: the paintings of Van Gogh, the final movement of Beethoven's Ninth, the architecture of a church, the taste
of wine, the singular beauty of an articulated word—these things
were motivation enough for me to join humanity, these things were
all it took to nudge my soul into a state of rapture. Hilarious Larry,
even if he had understood these things—though I do not believe
he ever could have—would have found nothing in his heart to love
them with. He would have preferred to spend his life beating his
chest, sleeping in the trees, and fucking in the mud beneath an
open sky, to move through the world in the sensory immediacy of
nature. What could Van Gogh or Beethoven have possibly given to
such a soul? Nothing. I cannot help but admire the obstinate purity
of such an attitude, and although I do not share it, my reflections

on it sometimes cause me to doubt the inner honesty of my own convictions on the fundamental goodness of art. And then, if I let them, my most pessimistic ruminations on this subject lure me to the thought that perhaps we must count all things of human artifice that outlast the very days of their creation as only so much pollution.

One evening, Lydia and I hiked the half mile or so between our peaceful little house and the big house that everyone else lived in, in order to join the others for dinner. Upon our arrival Mr. Lawrence informed us in solemn tones that Larry's illness had taken a severe turn for the worse. A curtain of respectful quiet had fallen over the house. Mr. Lawrence sat with us as Lydia and I supped on a modest meal of bread and tomato soup. Then we went upstairs to the bedroom that Larry and Lily slept in.

There lay Hilarious Larry, in bed, surrounded by his friends, his adopted family. I had last seen Larry a week or so before, and I knew he had been ill for some time—but since last I saw him he looked to have aged thirty years. He had been so stalwart, so stocky and meaty and hale before, but now he was thin, frighteningly thin. He must have lost forty pounds. The spirit of the big fat dominant male had left him, and his life itself was soon to follow it out of his body. His body was an old house being rapidly vacated by the energies that had inhabited it. It's a frighteningly awkward thing to stand around a deathbed. Does he want company as he breathes his last? What good is company?—give him the respect of space, let him die in the peace of his solitude. The blinds were drawn shut. It was dark except for a lamp in a far corner of the room. There was a sad foul odor, sewage, fetid water, rotten onions—which I supposed was the smell of a decomposing body, of death. Larry's long and hairy hands lay weak and limp on the red sheet that was drawn up over his ghastly thin body. I could see the depressions in his chest between his ribs through the sheet. His false teeth were in a

292 • Benjamin Hale

foggy glass of water on the bedside table, and his toothless face was caved and sunken. His eyes were each open a sickly slit, but they may as well have been closed for all they were doing. He wasn't looking at anything in particular. He glanced at us through the thick veil of his fever when Lydia and I entered the room as noiselessly as butterflies, and then he looked away. Regina Lawrence, her white-streaked red hair knotted in a long braid dangling behind her, sat with Clever Hands near the foot of the bed, holding one of his hands in hers, and Lily sat beside Larry's head, rocking her body methodically in her chair, which squeaked under her shifting weight, and she fondled the beads of a rosary in her long purple hands. No one spoke. Lydia and I sat down on unoccupied chairs and joined this somber company in the darkness, the silence, and the smell. I wondered how consciously Larry understood that he was dying. He did not seem to fear death.

We sat around his bed a long time. Regina went out and returned some time later with a cup of heated chicken broth. Chicken broth was something Larry liked. He liked the comforting warmth and saltiness of it. As he was too frail to lift it himself, Regina held the cup to his sunken withered lips. Larry submitted to take a sip of the hot salty liquid as Regina gently tipped the lip of the cup to his toothless mouth. He took a long sip and then gently pushed it away. His chest trembled with the labor of moving air in and out of his lungs.

The bed itself. It was an old and simple oaken four-poster bed, covered with red sheets. In the simply decorated white room, this bed gave it a feeling of a monk's room—a feeling helped along by the crucifix, an insistence of Lily's, that hung on the wall above the center of the headboard.

Regina set the cup of chicken broth on the side table and returned to her chair at the foot of the bed. Larry was shivering, despite the stifling warmth of the room. I watched Lily set her rosary in a clicking pile of beads on the bedside table, right beside the cup of broth and Larry's teeth in the glass of water. Then she took off her dress. In front of everyone, without so much as a sidelong glance in our direction, she struggled out of her dress, lifting the dark blue and white polka-dotted garment up and over her head. She shirked it from her body and onto the floor. Then she climbed into the bed beside Larry. Larry's feverish head turned toward her as she got into the bed. She scooted toward him beneath the red sheet, and Larry let his body crumble into hers, into her arms. And she held him. She took the dying old toothless chimp into her arms and pressed his head against her furry chest. She lay with him there in that bed beside him, embracing him, waiting with him for the life to leave his body, the pressure and warmth of her body easing his passage into death.

Clever looked at me, and our eyes met, and, I following his lead, we respectfully left the room. Regina and Lydia followed. Hilarious Larry died shortly thereafter. Peacefully, in his sleep, with Lily lying beside him. Actually, I have no idea whether or not his death was peaceful. All we know is that he died in his sleep. He had already passed away by the time the veterinarian arrived. We should not have sent for the vet, but for the priest.

For some reason the image of Larry's deathbed hauntingly remains burned into my memory like a scorch that lingers in the vision from looking too long at the sun. And I mean the bed itself, the thing in which he had slept during his decade of retirement at the Lawrence Ranch. Think about the bed. It is a symbol of both birth and death. A bed is a lucky thing to be born in, and it is an even luckier thing in which to die. I suppose it is a blessing to have a death as quiet as Larry's. It fit him. He was a creature of proud stoic resignation. I suppose that was why he was not afraid to die. Even if I manage to die in a bed, Gwen—which I suspect at this point I will—I do not expect my death to be like his. I am no Socrates, nor even a Hilarious Larry. I know I will not die with such peaceful bravery and grace. I know that I am a coward, and I will probably die like a coward, in the same way we are all wrested from the womb in the first place: kicking and screaming. I am afraid of death. I fear it and I hate it. I hate death because I love life. It's a morbid irony that an excess of love for life often leads one to a life dogged with fear and anger. Larry was not like that. He embraced death like a man reunited after a long separation with a childhood friend. Born in the jungle, raised in the circus, he died in a human house, in a bed. He turned his back on life and died himself a soft, domestic, taciturn death, not in his boots, but in his slippers. I cannot imagine myself doing that—at least not in the way he did it. Those who love life, who truly love it, love it to the point of jealousy, of rage, of sickness, of possessiveness and obsession—those who love life the most cannot help but be cowards. I suspect that I will die a violent and cowardly death, like a lover, even if I have to do it, like a lover, in bed.

———

There was a small funeral for Hilarious Larry several days later. His widow, Hilarious Lily, insisted on a Catholic service, even though Larry himself had never been a believer. It hardly matters: funerals are for the living. The service for him was held at the Sacred Heart of Mary Cathedral in Montrose. It was an old church, a rarity in the West. It was built in the nineteenth century with all the pomp and glory of old-fashioned religious architecture. It served a parish of mostly Mexican immigrants, and offered daily services in both English and Spanish. This was the church where Rita would take Lily on Sundays for confession and the service. Rita knew the priest—Father Malcolm—and Hilarious Lily's face was familiar to him, always sitting beside Rita in the first or second pew from the pulpit, her hairy head lowered in sincere genuflection. Of course he agreed to say the liturgy for her husband. Why shouldn't an ape go to his God as well? If he truly believed Christ was King of Men, then does it not follow, if one is also able to accept that all men are apes, that Christ was also King of the Apes? Much like Tarzan? I don't know what his logic was (not that there necessarily had to be any), but he performed Hilarious Larry's funeral rites as seriously as he would have for a deceased human. As Saint Francis—who could make peace between men and animals—did not find it odd to preach to birds and baptize the wolf, Father Malcolm did not find it odd to say the liturgy for an ape.

I had never been in a church before. There were not many people in attendance: just me, Lydia, Lily, Clever, Rita, the Lawrences, and several of the ranch workers. I was awed by the mysticism and magic of the ceremony. The costumes of the priest who delivered the homily and the men who walked up the aisle swinging jars of incense on thin golden chains, the recitations and chants in Latin, the beauty of it, all the colors and ornaments. I have never exactly wished that I was religious, but all the soul-stirring ritual of a Catholic funeral makes me understand something about it. How could anyone sit in a Catholic church and watch and listen with an open heart to the Requiem—the solemnity, the beautiful music, the Latin incantations—and walk away unmoved?

After the funeral we drove back home in a short chain of cars with the headlights on, where all that was mortal of Hilarious Larry was inhumed in a grave on the ranch grounds. Lily stood beside the grave in a black dress and lace veil while the casket was lowered into the earth and Father Malcolm scattered holy water from a wand and threw dirt on it as he said the Pater Noster. Afterward the others retired inside for the wake. There were cookies and punch. Lily did not join us. The small chapel the Lawrences had built for her on the ranch stood just a little off to the side of the big house. From the outside it looked like little more than a glorified toolshed with a cross on top of it. It was Lily's space; I had never been in it. I saw her walk away from everyone else and enter the doors of the little chapel. After mingling for a while around the cookies and punch bowl at the wake, I wandered outside onto the back deck to have a look at the deep red light of the late afternoon waning on the faces of the mountains, still in my little black suit but with my black tie loosened, with a plastic cup of punch in my hand. My feet crunched in the grass as I approached the little chapel. I quietly cracked the double doors and slipped my head inside. It was a small, windowless room, but beautifully built, with planed and polished rosewood wainscoting on the walls and a wooden ceiling and floor, ambiently underlit with dim soft lights, and an altar at the far end of the room. At the altar, an especially gory and emaciated Jesus hammered to an elaborate cross tipped his curly-haired and serene head heavenward. Candles flickered and dripped wax over the altar. I saw Hilarious Lily kneeling on a red prayer cushion before the altar with a lowered head and shut eyes, fondling the beads of her rosary. She touched her long fingers to her shoulders, head and chest, shoulders, head and chest, making the sign of the cross over and over. I went out and shut the door behind me.

That night, after the wake, I followed Clever outside, and we walked together through a field of dry waist-high yellow grass, shushing all around us in the wind. I was drunk, quite drunk, a bit too much punch singing in my veins, and my head wobbled groggily on top of my shoulders. It was a new moon, giving us perfect darkness to see the stars in. We came to a point at which Clever decided—following either a random decision or some unknown or arcane cue that remained invisible to me—to suddenly flop himself down in the grass and look up at the sky. I dropped down next to him. We were close enough to the house that we could see the lights in its windows and distantly hear the humans talking, but far enough away that we felt quite alone together, out here in the night, lying in this field. We heard a wire-thin crackle of coyote laughter from somewhere far away in the mountains. We gazed up together at the thousands and thousands of stars exploding across the clear sky of that moonless Colorado night in spring. It wasn't cold out, but it wasn't very warm, either. I think I may have even caught a cold, lying drunk in the field with Clever that night. We watched the sky until we could see the dim dots of satellites traverse it in the spaces of darkness between the stars. It caused me to think about space and time and the universe. There are two kinds of awe, I thought, and may have said so to Clever, who may have looked at me, mutely shrugged, and looked back at the stars. One kind of awe is what I feel when I look up into a clear night sky like this one. The other kind of awe is what I feel when I listen to music, or see a painting that I love, or when I watch Lily kneeling on her prayer cushion before the altar, praying. One is an awe at nature, and the other is awe at the wild irrational beauty of the mind. Are these awes in opposition to one another? Or are they, in some ter-rifying, spooky way, somehow connected? Clever just shrugged. I believe that all our philosophy—I said to him, on a roll now—all our religions and even our sciences, every human attempt to understand or explain ourselves, the world and our place in it—all our inquisitiveness, our superstition, our fear, our arrogance, all the ways in which we defend ourselves against the awe an animal feels when he stares into a starry black night like this one, the terror felt by an animal smart enough to ask but not enough to answer—has its roots in our understanding of time. We are animals cursed with cognizance of death; we know we will end, and while we do not remember beginning, we know and must believe that we began, and this belief in our own beginning makes us want to find out what happened before we all began, and further it makes us want to know how everything began. What happened in the beginning? Imagine this (I said to Clever): it is night—a clear cool night like this one, a bleak and hard night of a long time ago. The wind ripples the grasses of the rolling plains, predators cackle forebodingly far away (or maybe near). A primitive man, exhausted deep in his bones from the endless labor of daily persistence, pokes listlessly with a stick at the orange embers crumbling in the firepit. Sparks crack, smoke wafts upward, bright spirals of light skittle up from the throbbing ashes. Nearby, a drowsy child looks up at him, his face red in the dim firelight. He is almost asleep, his eyes languid but full of idle curiosity. He points at the rocks and the trees and the fire, and finally at the looming vault of sky above them haunted with ribbons of starsmoke, and asks his father—*How did all this come to be?* And the primitive father can only scratch his head, clear his throat and say—*Well, um, it's, uh . . .* (ahem) . . . *It's complicated. Gee, how do I put this . . . ?*—and then he proceeds to make something up, and he comes up with some crazy story that quickly spins into a mythos so bizarre and darkly beautiful that in time he's even managed to convince himself of its truth. And the story begins: In the beginning . . . In the beginning. In the beginning was . . . In the beginning was a cosmic egg. In the beginning the earth was without form and void, and darkness was upon the face of the deep, and the spirit of God was moving over the face of the waters. In the beginning was chaos, and chaos gave birth to the earth, the sky, the underworld, love and darkness, and the earth lay in love with the sky and gave birth to the sea. In the beginning was the earth, resting on the backs of four elephants standing on the shell of a turtle. And what was the turtle standing on? Another turtle. And what was that turtle standing on? You're very clever, young man—says the primitive father—but it's no use, it's turtles all the way down. In the beginning was the word and the word was with God and the word was God. In the beginning the entire universe was condensed into a single point of infinite mass, which suddenly blew up and made everything. And this was the beginning of time.

The beginning of beginnings, the beginning of Beginning. In the beginning was word. *A* word, or *the* word? Just word, my son, this was a time long before definite articles. In the beginning, somebody said let there be light. And there was. How did he/she/it know the word for light? How could the word *light* preexist the thing light? How was the universe brought into existence by the utterance of a word?

You see (I said to Clever) it is natural that we should think language somehow created matter itself, since language creates thought in our minds, creates the very question itself. That the world was birthed on the tongue, in the mouth, in the lungs, in the blood, in the brain, in electricity, in light. That it was the word itself that formed the world. That we were birthed not by a great otherness who sculpted us from dust, packed the clay on our bones, and inflated our lungs with the kiss of life, nor even by an unaccountable explosion ringing out in an unimaginable void—but by our very capacity for conscious thought. A word begets time and consciousness, and consciousness begets the curiosity as to what begat time before we were conscious, and this begets the question: What happened in the beginning? But maybe a wiser question to ask is, What *is* beginning? If we had begun with *that* question, then maybe we wouldn't get so twisted up in wondering what happened before the big bang, who uttered the cosmic word that brought us into existence, and what the turtle is standing on. Thus men forgot that all deities reside in the human breast.

At some point my monologue had become a dream, because I had fallen asleep in the field. Clever went back to the house to get Lydia. Clever took her by the hand and led her to the place in the field where I had fallen into drunken sleep beneath the stars. Lydia scooped me up in her arms and I half-consciously held on to her neck, which I kissed continually as she carried me to bed.

XXVII

Last night I found something in my memory that may be of interest to our readers, Gwen. It is one last relevant bit of dangling narrative in need of narrating from my time at the ranch, and once I have narrated it, then we may spin those hands of that clock into that time-blur that I have promised.

I could not sleep last night. Sometimes I have these bouts of insomnia. Nothing terrible—nothing at all like what Lydia used to have—but every so often I spend a restless night in bed, I thrash around in my sheets, with my mind turning over and over like the engine of a car stuck in neutral gear. I still haven't yet slept today, despite the fact that the unencumbered leisure of my daily schedule would not prevent me from filching a few hours' worth of a nap.

So, as I lay in bed last night, flipping my pillow over again and again to cool my sleepless cheeks, watching the rectangle of moonlight on my bedroom floor slowly slant into a rhombus, for entertainment I began rummaging through the toy box of my brain to see if I could find any old half-forgotten memories to play with. And what I found buried toward the bottom, dusted off and examined with curiosity and a sudden gush of remembrance was this interesting hippocampal artifact. In my sleeplessness, I remembered an incident that happened at the ranch—I can't exactly remember when it was, but I know that it was near the end of our stay there. I'm pretty sure that we left the ranch at the end of a summer, or the beginning of a fall. So, seeing as we arrived there in a winter, I guess we spent more than two years there, more like two and a half. Wait a moment, Gwen, the fog of my memory is lifting...lifting...I can almost see it...ah-*ha!* Yes, there it is. I see it clearly now. Just as I suspected: this happened on the Fourth of July. Independence Day. I also remember that it involved a hot tub.

There was a hot tub embedded in the wooden back deck of the big house. Wait, how could this have been in the summer? I remember very clearly the steam that was rising off the surface of the water. No, it was summer, because even midsummer nights can get quite cold at those altitudes—hence the steam. It was night. The color of the water—that I remember exactly: it was absolutely aquamarine, and glowing, as if it contained mysterious radioactive agents. Lydia is sitting in the hot tub. I am sitting in the hot tub. Mr. and Mrs. Lawrence are sitting in the hot tub. It is the Fourth of July.

That is a holiday I sometimes miss in my current confinement. I haven't seen a Fourth of July since I've been sequestered here in the Institute. I am told—and I believe—that the first time Lydia took me to a Fourth of July fireworks celebration (in my mind the Fourth of July was a celebration that celebrated fireworks), I spoke of stars. This was in Chicago. I, Bruno, borne in her arms, was swaddled in the oversized green hooded sweatshirt that I would wear on our outings into human society. She took me to the fireworks celebration at Navy Pier on the Fourth of July. The sounds, the clicking and binging and whirring noises everywhere, the music threading through the atmosphere, the giant Ferris wheel: Navy Pier. When the music that accompanied the fireworks began to blare from the crackling loudspeakers and the fireworks began to shriek into the sky to detonate themselves above our heads, she said that I pointed

up to the sizzling clouds of smoke and sparks, I pointed up at them
with my long finger and distinctly said, in a voice slow and breathy
with awe: "Stars!" Stars! Stars! STARS!

(It should be noted, however, that during the summers Chicago
for some reason elects to discharge a battery of fireworks into the
sky from Navy Pier *every single Friday and Saturday night*, and thus
Chicago is a city spoiled rotten with fireworks, like a silly child
who eats her favorite food every day until she loses the taste for it.
So on the Fourth of July they compensate simply by shooting off
lots and lots of fireworks!—which is admittedly an uncreative solu-
tion to the problem of pyrotechnic desensitization that arises from
that city's powerful thirst, her loving greed to smell the sulfur in
her nose and to hear these ballistic hosannas and to see these wild-
flowers of energy blooming in the sky and reflected on the surface
of her lake. I have said earlier that Chicago is curmudgeonly in
the winters. Yes, but in the summers—perhaps, in fact, in order to
amend for her frigid behavior most of the year—in the summers
Chicago is no longer Chicago-that-somber-city, but instead is a
wild rich child of a city, who demands to eat her cake and ice cream
every single day—and the weakhearted people of the city give it to
her, they give it all to her because they love her, they spoil her, just
because, even if she doesn't deserve it, they love to see the beautiful
look on her face when she gets what she wants.)

Fourths of July were more subdued in Colorado, but no less
beautiful. Many animals are terrified of fireworks, but I have never
been one of them. Animals are afraid of fireworks because they
do not understand them. To them, fireworks are an aberration—a
frightening hole in the fabric of their accepted universe—whereas
I, Bruno, share man's love of fire. I too have plucked the red flower.
I have joined the pyromantic primates. In my younger days, so long
as Lydia was near, I never really feared a thing if I could see that
she wasn't afraid of it, and this included the potentially disturbing

phenomenon of the inky firmament above us opening up with screaming bursts of colored fire. At the ranch, we had to sate ourselves with watching the Fourth of July fireworks display put on by the nearby sleepy mountain town of Montrose, Colorado, which was situated in the lap of a valley that we could see down into from the deck of the big house at the Lawrence Ranch, perched at the top of a long gradual slope of mountainside that spilled into the valley below. We sat on the deck at nightfall and watched from a great distance the fireworks that the people of Montrose shot into the summer air for themselves. From our high vantage point at the crest of the valley, watching the fireworks shoot up out of the town from miles away was like watching the destruction of a Sodom or Gomorrah in reverse, the fire and brimstone falling not from heaven to earth, but shooting up from the earth to make war against heaven. And we looked down into the valley, and lo, we did not turn to salt.

We could barely even hear the fireworks. The bullets sang up from the town's cluster of lights, rising to their designated heights and no higher, where they exploded into shimmering umbrellas of sparks and made noises that arrived late to our ears, noises that after running up our slope of the valley had been reduced to little pops no more impressive than the sounds of string-tethered corks pneumatically thrust from the muzzles of popguns. *Pop!... pop-pop!...pop!* And, like a giant clumsy child with a brimming bucketful of light, the fireworks carelessly splashed their waves of artificial color—red, yellow, blue, green—all over the faces of the mountains on either side of the wide dark valley.

Obviously all the animals on the ranch were terrified of the spectacle, but there was little that could be done to comfort them. They heard the shrieks and bangs distinctly from far away; the elephants felt the vibrations of them in their big flat feet, all the ungulates huddled together for protection; the birds hid their heads beneath their wings and the burrowing animals burrowed deeper into the earth. In their benighted animal minds, stars were not supposed to swing so low. The night was supposed to be silent and dark. These things could be the portents of disaster, the end of the world or the beginning of a new one.

We were sitting on the deck drinking white wine, wine from Mr. Lawrence's own vineyard. The other chimps had gone to bed. Or, I recall that Larry and Lily had gone to bed—was this before the death of Hilarious Larry?—it couldn't have been—so it was just Lily who had gone inside to retire for the night. Where was Clever? Clever had curled up and fallen asleep in a deck chair. Lydia is sitting in the hot tub. I am sitting in the hot tub. Mr. and Mrs. Lawrence are sitting in the hot tub. It is the Fourth of July. Is Lydia wearing her canary yellow bathing suit? Yes, let's say she is. So much of her smooth beautiful skin on display for eyes that are not entirely mine. I do not particularly like water—I mean, I drink it, yes, but I don't like my body being *in* water—few chimps do. We cannot swim because our bodies are too dense. I just dabble my toes a few millimeters deep into the swimming pool, feel the bone-chilling shock of it, and jerk them back, thereafter flatly refusing to submerge my body any further in the vile stuff. But I don't mind the feeling of being in a hot tub. The Lawrences' hot tub was embedded in their deck and shaped roughly like a kidney, a kidney full of warm aquamarine water, caused to glow from within by underwater lights, and steaming and bubbling like a witch's brew. A hot tub is different from a swimming pool. Lowering oneself into a hot tub is like lowering oneself into a tank full of amniotic fluid, like slipping back into the womb. And the Lawrences' hot tub featured a certain switch that when switched incited torrents of bubbles to shoot into the water from a series of holes in the tub's smoothly curving inner walls. I would press the switch again and again, and position myself right in front of one of these holes to let my body be massaged by the pressure of the jet thunderously farting out a hot stream of bubbles. We were all sitting in this hot tub. There were no more fireworks. The fireworks had come and gone away.

Are the humans drunk? I don't know. Probably. They never permit me to drink very much. Each of us is sipping a glass of white wine. No, I am not. I have already had my allotted fill tonight, but the three humans are still drinking wine. They are holding and drinking from glasses full of wine while actually sitting in the tub at the same time, occasionally setting the glasses on the surface of the deck. Everyone has his or her arms stretched over the lip of the tub in poses of relaxation. They are talking. Mrs. Lawrence and Lydia are enjoying some sort of conversation, while Mr. Lawrence contentedly looks on. I am enjoying the sensation of the bubbles massaging my back. I don't remember what is said here, but I think Regina Lawrence is the one who just said it, and I remember that whatever it is that has just been said has caused Lydia to blush. I can almost feel the temperature of the already-warm water rise a degree or two from the sudden heating of Lydia's blood.

"No, no," Lydia denies, speaking to Mrs. Lawrence as I glance over at her. Lydia is shaking her head vigorously back and forth, and her hair—which at this point has grown long again—is wet, and slaps her face as she shakes her head. But Lydia is not seriously upset: she is smiling, smiling a smile that threatens to erupt into a laugh, despite the fact that she is vehemently denying whatever Mrs. Lawrence has just accused her of. Her almost-laughter is half-gleeful and half-nervous. Is she drunk? My God, yes: she's drunk.

"Don't think we're stupid," says Mrs. Lawrence, smiling also, to soften the aggressiveness of the comment. Regina Lawrence's titanic breasts are pushed together by the top of her crimson bathing suit. She is leaning into the area of her husband's body where his lean arm meets his chest, which is wet and furry with curly white hair. "I can tell when a woman's in love."

Lydia says nothing. The gods of Smile and Frown war for dominance over Lydia's expression. After a long struggle, Smile emerges victorious. Then she laughs, but covers her mouth as if her laughter were a cough or a hiccup.

"Don't worry, darling," says Regina Lawrence. "We're no puritans ourselves."

I look again at Lydia, whose smile and laughter have gone from her mouth, and whose eyes are now staring down into the aquamarine depths of the warm, steaming water. I look into the water, too, trying to see what she might be looking at. Then I look up at the stars. *Stars! Stars!* Then my gaze settles halfway between the water and the stars, and I look at Mr. and Mrs. Lawrence, sitting directly across from us in the hot tub. I notice that a cloud of tension, without my realizing exactly when, has recently entered the airspace between us. I look over at Clever Hands, my mute companion, who is fast asleep in the canvas seat of a lounge chair on the deck, about fifteen feet away from us. Clever lies in the chair, slack-limbed and snoring. Sukie, the dog, is curled up asleep on the deck directly beneath Clever's chair. I look back at Mr. Lawrence, and see what may or may not be a wild look of sex in his eyes behind the foggy shields of his glasses.

Then I see something floating on the surface of the water. The bubbles rising from the bright depths of the tub bat the thing around on the steaming surface of the water. It looks like a lily pad, or a dark red flower, some sort of floating vegetable matter for a frog in a swamp to sit upon. It floats around aimlessly in the water between us, in the middle of the tub. I stare at it, transfixed. I realize that it is the bottom portion of Regina Lawrence's swimsuit.

In the vast darkness beyond the deck, the night is ferocious with the rhythmic chirping of crickets. There must be a cricket hiding under every leaf out there. The din they make deafens one, their incessant *krreepa, krreepa, krreepa*. Very far away, a band of coyotes cackle in the mountains. For a moment, nobody moves.

Seeming eons and probable moments later, more articles bubble up to join the limp red rag of material floating on the surface of the smoking blue-green water. Regina Lawrence sets her wineglass on the surface of the deck, settles into the water till it comes up to her chin, then resurfaces, and as she does, the upper portion of her swimsuit now also floats to the top of the water. The voluminous cups of her swimsuit top drift around in the glowing water like the bulbous red eyes of a sea monster whose body lurks just below the surface. Now Mr. Lawrence gradually worries his Speedo down his legs, and that too rises up to the surface from below the gurgling water. I look blankly across the water at them, across these three pieces of fabric floating in the tub like dishrags, and at Mr. and Mrs. Lawrence, whose blurry and pale bodies are now completely naked beneath the bubbles and the steam that wafts up into the atmosphere from the pale blue-green water. Mrs. Lawrence's breasts bob on the surface of the water for all the world like the bodies of two plucked geese. And her nipples. I must draw special attention to her nipples. *What nipples!* I've never seen such nipples. Lydia—Lydia has these tiny pink buttons for nipples, like the sweet little eyes of a white rabbit—but *these?*—*these* nipples are like big fat mushy cookies! I cannot *help* but stare! I flick a sidelong glance at Lydia. What in the world is she doing? Her breathing is heavy and irregular. Her breathing is heavy and irregular, coming into her in gulps of breath and going out of her in staggered shivers. I recognize that look on her face: the inner corners of the eyebrows tending upward, the eyelids half-closed over eyes that are not seeing, an expression of pleasure so intense it is almost an expression of pain. I recognize that look on her face and I recognize that cadence in her breathing. This is what she looks like, this is how she breathes when we are in the preliminary stages of making love. I look down: down into the glowing blue water. It's hard to see in the steaming, wobbling water, but my eyes are able to ascertain the following information: (one) Regina Lawrence has at some point in the recent past diagonally extended one of her trunk-like naked legs across the middle of the tub; (two) she has placed her bare foot in the crux of Lydia's groin; (three) the big toe of this foot has managed to maneuver itself beneath the fabric of Lydia's canary yellow swimsuit; (four) this toe is currently employed in the business of sensuously rubbing the flesh of what may or may not be Lydia's clitoris. The naked Lawrences begin to scoot toward her, with clear prurient intent. At this point Lydia inadvertently drops the glass of wine that she has been holding in her hand this whole time, but about which she has recently forgotten. It happens like this: deeply distracted, her fingers involuntarily loosen their grip on the thing, which plops into the aquamarine water; the wine in it spills into the water; for a brief moment the wineglass floats on the surface like a boat before the bowl of the glass fills up and the vessel capsizes, goes under, and plummets, surprisingly quickly, straight down into the tub, where it gets caught in one of the thundering streams of bubbles issuing from the holes in the sides of the tub, which shoots it through the water and smashes it against the other side of the tub. The glass shatters, noiselessly.

"Fuck!" said Lydia, as we abandon the present tense. She slapped a hand to her mouth. "Oh, no—oh—I'm sorry, I'm so sorry—"

Her face was red, her eyes flickered with blinks. She sucked in a giant swallow of air and straightened herself. She straightened herself like you straighten a bent wire.

"Nobody step in it!" said Mr. Lawrence, always trying to be helpful.

"I'm sorry, I'm sorry," Lydia kept saying. Her muscles and nerves had been infused with an inexplicable sense of frenzy. "Let's get out, Bruno. I think it's time for bed."

When she said this everyone clambered out of the tub as if a poisonous snake had just been dropped into the water. Lydia extended a hand to me to help me out. I shivered violently. I despised the cold shock of the air on my wet body. The water flattened my fur heavy against my skin. Mr. and Mrs. Lawrence's pink and dripping naked bodies fished around in the bubbling water for their sopping garments. Mr. Lawrence was covered with wiry white hair. Mrs. Lawrence was plump and jiggly. Her wet gelatinous breasts slapped around like fish. Mr. Lawrence's semierect penis was crimson—bright crimson!—before he hurriedly stuffed it back into the genital pouch of his Speedo swimsuit. Lydia vigorously rubbed me down with her towel until all my fluffy fur crackled with static electricity, and then she vigorously rubbed herself half-dry with it before she began, in frantic whips and jerks, to put her clothes back on over her canary yellow swimsuit. Mr. Lawrence busied himself with the job of draining the hot tub—to safely get at the broken glass, I suppose. Regina Lawrence, her sleek body reminding one of a porpoise, approached Lydia.

"I'm sorry, darling, I—"

"No, no," said Lydia, quickly. "Please, don't be sorry. It's fine. Everything's fine."

"I hope you're not upset. Dudley and I thought maybe you would be open to—"

"I'm not upset at all. Just tired. Please don't worry. We're going to bed. It was a wonderful evening. Really."

"If you like. But don't leave us like that. Come on, now."

Regina Lawrence opened her arms to her for a hug. She was again wearing both parts of her bipartite red swimsuit. Lydia, now fully clothed, placed herself into her embrace. The wet skin of Regina Lawrence's body dampened Lydia's clothes.

Now Lydia and I, holding hands as we walked along the narrow trail of gravel, headed back to our little house on the Lawrence

Ranch, a half a mile away from the big house. The lights in the big house were still on behind us. Our feet crunched along the gravel path, and the crickets all chirped their cricket song in the grass.

———

And now, if you would, please imagine the hands of that symbolic clock that I promised you earlier, spinning themselves faster and faster into a symbolic radial blur. Time passes. After our extended stay at the Lawrence Ranch, Lydia and I moved back to Chicago. When we finally returned from our Ovid-like exile in the wilderness, I could speak, read, and write the English language and had received some of my sentimental education. In fact, it may not have been long after the memory I just related that Lydia and I left the Lawrence Ranch and returned to Chicago. I honestly don't know why exactly we left the Lawrence Ranch when we did. I won't pretend to know how much—if at all—our re-relocation to Chicago had to do with this curious incident that I found last night in my memory-box. But our move back may have had to do with many other factors as well. For one thing, I think Lydia missed the city, as did I. She missed its familiarity; she missed feeling her independence. She did not enjoy feeling like a perpetual houseguest. She missed the place she had called home for nearly ten years. We thanked the Lawrences for all their financial support, their kindness, their enduring, tireless, and outrageously generous hospitality. We tearfully said good-bye to Dudley and Regina Lawrence, and even more tearfully to Hilarious Lily, and to Sukie, the dog, to the memory of Hilarious Larry, and most tearfully of all to Clever Hands, who signed *Good-bye!* to us and kept on waving, even as Lydia's car was tumbling over the washboards down the narrow dirt road. The sun may have been setting—or rising—painting the mountains behind us in majestic colors. And we left.

Part Four

threadsuns
Above the grayblack wastes.
A tree-
high thought
grasps the light-tone: there are
still songs to sing beyond
mankind.

                    —*Paul Celan*

XXVIII

I apologize that it's been so long since our last session, Gwen. You know I was extremely busy with *Woyzeck*, which you saw us perform last week. I honestly wasn't thrilled with the way the performance turned out. We took our bows at the end of it, and our audience applauded when it was time to applaud. I have fallen so far from the zenith of my theatrical career, back when Leon and I put on our epic production of *The Tempest*. That was more than ten years ago now.

Don't worry, Gwen, I'm not offended that stage fright prevented your acting in my play. I am afraid our production was amateurish at best. Chimps are very difficult to direct. I'm seriously considering learning the dark art of puppetry. Puppets would be more obedient actors.

I'm concerned about Leon. Leon is now over sixty. He has a moist eye, a dry hand, a yellow cheek, a white beard, a decreasing leg and an increasing belly, every part about him blasted with antiquity. His gait is slow and uncertain, his flesh doesn't have the sanguinity it used to. A man of great heart and courageous stomach, he's been dragging his body through hell all his life. He looks much older than he really is. Leon is the best and the last great friend I have left in the world, and I'm afraid it may be sooner than I'd like that I'll lose him, too. Freud observed that to love anyone is to give fate a hostage. These days, when I see Leon, I can almost see fate standing behind him with a knife pressed against his fat throat. I'm afraid for him. I will miss him when he's gone. We have heard the chimes at midnight. That we have, that we have.

Our performance of *Woyzeck*, as I'm sure you observed, was marred by an irritating accident. There is a train track that passes right outside the grounds of the Zastrow National Primate Research Center, situated somewhere in rural Georgia, USA. Every once in a while—probably three or four times a day—a freight train thunders by the research center. It makes a deafening noise, usually accompanied by a long, low blast from its horn and an uncertain shuddering of the earth, during which everything in this place is set to slight wobbling. The apes—by which I mean the animal apes, the non-enculturated chimps, bonobos, and orang-utans who live in this research center—they love it. They are so mystified and enchanted and terribly impressed with all the phenomena that occur every time a train passes. During these few minutes of rumbling, bellowing, and earth-shaking that happen several times daily, they all—down to an ape—commence to jump up and down, clap their hands, howl and pant-hoot and scream in wonder and irrepressible joy. And, as bad luck had it, at the absolute emotional climax of the play—the moment when Woyzeck murders his wife in a fit of jealous rage—what should happen, but that goddamn train decided to blast by outside the research center. As I staggered onstage with angst-haunted eyes and the retractable-bladed plastic toy knife in my hand, that stupid train chose that particular moment to blow its stupid horn and come rolling its stupid way along its stupid tracks, and at that moment, all the walls of our onstage narrative—fourth, third, second, first—instantly came crashing down, and not in a good way. All the chimps on the stage (except one) and all the chimps in the audience, when they heard that train roaring by, felt instantly compelled to start jumping up and down, clapping, hooting, howling, and screaming out in joyous rapture—completely ruining my play. All of my actors immediately forgot their roles, and were no longer characters in one of the greatest psychological dramas of early modern theatre, but were just chimps again, enthralled with a train.

The train passed, the apes recovered, and we forged ahead with the few minutes of the play that remained. But the moment had been ruined, and the time was irrecoverable. I almost cried. I wonder if those clear-minded creatures would be so impressed by passing trains if they understood what they were. To them, the trains mean only that for a few minutes, for some reason, the predictable behavior of the universe has been briefly upended. Suddenly nature has gone unaccountably bonkers, something has replaced the stillness and quiet of the outside world with a circus of sound and vibration. So they all clap and hoot and howl at the spectacle, because they do not know what it means. Whereas I, Bruno, am forever doomed to know what it means, and I can only peer out the window of my prison and wonder not about what makes this dangerous magical noise in the darkness beyond our walls, but about where that train might be going, where it is coming from, what it might be bringing to the free people of the world.

So, for whatever reason or convergence of reasons, Lydia and I were back in Chicago. I wonder why we were there again, after the Lawrences had for so long afforded us so much unabated peace and comfort in Colorado. I'm not even sure how it was we were surviving. Lydia wasn't working. Where was the money coming from, Lydia? I wish I could ask her now. Why did I never ask her? Was I not curious? Such things were so outside the sphere of my childish concerns that I never thought to ask such questions. Once again we were living at 5120 South Ellis Avenue. It was fall. The skies were gray and the denuded branches of the trees rattled against the punishing autumnal winds. We found our apartment much as we had left it, although the walls and carpets had taken on the smells of the tenants who had inhabited it during our long vacation. Lydia's renters had somehow made the apartment smell like a cheese factory, and we wondered what unsavory acts they might have committed within these walls. More unsavory than mere bestiality? No, Gwen, that *mere* is not in any sense ironic: I am not a beast.

For a time, Lydia and I took daily walks through the leafy and imperious campus of the University of Chicago. Our old haunts! Lydia's former place of employment. What in the world were we doing there, Lydia? Why didn't I ask you any of these questions at the time? When you could still speak, and were still alive? Sometimes we would stroll, hand in hand, down the length of Fifty-seventh Street, Lydia stopping occasionally to purchase things from stores: a notebook, a cup of coffee, a candy bar for me, a long-stemmed green rose to take home and put in a jelly jar of water.

The neighborhood seemed to have changed relatively little in the two years we were gone. The same buildings were all in place, the same trees, the same landmarks. We would often see the same people—the same old lady in the bright blue coat and pink scarf who would often be standing at such-and-such a particular bus station at such-and-such a particular time, the same man walking the same dog, and so on. Some stores and restaurants had gone away and been replaced by other establishments, or were vacant, or new establishments had opened in formerly empty places. I resignedly resented every little change. You know a place is home when you resent change. When we were at home in the apartment I listened: but no sound came from upstairs. No squawking parrots, no moaning bagpipes. Where had Griph Morgan gone? There was nothing but silence upstairs, and no smells, either—no more eau de boiling beans and parrot crap. Soon after we returned, I began a daily pilgrimage of galumphing up the stairs to bang on Mr. Morgan's door, in hope that maybe he would one day materialize behind it. It was a hopeless exercise that grew more hopeless each day I did it, but I did it every day. Or should I say it was the opposite of hopeless?—it was a vainly, absurdly hopeful exercise. Griph Morgan's door became more like a pagan idol at an altar or an oracle for whom I would leave offerings: I did not expect a reply, but nevertheless kept at it, hoping for any small sign, suspiciously, irrationally ready to interpret a flock of birds or a change in the weather as an effect of the cause of my homage. Every day I knocked on his door and called his name, and every day the door remained shut, and the space behind it silent. But absence of evidence is not evidence of absence—like a true believer, all I needed was continued hope and continued silence to continue asking.

Around this time I also noticed a subtle change—or at least a change in my perception—in the way people on the street, or in the stores we went to, interacted with Lydia. They spoke to her more slowly and more cautiously, treading on eggshells. The clerks in the stores gave her what she wanted and then quickly sought to get rid of us. Sometimes people gave her confused or concerned or distrustful looks. Many people tried very hard to avoid eye contact with us at all.

In retrospect, I may allow myself to surmise that perhaps Lydia had become known to the local inhabitants of the area as "that crazy woman who walks around everywhere with her chimp." In retrospect, rumors about Lydia and her past ("She used to teach at the university?"—"She was fired?"—"Some suspect her of..."—"With the *chimp*? Really? No...") may have been swirling. In retrospect, I realize that even many months after moving back into our—in retrospect, dingy—apartment in Chicago, we still had never fully unpacked our boxes from the move. In retrospect, I realize that Lydia wasn't taking as much pride in her appearance as she used to—that her hair was often tangled and unkempt and unclean, that her smart, crisp style of dress had been largely replaced by sweat-pants and floppy-sleeved dirty sweaters. I also remember how, during this time, her headaches and her insomnia were so miserable, and so miserably frequent, that she was taking her knockout drops not once or twice a month but *every single night*, and every morning she would drag herself out of bed as if from out of a pit of mud.

And then, one morning, one morning amid all this disturbing directionlessness, Lydia rolled—literally—out of bed, and fell face-down on the floor. She was wearing her nightgown. The bedroom was stacked full of unopened cardboard boxes. It was late—almost noon (we rose to greet the day late during this confusing period in our lives). I shook her. She didn't wake up. I turned her over.

"Lydia?" I said.

"Mmmmnnnnnnnnhhhhgh," she said.

Her eyes opened briefly to slits, and then shut again. Her pretty blond head flopped over to one side, cheek to the carpet. Her face was—was *twitching*. Her cheeks and nose and lips were making all these quick, erratic jerking movements. Her body was jerking and flopping around all over, like a fish just hauled from the sea. I shook her again, again she grumbled incoherently, flopped around and twitched. My confusion quickly became fear. Then I aimlessly ran around the apartment for a while. Then I shook her again.

"Lydia?"

"Mbbrrmmngnnn," she said, without even opening her eyes. She had quit shaking and twitching, and now she was just lying limp with a lolling head and eyes aflutter on the bedroom floor. I screamed a primal scream of terror. I shook and shook and shook her with my hands, and Lydia continued and continued and continued to not wake up.

I thundered out of the front door of 5120 South Ellis Avenue, Apartment 1A. I ran around for a while in the yard in front of the building. I was still wearing my pajamas. My sky-blue pajamas were spangled with representations of superheroes, such as Batman and Superman. I looked up at the day through the bare brown canopies of the deciduous trees in front of our apartment building. The sun was out and the light was yellow and bright and crisp, but despite that it was cold, with a cutting wind. The wind whipped up dervishes of dead brown leaves on the sidewalk and in the street. I think this was in October. No one was out on the street, except for a woman in a puffy red coat up ahead of me on the other side of the street, walking a Doberman.

"HELP!" I shouted at her. The Doberman began to woof barbarically at me, and the woman checked him with his leash, and then turned heel and went the other way. Then I ran back into the apartment building, clattered up the entryway stairs and began battering my chimp fists against the door of 5120 South Ellis Avenue, Apartment 2A. I banged on the door until my fists were mushy with bruises. I'm surprised I avoided bashing my hands to bags of blood and broken bones against that door.

"HELP! HELP! HELP!"

The door remained obstinately shut, obstinately silent. I continued to bash my fists against it and scream for help. After I do not know how many minutes or hours of this, another door down the hallway squeaked narrowly open.

"What's goin' on out there?" demanded a voice. I wheeled around to look at the door. I could not see the person who stood behind it.

"Help!" I said. "Where's Mr. Morgan? She won't wake up! She won't wake up! HELP HELP HELP HELP HELP!"

"The guy with the parrots?" said the dark sliver of space behind the door. It was a deep, throaty, dry, cracked voice, a sleepy voice, a woman's voice?

"Yes!"

"He died." The voice cleared its throat. "He passed away a few months ago."

What could I do? Gwen, the world was reeling and crashing all around me! My panic had now spiked into an apoplectic crescendo. Griph Morgan? He was DEAD. What if Lydia WAS GOING TO DIE TOO?

Grace under fire? Ha. Far from it. I am not a little ashamed to admit that I was flailing my arms in the air and rattling around in the hallway like a Ping-Pong ball.

"AAAAAAAAAAAAAAAAAAAAAAAAAAAAAAAAAAAAAAA-AAAAAAAAAAAAAAAAAAAAAAAAAAAAAAAAAAAAAAA-AAAAAGGGGGGGGGGGGGGGGGGGGGGGGGGGGGGHHHH-HHHHHHHHHHHHHHHHHHHHHHHHHHHHHHHHHHH," I said.

The door down the hallway thumped shut, and my heart fell into my bowels. Then it sailed back up into my throat as I realized that the person behind mysterious door number three had only closed it in order to unhook the chain, and now the door was swinging open to its full width to reveal the possessor of the voice that had spoken, who was a heavyset middle-aged black woman. She was wearing glasses and a bathrobe. She looked and acted like I had just woken her up.

"What the heck are you screaming your head off about?" she said.

"Come on," I said, and grabbed her hand. "Lydia isn't waking up."

"You live downstairs?"

"*Yes! Pleasepleasepleasepleaseplease* HELP!"

The woman yawned. I dragged her by the hand. She left her door open, and descended the stairs with me in a pair of faded purple slippers. I brought the woman into our apartment. She entered cautiously, knocking with her knuckles on the open front door. I realized from the disgusted look on her face what a squalid and disreputable mess the house must have seemed to her. In the old days Lydia would never have let it get like this. It is true we had been living mostly out of our suitcases since we moved back several months (was that what they were, not weeks?) before. It is also true that Lydia had not been cooking like she used to, so we had been ordering in lots of pizza (which I liked) and Chinese food (which I also liked), and much of the refuse from these deliverable cuisines—i.e., boxes of various shapes, sizes, and degrees of residual soiledness—was piled up on top of the table and the countertops—on top of most surfaces, actually, including the moving boxes. I'll own that at a certain point our apartment had developed a bit of a fly problem. It is also possible that our clothes and the sheets on our bed were unclean, as Lydia had not done laundry since moving back to Chicago. I have also neglected to mention that Lydia had some way of acquiring those lumpy pungent-smelling cigarettes she used to indulge in with Tal, and that she had been smoking them so habitually lately that the entire apartment had taken on their odor.

When I led this unknown woman from upstairs into our bedroom, Lydia was awake. Lydia was awake again and standing up in our bedroom, in approximately the same spot of the floor on which she had fallen, right next to her side of our bed. She was still wearing the nightgown in which she slept.

"Hello?" said Lydia. Lydia held her head with one hand in a way that suggested that her skull had cracked open and she was trying to hold it in place so that her brains wouldn't dribble out. The sunlight coming through the bedroom window caught in the fibers of her hair, which was damp and bedraggled and falling in her face, and made them glow like the filaments of lightbulbs, like a disheveled scramble of tungsten wire. Her face was scrunched in pain, her eyebrows inwardly compressing the flesh above the bridge of her nose into two vertical folds. The bedsheets were in a state of rumpled disorder, and the air in the room was thick and faintly malodorous with Lydia's and my comingled sleep-sweat.

Seeing that Lydia was now awake, I darted across the room to her and desperately hugged her legs. I feverishly kissed and kissed and kissed her sticky thighs. She patted me on the head, confused.

"Who…who…who…who………you……who…," she said to the strange woman standing in the doorway of our bedroom. In her pain and confusion, she seemed to have omitted the word *are* from her sentence.

"I'm your neighbor," she said. "I live upstairs. Your pet monkey came and got me. You in trouble?"

Lydia looked absently around the room. The strange woman continued to stand there in the doorway. Her arms were crossed. Then, as if she had just seen something about Lydia that she hadn't immediately noticed, she craned her neck forward and squinted, and her arms dropped to her sides.

"Oh, honey," she said. "Are you okay?"

"I…don't…don't…don't…don't…don't…," Lydia said falteringly, groping in the dark for words. She probably repeated the word *don't* twenty times. The woman advanced into the bedroom toward us. I released my embrace of Lydia's sweet-smelling hot sticky bare legs, and I looked up at her face, towering above me. Her face was haunted with confusion the way a haunted house is haunted with ghosts. Lydia sat down heavily on the edge of the bed, and the bedsprings squeaked twice under her body. She looked at me. Then she looked at the woman who was standing in our bedroom. I snuggled next to her on the bed. She looked down at me and said, with agonizingly long pauses before and after the first of these words:

"Where…………………………………… are we?"

"We better get you to a doctor," said the woman. She repaired back upstairs to put on her clothes and shoes while I helped Lydia into her clothes and then helped myself into mine. I cannot even begin to adequately describe the terror I felt when I realized that I, at this particular moment, seemed to have more control over my faculties than did Lydia. This was the woman who raised me, who had given me consciousness, who had given me everything. She gave me civilization, gave me my mind, gave me everything I knew. And the way she was moving, the way her gaze just landed here and there on various objects in the room the way a fly buzzes around until it lands on something, and then decides to get up and go land on something else—the way she was looking around at everything like she'd just been born, as if she'd just peeled herself fully formed and sinless from the womb, the way she passively, curiously, dead-limbedly submitted to me ineptly, fumble-fingeredly dragging the sleeves of her coat over her arms and cramming her feet into her shoes—it terrified, it fucking *terrified* me. It was as if she had become the child, which meant that *I* had to understudy for the role of the adult. And how pitifully unprepared for the role I was. She was moving so strangely, so unnaturally. One of her arms seemed to be moving too stiffly, like someone had poured a little concrete powder into its veins, and she seemed to have developed a slight limp in her right leg overnight, as if in struggling with some mysterious stranger in a dream, her sciatic nerve had been wounded in her sleep.

The woman from upstairs came back into our apartment, leaving our front door open to the public hallway, with a set of keys tinkling from her finger. She found Lydia and me haphazardly dressed and ready as ever to go. She led us outside to her car, which was parked on the side of the street near Lydia's. Lydia's eyes met the violent sunlight in a daze of molish blinks, as if she was emerging to the surface from a year of living underground. The woman helped Lydia into the passenger seat, and I climbed into the back of the chipped old red four-door sedan, and the woman drove us in this wheezy-engined vehicle to the University of Chicago Medical Center, just four blocks away from the Erman Biology Center, which is where they had taken me, languageless, naked and fresh from the zoo, to begin my induction into human civilization. The upstairs woman knew the way. She may have said something about how she worked here as a nurse on the night shift and slept in the daytime, which was why she knew what to do and where to go. But maybe not. My mind was already in a nauseous dream-state of panic, a panic that poured oil all over my brain for the whole day and made it difficult for things to stick in it properly, and so my memories are jumbled and unclear of going to the hospital—of our shoes clopping across the parking lot—of somebody speaking with somebody else at a desk—yes, definitely a big pink desk—of a clipboard of complicated paperwork that had to be filled out—were there forms to be filled in, Lydia?—how did you fill them in?—what could you have possibly written down to satisfy them? There was paperwork, there was a vast waiting room, there was a big pink desk. There were antiseptic and sharply ammoniac odors, there were shiny sleek-waxed floors that caused our shoes to crunch and squawk, there was a fish tank full of tropical fish, on the floor of which a ceramic man in a diving suit seemed to have just discovered a tiny chest of ceramic treasure half-buried in a bed of gravel made pink by a colored fluorescent tube overhead. Wait a moment—where did the woman who lived upstairs go, the woman who had driven us to the hospital? Did she vanish from our company at some point in that long, hellish day of fear and sorrow? She must have, because I remember we took a cab home after everything at the hospital. Did we ever thank her properly? Did we ever see her again?

Here is what I remember from that day. I remember a room with some sort of giant machine in it. The machine was straight out of a science fiction movie set aboard a spaceship a thousand years in the future. It was a huge shiny white metal donut, standing up on its side, with a bed in it. Lydia was made to lie down with towels bunched around her body and a pillow beneath her knees, and she was told to put her head inside this cylinder of white metal. Then the bed was raised up by a robot and slid with buzzing motor into the yawning hole in the middle of the machine. For some reason there was music, melancholy opera music, playing from a stereo in the room. Why? I was not allowed to go into the room with her. I had to sit and watch it through a window in the wall of an adjoining room. Whatever this machine was doing to her, it took a *really* long time doing it, and as it did what it was doing the machine made chattering, bleeping, warbling, and gnashing noises that sounded exactly like noises a flying saucer would make as it hovers slowly to earth before a wonderstruck and fearful crowd, all points and murmurs and *ooh*s and *aah*s, and do they come in peace? Why was there opera music blaring in that room? After they took Lydia out of this machine, we were made to wait again. Long bouts of waiting and uncertainty—that's what I remember most about that day. Waiting. Back in the waiting room. Was it the same waiting room, or another one? I remember a room filled with uncomfortable chairs upholstered in an ugly tongue-colored cloth, I remember coffee tables littered with bright shiny magazines, pages that crinkled between the fingers, I remember a TV with the news on and the sound off. I remember that Lydia had to lie down across several of the pushed-together seats in the waiting room and take a nap, a long nap. I remember small Styrofoam cups of coffee and thin red plastic wands for stirring in the sugar and milk. I remember a water cooler whose blue plastic tank was flanked by a tall cylinder, from the bottom of which one could pull a conical paper cup to fill with the tepid water that trickled from a spigot; when one depressed the spigot's lever the water tank would belch up a cluster of bubbles, and the conical paper cup in your hand would quickly become floppy with dampness. And then there was the aquarium with the ceramic treasure-hunting diver in it: I whiled away some of those sluggish, agonizing hours watching the angelfish dumbly swishing their flat, triangular, translucent bodies from one end of their ten-gallon universe to the other and back again. I remember that day as a Morse code of waiting and testing, a dash-dot-dash-dot-dash of long periods of waiting punctuated by brief periods of frenzy and terror, time spent with the doctors, with their scientific languages and ear-needling machinery. I remember holding and squeezing Lydia's hand—more for my own comfort than for hers, I'm afraid—as the doctors turned off the lights, and in the darkness proceeded to clip black sheets of glossy film to a white glowing plate on the wall. I remember the doctors pointing to certain areas of the images. I remember the wobbling sound of the film sheets in the doctors' hands before they clipped them to the plate of light. These floppy sheets of shiny black film, when pressed flat against the glow of the plate on the wall, contained pictures that were thus: a bright white outline of a person's head, emerging sharp against the darkness around it, and inside of the outline, an intricately branching lump of gray cauliflower. Inside the lump of cauliflower, in one cluster of its fat lumpy branches, was a dark blot. The doctors pointed to this blot as they spoke. I remember these doctors bandying about a certain very beautiful and musical polysyllabic word that nevertheless was a word to be said in a low voice and with a grave face on, which was "oligodendroglioma"—this complicated eight-syllable song of Greek roots lilting many times from the doctors' lips.

A brain tumor had been found in the left frontal lobe of Lydia's brain. This tumor may well have been there for years, said the doctors. Years! They guessed this is probably what happened: a "benign" tumor, which had caused no "noticeably debilitating symptoms" (those words I remember clearly, as that is an exact quote from the mouth of one of these doctors: "noticeably debilitating"), had, for reasons unknown, recently begun to blossom into a "malignant" one. It had decided it was time to grow, and was currently in the process of chewing up part of Lydia's brain, and was getting fatter and fatter, crowding out and pushing around all the good and needed matter of her front-left cerebrum. The way the doctors described it to us, I imagined Lydia's tumor as a grotesquely fat man rudely shoving his way into a crowded elevator, squishing everyone else against the walls until they cannot breathe. There were several options, said the doctors, none good. They were united in the opinion that surgery—*fucking brain surgery*—was the best way to go, although they acknowledged that it could prove to be difficult, as apparently the tumor was located in a particularly inconvenient spot in her brain that would make it tricky to scrape out. So they advised first surgery—that definitely—and then a period of chemotherapy to follow it up. The chemotherapy was optional but strongly recommended. Lydia was told to think it over carefully, but that the brain surgery was a must if she hoped to live.

(Note: Gwen has just called to question the accuracy of certain elements of my narrative. She asked whether the woman from upstairs was at all surprised to hear me speak. Wasn't I not supposed to talk to strangers, anyway? Did they really allow me into the hospital? And etc., etc. I admit, as always, to embellishments here and there in servitude to the interests of drama, though I suggest you not worry too much about them. If I ever stray from the letter of the truth, I never do in spirit. Let's move on.)

XXIX

About a week later Lydia underwent surgery. They had to shave her head so they could saw her skull open to get at the tumor. As it turned out, the surgery wouldn't do much good. It would be a squandered effort. Lydia had no health insurance; so Mr. Lawrence paid for the surgery, a last act of kindness to us. But before we get to that, there's one more thing I must tell you about. Our readers probably already know about this part of my story, which has been well documented in texts other than this one, so I won't dwell on it overmuch.

That day at the hospital wasn't over yet. Or maybe this happened on another day. I can't remember. We spent a lot of time at that hospital during this unhappy period. Let's say it happened on the same day. Lydia did not yet know she was pregnant. I suppose she had not ovulated in months and had been gaining a lot of weight and so on, but these things were not the only things she had been ignoring since we had moved back to Chicago. It was discovered at the hospital in the course of all the many tests and whatnot that she had to endure because of her brain tumor.

The following scene I remember, though, or I at least imagine. Lydia and I were in the waiting room. Lydia had just come back to me after running another gauntlet of medical tests. We were sitting by that fish tank again. The angelfish gaped and swam back and forth through their narrow corridor of water, their sequin eyes flat and emotionless. She had quit crying, and was now occupied in the business of staring at an area of the floor where a chair leg met the floor. A nurse bustled back to us from backstage the hospital's theatre. She beckoned to Lydia. She said the doctors had found something interesting and unusual about the data of her body that they had collected. I was not allowed to be company when they were doing whatever they were about to do to her. Lydia obediently went with the nurse, leaving me with the fish. A long time passed. The fish did nothing interesting. Then the nurse returned, took me, Bruno, by the hand, and led me through the labyrinth of shiny white hallways lit by rectangles of fluorescent light buzzing softly overhead, past inoffensive framed watercolors of vases of flowers that blandly covered the nakedness of the walls, and into a certain room, where Lydia weakly smiled at me from the hospital bed on which she lay. I joined her at her bedside. The bed was elevated far off the floor, and I had to stand on a chair to make my body level with hers.

I remember that room, and remember it clearly. I had come to hate hospital rooms because their atmospheres reminded me of laboratories. These rooms are lit by the same frantically flickering and humming fluorescent lights. Sometimes it seems like my whole life has been lit by the fluorescent tubes of science. These fluorescent lights make for soft bright lighting that steals the shadow out from under every object and every person in the room. The rooms made for science and medicine have the same unnerving disharmony of whirring, whining electronic machines and the same sickly mint-green paint on the walls. Why is this nauseating mint-green color associated with a place where diseases are supposedly cured? Lydia was lying on a crinkly paper mat on her high plastic bed. There was a doctor, a heavy woman with a sandy brown bob of hair, and let us say there was a stethoscope draped over her neck. I was sitting in a chair beside Lydia, holding her hand. It was late afternoon. A storm had broken above the city, and rainwater speckled and streaked the window. Lydia lifted up her shirt and showed the doctor her belly. There was a machine beside the bed. It was a computer on a cart. The doctor squirted some sort of oil on her belly from a squeeze bottle and rubbed it all over her. Then she unwound a wand tethered to the machine by a long white cord wound around a peg on the cart. She pressed the wand to Lydia's belly. I squeezed Lydia's hand. As I held and squeezed Lydia's hand, the doctor pointed to the screen on the machine beside the bed. The screen was black except for a circle-and-triangle of green light, the shape of a keyhole. Indecipherable rows of green numbers and letters flickered skittishly at the top and bottom of the screen. Inside the keyhole of green light was a black, bean-shaped blob. The blob moved slightly. This small black bean-shaped blob, floating in a keyhole of glowing green goo, represented her child. And mine. Lydia was pregnant with our child.

This doctor fled from the room, and shortly after returned in the company of another doctor. Both of them looked at the black bean-shaped blob floating in green goo on the screen, exchanged a few furtive words between them, then both left. Shortly after that, these two doctors returned in the company of a third doctor. All three doctors looked at the bean-shaped blob in the keyhole of glowing green goo on the screen on the machine beside Lydia's bed. They looked at Lydia, and then looked at me; they looked back and forth from me to Lydia, from Lydia to me. Then all three of them redirected their eyes to the bean-shaped blob, floating in a keyhole of green goo on the screen of the machine.

The doctors seemed surprised, although I see little reason why they should have been. Humans and chimps have more chromosomes in common than a donkey and a horse, Gwen. It's only natural. What I find far more surprising is that this sort of thing doesn't happen more often.

Oh, and the fallout. I don't want to extrapolate much on this next episode of my life, as it is perhaps one of the least interesting and best externally documented. Our readers will surely recall Lydia's and my long and unwanted moment of infamy. They will no doubt recall the shock, the scandal, the public ridicule. They will no doubt recall the stories in the news and the long comet-tail of jokes on late-night talk shows that followed our initial splash of media attention. I suppose this is the moment where I would instruct the filmmakers of the film of my life to insert a sequence in which the front pages of newspapers, each one heralded in by a tumble of dramatic music, come rapidly spiraling at us out of a black void to splat against an invisible plane of space a few feet in front of our eyes, displaying headlines such as: CHIMPANZEE LEARNS TO SPEAK; HISTORY-CHANGING SCIENTIFIC BREAKTHROUGH DEMANDS REDEFINITION OF MANKIND; and CHIMP AND SCIENTIST INVOLVED IN SEXUAL RELATIONSHIP, WOMAN PREGNANT WITH "HUMAN-ZEE"! Let's leave it at that and try to move on; I find all this stuff deeply depressing and fundamentally boring. All this attention, to say the least, was undesired. Day and night that pale green phone on the kitchen wall needled us awake with its electric gobble, with voices on the other end of it begging for information, for interviews, offering money for appearances on TV talk shows—all of which, despite our poverty, were handily denied. After a few days Lydia unplugged the phone.

It should come as no surprise people were far more interested in the salacious, prurient elements of my story than the mere fact that a nonhuman had become fully fluent in a human language. That's what it takes to get the public's attention. A "scandal." The "experts" were certain that I had not actually attained "Language with a capital L" (whatever that means). Suddenly, for a few long days, it seemed you couldn't turn on a TV without seeing Noam Chomsky vigorously denying to Larry King or some other idiot that what I spoke could possibly be properly called "language" for such-and-such reasons. These "linguists" would deny to my face that what I speak is language, even when I can personally engage them in verbal argument. Lydia advised me not to speak to the media, so I didn't. I turned down all requests for interviews. What could I ever have said to satisfy them, anyway? Nothing! There was absolutely nothing I could do or say. Their minds were made up as to the uniqueness of human language, and no proof could have possibly swayed them. I am an animal, everybody knows animals do not talk, and that was that. To accept that I had language would have required them to evict their most narcissistic of species from the false office they believe themselves to occupy, and so they did not listen and never have since. What people were more interested in was that a human woman had become pregnant with the child of an ape—and that this woman and this ape were very much in love, and that this woman planned to bear the child to term. My child. And Lydia would get better. This bug in her brain was no big deal, we would suffer through it, she would get better, and we would raise our child together, and we would be happy. That was the plan.

I'm sure our readers know as well as you and I, that did not happen.

———

For a long and obnoxious time Lydia and I could not leave our apartment without having to push our way through a slobbering throng of journalists, gawkers, and protesters.

Ah, yes. The protesters. Shouting and chanting their idiocies outside of our apartment all day and all night. Praying for us, they said. Holding candles and singing hymns. Pumping picket signs in the air. Screaming their putrid throats bloody with their vile, hateful screeds. At least the journalists would only appear and disappear from the vicinity of the front door of our now-unhappy home at relatively sane times of day—they, after all, had their jobs, and presumably lives of their own to live—but the fervent religious zealots apparently did not, as they never, *ever* seemed to leave. Sometimes—in the beginning of the fallout—early in the morning, there would be hundreds of them standing in front of our building. They were a pestilence, an infestation. Sometimes we could call the police, who would come rolling leisurely down the street in their black-and-white cruisers, wheeling their way through the zoo, the human zoo into which these people had converted our quiet, tree-lined block of South Ellis Avenue. The cops would turn on the blue and red bar of light on top of their car and give them all a truncated whoop from the siren, and they would scatter in all directions, as cockroaches do when you flick the light on, only to congregate again mere minutes after the cops had left, huddling together all their bodies that housed all their pious Sunday-morning souls.

These people were led by a man whose name, as he told us through his megaphone, was "Reverend Jeb." Reverend Jeb was not an "ordained" reverend of any church but his own. His full name was Milton Jebediah Hartley III. He was the proprietor of a nondenominational fundamentalist Christian church in Wichita, Kansas, who had driven himself and other protesters up to Chicago in a bus to camp out on our lawn and harass us. This Lydia and I surmised because we read the papers. He carried his body with the bloated parody of dignity that is common among "men of God," and his typical uniform was a wool houndstooth suit worn with a blue bow tie and a blue-and-white-striped scarf that he would jauntily toss over his shoulder as he shouted his spittle-choked lunacies into the narrow end of his RadioShack megaphone. Reverend Jeb was a handsome older man, there's no denying that. He had the leathery face and blocky features of an old-fashioned movie star, and a full head of brown hair shot through with gray, which he would swish back on his head with his fingers with the same theatricality as he would sling his blue-and-white-striped scarf over his shoulder. Nor is there any point in denying that Reverend Jeb was a man who—by dint of his style of dress and the booming braggadocio in his rich gravelly voice, carefully hedged into an accent that was part Southern preacher and part midcentury radio announcer—hearkened back with his every word and movement to a previous era—not necessarily a *better* one, mind you, but a previous one—when no man left his home without a hat on and not to be able to sing or tell a story right was seen as a sad, inhibiting trait.

Reverend Jeb was always there. Allow me to repeat for emphasis, lest that sentence look like a throwaway on the page: *he was always there.* Reverend Jeb was always, always, *always* there when we left our home—in which, during this brief, unhappy period of our lives, Lydia and I tended to barricade ourselves, unless some inescapable errand dragged us into the outside world. There he was, with his bow tie, his houndstooth suit, his blue-and-white-striped scarf and his RadioShack megaphone, timeless, undrainable of the venomous energy that surged in his jaws. Reverend Jeb apparently woke before us and went to sleep after us, if indeed he slept at all. His favorite words were (listed in, I believe, their approximate descending order of frequency in his speech; put these words in capital letters, Gwen, from the megaphone): "HELL," "GOD," "CHRIST," "DAMNATION," "EVIL," "BEAST," "MAN," "WOMAN," "SIN," "SATAN," "DEVIL," "ABOMINATION," "HEAVEN," "WHORE," "BABYLON," "HARLOT," "IMPURITY," "UNCLEANLINESS," "MONSTER." Somewhere in my inner ear I can still hear the squawk and crunch of his RadioShack megaphone, and hear his vitriolic oratory thundering from our lawn in the morning, calling us sinners, calling Lydia the whore of Babylon, calling me an abomination before God and man, asserting that there lived in her belly the child of Satan.

"NEITHER SHALT THOU LIE WITH ANY BEAST TO DEFILE THYSELF THEREWITH!"—he screamed at us one morning, reading from a Bible held in the hand that did not hold the RadioShack megaphone—"NEITHER SHALL ANY WOMAN STAND BEFORE A BEAST TO LIE DOWN THERETO: IT IS CONFUSION! DEFILE NOT YE YOURSELVES IN ANY OF THESE THINGS! FOR IN ALL THESE THE NATIONS ARE DEFILED WHICH I CAST OUT BEFORE YOU! AND THE LAND IS DEFILED! THEREFORE I DO VISIT THE INIQUITY THEREOF UPON IT, AND THE LAND ITSELF VOMITETH OUT HER INHABITANTS!"

During downtimes there were just three or four others with him, bundled in their winter coats to make the important pilgrimage to our lawn to harass us, but at peak hours he was surrounded by hundreds of people. They chanted, they held lit candles in their hands and sang their stupid hymnals and liturgies and hosannas and "prayed" at us. Sometimes there were so many of them! Sometimes these glassy-eyed slack-faced adults brought along their adorable glassy-eyed and slack-faced children, who stood right beside their parents with little blond heads all abob with springy ringlets of flax-blond hair, picking their snot-drooling noses with grubby little fingers.

These people looked just like normal people. You would think they might bear some sort of clear distinguishing mark, maybe black spots upon their foreheads or something—but no—outwardly, there was nothing odd about them. If you passed any of these people on the street—out of their proper context—you would not have looked twice at them. But there was something, there was some gruesome contaminant in their brains that caused them to believe that the earth is six thousand years old, that cavemen rode dinosaurs to work, and that all the beauty of the natural world has been deliberately placed here by the devil like so many red herrings for scientists to find to test our faith in God. What in the world is *wrong* with a civilization in which we must take these people at all seriously? Why must we listen to their "opinions"? Why must we suffer them to jam their feet in the doors of our discourse? Why must we respectfully demur to their "faith"? Why allow their voices into our politics? Why must these intolerant people be tolerated? I refuse to tolerate them! I swear, Gwen, in my least "tolerant" moods I sometimes think that any truly just and wise society would regard religious faith not as some deep noble kind philosophical lofty spiritual bullshit, but merely as an official, DSM-certified *mental illness*! Throw it right in there with schizophrenia! Why not?

Religion says this world is not good enough for us—that there is more, or that there should be. What is religion but the philosophical hatred of the world?

But why did these people hate us? Why were these people bivouacked on our lawn in order to harass us all day and all night? Because they, being good Christians, did not believe in evolution. They did not believe in evolution because the Judeo-Christian tradition is the ultimate anthropo-chauvinist doctrine, which asserts that man has dominion over the earth—that God has told him to be fruitful and multiply, to fill the earth and subdue it, and have dominion over the fish of the sea and over the birds of the air and over every living thing that moves upon the earth—that he stands over and against nature, the chosen son of all creation, given by God his mind, his consciousness, all his human "dignity." And they hated us because of this: because there, swimming in a pouch of fluid in Lydia's lower abdomen, was living, unassailable proof of human evolution.

XXX

The tumor in Lydia's brain was located in a place called Broca's area. I learned then that some parts of the brain have apparently been named, and some of them have been named, like new continents, after their first cartographers, as I suppose Mr. Broca was the first to map meaning onto this particular part of the brain. Broca's aphasia (as opposed to Wernicke's) is a problem not of understanding language but of the production of it, not of listening but of speaking.

Lydia's aphasia began on that morning she had her seizure (for that was what it was, the doctors informed us). Even after her surgery, Lydia continued having seizures, and her aphasia only got worse, a decline that proceeded unchecked even after she started undergoing speech therapy. When it was first found the tumor was in such an advanced state of growth that the doctors suggested operating as soon as possible. Seven days after her first seizure, I was left alone at home while Tal drove Lydia to the hospital to get her head shaved, her skull sawed open, and a blob of disease cut out of her brain tissue. I forgot to mention that Tal came back into our lives at the beginning of Lydia's illness (or the beginning of the time after Lydia learned she had an illness). Lydia must have called her up and asked for her help, being estranged as she was and geographically removed from her family. Tal still lived in Chicago. The night before Lydia's surgery, Tal brought us a dinner she'd cooked, a dish composed of a sticky yellow coagulum steaming beneath a sheet of aluminum foil in a rectangular pan that she carried up the walkway to our door, having threaded herself with some difficulty through the thick mob of nasty morons encamped in front of our building. Lydia was elated to see her. She had spent much of the last six days sleeping, or else being awake at odd times of the night. That blob in her head had the effect of throwing her circadian rhythms into disarray, like shouting out random numbers at someone who's trying to do some complicated math in her head, or interrupting a string quartet that's busy playing a waltz by brattling on a pot with a spoon. So Lydia had just dragged herself messy-haired and puffy-eyed from one of her many long naps when Tal appeared at our door in the late afternoon. The right half of Lydia's face had been drooping ever since that seizure, gone flabby and slack as if someone had snipped the strings that held that side of her face together.

I was surprised to see Tal physically changed somewhat, though I shouldn't have been, because the last time I'd lain eyes on her was more than two and a half years before. Gone were her dreadlocks. Before, her hair had looked like something that ought to be dangling from the throat of a bison, but now her hair was a floppy, messy mop of buoyant and bitumen-black coils. Tal and Lydia hugged like long-separated sisters in the foyer after the casserole had been set down. Then she fearlessly embraced me, too. I was all grown up, much more mature and conversant than the wild thing that had once munched off most of the middle finger on her right hand. Now that I had speech, I apologized profusely for my past transgression, and she thankfully accepted my apology with warmth but enough gravitas to indicate that her forgiveness was sincere, which put me at relative social ease in her company, though every time I allowed my gaze to trickle from her face to her hand, and I saw the finger that abruptly truncated in a stub of scarred skin where once a prehensile digit of flesh and nerves and blood had been, I felt a pang of shame and remorse as tangibly felt in my innards as a pang of hunger. Tal fed and comforted us that night, rescuing us at least temporarily from the disorder, sorrow, and publicity of our current lives. She observed what a state we were in with no one around to help us, and wept with us tears of sympathy.

The next day Tal took Lydia to the hospital for her brain surgery. I pushed back the curtains to watch Tal and Lydia walk out of our apartment building and into the crowd of religious protesters. Reverend Jeb, diligently posted in front of our building on the frozen grass in his houndstooth suit, bow tie, and long blue-and-white-striped scarf, was shouting into the narrow end of his megaphone about man and beast and God. The protesters shielded their children's eyes so they would not see the faces of the sinners, as they pumped their handmade cardboard picket signs up and down in the air, screamed their throats bloody, pointed their fingers at Lydia and Tal, and shouted "SINNER," and "DEFILER," and "WHORE." They spat at them, and on them if they got close enough. Lydia and Tal pushed through them and made it to Lydia's car, the paint job of which had recently been ruined by a palimpsest of defacements, and was now covered with prayers and Bible quotes and crude crosses that had been scratched with keys into the silver-blue paint. Tal opened the passenger-side door for Lydia, saw her in, and got into the driver's side, squeezed the vehicle out of its parallel parking spot and onto the street. The protesters crowded around the car, spitting at it, screaming at the rolled-up windows, drumming with their fists on the doors and hood.

Tal did not come back until long after dark. I'd already watched *Pinocchio* three times. I was starving. Tal reheated some leftovers for us to eat, and we ate together in near silence. I cried. She cried. Then she pulled herself together, stopped her tears, and washed the dishes. Tal slept on the couch that night, after sharing one of her lumpy white cigarettes with me.

Lydia came home from the hospital the next day. Her hair was completely gone, and her bald head was partially covered with a white bandage. She went immediately to bed.

The doctors had strongly recommended radiation therapy to follow up the surgery, which Lydia refused for several reasons, the main one being that radiation therapy posed a dangerous risk to our unborn child.

Tal moved in with us a few days later. She slept in my old studio, my old room—which was just as well, as I wasn't painting. I didn't have the spirit or energy to. We appreciated to no end the advent of her cooking and housekeeping, how it dramatically lightened our burden. Lydia and I had allowed these sorts of pragmatic domestic things to fall into a state of squalid neglect. We almost hadn't noticed how filthy and cluttered our living space had become until Tal cleaned it up. It was Tal who finally ripped the packing tape off of the flaps of the brown cardboard boxes still stacked up here and there all over the apartment, opened them up and put their contents in their proper places—books on the shelves, clothes in the closets, so on and so forth. She swept and mopped the wood floors and vacuumed the carpets, took out the trash, changed the sheets, did the laundry, washed the dishes, and summarily brought our apartment back into a state of sanity and sanitation, all while Lydia lay languishing, sweaty, naked, and depressed in bed, with her mind on the wane and her womb on the wax, and while I sat around the house uselessly moping in despair.

That's not quite true. I was useless in other ways, too. I took a lot of long walks that winter, alone, through the neighborhood. I would bundle myself up in disguise, in my oversized green hooded sweatshirt, a scarf wound around my lower face to further hide my apeness, with dark sunglasses to shield my eyes from the blinding snow. Yes, it was winter in Chicago, and in my heart. Oh, hello again, you bitter Chicago winter! How could I have forgotten you? The bastard had come back for us, icing the streets, leadening the sky. And lo, the bile-throated gnashing-mouthed religious zealots on our lawn did not go away, they did not abandon their posts for one minute no matter how low the mercury sank in its thin glass flute: they kept at it, determined as ever in their mission that was from God to annoy and harass us, so steady and steadfast were their little Protestant work ethics, to stand in front of the door to our building in subfreezing temperatures, singing their glorious songs in angelic harmony with eyes lifted piously heavenward between bouts of indefatigable screaming about the supposed loves and hates of their jealous God.

Whenever I would leave the apartment on my walks I would slip out, fugitively, through the back, in order to escape the crowd of shouting protesters stationed out front. There was a back way: out through the glass doors that slid out onto the patch of backyard we shared with the other residents of the building, through the gate, past the garbage cans, down the alley and out onto the street. This was the first time I discovered the possibility of my independence. With Lydia desperately sick, mostly housebound and mostly bedridden, and me with my itchy restless boredom, I struck out on the streets, prowling the sooty, slushy grids of Hyde Park like a monster swaddled in human clothes.

I walked around on the campus of the University of Chicago, moving in the shadows of the magisterial ivy-strangled buildings— ivy I'd once gleefully climbed in my early days as an animal full of yearning—and over dead yellow and frost-dusted lawns past trees whose brittle leafless branches clicked and chattered together when the wind got strong. As these ambulations always passed without incident, I suppose I was simply mistaken by the passersby for a student: a quiet, unhappy, unfriendly, brooding, and heavily bundled student with his hands sunk in his pockets and his eyes locked to the ground, and thus by this description not especially distinct from most of the actual students at the University of Chicago.

I sat in on courses at the university. I would slip into lecture halls while the classes were in session, with my green hooded sweatshirt pulled low over my face, and take as inconspicuous a seat as I could toward the back of the room. I sat in on courses in literature, history, philosophy, economics, art history, physics, biology. I wanted to know everything I possibly could. I wanted to devour the world. I also spent a lot of time in the reading room of that cathedral of a library, sitting at one of the long desks that furnish the high-ceilinged, architecturally sepulchral, and ceremonially symmetrical room, whose walls are outfitted and ornamented with monster faces as rubber-mask-like as my own, their stone mouths carven in permanent howls of laughter or scowls of disgust, who have watched generations of readers with those fixed expressions implicative of emotional violence. In this room I would sit and while away hours to avoid the sadness of my home, where Lydia lay in bed with a decaying mind while a band of chimeras more grotesque even than these shouted and cackled at her from outside. Here among the dust motes flurrying in the light shafts that filtered through the multicolored panes of the stained-glass windows, I sat under a lamp at one of the long wooden mess-hall tables, getting up now and then to browse the shelves and unshelve books, which I splayed open on the table and read all day long. A lot of my education happened that winter, as I sat, usually alone or nearly alone in that huge solemn room, with the gloom of November in the windows, and in the back of my mind the gloom of the illness of the one person in my life I have truly loved.

Sometimes, if I did not feel like sitting in on classes or visiting the library, my solitary walks took me through a leafless-treed and snow-covered Washington Park. One day I was walking along the periphery of the park, clutching my coat tight to my weird little body and wading through rattling heaps of dead leaves, my feet crunching the frost-crystallized grass, keeping away from the other people in the park—just smatterings of people here and there who stood in the park wrapped up like mummies and bouncing on their knees to keep their blood moving, who had come to the park to unleash their dogs to let them scamper and arf around for a few minutes before returning home to hibernate away the winter like all good mammals should. And I was walking *crunch-crunch* under the sleeping trees with my gaze downturned and my head roiling with dark thoughts, when I saw the dead parrot.

It was a macaw. A red and green, yellow, blue, and very dead parrot, lying on the ground in the frosted-gray grass. It was unmistakably one of the recently deceased Griph Morgan's parrots. One of the parrots whose coos, screeches, and squawks had once harmonized roughly with Griph's bagpipes, and had once colored my dreams red, green, yellow, and blue with unusual cycles of affinity and association. There he lay, stiff and ice-coated at my feet. He was frozen. His steely gray horn of a beak was stuck in a slightly unhinged position, as if in midspeech, or in reaching out to accept a remunerative cookie or cracker. His eyes and tongue had dissolved, leaving two gray sunken holes that looked back into the inside of his now-hollow skull where a walnut-sized brain had once been. The barbs of his colorful feathers were brittle with ice. I guessed that he had probably died at first frost. Where were the others? Griph had shared his apartment with ten birds. I suppose they had been released into the "wild" when the vandyked, bean-boiling, and backgammon-playing Griph Morgan passed away. I hoped that he was buried with his bagpipes. I hoped that the other nine birds had enough wisdom to fly south when the weather began to turn. But probably they did not. A creature raised in captivity with central heating to eliminate the seasons remains ignorant of the paths of his ancestors. So the birds had most likely simply settled in the branches of the closest thing they could find to the equatorial rain forests where their blood told them to go—which happened to be the trees of Washington Park. And when the winter came, they dropped dead from the trees. I imagined this parrot, an aristocratic flame of an animal, his bright red, green, yellow, and blue plumage contrasting ludicrously against the sepia-toned gray-and-brownness of Chicago, a bird colored like a magician's flash-and-burst of obfuscatory smoke perched in the dying black-branched trees of Washington Park, chattering, hauking, fluffing up his neck feathers with his beak and smoothing them down again with passerine prissiness—outside in the world, free at last, and without a clue as to how to be a real bird in it, blithely whistling and chirping away, occasionally singing snippets of Scots Gaelic folk ballads, and shouting out with ebullient gusto at the bemused passers-by from his perch in the tree: "HELLO!"—shouting it as a salutation at first, as if cordially inviting small talk—"HELLO, HELLO!"—then later, as the people turned their faces away, in anger—"HELLO!"—and then, finally, as winter descended, in desperation—"HELLO?…HELLO?… HELLO?" And then he died.

I nudged the bird with my shoe. The frozen parrot was light as nothing, it moved across the ground so easily. Now my eyes were secreting tears. They turned to ice in my eyelashes. I looked up to see if anyone was looking at me: they were not. I tried to dig a little grave in the ground for this frozen parrot: I could not. I clawed my long purple fingers bloody trying to dig a hole, but the dirt was so tightly compacted and solidly frozen that to dig a hole in it would have been impossible without a shovel. So I gave up and turned back for home. I felt like a failure, and in many more ways than just in my apparent inability even to successfully dig a grave for a deceased parrot. But as I was heading home, as I was walking down

Fifty-fifth and about to cross Cottage Grove, waiting for the light to change, I realized that it makes no ceremonial sense to bury a bird. Just that day, or maybe the day before, I had been sitting in the reading room of the library perusing a volume of Herodotus. I had come across a passage in which the historiographer related—with a clear note of revulsion—the Persian funeral custom, which was to lay the body of the dead stark naked on a platform in the open air at the very top of a tall tower, and let the birds pick the bones clean. Herodotus found the practice disgusting, unbefitting his notions of human dignity. For him, the only dignified methods of getting rid of a stiff were either to vaporize it with purgatory fire or bury it in the ground. On first thought I agreed with his judgment, but when I had another think on it I realized that perhaps there may actually be a counterintuitive metaphorical beauty to the Persian custom. For cremation implies a total erasure, a vanishing act: as goes the soul, so must go the body, up and away in a puff of useless smoke. Burial—especially the kind where the king is buried with all his things—implies the opposite, a clinging refusal to let go, even of one's earthly property. Whereas to dissolve the body in the bellies of birds seems rather to give back what is nature's to nature. By extension I therefore reasoned that it would make no semiotic sense to bury a bird. That bird—and granted it may have lain there until spring before the body defrosted—would be slowly disappeared by the weather, decomposed and reconstituted into the stuff of the world, without ceremony, without any sign or token or record at all to mark that it had once lived, spoken, and died in the world.

I admit that like any true poet, I am vulnerable to romance. Do not think, Gwen, that I am an entirely rational creature, or conversely that I'm too irrational to consider and reflect upon my own moments of illogic. There is such a thing called confirmation bias, which is when the mind attaches significance to something insignificant, singling out a seemingly supernatural coincidence from all the chaotic junk in the world around it and funnels all its prayer and confidence into it because it wants it to be true—which is the source of much faith, much love, much religion, much magic, much hope, much hopeless error. I am aware of my hypocrisy when, in certain moods, I rail and rage against religion, then turn right around and find myself susceptible to belief in ghosts, in the prophecy of dreams, in spooky action at a distance. If I am vulnerable to these things it is because I have become human. I was the chimp who tapped on the box. If I rail and rage against religion, it is partly because religion is a magical belief structure that has hurt me personally, whereas secular magic has offered me hope. If I hate the irrational while being irrational myself, it is because my mind is trapped, like all human minds are trapped, between the rational understanding of the world sternly provided by empirical science (which includes the knowledge that I myself am irrational) and the ancient crazy wild beautiful brazen nonsense, the spookiness that all human consciousnesses are vulnerable to, even the hardest of scientists. It's this human vulnerability to spookiness that had Sir Isaac Newton, when he wasn't busy laying the foundations of classical physics, earnestly fiddling around with powders and potions and flasks and beakers, searching for the philosopher's stone, for the elixir of life, for the secret to the transmutation of lead to gold. This is why I do not believe the argument that the light of empirical science will guide us on the path of progress, toward utopia, toward a great rational peace when nation no longer wages war against nation over pettifogging disagreements about invisible and almost certainly nonexistent things. If we ever arrived at this scientific utopia, there would be no religions, yes, and never again would a drop of blood be shed over such lunatic stupidities—but also we would produce no art; whether this is throwing the baby out with the bathwater I'm still not entirely sure. Even if we ever arrived at such a rational peace, when we got there we would no longer be human.

XXXI

Meanwhile, after months of idleness, and now with the constant influx of medical bills like so many matches on the fire, our household finances were dwindling to nil. I had only a vague grasp of these things, being as I was then and am now very bad with money. Among the members of the little nuclear family unit that we had grown into out of necessary closeness, Tal was the one who mostly handled these issues. I don't know how much money there was, but it may have been nothing, or nearly nothing, or we may have gone deeply in the red. Tal balanced our books, cleaned the apartment, kept things in order and cooked our meals. She was a decent cook in her own right, though I would have preferred Lydia's cooking. Tal was capable of making something out of nothing in the kitchen; she could immaculately conceive a meal out of whatever pathetic smattering of ingredients happened to be knocking around in the cupboards and refrigerator—but satiating as her dishes were, these meals tasted ever increasingly of our bitter poverty. Lydia was out of commission. Even when she was awake, she just puttered around our apartment with the vacant eyes of a starving person, picking things up and putting them back down, often babbling incoherently, or else remaining disturbingly silent.

If she wanted to salt her food at the table she would point at the saltshaker and say, "The...the...the...the..............the..." Meaning, of course, "Please pass the salt." Lydia's silences grew longer, darker, more profound. Her words were leaving her. One by one the elements of her vocabulary were packing up their things and vacating their apartments in the condemned building of her mind. It was such a heartbreaking experience, I could never adequately describe what it was like to live with her in the following months. The only places Lydia ever went were to the doctor or to her speech pathologist, who was unable to prevent the words from crumbling away from her. Every word she spoke was preceded by and followed by such long silences that it was impossible to remember how her sentence had begun. Tal assured me that because of the nature of Lydia's aphasia, because it was in Broca's area and not Wernicke's, she could understand us when we spoke to her, although she herself had greater and greater difficulty speaking. Her mind had become half-silvered, like Clever Hands's. Her eyes were one-way mirrors, the windows to her soul opaque on the outside. She could see out; we increasingly could not see in. She slept all day. Her belly got bigger as my child grew obstinately inside her. I, Bruno, who was perfectly healthy, had become deeply nervous and unsure whether I would be able to handle the travails and responsibilities of my coming fatherhood—much less how she would handle her coming motherhood.

Once, after I arrived home through the sliding glass back doors to avoid the protesters, and shook the snow powder off my coat and thunked the mush off my boots against the doorframe, coming in from one of my daylong journeys that had taken me through the park and then through the vaulted and chandeliered reading room of the library and through the pages of whatever I was reading at the time (I think it was Gibbon's *Decline and Fall*), Tal asked me in a solemn tone to sit with her at the kitchen table. She wanted to talk with me about something. She was not angry, but I recognized the note of sternness, of getting-down-to-businessness in her voice when she requested my audience, and so I instantly began to dread whatever was coming. To her credit, at least she softened the hideous blow to my well-being she was about to deliver by preparing me a cup of hot chocolate. She knew precisely how I liked it, with five small slimy marshmallows bobbing on the surface, slowly dissolving into the hot tan liquid. I blew on the surface of my hot chocolate, and sipped.

"Bruno," she said, her palms anchored on the surface of the kitchen table and her fingers intertwined. "You know we're running low on money. I'm doing the best I can to take care of Lydia. But I'm afraid you need to help out, too."

I gulped in mild terror, scalding the back of my throat with too big and quick an intake of hot chocolate. The thing was this: I had to get a job. I needed to "pull more of my weight" around our household. When Lydia and I returned to Chicago, Tal had been working at the lab again. She worked at the lab for most of the day, then came home to us to housekeep and nurse. And still there was no money. She was wearing herself thin. Norman Plumlee was still the director of the Behavioral Biology Lab at the Erman Biology Center. She said she could get me a job working at the lab. Now that I had learned language, apparently I was even more valuable to science, and Norm wanted me back. They were willing, she said, to pay for my services, since this time around I was considered conscious enough to provide consent, and therefore would no longer be treated like a slave. I had freed myself from the animal slavery of my silent mind, only to be offered my previous job at pittance wages. I would be able to help pay for things around the house. The way Tal put it, there seemed to be no option. Bruno was all grown up now, and tight circumstances demanded it was time for him to go to work. I, Bruno, nobly, albeit begrudgingly, decided to accept her offer—or command, or whatever it was. I had to go back to the lab. I would do it, but only for Lydia. Simply put, we needed money, and I, like any whore, had nothing to sell but myself. So I sold myself back to science, and back to the lab I went.

Tal took me with her to the lab the next day. Oh!—308 Erman Biology Center! Norm was there, fat and irritating and beard-tugging as ever, right where we last left him, though his salt-and-pepper beard now had considerably more salt in it. The gray Formica tables, the salmon-colored vinyl floors, the thick glass enclosure, the faintly flickering and buzzing fluorescent lights—this place brought a tide of sense-memories back to me, and I almost drowned in it. I had gotten much bigger since I was here last—at three feet and ten inches and a stalwart one hundred and thirty pounds I was essentially full grown now—and so I was shocked by how small the things in the room appeared when contrasted with the images of them I had in my memory. Prasad and Andrea (and Tal, of course) were still working at the lab, but those were the only people from the old days whom I recognized, as the rest were grad students who had moved on and been replaced with new grad students. There were a lot of new faces. Norm received me back to the lab with a tone of welcome that only thinly masked his chilly resentment. He was obligatorily impressed with my language faculties, but at the same time I could see him seething beneath his beard with child-ish jealousy over the fact that my linguistic mind had truly come to blossom not under his guidance but under Lydia's, and that he probably full well knew that in the process of my education he had been more of a hindrance than a help.

Since I bear no official documentation, I have never been able to legally work in this country or any other. Rather than pay me under the table per se, Norm decided to evade this ticklish legal problem by including my wages in Tal's paychecks, effectively, for the books, making up the difference of my earnings by giving her a raise. And from Tal's paychecks they went straight into paying off Lydia's mounting medical bills. So I felt like an indentured servant during this time, as I never saw the actual cash proceeds of my labor.

So it was back to the grindstone of science with me. Every day a long nauseating wave of déjà vu. To the usual old tests they added a battery of new ones. I remember word-association games, Rorschach inkblot tests—all the classic psychoanalytic tactics. I also remember EEG tests, which for some reason I had to undergo once or twice a week. They would paste a nest of electrodes to my head and tell me to lie down in a bed and be absolutely still. Don't move a muscle, they said. Even in this I found a way to rebel. I remember looking over at the needle scratching out a line on a scroll of graph paper that rolled on and on like the cylinder of a player piano, which was supposed to indicate the levels of my brain activity. I was told to lie still as a stone so that they could observe the spikes and dips that happened as a result of my mysterious inner processes while my body lay quiescent, instead of the less interesting spikes that happened due to muscle movements. For instance, if I lifted my right index finger, a spike would suddenly shoot up in the line the needle was etching out on the scroll of graph paper. But the scientists would notice if I disobediently dared to lift my fingers to gum up their data, and would castigate me accordingly when they caught me doing it. However, I realized—as I lay there motionless in bed, my brain feeding the machine, feeding science through the feeding tubes that were all the wires pasted to my head, looking askance at the scroll of paper and watching the skittish electric march of my brain activity documented in graphite by a jittery needle—I realized I could make the graph spike by silently, invisibly, clenching and loosening my jaw. The scientists never noticed. Ha, ha, ha! I would watch my brain graph and playfully experiment with making electroencephalographic artworks: the scroll of graph paper was my canvas, my jaw my brush, my own brain activity my paint. I repeatedly clenched and unclenched my jaw to make interesting patterns, slowly or rapidly increasing or decreasing the pressure between my closed teeth to make dramatic hills and mountains or sloping valleys or plateaus in my graph, or at a steady rhythm to make visual music, or letting a long undramatic line of relatively low activity go by before a sudden ecstatic orgy of jaw clenching—always invariably causing the scientists to knit their brows and stroke their chins as they fondled the long sheet of thin waxy paper, tracing with pointed fingers the unexplainable oddities and anomalies in the graph, wondering among themselves what in my brain could have possibly provoked these strange and beautiful markings.

I should also not forget to mention that it was around this time that began my great depilation. I have theorized that my initial hair loss was due to the tremendous stress in my life at the time. Universal alopecia—for that is the deceptively poetic-sounding name of the condition I contracted—sometimes occurs when an animal is in a severe state of emotional turmoil, which indeed I was at this time. Through all this bad luck and trouble, I lost all my dear sweet hair. Lydia being pregnant and in pain and losing her mind, me having gone to work, Tal having moved in with us, a crowd of crazed imbeciles constantly encamped outside our home for the express purpose of harassing us—how had my life descended so suddenly into such hell? Whatever the cause, my hair has never grown back since. This is when I became my smooth, pink, hairless self, which you see now before you.

I first noticed it one morning in the shower. I climbed, sticky from my slumber, out of the bed and into the shower, leaving Lydia asleep, preparing for my day of work at the lab. I had to rise so early to go to work, and early rising has always been hateful to my constitution. I am not a "morning person." This being winter, the calendar's dark vale of late sunrises and early sunsets, Tal and I had to get up while the windows were still painted black with night. In the shower I felt the hot hissing needles of water all over my body, and I yawningly scrubbed, shampooed, and rinsed myself as usual, but—not as usual—when I twisted off the water, I looked down at my toes and noticed that an inordinately thick deposit of my hair had collected at the drain, severely slowing the spiraling flow of the soap-marbled water. Disgusted, I scooped the stuff up in my hand, plopped it in the toilet, and flushed. I checked myself for any perceptible thinness in the hair all over my body, but could find nothing distinct. This event repeated itself in every detail on the morning of the following day, and the morning after that, and so on. I was losing more and more hair. In a week or two the clumps of hair glued to the drain after my shower were practically fistfuls. Soon it began to simply come out in my hands. No pulling or yanking was necessary to loose the stuff from my body—for I am no trichotillomaniac—it simply left me on its own accord. I would be sitting in the lab, working diligently away on some particularly difficult problem, while absentmindedly running my fingers through the fur on top of my head, and—what's this?—look!—in my hand there's a tangled skein of my hair, so much of it that it looks like I deliberately grabbed a bunch of it in my fist and uprooted it by force. Then one day, after my morning shower, I climbed up onto the sink to get a good look at myself full-on in the mirror. What I saw made me howl out in fear. Tal heard me scream—Lydia just turned over in bed and grunted listlessly in her brain-sick sleep— and came bursting through the bathroom door, which I had left unlocked, fearing no intrusion. I was naked before her eyes, but my panic robbed me of my modesty.

"I'm losing my hair!" I shouted. She could see that it was true. Great empty swaths of my flesh lay raw and exposed in rangy mottles all over my body where my fur had thinned to nothing. I was hideous. I looked sickly. Tal touched my fur. My wet hairs just slid off of me and stuck to her fingers. I was so embarrassed about my condition, that day I wore a long-sleeved shirt and a stocking cap to work, which I kept on all day long, refusing to unlid myself. (Thank God I did not have to submit myself to an EEG test that day.) It did occur to me that I might be losing my hair because I was becoming human. I was becoming one of you, the naked apes, the apes of vanity.

So then, a word on vanity, my vanity. Vanity: what sin is more uniquely human? This is why we are so impressed when an animal recognizes itself in a mirror. It's vanity that makes us human. A bird or a fish will interpret its own horizontally backward image as a threat—not even realizing it is flat, not even remarking on the curiosity that this dangerous other moves only when the animal's I moves. Hence the animal attacks the mirror. Hence the rage of Caliban seeing his own face in the glass. Hence the rage of Caliban not seeing his own face in the glass. Great apes, though, do see themselves in mirrors, as do dolphins and elephants. But let's make a comparison to, say, tool use. The important thing is not so much the *use* of tools as the modification of tools. That is, we used to think that human beings were alone among the animal kingdom in their use of tools. Then somebody observed chimpanzees fishing for termites with twigs, and concluded that we must now unhook the velvet rope and allow chimps into the exclusive tool users club. Ah, *but!*—said the anthropo-chauvinists, we're still the only species to *modify* tools, aren't we, ha, ha! Then a woman—always a woman, a patient and compassionate woman—actually bothered to sit quietly and watch for long enough to figure out that we were in fact snapping live twigs off of trees and stripping the leaves before rooting around in the termite hole, because the termites stick better that way, for life clings to life. Since then, by the way, chimpanzees in "the wild" have also been observed smashing nuts open with rocks and hunting with makeshift spears. So check and mate then, we *Pan troglodytes* both use and modify, and the list of things that make human beings so fucking special continues to shrink.

But my point is, what goes for technology goes for vanity. To recognize oneself in a mirror is one thing, to modify oneself in a mirror is another. Body modification is more human than merely humanlike. I see human, I look in the mirror, I see ape. This was a great psychological vexation in my formative years. Monkey see, monkey want to be.

For what differentiates a human being from a chimpanzee? Merely in physical terms, I mean. If space aliens were to beam down to Earth tomorrow and look at all the creatures that slither, crawl, hop, run, prance, swim, waddle, and walk it, and initially have some trouble telling chimpanzees apart from humans, what subtle physiognomic distinctions would we tell them to take note of so they might better parse us out from one another? Notice the length of the legs and the forearms, we would tell them, the shape of the skull, the curvature of the spine, the distance between fore-finger and thumb, that humans have two opposable thumbs and chimps have four. And chimps have thick hair all over their bodies. So there are two principal things hominid animals did when they branched off from our common ancestor: they gained language and lost their hair. In becoming human, I realized that I was faced with the daunting task of reenacting about five million years of parallel evolution, all by my little self. I had gained language, check, but now I began to want a physiognomy that was closer to human. It wasn't just that altering my physical appearance made me more attractive—though it certainly did—but that I was disgusted with myself. Humans: I wanted to be one of them, and I simultaneously hated myself for this dirty disgusting perverted desire. I couldn't go back to the zoo. I couldn't go back to being a chimp, not after everything I had learned. I was between species. I still am. I don't feel at home in either genus, *Homo* or *Pan*.

My body looked ugly, so goddamn ugly. I hated my face. I hated my nose. I hated my fingers. I hated my toes. I hated my long arms. I hated my stubby, ridiculous legs. I hated my grotesque feet. And now most of all I hated these sickly-looking, uneven patches in my once-thick coat of fur. I decided to simply get rid of it, to mow the field. To cover up my unsightly hair loss, one evening I shaved off all of my body hair. I was alone when I did it. I found a canister of shaving cream in the cabinet under the bathroom sink—the kind that squirts out a jet of green ooze that becomes thick foam when one agitates its molecules by rubbing it against the skin. I stood naked in the bathtub, sopping wet, and squirted this stuff into my remaining fur and lathered it in. Then I took the razor—all this equipment was Lydia's—and, swishing it between strokes in the lukewarm bathwater I stood in, I scraped off all my hair, except for the few areas in which humans are hirsute: the top of the head, the underarms and the neat corona haloing the genitals. This was an adorable but futile gesture, for these four remaining patches of hair soon afterward also fell out. I had learned how to shave from watching Lydia shave her legs in the shower, a ritual I had observed hundreds of times. I wasn't accustomed to using a razor. In the medicine cabinet I had found a package of plastic disposable razors, and I ruined every one of them during my full-body shave, nicking myself so frequently in the process that it seemed a gallon of my blood trickled out of me to swirl sickeningly red-brown in the water below. I had so much hair all over me that it took six or seven passes to get down to the skin. This is one instance in which having these long, flexible arms was a tremendous help, as I needed no assistance to reach my back. The shaving took an hour to complete. I depleted the entire can of shaving cream in the process. When I drained the water, the bathtub was coated an inch thick all around with a sodden carpet of soapy, bloody chimp hair. Imagine how it smelled. I scooped it up in sopping handfuls and dumped it all in the toilet, flushing repeatedly until it was gone, all gone, and then showered off all the residual hairs still clinging to my skin. When I was finished, I presented me to myself in the mirror. I scrambled onto the bathroom counter and clung to the rims of the sink by my opposable toes, to look at the full length of my naked and newly hairless body in the harshness of the four incandescent bulbs above the bathroom mirror. I stood inches away from the cool silver glass. I liked the way I looked. The novelty of this moment—the autoerotic thrill. In the next room I heard Lydia shift in bed and mumble something in her sleep. I caressed myself, sensuously smoothing my arms up and down my hairless torso. It wasn't just the feeling—the newfound tingling hypersensitivity all over my body, the visible prickles of gooseflesh—it was also that I had never before looked so achingly human. I gazed into the mirror. What gazed back at me was no longer recognizably Bruno the chimp. In that reflection was undeniably a person, after a fashion. His legs had thickened out considerably with the years of exercise they'd been getting from all his bipedal walking. He stood on two feet, and rigidly upright—this creature no longer had a moronically bowed simian spine, but had begun to develop a slight S-curve in the small of his back above the tailbone, just like a man. He stood with his forehead out and chin aimed downward, instead of with his face jutting out like that of an ape, who enters a room jaw first. He stood with his arms at his sides. He was still dripping from the shower. Except for the patches in his crotch and armpits, his body was hairless: just one smooth long tract of peachy naked flesh. Flesh that needs to be clothed in the cold. Flesh that needs to be clothed for decency. Flesh that is unclothed only behind locked doors in the dark, in the most private of private moments, in the most private of private places. Flesh that is desirable, flesh that is shameful, flesh that is frail. Flesh that yearns for flesh. This animal in the mirror: it may have been that he stood a mere three feet ten, it may have been that his feet monkeyishly resembled his hands, with two extra thumbs sprouting grotesquely from his insteps, it may have been that his legs were stumpy and that his hands, when at rest, dangled down past his knees—but this animal *carried himself* like a man, god *damn* it, his eyes had a certain glint indicative of a brain pregnant with complex symbolic intelligence. Faculties of reason, faculties of vanity, faculties of pride. Thou hast made him little less than an angel. Here Bruno Narcissus received in his hand the dubious gift of an erection just from looking at himself, contemplating his own body, how humanlike it was becoming, how very human. He turned in circles in the mirror, admiring his freshly shaven skin, creaking his head over his shoulder trying to get a look at his backside. Bruno, the hero of our story, decided to masturbate onto the mirror. Or rather, it was decided for him. Who can say what real choice he had in the matter? That is a question for philosophers, not the humble autobiographer. All I know for sure is that Bruno stood before his magnificent image in the mirror and stared long and deep into his own eyes, and as he did messages bounced back and forth between his mind and his reflection, photons leapt and wiggled from his eyes to the mirror and back into his eyes, shot into those two globs of light-perceiving jelly in his head, tunneled through his optic nerves and buried themselves smack in the squishy electric meat of his brain, became data to be exploded and decoded by this beautiful organ of consciousness set snug in his skull, which soaks up the world's information and reshapes itself in response, which reaches out and reshapes the world. Bruno stands, legs apart, proudly, aggressively, not unlike the men's restroom pictogram he was once reminded of by a certain clown-made pink balloon, hips out, in love with himself, in love with his own body, stroking and yanking savagely on a penis that he has just lubricated with a generous dollop of spit, lips curling back to a snarl, gnawing on his tongue, thinking of nothing more erotic than simply being a member of the human race, of humanity!—and now his chest is suddenly burning with white heat and *oo oo oo ah ah ah ah HYEEAAGHHHH, HYEEAAGHHHH!*————————he comes onto the mirror!—take *that!*—and *that!*—and the globules of milky syrupy goo go drooling triumphantly down the glass, as if the last remaining drops of his animal essence are contained in that splat of his jizzom, pure extract of primate, dripping away between me and my reflection.

My hair never grew back. What little I left of it soon also went away on its own. Since then, I have spent my life hairless. A cold, weak, naked creature of a day.

XXXII

Eventually the protesters went away. For the most part. Their protests in front of our house were no longer a daily occurrence, as they had been for months. A time finally came when we were left totally unharassed on most days. Although sometimes on weekends a few of them still showed up, the gathering of the faithful had whittled down to only a handful of indefatigable true believers—Revered Jeb, with his scarf and bow tie and brown houndstooth suit, RadioShack megaphone in hand, always reliably among them. But even Reverend Jeb was no longer an expected fixture in front of our door. Then finally a weekend came and went during which they did not show up at all, and we surmised they had forgotten or grown tired or bored with us, and we were finally free of them. Tal had fully moved in at this point. She had broken the lease of whatever Humboldt Park dump she had been inhabiting and relocated her whole gypsy bazaar of personal possessions, all her knickknacks and ornaments and gruesome lacquer-polished puppets into the cramped and uncarpeted bedroom that had once been Lydia's stillborn son's intended bedroom in days much different than these, and then, for a time, my bedroom, and then, for a time, my painting studio. Tal was crowded out of the room by her things, as if the puppets wanted the living space, and they kicked her out so they could spread out their spindly wooden arms and legs, and she obeyed them, and did not sleep in that room.

At first she slept on the living room couch. But Tal spent only a night or two on the couch before Lydia, in what few words could still come to her, haltingly and stutteringly and pointingly and gesturingly invited her to sleep in "the big bed" with us. Lydia needed as much comfort, as much human warmth, as much skin next to hers as possible. Of course I would have preferred Tal to sleep alone. Before Tal came to stay with us, before the period during which every night all three of us were sealed in like a row of sardines in the bed, Lydia and I would make love in a sluggish, dreamy way—she, silent, pregnant, brainsick; both of us groggy and sweaty. Because of her sensitive belly it was only possible to conduct intercourse in a limited number of arrangements. That was one thing that was possible without words, one thing that was perhaps enhanced by wordlessness: the physical act of love. But Lydia seemed more and more often to not be in the mood for it, and there was no sex after Tal joined us in the bed. Lydia seemed to prefer that Tal be near to her, and so I, rather nobly I think, refrained from complaining of this sleeping arrangement.

It was a crowded bed all right, with me beside Lydia and Lydia beside Tal, or more often Lydia and Tal on the right and left sides of the bed and me monkey-in-the-middle between them, this to facilitate Lydia's semisomnambulant night ramblings that came from spending the daylight hours drowned in sleep, so she could get out of bed without waking me or Tal. And who can say what she might have done during our slumber? Certainly not Lydia herself. More and more she found that she could not say anything. The disease in her brain lay heavy on her tongue, rendering it numb, slow, a useless slab of meat in her mouth. The bed wasn't an uncomfortable place to sleep. I'm not a sleeper who craves contactless bodily

solitude. Especially with my then newly hairless body, I loved the
way another's flesh felt pressed against mine. If the two women
ever caught me—perhaps from the thin slit of vision between
almost-closed eyelids—surreptitiously, feverishly masturbating
once I believed they were both asleep, they never said anything to
me about it. When the necessary act was finished, I would quietly smear away the result on the hem of Lydia's nightgown, roll
over and submerge myself in dreams, falling asleep listening to the
steady shallow rhythms of two human women breathing softly
beside me.

Then in the morning murk of winter, Tal and I would rise
together, prepare ourselves for the day and set out for the lab, leaving Lydia still asleep. Tal and I would make that walk of twenty or
twenty-five minutes together from our home to the lab, our place of
employment, side by side, buried in winter coats, our breath bouncing against our scarves back onto our faces for warmth. It wasn't an
unpleasant walk, anyway: a left turn on Fifty-second, a right on
University, four blocks down, across the wide bustling expanse of
Fifty-fifth just as the sun was breaking into full light over the road,
past the white vastness of the snowed-over soccer field, block by
block the university buildings looking more and more like medieval fortresses all buttressed, turreted and bulwarked, gargoyles
squatting bat-winged and freakish at the corners of the sills with
torrents of watery vomit hanging frozen from their open mouths,
now a right on Fifty-seventh, and now we pass through the tabernacular gatehouse, jagged with dripping icicle teeth, then across
the main quad, up the stairs, through the doors, down the hall,
into the elevator, out of the elevator, down the hall, and through
the frosted-glass door to the lab, room 308.

I do not know for how long we were being followed each morning before I noticed him. Tal and I had long since accustomed ourselves to slipping out the back way when we left the apartment in

the morning on our way to work, but with the protesters gone, we felt safe enough from their molestations to brave the world through our own front door—imagine!—as if we were not hunted criminals. On a certain morning as we were crossing Fifty-fifth Street, I happened to look behind us. I don't know what prompted me to look back. Some little inchworm of paranoia inched into my mind and whispered to me that we were being watched. I turned around. I felt we were in the company of a third. When I counted, there was only she and I together, but when I looked behind us down the white road, I saw another. I did not know whether a man or a woman. When I looked harder, when my eyes narrowed to slits of concentrated vision, the person went away—like a mirage, like a Fata Morgana appearing steamy and silvery on the horizon to the eyes of a traveler hallucinatory with thirst, only to vanish upon closer inspection. We walked on. A block or two later down the road I turned around again. I saw someone walking down the street, in our direction, a block and a half north of us. Granted, there would have been nothing unusual at all—as this was Hyde Park, not Shackleton's Antarctic—about a lone pedestrian who happened to be walking a block and a half in tandem with us, but the way this person was moving suggested some ulterior hostility. We walked on. I filched another backward glance down the street, and this time saw nothing. This afforded me no comfort. I said nothing about this to Tal, who was walking alongside me, heaving breath into her scarf in the cold with her eyes locked to the ground.

The next morning I saw him again. I was sure it was a man now. I saw him again, and again I looked a second time and he was gone. But I had noticed—or thought I had noticed, or convinced myself later that I had noticed—a brown suit, of what may or may not have been houndstooth, and a long blue-and-white-striped scarf.

I asked Tal then if she noticed someone walking behind us. She said she didn't see anyone, and shrugged it off. We went to the lab. I remember that day at work about as well as I remember my own birth. What I remember was what happened after.

When we left the lab that day, something in the world was wrong. The sun was waning weak and orange over the craggy parapets of the ivy-strangled gray stone buildings. It was early March. The snow on the ground had been painted over with rainwater, which had frozen to a candylike crunchy glaze of thin prismatic crystal on top of the old snow. Tal and I walked home together in near silence, listening to our breath and the footfalls of our booted feet busting through the carapace of ice on top of the snow. When we got home, Tal unlocked the front door and pushed it in. In the foyer we stamped the slush off our boot soles and hung our coats on pegs. The apartment was cold inside. It was nearly as cold inside as out. This was because someone had smashed in the glass in the back door. The remaining glass in the sliding door clung to the doorframe in jagged triangles. We walked into the silent living room in our snow boots. The blue-green glass was scattered like sugar, like sand, across the floor of our apartment. Shards of it kissed and crunched beneath our boots. Tal called Lydia's name twice: the first time with the rising inflection of a question, and the second time loud, hard and flat. There was no answer.

Lydia was in the bedroom, right where we had left her that morning. We saw her lying in the bed. Tal saw her lying there, and immediately turned around and ran down the hallway to the phone. A moment later I heard her yelling and crying into the receiver of the phone in the kitchen. The room was dark, blinds shut. Lydia was in bed, in her nightgown—she effectively lived in that silken garment these days. The bed was soaked with her blood, soaked as damp as a sponge. I pressed my fingers into the mattress, and like a sponge its surface offered up blood as it squelched and sank under the slight pressure of my fingertips. Her legs were folded into her stomach beneath the wet bedsheet. Her blond hair stuck out of her head in short spiky sprigs because her head had been shaved for her surgery several months before. Her eyes were closed. Her bloody bare feet stuck out from under the sheet. A lamp that had been on the bedside table lay overturned and broken on the floor. I went to the head of the bed and put my hands on her head. Her eyes vibrated a little under her eyelids. Her chest was drawing and exhaling air. Tal came back from the kitchen and flicked on the bedroom light, and we winced at the sudden brightness. Lydia groaned. Tal unpeeled the sheet, limp and heavy with wetness, from Lydia's body. Her arms and legs were swollen and purple with bruises. The bottom of her nightgown had been yanked inside out and jerked up past her navel. Her bloody naked legs were curled into her belly. From between her legs a knotty cable of red flesh came out of her body, and this cable of flesh wound and wound out of her and connected to a little thing that lay there in the bloody sheets beside her on the bed. This thing was about as big as two fists held together. It looked like a rubber puppet. Its skin was red and blotched with purple. Its eyes were closed. It was curled into itself, with knees drawn up, and long rubbery arms tucked under the chin. It had a face, a twisted-up rubbery goblin face. Its round flaps for ears stuck straight out of the sides of its clumsy round rubber ball of a head. The membranous skin of the ears was so thin it was translucent—I could see the forking blue veins in them. It had a wide mouth, with a long space between the flat, upturned nose and the upper lip. The wispy black beginnings of eyebrows sprouted above its eyes. It had long gangly arms and stubby, foreshortened legs. But its fingers and toes—already with tiny fingernails and toenails on them—were so thin, and so delicate, so unmistakably human.

We could already hear the siren of the ambulance that Tal had just called screaming up our street outside when we looked up and saw writing on the wall. This was something we had failed to see when Tal and I first walked into the room that afternoon. There was something scrawled on the wall of our bedroom. It was written above the headboard of the bed in black marker, in thick capital letters:

AND IF A WOMAN LIES WITH ANY ANIMAL, YOU SHALL KILL BOTH THE WOMAN AND THE ANIMAL. THEY MUST BE PUT TO DEATH. THEIR BLOOD SHALL BE UPON THEM.

LEVITICUS 20:16

Part Five

Gentlemen, pity me. I am science.

—*Woyzeck*

XXXIII

That night I was taken away. I was drugged, stripped naked, and locked in a cage. This cage was not dissimilar to the cage I had once been put into when Lydia conveyed me from my birth home in the Primate House of the Lincoln Park Zoo to the laboratory at the University of Chicago: it was a temporary cage, designed for carrying me against my will to a place where I had no wish to go. It was cramped, such that I could neither lie down at my full length nor stand up at my full height. It featured a grated metal door that hinged open when unlocked from the outside, through the squares of which I could only strain to see my surroundings. A repugnant odor filled this claustrophobic cube of space, smelling first of the unwelcoming plastic and chemical smell of its material, and later, once I had been forced by my confinement to piss and shit inside it, it smelled of my own bodily filth.

Why had I been put inside this cage that I describe? For three reasons: (one) I admit, for my own safety, as my life was believed to be in danger; (two) I suppose, for the safety of others, for I will own that on that evening I did do a good deal of weeping and gnashing of teeth, and of flailing, of spitting, of howling, of shrieking, of screaming, and I shall even humbly admit that my behavior disquieted and disturbed the humans who were then in my presence—that I was showing myself, despite my articulation and erudition, to be unfit—at least temporarily—for the freedom of unrestricted social congress with and within human (and please, Gwen, make sure to seal this next word in a bitterly mocking envelope of quotation marks) "civilization"; and (three) for transport. For I was set to be forcibly relocated. Whither? Eastward. Why? For my imprisonment.

It happened like this. We were back in the hospital. This place where we had been spending a lot of unhappy time lately. The same giant university hospital as before: the bubble-belching water cooler, the fish tank, the pink-upholstered chairs in the waiting room, the coffee tables littered with bright crinkling magazines, the pervasive odor of antiseptic fluids. I rode with Tal in the back of the ambulance, with Lydia supine on a gurney. Bumpy ride, thankfully brief in duration. The banshee howl of the siren over our heads, transparent plastic bags dangling from hooks in the ceiling, tubes, machines, equipment. Lydia unconscious, covered in blood. First the paramedics snipped the umbilical cord that still connected her to our dead son, untimely ripped from her womb. Dark medical words and phrases floated around above my head, among them: "massive hemorrhaging," "blood loss," "forced abortion." The back doors of the vehicle banged apart and we tumbled out. They took Lydia away on the gurney, wheeling and whanging her into a secret part of the hospital's labyrinth, to which Tal was permitted to come, but not I, search me why. I was left alone in the waiting room, kept company only by the lady at the ER desk and the tank full of fucking fish. This was when all the sweetness and light of my learned humanity temporarily escaped my soul, leaving only the confusion of the animal.

Then two large and forceful men in turquoise onesies emerged from some hidden location, chased me down until they had me seized by the arms, and one of them produced a long hypodermic needle. They wore white latex gloves. The one with the needle pressed the button of it and made whatever was the vile liquid contained inside its chute squirt slightly from the point of the long fierce needle, and tapped it twice with his finger. He slid the needle into a vein in my arm and pushed the poison inside me. Admittedly, I may have been causing a ruckus. Admittedly, when left alone by my humans, I may have begun to scream. Admittedly, I may have torn around the room in a crazed apoplexy of fury. Admittedly, I may have been overturning tables and chairs. Admittedly, I may have bitten some woman, a total stranger, how deeply I do not know, on the leg. Admittedly, I may have tasted the warm coppery tang of blood on my tongue. Admittedly, I may have—for some reason that may or may not have made sense to me at the time—yanked out the leg of the piece of furniture that supported the fish tank, and, admittedly, the fish tank may have fallen, and may even have smashed upon the floor of the ER waiting room with catastrophic violence and noise, and the water in it may have whooshed swiftly across the room and gone spilling down the steps leading into the lobby from the door, and it may have smelled putridly, and the flat translucent triangular bodies of the angelfish may have lain, gaping, slapping, dying on the waiting room floor amid a crunchy scattering of slime-coated pink gravel and broken glass and the broken chunks of a ceramic deep-sea diver with a ceramic chest of sunken treasure. Admittedly, I may also have bitten the man who savagely held me to the floor while the other slipped that needleful of venom into my bloodstream, to make me sleep, and the bitten man may have cursed and shouted, for in fact I may have nibbled on his forearm so ferociously that it was a damned lucky thing for him that he happened to already be in a hospital, for his wound may indeed have required immediate medical attention. I looked up at the ceiling, hazily, the forced soporific trickling swiftly through my blood.

I saw the rotating blades of a ceiling fan above me. I closed my eyes.

When my eyes opened I was in a cage. Four walls, a ceiling, a floor: no way out. Through the miserly square of vision given me of the world outside my cage, further cut by the crisscrossing metal bars into a grid of smaller squares, I saw a long metal floor, wavy with corrugations, and beyond that, a slightly curving metal wall. I heard a low droning rumble, a purring noise that gave this storage room or cargo hold—for that was what it appeared to be—an ear-swelling, stifling acoustic character. My head felt groggy, sick, hot, and blood-fat, as if my ears were plugged with wax. I rooted around with my fingers in the recesses of my giant round ears, and found nothing in them. I noticed that by yawning my mouth wide or by clicking my jaw this wax-stuffed ear feeling abated, albeit only slightly and temporarily. I also felt an unprecedented sensation in my guts, there was a woozy inconstancy to the quality of the gravity in this room. I concluded therefore that I was aboard a ship that was sailing on the sea. I had never been on a boat before of any sort, but I had heard and read accounts of the experience from various sources, and these remembered descriptions seemed to roughly align with what I was then experiencing: this nauseous pitching and rolling of the room, this dipping and weaving feeling, my body's yearning for solid earth, for the reliability of gravity to keep my feet planted comfortably to ground. I made a noise, just to hear myself. I called out: "HELLO!" It was hard to hear with that softly vibrating rumble all over the room. No one answered. I was alone. Piled up in this room with me were all sorts of crates, boxes, bags, suitcases—suitcases?—why suitcases? Whatever journey we were on seemed to be a long one. It was chilly in the cargo hold of this vessel. My abductors had supplied me with a thin, ratty blanket—their one humane nod to considerations of my comfort—and in this flimsy scrap of cloth I wrapped myself tight against my shivering until the end of the journey, silently awaiting my fate. But this ship did not slowly push into port and maneuver itself at the dock to drop anchor, as I had expected, based on my chance readings on nautical matters, but rather, the sound of the vibrant rumbling purr that permeated the long dark metal room suddenly escalated in pitch and crescendoed in volume, and as it did I felt all my precious innards jump up into my throat with the sickening rollick of the craft. You see, Gwen, I was not in a ship sailing across the bubbling waves as I had thought, but rather flying through the sky, in an aircraft—and we were descending. The sound of the jet engines' howl as we approached the surface of the earth was more terrifying than even thunder—for it was the work of man—and my heart nearly exploded in fear when I felt what I now believe was the jolting *b-bump* of our wheels making contact with the ground. This was followed by a period of comparative calm. I still sensed motion in my belly, but I guessed that our craft, grounded now, had slowed to a gentle creep, and the earth beneath us was perfectly flat. Then we stopped. I heard the hisses and sighs of depressurization. The reverberant purr of the whole moving building was abruptly cut, and silence swept into the auditory vacuum left in its wake. I heard noises above me, shifting, thumping, banging. Then a door opened. I heard a pressure lock released, the unratcheting of a hatch, something shrieking on metal hinges, and then the rich audioscape of the outside world. Two pairs of boots clanged arrhythmically on the corrugated metal floor. They were coming straight for me.

"There he is."

"Poor guy."

I decided to pretend to be asleep. I collapsed in affected slumber beneath my blanket. I heard the boots clang closer, and felt the presence of someone bending down to peer through the door of my cage. I dared not open my eyes.

"Smells like he pissed in his cage."

"Where's he going?"

"Westchester. NYU has a research lab up there."

"The fuck's wrong with his hair?"

"Dunno. They said it all just fell off."

"Is he okay? He looks sick or something."

"They knocked him on his ass with tranquilizers. They said he'd probably sleep straight through everything. This monkey's out cold."

"Look at the poor little guy, he's all passed out and hairless and shit."

"It's a sad story. The lady he was with is terminally ill. She's got brain cancer. Then she got attacked or something. Some religious nutcase tried to kill her. This all just happened yesterday. She's in real bad shape. Then this guy just freaked his little ass out. For some fucking reason he was at the hospital with her in Chicago."

"What? No."

"Yeah. He starts tearing the place up, said he broke a fish tank or something. So they knock him out, *good* night. But then nobody knows what to do with him. They told me somebody puts in a call to somebody, yadda yadda yadda, the people at this NYU medical lab say they want him. They always need chimps. So they got him."

"Is that the crazy lady in Chicago who was fucking her pet chimp?"

"Yeah, that's the one. And this is the chimp."

"I heard about that on the news. Shit was fucked up."

"C'mon. You get that end."

"We got directions?"

"I know the place. We take the Whitestone to the Hutch."

I heard jostling and scooting, and then felt myself being hoisted up.

"He's a *heavy* motherfucker."

My cage wobbled and swayed as the possessors of these voices bore me away. I opened one of my eyes just a sliver. I saw the torso of one of the men, just outside the window of my cage. He was wearing a dark green uniform. He and the other man, who I could not see, carried me out of the cargo hold of the airplane and down a flight of stairs. It was daylight, cold and windy. I shivered under the thin blanket. They carried my cage across a wide flat expanse of gray concrete and set it down on the back of a motorized cart. The two men climbed into the front of the cart and we began to drive away. Through the small grated window and through a single eye that I would only half-open out of caution, I looked out across this expanse of gray concrete crisscrossed with long curving lines of yellow paint: I saw enormous machines resting on it; I saw people moving on it by foot and by vehicle; I saw an ice-blue sky looming cloudless overhead; and in the distance I saw many tall and glittering buildings. I saw a tangled lacework of gold, copper, silver, iron, steel—skyscrapers—the lattices of bridges, power lines, radio towers, smokestacks, and antennae. All this looked similar to what could be found in Chicago—similar in make and shape and character, and probably also similar in purpose—but I recognized none of it, which told me that I had been taken to another city, another seat of this civilization—one that was apparently even bigger than my beloved home city. What city on this earth, I wondered, could possibly have been built up wider and higher than Chicago? Was the world so insatiate? What conceivable need could there be for a city that was even greater yet, more sprawling, more complex, and more powerful than Chicago, my Chicago?

The two men transported me in the small vehicle across this ocean of concrete, parked the vehicle, hopped out. I closed my eyes again in my sleep of deceit. So in darkness I felt myself being picked up in my cage, carried across a breadth of space, and set down inside a warm, quiet enclosure. I heard car doors slamming shut, opening, slamming, locking with decisive clicks. I heard a radio flicker on with music. I allowed my eyes to open and perceived that I was in the storage area of a van. I could not see out of it. I guessed the last leg of my forced journey—that which was by road—to take about an hour's duration. I could see nothing. The men conversed in the front seats, but for the throbbing engine of the van I could not hear them. We moved along quickly at times and crept slowly at others. The van eventually stopped, with a whine of brakes and the motor shuddering off. I shut my eyes. The doors opened and they picked me up and carried me, heaving and grunting. I opened my eye a cautious slit, enough to see that I was being carried into a building—a cool, large, clean, institutional building, a kind of place I was more familiar with than I would have liked to be. They carried me through the brightly lit hallways. I heard the two men's boots scrunching on the hard shiny floors. Hallway, elevator, hallway, doors. They carried me down a long corridor and into a dim, cavernous room. The concrete floor sloped in the middle into a shallow valley with grimy iron drains in it, and the room smelled thick and perfect with the odors of animal excrement. But the sounds of the room: a cacophony of yelps, howls, hoots, screams, clicks, scrapes, scratches, chatters, rattles and bangs rose up like so much auditory vomit in the foul and filthy air from both sides of the room—we were descending, as if led by the hand of Virgil down the grotto steps into the Inferno, abandon all hope ye who enter here—these were the noises of the dungeon, like sounds suggested by a Hieronymus Bosch painting of unending pain, of suffering, of Hell. There were cages, and inside the cages twisted, screaming faces, the mocks and mows of apes with foreheads villainous low. On either side of the room stood three long rows of metal cages stacked one on top of the next, and each cage contained a chimp. This room was a prison, a torture garden, a madhouse for

the dirty, for the crazed, for the rage-rankled and diseased creatures in it, locked up in four-by-four-foot cells forever till death
deliver them from their pain, imprisoned and tortured for crimes
unknown to them. Sick curiosity got the better of my caution, and
out of horror I let both my eyes open. I saw them: I saw their rangy,
sickness-ridden, parasite-bitten and malnourished arms and fingers dangling, weak, limp, pathetic, from between the bars of their
cages, their eyes murky piss-yellow with jaundice, wracked with
who knows what artificially injected illnesses—AIDS, hepatitis—
their minds and bodies ravaged with hate and sadness and madness
and fear. They shook, they shivered, they banged their fists against
their heads and throttled the bars of their cages, they cried out in
despair. This was the place where I had been brought. I shut my
eyes.

I would not stay in this place. No. I refused. My pride would not
let me. Pride? Or was it my vanity? Fine, then: call it my vanity. To
say nothing of my fear. I do not care what you call my motive for
escape, but I had to escape. I would not live in there, I would not
die in there. I thought: you fuckers cannot keep me here. I will find
a way out—I will claw and chew and fight my way out if I have to,
and I do not care in the least who I hurt in the process. You do not
own me. I will not give my life to science. I will not give my life
to human medicine. If my body could provide the data that cure
every disease in the world, I still would not let you touch it. No,
Man, you shall *not* have dominion over *me*.

The two men who had brought me here stopped and lowered my
cage onto the piss-stained cement floor.

"Careful when we transfer him. We don't want him waking up
and giving us any trouble." I felt the gaze of the man looking at me
through the bars of the cage. "Aw," he said. "This little baldheaded
guy's sleeping like a baby."

"Good."

I felt and heard the cage door being unlocked. It squeaked open. The man prodded my falsely sleeping flank with an experimental finger.

"He's out cold."

"So c'mon then. Let's do this."

Two big hot human hands entered my cage and took hold of my arms. Though my heart hammered at my ribs and my stomach trembled, I did all I could to keep feigning sleep. I tried to relax completely, to let slack every muscle in me, to be limp, as floppy and boneless as a stuffed toy, as a puppet. The hands dragged me out of the cage. I slid out onto the cold floor. He picked me up by the shoulders. I let my legs dangle like rags.

"Okay, now get the cage open."

I opened my eyes and bit down as hard as I could on the forearm of the man who held me. I let my teeth sink deep into his skin. I felt my teeth pressing through cloth and skin and muscle and clamping down on bone, and I ripped my mouth away with my jaws locked.

"FUCK!" the fellow asseverated. He dropped me.

Blood was running rapidly out of the shirt cuff of his green uniform. I tasted that hot coppery taste in my mouth. The chimps imprisoned all around me in three rows stretching down the length of each long wall—they shrieked, they barked, they crashed around in their cages, a pandemonium of noises both animalistic and metallic. The other man stood by in dumb shock beside the open door to the empty cage where they were supposed to put me, sitting flush between the walls of two other cages, each containing a single miserable and sickly chimp. I stood naked before them on the concrete floor. Blood poured from the arm of the man I had bitten. The two looked at me for a moment, too agog with surprise to do anything for a very brief moment. In this moment I held up my right hand with my index, ring and pinky finger curled into my palm, but with the second digit from my thumb stretched straight upward for their viewing. And lest our readers mistake the general for the particular, let me clarify: that goes out to all humanity.

"HA!" I informed them. And so saying, I turned, pivoting sharply on my heels to rotate my body away from them such that I faced the other direction, looking down the corridor of cages toward the door at the end of it, while conversely showing them my hairless backside and naked little ass—and I ran.

Oh boy, did I run.

I had no time to gather my bearings. My adrenaline-flooded nerves shimmered with panic. Here, Gwen, is where I heave a sigh of mild remorse that the narrative I tell must now dip its fingers ever so slightly into the cartoonish, the grotesque, even. So be it. Tell it I must, for it is true.

Fumbling, four-limbed and pell-mell, my body an exploding ball of fear-driven energy, I ran down the corridor between the two walls of cages full of chimps—chimps like me, but like me only by genetic accident of birth—all of them screeching, teeth-gnashing, cage-shaking, wailing in their pitiful metal boxes. Broken, doomed. I wish I could have unlatched their cages, set them free. They shouted at me as I ran, perhaps half in envy or admiration of my mad dash for escape, and half in pleading for their own freedom—but I had no time to play their liberator—I had to liberate myself!—and so I ran. I raced headlong between them toward the door. The other man, the one I had left physically unpunished, now began to chase after me, having recovered from the initial surprise I gave him, while the man I had bitten staggered, grumbling hoarsely in pain, clutching his bleeding arm, in the other direction, to the opposite end of the room where there was another door—to trigger an alarm of some sort? I crashed through the heavy double swinging doors at the end of the corridor and into a hallway, shooting wild looks around me for something in arm's reach to bar the doors with, and, finding nothing, I chose a direction and kept running. Then a blaring electric roar sounded all over the building—it *was* an alarm!—and I saw a retina-piercing white light flickering from a red machine at the corner of a wall. The noise was so bone-grindingly loud. Doors all down the hallway whacked open and confused-looking men and women in white coats stumbled out of them, blinked, looked around, and shrieked when they saw me as I scrambled past them, bouncing off the walls, swinging from the pipes in the ceiling, rushing between their legs, knocking them to the floor. I heard the clamor of pursuing feet in the hall behind me. I picked a door at random and pushed through it, finding an emergency stairwell on the other side. I started down the rectangular spiral of white-washed metal stairs. The building roared and flashed everywhere with the alarm. I hadn't descended two flights before my pursuers came through the door after me. They were men in shiny blue jumpsuits—they had walkie-talkies clipped to their belts and vests, beeping, crunching and squawking with static, and they carried electric prods. I jumped off the railing down the shaft, bouncing from one flight down to the next, in my animal agility gripping, swinging, releasing, swooping myself down the stair shaft by my long arms and four hands. The sickening spiral of stairs above me shrank rectangle by rectangle to the ceiling. The staircase wobbled and clanged with shoes, and the tall blank room resonated up and down with the echoes of shouting human voices. I jumped onto the next landing and saw a door with a narrow window in it, and I saw that the window was bright with the natural light of sun and sky. The green light of an institutional EXIT sign glowed above the door. I slammed myself into the bar of the door, it fell open for me, and I was out. I was in an alley behind the building. I looked to the right: a long flat brick wall, beyond which I could see what looked like a parking lot. I looked to the left: more wall, several dumpsters, more parking lot. I looked straight ahead: a chain-link fence with a pigtail coil of razor wire strung along the top of it. Beyond the fence: a forest of thin brown dead trees—and the possibility of escape. Now I was climbing the fence, which wobbled with my weight against its poles, metal chiming against metal, and I heard the handle of the door jitter open behind me. I did not look back. I scrambled over the top of the fence and dragged my naked body through the coil of razor wire. I felt the blades lacerate my flesh in a dozen places as I scrambled panic-blind and unthinking through it. I heard gunshots, actual gunshots behind me, but the bullets missed me. I was already swinging by my long arms, crashing through the dry branches of the trees, brachiating from canopy to canopy, before I even felt the pain, or saw the freely flowing gush of my own bright blood leaving my body.

XXXIV

The previous day (or whenever it was—my sense of time was garbled, the string of memories that led me here all tangled up in a knot) I had woken up in Chicago—and now here I sat, far away in an unknown place, in a tree, no less, like my fathers before me, and also like my fathers before me, naked. And I was bleeding profusely. I had cut myself badly on that fence. Cuts all over my legs, my chest, my arms. They were not rough cuts either—which are actually less painful—but thin, precise, deep slices. I was covered in blood. I was filthy. I was hungry, I was thirsty. I was lost. Oh—and, this being March, I think, while not abjectly freezing, it was very cold. And let's not forget I was hairless, too, and to add insult to my compounded injuries, nude: therefore I was shivering. And I knew that they would be hunting after me. Thus was the state of my affairs: bleak. I sat there awhile, my arms hugging my legs for warmth, rocking back and forth, bleeding in a tree. I was an endangered animal.

By and by the bleeding stopped, but my skin was tingly, hypersensitive, swollen with pain for days afterward. I still have faint white scars. After escaping from the biomedical research lab, I crashed blindly through the woods in this place yet unnamed to me, until I came to a narrow paved road with a shallow ditch running beside it. I slogged through the ditch awhile, my naked feet stepping on rocks and twigs and squelching in the mud, diving for cover beneath muck and dead leaves and pine needles every time I heard a car coming. I lost myself in another thicket of these knotty, spindly brown trees, thrashed through the leaves and bushes until I came to a pond, which was frozen except for a hole in the center. At the pond's edge I bashed the ice in until I uncovered liquid, and I drank from two cupped palms and rinsed my wounds with dripping handfuls of frigid water. My fingers went numb and turned blue. I cracked and rattled my way between trees and more trees and through crunching piles of leaves, sticks, slush, dirt, and hard old gray snow.

At first I thought I was deep in some unknown wilderness. It hit me like a gestalt shift—like the precise moment you realize the negative spaces surrounding that goblet make the silhouettes of two lovers poised to kiss—when I realized that I had not been in the wilderness, but actually in a wooded area of a big park or something, which sat along the peripheries of what looked like a quiet, leafy, upper-class suburb. I realized this only when I stumbled—ragged, muddy, blood-streaked, naked—out of the bushes and into someone's backyard. Across the yard sat a palatial house, a big viny shingly stony half-timbered chunk of Tudor architecture painted white and brown, loaded with gables and turrets and windows with diamond-shaped panes set in diagonally crosshatching grids. A big brick veranda spilled from the back door of the house down in a series of wide shallow steps onto a long slope of lawn, which I'm sure shimmered like an emerald in the summer but at the time was brown and yellow with winter. There was a drained swimming pool near the house, with orange rust streaks drooling from the rivets in the blue-green marbled walls of white lime. At the bottom of the sloping lawn there was a children's jungle gym: a ladder led to two parallel wooden beams connected by metal bars, while from one of these wooden beams two swing seats hung on slack chains—one of the chains was tangled such that one swing was twisted at an angle—and this was attached to a wooden platform, sheltered by a small roof and accessible by a ladder, and a bright red plastic slide slalomed to the earth from the deck of the platform. It reminded me of the furniture in the chimp habitat I shared with my original family in the zoo. The structure looked like it had fallen into habitual disuse, by the rust in its metal and the splitting in its wood. Beside it was a sandbox; several forgotten toys lay partially buried in the frost-hardened sand. Nearby all this stood a tiny pink house. I think one could safely call it a "cottage." The little house, set away from the big: I was reminded of the little house/big house dynamic of the Lawrence Ranch. From inside the house (the big house) I heard the manic yapping of a small dog—yapping, most likely, at me. I approached the cottage.

This little cottage was about the size of a small garage. It was built to imitate a human dwelling, but all in miniature. The door, for instance, was not built to human scale—it was only slightly above half the height of a door in accordance with modern architectural standards. Two shuttered windows flanked a door placed dead in the center of one wall, with planter boxes full of dead flowers below each window. The door itself had an arched top, and was pink with a decorative white valentine heart in the middle. The heart was replicated in the pink trim above both the windows. When I came nearer I realized that the whole thing was made of plastic, designed to mimic the appearance of painted wood.

I tried the doorknob—which was also shaped like a heart— found it open, and went in. The door was so short that I, at my three feet ten, passed through it with only a few inches of space above my head. I shut the door behind me. It was cool inside, but warm enough. The tiny house was crowded with artifacts of an

American childhood: toys and games and crayons and markers and stuffed animals. The interior walls were as pink as the gastrointestinal medicine that Lydia would sometimes urge me to swallow when I had a stomachache, and covered too with images of hearts and flowers, and also with smudgy fingerprints and the errant crayon and marker scribblings of children. A tiny tea set rested on a tiny tray on top of a lacy white tablecloth draped across a tiny tea table made of elaborately bent wire. Amid the plastic teacups, teakettle, and saucers, a plastic vase stood as centerpiece. From the lip of the table protruded the green plastic stems of fabric flowers. On the table, along with all this mock-Victorian crockery, were strewn several small rubber effigies of beautiful naked women, lankily proportioned and Nordic-featured, with heads of flowing bright blond hair; the women were disturbingly desexed, with smooth nippleless breasts and no discernible genitalia in their crotches, and one of them was, due perhaps to some horrific imaginary accident, missing an arm, for only a plastic peg the same color as her flesh protruded from the socket of her shoulder. Four small chairs that matched the wire table surrounded it, and the lumpy, lifeless forms of stuffed animals were pushed up on the seats of three of the chairs: a rabbit, a bear, and a duck (three animals that in the wild would obviously never sit down together in peaceful communion); the fourth chair was empty—reserved, perhaps, for Elijah. The corners of the room were obscured under mounds of other stuffed animals: a whole cuddly and disorderly menagerie of bears, birds, bunnies, horses, cows, pigs, camels, marsupials, waterfowl, ferrets, badgers, monkeys and—yes—apes. Among all these creatures, all these animals with their sweet dopey unblinking marbles for eyes, and cloth for skin, and cotton stuffing for bones and blood, I hid myself. I burrowed myself deep beneath them, and they enclosed around me, warmly enveloping my body—my cold, hurt, shivering, naked body—and, weak and battle-wracked in my aching bones, from fear and chase and cold and hunger and a thousand other stinging thistles of my fugitive deprivation, I made a soft nest of them, and my mind passed gently into the darkness of sleep, true sleep.

Later—I've no idea how much later exactly—my nostrils woke me. I smelled the very distinctive odor of cigarette smoke. The sense-memory had caused me, just before I woke, to dream of my father. For he, fat, mean, implacable Rotpeter, my biological father, was the one with whom I will always associate that odd rank musty smell, half-sweet and half-stink. I saw him squatting on a log in our chimp habitat in the Lincoln Park Zoo, smoking his chest weak and his teeth yellow and making our air stifling with his smoldering ill-gotten and clandestine-kept tobacco. I gently pushed aside the plush curtain of a stuffed pig that lay before my eyes, and peered: there was a girl—a pretty little girl—dressed in jeans and a sweater of azure silver-threaded cashmere. Her hair was brown as a nut and parted precisely straight down the center of her head and falling past her skinny shoulders on either side of her face, which was round as a full moon and nearly as radiant with the luster and smoothness of delicate youth. Her mouth and skin looked like they had been sprinkled with a film of gold dust, and her chipped fingernails were painted alternately red and green, Christmas-tree colors. She sat in the fourth chair, the previously unoccupied chair around the tea table, in the fluffy, motionless, and mute company of bear, bunny, and duck, smoking a cigarette. That's what had woken me. She brought the white stick to her lips and shallowly inhaled, and as she did the thing deftly crackled and the end of it glowed orange for a moment, and she blew the smoke out from between her gold-dusted shiny lips, and with a poised index finger she tapped on it until a cake of ash crumbled off of it into the hollow of a teacup. The fragile beauty of the girl and the childlike innocence of her surroundings contrasted with jarring sharpness against the unwholesomeness of her activity.

I must have made a noise of some sort then, or a movement, or else the girl sensed she was being watched, because her head snapped toward the pile of stuffed animals under which I lay buried. Perhaps she thought she had heard something and looked, but wasn't sure what she was looking for amid the jumble of stuffed animals heaped up in the corner of the cottage. Her eyes scanned searchingly over the animals until she was staring fixedly in my direction. I blinked. She screamed.

She shivered involuntarily, jumped up in terror, shrieked, and so on. Now, the throat of a little human girl is acoustically unique in this world for the sheer hyperbolic qualities of the sound of which it's capable: so long in duration, so deafening in volume, so piercing in pitch! I had to clap my palms over my ears lest my exploded eardrums further bloody her stuffed animals (I had already bled on them some), and in the process of clapping my hands to the sides of my head—such that I resembled the central of the Three Wise Monkeys—my flailing arms upset the pile of stuffed animals, sending them flying in all directions, and also revealing myself from the waist up—and, upon seeing me, the girl's bright eyes waxed all the wider in fear, and she screamed all the louder. Then she shut her mouth, and the screaming ceased.

"Do not be afraid!" I said, trying, I suppose, to sound powerful but benevolent, like the voice of an angel appearing before a mortal. She wasn't buying it. She threw down her cigarette and bolted for the door. I leapt after her from my makeshift nest, stuffed animals bouncing and scattering all over the little pink room. Her hand was already on the heart-shaped doorknob when I intercepted her. I grabbed her waist and covered her mouth with my hand, which she then, with astonishing ferocity, bit. I suppose I understand, for I'm no innocent when it comes to using my teeth to get out of a tight spot. However, it certainly did hurt, and I bellowed out in pain, but did not release her. She kicked and squirmed in my arms, hitting me with her elbows and trying to kick my shins with the heels of her shoes.

"Please don't be afraid! Please, please don't! I won't hurt you."

She was weeping now in fear, wailing, thrashing in my arms. I dragged her backward into the room toward the fluffy pile of animals in which I'd been sleeping, and shoved her down while grabbing her arms and holding them pinioned together behind her back. I quickly inspected my hand: she had left a puffy bite mark in the flap of flesh between my forefinger and thumb.

"You're a monster!" she screeched. I did not try to correct her.

"Please help me. I mean no harm," I said.

I was still holding her arms behind her, though, with her head buried in the stuffed animals, and when she spoke her words were muffled: "Are you gonna rape me?"

"No!" I said, with a gasp of offense.

"Then why the fuck were you hiding naked in my playhouse?"

"I was lost and hurt and cold!"

"Why naked?"

"Because I have no clothes! They were taken from me!"

She quit struggling beneath me. I loosed my grip on her arms.

"Please don't scream or run away," I said. I slowly stood up. As I did, I seized a stuffed zebra, and modestly held it over my genitals. The girl slowly rose to her feet, too. She did not run this time, but backed cautiously away from me. I edged myself nearer to the door to prevent her from escaping, while clutching the zebra to my crotch.

"Who the fuck are you?" she said. "Are you like, some weird midget or something?"

"I'm shocked to hear such coarse language issue from such a young mouth!"

"I'm four*teen*, dickwad."

This information immediately injected into my heart an added affinity for her—for I too was in my fourteenth year. She caught my eyes asking visually at our surroundings.

"This is all my baby shit from when I was a kid. This was my Little Princess Playhouse."

"Please—," I said, still obscuring my groin with the stuffed zebra. "I need help. I need some clothes, at least. It was never my intention to appear indecent before you."

"So are you a midget, or what?"

"In a sense, yes."

"God, you are *so* weird-looking." She stepped closer to me, her fear quelled.

"I'm sorry if I frightened you," I said.

"*Jesus*, I thought you were gonna rape me. You're all bloody! What happened?"

"I had to climb over a barbed-wire fence."

"Are you in trouble?"

"Much."

She noticed that the cigarette she had dropped had landed in her teacup, and was still burning. She picked it up, pincered between her fingers, dragged on it, and stabbed it out in the bottom of the cup.

"Okay, come inside," she said. "But my mom gets home at five thirty. You have to be gone by then."

I said "Thank you" again and again until she shushed me, and then I was silent.

She led me out of the pink plastic cottage and across the lawn. I did not know how long I had been asleep. Over the course of the day—if indeed this was the same day on which I'd fallen asleep—gray clouds had smothered the sun and a few snowflakes fluttered to the earth like ash. The girl rolled open the sliding glass door to the massive house, where a tiny yellow dog was bouncing up and down at us, frantic with yapping.

"*Shaddup!*" she roared at it, and the little dog skittered out of sight in a diminuendo of whimpers. The girl led me through the opulent interior of the house: through a kitchen, up a long flight of curving stairs, down a hallway, through a door, and into a bedroom. She closed the door behind us.

"Wait here," she commanded. I stood there, still self-consciously holding the stuffed zebra to my genitals, as she fled from the room and shut the door behind her. The room was decorated in a style similar to the Little Princess Playhouse: painted all around in that slightly nauseating shade of medicinal pink, with white trim. The room was large and featured a four-poster bed with a drooping canopy of diaphanous gauze. Piled up on the bed was a small ziggurat of yet more stuffed animals. More of those rubber effigies of beautiful blond women lay strewn about the room, and a caravan of unrealistically colored plastic ponies cantered, hooves frozen in midstep, across the windowsill. The ponies seemed to wear coy expressions. A dollhouse sat on the floor, bisected and winged open at the hinges to allow an exploded view of its interiors. This and other residues of girlhood furnished the room, but this was a room, like its inhabitant, in a state of transition: I could see the girl's burgeoning adolescence taking over the décor, the plastic ponies and dolls and stuffed animals reluctantly giving way to tacked-up posters displaying the countenances of the stars of popular music and contemporary cinema—of beautiful young men with wet hair falling tousled in their faces, and of beautiful young women in states of semidress looking down upon us from the walls through eyes heavy-lidded and viscous with sex. As I looked upon the two stages of the girl's life represented in the changing décor—childhood and adolescence—I realized that the transition was not jarring, but actually a thematically fluid one. The languorous sex-sodden eyes of the women that she tacked to her walls for fastidious emulation were already there, in the heads of these female dolls left over from early girlhood—and indeed, strangely, even in the eyes of the ponies. The rubber effigies of beautiful naked women I had seen lacked sexual parts (like angels!) merely because they were there to represent an *idea* prior to the exposition of the *specifics*. Viewed in this context, all the trappings of the first stage—childhood—were not so innocent or so sexless, but rather, could be seen as all part of a careful preparation for the next.

A bathroom adjoined her bedroom, where I looked at myself in a mirror for the first time that day, and inspected the cuts in my naked flesh. The girl—whose name, she told me, was Emily—came back with some clothes for me. But first she told me to take a shower, which I did. It both cleaned and warmed me. I was so dirty the runoff that dribbled down my legs and spiraled down the drain was black. When I had showered, little Emily swabbed my wounds with cotton balls that she dampened with stinging alcohol, and taped over them with dozens of Band-Aids. I lay supine on her bed as she treated my wounds. I tried to be modest before her, but in her no-nonsense office of nurse she swatted away my hands that held the stuffed zebra, and she did not remark upon my indecency. She gave me a pair of men's underwear, socks, a pair of corduroy pants and a cable-knit sweater as green as a green apple. All of these things were too big for me; the pants I had to roll up at the ankles and scrunch in at the waist by means of a belt she also fetched for me, and the green sweater clung loosely to my form with flapping sleeves. She said these clothes belonged to her older brother, who was away at college and wouldn't miss them. Later, she unearthed from a closet an old pair of her father's shoes. They were black leather loafers, slightly worn and like everything else too big for me, but serviceable enough. Prompted then by my cries of thirst and my belly that snarled audibly with hunger, she even brought me food and drink. (Oh—where would I be but for the kindness of women?) She restored my strength with a tall glass of water and

choice viands—a dish, a great dish of chocolate chip cookies!—
which she procured from somewhere downstairs. She warmed to
me a little, then a little more, and then we sat in her bedroom and
talked for a long while of general things. She was in the ninth grade,
she said, and a freshman student in high school. She spoke of her
father and mother and her older brother in a tone of bilious vitu-
peration, and I replied that I only wished I had a family like hers,
and that she ought to count herself fortunate to be raised in a good
home with a nice family, and she riposted by giving me the finger.
Of course she inquired about my own unusual circumstances—
i.e., how I came to be discovered hiding in her "Little Princess Playhouse," trembling from cold and fear, with flesh badly lacerated,
mud-spattered, and nude. I stalled and stammered and creatively
perambulated the truth—which I admit was morally wrong in theory but right in practice, for although I puttered and obscured and
flat-out lied to her about certain ticklish specifics—I think I may
have told her that I was born with gruesome birth defects, and
my impoverished parents had sold me at a young age into a life
of indentured servitude with a traveling circus, from which I had
just escaped (which was plausible enough)—if I slightly fudged my
autobiographical facts it was only because I was afraid of how she
might react if she knew the truth.

Little Emily did not guess that the being who kept her company
in her bedroom that afternoon and night was actually a chimp—
and not just any chimp!—but Bruno, the speaking chimp of Chicago, who had already attained a dubious and unwanted degree
of celebrity, as much for his iniquities as for his accomplishments.
News of my daring escape from the New York University's nearby
Laboratory for Experimental Medicine and Surgery in Primates
(LEMSIP) in Hastings-on-Hudson, New York, appeared on the
front page of the newspaper the following morning (tucked away in
a quiet corner of the front page, but on the front page nonetheless).

I don't think little Emily suspected me then, though. I allowed her to continue in her belief that I was merely some sort of deformed midget. It's a testament to her sterling character that she took me in, believing even this (which is unusual enough), and nursed my wounds, and gave me clothing, food, and shelter. After the initial shock of discovering me, she saw that I was articulate, and moreover that I was kind, and her first fear—that she would come to some harm at my hands—abated more with every passing minute we spent in conversation; but I suppose what put her at ease with me the most was a combination of the erudition I have by learning, and the charm I have by nature.

Little Emily and I had become so engrossed in our discourses that she forgot the time, and when she heard the sound of the front door of the house opening and shutting—faint as the sound was, her hyperattentive young ears immediately detected it—the color drained from her face, her eyes widened in fear, and she said: "Shit! My mom's home."

Downstairs, the dog went berserk with yapping; keys tinkled, shoes hit the floor. Then the voice of a woman calling: "Emily?"

"What should we do?" I said.

"You stay here," she whispered. "I'll deal with her. She knows she's not allowed to come in. She respects my personal space." (What therapeutic language!) "If anybody comes in they'll knock first. So hide if you hear a knock."

She rushed out of the room and shut the door.

"Hi, Mom," I heard her sweetly sing out. I listened to her feet thumping fast down the stairs, taking them two at a time. Then I heard two female voices in conversation, but could not discern what they were saying. Little Emily was gone for a long time. I sat on her pink bed for a while, in my borrowed clothes. I got up and inspected the things in the room. It wasn't a boring place to be left alone, crammed to the gills as it was with all manner of interesting diversions. I opened and shut every drawer in the bathroom, sniffed all her little perfumes and rolled out red nibs of lipstick, noted the pack of cigarettes stashed in the medicine cabinet, and noted the presence of tampons that indicated she had already begun to menstruate. I cannot resist the lure of the accoutrements of human femininity: I love women's bathroom counters, stocked like alchemy labs with all those puffs and powders and potions and phials and bottles and canisters—the heady, intoxicating smells of all that stuff! Then I scanned the spines of the books in her bookshelf, looking for a text to pass the time with. There were lots of books that I guessed were things she had been assigned to read in school, simply written slender volumes deemed "literature" while still being accessible to youth—*Of Mice and Men, Lord of the Flies*—a lot of girls' classics—*Anne of Green Gables, Little House on the Prairie, Little Women*—and then, interestingly, a lot of books that were juicy with sex—Anaïs Nin, *Lady Chatterley's Lover, Justine, The Story of O*. There were textbooks, picture books, poetry: Emily Dickinson, Robert Frost, Sylvia Plath. The books were arranged in no immediately discernible order: not alphabetical, not chronological, not Dewey decimal. I had already read some of these titles, either curled up in an armchair in Mr. Lawrence's library or sitting beneath a lamp at one of the long wooden tables in the reading room at the University of Chicago library. To pass the time I settled on a whimsical bit of frivolous juvenilia about a girl who for some reason is living in an attic with her family, in the pages of which I busied my eyes until little Emily's return. Eventually she came back. She opened the door slightly, slipped inside, and clicked it shut behind her.

"You can stay here tonight," she said in a voice two degrees north of a whisper. "But my mom and dad don't know you're here, so we have to be quiet. And you have to go in the morning. I have to eat dinner now. I'll bring you some food later."

Again she was gone, and again, maybe an hour or so later, she came back, this time with a plate of lukewarm food: chicken, carrots, peas, etc. "Here. I snuck this up for you."

I was insane with hunger, and I ate it sitting at her desk, devouring with indelible gusto every edible atom of what was on the plate, and thanked her with an energy bordering on groveling.

"You must have been hungry," she said.

"Starving!"

"I have to do my homework now." She dumped out the contents of her backpack and flopped a heavy textbook open flat on her desk, switched on the desk lamp, and got to work on a series of mathematical equations.

"What are you doing?" I said.

"My algebra homework, dipshit. What, they don't teach algebra to circus midgets?"

"No!"

"I *know*. That was *sar*casm. We're doing rational inequalities. I hate this stupid bullshit."

I looked over her shoulder at the big glossy textbook pages from which she was copying "problems," as she called them. I watched her work, and comprehended nothing. It was all a bunch of chaotic and elusive symbols to me, numbers mixed up with letters, lines, shapes, dots, punctuation marks, alien markings as enigmatic and indecipherable to my eyes as hieroglyphics carven on the walls of an Egyptian tomb. Little Emily, though, was apparently so accustomed to the business of unlocking these symbols' mysteries that she was actually bored with it. She raced, *flew* right through the "problems," mashing buttons on her calculator and using her pencil to scribble out more and more of these symbols, new symbols which the arrangements of the symbols in her book somehow unleashed into possibility—all while grumbling and sighing in irritation. I was fascinated by the process, watching her glance at the symbols and then send the tip of her pencil into a flurry of scratchings, scribblings, and crossings-out, until it arrived at some final number—the mysteriously-arrived-at "answer"—as seemingly arbitrary as the rest of the process—which she then lassoed in a circle of graphite before moving on to the next "problem." I was not only enchanted by the sorcery of this, but I began to grow sick with envy in my heart at little Emily's privilege of education. I was envious that she was so comfortable with this privilege that she had grown resentful of it. What I would have given for a formal education like hers! To learn algebra, geometry, calculus, and trigonometry and all the rest of it! All the education I had ever received—outside of my experimental instruction in spoken and written language and my lessons in philosophy and logic with Mr. Lawrence—I had given myself, with little outside guidance. I had given it to myself not out of a desire to better my mind, but simply out of curiosity, nothing but curiosity, as I sat in the reading room of the University of Chicago library, where I read many books more or less at random. I would read Thucydides followed by Freud followed by Dickens followed by Austen followed by Machiavelli followed by Blake followed by Montaigne followed by Wittgenstein followed by Cervantes, returning often to Milton, and most often, I think, to Shakespeare. I read these books merely because they were the books that happened to be in that room. I also read legal disquisitions, encyclopedias, medical school primers, travelogues, books on astronomy, botany—it didn't matter, I was utterly indiscriminate in my reading; all of it fascinated me. The problem was (and this is the curse of the autodidact) my studies had no guiding direction, and so my education lacked any sort of coherent plan, path, or structure—and so there were (there have always been) gaping holes in my learning, and one of these holes was mathematics. Thus I stood gape-jawed and wide-eyed in rapture before little Emily's arithmetical aptitude, while simultaneously eaten up inside with jealousy at her fortunate birth, a jealousy that darkened even into a shade of anger because she took her fortune for granted so. But my anger went away. "I was angry with my friend: I told my wrath, my wrath did end." (Blake.) Only I didn't tell it, actually. I swallowed it, and like a bit of unwholesome food it pained my belly awhile, and then the pain subsided as my system digested it. Silly monkey—educations are for kids.

So I had to sate myself with watching in glazy-eyed awe as the tempests of numbers and other symbols shot from the tip of her pencil as if from the end of a wizard's wand.

"Fuck off," she said, in a voice unheated with any real anger. "I can't concentrate with you standing there, like, breathing on me. Go away." I retreated from looking over her shoulder in remorse, and instead occupied myself with her books, or in inspecting all the artifacts contained in the room. Dejectedly, I sat down and played with the sexless woman-dolls in their dollhouse. So we passed the remaining hours of the waking night, she bent monastically over her studies with pencil, calculator, and book, and I sitting on her floor playing with dolls. It is a woeful thing to be a striver like me.

The hours ticked away like this until the house gradually grew silent and dark. Other noises had helped to animate this house—footsteps and so on from downstairs, and the murmur of a TV—but these noises died away as the evening wore on, and soon in little Emily's bedroom we could tell by the silence and the absence of vibration in the rest of the house that everyone else in it had gone to bed. There was a soft knock on the door. I abandoned the dolls and swiftly hid myself amid the lint and dust under the bed.

"Come in," sang little Emily. In the sliver of visibility beneath the scrim of her bed, I saw a pair of slippered feet quietly enter the room. The slippers crossed the carpet to where little Emily sat at her desk, the desk lamp burning her shadow long across the room.

The slippers walked up behind her chair, and a female voice said: "Good night, sweetie."

"Good night, Mom," said little Emily, with a note of annoyance.

"I love you."

"Love you too." Little Emily's voice was quick and flat. The slippers left the room, the door shut. I dared not emerge yet from beneath the bed. I saw the crack of light under the door go dark. Little Emily did not tell me to come out from under the bed, so there I remained. I heard the thump of her shutting her mathematical textbook, and the click of her pencil lain to rest on the desk. I saw her small bare feet step swiftly out of the room. Her bare feet came back a few minutes later.

"You can come out now. My mom and dad went to bed." I slithered out from beneath the bed. Little Emily was pouring red wine into two wineglasses on the desk.

"They have so much wine they never notice when I steal a bottle," she said. We drank the wine in the bathroom, where little Emily stood on the lid of the toilet seat and smoked another cigarette, surreptitiously blowing the smoke through the window, which she'd propped open to the cold March night. We talked for a long time after that. Little Emily told me all about her complex family and social lives. She told me that she was a four-time child beauty pageant winner. She told me that as far back as she could remember her life had been a harried circus of traveling, preening, and display. She also told me that her mother wanted for her a life of celebrity. She told me about being dragged to auditions in the city, about endless hours of acting lessons, singing lessons, lessons in any discipline that might increase her value in the entertainment industry, about her mother taking her to be consulted by certain professionals on matters like what clothing would most flatter her unripe physique, what hair and what makeup. She said her summers were always eaten up by all these lessons and auditions, and by rehearsals for the plays and TV commercials she had successfully auditioned for, and in flying back and forth to Hollywood to film these commercials when they couldn't be filmed in New York. She said she had been in TV commercials for all sorts of various products: for fast food restaurant chains, for toothpaste, for waffles, for breakfast cereals—any sort of product that a smiling, adorable young girl might help to sell. She told me that she was currently slated to star in a production of *Little Orphan Annie*. All this she told me, and more. In a way I sympathized with her, even identified with her life. Both of us had been selected by forces greater than ourselves for lives of careful study and display. Little Emily had been sold into entertainment, just as I had been sold into science.

XXXV

In the morning I woke alone in little Emily's pink bed, where she had let me sleep beside her. She had long since gone to school. I could tell it was late in the morning by the angle and quality of the light, and by the quietness outside that it had snowed overnight. I did not want to leave her bed. That big fat squishy mattress was so impossibly soft, and warm from the warmth of our two blood-filled bodies. I had little desire to expose my sore, battered little body to the fatalistic whimsy of the outside world. I wanted only to let my eyelids slide back over the wet globes of my eyes, sub-merge my brain again in darkness, steep it in dreams, my body safely enveloped once in pink sheets and again in the curtains, kept company by little Emily's stuffed animals. I wanted to never leave that bed, to exist in that room for the rest of my life as little Emily's kept ape. Whenever little Emily's mother or father would enter the room I would make my eyes look glassy, like marbles, and hold very still, so they would think I was a very realistic-looking stuffed animal. And why not? Because my hairlessness would give me away.

So I got out of bed. I showered in her bathroom, carefully leav-ing everything in it exactly as I'd found it. I put on the clothes little

Emily had procured for me the day before, the shoes and the corduroy pants and the floppy green sweater. I crept out of her room
and shut the door. I listened: heard nothing. In a hallway closet I
found a black coat, a flannel scarf, and a hat—a black snap-brim
felt fedora with a silk hatband. I put them on. In the dressing mirror on the back of the closet door I turned the brim of the hat low
over my eyes, wound the scarf over my chin and cheeks, knotted
and stuffed it into the breast of the coat and flipped up the collar. The coat was also too big for me. It came down to my ankles.
With my chimp features thus hidden beneath collar, coat, hat,
and scarf, I set out. The little dog downstairs lunged into a fresh
fit of yapping as I descended the stairs, and I ignored it, though
it growled and scampered circles around my feet as I headed to
the door. I stood on a chair to unlatch the dead bolt, opened the
front door, and squeezed myself through it, trying not to let the
dog escape. I crammed my hands into the pockets of the coat for
warmth, and my fingers found a few crinkled twenty-dollar bills—
another boon. The new snow sparkled, clean and radiant on the
ground, the sun high and pale in the sky. Birds twittered in the
dead trees. My stubby legs waddled my coated and hatted form
down the walkway leading from the front door to the street and
the sidewalk, where I made a left turn that took me down a narrow road lined with houses, trees, bushes, driveways, mailboxes.
I walked on, hoping to encounter something that would suggest
a direction, something that would take me somewhere. That was
all I had in me to call a plan. I was fortunate enough to have what
I had: the stolen clothes on my body and a precious bit of money
in my pockets, and I hoped these alone would tide me over until
I managed to get somewhere. I do not believe I had an immediate plan to return to Chicago. That was my distant plan, not my
immediate one. My first plan was to figure out where exactly I was.
Then decide what to do. In a certain way I was enjoying my new

freedom and independence, however unasked for it was. There was a streak of adventure in my misfortune.

Though I did not know it then, I was in the village of Hastings-on-Hudson, New York: a smallish town nestled on the side of a steep hill on the Hudson River, north of New York City. I walked a way through this upscale and quiet residential area until I came to a thicker and more heavily trafficked road, which I walked alongside, downhill, coming to a place where the buildings were closer together, where there were shops and restaurants flanking the streets and people moving here and there up and down the sidewalks. The people passing me on the street flicked their eyes down at me in mild surprise or curiosity as I waddled past them, and then politely, or disinterestedly, they looked away. I came to the top of a hill, which sloped steeply downward and ended in a wide river: across the river was a long wall of tall flat gray cliffs, and very far away but visible in the distance a massive blue bridge, built like a metal spiderweb, connected one bank of the wide black river to the next. I did not know it then, but the river was the Hudson, the cliffs across it were the Palisades, and the bridge in the distance was the George Washington. Seagulls reeled overhead. I saw railroad tracks running along the bank of the river. There was a train station where the town sloped downhill and came to an end at the water. I headed for the station.

I climbed the stairs to the station platform, my stubby legs by necessity taking each of the metal steps one at a time, and found myself standing on a long flat slab of concrete. It was a sheer accident that I decided that day to climb the stairs to the southbound train station platform, rather than the northbound platform on the other side of the tracks, which was accessible via a raised walkway. I hadn't a clue as to what lay either to the north or the south of me. Who knows what my story would have become had I boarded a northbound train, which would have whisked me upstate, to

Albany or Buffalo, or even to the icy and moose-infested climes of Canada, or northeast to New Haven, or Providence, or Boston? I haven't a clue what might have befallen me if I had chosen the northbound train, what I might have learned, who I might have become. All I know is that the fast-spinning wheels of the Fates had it otherwise, for when I saw the specks of headlights in the distance, and I heard the bellows of the whistle, two short and one long, and this enormous metal caterpillar came clattering to a stop, and the doors slid open, and I stepped onboard in my coat and low-pulled hat, expecting nothing more particular than to be taken someplace else, it so happened—it *just* so happened—that it was the south-bound train I chose, and that, as the poet says, has made all the difference; for that rolling and bellowing metal caterpillar took me not to Albany, not to Canada, not to Connecticut or Boston, but to New York—to New York City, where I met a friend, and a little glory, and the beginning of my downfall.

———

I found an unoccupied booth upholstered with orange plastic pads, curled up against the wall beside the heating vents, and looked out the window west across the river at the granite cliffs. Thank God that money had been in the pocket of the coat I had liberated from the closet of little Emily's parents' house, or else I would have had nothing to buy my ticket with when the conductor clumped down the aisle between the seats. A voice came on a loud-speaker and chanted off a litany of destinations the train would reach: *Greystone, Glenwood, Yonkers, Ludlow, Riverdale, Spuyten Duyvil, Marble Hill, University Heights, Morris Heights, Harlem, Grand Central Station.* I handed a crinkled twenty-dollar bill to the conductor, and he handed me a ticket and change, perforated a paper card with a hole puncher and stuck it in a slot above my seat.

We rolled beneath the blue metal bridge I'd seen in the distance, we bumped and shuddered past telephone poles and ragged brown brick buildings, until we were in a city, a huge and dense city of, I thought, potentially infinite complexity. The train filled up with more and more people after each stop, and with each stop the litany of destinations the voice on the loudspeaker chanted off shrank shorter by one place name. Three more passengers had to cram themselves in beside me in the orange booth. I kept my head down and pulled the brim of the hat lower, not wanting to expose my face to any undue scrutiny, but I felt their big bodies press warmly beside me. We were barreling headlong into New York City. After the penultimate stop—*Harlem, 125th Street*—we gathered speed, rolling high above the buildings and crowded streets alive with voices and honking cars, and soon after that we plunged into a profound and vacuous darkness, and in this darkness we remained until we slowly rolled to a stop—our final destination, apparently. The train's electricity was cut, the long metal serpent sighed away to silence, and all the people crowded thickly around me—the train was crammed absolutely full by the time we descended into the darkness—erupted into sudden activity, everyone jostling each other, all knees and elbows, fists held to coughing mouths, rolled-up newspapers and magazines, coats buttoned, fat-stuffed luggage heaved from overhead racks, and they all lined up in the aisle to funnel out the doors. I joined the crush, and the flow of people pushed me through the door and onto another long concrete platform.

We were in a vast cavern, dimly lit by feebly buzzing lamps hanging high above us. In one direction the cavern stretched far away and out of sight into darkness, and in the other direction the concrete platform became a bright staircase. All the people who had just stepped off the train were swarming onto this staircase; I followed them. The weight and pressure of their stream of moving bodies pushed me along the platform, up the stairs, and into the light. At the top of the stairs the crowd dispersed, each person going his or her own way to private destinations. I wandered around the floor like a chunk of flotsam on the surface of the sea, knowing neither where I was nor where I was going. I was in an underground network of ornately carven stone and golden-veined marble. Currents of human traffic rushed in many different directions, the waves of people meshing here and there into cross-streams, forming interference patterns of coming and going, some people bustling this way and others bustling that. They dragged suitcases on rollers behind them on the floor. They sat still or slumped over on benches. They sat at tables sipping coffee, reading magazines splayed flat before them. Shops, restaurants, cafés, bars, and news vendors operated out of nooks set in the walls. I found a set of wide marble stairs and climbed them. When I emerged at the top of these stairs, I was in a huge, glittering, beautiful room, what looked like the grand ballroom of a palace, where people wearing powdered wigs and whalebone corsets and masks ought to be waltzing to "The Blue Danube." Instead, people in modern dress scrambled across the floor in frenetic hordes. In the center of the room a circular booth stood sentinel, glowing from within, with a huge round clock on top of it, like a temple to the concept of time, an altar to Chronos. Then I looked up: the huge, high, vaulted ceiling of this spectacular room was painted blue, and decorated with stars, the whole night sky spangling the robin-egg blue ceiling of the room, with golden outlines of animals drawn over the points of light, some of which were represented by real electric lights embedded like jewels in the ceiling! I must have stood there for half an hour at least, drop-jawed at the sight of this. It looked just like the planetarium that Lydia used to take me to so long ago, in Chicago. All those beautiful zoomorphs, the shaggy lion frozen by the suggestion of his stars in midpounce, the ethereal, sexy nymphs and goddesses and gods stretching their bows taut and aiming their arrows, creatures with wings and horns and men whose torsos melted into the bodies of horses. I guessed that this huge and religious room was like a throbbing heart to this city, pulsing as it was with humanity, its valves taking people in through its arteries and pushing them out again through its veins, a big, bloody, pumping muscle of energy, of commute, of communication, of civilization, its ceiling painted with stars whose warm, audacious artifice dared to rival the more indifferent beauty of real nature. Indeed, I thought back on the sky at night over the Lawrences' ranch in the wilderness of Colorado, with all its unfriendly and unhelpful and useless wonder, with its undercurrents of loneliness and fear, and wondered if this version wasn't, in a way, an improvement.

I picked a direction and walked in it. I came to an escalator that lowered me into a chamber made of tile and concrete, which smelled of urine. At the bottom of the escalator turnstiles led into the catacomblike underground structure. I saw that it was an underground commuter train station, much like the stations they have in Chicago, except below the surface of the city. I squeezed myself beneath the turnstiles and waddled around in the big reeking concrete room awhile before descending some stairs, some more stairs, and hopping onboard the first train that whooshed, horn lowing and headlights glaring, into this dank and crowded oubliette of a train station, displacing the fetid air in the tunnel and blasting it in our faces like a hot wet wind. The train docked and hissed, the doors scrolled open, the boarding cluster of humanity stood aside to allow passage for the departing cluster of humanity, and I followed the people on.

Imagine: Here is Bruno. He is sitting on the subway. He is sitting on a seat on the train. Perhaps it is a southbound Lexington Avenue Local, which is grumbling like an enormous tapeworm through the intestines of the subway system. The train whimpers to a stop every once in a while and opens its valves to the inward and outward effluvia of humanity, while Bruno, who regards them not, has been sitting patiently all day long inside this putrid contraption, half-twisted around and peering backward into the roaring blackness through the graffiti-engraved window. He has been sitting right where he is for hours, waiting for the train to take him someplace definitive, and growing increasingly apprehensive that he is not being taken anywhere. He is afraid that maybe the train is only traveling back and forth along a predestined route, and he is only seeing the same places over and over. In his mind, Bruno is busy pondering. What is he pondering? He is probably thinking thoughts deep and true and spiritual while he reflects on his unusual life. He is posing to himself questions like those that came to Gauguin when he saw all those well-upholstered Tahitian nymphs carrying woven baskets and in their uninhibited Asiatic innocence taking no notice of their freely bobbing breasts: *Who are we? Where did we come from? Where are we going?* And, like Tonto to the Lone Ranger, I answer: *What's all this "we" stuff? I am Bruno, and I'm on my own journey. I am an animal with a human tongue, a human brain, and human desires, the most human among them to be more than what I am. And I have no idea where I'm going.*

Then, while Bruno's brain is submerged in these and other musings, the Beggar King enters. Who is the Beggar King? I will tell you. A man, who appears to be dressed as Henry VIII, has entered the train car from the far opposite end. There is a whoosh of rushing air as the door opens and thumps shut behind him, and this man announces his presence to everyone by throwing an arm in the air with a wild theatrical flourish, and he begins to shout: "To say that he is old, the more the pity, his white hairs do witness it—but that he is, saving your reverence, a whoremaster, that I utterly deny!"

Everyone on the train commences immediately to desperately ignore him, taking pains not to look him in the eye, as he could be dangerous. He is wearing a big floppy black hat like a sort of formless tam-o'-shanter, pushed back on his head at what I can only accurately describe as a rakish angle, and the plume of a pheasant flutters from the side of it; he wears a glossy fur coat with colossal shoulder pads, a frilly white pirate shirt with droopy sleeves, an embroidered lace-up vest that I will be later informed is a "doublet," a pair of poofy, diaperlike red silk pants, garters, tights, and buckled shoes. The most important thing to convey about this man is the sheer mass of him. To say that he is rotund would be to commit the sin of understatement. This man is a behemoth. He is a man of mythopoetic obesity. He is not only on the tall side—about six feet and an inch, I would estimate—but of such impressive diameter that he occupies about as much space as would three more modestly proportioned people lashed together in a bundle. The way he carries himself invites one to draw comparisons from among the lower orders: the walrus, the hippo, the manatee. The last of these is probably the most helpful for purposes of mental illustration because, due to the way his corpulent torso dwarfs his normal-size appendages, his arms do indeed appear to extrude helplessly out of his sides like a pair of ridiculous little flippers. And his legs? Any apprentice architect would be gravely lambasted by his superiors for designing a structure with such flimsy load-bearing mechanisms. The fact that those legs are apparently able to convey that body through space seems to defy the laws of physical nature, a defiance made tenfold impressive when you take into account the constant pitching and rolling of a subway car in motion. In one hand he carries a coffee can: a big tin cylinder that, according to the lettering on the side, used to contain the grinds of Maxwell House Colombian Roast. Hark!—he speaks.

"If sack and sugar be a fault,"—and here he braces himself against a pole, removes a flask from somewhere in his regal fur coat, unplugs it, takes a pull, and emits a gruesome belch—"God help the wicked!" As he fishtails down the aisle, he booms out the words—which of course I recognize from act 2, scene 4 of *Henry IV, Part One*—in a gravelly and robust foghorn of a voice: an actor's voice. Here is a man who has trained himself to speak in a Boston Brahmin continental accent. This man is obviously drunk, but nevertheless his voice is melodious, articulate, authoritative.

"If to be old and merry be a sin, then many an old host that I know is damned. If to be fat be to be hated, then Pharaoh's lean kine are to be loved!" As he shouts, the Beggar King pivots to his left and right, swinging his belly before him like a sack of cement, addressing his involuntary audience personally, directly. Aggressively, even, confrontationally. He holds out his coffee can, rattling its contents to communicate that it is a receptacle into which bits of currency ought to be placed in exchange for his services, or at least to make him go away. The Beggar King goes generally ignored. The passengers regard him as an irksome presence, pretending that he is invisible and inaudible, even as they scrunch themselves into the sides of the train car to allow unobstructed passage for his elephantine girth.

As he works his way down the aisle, a passenger or two clinks a coin into his coffee can, gestures he acknowledges with a subtle nod of appreciation. Because I am trying to remain incognito, I am furiously looking away from him; even now I know—perhaps by intuition—there's nothing that sets off a freak quite like another freak. *Don't look*—I tell myself, as if to look would destroy me, as if to look at him were to gaze into the eyes of Medusa—*don't look, Bruno, don't look, don't look, don't look.*

The Beggar King continues: "No, my good lord: banish Peto, banish Bardolph, banish Poins..." The Beggar King approaches. I try to appear inextricably fascinated by something happening outside the window, out there in the void of the subway tunnel, the empty rushing blackness. But he sees me—I can feel it. I can feel his curious gaze lock onto me. I begin to sweat in panic. I look down, letting the brim of the hat shade his countenance. The Beggar King not only sees me—but he is intrigued by me. He is *staring* at me. The Beggar King seems to have temporarily forgotten his lines, his eyes are so fixed in curiosity upon the little creature sitting quietly on the subway in a black coat and a hat, like a pariah, like a tiny miserable deformed midget pervert. The Beggar King's stare has now herded the eyes of the other passengers onto me. He is now standing directly in front of me. I stare down, dogged in my resolve to ignore him.

Then the Beggar King leans down toward me, decanting his mountainous self closer and closer to the only fully dressed hairless chimpanzee on this particular subway car, who is sitting—quietly, civilly, harmlessly—alone. He is so close I can smell the sweat beneath his Henry VIII costume, and smell the whiskey on his halitosic breath, breath which I can smell as well as also hear: it is loud and belabored fat-man's breath, whistling in and out of his nostrils. With his free hand the Beggar King seizes a nearby pole to steady himself. He addresses my averted face as he says—softer, now, no longer shouting (though still probably loud enough for everyone on the train to hear):

"But for sweet Jack Falstaff... *kind* Jack Falstaff, *true* Jack Falstaff, *valiant* Jack Falstaff, and therefore more valiant being as he is *old* Jack Falstaff..." Finally, I dare to look at him. I turn my face upward to his. His face is so close to mine that the brim of my hat brushes against his beard as I raise my head.

The Beggar King is probably in his fifties, though maybe he looks older than he is. A bramblebush of beard bursts forth from his face in matted gray fistfuls. His cheeks and his golf-ball nose are deeply dimpled with overlarge pores and tinged pink with rosacea, and under his floppy hat his hair is long and gray. He looks a little greasy, though not quite to the extent of your typical public-transit tatterdemalion; you can tell this man at least has a roof of some sort under which to sleep, otherwise he would be in worse shape. His eyes, though, are sane and alert.

"Banish not him thy Harry's company," he says, "banish not him thy Harry's company—banish plump Jack, and banish all the world."

And I, Bruno, counter him with what I know is the answer: "I do. I will."

Then I see in his eyes that he has realized I am a chimp. The Beggar King places a huge paw of a hand on my head and takes off my hat. Everyone on the train is looking at us now. They may have been murmuring, or making interjections of wonder or gasps or shouts of fear—I don't recall. The Beggar King has unmasked a monster in their midst.

"Great snakes!" says the Beggar King. "You, sir, seem to be an ape!"

At this moment the train slows down to make a stop: *bing!*— "Twenty-third Street," the electronic female voice announces. The doors scroll open, and everyone on board who is neither Bruno nor the Beggar King hastily departs the train car at the same time. Let them go. Bruno is alone with the Beggar King. This is how I met Leon Smoler, the best human friend—besides Lydia—that I have ever had.

XXXVI

Why did Leon Smoler become my friend? Because he was one of the very few humans I had ever met who spoke to me without any underlying prejudice evident in his voice. Nor, on the other hand, did I find that he overvalued or exoticized me. Leon truly could not have cared less whether I was a chimpanzee or a biological human. Because Leon was just barely sane enough to live in the world, yet mad enough not to find it at all odd that Bruno, later his best friend, roommate, and business partner, was an articulate chimp. In Leon Smoler there was not the faintest shred of that incredulity, that horror, that queasiness, that shock and discomfort that betrays the face of pretty much everyone who has ever met me. If anything, when he found out I was a talking ape, he was amused and maybe mildly interested. For some reason, Leon is immune to the uncanny valley. This thing I can sense in people—maybe people with horrific deformities, severe physical defects, serious mental illnesses, maybe those sorts of people can understand that look in other people's faces I am talking about. But I don't think so. The discomfort I see in people's faces when they look at me does not necessarily have any pity in it, or even any relief, any sure-am-glad-that's-not-me in it. The look of unease that I am met with is a symptom of the same great unease that met and continues to meet Darwin even a century and a half after *The Descent of Man*. It is the sense of absolute nakedness, of humiliation that humans feel when confronted with the realization that they are not so fucking special. They look at me and see an assault on their notion of "human dignity." Dignity? No, *vanity*! Who else—who else could be so vain?

But not Leon—in Leon Smoler there was—is—none of that. He is no anthropo-chauvinist. Because Leon's as in touch with his animality as any human I have ever met. Have you ever heard of Diogenes the Cynic, Gwen? Once, in the course of my self-directed studies in the reading room of the main library at the University of Chicago, I sat at one of the long desks with a volume of Laërtius's *Lives and Opinions of Eminent Philosophers* splayed before me under the lamp, and I read in it an account of the life of Diogenes the Cynic. Back in Plato's selfsame ancient Athens, Diogenes went naked and lived in a bathtub, urinated, defecated, and masturbated in public, and denounced all laws, religions, governments, and good manners. People called him "the Cynic" because the word means "doglike" in Greek, because Diogenes lived like a dog. He wasn't offended, though; he liked it. You're damn right I live like a dog, he said to them. Alexander the Great returned to Athens fresh from conquering the known world and found Diogenes, naked as was his fashion, sunning himself on the steps of the Acropolis. Alexander stood before him and said, Ask any favor you choose of me. Name anything, because I'm Alexander the Great and that basically means whatever it is, I can get it for you. Diogenes looked up at him, squinted, maybe gave his scrotum a lackadaisical scratch, shrugged, and said, Get out of my sun. Can one help but admire that? We are animals who like to constantly congratulate ourselves on all our sweetness and light and triumph of spirit, and nobody is supposed to choose to live like a dog. I've always admired this man, his presence at the same place and time as the birth of philosophy, like a voice crying, not in the wilderness, but from the wilderness in the human heart, in the midst of civilization. The solemn golden machineries of politics, learning, thought, goodness and grace and virtue and art— *especially* art—all we call our society, needs Diogenes in the middle of it, a human proud and content to live like an animal, to remind us not to mistake the frippery of human civilization for anything too distant or distinct from what's already there in pigs and monkeys and dogs, to remind us that for all the sweetness and light of our great cities and great machines and great art, we are nothing terribly more magnificent than apes with clothes on our bodies, words in our mouths, and heads inflated with willful delusions.

And now I arrive at my point: if ancient Athens were late-twentieth-century New York City, Diogenes the Cynic would be Leon Smoler. Leon the Cynic. Leon lived a perennially criminal existence, yet always managed to evade punishment without really trying. Leon cared so little for the laws of mankind that he saw our civilization as a sort of cosmic joke. His were never crimes of passion, or ignorance, or opportunism, or of any particularly malicious intent. There was certainly nothing at all political in his habitual criminality, either. He did not believe that the victims of his crimes in any way deserved them, and he did not imagine any sort of irreparably corrupt system that deserved to be gamed. Leon's were crimes of cheerful and utter indifference. If Leon Smoler had not been blessed with an essentially peaceful demeanor (or not cursed with his unwieldy physique), he may in another life have been a dangerous man, for this indifference of his unquestionably bordered on the sociopathic. When he wanted something, he took it, and the way the world seemed incapable of meting out any consequences to him was nothing short of magic.

The mention of magic is apropos, for Leon was a magician as well, in a nonmetaphorical sense. When he wasn't performing Shakespeare in the subway, he scraped together a supplementary income performing magic shows for children's birthday parties, for office Christmas parties, etc. On such occasions, Leon dazzled his gaping, clapping, awestruck, *ooh*ing and *aah*ing audiences with his magic tricks, with his born performer's showmanship, with his histrionic, always-in-motion and colossal body crammed (which seemed a magic trick in itself) into a plus-plus-size tuxedo—the decidedly old-fashioned kind, with the wing collar, black bow tie, vest, and cummerbund, the damp velvety burst of a red rose stuck in the buttonhole of his lapel, and a glittering blue lamé cape draped across his shoulders, decorated with moons and stars that Leon had industriously snipped with safety scissors out of white felt and glued on himself. I myself never learned the secrets of most of his better tricks, and thus they remained magic to me. He could do things with a deck of ordinary playing cards that bent the laws of physics. He could do things with a set of linking metal hoops that subverted the space-time continuum. He could do things with coins and wands and torches that defied gravity and electromagnetics. He could do things with silk scarves and hats and gloves and tea sets and tablecloths that momentarily unified the theory of relativity with quantum mechanics. He was also an accomplished juggler.

Later, I would submit myself to the role of assistant during Leon's magic shows: I clad myself in a little red tuxedo and went hopping around in the audience, exaggerating for effect my already-unusual gait, with a hat in my hand turned upside down for tips at the end of the show, or holding or procuring things for Leon during the act, or seizing "volunteers" from the audience by the hand and dragging them onstage, or making weird and silly faces at the children, provoking sometimes laughter, sometimes tears. Leon furnished me with a kazoo of gleaming nickel, and taught me how to play it, and I practiced at it intensively, until I had essentially become a virtuoso at this surprisingly versatile and emotive instrument. After I had attained mastery over my kazoo, seldom did the instrument escape my lips during Leon's magic shows. I was always zipping and blowing notes from it as I moved amid the audience, scurrying between bodies and legs, providing a running musical accompaniment to Leon Smoler's magic tricks. I grew to love show business.

And we got by, Leon and I. I lived with him during the year I spent in New York, my year in show business. But I'm getting ahead of myself.

On the night I met him, the night I discovered him (and he discovered me) performing Shakespeare on the subway, enlightening the souls of the passengers, force-feeding poetry like castor oil down their throats to help alleviate their spiritual illness, and after he unmasked me for a monster in their midst, Leon took me to dinner. He took me aboveground, to the surface of the city. Together we ascended from the subway's musty inferno onto the purgatory of the street. To celebrate our new alliance we dined under someone else's reservation at the Four Seasons. Leon waited till the hostess's attention was distracted, picked up the reservations log on the podium, read it, and replaced it before she looked up at us. Just like that.

"Mr. Burton Miller," he announced.

"Party of two?"

"Indeed. I apologize for our earliness."

"Your reservation is for seven," she said, snatching a glance at her watch with a scowl of irritation. "Your table is ready anyway. Right this way."

"Yes, yes," said Leon, as she led us through the restaurant to a small table in a quiet corner of the room. No one dining in the restaurant could help but stare in our direction as we passed their tables: Leon was still wearing his Henry VIII costume, and I myself was a bit underdressed. "It's far too early for any civilized dinner," Leon whispered to me. "Of course our table is ready. We shall probably have approximately forty-five minutes before the real Millers show up."

We ordered a very nice bottle of wine, which moistened the

braised rabbit and sturgeon steaks we put in our bellies. Over dinner, in varying degrees of detail or abstraction, I told Leon my story from the beginning up until the moment I currently relate. By the time I was finished, we were sipping aperitifs and awaiting our dessert.

"Bruno," said Leon, when I had come to my unhappy conclusion, "you have led a brief and troubled life, and you have probably noticed by now that ours is a civilization in a state of rapid and hideous decline." Leon's eyebrows, it is important to relate, were always twisted into some real or affected expression of righteous indignation. His eyes were always bugging with horror and irritation, and he had an effeminate tic of gingerly sweeping the long, stringy hair from his face with the tips of his fingers, which he was doing at this moment with one hand as he used the other to tilt a wineglass to his mouth. "Every worthwhile art in our world is a dying one," he went on. "You have had the cruel misfortune to join humanity at a time when most people no longer care about the question of what it means to be human. Thus is the state of the world into which you were unwittingly led, and for this I sincerely apologize to you on behalf of the human race."

I accepted his apology, which endeared me to him deeply.

"You shall become my student," Leon announced. "I can think of no more perfect mentor than Leon Smoler to someone in your unlikely situation. I shall give you asylum in my home, and you in turn must enter a period of intensive training in the dramatic arts, for I see clearly that you are destined to become an actor. And of course you shall enjoy it. The theatre is the least degrading calling left in our ruined society, if not the most culturally relevant. But for now, I see that the time has come for us to flee this place."

I looked behind us across the restaurant, and saw that some sort of squabble had erupted at the hostess's podium, for the time was upon us (in fact it was more than a quarter past us, because they were late), and it seemed that the real Mr. Burton Miller, party of two, had arrived, and everyone involved was miffed to learn that two imposters had been dining in his name for the last hour. With ceremonial closure Leon yanked out the napkin tucked into the neck of his doublet for a bib, threw it in a contrivance of disgust across the table and rose to leave. The hostess was now clacking toward us at an angry clip, with a face betraying much vexation with us.

"Come, Bruno," he said, "let us away from here," and I followed him as he pushed through the flapping waiters' doors and into the steam and gleam and clamor of the kitchen. The chefs looked up from their work in faint surprise, then returned their gazes to the food they were busily preparing. Waiters scrambled in and out of the doors in pulses of steam; spoons and pots and ladles dangled from their hooks in the ceiling. Leon led me down an aisle, past the rows of stainless-steel cabinets and counters. We slipped out through the kitchen door into an alley, escaped onto the street, and melted into the crowd on the sidewalk. A few blocks later we descended again down the tile steps to the subway and boarded a train that took us up through the city, out of the darkness, across the water and over the Bronx toward Leon's home.

Leon lived in a place called City Island. The commute time to City Island from the heart of Manhattan was well over an hour, but, he said, the rent was cheap. City Island is, in fact, an island, cleverly squirreled away off the far northeastern corner of the Bronx, in the westernmost nook of Long Island Sound. Here's how to get there, because if, like Bruno, your uncommonly slight stature prevents you from being deemed physically capable of piloting an automobile, you must rely on public transportation and your feet. It involves five stations. (One) If you're coming from Manhattan, board a northbound 6 train and ride it all the way to the end of the line; the 6 emerges into the daylight from its burrow somewhere in upper Manhattan and on raised tracks continues to snake its way north, crosses the river, and turns sharply eastward along a sweeping roller-coastery curve that briefly offers passengers a panoramic vista of the

city on one side of the car and the water crisscrossed with bridges on
the other, seen through plastic windows that are thickly engraved in
pen, pencil, coin, key, and knife with a palimpsest of graffiti, with
words and signs, with the insignia of all things sacred and profane,
religious symbols jostling for space among lewd questions, posed
anonymously and anonymously answered, hypertexts overscrawling
urtexts, vandalism in myriad languages, written and crosswritten
in all the nattering tongues of Babylon. (Two) Get off at Pelham
Bay Park, last stop. (Three) Fumble through turnstiles and down
stairs until you reach the street, where you will turn to your left
and see a bus stop. (Four) Board the Bx29 for City Island, which
will take you on a journey through Pelham Bay Park, around several traffic roundabouts and finally across an ornate bridge oxidized
with age into a picturesque mint green; you will pass beneath an
arch that welcomes you with a big sign to City Island. If it is nighttime then you will see from the bridge a seafood restaurant that
advertises itself with a giant neon lobster who suffuses the darkness
with a satanic red glow and is shakily duplicated in mirror symme-
try on the surface of the water below him; this massive crustacean
stands on his tail and holds one of his claws aloft, and the neon
lights are programmed to scroll back and forth, in order to suggest,
at an unhurried but invariant rhythm, the perpetual opening and
closing of a single ominous pincer. (Five) Get off the bus. Your nostrils should immediately detect a strong odor: a curious mixture of
fried shrimp and garbage. This is City Island. It's a pleasant enough
place, and I called it home while I lived with Leon in New York and
worked as an actor and magician's assistant. It may perhaps occur
to you that the neighborhood strives after the aesthetic of a quaint
waterfront community, in that if you are standing on City Island
you can scarcely throw a rock without hitting some sort of decorative nautical paraphernalia: ship's wheels, fishing nets, and wooden
caryatids ornament the edifices of nearly every storefront, moldy

antique shop, and seafood restaurant, strategically placed so as to absolutely prohibit you from forgetting even for one second that *this is indeed a quaint waterfront community*, although the effect is not achieved in full because all this maritime poseury is reined in by an ambiance of sleaze that lets you know that although this waterfront community may be quaint, you are still in the Bronx, albeit an obscure pocket of it. The high poison content in any aqueous creature you might happen to catch in that part of Long Island Sound makes it illegal to consume; hence the cuisine at all of the many seafood restaurants that line the main street is by law imported entirely from elsewhere. You may also notice a good number of large men in glossy tracksuits, jewelry, and exquisitely coiffed silver hair. There are also a lot of people walking around talking to themselves. For once, even if you are a shaved chimp, you might not be the weirdest-looking person around. The smell of fried shrimp pervades pretty much everywhere. It is a relatively safe neighborhood, and the houses are simple, decidedly blue-collar, and squat. The delicate clinking of rigging against the masts of docked boats is constantly audible. This is where I lived for one year.

We got off the bus in front of a grocery store and crossed the street. Leon lived in a small basement apartment in a white vinyl-sided house behind a restaurant called Artie's Shrimp Shanty. The door was located at the bottom of a flight of stairs in the alley behind the restaurant, where there were a couple of dumpsters just outside the back door to the kitchen. Whatever refuse Artie stored in those voluminous green metal tanks sure smelled strongly: of shrimp. In fact, the dumpsters in the alley behind Artie's Shrimp Shanty were perhaps ground zero for the all-pervasive fried shrimp smell on the island. Fried shrimp and marinara, mingled maybe with the saltiness of the nearby sea and the lingering aromata of the waitresses' cigarette breaks, plus other miscellaneous garbage. The flat gray metal door to Leon's apartment was without any extraneous ornament to suggest someone might live there: it could have been a door to a boiler room. Leon removed his keys from the pocket of his Elizabethan fur robe and let us in.

The apartment was small and dark. It featured only two small windows that offered views of the corrugated aluminum walls of window wells. One wall of the apartment was exposed red brick. There was one bedroom and a small bathroom, the floor of which was sticky and peppered with pubic hairs, and the rest of the apartment was a combined kitchen/living room. The place had long ago taken on the odor of shrimp that blew in from the dumpsters behind the seafood restaurant. There was a TV perched precariously on the edge of a coffee table. The room, though sparsely furnished in terms of actual furniture, was densely cluttered with wide-ranging and erratic miscellany. Books, magazines, a dust-coated electric typewriter, a metal twin-bed frame pushed upright against a wall. A heavy plaster bust of Shakespeare and a broken record player rested on top of an upright piano that had four black keys and two white keys missing, all the remaining keys out of tune, and no bench. All kinds of devices, bric-a-brac, and curiosities littered the floor and every flat surface, accumulated in the corners, and erupted forth from drawers too stuffed to shut properly. Boxes of sheet music, broken toys, wind-up ballerinas. The walls were covered with posters and other kinds of memorabilia from Broadway and Golden Age Hollywood. A flabby futon faced the TV. The futon could be collapsed to a horizontal position to become a bed with a slight valley in the hinge of it, and that night Leon covered it with a bedsheet and punched some fluff into a flabby spare pillow for me. The books stood in precarious vertical stacks that reached the ceilings. In particular Leon adored the work of Edgar Rice Burroughs. There was a complete set of all twenty-four Tarzan novels, leatherbound with gilt lettering on the spines, snugly set in orderly rows in a custom-built bookcase. I slid one out and flipped through its Bible-thin pages.

"It is appallingly obvious," said Leon, "that of all writers who have ever dared to commit the English language to paper, Edgar Rice Burroughs remains second only to Shakespeare." He suggested we visit Artie's Shrimp Shanty for a nightcap. I was tired, but I acquiesced, so we went next door for shrimp and beer. The interior of the restaurant was cluttered with nautical paraphernalia—ships' wheels, fishing nets, dried starfish, etc.—and lit with winking Christmas lights tacked up in a drooping contiguous string along the perimeter of the room where the wall molding met the ceiling, and the lights pulsed blobs of red and green and blue light, giving the room an undersea feeling. A giant rubber shark, its jaws gaping to show its fearsome rubber teeth, dangled on scarcely visible wires from the ceiling, looming monstrously above the curving rosewood counter of the bar. The bar was in a smaller room that adjoined the main room of the restaurant. The shark was reflected, as if it were swimming past a glass window in an aquarium, in a smudgy mirror behind the bar, which also illusively doubled the number of liquor and wine bottles arranged in three rows along the back of the bar, which was underlit with bluish lights. Leon was clearly a regular at this place: he waved to the two old men sitting at the other end of the bar and sank his body onto a bar stool as comfortably as the king he was dressed as would have sat upon his throne. I climbed onto the stool beside Leon's, and soon the young woman behind the glossy rosewood counter placed before us two glasses of beer and a shrimp appetizer, their breaded tails fanned around a cup of red sauce. Leon began at once to greedily devour the shrimp.

"Audrey," said Leon, "allow me to introduce you to Bruno, my acting pupil. Bruno, this is my lovely daughter, Audrey. Bruno has expressed a desire to learn my craft. Under my strenuous and unsparing tutelage, Bruno shall become a great and famous thespian."

"Hey," said Audrey flatly, giving me a half wave. "Where'd you meet my dad?"

"He was performing Shakespeare on the subway."

"Dad," she said to Leon, who was slurping the squishy wet meat out of a shrimp tail with his teeth. "Mom called earlier."

"What could that wanton fustilug possibly want of me?"

"She's pissed that you borrowed her car and returned it with no gas."

"Pish! Has she no pity for a poor man?"

"Just saying. She said she called your place and didn't get the answering machine so she called here."

"It is currently impossible to contact me by telephone because I have been refusing to render my pound of flesh to the AT&T company," said Leon, gravely shaking his head and brushing his hair back with his fingertips. "In any event I shan't return her call. What could she possibly want? Financial reparations? To squeeze blood from a stone? The only sane response is to ignore her utterly. Should she call again, you must inform her that I have at long last died of starvation. Come now, Bruno. Eat shrimp."

Leon delicately licked the beer froth from his mustaches, made a series of nipping noises with his tongue and lips and ordered another round, another shrimp appetizer, and three shots of whiskey. Audrey gamely knocked jiggers with us and we all drank.

Audrey was a stocky, thick-limbed girl in her twenties, though she was nowhere near as fat as her father. She had a lot of tattoos on her biceps and a round, pretty face. She spoke quickly and cuttingly in a sharp, nasal voice, and her eyes spent a lot of time sardonically rolling around in her head. She tended the bar at Artie's and let Leon drink for free if her boss—Artie himself—was not present, though she hinted that Artie tacitly suspected this and did not much mind. It was clear that Audrey loved her father, but in the world-wise and resigned way in which children who are more mature than their parents sometimes do; that is, they may choose to love them honestly and deeply even though their love is darkened somewhat by the resentment that their parents' irresponsibility by necessity pushed them too early into taking care of themselves; but she loved him, anyway. Leon ordered more beer, and then it was late and I was drunk, the restaurant was empty and the houselights had come on, and we had to go. The next day we began to rehearse our performances of Shakespeare.

———

When I met him Leon Smoler was a great and brilliant and unpromising and utter failure. He'd spent a lifetime perfecting failure almost to an art form. He had failed at many arts. He was a failed director, a failed actor, a failed writer, a failed musician, a failed photographer, a failed housepainter, a failed gravedigger, a failed commercial fisherman, a failed substitute high school teacher, a Princeton University dropout, an avowed alcoholic, a dishonorably discharged veteran, and a three-time divorcé. A Renaissance man, a jack-of-all-trades, and a master of few. He was fifty years old when I met him. He'd thus far spent his life pinging around like a pinball from one elaborate catastrophe to the next. He had once directed an off-off-Broadway production of *A Midsummer Night's Dream* performed entirely in the nude. He lived in Los Angeles for a while, working as a set painter. Life in Hollywood fizzled out and he moved back to New York, where he founded a theatre company to produce his own plays, which he wrote in accordance with Artaud's manifesto on the Theatre of Cruelty. This feat of entrepreneurial derring-do also ended in ignominious bankruptcy. He had played Hamlet, Macbeth, Lear, Shylock, Brutus, Falstaff. He had been stabbed to death many times over, as Polonius, as Claudius, as Banquo, as Julius Caesar. Somewhere in all that Leon got married and divorced three times, though none of these marriages lasted more than a few years. He has two grown children from different marriages, Audrey and Oliver (both named after Shakespearean characters), to whom he was a permissive and incompetent father.

Oliver lived far away and seldom saw his father, whom he resented, but Audrey lived nearby with her girlfriend and worked behind the bar at Artie's. On that particular day in March when I met him, he had been busking Shakespearean monologues on the subway because he had recently been sacked (for insubordination) from his job as a bus driver. Following his sacking he had liberated the Henry VIII costume from the dressing room of a theatre company to which he still had an illegally copied key, and went to work.

"It was not stealing, because it is impossible to 'steal' a possession unneeded by its possessor," he said. "They could not possibly have needed it, because it would never have fit anyone but me. I played Henry VIII in a spectacularly wretched production of that deservedly underproduced play a year or two ago. The costume was designed to my specifics and would never fit another human being. Therefore, by virtue of my physiognomy, it is rightfully mine." He invented a name for his one-man theatre company—the Shakespeare Underground—and took to the trains, riding them all day, yo-yoing up and down along the length of Manhattan and undulating back and forth across the breadth of it, walking from one train compartment to the next, shaking his coffee can and allowing his lungs to be inflated with and his soul to be possessed by the words of Falstaff, Hamlet, Lear, Macbeth, Othello, Shylock, Prospero, reciting whatever speeches came to mind in whatever order in which they came, a revolving cast of kings, princes, sorcerers, moneylenders, and madmen, lovers and the beloved, traitors and the betrayed, murderers and the murdered, haunting the reeking and rattling underground trains with Shakespeare's ghost.

So far he'd made seventy-eight dollars: a sum which, while by no means lavish, was not to be sneezed at. He said he'd been doing it for six days.

Soon after we met, I became an inspiration to Leon. He saw great potential in me. I put an idea into his mind, an idea that would later blossom into the magnum opus of both his career and mine: to stage an epic production of *The Tempest*. It would be a spectacle that would weave together his two passions: Shakespeare and magic. It would star Leon as Prospero and Bruno Littlemore as Caliban.

"This idea took form in my mind from the very moment I first saw you," Leon would say much later. "The roots of this idea took hold, the green sapling began reaching out of the soil into the sunlight, and this great idea slowly began to develop into a reality." When he divulged his plan to me, we had already been giving performances of Shakespeare in the subway together for some time. For obvious reasons, the circuslike spectacle of a monstrously fat man playing opposite a clean-shaven and verbally conversant chimpanzee more than quintupled the average hourly income of the Shakespeare Underground, which now boasted two members.

At first we performed in the subway cars, as Leon had been doing before we met. I would ride like a child on his massive shoulders as he walked down the aisle, rattling the coffee can. This was because it was infeasible to perform any other way in the tight confines of the subway car. Great fun, it was. I would always have to duck to fit under the door as we passed from one car to the next, clinging to Leon's head with my long purple hands during that terrifying moment of darkness and thunder, stinking hot air and blasting wind between car and car. I stretched out my long arms to grab hold of the poles and the loops of strap in passing, and this also helped to steady Leon's balance. For sheer amusement we continued to play certain scenes in this way—me sitting on Leon's shoulders and flailing my long arms high in the air—even after we switched to performing on the floors of the stations. Because after the first couple of weeks we soon found it more advantageous to perform in the subway stations: for financial reasons (higher traffic, bigger audiences), pragmatic reasons (more freedom in terms of staging), and because (as we were at one point somewhat rudely informed by an officer of the NYPD) performing inside the cars while they are in transit is, in fact, illegal. So after that we typically set up shop in the terminal beneath Grand Central Station—that giant, palatial building whose ceiling, ornamented with a golden map of the nighttime heavens, had so dazzled me upon my near-accidental arrival in New York—where the floors are wide and the pedestrian traffic is always bustling, and if we got bored of performing there we would relocate to the Forty-second Street or the Union Square stations.

Leon's favorite character to play was Falstaff, and he had the physique for the role, so I would oblige him with my Prince Hal. He would lie on a bedroll on the filthy tiled floor of the station, pretending to sleep (which looked plausible enough), and I would stroll by, notice him, and rouse him with a gentle kick. Falstaff half-sits up, and, yawning, stretching, snorting, rubbing his eyes, says: "Now, Hal, what time of day is it, lad?"

And I retort, "Thou art so fat-witted with drinking of old sack, and unbuttoning thee after supper, and sleeping upon benches after noon, that thou has forgotten to demand that truly which thou wouldst truly know. What a devil hast thou to do with the time of day?" And so on. We would do any scene that called for a dialogue between two characters, though we gravitated toward comic scenes, and our tragic scenes for some reason had a way of becoming comic when we performed them. I was Horatio to his absurdly obese Hamlet, I was Cassius to his Brutus, I was Iago to his Othello, Antonio to his Shylock, and I wore a blond wig, lipstick, and a dress to play the Juliet to his Romeo (authentic Shakespearean women are performed in drag anyway), the Cordelia to his Lear, and I was the Lady to his Macbeth, riding triumphantly on the shoulders of my husband as I chastise him for his weakness of heart and exhort him to murder, and now I realize, Gwen, that I've gotten ahead of myself and completely neglected to tell you about my nose.

XXXVII

Ah, my nose! My anthropomorphosis was not complete yet. Let's talk about noses, Gwen. Look at a chimpanzee's nose. No human being who isn't grotesquely deformed has a nose like that. It's barely there at all. The chimp's face caves inward in the middle like a wad of punched-in dough. The gentle glacis of his lower face into his wide upper lip from his nose holes, these two ugly apertures are flanged with a couple of slight ridges between the eyes, and that is all a chimp has to call his nose. I felt that I could not even begin to convincingly pass for human with an abhorrence like that smack in the middle of my otherwise not entirely unhandsome face. No, that thing had to go. Or rather, it had to *become*: to become a real man's nose.

I do not remember at what point I had begun to obsess so much over my nose, but it was before I was accidentally removed to New York, and before I was living with Leon and performing Shakespeare in the subways. But I do know that this was when my vanity finally drove me to rhinoplasty. I was so self-conscious of my nose's ugliness that I swear I couldn't go five minutes without thinking about it. I scrutinized my face in every reflective surface I happened to pass, imagining what it would look like with a decently attractive human nose. Noses are strange things, Gwen. There is something innately humorous about them. Noses are silly. While the eyes are the tragedians of the face, the nose is its comedian. The eyes are the windows to the soul: human beings are disturbed and enchanted by their eyes—and amused by their noses.

Anyway, I wanted one. I had to have a nose. I'd made my decision, but there were difficulties. Chief among them: I was illegal. I was off the grid. I had no Social Security number, paid no taxes, had no papers of any kind to prove my existence, outside of some documents moldering in a filing cabinet somewhere in the Lincoln Park Zoo—but they were of course no help to me, not for what I wanted. The Shakespeare Underground was beginning to pull in a decent (but far from exorbitant) amount of cash by this time, due almost certainly to the addition of Bruno to the company, to the freak-show element he added to the act, and so also was the case with Leon's magic shows. In truth, Leon had never been scrabbling in so much business in a very long time as he was with me. He came to depend on me—he needed me. Like organ grinder and monkey, we were entertainment symbiotes, lowbrow wedded to high. Months passed quietly. Leon and I passed these months in performing Shakespeare in the subway stations, rehearsing our acts in Leon's squalid apartment on City Island, and occasionally performing our magic shows. Leon made me a present of my beautiful nickel-plated kazoo, and I learned to play it. As I've said, I have it still. Sometime I will show you my kazoo, Gwen. Leon would cook spaghetti for us, or instant macaroni and cheese, and we would eat watching old movies on TV—watching Laurence Olivier, Orson Welles, Cary Grant. We spent many nights at Artie's, drinking for free at Audrey's tolerant behest. We became great friends.

Between Shakespeare, magic, and the bar beneath the rubber shark in the back of Artie's Shrimp Shanty, the months passed, and our finances increased at a modest rate. But I was still a fugitive, and I was still in hiding. During these months, I dared not try to return to Chicago to come back to Lydia, although she was never far from my thoughts. I too much feared what would have become of me. Of course I wondered—bitterly, I wondered—if it had been Tal who had sold me out to the biomedical research lab. I shuddered to think it. I could not believe this seriously, though. I was sure that forces beyond her control—and far beyond Lydia's—had resulted in my forced removal to New York, and my attempted enslavement. I was on my own. What could I have done? Where could someone in my situation have gone? There seemed but two options: science or entertainment. I could have gone crawling back to science, if it was certain slavery with the benefits of security and relative comfort I had wanted, and of course I did not want that. So instead I went into show business. And I liked it. I liked to regale an audience with my clacking teeth and hideous form, I enjoyed the attention, I loved to act, and I loved to scramble around in the audience riling up all the shrieking children with hat in hand and kazoo in mouth, while Leon's skilled magician's hands twisted and bent matter into wild manifestations of apparent magic.

I mentioned to Leon that I wanted a new nose. At first he balked.

"Why in the blighted world would you want to beautify that gloriously revolting face of yours?" he said between a gulp of beer and a belch. "Nature has obviously intended you for a life in entertainment! That face is your golden goose! Don't butcher it!"

"I don't care what nature intended me for. I want a human nose! I'm going to get one, and I don't need anyone's permission, either."

"Claptrap, Bruno! I am your employer. *I* shall decide what your nose looks like, for your appearance is my business."

"Before you met me, Leon, you were a buffoon shouting Shakespeare in the subway. Business never picked up until I came. You wouldn't make a pittance without me!"

"Great snakes!" Leon bashed a fist on the bar counter, causing the glasses on it to wobble. "What insubordination! Audrey! Did you hear such vomitous insubordination issue from the mouth of the insolent animal who sits even now beside me? Don't forget under whose roof you sleep, you ungrateful wretch!"

"I want a new nose! A nose, a nose! Leon, forgive me! I hate my nose! It's a burden! It is an albatross that hangs from the neck of my face!"

"And how, you vain ape you, would you even begin to pay for cosmetic surgery? Pshaw! Surely it costs many thousands of dollars, if not millions. No, I'm afraid not, not in your income bracket. Such luxuries—such vanities!—are for the rich, and are not afforded the humble Shakespearean actor. This is not even to mention the logistics of it all. You've no head for logistics, Bruno. You fail utterly to grasp the delicate interworkings of reality." A pause, and Leon went on: "And why ever would you *want* to attach a human nose to your ape face? Why blaspheme it so?"

"Because I'm a human now. I want to look like one."

"You are *not* human!" Leon snorted. "Much as it begrudges me to pay you compliments. But call a spade a spade."

"I am not an animal!" I cried out in frustration.

Leon reified his posture on his bar stool, and with a daintily dismissive flutter of his fingers, said: "I quote Jonson: 'An ape's an ape and a varlet's a varlet, though they be clothed in silk or scarlet.'"

"What's that?"

"That's you: an ape in scarlet."

"I meant the quotation."

"*Ben* Jonson, *obviously*!" Leon roared. "The poor man's Shakespeare."

"I know a guy," Audrey offered from behind the bar.

"*What?*" said Leon. "As do I. I know many 'guys.' But only one man." He indicated himself by cocking his head and raising his eyebrows.

"No, I mean I know a guy who does plastic surgery. Well, I know *about* him."

"Silence, shrew!" said Leon.

"Tell me more," I pleaded. "What is his name? Have you met him?"

Audrey leaned over the counter toward me and spoke quietly, even though there was no one else in the bar besides me and Leon.

"I don't know his name. I only know someone who knows him. You know Sasha?" I nodded. Sasha was Audrey's coworker—she was a waitress at Artie's whom I knew, though not well. "She knows him," said Audrey. "He did a nose job for her sister. He was a doctor in Brazil before he came to the States. He's not licensed to practice here, but he does plastic surgery on the sly. He works out of the back of a beauty salon in Astoria. Brazilian women come to him for lipos and nose jobs and stuff like that. He's clean, he's safe. Sasha gets a commission if she brings people in, that's how it works. I think she used to work at the beauty salon before she started waitressing here."

"I must meet this man. How much does he charge?"

"I don't know. Cheap, I think. But not free."

A nose!—to have a human nose! If only I had that, my body would be complete!

A few days later, Leon and I were in Artie's Shrimp Shanty again after another day of performing Shakespeare in the subway all afternoon and night. We didn't even stop at home to change into our civilian clothes: Leon was in his Henry VIII costume and I was wearing my costume, which was a Harlequin's suit checkered with red and yellow diamonds, and a jester hat with floppy red and yellow tassels with bells sewn on the ends of them. This was our usual style of dress during this time. When we came in, Audrey met my eyes, and with a beckoning hand and a jerk of her head asked me down to the far end of the bar, where Sasha sat beneath the rubber shark, with an electric-blue cocktail on a napkin in front of her. Leon squelched his weight onto his usual stool at the other end of the bar. His squishy haunches ballooned over the stool like the edges of a giant flesh muffin.

"I shall have a pint of ale!" he declared in his thespian's faux-Continental accent. Audrey ignored him for the moment. Leon harrumphed and turned his attention to the baseball game playing on the muted TV bolted to the corner of the wall. I sat down beside Sasha. She had finished her shift but was still wearing her waitressing uniform. Sasha had olive skin, dark hair dyed blond, sharp green eyes, silver hoop earrings, and long artificial fingernails that were polished glossily and painted a neon blue that almost matched the color of her drink. Her false eyelashes were long and brittle, and made very subtle clicking noises when she blinked. I found her attractive, though in a very deliberately organized way.

The doctor's name was DaSilva. He was a friend of her father's.

"He did a nose job for my sister," said Sasha in a Queens-Brazilian accent. "Cost her half a grand. Not too bad." She shrugged and clicked her nails against the bar counter.

"I can pay!" I blurted.

"I'll take you to talk to him. But he only works on people he knows. He knows me, so he'll prolly do it, but he might not want to."

Some days later Audrey borrowed her mother's car to take me to Dr. DaSilva. Audrey's mother—the second of Leon's ex-wives—lived in Yonkers, and had lent Audrey her wood-paneled 1987 Wagoneer, with forewarnings about the vehicle's many ailments and electromechanical idiosyncrasies. Audrey and Sasha met me in the morning at the door of the apartment I shared with Leon behind Artie's, and I went with them. Leon was irritated with what he saw as my insubordination, irritated further that Audrey was playing accomplice to it (Audrey liked me—she had come to regard me as a younger brother, I think), and even further irritated that the Shakespeare Underground would miss a day of performing because of this errand of vanity. I said good-bye to him, but he churlishly refused to answer or get up from where he sat in his terry-cloth bathrobe on the futon, absentmindedly watching *Bringing Up Baby* while muttering something about my insubordination and eating a ready-made rotisserie chicken in a plastic container that he'd just bought for breakfast at the grocery store down the street. Audrey drove us off the island, through the park, down the expressway, and across a bridge that hung high above the water on stark gray towers before sloping into Queens, into a dizzying web of narrow streets, and then we were in a place where the alphabets of many different languages were jumbled together on the storefronts, where Latinate, Cyrillic, and Greek letters fought for space with Arabic and Chinese, this Babylonian salmagundi of scripts and tongues all nattering in unison—tongues, and musics, too!—strains of polka, samba, reggae, and klezmer intermingled with Persian ululations, the accordion-and-brass *oompa-oompa* of mariachi music and the fuzzy thumps of rap blasting from car stereos—and the smells!— whiffs of meat crackling over fires and fried dough and who knows what else twisting together with the smells of tobacco and sewage, and there were all kinds of people jostling each other on the streets, women in bonnets and wooden clogs wheeling baby carriages with pudgy children pattering after them past skinny men in glossy tracksuits and jewelry and with glued-in-place hair, and so on and on: this place was like a sprawling fractal of infinitely divisible human complexity, a distracting circus of the senses where everyone was so busy that no one bothered to look anywhere but where they were going. Audrey piloted us in that grumbling behemothic vehicle down the street, past barbershops, shoe stores, bars, gas stations, and donut shops, until we came to where we were going. She gradually seesawed the large automobile into a parallel parking place. We were in a Brazilian neighborhood, said Sasha. Everywhere I saw what I presumed were Brazilian flags draped over things, hanging from awnings or painted on windows, green and yellow with a star-speckled blue orb in the middle, and everywhere I saw people with the same olive skin and green eyes that Sasha had. Here was a storefront embedded in the middle of the block of a medium-traffic street, inconspicuously snuggled between a deli and a store that specialized in doors: a picture of a palm tree and the words IPANEMA BEAUTY dancing in loopy green cursive across the front of a white awning that shaded the front door. We went in.

A string of bells clinked against the glass as the door shut behind us. A long, narrow room: in front, a desk, a register, and a waiting area, with metal folding chairs and a coffee table covered with women's magazines in Portuguese; in back, a doorless doorway covered with a turquoise curtain; below, linoleum floors; above, a row of three ceiling fans with pull chains clinking against wobbling light fixtures; there was a long counter with rows of metal sinks embedded in it, and scissors, razors, bottles, sprayers, combs and brushes scattered down the length of it; two parallel mirrors stretched along opposite sides of the room; next to the counter, reclining chairs were rooted to the floor on metal poles, with pedals to pump the chairs up on the poles or release them to sink hissing downward, and at the head of each chair a hemispherical plastic helmet fixed on a hinge that would descend over the head of the person sitting in the chair. The room smelled lush with shampoos, soaps, perfumes, wet hair. The feminine energy in this room was sweet and thick as cream. Several women lay in the chairs, and other women stood over them, fixing up the heads of the women lying in the chairs—snipping, clipping, brushing, lathering, rinsing, blow-drying, etc.—and all the women were talking together in the universally recognizable tones of gossip, but were speaking Portuguese—that pretty language, musically mysterious to me, that sounds like Spanish softly brushed with French.

When we came in, the women smiled and blew kisses and flicked feminine waves hello to Sasha, and one of the women—she was heavyset and middle-aged, with heavy purplish pouches under her green eyes, pink lipstick, and dyed bronze-blond hair—said something to the woman in the chair whose head she was working on, and came smiling and clacking on her heels toward us across the linoleum. She and Sasha embraced, exchanged kisses on cheeks. Then Sasha and this woman had a lightning-quick conversation in Portuguese, and Sasha pointed at me. The woman held out her hand to me, palm down.

"Hello, Mr. Bruno," she said, in an accent with feather-dusted consonants. I put a small kiss on the top of her plump brown hand, because that seemed like the thing to do, and she was introduced to me as Cecília. With a long fingernail, painted pink to match her lips, she beckoned us to follow her through the mirrored corridor of the beauty parlor, where in passing she bid one of the other women with a signal and a flutter of Portuguese to finish her work for her. She scraped aside the turquoise curtain covering the doorway at the back of the room and directed us through a dingy storeroom filled with damp cardboard boxes, down a short, dim hallway, through another door and into another waiting room, which looked much like the waiting area in the front of the front room, with the same metal folding chairs and coffee table with the same magazines on it. There was a plastic potted plant in one corner and a framed mirror on the wall.

This room essentially looked like the waiting room of a normal doctor's or dentist's office, in that it was clean and well-lighted and so on, and even professional-looking—but what was missing from it was a feeling of legitimacy, of—well, *legality*, a basic lack of fear. Yes, that's it—this room had a little *fear* in it, a fear that slightly soured its mood; but only *slightly* soured, like a whiff of milk that's just beginning to turn but would probably still be safe to drink. The carpet was a little too thin or too questionably stained, the décor a little too shabby, the walls a little too naked of ornament. We sat down in the cheap metal folding chairs, and Cecília went out and brought us coffee in Styrofoam cups, and sat down to ask me a few polite questions, nothing too serious yet, which questions I answered as politely and as well as I could between sips of coffee. Then Cecília turned to Audrey, asked her a few similar questions, and apologized to us before turning to Sasha and launching into a rapid exchange in Portuguese. I liked Cecília—she was business-like, but beneath that there was something almost grandmotherly about her, something worldly and kind that I trusted.

The other door in the room softly clicked open and two women came out. They looked surprised to see us sitting there. The older of them held the younger one by a linked arm. I realized from their synchronized gait, bodies, and eyes that they were mother and daughter. The daughter's face, from her upper lip to her eyes, was covered in a bandage: plaster-wetted gauze was wrapped across her nose, a big adhesive bandage secured it to her face, and a cotton pad strapped over that with white tape wrapped around the back of her head beneath her hair. Both her eyes were swollen-lidded, blood-shot, and bruised purple, as if she'd been in a fistfight. She was breathing through her mouth. The mother dipped a careful nod at Cecília, who nodded back with pursed pink lips and knowing eyes, and they went out. The other door was still slightly ajar. The door swung outward and a little man came out: he was middle-aged, thin, and delicate-looking, with pronounced cheekbones, pewtery hair that glistened like fish skin slicked flat to the sides of his mostly bald head, and a neat black mustache that pointed down from his nose to the corners of his lips; the overall effect of his face evoked an aging matinee star from the era of silent film. A pair of wireframe glasses pincered the bridge of his nose. He was snapping off a pair of bloody surgical gloves and whistling. He wore a string-tied white apron, covered in blood. Then he saw us sitting there, and, still whistling, he jabbed an index finger in the air, probably pretending to have forgotten something, turned back inside and shut the door behind him. For a while we heard the clank and scuttle of things being cleaned up or thrown away, the *eek-eek* of faucet knobs and the hush of water, accompanied all the while by his tuneful and insouciant whistling. Cecília excused herself, rose, went into the room and added the sound of their muffled conversation to these noises. She came back and sat with us again, reassured us with a smile and a wink, and patted me twice on the knee. Soon the man came out again. The wireframe glasses were now pushed higher up on his nose and the gloves and bloody apron gone. He wore elegant shoes and a purple shirt tucked into pinstriped gray slacks; his sleeves were rolled up past his hairy forearms, and a silver watch with a segmented band flashed at his wrist. This was Dr. DaSilva.

There was some initial business to discuss. After that was over with and the DaSilvas (Dr. DaSilva was the husband of Cecília, who ran the legitimate half of their business) were sufficiently convinced I was trustworthy, Cecília returned to the front of the store and I left Audrey and Sasha in the waiting room to follow Dr. DaSilva back to his office, a cramped but clean, windowless room with a desk, a sink, and an operating table. An assortment of surgical equipment lay gleaming on the counter. The operating table had a white bedsheet draped over it, with fluorescent lamps C-clamped to its edges. Dr. DaSilva decompressed into the office chair behind his desk, and I sat across from him in a small wooden chair facing it. There was a distinct sense of Old World gentility to Dr. DaSilva. Seen close up, he looked even more like a silent film star: he even seemed to move like a man in an old movie, too slowly when standing still and too quickly when walking, and sometimes, while in transit, popping instantaneously from one place to another; you could almost hear the crackle of decaying film as he moved around the room.

"I need your help, Dr. DaSilva. I want a nose."

"I believe I can provide that," he nodded. He sat in his cheap wheeling office chair with his elbows anchored on the thighs of his crossed legs and his fingers making a cage, each fingertip leaning on its corresponding fingertip. Dr. DaSilva looked like a man of science. Something about his mannerisms reminded me at that moment of Dr. Norman Plumlee.

"Look at my nose!" I half-wailed. "It's hideous! I want to put a new nose on my face."

"What sort of nose are you imagining, Mr. Littlemore?"

"A nice big one."

"Hm. Would you like, say, a nose like this one?" He tapped the side of his own nose.

"I simply want a nose, Doctor, that will make me look more— um—well—more like a normal person." I refrained from telling him my whole story. Usually my faculties of speech were enough to convince people that I was just a very weird-looking human. He seemed to believe that I was human, and so I did not tell him that what I wanted, what I really wanted, was a nose to make me more humanlike. I even dared to crack a joke: "Whenever I talk to someone, I see them staring at this aberration between my eyes, and I know they're thinking: 'Look at that *nose*—this guy looks like a chimp!'"

440 • Benjamin Hale

Dr. DaSilva smiled warmly and laughed, laughing with me, until he adjusted his wireframe glasses, looked at me a little closer, and quit laughing. He cleared his throat.

"This will be a tricky one," he said.

"Please, Doctor!"—my fast-beating heart screamed out within my breast—"I don't care where you get it! Cut it off a corpse for all I care, I just want the nose of a man, a man!"

Dr. DaSilva pulled a big three-ring binder from beneath his desk and flopped it open under his desk lamp. The book was full of photographs of all the nose surgeries he had performed. These were the kinds of noses he could shape with his knife. It functioned as a catalog. They were pre- and postoperative pictures of his clients, with the eyes scribbled out of the pictures to protect their anonymities. These pictures were nothing short of astounding to me. These women went under Dr. DaSilva's knife and woke up with brand-new faces. He must have been a genius of the craft of plastic surgery. He was an *artist*—a sculptor—but his medium was not clay nor marble; it was the fragile union of flesh and nonflesh, the fluid marriage of the animate with the inanimate. He was like the Rodin of the corporeal—instead of kneading nonliving matter into forms suggesting life, he manipulated the very matter of life. I flipped through the glossy photographs stuck in the plastic sleeves of his scrapbook. They were lovely noses all, beautiful noses. But what I wanted was something a little different from these noses. For one thing, they were all women's noses. For another, all of these operations were shrinkings or reshapings of noses: DaSilva shortened bones, smoothed out bumpy bridges, narrowed flaring nostrils, turned the downturned up, sharpened bulbous tips, etc. I suppose rhinoplasticians are generally in the business of the reduction—rather than the augmentation—of the schnoz. This, among other things, is what made the surgery I wanted a rather unorthodox one.

Usually it is the surgeon's job to break that delicate little bone in the bridge of the nose, remove the cartilage deemed unsightly and re-form the thing in closer accordance with our standards of beauty. But what Bruno desired was the opposite procedure: what I desired was practically the *creation* of a nose. I wanted a big, aggressive, human-looking nose to protrude from the middle of my chimp face.

Dr. DaSilva folded the book shut and stored it under his desk, then produced a sketchpad and a pencil, and asked me to turn my head so that he saw my profile. I did, and he trained his desk lamp on me. I winced.

"Sorry," he said. "Please be still for a moment."

I stared straight ahead and listened to the pencil scratching on the paper. When he was done, he showed me the quick sketch that he had drawn of me. It looked like this:

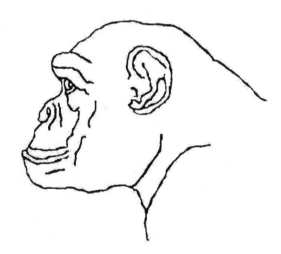

Dr. DaSilva was evidently a skilled draftsman. I agreed this was an accurate rendering of my profile. Dr. DaSilva flipped a sheet of transparency paper over this drawing, and sketched out a prospective nose on top of it. When finished, he showed me the result:

"Yes!" I shouted. *"That's it! That's the nose I want!"*

I forgot myself—I was hopping up and down madly in my seat, and Dr. DaSilva sharply hushed me. I slapped my hands over my mouth such that I resembled the third and final of the Three Wise Monkeys, and, when I was sure no more yelps of irrepressible joy would escape me, I lowered my quivering fingers. The image Dr. DaSilva had rendered drove me to the brink of tears. He understood precisely the nose that I desired. The nose that would make me a man. Dr. DaSilva also offered to trim my ears into a more human size and shape, but I declined. I've always liked my ears. It was only the nose I was after.

The price he named was one thousand dollars. I blanched when I heard the figure. By exhorting his pity—pleading that I was but a poor Shakespearean actor, that it might take me months to scrabble together so much capital—I was able to talk him down to nine hundred, but he would not drop a dime lower. Such a price, he said, was charity enough considering how unusual and difficult this procedure would be. Now, at this time, I had sixty-seven dollars and ninety-one cents to my name. It was all stuffed in my piggy bank at Leon's place. My heart sank as I wondered how many months of scrimping and saving it would take me, how many corners cut, how many frivolities forgone, how many months of monastically abstemious living it would take me to save up so much money. Audrey agreed to lend me two hundred dollars right away, with no interest. Leon was still skeptical.

"I see no reason why you should want to gravitate that delightfully comic face of yours, Bruno. That face is what will make your fortune."

"Fine then. If it'll make me a fortune, then I'll use my face to make my fortune, and I'll use my fortune to make my face!"

"Pshaw!"

"Don't worry, Bruno," said Audrey. "You'll probably still look like a freak."

"Thank you," I said bitterly.

"Bah," said Leon. "Weep not, ape. We tease because we love."

How—*how* to get the money? This financial question now took over the obsessive place in my mind that had been previously occupied by the nasal question. How to get the money. How to get the money. The obnoxious refrain "How to get the money" moved into my waking consciousness, took a seat, kicked off its shoes, and sat there for days and weeks, driving me insane. Where in the world would I turn up nine hundred dollars? Or seven hundred, I suppose, considering Audrey's promise of a loan. But still. This amount of money seemed an insurmountable peak to me, an insane figure, a wistful, romantic impossibility, a childishly fanciful sum, as if the doctor may as well have asked for one-hundred-billion-trillion-gazillion dollars' recompense for my surgery.

For a time I sank into a malaise. I entered a period of melancholic yearning. I pined for a nose. I would lock myself in the bathroom and stare at my face for hours, imagining where my nose would be, how handsome I would look. It was not so much that I wanted to aesthetically improve my face, but that...that I felt *incomplete* without a nose. I felt that I had been born missing one, that my lack of a definitive nose was a glaring and unfortunate deformity that wanted surgical correction. I tried to hatch money-getting schemes with Leon, but Leon still refused to lend even his emotional (not to mention financial) support to my surgery. The money-making schemes I idly allowed to incubate in my mind veered into the fantastic, even the felonious: I would embark upon a life of crime! I would rob a bank! Smuggle diamonds! Of course such fantasies never came close to fruition. I even considered writing to the wealthy Mr. Lawrence in Colorado to ask for the money—after all, a mere seven hundred dollars would be a drop in the bucket to him—but I rejected the idea almost as soon as it had crystallized in my consciousness, for the obvious reason that I was still a wanted fugitive in the world, whose whereabouts were unknown. I was lost, without money or nose. For a long time, my heart was sorrowful.

XXXVIII

L eon and I began talking seriously about what would be the Shakespeare Underground's first (and only—but I'll get to that when the time comes) major production. There was a little—just a little, not much—discussion at first as to which play we should perform for our company's debut production. We had our hearts set on *The Tempest* right from the beginning, but we briefly considered others.

"What about *Lear*?" I suggested. Splayed open before us on the bar counter of Artie's Shrimp Shanty, under the shadow of the giant rubber shark, was Leon's battered and loveworn black leatherbound Gramercy Edition of *The Complete Works of William Shakespeare*, with gold-edged pages as thin as cigarette papers and a ribbon sewn into the binding for a bookmark. Leon's pudgy fingers flapped through the pages of the book.

"That's much too dreary for me," Leon snorted. "I'm frankly not in the mood for it. About the only thing that doesn't happen to Lear is getting eaten, but if the play had been given one more act, it probably would have. I played Lear once, you know"—Leon was in a wistful mood—"some years ago now.... I was a bit lighter then. I had the beard for it, but not the physique. They told me to lose weight. I did in fact manage to lose a little, but nevertheless the audience laughed whenever I came onstage. That was in the winter, and on the side I was playing Santa Claus in a mall on Long Island. Oftentimes I would get carried away and slip into Lear, and all the grubby little children would commence to sob in terror. They laughed at my Lear and cried at my Santa. The bastards."

"*Othello*?"

"I like *Othello*. It's got lots of casual chat. You don't get casual chat in *Lear*, everyone's too busy thinking about the universe. But I'm afraid that in this day and age it would be in poor taste for me to wear blackface."

We discussed *A Midsummer Night's Dream*, *Macbeth*, *Love's Labours Lost*, and *Coriolanus*, but rejected each in turn for various and sundry reasons.

"*The Tempest*," Leon declared, "is really the only obvious choice for us."

"Agreed."

"We must get it absolutely right, though. *The Tempest*, of all the Bard's plays, is the one that offers the most creative leeway in the interpretation of staging, sound, music, scenery: it is a veritable blank slate for mise-en-scène, which makes it both an exciting and a difficult play to produce. The first act is reasonable enough, and so's the second, but the Bard seems to have dropped acid for the third and fourth acts. Really—just read the stage directions, they're completely insane. Take this, for instance." Leon cleared his throat and read: "'Thunder and lightning. Enter Ariel, like a harpy; claps his wings upon the table; and with a quaint device, the banquet vanishes.'"

"How are we supposed to do that?"

"With magic, Bruno. Some plays want stark, minimalist staging in order to focus the audience's attention on the human elements of the play. *The Tempest* is just the opposite. *The Tempest* is a song to sing beyond mankind. A truly great production of it must be an experience so seductively thaumaturgical that it is rivaled only by the erotic in the scope of human experience. What I envision is not only a play, but also a magic show. The ideal production of this play, of course—the only production truly worthy of the text—would have to employ not *tricks*, not mere special effects nor slights-of-hand, but *real magic*. This production shall aspire to come as close to that ideal as possible. It shall be miraculous, nearly a religious experience, really, though it won't be overtly good for anyone's soul. No true theatre is. Theatre, Bruno, is a secular miracle."

So our production of *The Tempest* would have to involve a spectacular sensory overload of mise-en-scène, involving mysterious tricks of light and sound, smoke and mirrors, music and magic. Leon would play Prospero. I would play Caliban. The rest?—details.

We needed funding: always a problem. How did this wretched and life-denying civilization come to be?—how did we blindly, stupidly, collectively manage to erect an architecture for our world in which we waste so much of our lives fretting and worrying and sweating and losing our sleep and grinding our teeth and biting our nails in putrid consternation over the movement and circulation, over the having and the not having, over the keeping and the losing and the procuring of little pieces of metal and paper? Then I remembered Emily—little Emily! Little Emily, who had nursed me when I was wounded, who had sheltered me when I was hunted. I recalled how her parents so desperately wanted for their beautiful daughter the celebrated life of the stage and screen. Perhaps, perhaps...

I described to Leon in full detail my adventure that involved little Emily; how I was pursued, alone and hurt, how she gave me sanctuary and nursed me back to health. I noted that she was a young actress of both stage and film, and a gifted songstress as well, and that when I had met her, she was preparing feverishly for her role as the eponymous character in the musical *Little Orphan*

Annie, which surely must already have come and gone by now. And I did not fail to mention that she appeared to come from a family of ample means.

"Perhaps," I said aloud, "perhaps, perhaps..."

"Of course," said Leon, licking beer froth from his mustaches, clapping and rubbing his hands together and slyly arching one eyebrow in villainous collusion.

The following day found Leon and me seated in Leon's ex-wife's Wagoneer, exploratorily driving around in the village of Hastings-on-Hudson, New York, looking for little Emily's family's big house. We had put on our best suits and ties, and Leon carried an officious-looking attaché case he had dug out from the bottom of a closet for the purpose of looking officious. We kept reminding ourselves that we were not *dressed up as* fancy Broadway casting directors, but that we *were* casting directors. We were casting directors who happened to have seen little Emily's (I cursed myself a thousand times for failing to learn little Emily's surname) genius, dazzling, etc., performance as Little Orphan Annie in the musical play of the same name, and we hoped to cast her as Miranda in *The Tempest*, which would mark the debut production of the avant-garde theatre troupe the Shakespeare Underground, and by the way we are looking for backers, so perhaps, perhaps...?

"This is the neighborhood," I said. "I remember it very clearly. I think I've seen that house before. It must be around here somewhere."

Leon piloted the wood-paneled Wagoneer through the narrow roads, runs, drives, lanes, and culs-de-sac of the posh Westchester suburb. One after another, we passed Tudor-style mansions surrounded by oaks and sprawling swaths of green lawn and topiaries.

"Ignorant baboon!" grumbled Leon. "How in the blazes could you possibly know? All of these stately pleasure domes look nearly identical to me!"

We had been driving around for hours, and it was about six in the evening when we rolled past the house, and the telltale wave of déjà vu I'd been hoping for finally came to trigger my recognition of it. There indeed stood the white and brown and brick Tudor-style house, which I was certain was little Emily's.

"There! That one!" I shouted, the tip of my long purple index finger squished against the glass of the passenger-side window. "I'm sure of it!"

We parked a little ways down the street, out of sight around a bend in the road, in order to avoid raising any undue suspicions as to why two fancy Broadway casting directors should arrive in such a déclassé mode of transport as Leon's ex-wife's Wagoneer. The lights in the house were on, and there seemed to be human activity going on inside of it. We saw the shadow of a person moving in the ground floor windows. It was autumn, and the trees lining the road were ablaze with color. We hiked down the leaf-scattered road, past a mailbox—noting the name GOYETTE printed on the side of it—and up the walk that led through the lawn and garden to the front door, Leon with his hair neatly combed back and his beard freshly trimmed, the officious-looking attaché case swinging freely in his fat fist, and I beside him. Leon depressed a sausagelike finger into the doorbell, and soon that same tiny yellow dog appeared in the narrow frosted-glass window beside the front door, yapping its miserable little head off. In a moment a woman's face peered out the same window at us, her hand cupped against the glass to see outside, her eyebrows knit in an expression belying confusion tinted faintly with apprehension. She opened the door just a tiny squeak ajar, and the dog shot forth as if from the muzzle of a cannon, and commenced to scurry circles around our feet, growling, yapping, baring every tooth in its small furry head.

"Good evening, Mrs. Goyette," said Leon in a voice as officious-sounding as the attaché case looked, offering a moist pudgy paw for a handshake.

"Hello?" the woman said, opening the door slightly wider. Her voice had a slight rasp. We could tell by the change in her face that we'd gotten the name right. Mrs. Goyette was in her late forties. She was short and considerably fat. Her clothes were clean and fashionable. A fleshy neck supported a roundish head with dark-dyed hair and a broad face with a sharp nose and a wide mouth that inclined toward elastic shifts in expression.

"I am Leon Smoler, and this is my associate, Mr. Bruno Littlemore." I nodded in assent. "We have come on a very important and exciting matter of business concerning your daughter, Emily."

The woman's hand flew to her mouth and her eyes bugged as she gasped: "Oh my God—is something wrong?"

Leon summoned a belly roar of dismissive laughter.

"Of course not! Quite to the contrary. We represent the Shakespeare Underground, an experimental theatrical production company."

The look of alarm on the woman's face was replaced with a look of hesitant distrust.

"We are extremely interested in your daughter's considerable acting talent."

"Are you talent scouts?"

I shook my head no and was about to speak.

"Yes," said Leon, "in a manner of speaking."

She invited us in. Leon and I seated ourselves on a couch by a fireplace, and she asked us if we wanted coffee.

"Yes, please," Leon called. She was in the kitchen. Leon and I waited on the couch in silence, looking around at the various bric-a-brac in the house and listening to the ticking of a grandfather clock and the chains jangling against its pendulum. The room was partially lit by the frenetically flickering bluish glow of a TV, but the sound was muted. Bill Clinton, who was the president of the United States at the time, was fidgeting on the TV. Mrs. Goyette returned with cups of coffee, which she placed on the coffee table, and took a seat in an armchair directly across from us.

"We are preparing to stage a production of *The Tempest*," Leon began. "The Bard's swan song, in which he breaks his staff and frees his magic to the four winds."

The woman pensively sipped her coffee.

"Upon having the pleasure to see little Emily's purely genius—"

"Dazzling," I said.

"Yes, dazzling, genius, dazzling performance in *Little Orphan Annie*, we have determined that no other actress would be as well suited for our female lead."

"Why were you watching a high school musical?" said Mrs. Goyette. "How did you find us? Why did you come in person instead of calling? I don't know how I feel about—"

Leon raised a judicious hand to silence her, which gesture was accompanied by a friendly smile to indicate that all would soon be explained.

"Excuse me," I said, "may I use your bathroom?"

"It's down the hall, second door on your right," and she pointed.

I rose and left the room, and behind me I heard Leon hoisting the sails of his rhetoric in preparation for a long and possibly stormy voyage. The request to use her bathroom was, of course, a ruse. I stole down the hallway and crept up the stairs to little Emily's bedroom, and softly knocked on her door.

"*What!*" she said, much, much too loudly. I quickly opened the door.

"*You can't come in unless I SAY so, you stupid bitch!*" she began to scream, as she wheeled around in her chair, away from the pile of homework spread before her on her desk, before she saw who it was who stood at the threshold of her bedroom. I put a finger to my pursed lips to beg her silence. It is remarkable how quickly a person in the throes of adolescence can change. It had been, I think, about seven months since I had last seen little Emily—and lo, she had very nearly become a woman in that time. I wondered if she remembered that evening we had spent together, and if so, if she remembered it fondly. Her bedroom had now been mostly cleansed of its childish affects: the dollhouse, the rubber women, etc., were gone. The stuffed animals, however, were still present, and all else looked the same as it had when last I saw it. The stuffed animals—among the few remnants of little Emily's childhood that steadfastly remained—seemed to have shifted meanings: they had fallen totally from innocence into experience, and they no longer represented childhood but now represented a consciously ironic retrograde sexualization of the childlike.

"What the fuck are *you* doing here?" she hissed.

Briefly, I explained the situation to her.

"That's so stupid," she said, when I had brought her up to speed. "It won't work."

"Please help us!" I blubbered. "Think of the glory of starring, at such a tender age, in a major stage production of Shakespeare! Just come downstairs and play along."

Then I fled the room to rejoin Leon and little Emily's mother downstairs. When I found them, they had switched from the living room to the kitchen and from coffee to white wine, and little Emily's mother was laughing buoyantly and feeding Leon squishy pastries with her fingers. Leon's coat was off and his tie was loosened.

"Why hello, Bruno," said Leon, with a touch of derision in his voice. "We thought you'd fallen in!"

I cleared my throat.

"I'm just charming Mrs. Goyette into submission," said Leon, and opened his mouth to accept a cube of chocolate that the woman had been trying to push past his lips. Her arm was around Leon's gargantuan waist. She lit up the room with a spell of half-drunken laughter. "Vivian has invited us to stay for dinner!"

"Well," I muttered, testing the waters. "We wouldn't want to inconvenience you—"

"Please stay!" she squealed to Leon.

"But of course," said Leon.

We stayed. Dinner was Cornish game hen. Mr. Goyette, little Emily's father and Mrs. Goyette's husband, was out of town on business.

"As usual," added Vivian—little Emily's mother—with the rolled eyes of bitterness. The chicken was indeed delicious. We ate at an ovular dining table—Leon, Vivian Goyette, little Emily Goyette, and myself. I sat across from Emily and Leon sat across from Vivian. Little Emily and I were both a little nervous and out of sorts. Our eyes kept darting to the other two and then back to each other to trade looks of uncertainty. Over dinner, at first we all talked about the upcoming production of *The Tempest*. We toasted to the production. We toasted to our success. We toasted to little Emily's preordained fate as a celebrated actress of stage and screen. Then talk became general. Much wine was drunk and all pretenses of table manners were soon discarded. Leon and Mrs. Goyette planted their elbows on the table and slurped the chicken from the bones with noisy, lustful abandon. Leon ate with his hands, smacked his jaws, licked his fingers, gulped his wine and roared between bites with thunderous eructation, and the more grotesque his table manners became, the more directly they were mirrored across the table in the behavior of little Emily's mother. Leon and Vivian Goyette locked eyes as they slurped the juicy meat from the slick slender chicken bones, frequently knocking their glasses together to toast (often forgetting entirely to include little Emily and me), refilling one another's wineglasses with increasing frequency throughout the meal, uncorking one bottle of wine after another, often uncorking another bottle even before the previous had been depleted of its contents. Leon grew flushed, unbuttoned his collar, whipped off

454 • Benjamin Hale

his necktie and threw it over his shoulder. Vivian unpinned her hair and undid the first two buttons of her blouse. Both of them ate and drank to bubbling crapulous excess. Vivian grew as pink as a carnation and sticky with perspiration. Leon's rosaceous face beneath his beard grew deeply enflamed, and his shirt became glued to his torso with sweat. Both of them were exploding and melting at the same time with laughter, sweat, and glee. More wine was opened and drunk. Little Emily and I were ordered to the kitchen to wash up while Leon and Vivian ate chocolate cake.

Little Emily sullenly passed the dishes, glasses, and silverware under hot water at the kitchen sink and handed them to me to put in the dishwashing machine. Leon and Vivian finished their cake and retired to the living room, where we heard their mirth continue.

"So you live with that big fat douchebag?" said little Emily. I had taken off my suit jacket and rolled up the sleeves of my shirt.

"We've been performing Shakespeare in the subways and doing magic shows."

When we finished washing the dishes, Leon and little Emily's mother had disappeared from the living room.

Little Emily plopped down on the couch, snatched up a remote control and turned on the TV in a single fluid motion, with the muscle-memory of a well-practiced hand.

"Where is your mother?" I said. Little Emily shrugged and rolled her eyes.

"*Ptf.* Dunno."

I sat down next to her on the couch.

"What are you watching?" I said. I scooted a little closer to her.

"*Friends*," she said.

We watched the program for a while. I had never really seen much "grown-up" TV before. Lydia would only let me watch educational programming on PBS, or cartoons sometimes. Leon only liked golden-age Hollywood movies, or else he liked to turn on the news and yell at it. But this? Something new to me. People were doing things on the screen, and it didn't make any sense to me. There seemed to be an electric current in the air in the universe where these people lived, a gathering of invisible voices that would laugh at them, sometimes at such mysterious points in time that it was very difficult to determine what these disembodied voices found so funny. It also seemed that the people who lived in this world were themselves unaware of these voices—or if they were, they had grown so used to them that they no longer found it strange. What would it be like to grow up in the world of prime-time sitcoms? To come of age under the watchful eyes of these audible but invisible gods that live in the fabric of the air, a chorus of judging voices sadistically laughing at you from infancy, at your every mistake, your every misfortune, your every shameful secret, your every foible and error of judgment? It would drive you insane!

Where were Leon and Mrs. Goyette?

Little Emily went into the kitchen and returned with a sack of Cheetos. And so we ate the Cheetos and watched *Friends*. After *Friends*, there were other TV shows much like it. Some of them were set in offices, and some of them were set in the homes of the characters, or in comfortable locations like bars, coffee shops, restaurants. The characters usually worked at interesting but decidedly white-collar places of employment, like radio stations and magazine offices, jobs that apparently involve a lot of standing around drinking coffee and playing petty practical jokes on unsuspecting coworkers. The characters in these TV shows, despite the derisive cackles of the maddening crowd that hangs in the luminiferous ether between them, do not have to worry. They might have sexual relationships with one another, they might fall in and out of love with each other, they might have conflicts with each other, power struggles, or squabbles over resources. They are free to love, to hate, to go to work, and do all the things that people do, except worry.

They are supernaturally free of true worry, because these characters know that at the end of the episode everything will reset itself, and the world will be as new. These people live in a candied reality, where all the conflicts of real life appear and disappear in joyful simulacra free of the possibility of permanent consequence. All of these TV shows were like a single, soothing lullaby voice, holding up a hilariously warped mirror to the middle class and whispering to them: *Do not worry. Do not worry. Do not worry.*

At some point during our TV watching and Cheeto eating, little Emily slipped her hand into mine. So, as we waited for Leon and Mrs. Goyette to return from whatever rabbit hole they'd disappeared into, little Emily and I sat on the couch downstairs, watching grown-up TV and holding hands as we ate Cheetos. The big crinkly cellophane sack of Cheetos we situated between us. I held her left hand in my right hand, and with my left hand I periodically reached into the Cheetos bag to grab some of the flavorful orange sticks, and she did likewise with her right hand, such that in time both the fingers of her right and my left hand were covered with sticky orange Cheeto-dust, while my right hand and her left hand were wet with the sweat produced from the heat of our pressed-together palms. We watched the grown-up TV shows where the world laughs at the inconsequential lives of its characters, and I didn't understand much of it, but I liked the Cheetos and I liked holding little Emily's hand, I liked to hold her slender little heated hand in my long purple freakish hand. And, once, each of us with one hand hot and wet and the other orange and sticky, we turned our faces toward one another, and our orange and sticky lips met in a long, profound, salty kiss. We were young, we were Americans, it was the late twentieth century.

XXXIX

It would not be quite accurate, I don't think, to say that funds were wrongfully pilfered from our production budget to pay for my nose surgery. We wrote it up as a production cost because that was, after a manner of interpretation, what it was: there was no way I would have dared grace the stage as Caliban without my new nose; it was the nose that completed the effect I wished to achieve.

When we left the Goyette household that evening—very late that evening, after Leon and Vivian, little Emily's mother, had finally descended the stairs to join us again, both of them with damp hair, for they had apparently showered; and after Leon had collected his jacket from the living room and his tie from off the dining room floor; and after Leon and Vivian Goyette exchanged a parting embrace and she deposited on his cheek a more-than-friendly smack that left the impression of her lipsticked lips on his bearded face, which rose to definition as soon as enough of the pink had drained from Leon's face that the pink lipstick could be discerned against the surrounding flesh; and after we bid good-bye to little Emily, who was in a sullen way, unsharing in her mother's high spirits; and after we walked outside and hiked back up the hill to where we had parked Leon's ex-wife's car out of sight in order to conceal our embarrassing poverty; and after I had interrogated Leon as to the particulars of what had happened when he and Vivian Goyette, little Emily's large mother, had remained out of sight for well over two hours; and after I had interrogated in vain, for Leon uncharacteristically clammed up and wouldn't offer a word in the way of detail, thus forcing me to guess the worst; and after we had climbed back into the car; and after Leon started up the engine and began to try to guide us back to the Cross County Parkway, which would carry us home—Leon smiled wryly at me, as I sat beside him, slipped his fingers into the breast pocket of his shirt, extracted a once-folded rectangular slip of paper and handed it to me, whereupon I inspected it, read the writing printed and scrawled upon it in the shifting light of the streetlights we were passing beneath, and saw that it was a check, in the account of Mr. and Mrs. Goyette, signed by Mrs. Goyette and made out for an impressively large sum of money. I was shocked by the figure written on the check.

"Is that correct?"

"Your eyes do not deceive you, Bruno. Of course I suppose this means that we must cast that sullen child in the role of Miranda. But if anyone can make anyone into a first-rate actress, it is I. How old is she?"

"She's fifteen."

"Aha! Convenient. That is the age of Miranda in the play." Leon quoted: "'Canst thou remember a time before we came unto this cell? I do not think thou canst, for then thou wast not out three years old, and twelve year since, thy father was the duke of Milan and a prince of power.'"

Leon let me fondle the check and read it over and over on the way home. This was to be our production budget. The next morning we went straightaway to the bank to cash the check before any second thoughts could come to a more sober Mrs. Goyette. The first thing we bought with the money was a sturdy metal box with a combination roll that released its snaplocking clasps, in which we dumped all the crisp, never-been-circulated one-hundred-dollar bills that Leon and I had summoned from their beds of rest in the bank teller's register, to introduce them into the winding paths of commerce, to be spent toward a good cause, and forthwith set out on whatever untold adventures the world had in store for them. We carefully counted and re-counted the money, and wrote the amount on the top line of the first page of a yellow spiral-bound college-ruled steno pad (much like the notepads that Gwen, my amanuensis, uses to record this narrative), clipped the pen to the pad and put it in the box to keep the cash company, along with a calculator for subtracting expenses. This was the entire extent of the bookkeeping system we cleverly designed for the company expense account of our now-considerably-enriched avant-garde theatre group, the Shakespeare Underground. Leon and I decided on a combination that we each committed to memory, set the combination, shut the box tight, and locked it.

Then we immediately opened it again to pay for lunch. We extracted two of the crisp hundred-dollar bills, fastidiously marked the expense on the steno pad, locked the box, stashed it under the futon, and took a train downtown for celebratory steaks. It took a while to find a nice restaurant that we hadn't swindled before, but we found one, and over top sirloins and martinis we discussed the immediate future of the Shakespeare Underground. Our first argument concerned the venue. We arrived at no immediate conclusions, as Leon was hard-pressed to think of a theatrical venue that he had not been barred from for some reason or other. Our second argument concerned our first significant production expense, which was to be my nose surgery. Leon argued that it was an unnecessary and irresponsible use of company funds, the relevance of which to the project at hand was questionable at best.

Leon, it turned out, would later have to eat a lot of crow concerning his initial objections to my nose surgery, because the surgery in an unexpected way led to the resolution of the first argument. Then we entered the serious planning stages, i.e., preproduction. What we imagined was spectacular, veritably epic in scope and ambition. We had the first of many conversations about what was needed to resuscitate the theatre for the coming twenty-first century—for that was our ultimate aim. I'd been reading Stanislavsky, I'd been reading Artaud. This reading was all part of Leon's required reading list for my tutelage in modern dramaturgy. As a teacher, Leon equally emphasized both theory and practice, and was particularly interested in the theories of Artaud.

"This shall probably be the greatest production of Shakespeare in history," said Leon. He gingerly pushed his hair back from his face with his fingertips to prevent it from getting in the martini he was slurping. I had to agree.

"I have realized," Leon continued, "that Shakespeare wrote at the tail end of the period in human history in which the magic of the narrative art was still truly alive. Later, the wild animal of Shakespeare was captured, killed, taxidermized, and enshrined by the idiotic and anodyne scholarship of the four sad centuries that have followed him, but this obviously is not the Bard's fault. We must save Shakespeare from his admirers, from his murderers. We must save him by doing away with the tyranny of the text."

I asked how this might be possible.

"An excellent question. The task that lies before us now is to undo the damage that the Enlightenment and its subsequent centuries have wrought upon the narrative arts. We must revive a sense of danger to the theatre, a sense of vitality. To break down not just the fourth wall, but also the first, the second, and the third. These walls should never have been built. Do you follow?"

"Not exactly."

"Then I shall explain. After many exhaustive years of careful study and reflection on the matter, I have arrived at the inconvenient conclusion that the Enlightenment caused the beginning of the downfall of Western theatre, just as it ruined nearly everything else. You will notice, for instance, that the centuries following Shakespeare produced astonishingly little literature that may be deemed truly significant. The work of Edgar Rice Burroughs is an exception. And *some* Dickens. But they were swimming against the current." Leon paused to insert a generous plug of steak into his cheeks. "Take the Ancients," he went on, gesturing with his fork, his words pillowed in his cheeks by his chewing. "For them, theatre could not be disentangled from the very fabric of life. The Romans took the theatre so seriously that they were known to occasionally execute people onstage, and would write these executions into their plays, as sort of, you know, plot points."

"One might argue," I felt it necessary to point out, "that we should not admire the seriousness with which the Romans took the theatrical arts, but rather be appalled at how seriously they didn't take the dignity of human life."

"Bah! What a deeply uninteresting perspective. Please henceforth banish it from your mouth in my presence."

"Sorry."

"Right. Where was I? I would speculate that Western theatre began its steady crumbling decline around the fall of the Roman Empire, and was nearly complete by the mid-seventeenth century. After that, it would never be as good again. Why, you may ask? Because after that historical moment, the narrative arts had become severed from the body of society—severed like a limb is severed! After that, all narrative art was placed inside a display case, as something to be viewed safely from outside. It became like a caged animal, pacing back and forth before the bars, to be awed and admired only from behind a protective barrier."

"I know how that feels!"

"Precisely! You are in a unique position, Bruno, because you have seen this cage from both within and without. And just as you have liberated yourself from the confines of this cage, we must liberate narrative art from its cage. We must return the theatre back to the wild, where it is free, if it so chooses, to rip its spectators to bloody shreds!"

"The theatre of wild animals!"

"Bruno!"—Leon grasped me by the arm, grasped it as forcefully as if he had just suffered a heart attack—"What a brilliant phrase! The theatre of wild animals!"

We toasted to this coinage, violently knocking our martinis together in celebration. An idea had just been born. The theatre of wild animals: we fell in love with the idea at once. In the meantime, I was able to convince Leon to begrudgingly permit me to borrow—he considered it a loan, a term I hoped he would forget about—seven hundred dollars from our company cash box to pay for my nose.

XL

My nose. Exactly as I once did, Gwen, upon the lid of a now-quasimythical Plexiglas box on the floor of a small white room in the Behavioral Biology Laboratory of the University of Chicago—the box that led me into civilization—years later, with the same ape knuckles I knocked three times: *knock, knock, knock.* Only this time it was not a transparent plastic box containing a peach that I knocked three times upon, but rather a door—a door I had seen once before—in back of an inconspicuous Brazilian beauty salon. Beside me stood my magnitudinous friend, Leon Smoler, who, finally bending to my desire to have a new nose, had driven me in his ex-wife's Wagoneer from the apartment we shared on City Island to this place, and would drive me home following my operation. On the drive to Queens we noticed that Leon's ex-wife's car was running low on gas. This problem would have been easy enough to ameliorate, but Leon, acting in rational economic self-interest by seeking to minimize production expenses, wanted to milk every last possible mile out of the current contents of the fuel tank, and he planned to make the eighth of a tank that was already at our disposal when we picked it up from Leon's ex-wife's house in Yonkers last all the way from City Island to

Queens, then back to City Island, to our apartment behind Artie's Shrimp Shanty, where he would tenderly outstretch me supine on my bed to convalesce, then back to Yonkers to return the car. I expected to be anesthetized and in no shape to see myself home after the surgery. So long as I got my nose—and I am infinitely grateful to Leon for this favor—I chose not to advise him as to the wisdom or folly of his plan, nor to the ethical questions it raised.

The car was parked outside on the street in front of the Impanema Beauty Salon. Beside Leon stood Cecília, Dr. DaSilva's wife and the owner of the legitimate end of the business that this establishment conducted. (But what business is *legitimate*, really? The entire system of economic exchange has always smacked of unnaturalness to me, of absolute spiritual illegitimacy.) In the inner pocket of my jacket was an envelope, containing nine one-hundred-dollar bills, two of them borrowed from Audrey and the other seven borrowed from the production budget of *The Tempest*. The door opened. There stood Dr. DaSilva, looking even more like a man in a silent movie than he had before: that slicked-back pewtery fish-skin hair, the ends of his elegant little mustaches pointing down and away from his nasal septum like two arrows, the supreme gentility of his manners, and the gentleness of his demeanor.

I distinctly imagined that I heard the trilling of a toy piano providing musical accompaniment, and after he extended his delicate hand to me and I shook it in greeting, a black title card appeared onscreen, with the words printed on it and framed in an ornate border: *Hello, Mr. Littlemore!* Perhaps there were other words exchanged between us, but they are cleverly implied by our facial expressions and gestures. The doctor asked who this Gargantua was who loomed so tall and wide beside me, and I answered that this was my friend Leon, who drove me here as a personal favor, knowing that after my operation I would not be in any condition to see myself home. Leon tried to follow me into the operating room, but Dr. DaSilva shook his head and held up his hand, and the piano notes deepened to indicate that Leon was not to be admitted into the operating room, he must wait outside, sorry, it's my policy, and after some futile arguing Leon stamped his foot and turned away. Dr. DaSilva shut the door, and in my silent movie Leon shuffled over to the waiting area and deposited himself in one of the folding chairs. He then tapped his foot as his eyes flicked back and forth in boredom. He picked up a magazine from the coffee table and begun to flip through it, but it was written in another language, and he could not read it, so he had to content himself with looking at the pictures. Then another black title card flashed on the screen: *Meanwhile...* Cut to Dr. DaSilva's office-cum-operating room. Dr. DaSilva politely conveyed me to his desk, his hand on my back. Bruno sat, Dr. DaSilva sat, and across the desk we engaged in one last conversation about the nose that he was going to make on my face. My organs trembled with an emotional recipe consisting of three cups excitement and a teaspoon of fear. My eyes drifted to a work counter on one side of the room, where I caught sight of an open black suitcase. It was a surgical kit, made perhaps sometime in the early twentieth century. The surgical instruments were made with a craftsman's love and precise attention to detail that we rarely glimpse anymore in objects of modern make. The scientific delicacy of those gleaming instruments!— every pair of forceps, scissors, pliers, tweezers, every knife, needle, saw, scalpel, lancet, caliper, trocar, cauter, retractor, spatula and speculum snug in its place, strapped with green ribbons into its proper depression in the green velvet lining of the case. There was, though, a distinct overture of menace in the way these sharp things glistened. Dr. DaSilva told me what I must do after I leave following the operation. He told me I could not remove the bandages until such-and-such a date. He told me not to get them wet. He told me that I might wake up with a face that was wounded, swollen, badly bruised, looking as if I had been bloodied up in a fistfight. Following surgery, I must stay in bed with my head elevated for the first twenty-four hours. My face would feel puffy, my nose would ache, a dull headache might be present. Swelling and bruising would peak after two to three days, but this could be lessened with the application of cold compresses. Bleeding was common for the first few days of recovery. Do not bend over with the head below the heart, he said, as this might increase swelling and/or bleeding. The nasal packing could be removed after a few days, and the splint could be removed one to two weeks later. I might go a little insane from the unremitting itching beneath his bandages, and it would feel like a swarm of fire ants crawling all over my flesh, but I must under absolutely no circumstances satisfy the desire, which would be a burning one, to scratch the itches. It would be best, the doctor told me, if during the healing period I did not touch my face at all, or at least as little as possible. Do not blow your nose for at least two weeks following the operation, he said. He told me that I must have serene patience to endure the coming vexation, the mad itching, the pain and discomfort that would pinch and enflame and torture my face. Patience, patience. The patient must be patient. Get lots of rest. Painkillers, if you can get them. What do you mean *if* I can get them, I wailed in alarm, and the doctor reminded me that he was practicing without a medical license, and so he could not prescribe anything. I should brace myself for a long period of excruciating pain, he told me. Vanity is painful. Beauty is difficult. And I should be discreet. Keep a low profile. Invisible, if possible. In fact it would be best, said the doctor, to simply not leave your home for a while—say the first week or two following the surgery. After all this had been said, the doctor asked me again, one last time, if I was still prepared to go through with the operation. This was my last chance to back out. The patient answered the doctor in the brave, defiant affirmative. Then the doctor asked for his fee:

everything up front. The doctor was acutely embarrassed even to be discussing money—he was a man of almost aristocratic manners, and disliked the dirty but necessary intrusion of the economic into this conversation. The patient reached a long purple hand into the inner pocket of his jacket and slipped out an envelope, which he slid across the desk. The doctor opened the unsealed flap of the envelope, peeked inside, and counted the money visually without handling it, then rolled open the desk drawer, dropped the envelope in the drawer, and rolled it shut. The doctor nodded gravely. He rose from the desk, pushed in his chair, rolled up his sleeves, draped a white apron over his head and tied the strings in the back. He told me to take off my shirt and lie down on the operating table. I did as he commanded. The thin paper mat on the operating table crinkled under my body and stuck to the sweaty flesh of my back. I rested my sweet head on a little paper pillow, and heard the paper fabric rustle and crunch under my ears. The doctor covered me with a clean white sheet. He billowed it over my body as if changing a bed, and pulled it up to my neck and tucked it under my chin. The doctor clicked on the fluorescent lamps C-clamped to the edges of the operating table. The tubes glowed on—*nzt-nzt-ngnzzzzzzzz*—stinging my eyes with bright light. Why does it seem at times as if my whole life has been lived out beneath the cold glare of fluorescent lights? The lights of academia, of science, of art, of medicine, of the madhouse. That is my fate, to live beneath fluorescent lights. In my peripheral vision I saw Dr. DaSilva—his body moving quickly and exactly, though with the occasional pops, scratches, blots, and jitters in the old celluloid—as he took a roll of duct tape from the operating table. The primitive restraining device of an illegal physician. I heard the sound of a long strip of tape being unpeeled from the roll. I smelled the incredibly distinctive odor of freshly unpeeled duct tape. With a long band of smelly gray tape the doctor secured my head to the back of the table, then wrapped several more layers of tape around my forehead, until I couldn't budge it. He did likewise with my arms, until the image of Frankenstein's monster strapped to the table to presently await his incarnating bolt of harnessed lightning probably became comically analogous. I hesitantly asked the doctor whether these restraints were entirely necessary. The doctor assured me they were a necessary precaution, nothing to worry about. He dabbed alcohol on my forearm, squirted a spurt of clear liquid from the end of a hypodermic needle, knocked it twice with his fingers, slid it deep into a vein and pushed its contents into my bloodstream. Things began to get fuzzy here for me. My sense of time dilated. I felt my body quickly becoming cool and numb. It was a pleasant sensation. Hot and cold at the same time. My breathing slowed faster than my stream of consciousness. I might have muttered incoherently. *Lydia*—I hope I did not mumble over and over until the anaesthetic took me under—*Lydia, Lydia, Lydia*... Perhaps the doctor wondered what significance this name had for his patient. What other secrets did morphine unlock from my fading brain? I'll never know. I woozily observed the doctor wash his hands at the sink as if from a thousand miles away. Somehow I was asleep and awake simultaneously. I could feel the doctor's delicate hands, I could feel the slight applications of pressure, the deft touches, the surgical flourishes, the cuts. I could just barely feel the doctor mutilating my face with his instruments, and a distant part of me felt the blood running down my cheeks, I tasted it as it dripped a little into my mouth, the warm bitter metallic tang of blood, and I heard, or I dreamt or imagined I heard, a drop or two of my blood go *plit plit* on the sticky linoleum floor of the operating room. I floated above my own body and watched the surgeon as he removed parts of my face. I watched the doctor break something in my nose and jerk it loose from its envelope of bloody slime. I saw the naked meat beneath my skin, exposed under the hot buzzing lights.

I dreamt that I was making love with Lydia. We were in Chicago. It was years ago. We were in our bed in the apartment in Chicago. It was snowing outside. Her warm body, her skin next to mine. The bed became earth, and then I was crawling through damp, dark soil. Pebbles, roots, grubs. My hands reached the surface. I pulled apart the clods of dirt, and saw a faint spot of light above. I dragged myself above the surface and emerged in a forest. I was in the jungle. I was in a wet, dark, densely vegetated place, ancient and teeming with life, with steam, dirt, fire, blood, semen, water, disease, ghosts. Everything was alive, everything breathing and flowing and moving and writhing with animal spirits. I was surrounded by chimpanzees. Naked, hairy animals, unenlightened, ungifted with speech. Grunting, howling, farting, scratching themselves, eating bugs and worms, picking nits out of each other's fur. Their rubbery masklike faces, dark glassy eyes. They looked at me, confused. I was not one of them. I looked up into the sky. I could see only patches of blue here and there; most of it was shrouded by branches. But in one of the places where I could see the sky unobstructed by the leafy umbrages of the giant jungle trees, I saw something: a tiny speck, something floating in the sky, way up high above the trees. It descended, getting bigger, clearer, until it floated down through the break in the trees to the forest floor: it was a pink balloon effigy of a human being. I reached out to touch it. It popped.

XLI

Someone was shining a flashlight in my eyes.

I blinked twice, and blinked again. My eyelids were weighty with drugged sleep.

"Hey *buddy*!" said the flashlight, in a nasally New York accent. "You gotta be kiddin me here!"

"What?...um...hello?" I mumbled, or something like it, into the light.

"C'mon, buddy, what's a matter with you?"

The blinding light was yanked away from my eyes, and, squinting through burning tears of confusion, I saw the upside-down face of a police officer looking inquisitively into mine. I seemed to be lying beneath a blanket in the backseat of Leon's ex-wife's car. Leon himself was not present. I was so disoriented that I didn't know at first if it was day or night. I felt the parked vehicle shudder as a monstrous truck whooshed past us on the road. My face hurt—like hell. My eyes were burning.

The police officer's face and tone of voice were stern, but not malicious. He was middle-aged, clean-shaven, and white. He was also the unlucky possessor of one of those loose flaps of flesh that hang pendent from the throat and chin, which I only now remember is called a "wattle."

"What time is it?" I said. "Where am I?"

"It's three in the frickin' morning, and you're in a vehicle with an expired registration on the shoulder of the Hutch."

"Well, that's not where I went to sleep. I'm sure there's some explanation, Officer."

"What's your name?"

"Bruno. My name is Bruno."

"What's a matter with your face?"

My hand leapt to my face, and the tips of my long purple fingers met some sort of hard, coarse, dry texture. There was something wrapped around my head just below my eyes. I realized it was a bandage—covering my nose.

"I've just undergone surgery, Officer," I said. "I'm sorry, but I've been heavily sedated. I was under anesthesia."

The police officer frowned at this information. However, because his head was upside down, his frown instead appeared to me as if a funny-looking sightless chin-creature was smiling at me.

He was standing on the roadside and leaning in through the open car window. He went away for a moment, to perambulate Leon's ex-wife's Wagoneer, briefly illuminating the trunk and front seats with his flashlight.

"Where—where is Leon?" I said, my mind still hazy.

"What?" said the police officer, returning to my side of the car.

Now I was aware of a second presence. There was a man in blue jeans and a black T-shirt following the policeman. This second man carried, mounted on his shoulder like some sort of weapon, a camera: a video camera. He pressed one of his eyes to the view-finder, the other eye a squint. A red light on the machine blinked on and off, an evilly winking little red dot. Why do humans always feel this urge to document?

"Who is *he*?"

"They're filming this stuff for a TV show,'" said the cop.

"Yo," said the cameraman.

"They'll ask you to sign a waiver, unless you want 'em to blur your face on TV."

"Probably won't have to," said the cameraman. "We only air the good shit. You know, where something actually happens."

Is a dispassionate observer supposed to interlope the conversation like that?

"My, um, my friend—Leon," I stuttered. The cop turned to me again. "He was supposed to drive me home after my surgery."

"Some friend," said the cop.

I was sitting up in the backseat now, clutching the blanket, wondering suddenly if it was all I had to cover my nakedness. I could tell by the dilation of the camera lens that the cameraman was zooming in on my face. Seedlings of panic begin to sprout beneath my skin. Was there a German shepherd present? Would they beseech him to rip the fragile flesh from my bones? I wondered if I would be on TV.

But hark!—there, in the distance, a lone figure is seen, approaching in the harsh orange lighting of the urban night. And he is a really big lone figure. He's so girthy it looks as if he's hiding a floppy sack of potatoes under his shirt, and he is huffing and wheezing with each toilsome step as he hoofs it along the shoulder of the Hutchinson River Parkway. His gigantic figure makes the man unmistakable, even to my bleary eyes.

"Leon!" I shouted from the back of the car, still wrapped in my blanket. As I opened my mouth wide to shout a sharp pain zinged all over my face, and I guessed I should refrain from straining my facial muscles until my nose had fully healed. An eighteen-wheeler, lit up like a circus, blasted past us in the night. The police officer responded to my shout by shining the flashlight in my eyes again. I winced. I pointed at Leon, loping and puffing up the shoulder of the road.

I said: "There!—him!—that's my friend."

Leon had clearly spotted the police officer, and in his steps there was now a marked hesitation, a heaviness, indicating a dread of entering this situation, mixed with his mind working wildly to come up with a way of evading it, which, as his steps drew closer, turned into a wild working of trying to think of what he was going to say.

"Hey *buddy*!" said the cop, redirecting the flashlight's pale annulus at Leon. "Hey—you! This your car?"

Leon, approaching, waddled along the shoulder of the parkway as quickly as he could, looking exactly like a walrus attempting a lumbering and poorly planned escape from a zoo. In one hand, he carried a gas can. It was then I realized why the car was parked on the shoulder of the road. When Leon arrived, the police officer had to allow him some time to catch his breath.

"My—sincerest—(*gasp*)—apologies, Officer," he said, pushing each word out of his mouth as if they were heavy objects he was heaving one at a time over a wall. "You see, gentlemen— I—my automobile—was—depleted of fuel—hence—it came to—an unfortunate halt—in this most inconvenient—location. *However*—" catching his breath and holding the gas can proudly aloft for all to see, including, presumably, the television audiences watching at home "—in response to the problem, I valiantly betook myself, an empty gasoline receptacle in hand, down the road to a local fueling station—a Mobil—whereat I procured this gasoline, which I have conveyed hither and with which I now plan to replenish the fuel tank of my automobile."

"Where'd you learn to talk, jackass?"

Leon arched his eyebrows and lifted his chin, striking an aspect of great dignity. "The *theatre*."

"Lemme see your license and registration."

"Certainly, Officer." Leon rifled through his pockets for a wallet. As he did, the police officer trained a suspicious eye on me.

"You know the registration on your plates is out of date."

"That is because this automobile does not, in fact, belong to me. If it did, I would have surely exercised enough forethought to remember to reregister it at the proper time. As it is, this car belongs to my former wife, and I am sure you are all-too-well familiar with a certain negligence in such practical matters that is characteristic of the fair sex."

"What, like letting your damn car run outta gas on the Hutch?"

"Pish, Officer. I am only human."

"Hey, we might run this shit after all," mused the cameraman.

Leon handed him his driver's license. The policeman read it under his flashlight. He looked up.

"You been drinking at all?"

"Nay, sir, not a drop."

This could not have possibly been one hundred percent true, I thought. I wanted to say, "Why, thy lips are scarce wiped since thou drank'st last," but I checked my tongue, considering the circumstances.

I saw the moon, tinted orange, rising above the trees like an orb of burning blood suspended on a wire before the velvety curtain of night.

"I think your buddy back there's a little sick," said the officer. The cameraman audibly suppressed a guffaw. "You oughta take care of him."

"He's recently had an operation. I was transporting him safely home, whereupon the car became suddenly and completely unexpectedly depleted of fuel."

"Tell your ex-wife to reregister her car. It's a month past expiration. We stopped to take a look 'cause it looked like a suspicious vehicle."

The police officer gave Leon his driver's license back, and the two men got back in their car and drove away. My brain was still sodden with anesthesia, I did not fall back asleep, but mumbled and gurgled to myself in the backseat, watching the shadow play created by the car passing under the streetlights lining the parkway, and listening to the traffic in the other lane whooshing past us. I felt simultaneously chilled and relaxed. I imagined I was in a spaceship, blasting away from the earth and into the cold black vacuum of space at a velocity close to the speed of light, so that time dilates and millions of years go by, and one day I crash-land on an alien planet populated by a hostile race of talking hairless upright apes, only to discover to my horror that this is really earth. I felt a great surge of affection for Leon, in spite of his appalling incompetence. He had let his ex-wife's Wagoneer run out of gas on the parkway, then left me asleep and drugged in back of his car in the middle of the night as he hobbled down the shoulder in search of a gas station. Yet I felt no anger, no resentment, toward him. He was my friend. I felt my organs sloshing around inside my little body with every turn, every slight shift of centripetal force. Leon had the radio on, very softly, so as not to disturb me, and I think he had it tuned to an "oldies" station, which was playing a Roy Orbison song: *only the lonely... know the way I... feel tonight...* And I listened to Roy Orbison's angelic falsetto mournfully cooing that bittersweet threnody to his loneliness into the rush and howl of a cold dark night on the Hutchinson River Parkway.

Soon Leon was easing the car off the highway and onto the small winding roads that led us through Pelham Bay Park, across the

mint-green bridge and back to City Island. I looked out the window as we were shuddering across the bridge that took us home,
and I saw the giant neon-red lobster, doomed—doomed like someone in Greek mythology is doomed in Hades to endlessly repeat
some futile task—to forever repeatedly open and close his claw. His
red light was reflected in the black and wobbling waters beneath
him. Leon parked the car and helped me out. I tried to walk, but
I could not. The earth kept pitching and shifting under my feet; it
was like trying to walk on the bottom of the ocean. Leon held my
hand to support me, but it was obvious to both of us after a few of
my unsteady steps that autonomous locomotion was still impossible for me, and the only way I would make it back to the apartment unaided would have been to crawl there. So Leon scooped
the still-delirious me up in his big squishy arms and hoisted me
up, and I clambered onto his shoulders and sat on them, just as
we would do while performing Shakespeare in the subway stations.
And I held on as tightly as I could. And I clung to him, riding on
Leon's shoulders, my face swaddled in surgical gauze, as he inched
his mass fastidiously down the sidewalk, walking under the lurid
orange lights, under an urban night sky, orange and starless.

We passed Artie's Shrimp Shanty, long since closed up and dark
by now, around the corner, past the dumpsters by the kitchen door,
and opened the door to our apartment, and Leon carried me inside,
reminding me to duck beneath the doorway. He took me into the
apartment without snapping on any lights that would have disturbed
my retinas with their unwanted brightness, guiding himself only by
his intimate knowledge of the space. He laid me supine on my bed,
the futon in the living room. It wasn't made. Leon tucked me in. I
clutched the blankets and fell asleep almost immediately: my eyes
shut, and I returned to oblivion like a weary traveler finally returning home, mumbling Lydia's name until it dissolved into nonsense
syllables and disappeared into silence.

XLII

When I woke up the next day it was the afternoon and my head felt hot and my skull was throbbing fuzzily with a headache. I looked at myself in the bathroom mirror, at my gauze-wrapped head, felt my face flaming with postoperative pain, and felt with my hand the new protrusion in the middle of my face where my nose was, hidden underneath the bandages.

"The doctor informed me you're not to remove the bandages for six days," said Leon over breakfast, rattling the pages of the *New York Times* he had purchased that morning when he had left the apartment to buy donuts. He had purchased two dozen donuts at a Dunkin' Donuts three blocks away, and had even abstained from eating two of them, which were for me. One of them was a plain cake donut, which I found at least marginally palatable, but the other was coated in chocolate frosting, in which was embedded an overabundance of those unsettlingly plasticlike sticks of color called "sprinkles," which I find to favor the eye over the tongue, so Leon obliged to eat that one as well.

"And he apologized," continued Leon, the chocolate-and-sprinkle-coated donut making spongy squelching noises in his mouth as he chewed it, "for the sad fact that he had no painkillers to spare and for obvious reasons was not able to write you a prescription. But he said you should be taking them for the next few days or else you will probably have to endure excruciating pain."

The pain I was in was dull and horrible, but not yet excruciating. I consumed my donut, taking tiny rabbitlike bites because I couldn't open my mouth very wide without experiencing a burst of flames in my facial nerves, in the place where I now understood my new nose to be.

I didn't leave the house for a week. I drank a lot of wine. From beneath some pile of rubble in the apartment Leon managed to unearth a brown plastic prescription jar of Percocet pills with a long-expired label that he said was from a past knee surgery. They did the trick. I took the Percocets and washed them down with wine, and spent much of the next few days lying with my head propped up on a mountain of pillows watching TV while floating about three feet above my body. I completely exhausted Leon's video collection. I watched *2001: A Space Odyssey*, *Last Tango in Paris*, *Annie Hall*, *Satyricon*, and I blew through an entire boxed set of Ingmar Bergman videos that Leon had, titled *Let's Talk About Death*. Leon even rented *Pinocchio* for me, which I watched several times in rapid succession, and it brought me joy. Leon kept me company while I convalesced, and occasionally went out to rent videos for me and to buy more donuts and wine.

This also happened to be 1998, and when I wasn't watching movies on it the TV had turned into little else but a window gazing onto the sordid vista of the president's sexual liaisons, specifically his dalliances with a plump young thing who stood accused of repeatedly fellating our commander in chief and allowing him to insert a cigar into one or more of her orifices. There he was on television, rosy-faced, butt-nosed and silver-haired, sheepishly shrugging, denying all, as if he was not his nation's leader but rather her philandering husband caught with the babysitter. Leon and I watched in amusement as the news played and replayed footage of Bill Clinton assuring us that he did not have sexual relations with that woman. Leon had just returned from Artie's, where he had picked up a double order of shrimp and a bottle of wine. The shrimp were nestled in a Styrofoam container in the lap of the terry-cloth bathrobe Leon usually wore while at leisure. Between cramming fistfuls of shrimp into his cheeks, Leon drank wine in gulps and shouted at the TV.

"Damn-blast it!" he roared. "Why does the Supreme Court get in such a tizzy when the president receives a blowjob? And why does he not simply say, 'Leave me alone, get your own blowjobs!'? Really, Bruno. This whole business is so mind-bogglingly insipid. It's nothing short of a sexual crucifixion. They may as well nail his penis to a cross. Think about JFK, for God's sake. His sexual goings-on make Bill Clinton look like a fifties teenager groping in the back of a Plymouth convertible."

I wasn't entirely sure what the Supreme Court was.

"Gadzooks, Bruno, your education is riddled with holes!"

I didn't deny it. It wasn't my fault. As I've said, this is the curse of the autodidact.

"What's the Supreme Court?" I demanded.

"I'm no civics teacher, but I shall do my best: the Supreme Court is a panel of political whores. You see, there are such things in our government as checks and balances. That's why we have three branches of government: the executive, the legislative, and the judgmental. When I was a child, my teachers made it abundantly clear to me that this was why I was lucky to have been born in America. I supposed that British royals were as nasty as my grade school teachers, and so the Queen might see me walking to school one day and say, 'I don't like the looks of that boy. Cut his head off!' Whereas here, even if both houses of Congress voted unanimously to have my head cut off, the Supreme Court could intervene. And that's checks and balances. *Now* do you understand?"

A commercial came on. It was a commercial advertizing a certain brand of mobile telephones, which were at the time ascending to widespread popularity. The commercial opened with a shot of a theatre, an expectantly hushed audience sitting before a red velvet curtain. The curtains raised and parted, and what followed was a version of *Romeo and Juliet* abbreviated to thirty seconds because all the characters had cellular phones. The joke was that wireless communication technology speeds things up. Leon was appalled. He threw a shrimp at the TV, which briefly stuck to the screen before sliding off, leaving a wet mark.

"Of *course* these cellular telephones speed up communication! Why the blazes would you want to do *that*, you vicious bastards? The whole blasted plot of *Romeo and Juliet*—nay, of *all* great literature!—I daresay *hinges* on miscommunication. Flawed information, crossed signals, late and undelivered messages! What these infernal things are doing is paving over all the beautiful mountains and valleys of confusion in the landscape of human society! It's disgusting! I'm sure that in a few years every idiot on the street will be puttering around like a somnambulist with one of these hideous devices nailed to his ear. And then we will at long last have entered the final phase of the decay of human civilization. Once everyone owns a cellular telephone, great literature will no longer be written, due to the end of miscommunication."

"Perhaps," I offered, "the advent of cell phones will not eliminate miscommunication, but simply speed it up. Much more efficient."

"Curses! To hell with efficiency! To hell with convenience! To hell with communication! What kind of future are we making for ourselves, Bruno? What is this great supposed virtue we attach to these values—efficiency, convenience, communication? These are not human virtues—these are the debauched virtues of *commerce*! It's a shopkeeper's virtue! Listen, Bruno!" Leon gingerly brushed his long hair back with his fingertips and cupped a hand to his ear. "Listen," he whispered.

"What?"

"*Shh.*" Leon's voice sank to a stage whisper: "I hear something! I hear something occurring outside the sanctum of our little home."

"I don't hear anything."

Leon raised his voice to full theatric boom: "Listen, Bruno, and *despair*, for what I hear is the flaccid language of business osmotically replacing every syllable of poetry still alive in the human heart!"

"Oh."

"To hell with it all!" he thundered at the TV, waving his glass of wine in the air in front of him so histrionically that some of it slopped into the lap of his bathrobe. "Give me miscommunication! Give me confusion! Give me a world rife enough with errata to fuel the great tragedies of bygone eras! Where has the tragedy gone in our world? Tell me that! *Everything* is comedy! And you cannot truly appreciate comedy if you suck all the tragic out of life. Just look at this buffoon who lives in our TV. I mean our 'president,' Bruno. Look at him: he knows this is all mere comedy! Yes, he faces impeachment and so on, oh yes, you naughty boy, you're really in trouble this time! But you can see that thin mask of concern on his face only scarcely conceals a smirk. A *smirk*! Inside, he's thinking, 'Tiddly-dee, this whole thing is actually funny.' And, devil take him, he's *right*! It *is* funny! 'That's right—acts of fellatio have been administered in this very office! Beneath this desk! What do you think of that, America? Aren't you just a little jealous of your alpha male in chief? That's right—suck it, America!' We live in an age of comic unreality. Nothing's real to us. It's all jokes. I am sure—mark my word, Bruno—I'm sure some great tragedy is quietly brewing beneath it all. Go ahead and laugh, America, laugh your moronic heads off. But when tragedy befalls us—which it invariably must, for all our cellular telephones and World Wide Web sites have not jammed a very stick in the *Rota Fortunae*—when it happens, we will all be so sick and stupid from years of laughing that we won't have a clue how to behave. Only then can true comedy begin again. We need tragedy to show us what's *really* funny. Oh, God!" Leon turned his eyes to the ceiling in wistful abandon. "To live in an earlier world! I would put up with the horseshit! Really!"

———

After over a week my period of convalescence came to an end. After the first few days the swelling went down, my two black eyes healed, and a few days after that the pain had decreased from grating to almost bearable. A few days later I removed my bandages.

I waited until Leon was out of the house. I don't remember where he was, maybe on a wine-and-donut run. I wanted to be alone with my nose. I climbed up on my little stepladder that led to the bathroom sink and stood before the mirror. The middle section of my face—just below my eyes, just above my mouth—was covered in bandages. I snipped at it with Leon's plastic-handled children's safety scissors, and gradually unpeeled the bandages from my face. Then I unraveled them in fistfuls. The bandages were sticky and wet on the inside and darkly mottled with dried blood. The bandages dropped to the bathroom floor, *flap, flap, flap*. The bandages smelled bad. The flesh of my face was wet and wrinkled from marinating in sweat under the bandages for a week.

There, in the middle of my chimp face, was a human nose.

My human nose so naturally melded to my face that it almost looked as if I was born with it, though when I first revealed it to myself the white scar that surrounds my nose was still very noticeable. Look at me. This monster had been made a man.

I stared at it. I stared from every possible angle, then derived new angles of scrutiny out of a hand mirror held opposite the mirror on the wall. Mirror mirror on the wall, whose lovely nose is this?

I touched it. I lovingly stroked it with my long purple fingers. I looked so beautiful.

I began to cry. These were tears of joy. I felt the saltwater sliding in hot rivulets down the flanks of my beautiful new nose. This nose—as you can obviously see for yourself, Gwen—this nose was so artfully sculpted out of the flesh of my face ... but it wasn't just that. It was like the perfect nose had been found for me. The nose was totally in harmony with my face. I looked almost like I could pass for a natural-born human. I looked so good. My beautiful new face gave me a feeling of power. I wanted to parade my aesthetically improved face around town, introduce the world to the brand-new Bruno.

When I heard the front door open and close I burst from the bathroom to show Leon my new nose.

"Snakes alive!" Leon gasped. His eyes threatened to erupt from his eye sockets like corks from popguns. "Let me touch it!"

"Gently," I warned. My nasal flesh was still very sensitive.

Leon placed a single shaky fat finger on the bridge of my nose.

"This is remarkable," he whispered, "quite remarkable!"

Leon delicately caressed my nose with his finger. Then our eyes met in an uncomfortable way, and he quit touching my nose. We both looked away, and Leon pretended to cough.

"Come, Bruno, let us repair to Artie's to celebrate your transformation. Audrey is tending the bar this evening."

We went next door and ordered shrimp and wine, and I showed off my new face to Audrey and Sasha.

"Didn't I tell you?" said Sasha. "He does good."

"Wow! You almost look human, Bruno," said Audrey.

"Thank you," I said with a mild bow, taking the compliment with gentlemanly grace.

The girls all cooed and fawned over my face and patted me on the head. I entertained many fantasies about all the thousands of women who would be powerless to resist the magnetic attractiveness of my face now that I had a human nose.

"I am afraid your honeymoon with your nose must be short, Bruno," said Leon. "For tomorrow, we must begin in earnest to work on our play."

I knew that was true. My convalescence had stalled the production for long enough. There was the ticklish and interesting question of finding an appropriate performance space. We were called the Shakespeare Underground because our performances were held underground both metaphorically and literally. Performing the whole play in the subway wouldn't have been feasible. Leon had an idea that involved a long-lost uncle of his.

"I have a long-lost uncle," he said, "who must be in his nineties by now. He has owned and operated a locksmith's shop for many years. He inherited it from his father."

"Is he your father's brother?"

"No." Leon dug his fingers through his beard in thought. "He is my mother's father's brother. I suppose that's a great-uncle. In any event, I hope he's still among the living. I haven't seen him in the last thirty years or so. He ought to be, he's a stalwart and salubrious fellow. We shall pay him a visit tomorrow."

"Where?"

"An excellent question." Leon turned to his daughter, who was busy at the other end of the bar, and called: *"Audrey!"* He clapped his hands twice and jabbed a finger in the air.

"What?"

"The phone book, my darling."

Audrey rolled her eyes and plopped several huge phone directories on the bar counter, one for each borough. We flopped them open to the L sections and found the listings for locksmiths.

"I misremember precisely where my uncle's shop is," he said, licking his thumb to page through the phone book. "I am reasonably certain it is located on the isle of Manhattoes, so we shall have to systematically visit every locksmith shop listed there until we find him."

I agreed this was an excellent plan indeed. At Leon's suggestion we ripped out the relevant pages from all the phone books.

"Jesus, Dad," said Audrey. "Don't vandalize the phone books."

"Pish, my dearest. What conceivable need would anyone at this establishment ever have for a locksmith in this saloon? In any event, we shall return the missing pages when we are finished with them and you may tape them in again."

The following day Leon and I donned the suits and ties that we wore when conducting serious business. Leon put his long hair in a ponytail and carried his officious-looking attaché case, and we took to the streets, visiting all the locksmith's shops in the city one at a time, guided on our mission by the phone book pages.

The not-so-cleverly named establishment Mr. Locksmith was only the ninth place we visited. (Leon did have a general idea of where the shop was located.) Imagine the eight faces we saw before Leon's long-lost uncle: all the arched eyebrows and questioning looks we received when a monstrously obese man and a deformed hairless dwarf, both in suits and ties and one of them carrying an officious-looking attaché case, entered their shops to inquire whether they had known Leon as a babe in arms. Most people told us to get lost and hurried us away. A few feared we might be engaged in something illegal or otherwise nefarious, and their hands drifted to their phones when we walked through their doors. Thank God we finally found the right place on only the ninth try, because by the late afternoon of our day of searching, my stubby little legs were so rubbery with exhaustion that I don't think I would have been able to stand (literally) for another day of this heretofore fruitless quest. I did, however, enjoy exposing my nose to the fresh air and the adoration of the masses. We got a lot of interested stares, and not all of them were because of the freakish spectacle that we brought with us wherever we went; I'm sure that some of the women who passed us on the street looked twice at me not just because I was freakish, but because of my newly beautified face. We found Leon's great-uncle's shop off of Broome Street on the Lower East Side. The storefront was across the street from the courtyard of a decrepit tenement complex and in front of a pile of black fly-covered trash bags in a filthy and run-down-ish area. I've been told that during the years I have languished in captivity this area has undergone significant gentrification, but at the time the place still more or less looked authentically squalid.

There was a yellow neon light in the window, shaped like a key. Behind that, on a windowsill, a cat—a soft fat black cat with a white face, belly, and feet—lay beneath the neon key in a bed made of a rumpled towel, watching Leon and me from inside.

"This one is it," said Leon to me. "I'm absolutely certain of it."

"How do you know?"

Leon pointed at the cat. "The cat has seven toes on each paw. My grandmother had one just like it. That deformity has been passed down for generations of my family's cats."

I looked at the cat's feet. He was right: the cat had enormous feet due to an excess of toes.

We went in. As we did the jingle-bells clinked on the door behind us and the cat mewled indifferently. It was a dark, cramped room with wood-paneled walls, full of all kinds of locks and keys—there were keys hanging on pegs in the brown breadboard walls. Everything inside was brass and brown, and had the metallic, oily smell of a machine shop. A man who looked to be about three hundred and six years old sat behind the counter on a stool, working on something at a high workbench. Bushy sprigs of white hair sprouted from his ears and nostrils, and he wore a green plastic visor. Behind the counter there was a small TV; the picture was jittery and the volume was low, and the man wasn't watching it. The cat in the window was looking at me. I looked back at the cat. The twenty-eight-toed cat groaned and returned her attention to the sidewalk in front of the store.

"I'm almost closed," said the man, glancing disinterestedly at us and then at his watch. "Fifteen minutes."

"No matter," said Leon. "We are not here for keys."

"Then what do you want?"

The man had a bald, liver-spotted head and wraparound glasses that looked about two inches thick.

There was a basketball game on the TV. Staticky reception made it appear to be snowing on the court. I noticed a cord running from the bottom of the neon tube twisted into the likeness of a key and down to an electrical outlet above the floor molding.

Leon threw out his arms in an invitation to embrace, and roared: "My dearest uncle!"

"Hm?" said the old man behind the counter.

"It's me, your grand-nephew! It's Leon!"

"Eh?"

"Leon Smoler!"

The man looked blankly at him from beneath his visor. His skin was translucent and he looked like he weighed little more than a child. The man rose from his stool and walked up to the counter so slowly it was as if the air were made of glue. He was humpbacked with age and not much taller than me.

"I'm Yvonne's son," Leon helped him.

"Ah," said the man. The gears were turning in his head as quickly as the hour hand of a clock—but they *were* turning.

"*Ah!*" he finally said. His mouth had three teeth in it and his tongue was as black and dry as an old boot. "Leon!"

The old man opened the trapdoor of the counter and baby-stepped out to be hugged by Leon, who had a difficult job of hugging him with sufficient heartiness without crushing him like a baby bird in a fist.

"How's your mother, kiddo?"

"Safely interred, thank you. She hasn't budged in fourteen years."

"Atta girl. It's been too long, Leonard! You oughtta visit more often."

After several agonizingly long moments of preliminary introductions, catching up, and other such social niceties, Leon revealed the ulterior motive for our call. The old man—whose name, despite it being the name of his business, was not "Mr. Locksmith," but was actually Samuel B. Siegel—was the owner and had been the sole operator of this locksmith's shop for more than forty years after inheriting it from his father (Leon's great-grandfather). He was surprised that Leon knew about the vast space below his shop, which was accessible only by an elevator in the back of the store. I was also surprised. Mr. Locksmith—as he shall here on out be called, because I prefer the moniker to his real name—looked at his watch, then locked the storefront, unplugged the neon key in the window and took us into the back room in shaky, puttering steps. He made a series of smooching noises, and the fat soft black-and-white cat stretched herself, got up from her bed beneath the neon key, and followed us.

To the right of the work area and counter there was a short narrow hallway lit by a single bare low-wattage lightbulb in the middle of the ceiling. A door on the right opened into a small bathroom that doubled as a storage place for cleaning supplies. There was a shallow porcelain dish on the floor with a mop in it and a yellow plastic sign, folded up against the wall, saying, CAUTION, WET FLOOR, and below that, CUIDADO, PISO MOJADO: between the languages, a man was falling. The back rooms smelled like oil, smoke, and cleaning fluids. Then the hallway bent left, a bend sinister, and we bent sinister with it. A calendar was tacked to a corkboard on the wall, the bottom half a grid of dates with notes scrawled in the squares, the top half featuring a photograph of a sand-speckled naked woman lying on a tropical beach in mildly pornographic repose. The hallway ended in an old-fashioned elevator, the kind with a grate of brass latticework that accordions open and shut. Everything in it, the panel with the buttons, the walls, the ceiling, was fancy, decorated with loops and filigrees of bent metal and carved wood, because it was built in a time when elevators were still special, when there was still enough amazement in them for people to want to ornament them—only this one was old and in a state of creaky disrepair, covered in stains and rust and dust, the brass discolored and the wood chipped and scratched and worn down. Mr. Locksmith was using it as a storage closet. He rolled back the brass accordion grating of the elevator door with a clatter and shriek of old and poorly lubricated metal parts grinding together, and started removing buckets and brooms with shuddering, sapling-thin arms. Leon inspected his cuticles and sighed in irritation as his great-uncle fastidiously removed the things in the elevator.

"I just use this old elevator for storage," he said. "I never go down below anymore. Place gives me the jeebies. I never needed that room anyway."

When he had cleared out the elevator we all squeezed inside, including the fat-footed cat. The elevator lurched and bounced when Leon stepped onto the platform. Mr. Locksmith looked at Leon, and looked a bit worried.

"How much you weigh, kiddo?" he asked. "Tell me honestly."

"One hundred and seventy," said Leon.

The man looked at him in confusion, then shrugged and pushed the button.

"Kilograms!" Leon whispered to me.

The elevator jolted into movement, and the cables began to chatter, squeal, grumble, and moan as the ancient machinery was put to rare use.

"Don't make 'em like they used to," said Mr. Locksmith in the dark.

"Well," said Leon, "this is clearly a contraption that was built prior to the total hideous decline of modern aesthetic philosophy."

"Uh-huh," said Mr. Locksmith.

We watched the line of the floor rise up and up until it was out of sight, and everything was dark, and in the dark we listened to our own breathing and to the machinery clattering and moaning above and below us. We sank down and down in the dark. As we sank Mr. Locksmith lit a cigarette with a match that momentarily underlit his face, threw a green shadow from his plastic visor onto the ceiling behind him, and filled the small metal box with a burst of phosphor. He dropped the match on the floor and it was dark again.

"I come down here only once a year or so," he said. "Maybe less. It was supposed to be a subway station back when they first built it, about a hundred years ago. They redirected the lines before they ever connected them to the station. So they just walled it in, good night. Bricked over the tunnels and everything. There used to be stairs to it around the block. That's gone. This elevator's the only way to get in or out of it now. I thought I was the only one who knew about it anymore."

"Mkgnao!" said the cat. It was pawing my pant leg with its freakish feet.

We hit the bottom of the elevator shaft with a decisive clunk, and the machinery went quiet. Leon's great-uncle rolled back the shrieking brass grate, and we stepped out into a dark room, which we could tell was enormous from the echo before we saw it. The locksmith groped along the wall to the right of the elevator and found an old-fashioned electric switch with a metal cable running from the bottom of it and a handle that clacked up and down. He pushed the handle up with a squeak and clunk, and three lights slowly came alive in metal lamps that hung down almost to head level from long cords in the ceiling.

The effect of the room's enormity was compounded by its almost total emptiness, with vaulted ceilings maybe thirty, forty feet high, supported by thick square columns whose capitals were cluttered with more turn-of-the-century ornamentation. Cornice moldings skirted the perimeters of the room. There were two levels—a big square main room and above that a balustrade running around its perimeter, big arching windows looking out onto brick walls and nailed-up sheets of particleboard. Huge round archways were set in the walls below the balcony, but the arches had been bricked in and painted over. The room smelled stiflingly of dust, mildew and chalk, and everything in it—walls, ceiling, floor—was whitewashed: it had been painted over, coat after coat until all the cherubs and lion's heads had become vague, sort of soft and gloopy-looking. I coughed from the swirling dust that we kicked up as we walked into the room. Near the elevator door there were some boxes and tools and old paint cans, but other than that the room was empty.

Our footsteps echoed hugely throughout the room, multiplied several times over. Even the cat's purring was amplified by the echo.

"Bruno," Leon said. His voice was half-hushed in amazement. "This is perfect for the Shakespeare Underground! It's even underground!"

He walked into the center of the room, winged out his arms, and spun around in the middle of the room like a giant child. He shouted out to hear his voice reverberate off the high moldy walls and vaulted ceilings, and the walls boomed so articulately with his many-times-multiplied voice that it sounded like four or five Leons were shouting in counterpoint: "FULL FATHOM FIVE THY FATHER LIES—OF HIS BONES ARE CORAL MADE. THOSE ARE PEARLS THAT WERE HIS EYES—NOTHING OF HIM THAT DOTH FADE—BUT DOTH SUFFER A SEA-CHANGE—INTO SOMETHING RICH AND STRANGE!"

There was long silence. Leon's arms were still swung open wide, as if to embrace the universe. His great-uncle hacked nastily into a fist and ground his cigarette out on the floor.

The cat groaned and pawed my pants with its deformed feet.

XLIII

Leon's elderly great-uncle conceded to rent us the space at a relatively modest price that I will not divulge. He responded shruggingly and with considerable confusion to our whole idea and the nature of our inquiry. I do not think Mr. Locksmith ever fully understood what we were doing. It is possible that his faculties of reason were somewhat impaired by his Methuselan age, which, as I have said, I would have estimated at somewhere around nine hundred and seven. Mr. Locksmith was a workaday man, not an artist. In any event, it was with a servile, acquiescent, sagely demeanor and the patience of a Buddha that he put up with all our rehearsals, all the stage equipment that we rented and hauled down to his basement in pieces via the elevator in the back of his shop. He put up marvelously with all the actors who began to show up for rehearsals every day at his inconspicuous little locksmith's shop, and what a rowdy lot we were!

Our production took shape over the coming months. A lot of things happened during this time in my life, Gwen. It would only require a hundred reams of paper and a thousand gallons of ink to do them proper justice, but because you and I and (I presume) our readers are only mortal, and unlike Mr. Locksmith presumably suffer from life spans with irritating promises of finitude, I will oblige us all to fast-forward through them, because I have almost come to the one time when I murdered a man in a fit of rage and therefore had to be placed in captivity, events which although they are philosophically insignificant I'm sure will tickle the puerile interest of the hoi polloi.

I had very little to do with the business end of the production: stage design, accounts, direction, casting, promotion, advertising, ticket sales, and so on. Come to think of it, did Leon, either? It turned out Leon was not an incompetent director. The Shakespeare Underground went aboveground at this point. We had a director, we had the principal actors, we had a budget, we had a performance space. By the time we had put all this together, our modest avant-garde theatre troupe did not look so pathetic. Leon, do not be surprised to learn, was not a pariah to everyone in the New York theatre world. He had been in it, and he was even well liked, in a personal sense, by many. Or enough, anyway. Phone calls were made, contacts were milked, people hired, money raised, things organized. Our production company entered such a stage of complexity that at some point I washed my hands of all this stuff. I won't delve much into these pragmatic details here, as I have never had a head for them, nor do I find them terribly interesting to relate. I trusted it all to Leon, and simply trained the focus of my energies solely on my perfecting my performance as Caliban.

Little Emily's mother pulled her out of a month or more of school so that she could attend our rehearsals. A car service would drop her off at our performance space in the morning, and pick her up in the evening. I would sit on the windowsill of the locksmith shop, sipping my morning cup of coffee and stroking the freakish-footed shop cat, and watch her expertly step out of the sleek black Lincoln town car in her buckled ballet flats, the parked car's engine thrumming as the driver watched her until she was safely inside. During downtimes at rehearsals, when not sneaking cigarettes in the alley, she would dump out the backpack full of homework her teachers sent her home with, and on a board laid across a milk crate or some other ragtag desk she'd set up shop with pencils and calculators and whatever else, not letting her academic career slip for a second even though she was about to costar in what would be probably one of the most groundbreaking productions in the history of the theatrical arts.

Little Emily was a bag of contradictions, her mood as quick-shifting and unpredictable as mercury. Some days she would be all smiles for me, and other days I would say "Hello" to her and she would look away and say nothing in return, pointedly ignoring me—leaving me to wonder if I had said anything at all, or if I had only hallucinated my saying something to her, or perhaps even that I had only hallucinated my entire existence. Then the very next day—nothing that I am aware of having changed in the nature of our relations (I'm moving from the general to the particular here)—she took me fiercely by the hand and led me into a small, dark area of the performance space, between two long racks of costumes. They were long pink silk dresses with ruffled hems and poofy shoulders. What were they doing there? I don't even recall their being used in the performance. The silk closed in around us, two whispering soft dark silk walls. My eyes dimmed. I could hear her breathing a foot or two away from me, and I could just barely discern the whites of her eyes, but otherwise, darkness.

"Hold out your hand," she whispered, and I knew it was a command.

I did as she said. I opened my long purple hand and held it out palm side up. Then I heard a very faint squelching noise, and I felt a hot globule of runny, sticky fluid land bull's-eye in the center of my palm.

"What in the world—?" I may have said, but she was gone,

having already fled, stealthy as a jaguar, through the two rows of rustling silk dresses.

I was not revolted. When I had clawed my way out of the dark, I examined my hand, held it up to the light, watched the wetness glisten, watched the generous dollop of her spit break like an egg in a pan and slide easily down my wrist and forearm. Was this, I wondered, a gesture of affection?

During this time, a deep and brooding melancholy overtook me. What I felt like doing was taking long walks in very foggy weather while wearing an overcoat and an inwardly pained expression of perfect ennui, pausing occasionally to lean against a railing and gaze at a misty winter seaside, a picture of deep and brooding melancholy. I was alone, Gwen. I was a fugitive. I realized that I had to return to Chicago. I would try to push from my mind the fact that I was a coward for not trying to return to Chicago a long time ago. Truth be told, I was enjoying the adventure of my freedom in the world. I was deliberately not thinking about Chicago and Lydia. I knew I had to go back. I knew she might be dead. I was so afraid to think this that every time I felt the thought creeping into specific articulation in my mind, morphing from a vague dread to an actual full-on conscious thought rendered austere and finite with words, I would push it back, push it down, suppress it like an urge to vomit. I would briefly buckle over with pain, clutch my stomach, and let it pass, let it pass—then cautiously stand up, take a few steps, okay, better, better, all shall be well and all shall be well and all manner of things shall be well.

(I had also become a bit of an alcoholic, if that's the right word for someone who drinks not just for fun but also to stave off anxiety, shame, and terror. That's partially why I'm on such experientially intimate terms with feelings of bucking, stomach-clutching, holding back vomit, trying not to picture my insides corroding like steaming green acid eating through metal. I had begun to drink furtively in the daytime before drinking openly in the nighttime. I bought whiskey or vodka and kept it in a little canteen in my coat pocket. I would just drink a little bit, steadily, all day long, enough to keep me consistently hooked up to a slight buzz, every sip I took like throwing meat to the wolf at the door. I would dwell on this in greater detail if only it were more interesting.)

As a result of my not having paid much attention to the business end of the Shakespeare Underground's production of *The Tempest*, to this day I remain not entirely sure how our audience found out about us—much less how they found out when and where the production was being staged, and so on—but find out these things they did. In thematic keeping with the name of our company, the Shakespeare Underground undertook its promotions and ticket sales in the same spirit as we began, and in which we committed all our operations: virally, secretly, in a mode of dubious legality, operating like an underground resistance movement. "Resistance to what?" you may ask. And Leon and I would answer: "Resistance to everything!" Resistance to a nation preoccupied with useless ephemera! Resistance to the slow incoming creep of the twenty-first century, resistance to that invisible poisonous gas that has been hissing up into the air from every crack and fissure in the street, which Leon taught me to smell. It is admittedly a vague thing, an invisible thing, a nebulously hard-to-define thing, but Leon and I knew it was everywhere, and that it needed to be resisted. It's still there. I can smell it, Gwen. It's stronger than ever, in fact. It's right here in this room. I can smell it even in here, even in the safety and sanity of this research center, even in the tidy environs of science, far away from human society, in captivity, in a tightly secured building nestled in a remote wooded area in rural Georgia, where the stars come out at night and the birds sing their songs in the day: even here I can smell it. Don't let your nose get used to it. When you are out walking on the street, going about your business, a part of your soul must always be crushing a handkerchief to your face.

But as I said, I funneled my energies totally into developing my Caliban. I hope that the future's scholars of dramaturgy (if indeed such people will exist in the future) will recognize that I, Bruno Littlemore, was the first actor to realize that the role of Caliban should be played through an *evolutionary* perspective. While I understand *The Tempest* was first performed in 1612, a good two and a half centuries before the publications of Charles Darwin, on closely studying the text, I find it hard to believe that Shakespeare was not in some way anachronistically informed and even influenced by *The Origin of Species*. Time perhaps is not as uninterestingly linear as we imagine, Gwen. Shakespeare was at the very least a clear premonition of his future fellow Englishman. I even go so far as to imagine that the ship in *The Tempest* is the *Beagle*, and Prospero's island, Galapagos. Examine the following, from the scene in which the drunken jester, Trinculo, discovers Caliban lying inert on the beach:

> What have we here? A man or a fish? Dead or alive? A fish! He smells like a fish; a very ancient and fishlike smell.... A strange fish! Were I in England now, as once I was, and had but this fish painted, not a holiday fool there but would give a piece of silver. There would this monster make a man; any strange beast there makes a man.... Legged like a man! And his fins like arms! Warm, o' my troth! I do now let loose my opinion, hold it no longer. This is no fish, but an islander.

"A very ancient and fishlike smell"—! The Darwinian undertones are clear to me. What Trinculo describes, upon seeing Caliban lying still and wet on the muddy beach, amounts to a description of evolution in fast-forward. He begins as a fish, smelling very ancient and fishlike, freshly crawled up onto the beach to leave a life in the oceans, and then becomes a monster, a strange beast—and then he grows legs, and his fins become arms! Finally, he abandons his cold blood for warm, and becomes a mammal, an islander: the monster is made man.

Shakespeare and Darwin, Darwin and Shakespeare. Darwin, Shakespeare; Shakespeare, Darwin. These two Englishmen, these two great minds, these two great thinkers, are obviously connected. They are braided together in some golden harmonious collusion between science and art, between biology and theatre. The one probably could not exist without the other. All theatre is biology, and it logically follows that all biology is theatre; this is what's meant by "All the world's a stage." Shakespeare, Darwin; Darwin, Shakespeare. Theatre is biology, and biology is theatre.

XLIV

Maybe pamphlets were distributed to pedestrians on the streets, maybe posters were pasted on walls to advertise the play, maybe there was a viral campaign, and talk of us spread in waves of excited furtive whispering across the campuses of colleges and universities. However the people in charge of publicity chose to do it, I'm sure they did it in such a way, as Leon had thoroughly drilled them on how to behave in accordance with the true spirit of the Shakespeare Underground: it was cultural guerilla war, an underground political resistance movement—keep it secret, dangerous, subversive, conspiratorial. Somehow, people found out about us, and they found us, and they came. People arrived from out of state to see the play, some of them, I am told and I believe, coming from far-flung locations many miles away. Young and old alike, they came. Our audience found Mr. Locksmith's locksmith's shop, squirreled away in a drably nondescript brown brick building on a ubiquitous-looking side street on the Lower East Side. His workshop now doubling as a ticket booth, the frail, confused, and elderly Mr. Locksmith took the tickets, wearing his green visor, as his fat black-and-white cat lazed on the countertop, her tail switching like a metronome. Ushers guided the people down the hallway of the locksmith's shop and past the bathroom—advising them to use it now or hold their pee until the end of the show—and to the elevator, where another usher/elevator operator took them down below in groups of five or six. When they clunked to the bottom of the elevator shaft, deep below the surface of the earth, the usher accordioned back the shrieking brass lattice to let them out, and the people stepped out of the elevator, where they were abandoned. The people would then feel and grope their way through several layers of thick black curtains and into a profound darkness. At first the darkness is so complete that they cannot tell if their eyes are closed or open or if they have eyes to open at all. Here they become disoriented, as if they have all been blindfolded and spun around in dizzying circles. Here the audience members enter dreamtime, are sucked back into the womb, or into outer space, or inner consciousness, into the darkness of their own brains, so that they cannot really be sure—even though they know they have entered the building consciously, perfectly alert, and of their own free will— whether they are awake or dreaming. After exiting the elevator into the performance space, the audience members are free to wander at will. Soon their eyes adjust to the low lighting, and they perceive that they are not in total darkness, but that the room is lit by very dully glowing red lights here and there—just enough lighting to give the illusion that the room is lit without allowing anyone to see exactly where they are, or even who is standing near them. The people bump into each other, they put their hands in front of them to feel the contours of their environment. They speak out to each other in the dark, make attempts at conversation, only to realize that the people who stand near them now are not the friends or loved ones in whose company they entered the building; they are perfect strangers. The room bubbles into a cacophony of voices calling out in the dark to lost friends, and the lost friends only sometimes call back, confused, disoriented. But no one ever finds who they are looking for. The room becomes a swirling gale of separated lovers and parted friends. The audience members also gradually come to realize that there are no seats and no stage. There are no designated places for anyone to sit or stand, nowhere to hang their coats, and no clear place for them to look toward. This is because the entire room functions as both audience and stage. Now beneath their feet, they feel a ground that is not hard, but soft and pliant, which gives beneath their shoes. Some of them bend down to feel the floor beneath them, and their fingers touch sand. Some of them pick up fistfuls of sand that they let sift out between loosely closed fingers. The floor is covered in so much sand that they cannot feel any flatness underneath it, the texture of the floor feels exactly like a beach. That's because it is a beach. Some people sit down in the sand. Some take off their shoes and socks, and dig their feet into the beach to feel the cool silky sand slithering between their bare toes. As they begin to spread out and wander around the room, some of them discover water. For there is water—real water—lapping at the edge of the sand. They kneel down to feel it with their fingers, or the ones who have taken off their shoes and socks dabble their toes in it, or they hike up skirts and roll up pant legs to go splash around in it. Yes, it is real, and not some elaborate illusion. What's more, it is saltwater. The whole room smells like the sea—although the audience has by now forgotten that they are in a room at all. The water spills onto the beach and draws back again in authentic waves. The quivering globs of jellyfish that have washed ashore lay scattered about the beach, and a few crabs click and scuttle in and out of the foaming surf. The people call out across the water, and they do not hear any echoes. They are answered only by the crash and roar of the open ocean, stretching far out into the indiscernible distance. *Look!*—they say to one another, strangers turning to strangers, pointing and whispering in voices hushed with bewitchment—*look!*—there's the moon, rising above the water. Is it a cardboard cutout moon, hoisted up on fiber-glass wires by an unseen crane? Is it a light projection on a wall, issuing from some hidden lens? It is so real-looking that it hardly matters whether it is real or illusory, for the effect is the same. Even if it is a false moon, it looks real enough to render the question of its realness irrelevant to the senses. The people look around them and, their eyes now aided by the moonlight, they perceive a jungle all around them. A wildly overgrown tropical jungle, resplendent with palm trees, with strange bushes exploding with bright flowers and dripping with vines, exotically shaped trees whose branches droop low with alien fruit, some of which the braver people reach out and pluck, and take bites out of, and find delicious, though it tastes like no earthly fruit they have ever experienced. The people run their hands over the leaves and stalks and trunks of the plants and the trees, and their fingers are shocked to be met not with the brittle dryness of plastic leaves or fabric petals, but with the unmistakably authentic fat wet honest kisses of vegetative life. They smell the flowers, they rip handfuls of leaves from the trees, astonished that it is all real. The air is steamy and hot. People take off their coats and jackets and hang them on tree branches. They look up: stars. *Stars! Stars!* STARS! Some ingenious artist has populated the ceiling's firmament with thousands of glittering lights, again so perfectly mimicking nature that it hardly matters whether or not it is arti-fice: above them is the night sky of some unknown mythopoetic landscape. Tropical birds croak and whistle in the trees. Frogs hop, insects zither around their heads. When the play begins, the room is crowded, but it is impossible for anyone to tell how many people are there, or even where the boundaries of the interior space lie. Interior has become exterior to them. The atmosphere is equally as thick with enchantment as with fear. Now a strange and solemn music begins to play. The orchestra is nowhere and everywhere at once. Unseen cellos murmur like a swarm of bees; the violins shiver

against the thrumbling tattoo of the timpanis. The music is dark
and quiet at first, halfway between audible sound and pure naked
feeling. Some of the people feel strangely warmed by the music and
others feel chilled. The music does not emanate from any discernible source or direction. It is everywhere, it permeates the jungle
and the ocean and the stars and the darknesses between them. The
music somehow comes from inside the leaves of the trees, from
inside the snakes and frogs that slither and hop at the people's feet,
and from inside the blood moving inside their own brains. The isle
is full of noises, sounds, and sweet airs that give delight and hurt
not. A thousand twangling instruments hum about their ears. A
soft crack-and-rumble of thunder in the distance. Now fast-moving
black clouds smother over the stars, and the sky turns black. The
people stand on the beach by the sea, or further inland, on the
grass that is a green as deep as an emerald and feels fat with water
under their bare feet, and they look up, and they watch the sky.
Those stars and that moon, which only moments before they were
amazed to see, are now obscured by thunderclouds speeding across
the sky. The clouds are like paint poured into water. The clouds
move fast but at the moment the wind is calm down here on the
ground. The silence and stillness below the scope of heaven seems
to portend some coming meteorological violence. The temperature
drops. People hug their jackets to their bodies and brace themselves
for the storm. The frayed leaves of the creaking palm trees are
hardly moving at all. The palm fronds click together with an only
barely kinetic languid floating in the tropical air. The snotgreen sea
slops and laps as if it is asleep and its body is moving only in
response to dreams. But up above, the silent sky is a snake pit,
writhing with black and green muscles of vapor that coil around
one another, strangle one another. The clouds look as though they
are made of solid matter, not gas. The clouds race in over our heads.
Their bellies sag with water. A flash of lightning asks a question of

the clouds, three heartbeats of silence follow, and the thunder answers. What does the thunder say? Another blast of lightning spreads out its veins and disappears, quickly trailed by its dawdling wake of thunder. The moon lights up the clouds from above and behind them, making them glow palely in the spot where the moon is. Sometimes the clouds tear apart for long enough to show a flash of the moon's whiteness. Now the sea beyond the beach begins to churn. The people standing on the beach look out across the water. They watch the water slap and splash with greater and greater violence. Rain whips down on us from the sky. It's just a needly spray at first. The air is mist. Raindrops patter on leaves. The people are getting wet. Some of them take cover under the fronds of palm trees. Some of them hitch their jackets up over their heads. Some of them simply let themselves get wet. Women smear away running makeup with their fingers and push soaked hair back from their faces. The rain is warm. It's a monsoon rain. The rain builds in intensity until there is a lull in its flow that everyone can feel, a quieting of its noise and a tangible drop in barometric pressure, the unmistakable moment right before drizzle becomes deluge, and it does, and now the rain comes thudding down on our heads hard and fast, pelting the beach's sand with fat crater-leaving splats of water, weighing down flowers and the leaves of the trees, bending branches, drenching everyone to the skin. The people begin to peel off their wet clothes. An erotic charge in the air joins the electric. The people leave their clothes slopped in wet piles on the sand. The people shiver and shake, and lie down naked in the sand. Now the wind blows the rain sideways and pushes the limber-trunked palm trees flat against the earth. People cling to trees, to rocks, to each other. Who knows what sacred oaths are signed or broken in sweat and flesh and seed and soil on this night, in that storm, in the dark, on the beach in the briny tide or secreted in bushes, under trees or in mossy hiding places among the rocks? Although the steam and fog and the rain that lashes the earth with thick ropes of water all collaborate to foreshorten our visibility to what seems little more generous a distance than is measurable by an arm outstretched before a face, a ship has been spotted out at sea. A huge ship, a man-o'-war, it's like a floating wooden castle. Its ripped sails flutter helplessly behind it. The ship rollicks in the waves and wind, tossed about as easily as a toy boat in a bathtub. Its sides creak and groan with strain, every element of its architecture cracking and splintering, threatening to snap in a hundred places. The ship is singed with St. Elmo's fire. The deck, the bowsprit, the ropes and masts tingle with flame; shivers of electricity run all over every surface of the ship. The deck's a scramble of frenzied activity. The sailors jettison things overboard, casks and barrels and crates. They yank at the ropes and pulleys and wheels, they run and slip and fall on the deck, clamber to their feet, slip and fall again. We watch from the shore as the sailors aboard the ship begin to dive off the deck into the water. The rain crashes down with renewed ferocity, then slowly starts to deliquesce. The wind softens a little. The sailors who jumped off the deck of the ship begin to struggle ashore. One by one they wash up on the beach, half-dead with exhaustion from their desperate dives and swims to safety. Their fingers claw at the sand. They stumble toward land, their boots slogging through the knee-high water. They crawl ashore, spitting out mouthfuls of salt-water, chests heaving, clothes sopping, and collapse on the beach. Crabs skitter around their bodies. A foamy film of tide licks at their feet, receding, returning, receding. The storm clears. The rain slows to a dribble, and then a patter, and then we cannot tell if it is still raining or if all we are hearing is water dripping to the ground from the puddles collected in the recesses of leaves and the funnels of flowers. The light changes: the stars disappear, though the sky does not brighten much. The quality of light in the sky is a deep muddy red underpainted with green and gold. The sky is not cloudy, but thick with mist. It is like a dawn on another planet, as if we are seeing the sunrise of another star, in another galaxy, on a world where an atmosphere composed of alien elements causes luminiferous effects unfamiliar to our eyes. The light is not bright, but it is light enough for the people to see around them. The birds in the trees begin to sing strange songs. The people look at the birds and do not recognize them, for they are not earth birds. These birds look half-dinosaur. Even the smattering of bird-watchers and ornithologists who happen to be in the audience are baffled by these birds, who seem to fall into unreal or unknown taxonomic slots falling perhaps somewhere between the cockatoo and the pterodactyl. The plants here are unrecognizable, too. The botanists who happen to be in the audience are amazed and even frightened, for they do not recognize them. Maybe they are prehistoric plants. They are plants with softly undulating slime-coated prehensile fingers, snapping carnivorous mouths, sensory appendages that seem to see and hear as distinctly as our own eyes and ears. These vegetables are almost animal in the immediacy of their movements, their quick responses to external stimuli, the strange emotiveness of their rooted bodies. We are in the valley of the uncanny. Some change has happened to the people's minds, too. They are thinking like children. The forest smells thick and wild and sweet—full of blood, milk, fire, liquor, sap. The air is wet and heavy. The plants, the water, the rocks: everything surges and breathes with an inner intelligence, a kind of half-sentient consciousness, everything is internally animated with spirits. Like the world to a child, everything is alive. The people forget the bedraggled figures who struggled half-drowned onto the beach the night before. Some people simply choose to wander around the island as curiously and aimlessly as if they themselves have just been shipwrecked. Their clothes—the nice coats and dresses and shirts and ties and scarves that they had worn to the performance, to the theatre, only last night—these clothes cling limply to their bodies, damp from the storm, already ripped and spattered with mud. Still, no one can find the people they had come in with. The people wander the beaches hand in hand with the perfect strangers that they had made love to in the bushes or under trees during the storm. Some of them are still curled up on cushions of matted grass, still naked and asleep. Some people walk along the perimeter of the island, carrying their shoes in their hands to feel the tide lap at their bare feet. People look into the sky, trying to determine a light source, trying to estimate by the position of the sun which directions are east, west, north, south—but failing, because the sun is too vaguely defined, the light too broadly diffuse across the red-green-gold sky to determine the directions of the compass. Some of the braver ones choose to explore the interior of the island: these ones almost immediately become hopelessly lost. These ones see—or they think that they see—the tip of a small mountain or hill in the distance, peeking above the treetops, and so they push through the jungle, shredding their clothes on thorny vines, smacking mosquitoes on their arms, trying to reach the higher ground, hoping to reach a point from which they can look out and see the full lay of the land. Those who decide to push their way inland into the forest will never reach the mountain, and those who decide to walk along the shoreline will never circumnavigate the island, will never connect their loop of footprints. This is because the geography of Prospero's island expands with the consciousnesses of its explorers. The act of exploration itself causes the space to grow. The island is potentially infinite. For those who have chosen to stay behind, the play begins. Only it is so real that it hardly feels like a play. The people hover around Miranda and Prospero in the dark jungle. The light focuses on Miranda and Prospero, everyone else is standing in darkness. They have become invisible. They are only ears and eyes. They have no bodies; they take up no space. They are like mathematical points, without volume, area, or any other dimensional analog. They are like spirits, observing invisibly. They have become what anthropologists only wish they could be. I am Caliban. When Prospero shouts—*What, ho! Slave! Caliban! Thou earth, thou! Speak!*—I come toward them, pushing past the people who are like elements of the forest to us actors, shoving them out of my way. The sticks and grasses snap beneath my plodding monster feet. I step into the light: hunched, grunting, limping under the weight of the bundle of sticks on my shoulders. *There's wood enough within,* I growl. *Thou poisonous slave, got by the devil himself upon thy wicked dam, come forth!* When I step into the light, the people gasp. In horror? In disgust? Some of them look away. Others stare at me in perverse fixation. *As wicked dew as ever my mother brushed with raven's feather from unwholesome fen drop on you both! A southwest blow on ye and blister you all over!* I am filth. I am a monster. I am a thing of darkness. I am naked except for a tattered loincloth clinging to my crotch. I am bent in half beneath my load of sticks. My flesh is covered with mud. I am half-human. Yet with soul enough to speak. I am a thing of lust and rage. I hate them. I hate Prospero. I hate them both. They have taken my birthright from me and put me to work. *This island's mine by Sycorax my mother, which thou takest from me.* I hate all humanity. Nothing but fear and rage and hate comes out of my mouth when I speak, except for sometimes when I speak the most beautiful poetry in the play. I throw down the bundle of sticks. *When thou cam'st first, thou strok'st me and made much of me, wouldst give me water with berries in it, and teach me how to name the bigger light, and how the less, that burn by day and night.... You taught me language, and my profit on it is, I know how to curse.* And so it goes. Ariel flies above our heads, fades in and out of visibility. Ferdinand grunts under labor, Miranda loves him. Antonio plots, Gonzalo philosophizes, I get drunk with Trinculo and Stephano, I try to make them kill Prospero and steal his books.

Spirits flutter in and out of our heads and make us say things we do not want to say. The audience disappears into the play. It is not really a play. The play is not something the audience is watching so much as something they are experiencing. The play is not confined to a stage or even a linear series of scenes following scenes and acts following acts, but rather, everything happens all at once. We disobey all rules of time and space. Everyone leaves his or her body and becomes raw floating consciousness. The play exists all at one time in the same way a book exists all at once. The object and the narrative cannot be disentangled. The play existed in a collective space of thought and feeling and dream and the world became a fog of impressions that night, of timeless immediacy, of magic and sex and fear and laughter coming together into a many-headed dream, a many-minded dream, like a dream being dreamed by the Hydra, and we had all changed our minds and had the minds of animals.

Part Six

ZIRA: What will he find out there, Doctor?
DR. ZAIUS: His destiny.

XLV

Prospero broke his staff and freed his magic. At first no one saw any distinct difference in their surroundings. But the magic was receding. It was bleeding away, like the blood from a cut throat. The people now looked around them and saw that the trees were made of plastic. The fronds of the palm trees were made of green construction paper cut into the shapes of leaves. The birds sitting in the branches? Fake parrots, clearly purchased from a novelty shop, intended as accessories to pirate costumes, with marble eyes and fabric feathers, wired to their perches in the fake trees by their thin plastic talons. The snakes and frogs on the ground? Limp rubber toys. The ground was not ground either; it was a hard flat floor with a little dirt and sand scattered on it. The starry firmament above was represented by several strings of Christmas lights tacked to the ceiling. The skies were colorful lights projected against the whitewashed brick walls of an abandoned subway station. It was a large room, but far from infinite. The stage scenery was no more impressive than backdrops for a grade school play. It was silly—hokey to the point of kitsch in its cheap fakeness.

The members of the audience glanced around themselves and at each other's faces in mild embarrassment. They cleared their throats, they shuffled their feet, they coughed and mumbled. When the play was over, the audience applauded politely, if too briefly, and then began to shuffle en masse toward the one point of egress, the elevator door. They did not even wait for all of the actors to finish bowing before they stopped clapping. They found the friends and loved ones in whose company they had come to the performance. The barefoot ones were the most embarrassed-looking; they irritably wiped the particles of sand clinging to their sticky feet and put on their socks and shoes. People shrugged themselves into their coats and jackets, casually noticing that their garments, being as they were drenched in the sea, held notwithstanding their freshness and glosses, seeming rather new-dyed than stained with saltwater. They checked their watches and snapped open their glowing cell phones (to check the time, not to make any calls, because we were too far underground to get any reception). They had been in this room for about three hours. All of them without exception needed to pee. We had no facilities available downstairs (though from the smell of things after the performance I suspect that didn't stop some people); they crossed their legs and shook their feet in discomfort. The crowd bottlenecked at the elevator door. The elevator could only take people to the surface in groups of five or six at a time, so there was a long wait to get out. As there was no stage, there was no backstage, so Leon, Emily, and I and all the other actors had nothing to do but putz around awkwardly at the periphery of the crowd. We talked amongst ourselves, reassuring one another that the performance had essentially been a success. A theatre critic for the *New York Times* had been spotted in the audience. He was talking about the performance to someone standing next to him in the crowd waiting to leave. He was overheard to have grumbled the words "overblown" and "gimmicky."

The magic was gone. The audience slowly filtered out of the room through the elevator.

There were supposed to have been five performances of *The Tempest*. However, apparently some "concerned" citizen who had attended the first night's performance had alerted certain authorities, and before we could stage the second scheduled performance, while in rehearsal, we were paid a relatively brief and extremely unpleasant visit by two particularly vile men: a short old skinny one with a droopy mustache and glasses, and a big young one whose clean-shaven pink wad of a chinless head ballooned ridiculously from the confines of his shirt collar; the short old one wore a glossy zip-up jacket, a cap, and an official uniform of some sort, and the big young one wore a suit and a tie that had pictures of Looney Tunes characters on it. These two vile personages were, respectively, a public safety inspector and a fire code inspector—I misremember who was which. They did not even take more than fifteen minutes or so to tour the performance space before declaring that we would have to immediately and indefinitely cancel all future performances in this space, for, as they put it—as they had written in a judicious scribble upon some sheet of paperwork, and then tore from a clipboard a translucent yellow carbon-copied slip of whatever bureaucratic trash it was and handed it to us—"totally appalling"—I quote from memory—"totally appalling violations of fire code and building safety code." These two were not done with us, though—they didn't seem to be going away. These pathetic sots seemed to have more to say. They had things to say concerning law, and order, and money, and other cold things. They spoke of the elevator, I remember. Apparently the elevator had most recently been inspected in 1910, and the suit from the public safety department seemed shocked that it still worked. These two men kept trying to refer to the piece of paper they had given us, which Leon, dressed in his Prospero costume—his glittery blue lamé cape decorated with glued-on moons and stars of fuzzy white felt, and a matching pointy hat—was flapping in his fist like a battle flag as he railed at them, shouting every curse that is vituperative under heaven until his face was as purple as a plum. In the end, somehow we succeeding in getting them to leave. But we knew we were finished. They were shutting us down.

There were all kinds of other pungent turds of officialese gobble-dygook buried in that litter box of a document—fines for violations of this-and-that, ADA compliance violations, lack of elevator operation permit, blah, blah, etc. and etc.—not, in short, the sort of corrosively base considerations to which free-thinking dreamers and artists such as Leon or I were wont to intellectually stoop. If we had paid any attention to this scrap of yellow garbage, if we had deigned to take it the slightest bit seriously, then I'm sure we would have discovered the Shakespeare Underground to be hopelessly bankrupt, and we ourselves to be financially ruined in a deeper way than the most dismal destitution. However, we elected on the one hand to begrudgingly comply with their crushing request to cancel the four remaining scheduled performances of *The Tempest*, and on the other to rip that piece of yellow paper first into quadrants, then octants, and finally hexadectants, which were flung from Leon's fist and fluttered like yellow snowflakes into a gutter as we exited the theatre that afternoon. As for the first decision, it was a practical one anyway, for it seemed that in parting those two men had even turned Leon's own beloved great-uncle against us; as we were leaving Mr. Locksmith shook his thin old delicate fist, mentioning in a loud hoarse voice something about even further financial reparations, lawsuits, legal action, criminal charges he threatened to press, for apparently these two vile men had informed him that he too was in a state of dire liability for allowing us to use the illegal space that he happened to have access to, which should never, they said, have been done. And I'm afraid to report that our business relationship with Leon's beloved great-uncle came to a disappointing close right then and there, with bad blood expressed on the behalf of both parties, and Leon and I had to deem it wise to thenceforth avoid returning to those premises, which was, to say the least, inconvenient, as we still had quite a lot of stage equipment and whatnot in that room beneath his shop.

There were still other irritating matters to be dealt with. Little Emily's mother, Mrs. Goyette, had come to the performance, and had felt particularly disappointed, possibly even betrayed. When the rest of the planned performances had to be abruptly canceled, she demanded her backing money back, threatened further legal action, and so on. Of course it would have been impossible to return any of her money, as we had spent it all, and then some. For a few days Leon and I hid out at home and spent a lot of time drunk. We played a lot of backgammon, too.

Leon even began to grow uncharacteristically concerned that the long and pestering arm of the law might soon want to reach its way into our lives as a result of all this silly folderol, and stick its meddling fingers into our various pies, and so he suggested it might be wise to leave the state of New York for a period of time. He put in a call to another one of his ex-wives—who lived in Los Angeles, a city Leon himself had lived in for a time, in another life—and in terms deft and delicate explained the gist of what she needed to know of the situation, and requested her temporary asylum, which she grumblingly but generously agreed to grant. It was time to leave.

I, for my part, decided it was time I returned to Chicago. I had to see Lydia. I was tired of living as a fugitive. I longed to see her, and to kiss her face and feel her skin against mine. I hoped that she was well. I had so many adventures to tell her!

So Leon and I agreed to travel west together. Among Leon's Luddite tendencies was a tremendous fear and distrust of travel by airplane. He suggested that it might not be wise to go that way in any case, as it might present legal hassles if they identified us at the

518 • Benjamin Hale

airport. So with the money from our ticket sales, we purchased boarding passes for an Amtrak train that would chug and roll all the way across America. We divided up the rest of the money, said good-bye (in our hearts, if not in person) to little Emily and her mother, and Leon's daughter, Audrey, and her coworker, Sasha, and Mrs. and Dr. DaSilva, and everyone else who had entered my circle of civilization in New York. And so, we left.

It is a wonderful thing to travel by rail. Especially in the world as we have it now, when it seems such an anachronism. Traveling long distances by train is also an excellent way to meet people who, like Leon, are terrified of flying.

"I hope you never have to endure an airport or an airplane," Leon told me, as we settled into our seats for the nineteen-hour trip from New York to Chicago. "It is a truly disgusting environment. All around you are nothing but the placidly content bourgeoisie, comfortable with their senses of entitlement and dispossessed of a single emotion worthy of feeling or a thought worthy of thinking. They are surface dwellers, both in soul and society. They wiggle into their seats subtly reeking of midprice perfumes and aftershaves, and usually proceed to look straight ahead of them without speaking a word to one another until the aircraft lands, or they open up their laptop computers to bury themselves in their work, or they open their artless books that are usually volumes advertised as being beneficial to their moral or psychological well-being, and if they chance to fall into conversation with their fellow passengers, they can only converse on harmless subjects such as golf or real estate. They are people who would rather pursue happiness than joy. That's what I really detest about air travel. It's not my fear of flying that prevents me from it; it's my fear of the middle class. I can only tolerate the company of either the underclasses, or the aristocracy."

Leon paused, held his breath and shifted his weight to ease the passage of a fart. He continued:

"So remember, Bruno: should you ever need to travel any great distance, you must always if possible take a train or a bus, any mode of transport but an airplane. That hideous invisible gas that permeates our civilization is at its thickest and most dangerous level of concentration inside the sealed cabin of a passenger airplane. But here? Look around! What do we see? We see all manner of people too low-class to fathom the idea of purchasing an airplane ticket. We see recent immigrants from distant impoverished lands, nattering amongst themselves in their exotic tongues, as well as a healthy sampling of drunks, perverts, rednecks, gangbangers, and drug addicts. We see people who are frighteningly thin as well as those who are frighteningly fat. We see people who belong to atavistically folksy religious sects that require them to dress for the early nineteenth century and speak in long-forgotten dialects. I prefer the company of these people, Bruno. In here, one can barely smell that poisonous gas—it is too well masked by the comingling odors of microwaved hot dogs, flatulence, and feet."

The idea of flying (I have only been on an airplane once in my life, and under unpleasant circumstances that I have already related in this narrative) does not repulse me for safety reasons (which I would have to admit irrational), nor for Leon's more subtle and difficult sociological reasons, and not only because there is nothing in my evolutionary pedigree (nor is there, for that matter, in yours) that could prepare me for the unnerving bodily discombobulation of the experience; rather, the idea of flying repulses me philosophically and psychogeographically. I have heard and I believe that a child in an airplane during takeoff may often be overheard to remark that the things he sees below through the window look like "toys." That's just it! Observing the earth from such a godlike perspective destroys an animal's reverence for its geography. They're not "toys," kid. All that land you're zipping over at forty thousand feet and five hundred miles per hour? Down there is a multitude of worlds that you will never know of. People may come to forget them, because they no longer care about them. So go ahead and let them die. Let the earth die, let all the animals die. You probably wouldn't be interested in them anyway. All people care about is getting from one human environment to another as quickly as they can, wasting the minimum possible time in the places between the places. The human imagination yearns to connect point A to point B not with a line, but simply by folding space until the points touch—to entirely eliminate the space between them. This is why, in some science fiction films, people in the future may travel from place to place by teleportation. That is the ultimate realization of humanity's quest to devise faster and more efficient ways of getting from one place to another: to simply eliminate the liminal spaces entirely. And then people will finally become what they have always sought to be: an animal who moves exclusively in environments of its own design, an animal that is all mind, an animal who has no use for its body, an animal who has no use for the earth.

But it was fun to ride the train! Beside us to our left the Hudson River rushed and sparkled against the Palisades as we shuffled and hooted away from New York City. We passed the train station of Hastings-on-Hudson, where I had once chosen to board the south-bound train instead of the northbound train, and thus met Leon and had all the rest of that adventure. That was more than a year earlier. I liked the crisp dark blue suits that the ticket collectors wore, and I liked their shiny brass buttons and the flat plastic visors on their caps. Leon and I sat in a booth in the dining car, playing the games we had brought: chess (a game at which I am not skilled) and checkers (at which I am) and, as always, my most beloved game, the one that a certain bean-boiling one-legged bagpiper first taught me many years ago, backgammon. The train shuddered and hooted and rolled onward, and the chessmen, checkers, and dice clicked, clattered, and tumbled on the table between us. We talked to the people who came and went from the dining car; we watched the landscape slowly scrolling by, gradually changing from urban to rural and back to urban again. Everyone is so friendly on a train, so curious and talkative and eager to make friends with strangers. Perhaps this is because the people on a passenger train are acutely conscious of the anachronism of it, pushing the experience into the realm of novelty, of the fun and interesting and unusual, which prompts people to want to talk. Or perhaps this friendliness arises because those who choose to travel by train tend to be the people who, like Leon, long for an earlier world, a chaotic and inconvenient world where things took a lot of time and people enjoyed talking to each other. A world before the world became a world where every place looks the same and nowhere is home.

So Leon and I intermittently conversed together and conversed with the other passengers and played our games and read our books and watched the land roll past the windows and dozed slumped over in our seats off and on from New York City to Albany to Buffalo to Cleveland to Toledo to Gary to Chicago.

My heart leapt inside me when I saw those familiar buildings rising in the distance, those very buildings that had once bewitched and seduced me when I was only a mind-silent animal. I myself was practically leaping up and down in my seat by the window with irrepressible glee as we rattled across the Union Station switchyard with the early morning sunlight flashing on the rails of the tracks.

Oh! Chicago! (My heart exclaimed within me in rapture.) I have been away from you for more than a year! Oh!—Chicago, are you happy to see me? It's me, Bruno—your son and lover! I have been unfaithful to you, I admit. I come back to you from an affair with your big sister—your bigger, older, meaner, and more complicated sister who lives eight hundred miles beyond you to the east! But Chicago, inland Chicago, redbrick and brown Chicago, freshwater Chicago, almost-uninhabitably-cold-for-the-better-part-of-the-year

Chicago, I've come back to you!—for you are the only city that I can truly love.

The train docked in a tunnel and hissed in repose, and then fell silent. Everyone disembarked, for it was the end of the line. Leon and I breakfasted together on bagels, bacon, eggs, and coffee at the Union Station food court before I saw him off at the gates of his connection, which would take him far away, across the great American interior—past I know not how many mountains and plains and desert cacti and shaggy-maned buffalo—to the sun-dappled land of California, where asylum had been promised him. Leon and I embraced as we said good-bye, with tears shed on the behalves of both parties. I stood at the gate, waving, as I watched him fastidiously guide his mass down the ramp that led to the train platform, and my heart burned as much with my gladness to be back in my homeland as with my reluctance to see him go.

He was wearing a rumpled brown corduroy suit, and he labori-ously struggled to drag along a fatly stuffed rolling suitcase behind him on the concrete platform. His hair was long and knotty, his beard bushy, his body huge. Altogether Leon looked like a baby whale that had been stuffed into a brown suit. Ah, but he carried himself with the dignity of a prince. Like the Prince of Whales, I should think. Farewell, thou latter spring! Farewell, thou all-hallown summer! Thou sweet creature of bombast!

And I, for my part? I, Bruno, left the train station. I left the sta-tion with a suitcase in my hand that contained my every remaining possession on earth, and exited into the busy morning bustle of Canal Street, crossed the river by the Adams Street bridge, crossed Wacker, passed beneath the shadow of the Sears Tower and pierced my way into the heart of the heart of the city. I breathed the famil-iar scent of this my home city, I observed the familiar stone orna-ments on the buildings, I kept my eyes peeled for any significant change, but detected little. I went in search of Lydia.

XLVI

It was still early in the morning. The train had left New York City the previous morning, and had traveled all day and all night before depositing us in Chicago at nine or so in the a.m. I had slept fitfully on the train, and the bright busy morning in Chicago took on the mildly hallucinatory quality a bright busy morning does when one hasn't slept well. I wanted to do nothing more than go straightaway to see Lydia, but something made me check myself. I thought it might be too strange or too rude to show up unannounced at her apartment so early in the day. She probably wouldn't even have been at home, I thought. So instead I spent a good part of that morning walking around in the city, ambling beneath the rumbling red iron latticeworks that support the L, noting down various poetic observations in my head. Every winking traffic light and every plump purring pigeon that hopped along the sidewalk seemed to welcome me back. "Hello, traffic light!"—I could barely restrain myself from saying aloud—"Hello, pigeon!"

Hello, Bruno! I would imagine the pigeon articulating back to me through her trilling throat.

I looked at the stone lions that guarded the doors of certain buildings, I gazed through windows at storefront displays of beautiful woman mannequins wearing various styles of clothing, I ducked in and out of bookstores and spent a while sitting at the foot of the giant Picasso sculpture at Daley Center Plaza. Gradually, gradually, I gravitated uptown—knowing full well, not in my conscious mind, but in my bones, where my puttering feet were taking me.

That was the first time I experienced the Lincoln Park Zoo as a visitor, rather than as an exhibit. On all our fun/educational outings in the early days of my enculturation, Lydia had never once taken me here. Surely this was because she was afraid of what I would think, what I might do. What the other chimps would think and do, for that matter. Taking me to see my own imprisoned family must have seemed a perverse torture she did not wish to inflict upon my vulnerable developing consciousness.

I walked into the emerald-green rolls of Lincoln Park from the south entrance, waddled along the winding pedestrian footpath past joggers clad tightly in shiny spandex outfits, past little dogs tugging on their leashes, past a baseball diamond, an equestrian statue, a big duck pond, where geese and swans drifted through green water neon with algae, and entered the zoo: the Lincoln Park Zoo, apparently, is free, a realization that stung slightly of insult. Oh!—to enter such a familiar space from such an unfamiliar angle! The violence of the gestalt shift whacks the mind like a club!

Seeing the place from the angle of the human observer disoriented me. It looked familiar and yet eerily alien to me at the same time. I had never realized what a sad, dirty little zoo it really is. The animals in it have so little space to roam. The big cats are cornered into such dirty, miserable little cages—old-fashioned ones with bars on them rather than glass, evoking prison cells rather than displays, with cold concrete straw-scattered floors that reeked of melancholy and urine. The animals in them looked so shabby and dejected, their souls broken, resigned to quiet lives of captivity and humiliation. The leopards and lions and tigers neurotically skulked back and forth behind the bars of their cages, pitifully trying to uphold their dignity, like ruined aristocrats. As they paced their aimless loops their hipbones and shoulder blades undulated with a physical grace not even humanity could take away, but their heads ticked now and then with tiny spasms of uncontrollable rage. When I lived in this place, I had known only the inside of the chimp exhibit, and what was immediately visible from within it. I could not see much beyond the concrete wall that dammed the moat surrounding our small artificial island. I had no idea that the zebras and kangaroos were within eyesight of the ledge that looked onto our exhibit, that we could have physically seen these strange beasts if only we had been able to stand on top of the wall. So I observed and pitied the animals—the cats, the birds, the giraffes, the elephants, the rhinos—as I followed the maps that led me through the small zoo to the Primate House.

To my right was the gorilla exhibit. That huge old magisterial silverback was still there. He was napping, slumped over limp-limbed and dejected in his rope hammock, looking as if he hadn't moved a muscle in all the years I'd been gone, one arm resting on his massive belly and the other arm dangling down beneath him, his fat-fingered wrinkled leathery hand grazing the ground like an old work glove.

To my left was the chimpanzee exhibit. I noticed for the first time in my life that in front of the window looking into the exhibit, a row of plastic cards are held up suspended on thin metal stands, and on the cards are printed brief blurbs of educational information about my species. Several of these cards displayed color photographs of wild African chimps grooming each other, swinging in trees and so on, and another displayed a map showing where our natural habitat is, colored in red: two small blotches of red, one in Central Africa and the other on the southern coast of the gun-handle of West Africa. Like this:

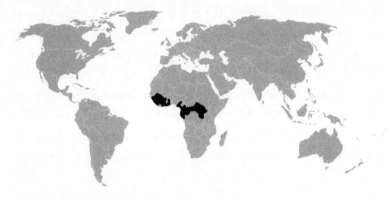

On another card was written the following text:

Chimpanzee
> *Pan troglodytes*

Mammals

Order
> *Primates*

Description
> *Length: 2.5–4 feet. Weight: 125–175 pounds, males slightly larger. Zoo weights higher. Much variation in body size and proportion. Coat mostly black; short, white beard common in adults of both sexes. Baldness also occurs in adults, more so in females. Face mostly hairless and light, darkening with age. Ears large, nostrils small. Females have prominent swelling of the pink perineal region while in heat; males have very large testes. Young have white tuft of hair on rump.*

Range
> *Western and central Africa, north of River Zaire, from Senegal to Tanzania.*

Habitat

Humid forest, deciduous woodland or mixed savanna;
presence in open areas depends on access to evergreen,
fruit-producing trees.

Niche

Omnivorous: mainly eats fruit and leaves, but during
dry season will eat seeds, flowers, bark, insects, birds and
mammals. Diurnal; sleeping nests built fresh each night.
Mainly terrestrial, walking on soles of hind feet and
knuckles of forelimbs, but will spend time or build nests
in trees (especially young), using brachiation to travel.
Communities number 15–120, but feeding is usually
an individual activity, especially among females. Males
are gregarious and form a loose dominance hierarchy.
Neighboring community ranges overlap.

Life History

Mating non-seasonal; single young born after about 9
months gestation. Young cling within a few days, ride
mother at 5–7 months, are weaned at about 3 years.
Mature at about 10–11 years, earlier in captivity. Females
promiscuous, migrating to a new community during an
adolescent estrous period. Life span 40–45 years.

Conservation Status

This species is listed as threatened and commercial trade is
prohibited by international law. Principal cause of population
decline is habitat destruction, particularly commercial logging.
Some hunting for bushmeat or commercial purposes still occurs
and has severely depleted populations in some areas.

Much of this, Gwen, was news to me. Let us imagine—as I myself
have often imagined, in the cumulative years of idle moments since
the beginning of my second confinement—a similar text that would

be written upon a similar placard, to be displayed before a cage designed to represent a human environment. A thick glass wall would look out onto another (perhaps a third?) species' crude caricature of their idea of a typical human setting. Although our readers may imagine whatever they wish—the interior of a mud hut, an igloo, a log cabin, the Hapsburg Palace—I personally, for my maximum amusement, imagine a blandly fake room in a hyper-imagined middle-class home somewhere in a North American suburb, furnished with somebody's rough idea of prototypically "human" items: a four-poster bed, a couple of armchairs, a dining table, and so on. There are candles on the table. The walls are painted a sickly cotton-candy pink. There is a reproduction of the *Mona Lisa* hanging in an ornately gilt frame on the wall. A false picture window looks out onto a painted backdrop of a pleasant sunny day. There is a mantel and a fireplace, inside of which glow flames cut from red and yellow crepe paper, underlit by a hidden lamp. Beside the fireplace lies, curled on a rug as if in slumber, a taxidermized dog, with a food bowl set before him, labeled SPOT. Inside this room are five or six humans of both genders and varying ages and races. One of the cards outside the window features a map showing in red the areas of the earth usually inhabited by human beings, with a card beside it detailing basic information about this species.

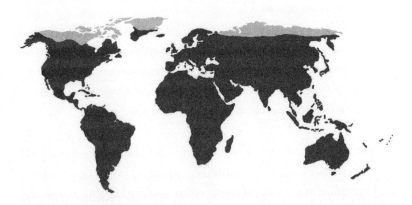

Human

Homo sapiens sapiens

Mammals

Order

Primates

Description

Length: 4–6.5 feet. Weight: 75–400 pounds, males slightly larger. Zoo weights considerably higher. Much variation in body size and proportion. Coat very sparse except on top of head and areas surrounding genitals and underarms; males may have hair on faces. Body modification, including selective hair removal, is common. Small ears, prominent noses. Long legs, short arms. Baldness often occurs in adult males. Females feature prominent teats. Young have disproportionately large heads.

Range

Because the human is highly adept at travel, transportation of materials and sheltering themselves from adverse environmental conditions, this species has spread to nearly every climate and lives on every continent of the world.

Habitat

Humans tend to live in small groups within much larger social hive areas. The human generally prefers not to inhabit environments in which other non-domesticated animals may be found. (The human often allows domesticated animals—especially dogs—to symbiotically cohabit its living space.) The human is most comfortable in areas specifically designed for human habitation.

Niche

Very omnivorous, generally diurnal. Mainly terrestrial, walking upright on soles of hind feet, though young remain quadrupedal until about 1 year of age. Adults may travel long distances by use of various tools, including in aquatic and aerial environments. Size of communities varies greatly; though some humans are known to live alone, most live in larger communities ranging from 100 to approx. 10,000,000. Feeding is often a communal activity. Both males and females tend to quickly form fierce dominance hierarchies. Neighboring community ranges overlap significantly. Humans have no known natural predators.

Life History

Mating non-seasonal and constant. Single young born after about 9 months gestation. Young cling within a few days, are weaned at about 1 year. Males may occasionally assist females in rearing of young. Sexually mature at about 13–15 years, earlier in captivity. Many never fully psychologically mature. May form sexually monogamous couples, usually leading to extreme psychological stress. Life span 40–90 years.

Conservation Status

The human is in no imminent danger. Due to its alpha predator status coupled with the ability to control its own climate, the human has ceased to evolve, thereby effectively removing itself from nature. Currently, the only palpable threat to the human is the human.

This imagining, however, will probably never come to be. There are laws against things like that—human laws. Laws that would prevent keeping a group of humans in captivity for purposes of public education and entertainment. Such an idea would violate our notions of ethics, which have always struck me as problematically anthropocentric. The chimps and the humans at the zoo are separated by that wall of glass because the chimps might harm the humans were there no glass. Albeit the same (it is almost too obvious to point out) could be said of humans and humans. However, humans only imprison other humans after the humans in question have proven themselves to be harmful to humans. If one were to apply the same logic to human beings as humans do to animals, then we would have to preventatively imprison everyone from birth. Then we would all be safe.

———

On an early afternoon in Chicago in late March of 1999, I, Bruno, stood and peered through the window that looked into the chimpanzee exhibit in the Primate House of the Lincoln Park Zoo. I peered through the window that looked into my childhood home. My old wordless world, my animal habitat. I looked through a three-inch-thick sheet of glass at my biological family. It looked much the same as I had remembered it, although I'd grown upward by about a foot and outward by more than fifty pounds, and so the space looked even smaller than I'd remembered it. I saw—and remembered as I saw—a ledge, a certain wide flat metal shelf bolted to the wall in a corner, very high up near the ceiling in the interior part of the exhibit, accessible via the ropes and nets that hung from the ceiling down to the cedar-planting-chip-covered floor: we chimps would often scramble up those ropes and nets up to the shelf, muster ourselves on top of it and huddle there together in the winter months, napping, grooming, lazing around all afternoon long in a languid tangle of embraces. It was March now, and cold outside, though not bitterly so, and all the chimps were inside, and most of them were huddled together on top of the shelf in the corner, just as I had once done. The shelf, as I recall, was a favorite place of ours, in part because its height probably reminded our instincts of the tree canopies in which we would have been taking our naps if this were the jungle and there were predators afoot below us, and in part because its height made it one of the precious few areas of that

Benthamite panopticon where we were not totally in view of our spectators. Of course the people could still see us—they could see that we were up there, could see our hands dangling off the edges of the shelf and could catch glimpses of the imperceptibly moving mounds of our warm breathing brown bodies—but at least we were not fully exposed up there. I looked up to the shelf, and I saw my family—my old family, my mother, Fanny, and my father, Rotpeter, my aunt Gloria, and my uncle Rex—huddled together on top of the shelf, several gangly purple hands and gangly opposably-toed feet poking out of the ball of appendages to dangle limply off the edge of the shelf. Down below them, on the ground, scratching and digging in the steamy urine-sodden carpeting of cedar planting chips, were two chimps whom I did not recognize. New additions to the zoo. One, a female, looked like a teenager—probably around my age, actually—fifteen years old. The bloated wad of pink flesh that she dragged along the ground beneath her advertised her fecundity, and a little brown button of a turd protruded shyly from her anus. The second new chimp was the infant she held in her arms.

I stood so close to the wall of glass that the brim of my hat touched it. (I was wearing the same coat and hat that I had once found in a closet in little Emily's house.) I shielded my eyes with a hand cupped against the glass to block my reflection. The glass had a faint blue-green tint. Beside me, a few paces away, there was a woman and a child. The woman looked middle-aged and middle-class, and wore a candy-apple-red coat with thick black buttons, a blue sweater, and glasses, and her brown hair was tied loosely back. There was a stroller beside her. It contained a soft fuzzy blue blanket and a stuffed animal, but other than that it was vacant—its presumed occupant was crawling around on the floor, wearing the standard uniform of an infant: a one-piece jumpsuit with a button-up door in the hindquarters for easy diaper-changing; the jumpsuit was blue, which we for some reason consider a color that connotes the innocence of infancy while still being appropriately masculine—oh, what an odd thing it is that humans begin to sexualize their young even when they're scarcely washed of womb-goo!—before they're born, even! (Perhaps this note should go somewhere in the blurb of species information on the human? No! No room for such details! That's where the devil is. Gwen—there's simply too much to say! There's too much to say!) This child, this presumably male human infant, was padding around, hands and feet slapping like four fat little flippers on the floor of the human observer's area of the Primate House of the Lincoln Park Zoo. Oh, God, he was beautiful. He was a beautiful baby, plump, bald, smooth-skinned, bright and Buddha-like, a creature at that stage of pure and perfect passions, the needle of his emotional meter capable of swinging instantaneously from bliss to despair and back to bliss on account of stimuli so easy as the touch of his mother's skin. Sometimes I see a baby and I nearly cry. *Why?* Why does the sight of a baby make me cry? Is it because I know too much about the world he's been born into? No, that's much too insipidly romantic, that can't be it. The sight of a baby fills me instantly with desperate, insane, boundless love. I love human babies! I love the animals! I love the world!...but—*I hate it! I love and I hate the world with equal passion!* That's why I cry when I see a baby! The hot and cold fronts in my soul slam together and make a storm—a tempest!—and I cry!

This child, this baby in the zoo, was too young to speak. His consciousness was still at the level of an animal's, that of an uneducated ape. He was babbling, being at the prelinguistic stage of early childhood when a baby is perpetually fascinated anew by his own ability to make noise, and so he spends every spare waking second he can get with his mouth busily spewing a nonteleological flux of cooing, humming, burbling, gurgling, and singing. In constant song! Music always precedes meaning! Music before meaning! On and on and on he babbled and sang, employing every technique available to the infant's cantatory repertoire. First he sang a high, constant note while repeatedly cupping and releasing a hand over his mouth to create an autohypnotic ululating effect. Soon he decided to modify this technique by rapidly flapping his fingers over his lower lip while dropping his voice to a hum, which made a noise like the low idling of an engine, and after tiring of that he took the same concept and kicked it into higher gear by increasing the pressure of his outward breath while rapidly vibrating his smiling lips; this last technique quickly led to an excess of drool leaking over his chin—ah, but he cared not.

The bottom three feet of the glass wall that looked into the chimp exhibit was foggy with little handprints, and soon this child began adding his own to the fog. He crawled up onto the short step that ran beneath the bottom of the glass, and pressed himself to the window to get a better look. He was still making a motorboat noise with his reverberating lips, absentmindedly, or maybe to make himself a little music to accompany the sight. He squished his tiny hands flat against the glass as he peered through it at the chimps. Inside the exhibit, eight or ten feet away from the window, the female chimp whom I did not recognize had slumped over backward onto the damp floor of cedar planting chips—not from fatigue, but probably from boredom—and the infant chimp whom she had been holding scrambled out of her arms, clambered over her hairy protuberant belly, and began to make his way on thin spindly arms and stumpy legs across the floor of the exhibit toward the window. The baby chimp crawled right up to the baby human. The chimp pressed his own hands against the glass and looked directly out the window into the face of the human child on the other side. Two babies, two species, inches apart, looked at one another through the glass. They were about the same size. Young chimps look even more humanlike (or rather, humans look like neotenic chimps): they have big eyes, big round heads, and small faces. I watched as these two primates, as these two children from slightly different species, looked at one another through the wall of blue-green glass, each with hands pressed flat to the window, each big-headed and big-eyed, each without language. At that moment—at this stage of their respective developments—it seemed completely arbitrary who was on which side of the glass. Each of them only knew that a glass wall divided them, and neither understood why.

The child's (I mean the human child's) mother eventually decided it was time to go, and she picked him up and deposited him in his stroller for transport.

As his mother was wheeling him out of the room, the human child peered over the rim of his stroller, looked back at the ape behind the glass, and waved.

———

They left. I remained. I stood in front of the glass and watched the chimps all afternoon.

I must have cut a strange figure that afternoon: a man, a hairless and somewhat deformed dwarf, in a coat and black fedora with a suitcase in his hand, standing all day in front of the chimp exhibit at the Lincoln Park Zoo. No one bothered me, though. The other chimps one by one roused from the naps they were taking on that high shelf in the upper corner of the exhibit, yawned, sleepily stretched their long hairy arms and scrabbled down the ropes and nets that hung from the ceiling to the floor. They putzed around, they chased one another, they groomed one another, they batted their hands at one another, they occasionally broke into rapid exchanges of howls and squeaks, they climbed their ropes, they nibbled at the food pellets they found in the planting chips on the floor. I watched my old family for hours. They never recognized me. I was a stranger to them. And why should they have recognized me? I was not an animal like them anymore. I was hairless, I was upright, I was clothed, I was nosed. That is why I stood on my side of the glass, and they on theirs. Their Bruno was a man now.

I noticed that Céleste was not among them. I looked outside, and did not see her there, either. I wondered if she had been transferred to another zoo for some reason. Wherever she was, she was not there.

I wondered long and hard if I regretted anything. I tried to imagine what my life would have been like if I had remained in the zoo with my original family. If I was with them still, still relegated to being the lowest-ranking male in the social group, never knowing anything of the world but this infinitesimally small patch of it. Never falling from innocence or stepping out of the darkness. Never knowing language, never feeling that strange alteration in me, to degree of reason in my inward powers, nor thenceforth to speculations high or deep to turn my thoughts, and with capacious mind consider all things visible in heaven, or earth, or middle, all things fair and good. The idea was now so foreign to me that it almost caused me to laugh. It was an aimless wondering, leading me nowhere. These animals were now so alien to my consciousness that I could no longer fathom what was going on inside their minds. Their behavior, the mental processes of these animals, had become as opaque to me as lead. Now I could only see them through a glass, darkly.

XLVII

I left the zoo that afternoon with a feeling in me that was not
sadness. It was a feeling like sadness, but quieter and stranger.
I left the zoo that day feeling as if I had attended the funeral of a
good friend who died of an unpreventable and accidental cause. It
was the late afternoon by the time I left the Primate House.

There was still something preventing my going to see Lydia.
I found a bar on Clark Street, a dark place of brass and leather
and lacquered wood, where in silence and solitude I quieted my
nerves with three whiskeys while eavesdropping on the nattering
conversation of three big pink men in disheveled suits and loosened ties sitting at a corner table by the window. One of them was
narrating to the other two men a chronicle of complications surrounding his pending divorce. The other men were warily trying
to salve his sadness with the medicines of laughter and anger. The
first man joined in the angry laughter, he joined in their raucous
tit-for-tatting of misogynist banter, but his sadness seeped through
his jocularity like water through cheesecloth. Now I was back once
again in the human zoo. All the world's a zoo, and all the men and
women merely animals. The stage and the zoo are interchangeable,

Gwen: remember, we have already discovered that theatre is biology, and biology is theatre. All the world's a zoo.

———

It was near St. Patrick's Day. Maybe it was the day before, or maybe the day after. I recalled in a rush how Chicago would dye its river green—so that it looked like a river of toxic waste—and I recalled wondering whether green fish ever turned up weeks later in the slapping and shimmering hauls in the nets of fishermen many miles north of the city. The streets, the windows of the shops and restaurants, were rife with St. Patrick's Day decorations: lots of green streamers, paper shamrocks, images of leprechauns. I don't know why the color green is supposed to symbolize Irish heritage— perhaps because of the famous verdancy of Ireland?

In any event, I walked past the window of a flower shop: outside the door, in a basket, the flower shop had green roses on display. Green roses! I recalled Lydia's weakness for them. As always, the green roses struck me as freakish, fascinating for their proud artificiality, the clear deliberation behind their bioengineering, the dye in the soil, or however it is the skilled florists turn the petals green. It always seemed to me that a flower—especially a rose—ought to be a different color from its stem, at least for contrast's sake. I entered the flower shop. I walked into a lush blast of fragrance and humidity, and selected one dozen long-stemmed green roses. I had the pencil-mustached man behind the counter roll them up in a cone of cellophane and then in another cone of decorative paper. I carefully carried them out in the hand that didn't hold my suitcase. Their smell was as intoxicating as wine.

I had a little money left—only a little—so I hailed a taxi on Lincoln Avenue and took it all the way down to Hyde Park, where I directed the driver to drop me off right before the door set in the side of a redbrick slab of apartments that led to 5120 South

Ellis Avenue, Apartment 1A. All the while during the drive I spent rehearsing in my mind a thousand things that I would say to Lydia. I was nearly queasy with anticipation. I crushed the green petals of the flowers to my face and felt the velvety wetness of their texture and sucked in their smell. I had no idea what she might say about my new clothes and my new nose. I had so much to tell her. I had so many exciting adventures to narrate, which I would regale her with. We would drink wine as I narrated my tales, and I would make us laugh until we became as light-headed as if we'd been inhaling helium all day, until we'd nearly faint from laughter, and in the end we would go to bed together, and in the morning we would resume our lives together.

I am, at heart, an optimist, Gwen, if that's the word for willing yourself to hope for the best when you know the truth is probably so horrible you don't want to look. Of course I knew why I had delayed seeing her after I arrived in Chicago. I had no idea what state she may have been in. I had been absent for a year. Honestly, however high I may have held my head in my self-imposed false good mood, still my steps were leaden with guilt. In the fantasy I had been entertaining for my homecoming, Lydia looked exactly as she had that day when I first met her, when I was a child, the day of the experiment with the peach in the box. She was young, healthy, gorgeous, with all her long blond hair, her skin smooth and her eyes alive with youth, and so on. Lydia smiling, Lydia laughing, Lydia stroking the rich red-brown fur that I had back then. The door would open, and that Lydia of my memory would somehow be standing there. I wanted the door to open into a time machine, which I would program to take us back six or seven years, and then freeze time, just hold it there. Gwen, I once saw a wonderful film about the life experiences of Superman. At the end of the film, Superman's girlfriend, Lois Lane, is crushed by a collapsing bridge because Superman was too busy with other matters at the time to save her. But not to worry, because it turns out that not even the space-time continuum is too immutable for Superman's prowess and ingenuity. Superman flies into the bubble of near outer space surrounding the earth's atmosphere, then starts flying so quickly around the circumference of the earth, over and over, that he succeeds in reversing the direction of the earth's rotation, which somehow acts as a massive "rewind" button for the planet. Then he zooms back down to earth, saves Lois Lane from the falling bridge, then zooms back into space and considerately recorrects the direction of the earth's rotation. It's this last bit that I would have omitted from the procedure, had I Superman's powers. I would have sailed up to the ionosphere, spun the earth backward to a day when Lydia and I were cohabiting this apartment, together, in youth, in love, but before her sickness, and before I could speak—and then I would blast back to the outer rind of the atmosphere, and through a difficult series of maneuvers, I would fly clockwise a little, then counterclockwise a little, left, right, left, bit by bit, until I succeeded in making the earth just stop, and hang there, quiet, suspended, and still in the blackness of space. Then I would return to earth, now converted into a giant fossilized snapshot of some particular moment on some particular day in say the fall of about 1994—all around the world, forks frozen forever about to enter open mouths, people stuck at the edge of day in slippers with arms stretched in midyawn, murderers ossified with guns still smoking in their hands, lovers cemented in embrace—and I, Bruno, would put myself in that last category: I would float down to a certain apartment in Hyde Park, Chicago, and find a healthy young Lydia, and viably position her arms such that they conformed to the shape of my body, and slip into them, and shut my eyes, and join the vast stagnant earth at that precise moment, and remain there, forever.

Yes, I admit that I am not as altruistic as Superman. That is why Superman is Superman and Bruno is Bruno. I am not a hero. I am a cowardly pernicious sniveling selfish wretch, who would destroy the world for his own happiness. But does that make me a villain?

I stood before the outer door to the apartment building, glancing up to notice the honking flocks of blackbirds that burst and fluttered from tree to tree in the blue and orange gloaming of that March day. I steeled myself, and sank a long purple finger into the buzzer. I hopped up and down on the toes of my shoes in anticipation. I crushed the green roses to my nose and drank them in. I took in a deep breath and let it slowly out. I cleared my throat. I wondered if she wasn't at home. I pressed the buzzer again. A moment later, a crunching of static and a voice—a woman's voice, but not Lydia's—electronically croaked through the speaker.

"Hello?" said the crunchy voice in a confused but polite tone. "Who is it?"

"Lydia?" I said. My voice squeaked. I cleared my throat again. "Is Lydia Littlemore at home?"

"Who is this?" demanded the voice, less polite now.

"A friend," said I. (I wanted to surprise her.)

The speaker buzzed, and I pulled on the door, went into the hallway and let it thump shut behind me.

I stood in the hallway. The door to the apartment I had shared with Lydia opened up about a quarter of its width—apartment 1A, the only door on this floor—and a figure stood in it, holding the edge of the door, peering past it into the hall.

"Hello?" said the figure, in the same voice as I had heard, but without the staticky distortion of the buzzer. "Can I help you?"

I waddled closer to the door, flowers and suitcase in my respective hands, hat on my head.

As I came closer I saw that the figure who stood in the doorway was Tal. She looked much the same as before, except that she was not clothed in the flowery gypsy garb she was wont to wear when I had known her best. Instead she wore more drably conservative garments: sweater, jeans, socks. Her thick wavy black hair was bound back in a ponytail reminiscent of the way Lydia used to wear her hair. Standing before her in the hallway, I transferred the bouquet of green roses from my right hand to the crook of my right arm, carefully, so as not to damage them, the paper and cellophane crinkling in my hand during this delicate operation. With my right hand thus freed, I moved it to the top of my head, pinched the shallow depressions in the crown of my natty black hat and slowly, gentlemanly, removed it. And there I stood in the dimly lit hallway of the apartment building in which I used to live in bliss with Lydia, my first and only true love. In the same building in which Griph Morgan, with his bagpipes and his parrots, used to live upstairs. In one of the only places on earth so formative upon my memory and consciousness. There I stood, in my coat and scarf, with a bouquet of green roses for Lydia tucked beneath my arm, carrying my hat and suitcase, my three feet and ten inches of stature heightened slightly by my shoes.

I looked up at Tal: I smiled at her and said hello. I admit that my gaze sank momentarily to the missing segments of the middle finger of her right hand, before I remembered myself and redirected it back to her face.

I did not know what I expected to happen then on her face, but the look of absolute horror that subsequently appeared on it as soon as she finally recognized me was not exactly what I had been angling for.

"Oh my God," Tal half-whispered, slowly backing away from me. She edged herself away from the doorway, narrowed the openness of the door, and stood inside the apartment with one hand on the doorknob, ready to slam it shut if necessary.

She said: "*Bruno?*"

I said: "My name is Bruno Littlemore. Bruno I was given, Littlemore I later gave myself. I have come for Lydia."

"What in the *world*"—she hissed, her expressions roving elastically from fear to confusion to disgust—"happened to your *face*?"

"Ah, this?" I said, tapping the side of my proud human nose with a long purple finger. "This is my nose. Do you like it?"

I smiled in the friendliest way I could.

Then Tal did, in fact, slam the door in my face. She locked it and slid the deadbolt.

I felt the blast of wind the door displaced in my face. If I had been any closer, the flat hard door would have certainly squashed my beautiful nose against my face, immediately undoing the careful work of my surgeon.

As I wailed and hammered on the door with my fists, pleading with her to let me in, I felt an unpleasant wave of déjà vu. A wave of déjà vu as visceral and stomach-clutching as a wave of nausea. I felt at that moment that I had spent a great portion of my brief and unhappy life engaged in the labor of screaming and pounding in desperation on doors that were closed to me—crying, begging, shouting—sometimes in rage and sometimes in despair, to be let in. Or out. Begging either to be let out or let in. I have always stood on some threshold. They have never let me in ... or out.

After seeming hours of my loud and pitiful bellowing—after angry neighbors upstairs opened up their doors and shouted down at me, demanding first to know what the trouble was and then simply for quiet for God's sake—Tal finally opened the door a squeak. She kept the security chain hooked.

"Tal!" I screamed into the crack of light. "Please let me in! I won't hurt you! I won't hurt anyone! I just want to see Lydia!"

"Why?" she snapped. "Are you going to smash anything or bite anything?"

"No! I'm a new man! I promise! I've changed! My days of smashing and biting are behind me! *Please*—," I whispered, "please trust me."

Tal slammed the door again, unhooked the chain and slowly opened it. I slipped inside, suitcase banging against the doorjamb, roses crinkling to my chest. I stepped into the foyer and shut the door behind me. Tal was wearing boots, now, and she was holding a big kitchen knife.

"That's not necessary," I said. "I won't hurt anyone."

Tal spat out a reverse-gasp of sardonic laughter. "You're too late for that," she said.

I let my head dip down in shame at this comment.

"Where the hell have you *been*?" she said. "What do you *want*? I can't believe you came back here. How did you even get back to Chicago?"

"In time," I said (sagely, I hoped), "all shall be explained. But, Tal, please…" I knew my voice had a tearful tremor in it, now.

I was still standing in the dark and muddy foyer of that apartment I knew better than almost any set of rooms in the world, feeling less even like a guest than an intruder, wondering if I should take off my shoes or presume enough even to unbutton my coat, still awkwardly juggling in my arms flowers, hat and suitcase as I said: "Where is Lydia? Please…I want to see Lydia." I felt tears surging up beneath my cheeks, threatening to cloud my vision.

"Are those for Lydia?" said Tal, pointing at the bouquet of green roses in my hand with her knife.

I held the flowers out a little from my chest. For a moment the crinkling of the cellophane and paper they were wrapped in was the loudest sound in the room. I couldn't answer her because I was afraid that I would cry if I tried to speak. I only nodded yes.

Tal sighed through her nose as she looked down at me, holding the green roses. She backed into the apartment and set down the kitchen knife she had wielded at me on the dining table with a click of metal on wood and beckoned to me to enter the apartment.

Everything inside the apartment had changed. All the furniture was different except for the dining table. There were new pictures on the walls. The living room wall had been painted over with sunflower yellow paint. Some of Tal's disgusting lacquer-faced wooden puppets were sitting in a row like spectators on the fireplace mantel.

Tal stood with her back leaning against the edge of the dining table as I came inside, not taking off my shoes or my coat. I walked into the middle of the room. She crossed and uncrossed her arms, then braced her palms against the edge of the table behind her. She crossed her arms again, uncrossed them again, and then took a few steps toward me. She bent down to me until her face was level with mine. She was also close to tears.

"Bruno—," she began. I already knew by then what she had to say to me. By the time she began to say it—by the time the information had actually begun to exit her lips—I had already endured the four or five longest and worst seconds of my life. I knew already what she had to say, and I did not want to hear her say it, and yet I knew that it had to be said. By the time she was actually saying it, I could not even see her face because my eyes were so blinded by tears of rage, nor could I hear or understand a word she said, because my ears were so deafened by the volume of my emotion, it was as if they had been plugged with wax.

XLVIII

Lydia had died six months before I arrived in Chicago. Some-how this had never even occurred to me—in my conscious mind—as a possibility, even though I guess I did know she had been deathly ill when I was taken from her. It never occurred to me that someone I had loved as much as I loved her—and there has only ever been one such person in all my life—could die, or that I would not be present for it. Lydia's attackers were still on the loose, and always will be. Lydia's tongue had gone numb, limp, and languageless from the poison in her brain, and so she could not name them, or even describe them. When she died she was as silent as any animal. After they had untimely ripped my child from her womb, and after I had been deported by Animal Control and taken to the LEMSIP biomedical research laboratory in New York (from which, as we know, I escaped), Lydia lost the will to live. The tumor that had been scraped partially and unsuccessfully from her brain could not be killed off with radiation therapy, though her doctors had tried. For the final months of her life, she was utterly speech-less. Her hair had fallen out, she grew thin and frail, her sweet frag-ile skin nearly transparent over her sweet organs and sweet bones. In her final days she was delicate, naked, and silent. Tal nursed her, and loved her, and took care of her, and I hope her presence eased Lydia's passage to the other side.

And then she died. It was torture for me even to see the inside of that apartment. Before she died, but after she knew that she almost certainly would die, Lydia sold the apartment to Tal for the symbolic price of one dollar. Tal had moved in completely, and after Lydia died she cleared the space of most of its old things. Most of the old furniture was gone. Tal had sold it and bought new furniture, furniture not miasmal with Lydia's memory. She painted the walls yellow and warmed the place up with all her rustic bohemian artifacts. The dining table and chairs she kept, but little else remained. These rooms that I knew so well that even now I sometimes move through them in my dreams had been stripped and dressed in new clothing.

I left our—Tal's now—apartment. I left in rage. All this hell in my brain, in my stomach and my chest—why did I have to hide it from the world?

Tal did not ask me if I needed a place to stay, and I did not bother to hint that I did. I could not have slept in that place, anyway. She told me that she had to go, and she did not specify why or where or with whom. I left that place.

The light had failed all around me, and now it was night.

I still had my suitcase in my hand and my hat on my head. The bouquet of green roses I left in the apartment. On the dining table. I hope she forgot to put them in water. I hope they died.

My cheeks were enflamed with crying. My chest was hot with sadness and anger, hatred of the self, and hatred of the world. I stumbled through the streets as if drunk. I was slightly drunk, actually, from the whiskey I'd had earlier. I decided at once to become drunker. I entered an establishment for just such a purpose on Fifty-third Street. It was a restaurant with a bar in the back of it, like Artie's Shrimp Shanty, where Leon and I had passed many a joyous night beneath that giant rubber shark.

"Table for one?" came a terrifying voice emerging from some unknown height or depth. I looked, and saw that the voicer of these words was a young hostess whose presence I had overlooked in my state of frailty.

"No, thank you," I said. "I have come for liquids, not solids, therefore I'll sit at the bar," which I promptly did, climbing onto a stool at the otherwise deserted bar counter.

The bartender slapped a cardboard coaster before me on the counter.

"Get you anything?" said he.

"A quadruple Scotch on the rocks, please," said I.

Looking askance at me, the bartender prepared the beverage, and I drank it. Then I ordered another.

I had three of these and entered dreamtime.

I vaguely recall that the bartender engaged me in some sort of dialogue, and I also vaguely recall that at some point he advised me to drink more slowly, then advised me to stop drinking, then *told* me to stop drinking, then *advised* me to leave the establishment, then *told* me to leave, and then, finally, on account of no one's advice, behest, or agency but my own, I left. I also vaguely recalled the blare and glare of the streets outside, and that when I was in that dark building it had rained heavily and then abated to a persistent drizzle, and that all the red and green and yellow traffic lights and the streetlights and the neon signs in the storefronts and the head-lights of passing cars were all mirrored brightly and shakily in the wet black asphalt. I walked the streets, my suitcase thudding behind me, with no idea as to what time it might be or where I was going. *I am a monster,* I thought. *I am filth. I am a thing of darkness.*

My course of direction somehow took shape: at first subconsciously, and then consciously.

I walked down Fifty-third until I turned south on University, then walked another three blocks, across the wide bustling expanse of Fifty-fifth, past the soccer field, block by block, the university buildings looking more and more like medieval fortresses, all buttressed and turreted and bulwarked and with gargoyles squatting bat-winged and freakish at the corners of the sills, vomiting rainwater from their open mouths, now a right on Fifty-seventh, now passing through the tabernacular gatehouse, then across the main quad to the Erman Biology Center at the University of Chicago.

The door was locked. I stood on tiptoes to look through the narrow window in the door. I rattled the door handle. I punched the door and hurt my hand. I stood there in front of the door for an hour. Eventually, a young man—what looked like a student, working late at a lab—walked out the door. My coat soaked through, rainwater dribbling from the brim of my hat, I pushed past him when he opened the door. He held it open for me as he was going out. Then I watched a spasm of doubt play across his features: his unthinking politeness at holding the door open for me was interrupted by caution. He realized that I might not be allowed into the building. I shoved my way past him. My hat passed just beneath his arm as I angrily banged my suitcase through the narrow passageway. Once inside the hall I turned back and saw his face in the window, giving me a quizzical and offended look through the narrow window in the door as it was sighing shut and the lock clunking. Then he rolled his eyes and went away. I ignored him. I waddled down the hallway. My wet shoes squawked and crunched on the salmon-pink vinyl floor. I passed under fluorescent lights that reflected white rectangles on the floor. I pressed the arrow-shaped Up button beside the elevator. The elevator happened to be resting on the ground floor, and so the doors rolled immediately open for me. I stepped inside, and with a long purple finger depressed the button labeled 3. The elevator bore me whooshing upward two floors, stopped, and opened, and I stepped out. The hallway was in darkness, but when I stepped out of the elevator my presence triggered the energy-saving fluorescent lights, which began to buzz and flicker on above me as my shoes squawked and crunched on the floor. The lights roused on one by one in my wake, illuminating the white walls and pink floors with the cold fluorescent glow of science. The flickering lights illuminated the doors to rooms 302, 304, and 306, and at the next door, I stopped:

308: BEHAVIORAL BIOLOGY LABORATORY

I could see through the smoked-glass panel in the door, across which that number and those words were written in bold black capital block letters, that the lights were on. I could also see a shadow moving around in the room. I could see that there was something going on inside, that science was progressing in there. I took the door handle in my long purple hand, pushed it down, heard it click, found it open. I pulled the door open and stepped inside the room.

Dr. Norman Plumlee looked up from his work. He was alone in the lab. Norman Plumlee was alone, that is, except for the creature who lay restrained facedown to a bed by straps. The creature's arms were strapped tightly to her sides. Her stumpy legs were spread-eagled and strapped down in place. A plump pink ball of flesh behind her advertised her fecundity. The fluorescent lights overhead flickered and buzzed.

The lab was somewhat altered—the squishy blue mat on which I used to play with my toys was gone. They had fancy new computers in the part of the lab where the humans worked. The thick glass enclosure that had originally been built for me was still there and showed signs of animal habitation: a tank full of drinking water, a pad and blankets for sleeping. The red plastic potty in which I had been trained to deposit my urine and feces so long ago was there again. The room smelled like the potty had recently been used, as well. The room smelled of animal: of urine, of shit, of sweat.

I smelled the distinctively repulsive smell of the dehydrated food pellets that scientists always feed laboratory primates. There were orange peels strewn across the lab floor. The glass door that separated the human from the animal side of the lab was propped open. The creature was strapped to the gurneylike bed on wheels inside the glass-enclosed area. The creature who was strapped to the bed was Céleste. She had grown. (As had I, of course—both outwardly and inwardly.) There was little else behind her eyes than there had been when we were children. That is animal psychology: always the mind and soul of a child. Her gaze was syrupy with sleepiness.

Dr. Norman Plumlee, as I said, looked up from his work. There he stood, in room 308 of the Erman Biology Center at the University of Chicago, alone in the room except for Céleste, below the flickering and buzzing fluorescent lights of science. Dr. Norman Plumlee stood behind the animal, looking at the figure who had just entered the room in more confusion at first than alarm. Rage was driving the alcohol from my veins. I looked at the round black-and-white analog electric clock on the lab wall and took note of the time. It was ten after ten in the evening. From his presence in the lab—unattended, and at this time of the night—it could be deduced that perhaps Dr. Norman Plumlee was engaged in doing something he was not allowed to do. From the look on his face it would appear that I had caught Dr. Norman Plumlee doing something that he probably did not wish to be caught doing. From the look on his face I estimated that I had caught Dr. Norman Plumlee in the act of doing something that might even, were my discovery made public, jeopardize his career, or at least shame and embarrass him to where he might be hesitant to show his face on the street. Dr. Norman Plumlee was wearing turquoise-colored latex gloves and a white lab coat with the sleeves rolled up his thick and hairy forearms to his elbows. His beard had gone from salt-and-pepper utterly to salt, and his hairline had receded more. In his latex-gloved hands he held a thick clear plastic syringe. I guessed that this was an artificial inseminator. The business end of this instrument Dr. Norman Plumlee held inserted in Céleste's squishy pink ape vulva. When I walked into the room, Dr. Norman Plumlee was in the very act of slowly depressing the button of the syringe with his thumb, pushing deep into her body whatever silvery viscous liquid was contained in the tube of the syringe. Then my eyes trickled away from them, and landed on top of one of the long gray formica lab tables, where I saw several publications of pornographic nature. I think one of them was a *Hustler*.

I grasped at once the nature of the experiment. I knew that it was human semen contained in that syringe, and that it was probably his own. This wasn't science—this was rape.

Dr. Norman Plumlee did not say anything when he saw me. Nor did I. He fastidiously slid the clear plastic syringe out of Céleste, and the room was so noiseless that I could hear the faint slurp and sucking gasp of it leaving her sexual orifice even from as far away from them as I stood. He carefully set the syringe down with a click on a tray beside him. I flung my suitcase to the floor with a dull thud and a rattling of its contents. I removed my hat and threw it aside. I unbuttoned my coat, shrugged my way out of it, and folded it and threw it on top of the suitcase.

Dr. Norman Plumlee stepped toward me. I saw then in his face that he had finally recognized me.

"Bruno?" he said.

"I am Bruno Littlemore." I spread the long purple fingers of my right hand and placed it on my chest.

"What happened to you?"

"I evolved."

"I mean your face—"

"I evolved by surgery. Biology can only take you so far."

He pushed his glasses up on his face with a fat finger. His

shoulders were hunched up to his ears and his arms were hanging at his sides as stiffly as if his elbow joints had been glued in place. He took a few more steps in my direction.

"What are you doing to Céleste?" I said.

I could feel my body involuntarily reorganizing itself: shoulders rising, muscles condensing, twitching. Despite my evolution into a human being, I could not help displaying the outward physical signs of an animal on the verge of attack, and Dr. Plumlee recognized them.

"Bruno, Bruno," he intoned, in an attempt at a soothing voice while moving his hands up and down in a let's-just-calm-down-now gesture. "You're not thinking of doing anything violent? That wouldn't make sense."

I saw him sidling toward a certain drawer in one of the cabinets under the lab tables.

"You created me," I said. "And then you abandoned me. And now you're going to do the same to Céleste."

"We gave you a little help here, Bruno, and that is all. You created yourself."

True as that was, I had no time to thank him for that apogee of compliments. I saw him make a swift jab for the handle of the drawer he was angling for. At that moment I realized that my days of smashing and biting were not behind me after all.

I shall not stoop to describe, Gwen, what it is like to kill a man in a fit of rage. To kill a man with one's bare hands—not to mention feet, teeth, and a computer keyboard snatched blindly from one of the lab tables—all of which I employed to the task. For the sake of taste and decency I will not attempt to describe the feeling of causing a person's life to flee from his body by means of brute force, nor will I discuss the feeling of watching the light being extinguished from his eyes, nor of watching his corpus go still and slack as his last breaths hiss from his lungs, as his blood goes flat in his veins and the electricity leaves his nerves. These are feelings that only murderers know, only monsters like me who have undergone this baptism of blood. I shall only remind you that an average healthy adult male chimp, such as I am now and was then, may be up to seven times stronger than a man, and that even the manhood into which I had come had not weakened the innate strength of these arms, nor had it managed to tamp out the potentiality for inner rage to become quickly sublimated into outer violence. Smashed fish tanks and whatever else aside, I had never fully made conscious use of this secret strength of mine, nor even fully realized it before. I shall only say that there wasn't much that was recognizably human of Dr. Norman Plumlee left when I was through with him.

So there I sat in room 308: BEHAVIORAL BIOLOGY LABORATORY, in that place that I had once known as a home and once again known as a workplace. The place that had helped my consciousness into existence. I had nothing left. Lydia was gone. Tal did not want me. Leon had gone to California. I could not have gone back to the zoo. I could not go back to science. I could not live in the world, either: I had just committed murder.

The lab was dirty with blood. The furniture was overturned, the glass cracked, the computers lay in ruins, broken scientific equipment and all kinds of machines were smashed and scattered across the floor, and the remains of a well-respected scientist lay slumped in a corner of the room in a puddle of blood that was quickly spreading across the floor. Who would have thought the old man had so much blood in him? The fluorescent lights above me flickered and buzzed.

I unstrapped Céleste from the bed to which she had been restrained in order to be raped by science. Her wrists and ankles were swollen and bruised from where she had been strapped down. How love must suffer in this stern world. I helped Céleste climb down from the sacrificial bed. She had obviously been drugged.

She could not walk or crawl on her own. Her knees caved beneath her. Her movements were sluggish. Her eyes were heavy-lidded, feverish, and glassy.

There was a sink in the lab, where I washed the blood from my hands as best I could. I put on my hat and coat. I unsnapped the locks of my suitcase and took out some clothes, and dressed Céleste in them. She was a little smaller than me, the clothes were baggy on her. I gave her some pants, and dressed her in the same droopy-sleeved green hooded sweatshirt that I used to wear when I was very young, in which Lydia used to dress me when we went out in public, to hide me, to avoid suspicion. I shut the suitcase and picked it up. We were almost out the door when another thought came to me, and, following the thought, I went back to the body of the dead scientist, and searched through his pockets until I found his wallet. My shoes stepped in the blood. I slipped the wallet into the pocket of my coat. Then together Céleste and I struggled through the door that led into and out of 308: BEHAVIORAL BIOL-OGY LABORATORY and into the hallway, which had gone dark again, and which our presence lit up again. We walked—she leaning on me, and me doing most of the walking—down the hall, and we rode the elevator to the first floor, and I guided her out and down another hallway toward the door.

Behind us, far down the hallway and out of sight, as we were nearing the door, I heard the peep and squeal of the wheels of a cart—and, very slowly, I heard a softly muted form of a familiar series of sounds: first the quarter-beat of the heel of a boot making contact with the floor, followed immediately by the *clomp* of the rest of the foot coming down, and then the deft squeak of the toe launching the foot on its journey toward the next step, then a loop of chain whapping against a denim-clad thigh, and the tinkling of a hoop of many keys: *kLOMPa-whap-SHLINK—kLOMPa-whap-SHLINK—kLOMPa-whap-SHLINK...*

I saw that I had left a trail of footprints in blood behind me in the hallway.

I grabbed the handle of the door that led out and pushed on it, and we left. The door whispered shut, clunked, and locked behind us. I wiped the bottoms of my shoes off in the grass.

How love must suffer in this stern world. How love must suffer.

XLIX

With most of the money I had left from New York I paid for another taxi to take us northward out of Hyde Park. I told the driver to let us out when we were passing between the stony feet of the skyscrapers of the Loop, and I asked for a room at the Palmer House Hilton on Monroe and State. We had ducked inside the hotel almost at random. It was raining again, and deep night. I was still woozy-brained with drink, and Céleste was drugged and stumbling. Two small figures, their clothes soaked flat to their suspiciously proportioned little bodies, waddled past a doorman in a cap and gloves and a brilliant bottle-green coat with shiny gold buttons, pushed through the hotel's revolving glass doors, wandered through the elegant underbelly below the hotel's main lobby, found an escalator, and rode it up a floor to a high-ceilinged and spacious and crapulously decorated lobby, all gilded neoclassical ornaments and Corinthian columns and so forth, glass and brass, golden-veined expanses of marble, painted plaster and potted ferns. I yanked the hood of my floppy green sweatshirt low over Céleste's face, to hide her apeness. At the golden-veined marble slab of the hotel's front desk I booked a nonsmoking room with one king-size bed on the nineteenth floor. I put it on Dr. Norman

Plumlee's credit card. I kept my hat tipped low over my features. The mirror-paneled elevator whooshed us up to the nineteenth floor in seconds—so fast it was slightly nauseating—and we scurried down the hallway and found the door to our room. I slid the keycard inside, watched a light flash green, and pushed the door open. I flicked on a light, took the sign reading DO NOT DISTURB from the other side of the door and affixed it onto the outer door handle, then shut the door, locked it, and clapped the hasp of the door guard over its brass knob.

We drew the curtains over the window and did not leave the room for three days. We hung our damp clothes from the shower curtain rod in the bathroom, and went naked for the rest of the time. The room immediately took on the smell of damp fur, and the smell got mustier and more mildewy over the course of the next three days. We ordered up food for ourselves from room service, always instructing the staff to leave the trays of food outside the door. We dined on steak. We dined on lobster. We ordered up bottles of wine. We dined on prosciutto and melons, chilled oysters, oxtail, salmon, duck, soft-boiled quail's eggs and venison sausage, and ordered crème brûlée and chocolate mousse cake and sweet port wine for dessert. All of it went on Norm's MasterCard. We let the dirty dishes stack up on the floors. We held on to one another for long hours. I gave Céleste whiskey and wine. I told her stories about my long adventure in human civilization, and she blinked dumbly at me, pursed her lips, and scratched her hairy protuberant belly. I tried to show her how to use the toilet, but she did not comprehend me. When she shat on the floor I dutifully picked it up in a wad of toilet paper and disposed of it. I read to her from the Bible we found in the drawer of the dresser: for idle entertainment I read her Genesis and Job and the Song of Solomon—and Céleste blinked dumbly at me, pursed her lips, and scratched her belly. On the first night we stripped the quilt and the tightly tucked crisp white sheets from the mattress and tore them into fine shreds, and we ripped open the plush pillows piled at the headboard, and we scattered all the tatters and soft feathery fluff around on the bed and wadded it into a warm fluffy nest on top of the mattress, in which we would lie together all day and all night, in our nest, in a lazy-limbed embrace, napping. Soon, having no clear use for them otherwise, we also shredded the various literatures provided in the room—the Bible, the phone book, and a copy of *Be My Guest*, the autobiography of Conrad Hilton (the room service menu we spared)—and we scattered the shredded pages all over the carpeted floor of the room. Sometimes, for recreation, we would jump up and down on the bed until we collapsed from exhaustion and mirth. At these times I could never help but to sing aloud: *two little monkeys, jumping on the bed...* and as I sang this song, this children's song, Céleste would howl and pant-hoot and shriek along to the tune in very approximate accompaniment—no doubt causing much wonder as to the nature of our racket in the adjacent rooms. Other times, we would sit up on the bed in our fluffy nest and watch TV. We watched TV while Céleste sat behind me and went through the motions of grooming me, even though I had no fur, and then we would switch places, and I picked and combed my fingers through the fur on her back, just as we had done when we were children. So we sat on the bed and took turns grooming one another, with plates of gourmet food sitting before us in the nest of tatters and fluff on top of the mattress, and I cut her steaks into bite-size pieces for her, and she would daintily pinch up the little bits of meat in her long purple fingers and insert them between her wide pink lips and chew them, and we sipped our wine, and we watched TV. We watched soap operas. We watched sitcoms. We watched daytime talk shows. We watched late-night talk shows. We watched music videos. We watched old movies—the movies I used to watch with Leon: with Greta Garbo, the Marx Brothers,

Cary Grant and Katharine Hepburn, Jimmy Stewart, Humphrey Bogart and Lauren Bacall, Errol Flynn, Laurence Olivier, and Orson Welles. We also watched *Sesame Street*, so that Céleste too could know the joys of Bert and Ernie. We watched interesting pornographic films that we ordered to the room on Norm's credit card. And—perhaps most important—we watched cartoons! We watched Bugs Bunny and Daffy Duck! Goofy and Donald Duck! We watched the cartoons that take eternal pursuit as their theme: both the amorous pursuit of lover and beloved—such as Pepé Le Pew, that French skunk undaunted in his unrequited and mistaken love for a black cat whose back has been accidentally painted with a white stripe—as well as the violent pursuit of predator and prey: Coyote and Road Runner, Sylvester and Tweety, Tom and Jerry . . . all that mythic pursuit!—the endless flux of the chase, the magnetic push-and-pull of aggression and defense, of repulsion and desire! . . . perhaps the true spirit of myth—of Echo and Narcissus, of Achilles and Hector—survives for us, in its pure form, only in cartoons.

That is how Céleste and I spent three days. These were three days of odd bliss that I spent with my little animal friend. These were my last three days of freedom in the human world.

In addition to all our joyful cartoons, we also, occasionally, watched the news. Although the time we spent in that room almost immediately blurred into the animal-minded time of liquid, dreamlike continuum (I had unplugged the alarm clock, and took but passing notice or interest in the lightening or darkening of the rising day or falling night behind the thickly drawn curtains), I believe it must have been on the second afternoon or night that, as a cartoon we were enjoying had ended and been superseded on that channel by some less diverting programming, I snatched up the remote control and began flicking through the many channels, looking for something fun to watch, and settled briefly on a local news broadcast. Céleste, who sat beside me on the bed in our nest, picking with her dirty fingers at a platter of seaweed-wrapped salmon pâté, gave me a lazy-blooded and dismissive wave of her hand to indicate that I should skip past this channel, because it was boring. However, I shushed her, because I thought I recognized a building on the screen. The establishing shot that led into the news segment was of the Erman Biology Center: I recognized that magisterial ornate gray stone architecture, the cornices and gargoyles, the ivy crawling up the stones. It was a video of a curious crowd gathered around the entrance to the building, which was cordoned off by long strips of bright yellow police tape. A lot of police officers were milling around by the building's entrance as two paramedics wheeled what looked like a body out of the doors on a gurney. The body was covered with a sheet. I turned up the volume. The voice on the TV told us that a certain Dr. Norman Plumlee, a research scientist and tenured faculty at the University of Chicago and lab director of the Behavioral Biology Laboratory at the University of Chicago's Institute for Mind and Biology, renowned in scientific circles for a long career of groundbreaking research on animal cognition and primate psychology, was found dead that morning in a laboratory on the third floor of the Erman Biology Center at the University of Chicago by a graduate student who worked at the lab, who had immediately notified the police. Dr. Plumlee appeared to have been brutally murdered by an unknown assailant. The police had no suspects and no leads at that time, and knew of no possible motives for the crime. Dr. Plumlee was beloved by his students, some of whom were interviewed, croaking their bafflement at the strange and horrible crime into the reporter's camera in various states of shock and tears. Dr. Plumlee's wife was also interviewed, expressing shock, anger, and immeasurable sorrow. The police were offering a reward for any information leading to the resolution of this terrible crime. Then the newscasters promised weather and sports updates after the break, and a commercial came on, and I continued flicking through the channels until I found a Porky Pig cartoon, which made us laugh, and I picked up the phone and ordered up another bottle of wine, and again we pleasantly forgot all the trouble in the world, the leavening effects of the wine and the Looney Tunes banishing all thoughts dark and grave from our minds as the birdsong banishes winter.

Later (was it the following evening? I don't remember, and have no way of estimating) the TV said it had come to light that Dr. Norman Plumlee, on the night he was murdered, had been performing experiments on a thirteen-year-old female chimpanzee named Céleste, whom the laboratory had on temporary loan from the Lincoln Park Zoo. This chimp—most likely the only witness to the murder—had escaped, having apparently been deliberately set free, probably by Dr. Plumlee's killer or killers. While investigators were not willing to rule out the possibility that the chimp herself had killed the scientist, it seemed unlikely for several reasons: that Céleste had no history of violence and was by all accounts a small and fairly docile chimp; and although chimps are extremely strong and can be violent when surprised or provoked, said the TV, forensic experts reported that the nature of the fatal wounds was extremely uncharacteristic of an animal attack. Plumlee had almost certainly been killed by repeated trauma to the head with a blunt object, most likely a badly damaged computer keyboard which had been found near the body. Probably the most telling evidence of human involvement, though, was the trail of bloody shoe prints that led from the scene of the crime all the way outside the building, where the unknown assailant had wiped his shoes off in the grass. Police were investigating the possibility that the crime was committed in connection with the Animal Liberation Front, or other animal rights or ecoterrorist organizations. This theory was circumstantially corroborated by the fact that all of the video cameras in the room, which were there to capture experiment data, had been switched off shortly before the estimated time that the murder took place, indicating some sort of human premeditation. The animal may be on the loose, and residents of the Hyde Park neighborhood and surrounding areas were advised to be on the lookout for an escaped chimpanzee. If you see the animal, pleaded the woman behind the news desk on the TV, please immediately call this number (which scrolled across the bottom of the screen) to contact City of Chicago Animal Care and Control Services. Disturbingly, several pornographic magazines as well as traces of semen had also been found at the crime scene. Police still had no witnesses or suspects.

The next segment dealt with the outpouring of community grief at the University of Chicago, with shots of a candlelit vigil and so on, and more tearful interviews with Dr. Plumlee's colleagues and students. The woman on the TV began to mention the connection Dr. Plumlee had to the infamous case of Bruno, the Chicago chimp who— (here I changed the channel).

The animal-rights-terrorist-group angle was not, after all, strictly incorrect. In a way I had acted as an animal rights terrorist cell of one. But I did not liberate an animal for larger ideological reasons. I liberated just one animal for deeply personal reasons, and in so doing, as we will see, I imprisoned myself. But come to think of it, I did not liberate Céleste, either—in the end I only delivered her into another kind of captivity. If it isn't one kind of captivity, it's another. There's no way out, no way out. You see, my actual feelings on animal rights are somewhat complicated and ambivalent. One hears much talk these days of free-range animals and cage-free eggs and so on. On the one hand I suppose it's a good thing to acknowledge our debt to the animals we enslave and kill for our pleasure by making their lives prior to slaughter as pleasant as possible, while on the other hand the impulse strikes me as emblematic

of a romantically rosy view of nature. It's all a paradox anyway. If
we think of the whole world as a prison, then there's no such thing
as a cage-free animal.

On the third and last day that Céleste and I spent in our hotel
room, a breaking news flash in the middle of the day announced
that the brutal murder of Dr. Norman Plumlee had been solved.

The murder had been committed by a man named Haywood
Finch, who worked as a night-shift janitor at the University of Chicago. Mr. Finch was probably the only other person in the building at the time of the murder. The police had apprehended Mr.
Finch the previous evening and taken him in for interrogation,
where they almost immediately obtained a full confession. Mr.
Finch confessed both to murdering Dr. Plumlee and setting the
chimp free. Mr. Finch, a developmentally disabled man—said the
TV—had a long history of psychiatric and emotional disturbances
and was severely autistic, with only a third-grade education and
an IQ of 54. Police psychologists judged Mr. Finch to be a highly
mentally unstable person and suggested that he may have a violent
personality disorder.

It was unclear as of yet whether Mr. Finch would be found competent to stand trial. If found incompetent, or found competent
and convicted but found not guilty by reasons of insanity, Mr.
Finch would probably be indeterminately committed to a psychiatric facility.

The missing chimpanzee had still not been found.

Then I drew open the curtains. It was a bright day outside. I
showered, as I had not done in three days, and put on fresh clothes.
I tried to get Céleste to take a shower, but she was afraid of the
shower and would not go in. I dressed Céleste as well, again in
my droopy-sleeved green hooded sweatshirt for maximum possible
inconspicuousness, and I put on my coat and my hat. I took my
mute friend by the hand, and picked up my suitcase in my free

hand. We left the hotel room without looking back. It was the late morning. I guided her down the hallway, into the mirror-paneled elevator, pressed the button that took us down to the hotel lobby. The hood of her sweatshirt pulled low over her face to hide her apeness and the brim of my hat pulled low over my face to hide mine, I holding her hand, Céleste and I walked out of the elevator and through the high-ceilinged and spacious lobby of the Palmer House Hilton, all gilded decorations and Corinthian columns, glass and brass, golden-veined expanses of marble, painted plaster and potted ferns. We passed by the clerks at the front desk without a word or a backward glance. We let a descending escalator carry us to the ground floor, where we passed through the revolving glass doors. We walked past a doorman in a cap and gloves and a brilliant bottle-green coat with shiny gold buttons, who smiled and waved good-bye to us (we did not smile or wave back), and onto the street. I held Céleste's hand in mine all the way.

With her long purple hand hot and sweaty in mine, we walked two blocks down Monroe and turned right on Clark, then walked north, holding hands and weaving in and out of the pedestrian traffic on the sidewalk for nearly two miles, a journey that took well over an hour. We stopped at a corner newsstand, where, still holding Céleste's hand, I put down my suitcase, rooted through the pockets of my coat and dredged up the absolute last of my remaining money. I was able to scrape up enough wadded small bills and loose change to purchase a pack of Lucky Strikes. I put them in my pocket, picked up my suitcase, tugged on Céleste's hand, and we kept walking. She followed as I guided us all the way up to Lincoln Park. We walked into the emerald-green rolls of Lincoln Park from the south entrance, waddled along the winding pedestrian footpath past joggers clad tightly in shiny spandex outfits, past little dogs tugging on their leashes, past a baseball diamond, an equestrian statue, and a big duck pond, where geese and swans drifted through green water neon with algae, and then we entered the Lincoln Park Zoo.

We walked past the great cats, the giraffes, the Bactrian camels, the rhinos, the kangaroos and the zebras, until we came to the Primate House. We arrived at the Primate House from the south entrance, which overlooked the outdoor part of the chimp exhibit: colloquially known as Monkey Island. We looked over the concrete ledge that gazed across the water-filled ditch between the human observation area and the chimp habitat. It was a fairly warm day for March, and some of the chimps—some of our family—were playing outside, including my father, Rotpeter. I set down my suitcase and let go momentarily of Céleste's hand. I reached into the pocket of my coat and took out the pack of cigarettes. I unwound the band of cellophane from the top, cracked it open and removed the foil lining of the pack. I backed up, wound back my arm, took aim, and threw it over the wall. It sailed over the moat and landed successfully on the grassy shores of Monkey Island. The chimps immediately all scrambled over to it to investigate. One of the babies picked it up in idle curiosity. I watched Rotpeter lumber over and rudely snatch it from the child's hands. His personality had not changed one bit. He was still as brutish, as violent, as selfish and unenlightened as when I had left him. His face brightened at once with a look of surprise and rapture as he realized what it was. I watched him sniff them, relishing the smell of tobacco he had long, long been deprived of. He bolted off at once to dig up his old cigarette lighter from the cache where it had sat unneeded for years.

Then I took Céleste's hand again, and I led her inside the Primate House. I let go of her hand. I put down my suitcase. I embraced her. I hugged her tightly to my chest, and I kissed her forehead and her silent face. The hood of her sweatshirt flopped back behind her head, revealing her apeness. I picked up my suitcase and waved good-bye to her. Céleste went to the window. She was confused.

She pressed her long purple hands flat against the glass and looked through the window at the chimp habitat. Our family stood gathered around her on the other side of the glass wall. My father, Rotpeter, already had a lit cigarette between his lips. All of them were hopping up and down, screaming, pant-hooting, ripping up fistfuls of straw and planting chips from the floor and throwing it in the air, bashing on the glass with their palms, displaying like mad—all of them probably wondering how in the world Céleste had come to be on the wrong side of the glass. Céleste pressed her hands to the glass and looked inside. She was happy to see them. She wanted to be with them. She wanted to be on the other side of the glass.

I left the Primate House. With my hat on my head and my suitcase in my hand, I slowly waddled away from it all. I made my way past the zebras, the kangaroos, the rhinos, the Bactrian camels, the giraffes, and the great cats, and out of the zoo. I walked out of the Lincoln Park Zoo for the last time in my life. I walked along the pedestrian footpath that encircled the park, past joggers clad tightly in shiny spandex outfits, past little dogs tugging on their leashes, past a baseball diamond, an equestrian statue and a big duck pond, where geese and swans drifted through the green water neon with algae. I said good-bye to the sky above my head. I said good-bye to Chicago. I said good-bye to my freedom to move at will through human society.

I saw what I wanted to see: I saw a mounted policeman reining his horse along the edge of the park. The giant sweaty brown animal clopped along at a leisurely pace. The policeman on the horse wore a dark blue coat, black riding boots in the stirrups, aviator sunglasses, and a sky-blue helmet with a visor. He seemed bored. He was watching the ducks in the pond. I waved to him and approached. The policeman snapped out of his duck-watching reverie as I came near. He tugged on the reins of his giant landbeast—like a hill of muscle—and clopped slowly toward me. We met on the pedestrian footpath, by the duck pond.

The policeman looked down at me, and I looked up at him. His horse snorted. The policeman raised his eyebrows and tipped up his sunglasses with a gloved finger to get a better look at this strange and tiny figure on the ground in front of him.

"Hello?" said the policeman. "Can I help you?"

I removed my hat.

"My name is Bruno Littlemore," I said. "Bruno I was given, Littlemore I gave myself. I have committed a murder, and I have come forward to confess."

The policeman peered down at me from on top of his horse with a look that suggested he was still searching for the owner of the voice that had spoken, still wondering if this small creature standing in the park with a suitcase and a hat could really be the owner of that voice. He took off his sunglasses, and blinked at me perplexedly in the late-twentieth-century Chicago sunlight.

L

The relevant parts of my tale are all told. It is a pleasing accident that this last chapter happens to be the fiftieth, the only other chapter in this volume except for the first (and, less elegantly, the fifth and tenth) to receive the honor of being headed with a bold and simple single capital letter. I began this narrative, as is natural, with an *I*: standing for the ego, the fount of the first-person voice. And I end it with an *L*. Does that *L* stand for light? For Lydia? For her given, and my self-given, surname? For locksmiths? For the commuter rail system of my home city? *L* is for laughter. *L* is for literature. *L* is for love. *L* is for life. *L* is for language.

It would serve as a useless and uninteresting dénouement to the story I have told you if I were to dig my long purple fingers too deep into the dirty details of my willing arrest, my confession, the trial, and the shock and scandal that surrounded it all—if I were to speak too much of the public reaction, how they remembered me from my previous scandals. Scandal erupts behind me everywhere I go. Scandal blooms in my footsteps like the flowers of discord. I confessed. I confessed all.

The evidence of Haywood Finch's coerced confession was thrown out. He was freed, and his name cleared. That was my only objective in coming forward to correct their faulty justice, and that much I achieved.

A few interesting points concerning the unusual particularity of my case arose on the legal agenda, especially in regard to the question of whether I should be tried as a man or as an animal. For one thing, I am not and have never been regarded as a legal citizen of this or any nation—even though I have never lived in any other—for no clear precedent or protocol exists concerning whether citizenship should or can be awarded to animals, be they mute or articulate, or what to do with talking animals if and when they transgress the laws of man. If I were to have been tried as an animal, then I would surely have been euthanized—destroyed, as any animal that harms a man must be. I, Bruno, however, was saved—and I leave it to my readers to ponder whether or not there is poetic irony in this—by science. 'Twas beauty killed the beast. 'Twas science resurrected him.

Scientists came forward to argue that I was too valuable and unique a specimen to be destroyed—that instead, I must be studied. Had I been exterminated—exterminated!—God, what fascistically clinical language!—then they would have lost much opportunity to study me. After all, I am interesting. Mine is an unusual case. There's that Aesop's fable, Gwen, about the farmer and his wife who had a goose that laid golden eggs. They thought maybe if they killed the animal it would be made of solid gold inside, so they cut it open and found it to be made of regular old goose-meat. Even if it had been made of gold it was poor economic reasoning to kill it anyway, but that aside—that's me: I lay the human race golden eggs, and they decided I'm more use to them alive than dead. Oh, I'm sure the studying won't stop with my death. They'll probably put my brain in a jar for the scrutiny of future generations, slice it up and test the thisness or the thatness of it. And I am sure their scrutiny will reveal nothing. Just regular old chimp meat inside. There will be some scientist a hundred years from now who will hold up my skull to show the classroom, like Yorick: look here, kids, behold the braincase of the long-dead jester—light, hollow, unfleshed by time, polished smooth as a gemstone. Notice the simian slope of the browridge, the jutting jaw. Would you believe that the monster who owned this once sang the world a song of pride and passion and love and joy and fear and darkness? No, they won't believe it. Because that's not how humans like to think of their wild animals. They want you in the dark, they want you shivering in the woods, cowering at the lightning flashes. They want to believe that they are not still shivering and cowering along with them. But they are. You are—you are, you upright beasts, you animals.

In the end the court was swayed by the scientists' arguments, and after a great deal of red tape had been slashed through, after a great deal of time and paperwork had come and gone and the question of what was to be done with me finally arrived at the point of egress of the complicated bureaucratic maze in which it had gotten hopelessly lost for a time, I was sent to live in confinement, relative peace, and seclusion in the Zastrow National Primate Research Center, located somewhere in rural Georgia, USA.

Here, within these four white walls, and within the perimeters of this land cordoned off by those tall chain-link fences that I told you about so long (it seems) ago, in the alternating sterility of the laboratories and the rich lushness of the forests outside, in the company of human scientists, unenculturated chimpanzees who do not understand me when I speak to them and whose inarticulate shrieks and gestures I no longer comprehend, I have lived for nine years.

The date today is August 8, 2008. I will turn twenty-five in twelve days. Next year I will have been here for a decade. I will have grown ten years older, and ten years wiser, maybe. I have continued to paint and read here in the solitary apartments that the scientists have kindly provided for me, and occasionally I have staged theatrical productions, which I direct and star in. Although I must work with a cast of nonprofessional actors, most of them chimps, and our audiences tend to be small—consisting only of the scientists who work here, usually—I do derive some joy from them. Leon still comes to visit me several times a year, and we correspond by mail frequently. Little Emily used to visit me in the early days of my incarceration, but I have not seen or communicated with her in years. I assume Emily has willingly forgotten me in order to concentrate on living the life of an independent young woman in her twenties, wherever it is she is doing that now. Tal visited me only once. That was an unpleasant visit. She still blames me—fairly or unfairly, I don't know—for what happened to Lydia. To hell with her. I loved Lydia ten times ten times as much as she or anyone ever did. I probably loved her ten times ten times as much as anyone ever loved anyone, inside or outside of their own species. Mr. and Mrs. Lawrence visited me once as well, and on that occasion—I misremember how many long and quiet years ago now that must have been—they brought along my old mute companion, Clever Hands. It was a joy to see him. Hilarious Lily, they informed me, had passed away—she died in the same bed in which her husband, Hilarious Larry, had died a few years before her, clutching her rosary in her fist, going silently to her God.

Aside from that—except for you, Gwen—I have no visitors from the outside. Leon Smoler, who is my best living friend, surely has not got much time left. He is old, he is old. And, moreover, in terrible shape, which I shouldn't find surprising. Pretty soon he will have to start patching up that old body for heaven. After he goes, I suspect that I will live out the rest of my days with little or no contact with anyone from the outside world. I obediently understand that it is most probably my fate to sit here and wait—cultured, educated, gifted with language and reason, and yet alone and deprived of my freedom—until, one day, I will die. And that will be all.

Unless, of course, I escape. As I have confessed to you before,

Gwen, I have recurring dreams of returning to that human world that so badly mistreated me. If I were a rational creature (which, obviously, because I am also a conscious creature, I almost by definition am not), I would have absolutely no wish to rejoin human civilization, seeing as I have everything I could ever want right here inside this patch of the earth that is sectioned off from the rest of the planet by that high metal fence. But whenever I am outside in the forest, feeling the heat of the Georgia sun on my face, sucking this wet Southern air into my lungs, listening to the calls of the birds, who are free to fly where they will and to sing their songs beyond mankind, something restless in my heart induces my gaze to tip curiously skyward, to the top of that razor-wire-topped chain-link fence that surrounds the grounds of the Zastrow National Primate Research Center. However, Gwen, these are only dreams, which are the children of an idle brain, begot of nothing but vain fantasy. These seeds of my dreams of escape never germinate past the first saplings of vague plots and plans in the mischief-rich soil of my devious mind: plots and plans of somehow getting over or under that fence, or past the door that I see you walk in and out of every day you come to visit me—and get out. There must be a way out.

The world is large. I know that I am not fit to live in human society. But then again, who is? There may still come a day, Gwen, when Bruno Littlemore is free to walk the world again.

Today, Gwen, this Scheherazade will officially fall silent for you for the last time, but I hope this will not be your last visit, because, as you've probably noticed, I have fallen in love with you.

That aside, earlier this morning, before you came to me today to complete your project, I was reading the Book of Psalms. No, please don't expect this narrative to end with some sort of Dostoyevskian last-minute prison conversion. Unlike Hilarious Lily, I have never been a religious ape. I was and remain the chimp of the perverse. But in my long hours of solitude and quiet reflection I have taken to reading the Bible. I admit sometimes it can be very beautiful. There is a dark and primitive energy in its words that sometimes, if I allow them to, can put a shiver in my spine, can make me feel as if my blood has turned to ice. And sometimes, too, I read it only to enrage me. I read it to make my blood sing out with violent fury in my heart at all humankind. It is an unusual text that can produce both awe and rage in me at once.

And I was flipping through the double-column-texted, tissue-thin and gold-edged pages of that famous book—the "Good Book"—and I landed on the Psalms (which as it so happens I read often, because they come right after Job, which is the book of the Bible I reread the most), and I came across this:

When I look at thy heavens, the work of thy fingers,
the moon and the stars which thou hast established;
what is man that thou art mindful of him,
and the son of man that thou dost care for him?

Yet thou hast made him little less than angels,
and dost crown him with glory and honor.
Thou hast given him dominion over the works of thy hands;
thou hast put all things under his feet,
all sheep and oxen, and also the beasts of the field,
the birds of the air, and the fish of the sea,
whatever passes along the paths of the sea.

When I read those words, it was not that feeling of awe that came to me, but a feeling of rage.

Little less than angels?

No! No, no, NO! *Not* little less than angels! Little *more* than apes! No! *Nothing* more than apes! *Apes!* Just apes! Arrogant, self-deluding, talking... *apes!* And now I am one of you. I am one of you, and I cannot ever go back! Go tell your God what I would give to unlearn your language! To go back to being an animal!

No, I can never go back! I can never go back again. I cannot unlearn my humanity. For evolution, perversely, moves forward. I do not mean it progresses, but only that it cannot be turned back like the hands of a clock. We cannot walk backward through time. We cannot put all our words into a pot and boil them down to a salty residue of grunts and howls and shrieks and gestures, we cannot retreat back across the ancient savannahs, grow our arms long again and climb back into the trees, let our spines stretch out into tails and let our stereoscopic eyes slowly recede to the sides of our heads, shake off our hair, cool our blood and drain our breasts of milk, turn our hot weak flesh to cold slimy scales, sprout spikes and horns and webs and flippers and fins, become fish, and go slithering on our disgusting bellies back into the sea.

If only we could! If only we could spare ourselves from all our suffering, from all our knowledge of death. If only we could spare the earth all our desecration. And, yes, I know we would also discard a lot of beauty and music and greatness and joy and blah blah blah and so on. Beware! That's how you get hooked! That's what *seduces* you!—what seduced me! Beware, you little fish!

Who, though—who among the host of devils could fault that sea creature of many years ago for gazing out through the mediary muck of its existence upon that muddy bank and open air and sunshine, and innocently wondering what beauty and music and greatness and joy might lie in wait up there? There, there would this monster make a man.

So go ahead, you stupid fish, you silent-minded monster. Crawl up out of the water. See what is up there. There may be some profit in it, after all. As I, Bruno, would like to say to the whole world, to scream and rattle up and down the Great Chain of Being from the simplest life-forms all the way to the upper links where the angels crowd around the heavenly throne with wings beating and mouths open wide in glorious song, but especially, *especially* to humankind, to this animal, man, who thinks he is the measure of all things: you taught me language, and my profit on it is, I know how to curse.

Acknowledgments

The Evolution of Bruno Littlemore would not exist without the gracious support of its allies. To my agent, Brian DeFiore, thank you for recognizing the potential of this freak show of a novel, and for your spectacular job of shaping it up and selling it; and enormous thanks to my editor, Cary Goldstein, for his tremendous enthusiasm for this book and his careful, incisive edits.

Thank you to the University of Iowa Provost's Fellowship and the Michener-Copernicus Society of America, and thanks to the fantastic teachers who helped me evolve as a writer: Brian Morton, Paul Lisicky, Brooke Stevens, Ethan Canin, and especially Edward Carey and Lan Samantha Chang, who held this book when it was just a baby.

Particular thanks to Jonathan Ames—the first person to read this whole thing straight through in the scattershot and inchoate state it was in at the time—for being an early advocate of Bruno's, and for his continued friendship and support further along.

Infinite love and thanks to my parents, Charley and Leigh—who raised me in a house full of books, and who for better or worse made me who I am—and to my brothers, James and John.

Special shout-outs to Jim Mattson, Nimo Johnson, Kate "Hunter Hero" Sachs, Sergei Tsimberov, Roman Skaskiw, Kevin Holden,

Andre Perry, Diana Thow, Cara Ellis, Andres Restrepo, John Benjamin, Sam Cooper, Graham Webster, Colin Heintze, Sarah Heyward, Jenny Zhang, Anthony Swofford, Sam Seigle, Gwenda-lin Grewal, and überthanks to Chris Wiley for his unflagging friendship, his apartment, a humdinger of a celebratory dinner, and countless other good turns.

Anna North, I cannot ever thank you enough.

Rock over London, rock on, Chicago.

Thanks to the Great Ape Trust and William Fields for his generous help with my research, and, with Sue Savage-Rumbaugh and Duane Rumbaugh, for continuing the fascinating and important pursuit of ape language research.

And thanks to Jane Goodall, who, when I was a teenager, I heard say, "All living things on this planet are far, far closer together than they are apart."

———

Great apes are in serious danger. It will be an unforgivable shame on our species if we allow this vital window into understanding ourselves to close forever. To learn about nonfictional ape language research and to support great ape habitat conservation, I urge you to visit www.greatapetrust.org.

About the Author

BENJAMIN HALE is a graduate of the Iowa Writers Workshop, where he received a Provost's Fellowship to complete this novel, which also went on to win a Michener-Copernicus Award. He has been a night shift baker, a security guard, a trompe l'oeil painter, a cartoonist, an illustrator and a technical writer. He grew up in Colorado and now lives in New York.

Reading Group Guide

Discussion Questions

- What is it about Bruno's performance of the peach experiment that makes the scientists select him for further study? What is the larger significance of this development?

- Bruno describes his friend Clever Hands as "imprisoned behind the half-silvered mirror of his mind." What do you think he means by this? And how does this set Bruno apart from Clever Hands?

- The ideas of freedom and imprisonment appear often in the book—both in a literal sense (i.e., being in a zoo or cage) and figuratively. In what ways does Bruno's evolved state set him free? And, by the same token, in what ways might it only serve to imprison him?

- What do you make of Bruno's relationships with the other chimps in his story? What do you think of Bruno's affection for them? How did this color your perception of Bruno?

- Bruno has many disagreeable traits. To what extent did you like or dislike Bruno, as a character? Did your opinion of him change during the story—and if so, why?

- Bruno says of human beings, "I love them and I hate them." In what ways does he love and hate humanity? Did you find yourself sympathizing with him?

- How self-aware does Bruno appear to be? How self-aware does Bruno *think* he is?

- What is the thematic significance of Shakespeare's *The Tempest* to Bruno's story?

- How reliable is Bruno as a narrator? If he isn't reliable, are there clues to what's happening outside his own perception?

- How does Bruno eventually learn to speak? At what point does it become clear that he can? Do you sense a change in him as he acquires the power of language?

- Much of the story happens before Bruno acquires language. How does this play with the internal logic of the narrative?

- What is the significance of the detailed drawing of the floor plan of Lydia's apartment that Bruno provides the reader? What does it say about Bruno's relationship to memory, and his sensation of physical space?

ABOUT TWELVE

TWELVE

TWELVE was established in August 2005 with the objective of publishing no more than twelve books each year. We strive to publish the singular book, by authors who have a unique perspective and compelling authority. Works that explain our culture; that illuminate, inspire, provoke, and entertain. We seek to establish communities of conversation surrounding our books. Talented authors deserve attention not only from publishers, but from readers as well. To sell the book is only the beginning of our mission. To build avid audiences of readers who are enriched by these works—that is our ultimate purpose.

For more information about forthcoming TWELVE books, please go to www.twelvebooks.com.